ABOUT THE AUTHOR

Stephen King was born in Portland, Maine, in 1947. He won a scholarship award to the University of Maine and later taught English, while his wife, Tabitha, got her degree.

It was the publication of his first novel *Carrie* and its subsequent adaptation that set him on his way to his present position as perhaps the bestselling author in the world.

Carrie was followed by a string of bestsellers including *It*, *Misery*, the *Dark Tower* series, *On Writing: (A Memoir of the Craft)*, and *Cell*. Some of his books have also been adapted into first rate films including *The Shawshank Redemption* and *The Green Mile*.

Stephen King is the 2003 recipient of *The National Book Foundation Medal for Distinguished Contribution to American Letters*. He lives in Bangor, Maine, with his wife, novelist Tabitha King.

PRAISE FOR STEPHEN KING

'Storytelling – the ability to make the listener or reader need to know, demand to know, what happens next – is a gift . . . Stephen King, like Charles Dickens before him, has this gift in spades' – *The Times*

'An incredibly gifted writer' – *Guardian*

'Splendid entertainment . . . Stephen King is one of those natural storytellers . . . getting hooked is easy' – Frances Fyfield, *Express*

STEPHEN KING

'SALEM'S LOT

ILLUSTRATED EDITION

Photographs by Jerry N. Uelsmann

HODDER

Copyright © 1975 by Stephen King
Introduction copyright © 2005 by Stephen King

Photographs copyright © 2004 by Jerry N. Uelsmann

First published in Great Britain in 2006 by Hodder & Stoughton
A division of Hodder Headline

This paperback edition published in 2007

The right of Stephen King to be identified as the Author
of the Work has been asserted by him in accordance with the
Copyright, Designs and Patents Act 1988.

A Hodder paperback

1

A CIP catalogue record for this title is available from the British Library

ISBN 978 0 340 95147 7

Typeset in Bembo by Palimpsest Book Production Limited,
Grangemouth, Stirlingshire

Printed and bound by Clays Ltd, St Ives plc

Hodder Headline's policy is to use papers that are natural,
renewable and recyclable products and made from wood grown
in sustainable forests. The logging and manufacturing processes
are expected to conform to the environmental regulations
of the country of origin.

Hodder & Stoughton
A division of Hodder Headline
338 Euston Road
London NW1 3BH

For Naomi Rachel King
'. . . promises to keep.'

CONTENTS

INTRODUCTION TO 'SALEM'S LOT
By Stephen King

My father-in-law is now retired, but when he was working for Maine's Department of Human Services, he had a very cool sign in his office. It said ONCE I HAD NO CHILDREN AND EIGHT IDEAS. NOW I HAVE EIGHT CHILDREN AND NO IDEAS. I like that because once I had no published novels and roughly two hundred ideas about the art and craft of writing fiction (two hundred and fifty on a good day). Now I have just about fifty published novels to my credit and only one surviving idea about fiction; a writing seminar as taught by yours truly would probably last about fifteen minutes.

One of the ideas I had in those good old days was that it would be perfectly possible to combine the overlord–vampire myth from Bram Stoker's *Dracula* with the naturalistic fiction of Frank Norris and the EC horror comics I'd loved as a child . . . and come out with a great American novel. I was twenty-three, remember, so cut me a break. I had a teaching certificate upon which the ink had hardly dried, I had published eight short stories and I had a perfectly insane amount of confidence in my own ability, not to mention a totally ridiculous sense of my own importance. I also had a wife with a typewriter who liked my stories – and those last two things, which I took for granted then, turned out to be the most important things of all.

Did I really think I could combine *Dracula* and *Tales from the Crypt* and come out with *Moby-Dick*? I did. I really did. I even planned a section at the front called 'Extracta,' where I would include notes, clippings, and epigrams about vampires, as Melville does about whales at the front of his book. Was I daunted by the fact that *Moby-Dick* only sold about twelve copies in Melville's lifetime? Not I; one of my ideas was that a novelist takes the long view, the *lofty* view, and that does not include the price of eggs. (My wife would not have agreed, and I doubt if Mrs Melville would have, either.)

In any case, I liked the idea of my vampire novel serving as a balance for Stoker's, which has to go down in history as the most *optimistic* scary novel of all time. Count Dracula, simultaneously feared and worshipped in his dark little European fiefdom of Transylvania, makes the fatal mistake of taking his act and putting it on the road. In London he meets men and women of *science* and *reason*, by God – Abraham Van Helsing, who knows about blood transfusions; John Seward, who keeps his diary on wax phonograph cylinders; Mina Harker, who keeps hers in shorthand and later serves as secretary to the Fearless Vampire Hunters.

Stoker was clearly fascinated by modern inventions and innovations, and the underlying thesis of his novel is clear: in a confrontation between a foreign child of the Dark Powers and a group of fine, upstanding Britishers equipped with all mod cons, the powers of darkness don't stand a chance. Dracula is hounded from Carfax, his British estate, back to Transylvania, and finally staked at sunset. The vampire-hunters pay a price for their victory – that is

Stoker's genius – but that they will come out on top is never in much doubt.

When I sat down to write my version of the story in 1972 – a version whose life-force was drawn more from the nervously jokey Jewish-American mythos of William Gaines and Al Feldstein than from Romanian folk-tales – I saw a different world, one where all of the gadgets Stoker must have regarded with such hopeful wonder had begun to seem sinister and downright dangerous. Mine was the world that had begun to choke on its own effluent, that had hooked itself through the bag on diminishing energy resources, and had to deal not only with nuclear weapons but nuclear proliferation (big-time terrorism was, thankfully, at that time still over the horizon). I saw myself and my society at the other end of the technological rainbow, and set out to write a book that would reflect that glum idea. One where, in short, the vampire would end up eating the fearless vampire-hunters for lunch. (Which he, as a vampire, would eat at midnight, of course.)

I was about three hundred pages into this book – then titled *Second Coming* – when *Carrie* was published, and my first idea about novel-writing went west. It would be years before I would hear Alfred Bester's axiom 'The book is the boss,' but I didn't need to; I learned it for myself writing the novel that eventually became *'Salem's Lot*. Of course, the writer *can* impose control; it's just a really shitty idea. Writing controlled fiction is called 'plotting.' Buckling your seatbelt and letting the story take over, however . . . that is called 'storytelling.' Storytelling is as natural as breathing; plotting is the literary version of artificial respiration.

Given my dim view of small New England towns (I had grown up in one and knew what they were like), I had no doubt my version of Count Dracula would emerge completely triumphant over the puny representatives of the rational world arrayed against him. What I didn't count on was that my characters weren't content to *remain* puny representatives. Instead they came alive and began to do things — sometimes smart things, sometimes foolishly brave things — on their own. More of Stoker's characters are around at the finish of *Dracula* than at the end of *'Salem's Lot*, and yet this is — against its young author's will — a surprisingly optimistic book. I'm glad. I still see all the nicks and dings on its fenders, all the scars on its hide that were inflicted by the inexperience of a craftsman new at his trade, but I still find many passages of power here. And a few of grace.

Doubleday had published my first novel, and had an option on my second. I had completed this one and another, what I thought of as a 'serious' novel, called *Roadwork*. I showed them both to my then-editor, Bill Thompson. He liked them both. We had a lunch at which nothing was decided, then started to walk back to Doubleday. At the corner of Park Avenue and 54th Street — something like that — we were stopped by a DON'T WALK light. I finally pulled the pin and asked Bill which one he thought we should publish.

He said, '*Roadwork* would probably get more serious attention, but *Second Coming* is *Peyton Place* with vampires. It's a great read and it could be a bestseller. There's only one problem.'

'What's that?' I asked, as DON'T WALK changed to WALK and people started to move around us.

Bill stepped off the curb. In New York you don't waste the WALK, even when decisions of moment are being made, and this – I might have sensed it even then – was one that would affect the rest of my life. 'You'll be typed as a horror writer,' he said.

I was so relieved I laughed. 'I don't care what they call me as long as the checks don't bounce,' I said. 'Let's publish *Second Coming.*' And that was what we did, although the name was first changed to *Jerusalem's Lot* (because my wife, Tabby, said that *Second Coming* sounded like a sex manual) and then to *'Salem's Lot* (because the Doubleday brass said *Jerusalem's Lot* sounded like a religious book). I was indeed typed as a horror writer, a tag I have never confirmed or denied, simply because I think it's irrelevant to what I do. It does, however, give bookstores a handy place to shelve my books.

Since then I have let go of all but one of my ideas about fiction-writing. It's the one I came to first (around age seven, as I recall), and the one I'll probably hold onto until the end: it's good to tell a story, and even better when people actually want to listen. I think *'Salem's Lot*, for all its flaws, is one of the good ones. One of the scary ones. If you've never heard it before, let me tell it to you now. And if you have, let me tell it to you again. So turn off the television – in fact, why don't you turn off all the lights except for the one over your favorite chair? – and we'll talk about vampires here in the dim. I think I can make you believe in them, because while I was working on this book, I believed in them myself.

Center Lovell, Maine
June 15, 2005

AUTHOR'S NOTE

No one writes a long novel alone, and I would like to take a moment of your time to thank some of the people who helped with this one: G. Everett McCutcheon, of Hampden Academy, for his practical suggestions and encouragement; Dr John Pearson, of Old Town, Maine, medical examiner of Penobscot County and member in good standing of that most excellent medical specialty, general practice; Father Renald Hallee, of St John's Catholic Church in Bangor, Maine. And of course my wife, whose criticism is as tough and unflinching as ever.

Although the towns surrounding 'salem's Lot are very real, 'salem's Lot itself exists wholly in the author's imagination, and any resemblance between the people who live there and people who live in the real world is coincidental and unintended.

S.K.

PROLOGUE

Old friend, what are you looking for?
After those many years abroad you come
With images you tended
Under foreign skies
Far away from your own land.

— GEORGE SEFERIS

1

Almost everyone thought the man and the boy were father and son.

They crossed the country on a rambling southwest line in an old Citroën sedan, keeping mostly to secondary roads, traveling in fits and starts. They stopped in three places along the way before reaching their final destination: first in Rhode Island, where the tall man with the black hair worked in a textile mill; then in Youngstown, Ohio, where he worked for three months on a tractor assembly line; and finally in a small California town near the Mexican border, where he pumped gas and worked at repairing small foreign cars with an amount of success that was, to him, surprising and gratifying.

Wherever they stopped, he got a Maine newspaper called the Portland *Press-Herald* and watched it for items concerning a small southern Maine town named Jerusalem's Lot and the surrounding area. There were such items from time to time.

He wrote an outline of a novel in motel rooms before they hit Central Falls, Rhode Island, and mailed it to his agent. He had been a mildly successful novelist a million years before, in a time when the darkness had not come over his life. The agent took the outline to his last publisher, who expressed polite interest but no inclination to part with any advance money. 'Please' and 'thank you,' he told the boy as he tore the agent's letter up, were still free. He said it without too much bitterness and set about the book anyway.

The boy did not speak much. His face retained a perpetual pinched look, and his eyes were dark – as if they always scanned some bleak inner horizon. In the diners and gas stations where they stopped along the way, he was polite and nothing more. He didn't seem to want the tall man out of his sight, and the boy seemed nervous even when the man left him to use the bathroom. He refused to talk about the town of Jerusalem's Lot, although the tall man tried to raise the topic from time to time, and he would not look at the Portland newspapers the man sometimes deliberately left around.

When the book was written, they were living in a beach cottage off the highway, and they both swam in the Pacific a great deal. It was warmer than the Atlantic, and friendlier. It held no memories. The boy began to get very brown.

Although they were living well enough to eat three square meals a day and keep a solid roof over their heads, the man had begun to feel depressed and doubtful about the life they were living. He was tutoring the boy, and he did not seem to be losing anything in the way of education (the boy was bright and easy about books, as the tall man had been himself), but he didn't think that blotting 'salem's Lot out was doing the boy any good. Sometimes at night he screamed in his sleep and thrashed the blankets onto the floor.

A letter came from New York. The tall man's agent said that Random House was offering $12,000 in advance, and a book club sale was almost certain. Was it okay?

It was.

The man quit his job at the gas station, and he and the boy crossed the border.

2

Los Zapatos, which means 'the shoes' (a name that secretly pleased the man to no end), was a small village not far from the ocean. It was fairly free of tourists. There was no good road, no ocean view (you had to go five miles further west to get that), and no historical points of interest. Also, the local cantina was infested with cockroaches and the only whore was a fifty-year-old grandmother.

With the States behind them, an almost unearthly quiet dropped over their lives. Few planes went overhead, there were no turnpikes, and no one owned a power lawn mower (or cared to have one) for a hundred miles. They had a radio, but even that was noise without meaning; the news broadcasts were all in Spanish, which the boy began to pick up but which remained – and always would – gibberish to the man. All the music seemed to consist of opera. At night they sometimes got a pop music station from Monterey made frantic with the accents of Wolfman Jack, but it faded in and out. The only motor within hearing distance was a quaint old Rototiller owned by a local farmer. When the wind was right, its irregular burping noise would come to their ears faintly, like an uneasy spirit. They drew their water from the well by hand.

Once or twice a month (not always together) they attended mass at the small church in town. Neither of them understood the ceremony, but they went all the same. The man found himself sometimes drowsing in the suffocating heat to the steady, familiar rhythms and the voices which gave them tongue. One Sunday the boy came out onto the rickety back porch where the man had begun work on a new novel and told him hesitantly that he had spoken to the priest about being taken into the church. The man nodded and asked him if he had enough Spanish to take instruction. The boy said he didn't think it would be a problem.

The man made a forty-mile trip once a week to get the Portland, Maine, paper, which was always at least a week old and was sometimes yellowed with dog urine. Two weeks after the boy had told him of his intentions, he found a featured story about 'salem's Lot and a Vermont town called Momson. The tall man's name was mentioned in the course of the story.

He left the paper around with no particular hope that the boy would pick it up. The article made him uneasy for a number of reasons. It was not over in 'salem's Lot yet, it seemed.

The boy came to him a day later with the paper in his hand, folded open to expose the headline: 'Ghost Town in Maine?'

'I'm scared,' he said.

'I am, too,' the tall man answered.

3

GHOST TOWN IN MAINE?
By John Lewis
Press-Herald Features Editor

JERUSALEM'S LOT — Jerusalem's Lot is a small town east of Cumberland and twenty miles north of Portland. It is not the first town in American history to just dry up and blow away, and will probably not be the last, but it is one of the strangest. Ghost towns are common in the American Southwest, where communities grew up almost overnight around rich gold and silver lodes and then disappeared almost as rapidly when the veins of ore played out, leaving empty stores and hotels and saloons to rot emptily in desert silence.

In New England the only counterpart to the mysterious emptying of Jerusalem's Lot, or 'salem's Lot as the natives often refer to it, seems to be a small town in Vermont called Momson. During the summer of 1923, Momson apparently just dried up and blew away, and all 312 residents went with it. The houses and few small business buildings in the town's center still stand, but since that summer fifty-two years ago, they have been uninhabited. In some cases the furnishings had been removed, but in most the houses were still furnished, as if in the middle of daily life some great wind had blown all the people away. In one house the table had been set for the evening meal, complete with a centerpiece of long-wilted flowers. In another the covers had been turned down neatly in an upstairs bedroom as if for sleep. In the local mercantile store, a rotted bolt of cotton cloth was found on the counter and a price of $1.22 rung up on the cash register. Investigators found almost $50.00 in the cash drawer, untouched.

People in the area like to entertain tourists with the story and to hint that the town is haunted – that, they say, is why it has remained empty ever since. A more likely reason is that Momson is located in a forgotten corner of the state, far from any main road. There is nothing there that could not be duplicated in a hundred other towns – except, of course, the *Mary Celeste* – like mystery of its sudden emptiness.

Much the same could be said for Jerusalem's Lot.

In the census of 1970, 'salem's Lot claimed 1,319 inhabitants – a gain of exactly 67 souls in the ten years since the previous census. It is a sprawling, comfortable township, familiarly called the Lot by its previous inhabitants, where little of any note ever took place. The only thing the oldsters who regularly gathered in the park and around the stove in Crossen's Agricultural Market had to talk about was the Fire of '51, when a carelessly tossed match started one of the largest forest fires in the state's history.

If a man wanted to spin out his retirement in a small country town where everyone minded his own business and the big event of any given week was apt to be the Ladies' Auxiliary Bake-off, then the Lot would have been a good choice. Demographically, the census of 1970 showed a pattern familiar both to rural sociologists and to the long-time residents of any small Maine town: a lot of old folks, quite a few poor folks, and a lot of young folks who leave the area with their diplomas under their arms, never to return again.

But a little over a year ago, something began to happen in Jerusalem's Lot that was not usual. People began to drop out of sight. The larger proportion of these, naturally, haven't disappeared in the real sense of the word at all. The Lot's former constable, Parkins Gillespie, is living with his sister in Kittery. Charles James, owner of a gas station across from the drugstore, is now running a repair shop in neighboring Cumberland. Pauline Dickens has moved to Los Angeles, and Rhoda Curless is working with the St Matthew's Mission in Portland. The list of 'undisappearances' could go on and on.

What is mystifying about these found people is their unanimous unwillingness – or inability – to talk about Jerusalem's Lot and what, if anything, might have happened there. Parkins Gillespie simply looked at this reporter, lit a cigarette, and said, 'I just decided to leave.' Charles James claims he was forced to leave because his business dried up with the town. Pauline Dickens, who worked as a waitress in the Excellent Café for years, never answered this reporter's letter of inquiry. And Mrs Curless refuses to speak of 'salem's Lot at all.

Some of the missing can be accounted for by educated guesswork and a little research. Lawrence Crockett, a local real estate agent who has disappeared with his wife and daughter, has left a number of questionable business ventures and land deals behind him, including one piece of Portland land speculation where the Portland Mall and Shopping Center is now under construction. The Royce McDougalls, also among the missing, had lost their infant son earlier in the year and there was little to hold them in town. They might be anywhere. Others fit into the same category. According to State Police Chief Peter McFee, 'We've got tracers out on a great many people from Jerusalem's Lot – but that isn't the only Maine town where people have dropped out of sight. Royce McDougall, for instance, left owing money to one bank and two finance companies . . . in my judgment, he was just a fly-by-nighter who decided to get out from under. Someday this year or next, he'll use one of those credit cards he's got in his wallet and the repossession men will land on him with both feet. In America missing persons are as natural as cherry pie. We're living in an automobile-oriented society. People pick up stakes and move on every two or three years. Sometimes they forget to leave a forwarding address. Especially the deadbeats.'

Yet for all the hardheaded practicality of Captain McFee's words, there are unanswered questions in Jerusalem's Lot. Henry Petrie and his wife and son are gone, and Mr Petrie, a Prudential Insurance Company executive, could hardly be called a deadbeat. The local mortician, the local librarian, and the local beautician are also in the dead-letter file. The list is of a disquieting length.

In the surrounding towns the whispering campaign that is the beginning of legend has already begun. 'Salem's Lot is reputed to be haunted. Sometimes colored lights are reported hovering over the Central Maine Power lines that bisect the township, and if you suggest that the inhabitants of the Lot have been carried off by UFOs, no one will laugh. There has been some talk of a 'dark coven' of young people who were practicing the black mass in town and, perhaps, brought the wrath of God Himself on the name-sake of the Holy Land’s holiest city. Others, of a less super-natural bent, remember the young men who ‘disappeared’ in the Houston, Texas, area some three years ago only to be discovered in grisly mass graves.

An actual visit to ’salem’s Lot makes such talk seem less wild. There is not one business left open. The last one to go under was Spencer’s Sundries and Pharmacy, which closed its doors in January. Crossen’s Agricultural Store, the hardware store, Barlow and Straker’s Furniture Shop, the Excellent Café, and even the Municipal Building are all boarded up. The new grammar school is empty, and so is the tri-town consolidated high school, built in the Lot in 1967. The school furnishings and the books have been moved to make-do facilities in Cumberland pending a referendum vote in the other towns of the school district, but it seems that no children from ’salem’s Lot will be in attendance when a new school year begins. There are no children; only abandoned shops and stores, deserted houses, overgrown lawns, deserted streets, and back roads.

Some of the other people that the state police would like to locate or at least hear from include John Groggins, pastor of the Jerusalem’s Lot Methodist Church; Father Donald Callahan, parish priest of St Andrew’s; Mabel Werts, a local widow who was prominent in ’salem’s Lot church and social functions; Lester and Harriet Durham, a local couple who both worked at Gates Mill and Weaving; Eva Miller, who ran a local boardinghouse . . .

4

Two months after the newspaper article, the boy was taken into the church. He made his first confession – and confessed everything.

5

The village priest was an old man with white hair and a face seamed into a net of wrinkles. His eyes peered out of his sun-beaten face with surprising life and avidity. They were blue eyes, very Irish. When the tall man arrived at his house, he was sitting on the porch and drinking tea. A man in a city suit stood beside him. The man's hair was parted in the middle and greased in a manner that reminded the tall man of photograph portraits from the 1890s.

The man said stiffly, 'I am Jesús de la rey Muñoz. Father Gracon has asked me to interpret, as he has no English. Father Gracon has done my family a great service which I may not mention. My lips are likewise sealed in the matter he wishes to discuss. Is it agreeable to you?'

'Yes.' He shook Muñoz's hand and then Gracon's. Gracon replied in Spanish and smiled. He had only five teeth left in his jaw, but the smile was sunny and glad.

'He asks, Would you like a cup of tea? It is green tea. Very cooling.'

'That would be lovely.'

When the amenities had passed among them, the priest said, 'The boy is not your son.'

'No.'

'He made a strange confession. In fact, I have never heard a stranger confession in all my days of the priesthood.'

'That does not surprise me.'

'He wept,' Father Gracon said, sipping his tea. 'It was a deep and terrible weeping. It came from the cellar of his soul. Must I ask the question this confession raises in my heart?'

'No,' the tall man said evenly. 'You don't. He is telling the truth.'

Gracon was nodding even before Muñoz translated, and his face had grown grave. He leaned forward with his hands clasped between his knees and spoke for a long time. Muñoz listened intently, his face carefully expressionless. When the priest finished, Muñoz said:

'He says there are strange things in the world. Forty years ago a peasant from El Graniones brought him a lizard that screamed as though it were a woman. He has seen a man with stigmata, the marks of Our Lord's passion, and this man bled from his hands and feet on Good Friday. He says this is an awful thing, a dark thing. It is serious for you and the boy. Particularly for the boy. It is eating him up. He says . . .'

Gracon spoke again, briefly.

'He asks if you understand what you have done in this New Jerusalem.'

'Jerusalem's Lot,' the tall man said. 'Yes. I understand.'

Gracon spoke again.

'He asks what you intend to do about it.'

The tall man shook his head very slowly. 'I don't know.'

Gracon spoke again.

'He says he will pray for you.'

6

A week later he awoke sweating from a nightmare and called out the boy's name.

'I'm going back,' he said.

The boy paled beneath his tan.

'Can you come with me?' the man asked.

'Do you love me?'

'Yes. God, yes.'

The boy began to weep, and the tall man held him.

7

Still, there was no sleep for him. Faces lurked in the shadows, swirling up at him like faces obscured in snow, and when the wind blew an overhanging tree limb against the roof, he jumped.

Jerusalem's Lot.

He closed his eyes and put his arm across them and it all began to come back. He could almost see the glass paperweight, the kind that will make a tiny blizzard when you shake it.

'Salem's Lot . . .

PART 1

THE MARSTEN HOUSE

No live organism can continue for long to exist sanely under conditions of absolute reality; even larks and katydids are supposed, by some, to dream. Hill House, not sane, stood by itself against its hills, holding darkness within; it had stood for eighty years and might stand for eighty more. Within, walls continued upright, bricks met neatly, floors were firm, and doors were sensibly shut; silence lay steadily against the wood and stone of Hill House, and whatever walked there, walked alone.

– Shirley Jackson, *The Haunting of Hill House*

CHAPTER ONE
BEN (I)

By the time he had passed Portland going north on the turnpike, Ben Mears had begun to feel a not unpleasurable tingle of excitement in his belly. It was September 5, 1975, and summer was enjoying her final grand fling. The trees were bursting with green, the sky was a high, soft blue, and just over the Falmouth town line he saw two boys walking a road parallel to the expressway with fishing rods settled on their shoulders like carbines.

He switched to the travel lane, slowed to the minimum turnpike speed, and began to look for anything that would jog his memory. There was nothing at first, and he tried to caution himself against almost sure disappointment. *You were nine then. That's twenty-five years of water under the bridge. Places change. Like people.*

In those days the four-lane 295 hadn't existed. If you wanted to go to Portland from the Lot, you went out Route 12 to Falmouth and then got on Number 1. Time had marched on.

Stop that shit.

But it was hard to stop. It was hard to stop when —

A big BSA cycle with jacked handlebars suddenly roared past him in the passing lane, a kid in a T-shirt driving, a girl in a red cloth jacket and huge mirror-lensed sunglasses riding pillion behind him. They cut in a little too quickly and he overreacted, jamming on his brakes and laying both hands on the horn. The BSA sped up, belching blue smoke from its exhaust, and the girl jabbed her middle finger back at him.

He resumed speed, wishing for a cigarette. His hands were trembling slightly. The BSA was almost out of sight now, moving fast. The kids. The goddamned kids. Memories tried to crowd in on him, memories of a more recent vintage. He pushed them away. He hadn't been on a motorcycle in two years. He planned never to ride on one again.

A flash of red caught his eye off to the left, and when he glanced that way, he felt a burst of pleasure and recognition. A large red barn stood on a hill far across a rising field of timothy and clover, a barn with a cupola painted white – even at this distance he could see the sun gleam on the weather vane atop that cupola. It had been there then and was still here now. It looked exactly the same. Maybe it was going to be all right after all. Then the trees blotted it out.

As the turnpike entered Cumberland, more and more things began to seem familiar. He passed over the Royal River, where they had fished for steelies and pickerel as boys. Past a brief, flickering view of Cumberland Village through the trees. In the distance the Cumberland water tower with its huge slogan painted across the side: 'Keep Maine Green.' Aunt Cindy had always said someone should print 'Bring Money' underneath that.

His original sense of excitement grew and he began

to speed up, watching for the sign. It came twinkling up out of the distance in reflectorized green five miles later:

ROUTE 12 JERUSALEM'S LOT
CUMBERLAND CUMBERLAND CTR

A sudden blackness came over him, dousing his good spirits like sand on fire. He had been subject to these since (his mind tried to speak Miranda's name and he would not let it) the bad time and was used to fending them off, but this one swept over him with a savage power that was dismaying.

What was he doing, coming back to a town where he had lived for four years as a boy, trying to recapture something that was irrevocably lost? What magic could he expect to recapture by walking roads that he had once walked as a boy and were probably asphalted and straightened and logged off and littered with tourist beer cans? The magic was gone, both white and black. It had all gone down the chutes on that night when the motorcycle had gone out of control and then there was the yellow moving van, growing and growing, his wife Miranda's scream, cut off with sudden finality when—

The exit came up on his right, and for a moment he considered driving right past it, continuing on to Chamberlain or Lewiston, stopping for lunch, and then turning around and going back. But back where? Home? That was a laugh. If there was a home, it had been here. Even if it had only been four years, it was his.

He signaled, slowed the Citroën, and went up the ramp. Toward the top, where the turnpike ramp joined Route 12 (which became Jointner Avenue closer to town),

21

he glanced up toward the horizon. What he saw there made him jam the brakes on with both feet. The Citroën shuddered to a stop and stalled.

The trees, mostly pine and spruce, rose in gentle slopes toward the east, seeming to almost crowd against the sky at the limit of vision. From here the town was not visible. Only the trees, and in the distance, where those trees rose against the sky, the peaked, gabled roof of the Marsten House.

He gazed at it, fascinated. Warring emotions crossed his face with kaleidoscopic swiftness.

'Still here,' he murmured aloud. 'By God.'

He looked down at his arms. They had broken out in goose flesh.

2

He deliberately skirted town, crossing into Cumberland and then coming back into 'salem's Lot from the west, taking the Burns Road. He was amazed by how little things had changed out here. There were a few new houses he didn't remember, there was a tavern called Dell's just over the town line, and a pair of fresh gravel quarries. A good deal of the hardwood had been pulped over. But the old tin sign pointing the way to the town dump was still there, and the road itself was still unpaved, full of chuckholes and washboards, and he could see Schoolyard Hill through the slash in the trees where the Central Maine Power pylons ran on a northwest to southeast line. The Griffen farm was still there, although the barn had been enlarged. He wondered if they still bottled and sold their own milk. The logo had been a smiling cow under the name brand: 'Sunshine Milk from the Griffen Farms!' He smiled. He had splashed a lot of that milk on his corn flakes at Aunt Cindy's house.

He turned left onto the Brooks Road, passed the wrought-iron gates and the low fieldstone wall surrounding Harmony Hill Cemetery, and then went down the steep grade and started up the far side – the side known as Marsten's Hill.

At the top, the trees fell away on both sides of the road. On the right, you could look right down into the town proper – Ben's first view of it. On the left, the Marsten House. He pulled over and got out of the car.

It was just the same. There was no difference, not at all. He might have last seen it yesterday.

The witch grass grew wild and tall in the front yard, obscuring the old, frost-heaved flagstones that led to the porch. Chirring crickets sang in it, and he could see grasshoppers jumping in erratic parabolas.

The house itself looked toward town. It was huge and rambling and sagging, its windows haphazardly boarded shut, giving it that sinister look of all old houses that have been empty for a long time. The paint had been weathered away, giving the house a uniform gray look. Windstorms had ripped many of the shingles off, and a heavy snowfall had punched in the west corner of the main roof, giving it a slumped, hunched look. A tattered no-trespassing sign was nailed to the righthand newel post.

He felt a strong urge to walk up that overgrown path, past the crickets and hoppers that would jump around his shoes, climb the porch, peek between the haphazard boards into the hallway or the front room. Perhaps try the front door. If it was unlocked, go in.

He swallowed and stared up at the house, almost hypnotized. It stared back at him with idiot indifference.

You walked down the hall, smelling wet plaster and rotting wallpaper, and mice would skitter in the walls. There would still be a lot of junk lying around, and you might pick something up, a paperweight maybe, and put it in your pocket. Then, at the end of the hall, instead of going through into the kitchen, you could turn left and go up the stairs, your feet gritting in the plaster dust which had sifted down from the ceiling over the years. There were fourteen steps, exactly fourteen. But the top one was smaller, out of proportion, as if it had been added to avoid the evil number. At the top of the stairs you stand on the landing, looking down the hall toward a closed door. And if you walk down the hall toward it, watching as if from outside yourself as the door gets closer and larger, you can reach out your hand and put it on the tarnished silver knob—

He turned away from the house, a straw-dry whistle of air slipping from his mouth. Not yet. Later, perhaps, but not yet. For now it was enough to know that all of that was still here. It had waited for him. He put his hands on the hood of his car and looked out over the town. He could find out down there who was handling the Marsten House, and perhaps lease it. The kitchen would make an adequate writing room and he could bunk down in the front parlor. But he wouldn't allow himself to go upstairs.

Not unless it had to be done.

He got in his car, started it, and drove down the hill to Jerusalem's Lot.

CHAPTER TWO
SUSAN (I)

He was sitting on a bench in the park when he observed the girl watching him. She was a very pretty girl, and there was a silk scarf tied over her light blond hair. She was currently reading a book, but there was a sketch pad and what looked like a charcoal pencil beside her. It was Tuesday, September 16, the first day of school, and the park had magically emptied of the rowdier element. What was left was a scattering of mothers with infants, a few old men sitting by the war memorial, and this girl sitting in the dappled shade of a gnarled old elm.

She looked up and saw him. An expression of startlement crossed her face. She looked down at her book; looked up at him again and started to rise; almost thought better of it; did rise; sat down again.

He got up and walked over, holding his own book, which was a paperback Western. 'Hello,' he said agreeably. 'Do we know each other?'

'No,' she said. 'That is . . . you're Benjaman Mears, right?'

'Right.' He raised his eyebrows.

She laughed nervously, not looking in his eyes except in a quick flash, to try to read the barometer of his intentions. She was quite obviously a girl not accustomed to speaking to strange men in the park.

'I thought I was seeing a ghost.' She held up the book in her lap. He saw fleetingly that 'Jerusalem's Lot Public Library' was stamped on the thickness of pages between covers. The book was *Air Dance*, his second novel. She showed him the photograph of himself on the back jacket, a photo that was four years old now. The face looked boyish and frighteningly serious – the eyes were black diamonds.

'Of such inconsequential beginnings dynasties are begun,' he said, and although it was a joking throwaway remark, it hung oddly in the air, like prophecy spoken in jest. Behind them, a number of toddlers were splashing happily in the wading pool and a mother was telling Roddy not to push his sister so *high*. The sister went soaring up on her swing regardless, dress flying, trying for the sky. It was a moment he remembered for years after, as though a special small slice had been cut from the cake of time. If nothing fires between two people, such an instant simply falls back into the general wrack of memory.

Then she laughed and offered him the book. 'Will you autograph it?'

'A library book?'

'I'll buy it from them and replace it.'

He found a mechanical pencil in his sweater pocket, opened the book to the flyleaf, and asked, 'What's your name?'

'Susan Norton.'

He wrote quickly, without thinking: *For Susan Norton,*

the prettiest girl in the park. Warm regards, Ben Mears. He added the date below his signature in slashed notation.

'Now you'll have to steal it,' he said, handing it back. '*Air Dance* is out of print, alas.'

'I'll get a copy from one of those book finders in New York.' She hesitated, and this time her glance at his eyes was a little longer. 'It's an awfully good book.'

'Thanks. When I take it down and look at it, I wonder how it ever got published.'

'Do you take it down often?'

'Yeah, but I'm trying to quit.'

She grinned at him and they both laughed and that made things more natural. Later he would have a chance to think how easily this had happened, how smoothly. The thought was never a comfortable one. It conjured up an image of fate, not blind at all but equipped with sentient 20/20 vision and intent on grinding helpless mortals between the great millstones of the universe to make some unknown bread.

'I read *Conway's Daughter*, too. I loved that. I suppose you hear that all the time.'

'Remarkably little,' he said honestly. Miranda had also loved *Conway's Daughter*, but most of his coffeehouse friends had been noncommittal and most of the critics had clobbered it. Well, that was critics for you. Plot was out, masturbation in.

'Well, I did.'

'Have you read the new one?'

'*Billy Said Keep Going*? Not yet. Miss Coogan at the drugstore says it's pretty racy.'

'Hell, it's almost puritanical,' Ben said. 'The language

is rough, but when you're writing about uneducated country boys, you can't . . . look, can I buy you an ice-cream soda or something? I was just getting a hanker on for one.'

She checked his eyes a third time. Then smiled, warmly. 'Sure. I'd love one. They're great in Spencer's.'

That was the beginning of it.

2

'Is that Miss Coogan?'

Ben asked it, low-voiced. He was looking at a tall, spare woman who was wearing a red nylon duster over her white uniform. Her blue-rinsed hair was done in a steplike succession of finger waves.

'That's her. She's got a little cart she takes to the library every Thursday night. She fills out reserve cards by the ton and drives Miss Starcher crazy.'

They were seated on red leather stools at the soda fountain. He was drinking a chocolate soda; hers was strawberry. Spencer's also served as the local bus depot and from where they sat they could look through an old-fashioned scrolled arch and into the waiting room, where a solitary young man in Air Force blues sat glumly with his feet planted around his suitcase.

'Doesn't look happy to be going wherever he's going, does he?' she said, following his glance.

'Leave's over, I imagine,' Ben said. Now, he thought, she'll ask if I've ever been in the service.

But instead: 'I'll be on that ten-thirty bus one of these days. Good-by, 'salem's Lot. Probably I'll be looking just as glum as that boy.'

'Where?'

'New York, I guess. To see if I can't finally become self-supporting.'

'What's wrong with right here?'

'The Lot? I love it. But my folks, you know. They'd always be sort of looking over my shoulder. That's a bummer. And the Lot doesn't really have that much to offer the young career girl.' She shrugged and dipped her head to suck at her straw. Her neck was tanned, beautifully muscled. She was wearing a colorful print shift that hinted at a good figure.

'What kind of job are you looking for?'

She shrugged. 'I've got a B.A. from Boston University . . . not worth the paper it's printed on, really. Art major, English minor. The original dipso duo. Strictly eligible for the educated idiot category. I'm not even trained to decorate an office. Some of the girls I went to high school with are holding down plump secretarial jobs now. I never got beyond Personal Typing I, myself.'

'So what does that leave?'

'Oh . . . maybe a publishing house,' she said vaguely. 'Or some magazine . . . advertising, maybe. Places like that can always use someone who can draw on command. I can do that. I have a portfolio.'

'Do you have offers?' he asked gently.

'No . . . no. But . . .'

'You don't go to New York without offers,' he said. 'Believe me. You'll wear out the heels on your shoes.'

She smiled uneasily. 'I guess you should know.'

'Have you sold stuff locally?'

'Oh yes.' She laughed abruptly. 'My biggest sale to date was to the Cinex Corporation. They opened a new triple cinema in Portland and bought twelve paintings at a crack to hang in their lobby. Paid seven hundred dollars. I made a down payment on my little car.'

'You ought to take a hotel room for a week or so in New York,' he said, 'and hit every magazine and publishing house you can find with your portfolio. Make your appointments six months in advance so the editors and personnel guys don't have anything on their calendars. But for God's sake, don't just haul stakes for the big city.'

'What about you?' she asked, leaving off the straw and spooning ice cream. 'What are you doing in the thriving community of Jerusalem's Lot, Maine, population thirteen hundred?'

He shrugged. 'Trying to write a novel.'

She was instantly alight with excitement. 'In the Lot? What's it about? Why here? Are you—'

He looked at her gravely. 'You're dripping.'

'I'm—? Oh, I am. Sorry.' She mopped the base of her glass with a napkin. 'Say, I didn't mean to pry. I'm really not gushy as a rule.'

'No apology needed,' he said. 'All writers like to talk about their books. Sometimes when I'm lying in bed at night I make up a *Playboy* interview about me. Waste of time. They only do authors if their books are big on campus.'

The Air Force youngster stood up. A Greyhound was pulling up to the curb out front, air brakes chuffing.

'I lived in 'salem's Lot for four years as a kid. Out on the Burns Road.'

'The Burns Road? There's nothing out there now but the Marshes and a little graveyard. Harmony Hill, they call it.'

'I lived with my Aunt Cindy. Cynthia Stowens. My dad died, see, and my mom went through a . . . well, kind of a nervous breakdown. So she farmed me out to Aunt Cindy while she got her act back together. Aunt Cindy put me on a bus back to Long Island and my mom just about a month after the big fire.' He looked at his face in the mirror behind the soda fountain. 'I cried on the bus going away from Mom, and I cried on the bus going away from Aunt Cindy and Jerusalem's Lot.'

'I was born the year of the fire,' Susan said. 'The biggest damn thing that ever happened to this town and I slept through it.'

Ben laughed. 'That makes you about seven years older than I thought in the park.'

'Really?' She looked pleased. 'Thank you . . . I think. Your aunt's house must have burned down.'

'Yes,' he said. 'That night is one of my clearest memories. Some men with Indian pumps on their backs came to the door and said we'd have to leave. It was very exciting. Aunt Cindy dithered around, picking things up and loading them into her Hudson. Christ, what a night.'

'Was she insured?'

'No, but the house was rented and we got just about everything valuable into the car, except for the TV. We tried to lift it and couldn't even budge it off the floor. It was a Video King with a seven-inch screen and a magnifying glass over the picture tube. Hell on the eyes. We only got one channel anyway — lots of country music, farm reports, and Kitty the Klown.'

'And you came back here to write a book,' she marveled.

Ben didn't reply at once. Miss Coogan was opening cartons of cigarettes and filling the display rack by the cash register. The pharmacist, Mr Labree, was puttering around behind the high drug counter like a frosty ghost. The Air Force kid was standing by the door to the bus, waiting for the driver to come back from the bathroom.

'Yes,' Ben said. He turned and looked at her, full in the face, for the first time. She had a very pretty face, with candid blue eyes and a high, clear, tanned forehead. 'Is this town your childhood?' he asked.

'Yes.'

He nodded. 'Then you know. I was a kid in 'salem's Lot and it's haunted for me. When I came back, I almost drove right by because I was afraid it would be different.'

'Things don't change here,' she said. 'Not very much.'

'I used to play war with the Gardener kids down in the Marshes. Pirates out by Royal's Pond. Capture-the-flag and hide-and-go-seek in the park. My mom and I knocked around some pretty hard places after I left Aunt Cindy. She killed herself when I was fourteen, but most of the magic dust had rubbed off me long before that. What there was of it was here. And it's still here. The town hasn't changed that much. Looking out on Jointner Avenue is like looking through a thin pane of ice — like the one you can pick off the top of the town cistern in November if you knock it around the edges first — looking through that at your childhood. It's wavy and misty and in some places it trails off into nothing, but most of it is still all there.'

He stopped, amazed. He had made a speech.

'You talk just like your books,' she said, awed.

He laughed. 'I never said anything like that before. Not out loud.'

'What did you do after your mother . . . after she died?'

'Knocked around,' he said briefly. 'Eat your ice cream.' She did.

'Some things have changed,' she said after a while. 'Mr Spencer died. Do you remember him?'

'Sure. Every Thursday night Aunt Cindy came into town to do her shopping at Crossen's store and she'd send me in here to have a root beer. That was when it was on draft, real Rochester root beer. She'd give me a handkerchief with a nickel wrapped up in it.'

'They were a dime when I came along. Do you remember what he always used to say?'

Ben hunched forward, twisted one hand into an arthritic claw, and turned one corner of his mouth down in a paralytic twist. 'Your bladder,' he whispered. 'Those rut beers will destroy your bladder, bucko.'

Her laughter pealed upward toward the slowly rotating fan over their heads. Miss Coogan looked up suspiciously. 'That's *perfect!* Except he used to call me lassie.'

They looked at each other, delighted.

'Say, would you like to go to a movie tonight?' he asked.

'I'd love to.'

'What's closest?'

She giggled. 'The Cinex in Portland, actually. Where the lobby is decorated with the deathless paintings of Susan Norton.'

'Where else? What kind of movies do you like?'

'Something exciting with a car chase in it.'

'Okay. Do you remember the Nordica? That was right here in town.'

'Sure. It closed in 1968. I used to go on double dates there when I was in high school. We threw popcorn boxes at the screen when the movies were bad.' She giggled. 'They usually were.'

'They used to have those old Republic serials,' he said. '*Rocket Man. The Return of Rocket Man. Crash Callaban and the Voodoo Death God.*'

'That was before my time.'

'Whatever happened to it?'

'That's Larry Crockett's real estate office now,' she said. 'The drive-in over in Cumberland killed it, I guess. That and TV.'

They were silent for a moment, thinking their own thoughts. The Greyhound clock showed 10:45 AM.

They said in chorus: 'Say, do you remember—'

They looked at each other, and this time Miss Coogan looked up at both of them when the laughter rang out. Even Mr Labree looked over.

They talked for another fifteen minutes, until Susan told him reluctantly that she had errands to run but yes, she could be ready at seven-thirty. When they went different ways, they both marveled over the easy, natural, coincidental impingement of their lives.

Ben strolled back down Jointner Avenue, pausing at the corner of Brock Street to look casually up at the Marsten House. He remembered that the great forest fire of 1951 had burned almost to its very yard before the wind had changed.

He thought: Maybe it should have burned. Maybe that would have been better.

3

Nolly Gardener came out of the Municipal Building and sat down on the steps next to Parkins Gillespie just in time to see Ben and Susan walk into Spencer's together. Parkins was smoking a Pall Mall and cleaning his yellowed finger-nails with a pocketknife.

'That's that writer fella, ain't it?' Nolly asked.

'Yep.'

'Was that Susie Norton with him?'

'Yep.'

'Well, that's interesting,' Nolly said, and hitched his garrison belt. His deputy star glittered importantly on his chest. He had sent away to a detective magazine to get it; the town did not provide its deputy constables with badges. Parkins had one, but he carried it in his wallet, something Nolly had never been able to understand. Of course every-body in the Lot knew he was the constable, but there was such a thing as tradition. There was such a thing as respon-sibility. When you were an officer of the law, you had to think about both. Nolly thought about them both often, although he could only afford to deputy part-time.

Parkins's knife slipped and slit the cuticle of his thumb. 'Shit,' he said mildly.

'You think he's a real writer, Park?'

'Sure he is. He's got three books right in this library.'

'True or made up?'

'Made up.' Parkins put his knife away and sighed.

'Floyd Tibbits ain't going to like some guy makin' time with his woman.'

'They ain't married,' Parkins said. 'And she's over eighteen.'

'Floyd ain't going to like it.'

'Floyd can crap in his hat and wear it backward for all of me,' Parkins said. He crushed his smoke on the step, took a Sucrets box out of his pocket, put the dead butt inside, and put the box back in his pocket.

'Where's that writer fella livin'?'

'Down to Eva's,' Parkins said. He examined his wounded cuticle closely. 'He was up lookin' at the Marsten House the other day. Funny expression on his face.'

'Funny? What do you mean?'

'Funny, that's all.' Parkins took his cigarettes out. The sun felt warm and good on his face. 'Then he went to see Larry Crockett. Wanted to lease the place.'

'The *Marsten* place?'

'Yep.'

'What is he, crazy?'

'Could be.' Parkins brushed a fly from the left knee of his pants and watched it buzz away into the bright morning. 'Ole Larry Crockett's been a busy one lately. I hear he's gone and sold the Village Washtub. Sold it a while back, as a matter of fact.'

'What, that old laundrymat?'

'Yep.'

'What would anyone want to put in there?'

'Dunno.'

'Well.' Nolly stood up and gave his belt another hitch. 'Think I'll take a turn around town.'

'You do that,' Parkins said, and lit another cigarette. 'Want to come?'

'No, I believe I'll sit right here for a while.'

'Okay. See you.'

Nolly went down the steps, wondering (not for the first time) when Parkins would decide to retire so that he, Nolly, could have the job full-time. How in God's name could you ferret out crime sitting on the Municipal Building steps?

Parkins watched him go with a mild feeling of relief. Nolly was a good boy, but he was awfully eager. He took out his pocketknife, opened it, and began paring his nails again.

4

Jerusalem's Lot was incorporated in 1765 (two hundred years later it had celebrated its bicentennial with fireworks and a pageant in the park; little Debbie Forester's Indian princess costume was set on fire by a thrown sparkler and Parkins Gillespie had to throw six fellows in the local cooler for public intoxication), a full fifty-five years before Maine became a state as the result of the Missouri Compromise.

The town took its peculiar name from a fairly prosaic occurrence. One of the area's earliest residents was a dour, gangling farmer named Charles Belknap Tanner. He kept pigs, and one of the large sows was named Jerusalem. Jerusalem broke out of her pen one day at feeding time, escaped into the nearby woods, and went wild and mean. Tanner warned small children off his property for years afterward by leaning over his gate and croaking at them in ominous, gore-crow tones: 'Keep 'ee out o' Jerusalem's wood lot, if 'ee want to keep 'ee guts in 'ee belly!' The warning took hold, and so did the name. It proves little, except that perhaps in America even a pig can aspire to immortality.

The main street, known originally as the Portland Post Road, had been named after Elias Jointner in 1896. Jointner, a member of the House of Representatives for six years (up until his death, which was caused by syphilis, at the age of fifty-eight), was the closest thing to a personage that the Lot could boast – with the exception of Jerusalem the pig and Pearl Ann Butts, who ran off to New York City in 1907 to become a Ziegfeld girl.

Brock Street crossed Jointner Avenue dead center and at right angles, and the township itself was nearly circular (although a little flat on the east, where the boundary was the meandering Royal River). On a map, the two main roads gave the town an appearance very much like a telescopic sight.

The northwest quadrant of the sight was north Jerusalem, the most heavily wooded section of town. It was the high ground, although it would not have appeared very high to anyone except perhaps a Midwesterner. The tired old hills, which were honeycombed with old logging roads, sloped down gently toward the town itself, and the Marsten House stood on the last of these.

Much of the northeast quadrant was open land – hay, timothy, and alfalfa. The Royal River ran here, an old river that had cut its banks almost to the base level. It flowed under the small wooden Brock Street Bridge and wandered north in flat, shining arcs until it entered the land near the northern limits of the town, where solid granite lay close under the thin soil. Here it had cut fifty-foot stone cliffs over the course of a million years. The kids called it Drunk's Leap, because a few years back Tommy Rathbun, Virge Rathbun's tosspot brother, staggered over the edge while looking for a place to take a leak. The Royal fed the mill-polluted Androscoggin but had never been polluted itself; the only industry the Lot had ever boasted was a sawmill, long since closed. In the summer months, fishermen casting from the Brock Street Bridge were a common sight. A day when you couldn't take your limit out of the Royal was a rare day.

The southeast quadrant was the prettiest. The land rose again, but there was no ugly blight of fire or any of the topsoil ruin that is a fire's legacy. The land on both sides of the Griffen Road was owned by Charles Griffen, who was the biggest dairy farmer south of Mechanic Falls, and from Schoolyard Hill you could see Griffen's huge barn with its aluminum roof glittering in the sun like a monstrous heliograph. There were other farms in the area, and a good many houses that had been bought by the white-collar workers who commuted to either Portland or Lewiston. Sometimes, in autumn, you could stand on top of Schoolyard Hill and smell the fragrant odor of the field burnings and see the toylike 'salem's Lot Volunteer Fire Department truck, waiting to step in if anything got out of hand. The lesson of 1951 had remained with these people.

It was in the southwest area that the trailers had begun to move in, and everything that goes with them, like an exurban asteroid belt: junked-out cars up on blocks, tire swings hanging on frayed rope, glittering beer cans lying beside the roads, ragged wash hung on lines between makeshift poles, the ripe smell of sewage from hastily laid septic tanks. The houses in the Bend were kissing cousins to woodsheds, but a gleaming TV aerial sprouted from nearly every one, and most of the TVs inside were color, bought on credit from Grant's or Sears. The yards of the shacks and trailers were usually full of kids, toys, pickup trucks, snowmobiles, and motorbikes. In some cases the trailers were well kept, but in most cases it seemed to be too much trouble. Dandelions and witch grass grew ankle-deep. Out near the town line, where Brock Street became Brock Road, there was Dell's, where a rock 'n' roll band played on Fridays and a c/w combo played on Saturdays. It had burned down once in 1971 and was rebuilt. For most of the downhome cowboys and their girlfriends, it was the place to go and have a beer or a fight.

Most of the telephone lines were two-, four-, or six-party connections, and so folks always had someone to talk about. In all small towns, scandal is always simmering on the back burner, like your Aunt Cindy's baked beans. The Bend produced most of the scandal, but every now and then someone with a little more status added something to the communal pot.

Town government was by town meeting, and while there had been talk ever since 1965 of changing to the town council form with biannual public budget hearings, the idea gained no way. The town was not growing fast enough to make the old way actively painful, although its stodgy, one-for-one democracy made some of the newcomers roll their eyes in exasperation. There were three selectmen, the town constable, an overseer of the poor, a town clerk (to register your car you had to go far out on the Taggart Stream Road and brave two mean dogs who ran loose in the yard), and the school commissioner. The volunteer Fire Department got a token appropriation of three hundred dollars each year, but it was mostly a social club for old fellows on pensions. They saw a fair amount of excitement during grass fire season and sat around the Reliable tall-taling each other the rest of the year. There was no Public Works Department because there were no public water lines, gas mains, sewage, or light-and-power. The CMP electricity pylons marched across town on a diagonal from northwest to southeast, cutting a huge gash through the timberland 150 feet wide. One of these stood close to the Marsten House, looming over it like an alien sentinel.

What 'salem's Lot knew of wars and burnings and crises in government it got mostly from Walter Cronkite on TV. Oh, the Potter boy got killed in Vietnam and Claude Bowie's son came back with a mechanical foot — stepped on a land mine — but he got a job with the post office helping Kenny Danles and so *that* was all right. The kids were wearing their hair longer and not combing it neatly like their fathers, but nobody really noticed anymore. When they threw the dress code out at the Consolidated High School, Aggie Corliss wrote a letter to the Cumberland *Ledger*, but Aggie had been writing to the *Ledger* every week for years, mostly about the evils of liquor and the wonder of accepting Jesus Christ into your heart as your personal savior.

Some of the kids took dope. Horace Kilby's boy Frank went up before Judge Hooker in August and got fined fifty dollars (the judge agreed to let him pay the fine with profits from his paper route), but alcohol was a bigger problem. Lots of kids hung out at Dell's since the liquor age went down to eighteen. They went rip-assing home as if they wanted to resurface the road with rubber, and every now and then someone would get killed. Like when Billy Smith ran into a tree on the Deep Cut Road at ninety and killed both himself and his girlfriend, LaVerne Dube.

But except for these things, the Lot's knowledge of the country's torment was academic. Time went on a different schedule there. Nothing too nasty could happen in such a nice little town. Not there.

5

Ann Norton was ironing when her daughter burst in with a bag of groceries, thrust a book with a rather thin-faced young man on the back jacket in her face, and began to babble.

'Slow down,' she said. 'Turn down the TV and tell me.'

Susan choked off Peter Marshall, who was giving away thousands of dollars on 'The Hollywood Squares,' and told her mother about meeting Ben Mears. Mrs Norton made herself nod with calm and sympathetic understanding as the story spilled out, despite the yellow warning lights that always flashed when Susan mentioned a new boy – men now, she supposed, although it was hard to think Susie could be old enough for men. But the lights were a little brighter today.

'Sounds exciting,' she said, and put another one of her husband's shirts on the ironing board.

'He was really nice,' Susan said. 'Very natural.'

'Hoo, my feet,' Mrs Norton said. She set the iron on its fanny, making it hiss balefully, and eased into the Boston rocker by the picture window. She reached a Parliament out of the pack on the coffee table and lit it. 'Are you sure he's all right, Susie?'

Susan smiled a little defensively. 'Sure, I'm sure. He looks like . . . oh, I don't know — a college instructor or something.'

'They say the Mad Bomber looked like a gardener,' Mrs Norton said reflectively.

'Moose shit,' Susan said cheerfully. It was an epithet that never failed to irritate her mother.

'Let me see the book.' She held a hand out for it.

Susan gave it to her, suddenly remembering the homo-sexual rape scene in the prison section.

'*Air Dance*,' Ann Norton said meditatively, and began to thumb pages at random. Susan waited, resigned. Her mother would bird-dog it. She always did.

The windows were up, and a lazy forenoon breeze ruffled the yellow curtains in the kitchen — which Mom insisted on calling the pantry, as if they lived in the lap of class. It was a nice house, solid brick, a little hard to heat in the winter but cool as a grotto in the summer. They were on a gentle rise of land on outer Brock Street, and from the picture window where Mrs Norton sat you could see all the way into town. The view was a pleasant one, and in the winter it could be spectacular with long, twink-ling vistas of unbroken snow and distance-dwindled buildings casting yellow oblongs of light on the snow fields.

'Seems I read a review of this in the Portland paper. It wasn't very good.'

'I like it,' Susan said steadily. 'And I like him.'

'Perhaps Floyd would like him, too,' Mrs Norton said idly. 'You ought to introduce them.'

Susan felt a real stab of anger and was dismayed by it. She thought that she and her mother had weathered the last of the adolescent storms and even the aftersqualls, but here it all was. They took up the ancient arguments of her identity versus her mother's experience and beliefs like an old piece of knitting.

'We've talked about Floyd, Mom. You know there's nothing firm there.'

'The paper said there were some pretty lurid prison scenes, too. Boys getting together with boys.'

'Oh, Mother, for Christ's sake.' She helped herself to one of her mother's cigarettes.

'No need to curse,' Mrs Norton said, unperturbed. She handed the book back and tapped the long ash on her cigarette into a ceramic ashtray in the shape of a fish. It had been given to her by one of her Ladies' Auxiliary friends, and it had always irritated Susan in a formless sort of way. There was something obscene about tapping your ashes into a perch's mouth.

'I'll put the groceries away,' Susan said, getting up.

Mrs Norton said quietly, 'I only meant that if you and Floyd Tibbits are going to be married—'

The irritation boiled over into the old, goaded anger. 'What in the name of *God* ever gave you that idea? Have I ever told you that?'

'I assumed—'

'You assumed wrong,' she said hotly and not entirely truthfully. But she had been cooling toward Floyd by slow degrees over a period of weeks.

'I assumed that when you date the same boy for a year and a half,' her mother continued softly and implacably, 'that it must mean things have gone beyond the hand-holding stage.'

'Floyd and I are more than friends,' Susan agreed evenly. Let her make something of *that*.

An unspoken conversation hung suspended between them.

Have you been sleeping with Floyd?
None of your business.
What does this Ben Mears mean to you?
None of your business.
Are you going to fall for him and do something foolish?
None of your business.
I love you, Susie. Your dad and I both love you.

And to that no answer. And no answer. And no answer. And that was why New York – or someplace – was imperative. In the end you always crashed against the unspoken barricades of their love, like the walls of a padded cell. The truth of their love rendered further meaningful discussion impossible and made what had gone before empty of meaning.

'Well,' Mrs Norton said softly. She stubbed her cigarette out on the perch's lip and dropped it into his belly.

'I'm going upstairs,' Susan said.

'Sure. Can I read the book when you're finished?'

'If you want to.'

'I'd like to meet him,' she said.

Susan spread her hands and shrugged.

'Will you be late tonight?'

'I don't know.'

'What shall I tell Floyd Tibbits if he calls?'

The anger flashed over her again. 'Tell him what you want.' She paused. 'You will anyway.'

'Susan!'

She went upstairs without looking back.

Mrs Norton remained where she was, staring out the window and at the town without seeing it. Overhead she could hear Susan's footsteps and then the clatter of her easel being pulled out.

She got up and began to iron again. When she thought Susan might be fully immersed in her work (although she didn't allow that idea to do more than flitter through a corner of her conscious mind), she went to the telephone in the pantry and called up Mabel Werts. In the course of the conversation she happened to mention that Susie had told her there was a famous author in their midst and Mabel sniffed and said well you must mean that man who wrote *Conway's Daughter* and Mrs Norton said yes and Mabel said that wasn't writing but just a sex book, pure and simple. Mrs Norton asked if he was staying at a motel or—

As a matter of fact, he was staying downtown at Eva's Rooms, the town's only boardinghouse. Mrs Norton felt a surge of relief. Eva Miller was a decent widow who would put up with no hanky-panky. Her rules on women in the rooms were brief and to the point. If she's your mother or your sister, all right. If she's not, you can sit in the kitchen. No negotiation on the rule was entertained.

Mrs Norton hung up fifteen minutes later, after artfully camouflaging her main objective with small talk.

Susan, she thought, going back to the ironing board. Oh, Susan, I only want what's best for you. Can't you see that?

6

They were driving back from Portland along 295, and it was not late at all — only a little after eleven. The speed limit on the expressway after it got out of Portland's suburbs was fifty-five, and he drove well. The Citroën's headlights cut the dark smoothly.

They had both enjoyed the movie, but cautiously, the way people do when they are feeling for each other's boundaries. Now her mother's question occurred to her and she said, 'Where are you staying? Are you renting a place?'

'I've got a third-floor cubbyhole at Eva's Rooms, on Railroad Street.'

'But that's awful! It must be a hundred degrees up there!'

'I like the heat,' he said. 'I work well in it. Strip to the waist, turn up the radio, and drink a gallon of beer. I've been putting out ten pages a day, fresh copy. There's some interesting old codgers there, too. And when you finally go out on the porch and catch the breeze . . . heaven.'

'Still,' she said doubtfully.

'I thought about renting the Marsten House,' he said casually. 'Even went so far as to inquire about it. But it's been sold.'

'The *Marsten* House?' She smiled. 'You're thinking of the wrong place.'

'Nope. Sits up on that first hill to the northwest of town. Brooks Road.'

'Sold? Who in the name of heaven—?'

'I wondered the same thing. I've been accused of having a screw loose from time to time, but even I only thought of renting it. The real estate man wouldn't tell me. Seems to be a deep, dark secret.'

'Maybe some out-of-state people want to turn it into a summer place,' she said. 'Whoever it is, they're crazy. Renovating a place is one thing – I'd love to try it – but that place is beyond renovation. The place was a wreck even when I was a kid. Ben, why would you ever want to stay there?'

'Were you ever actually inside?'

'No, but I looked in the window on a dare. Were you?'

'Yes. Once.'

'Creepy place, isn't it?'

They fell silent, both thinking of the Marsten House. This particular reminiscence did not have the pastel nostalgia of the others. The scandal and violence connected with the house had occurred before their births, but small towns have long memories and pass their horrors down ceremonially from generation to generation.

The story of Hubert Marsten and his wife, Birdie, was the closest thing the town had to a skeleton in its closet. Hubie had been the president of a large New England trucking company in the 1920s – a trucking company which, some said, conducted its most profitable business after midnight, running Canadian whisky into Massachusetts.

He and his wife had retired wealthy to 'salem's Lot in 1928, and had lost a good part of that wealth (no one, not even Mabel Werts, knew exactly how much) in the stock market crash of 1929.

In the ten years between the fall of the market and the rise of Hitler, Marsten and his wife lived in their house like hermits. The only time they were seen was on Wednesday afternoons when they came to town to do their shopping. Larry McLeod, who was the mailman during those years, reported that Marsten got four daily papers, *The Saturday Evening Post, The New Yorker*, and a pulp magazine called *Amazing Stories*. He also got a check once a month from the trucking company, which was based in Fall River, Massachusetts. Larry said he could tell it was a check by bending the envelope and peeking into the address window.

Larry was the one who found them in the summer of 1939. The papers and magazines – five days' worth – had piled up in the mailbox until it was impossible to cram in more. Larry took them all up the walk with the intention of putting them in between the screen door and the main door.

It was August and high summer, the beginning of dog days, and the grass in the Marsten front yard was calf-high, green and rank. Honey-suckle ran wild over the trellis on the west side of the house, and fat bees buzzed indolently around the wax-white, redolent blossoms. In those days the house was still a fine-looking place in spite of the high grass, and it was generally agreed that Hubic had built the nicest house in 'salem's Lot before going soft in the attic.

Halfway up the walk, according to the story that was eventually told with breathless horror to each new Ladies' Auxiliary member, Larry had smelled something bad, like spoiled meat. He knocked on the front door and got no answer. He looked through the door but could see nothing in the thick gloom. He went around to the back instead of walking in, which was lucky for him. The smell was worse in back. Larry tried the back door, found it unlocked, and stepped into the kitchen. Birdie Marsten was sprawled in a corner, legs splayed out, feet bare. Half her head had been blown away by a close-range shot from a thirty-ought-six.

('Flies,' Audrey Hersey always said at this point, speaking with calm authority. 'Larry said the kitchen was full of 'em. Buzzing around, lighting on the . . . you know, and taking off again. Flies.')

Larry McLeod turned around and went straight back to town. He fetched Norris Varney, who was constable at the time, and three or four of the hangers-on from Crossen's Store — Milt's father was still running the place in those days. Audrey's eldest brother, Jackson, had been among them. They drove back up in Norris's Chevrolet and Larry's mail truck.

No one from town had ever been in the house, and it was a nine days' wonder. After the excitement died down, the Portland *Telegram* had done a feature on it. Hubert Marsten's house was a piled, jumbled, bewildering rat's nest of junk, scavenged items, and narrow, winding passageways which led through yellowing stacks of newspapers and magazines and piles of moldering white-elephant books. The complete sets of Dickens, Scott, and Mariatt had been scavenged for the Jerusalem's Lot Public Library by Loretta Starcher's predecessor and still remained in the stacks.

Jackson Hersey picked up a *Saturday Evening Post*, began to flip through it, and did a double take. A dollar bill had been taped neatly to each page.

Norris Varney discovered how lucky Larry had been when he went around to the back door. The murder weapon had been lashed to a chair with its barrel pointing directly at the front door, aimed chest-high. The gun was cocked, and a string attached to the trigger ran down the hall to the doorknob.

('Gun was loaded, too,' Audrey would say at this point. 'One tug and Larry McLeod would have gone straight up to the pearly gates.')

There were other, less lethal booby traps. A forty-pound bundle of newspapers had been rigged over the dining room door. One of the stair risers leading to the second floor had been hinged and could have cost someone a broken ankle. It quickly became apparent that Hubie Marsten had been something more than Soft, he had been a full-fledged Loony.

They found him in the bedroom at the end of the upstairs hall, dangling from a rafter.

(Susan and her girlfriends had tortured themselves deliciously with the stories they had gleaned from their elders; Amy Rawcliffe had a log playhouse in her back-yard and they would lock themselves in and sit in the dark, scaring each other about the Marsten House, which gained its proper noun status for all time even before Hitler invaded Poland, and repeating their elders' stories with as many grisly embellishments as their minds could conceive. Even now, eighteen years later, she found that just thinking of the Marsten House had acted on her like a wizard's spell, conjuring up the painfully clear images of little girls crouched inside Amy's playhouse, holding hands, and Amy saying with impressive eeriness: 'His face was all swole up and his tongue turned black and popped out and there was flies crawling on it. My momma tole Mrs Werts.')

'. . . place.'

'What? I'm sorry.' She came back to the present with an almost physical wrench. Ben was pulling off the turnpike and onto the 'salem's Lot exit ramp.

'I said, it was a spooky old place.'

'Tell me about when you went in.'

He laughed humorlessly and flicked up his high beams. The two-lane blacktop ran straight ahead through an alley of pine and spruce, deserted. 'It started as kid's stuff. Maybe that's all it ever was. Remember, this was in 1951, and little kids had to think up something to take the place of sniffing airplane glue out of paper bags, which hadn't been invented yet. I used to play pretty much with the Bend kids, and most of them have probably moved away by now . . . do they still call south 'salem's Lot the Bend?'

'Yes.'

'I messed around with Davie Barclay, Charles James – only all the kids used to call him Sonny – Harold Rauberson, Floyd Tibbits—'

'Floyd?' she asked, startled.

'Yes, do you know him?'

'I've dated him,' she said, and afraid her voice sounded strange, hurried on: 'Sonny James is still around, too. He runs the gas station on Jointner Avenue. Harold Rauberson is dead. Leukemia.'

'They were all older than I, by a year or two. They had a club. Exclusive, you know. Only Bloody Pirates with at least three references need apply.' He had meant it to be light, but there was a jag of old bitterness buried in the words. 'But I was persistent. The one thing in the world I wanted was to be a Bloody Pirate . . . that summer, at least.

'They finally weakened and told me I could come in if I passed the initiation, which Davie thought up on the spot. We were all going up to the Marsten House, and I was supposed to go in and bring something out. As booty.' He chuckled but his mouth had gone dry.

'What happened?'

'I got in through a window. The house was *still* full of junk, even after twelve years. They must have taken the newspapers during the war, but they just left the rest of it. There was a table in the front hall with one of those snow globes on it – do you know what I mean? There's a little house inside, and when you shake it, there's snow. I put it in my pocket, but I didn't leave. I really wanted to prove myself. So I went upstairs to where he hung himself.'

'Oh my God,' she said.

'Reach in the glove box and get me a cigarette, would you? I'm trying to quit, but I need one for this.'

She got him one and he punched the dashboard lighter.

'The house smelled. You wouldn't believe how it smelled. Mildew and upholstery rot and a kind of rancid smell like butter that had gone over. And living things –

rats or woodchucks or whatever else that had been nesting in the walls or hibernating in the cellar. A yellow, wet smell.

'I crept up the stairs, a little kid nine years old, scared shitless. The house was creaking and settling around me and I could hear things scuttling away from me on the other side of the plaster. I kept thinking I heard footsteps behind me. I was afraid to turn around because I might see Hubie Marsten shambling after me with a hangman's noose in one hand and his face all black.'

He was gripping the steering wheel very hard. The levity had gone out of his voice. The *intensity* of his remembering frightened her a little. His face, in the glow of the instrument panel, was set in the long lines of a man who was traveling a hated country he could not completely leave.

'At the top of the stairs I got all my courage and ran down the hall to that room. My idea was to run in, grab something from there, too, and then get the hell out of there. The door at the end of the hall was closed. I could see it getting closer and closer and I could see that the hinges had settled and the bottom edge was resting on the doorjamb. I could see the doorknob, silvery and a little tarnished in the place where palms had gripped it. When I pulled on it, the bottom edge of the door gave a scream against the wood like a woman in pain. If I had been straight, I think I would have turned around and gotten the hell out right then. But I was pumped full of adrenaline, and I grabbed it in both hands and pulled for all I was worth. It flew open. And there was Hubie, hanging from the beam with his body silhouetted against the light from the window.'

'Oh, Ben, don't—' she said nervously.

'No, I'm telling you the truth,' he insisted. 'The truth of what a nine-year-old boy saw and what the man remembers twenty-four years later, anyway. Hubie was hanging there, and his face wasn't black at all. It was green. The eyes were puffed shut. His hands were livid . . . ghastly. And then he opened his eyes.'

Ben took a huge drag on his cigarette and pitched it out his window into the dark.

'I let out a scream that probably could have been heard for two miles. And then I ran. I fell halfway down-stairs, got up, and ran out the front door and straight down the road. The kids were waiting for me about half a mile down. That's when I noticed I still had the glass snow globe in my hand. And I've still got it.'

'You don't really think you saw Hubert Marsten, do you, Ben?' Far up ahead she could see the yellow blinking light that signaled the center of town and was glad for it.

After a long pause, he said, 'I don't know.' He said it with difficulty and reluctance, as if he would have rather said *no* and closed the subject thereby. 'Probably I was so keyed up that I hallucinated the whole thing. On the other hand, there may be some truth in that idea that houses absorb the emotions that are spent in them, that they hold a kind of . . . dry charge. Perhaps the right personality, that of an imaginative boy, for instance, could act as a catalyst on that dry charge, and cause it to produce an active manifestation of . . . of something. I'm not talking about ghosts, precisely. I'm talking about a kind of psychic television in three dimensions. Perhaps even something alive. A monster, if you like.'

She took one of his cigarettes and lit it.

'Anyway, I slept with the light on in my bedroom for weeks after, and I've dreamed about opening that door off and on for the rest of my life. Whenever I'm in stress, the dream comes.'

'That's terrible.'

'No, it's not,' he said. 'Not very, anyway. We all have our bad dreams.' He gestured with a thumb at the silent, sleeping houses they were passing on Jointner Avenue. 'Sometimes I wonder that the very boards of those houses don't cry out with the awful things that happen in dreams.' He paused. 'Come on down to Eva's and sit on the porch for a while, if you like. I can't invite you in – rules of the house – but I've got a couple of Cokes in the icebox and some Bacardi in my room, if you'd like a nightcap.'

'I'd like one very much.'

He turned onto Railroad Street, popped off the headlights, and turned into the small dirt parking lot which served the rooming house. The back porch was painted white with red trim, and the three wicker chairs lined up on it looked toward the Royal River. The river itself was a dazzling dream. There was a late summer moon caught in the trees on the river's far bank, three-quarters full, and it had painted a silver path across the water. With the town silent, she could hear the faint foaming sound as water spilled down the sluiceways of the dam.

'Sit down. I'll be back.'

He went in, closing the screen door softly behind him, and she sat down in one of the rockers.

She liked him in spite of his strangeness. She was not a believer in love at first sight, although she did believe that instant lust (going under the more innocent name of infatuation) occurred frequently. And yet he wasn't a man that would ordinarily encourage midnight entries in a locked diary; he was too thin for his height, a little pale. His face was introspective and bookish, and his eyes rarely gave away the train of his thoughts. All this topped with a heavy pelt of black hair that looked as if it had been raked with the fingers rather than brushed.

And that story—

Neither *Conway's Daughter* nor *Air Dance* hinted at such a morbid turn of mind. The former was about a minister's daughter who runs away, joins the counterculture, and takes a long, rambling journey across the country by thumb. The latter was the story of Frank Buzzey, an escaped convict who begins a new life as a car mechanic in another state, and his eventual recapture. Both of them were bright, energetic books, and Hubie Marsten's dangling shadow, mirrored in the eyes of a nine-year-old boy, did not seem to lie over either of them.

As if by the very suggestion, she found her eyes dragged away from the river and up to the left of the porch, where the last hill before town blotted out the stars.

'Here,' he said. 'I hope these'll be all right—'

'Look at the Marsten House,' she said.

He did. There was a light on up there.

7

The drinks were gone and midnight passed; the moon was nearly out of sight. They had made some light conversation, and then she said into a pause:

'I like you, Ben. Very much.'

'I like you, too. And I'm surprised . . . no, I don't mean it that way. Do you remember that stupid crack I made in the park? This all seems too fortuitous.'

'I want to see you again, if you want to see me.'

'I do.'

'But go slow. Remember, I'm just a small-town girl.'

He smiled. 'It seems so Hollywood. But Hollywood good. Am I supposed to kiss you now?'

'Yes,' she said seriously, 'I think that comes next.'

He was sitting in the rocker next to her, and without stopping its slow movement forth and back, he leaned over and pressed his mouth on hers, with no attempt to draw her tongue or to touch her. His lips were firm with the pressure of his square teeth, and there was a faint taste-odor of rum and tobacco.

She began to rock also, and the movement made the kiss into something new. It waxed and waned, light and then firm. She thought: He's tasting me. The thought wakened a secret, clean excitement in her, and she broke the kiss before it could take her further.

'Wow,' he said.

'Would you like to come to dinner at my house tomorrow night?' she asked. 'My folks would love to meet you, I bet.' In the pleasure and serenity of this moment, she could throw that sop to her mother.

'Home cooking?'

'The homiest.'

'I'd love it. I've been living on TV dinners since I moved in.'

'Six o'clock? We eat early in Sticksville.'

'Sure. Fine. And speaking of home, I better get you there. Come on.'

They didn't speak on the ride back until she could see the night-light twinkling on top of the hill, the one her mother always left on when she was out.

'I wonder who's up there tonight?' she asked, looking toward the Marsten House.

'The new owner, probably,' he said noncommittally.

'It didn't look like electricity, that light,' she mused. 'Too yellow, too faint. Kerosene lamp, maybe.'

'They probably haven't had a chance to have the power turned on yet.'

'Maybe. But almost anyone with a little foresight would call up the power company before they moved in.'

He didn't reply. They had come to her driveway.

'Ben,' she said suddenly, 'is your new book about the Marsten House?'

He laughed and kissed the tip of her nose. 'It's late.'

She smiled at him. 'I don't mean to snoop.'

'It's all right. But maybe another time . . . in daylight.'

'Okay.'

'You better get in, girly. Six tomorrow?'

She looked at her watch. 'Six today.'

'Night, Susan.'

'Night.'

She got out and ran lightly up the path to the side door, then turned and waved as he drove away. Before she went in, she added sour cream to the milkman's order. With baked potatoes, that would add a little class to supper.

She paused a minute longer before going in, looking up at the Marsten House.

8

In his small, boxlike room he undressed with the light off and crawled into bed naked. She was a nice girl, the first nice one since Miranda had died. He hoped he wasn't trying to turn her into a new Miranda; that would be painful for him and horribly unfair to her.

He lay down and let himself drift. Shortly before sleep took him, he hooked himself up on one elbow, looked past the square shadow of his typewriter and the thin sheaf of manuscript beside it, and out the window. He had asked Eva Miller specifically for this room after looking at several, because it faced the Marsten House directly.

The lights up there were still on.

That night he had the old dream for the first time since he had come to Jerusalem's Lot, and it had not come with such vividness since those terrible maroon days following Miranda's death in the motorcycle accident. The run up the hallway, the horrible scream of the door as he pulled it open, the dangling figure suddenly opening its hideous puffed eyes, himself turning to the door in the slow, sludgy panic of dreams—

And finding it locked.

CHAPTER THREE
THE LOT (I)

The town is not slow to wake – chores won't wait. Even while the edge of the sun lies below the horizon and darkness is on the land, activity has begun.

2

4:00 AM

The Griffen boys – Hal, eighteen, and Jack, fourteen – and the two hired hands had begun the milking. The barn was a marvel of cleanliness, whitewashed and gleaming. Down the center, between the spotless runways which fronted the stalls on both sides, a cement drinking trough ran. Hal turned on the water at the far end by flicking a switch and opening a valve. The electric pump that pulled water up from one of the two artesian wells that served the place hummed into smooth operation. He was a sullen boy, not bright, and especially irked on this day. He and his father had had it out the night before. Hal wanted to quit school. He hated school. He hated its boredom, its insistence that you sit still for great fifty-minute chunks of time, and he hated all his subjects with the exceptions of Woodshop and Graphic Arts. English was maddening, history was stupid, business math was incomprehensible. And none of it mattered, that was the hell of it. Cows didn't care if you said ain't or mixed your tenses, they didn't care who was the Commander in Chief of the goddamn Army of the Potomac during the goddamn Civil War, and as for math, his own for chrissakes father couldn't add two-fifths and one half if it meant the firing squad. That's why he had an accountant. And look at that guy! College-educated and still working for a dummy like his old man. His father had told him many times that book learning wasn't the secret of running a successful business (and dairy farming was a business like any other); *knowing* people was the secret of that. His father was a great one to sling all that bullshit about the wonders of education, him and his sixth-grade education. He never read anything but *Reader's Digest* and the farm was making $16,000 a year. Know people. Be able to shake their hands and ask after their wives by name. Well, Hal knew people. There were two kinds: those you could push around and those you couldn't. The former outnumbered the latter ten to one.

Unfortunately, his father was a one.

He looked over his shoulder at Jack, who was forking hay slowly and dreamily into the first four stalls from a broken bale. There was the bookworm, Daddy's pet. The miserable little shit.

'Come on!' he shouted. 'Fork that hay!'

He opened the storage lockers and pulled out the first of their four milking machines. He trundled it down the aisle, frowning fiercely over the glittering stainless-steel top.

School. Fucking for chrissakes *school*.

The next nine months stretched ahead of him like an endless tomb.

3

4:30 AM

The fruits of yesterday's late milking had been processed and were now on their way back to the Lot, this time in cartons rather than galvanized steel milk cans, under the colorful label of Slewfoot Hill Dairy. Charles Griffen's father had marketed his own milk, but that was no longer practical. The conglomerates had eaten up the last of the independents.

The Slewfoot Hill milkman in west Salem was Irwin Purinton, and he began his run along Brock Street (which was known in the country as the Brock Road or That Christless Washboard). Later he would cover the center of town and then work back out of town along the Brooks Road.

Win had turned sixty-one in August, and for the first time his coming retirement seemed real and possible. His wife, a hateful old bitch named Elsie, had died in the fall of 1973 (predeceasing him was the one considerate thing she had done in twenty-seven years of marriage), and when his retirement finally came he was going to pack up his dog, a half-cocker mongrel named Doc, and move down to Pemaquid Point. He planned to sleep until nine o'clock every day and never look at another sunrise.

He pulled over in front of the Norton house, and filled his carry rack with their order: orange juice, two quarts of milk, a dozen eggs. Climbing out of the cab, his knee gave a twinge, but only a faint one. It was going to be a fine day.

There was an addition to Mrs Norton's usual order in Susan's round, Palmer-method script: 'Please leave one small sour cream, Win. Thanx.'

Purinton went back for it, thinking it was going to be one of those days when everyone wanted something special. Sour cream! He had tasted it once and liked to puke.

The sky was beginning to lighten in the east, and on the fields between here and town, heavy dew sparkled like a king's ransom of diamonds.

4

5:15 AM

Eva Miller had been up for twenty minutes, dressed in a rag of a housedress and a pair of floppy pink slippers. She was cooking her breakfast – four scrambled eggs, eight rashers of bacon, a skillet of home fries. She would garnish this humble repast with two slices of toast and jam, a ten-ounce tumbler of orange juice, and two cups of coffee with cream to follow. She was a big woman, but not precisely fat; she worked too hard at keeping her place up to ever be fat. The curves of her body were heroic, Rabelaisian. Watching her in motion at her eight-burner electric stove was like watching the restless movements of the tide, or the migration of sand dunes.

She liked to eat her morning meal in this utter solitude, planning the work ahead of her for the day. There was a lot of it: Wednesday was the day she changed the linen. She had nine boarders at present, counting the new one, Mr Mears. The house had three stories and seventeen rooms and there were also floors to wash, the stairs to be scrubbed, the banister to be waxed, and the rug to be turned in the central common room. She would get Weasel Craig to help her with some of it, unless he was sleeping off a bad drunk.

The back door opened just as she was sitting down to the table.

'Hi, Win. How are you doing?'

'Passable. Knee's kickin' a bit.'

'Sorry to hear it. You want to leave an extra quart of milk and a gallon of that lemonade?'

'Sure,' he said, resigned. 'I knew it was gonna be that kind of day.'

She dug into her eggs, dismissing the comment. Win Purinton could always find something to complain about, although God knew he should have been the happiest man alive since that hellcat he had hooked up with fell down the cellar stairs and broke her neck.

At quarter of six, just as she was finishing up her second cup of coffee and smoking a Chesterfield, the *Press-Herald* thumped against the side of the house and dropped into the rosebushes. The third time this week; the Kilby kid was batting a thousand. Probably delivering the papers wrecked out of his mind. Well, let it sit there awhile. The earliest sunshine, thin and precious gold, was slanting in through the east windows. It was the best time of her day, and she would not disturb its moveless peace for anything.

Her boarders had the use of the stove and the refrigerator – that, like the weekly change of linen, came with their rent – and shortly the peace would be broken as

Grover Verrill and Mickey Sylvester came down to slop up their cereal before leaving for the textile mill over in Gates Falls where they both worked.

As if her thought had summoned a messenger of their coming, the toilet on the second floor flushed and she heard Sylvester's heavy work boots on the stairs.

She heaved herself up and went to rescue the paper.

5

6:05 AM

The baby's thin wails pierced Sandy McDougall's thin morning sleep and she got up to check the baby with her eyes still bleared shut. She barked her shin on the night-stand and said, '*Kukka!*'

The baby, hearing her, screamed louder. 'Shut up!' she yelled. 'I'm coming!'

She walked down the narrow trailer corridor to the kitchen, a slender girl who was losing whatever marginal prettiness she might once have had. She got Randy's bottle out of the refrigerator, thought about warming it, then thought to hell with it. If you want it so bad, buster, you can just drink it cold.

She went down to his bedroom and looked at him coldly. He was ten months old, but sickly and puling for his age. He had only started crawling last month. Maybe he had polio or something. Now there was something on his hands, and on the wall, too. She pushed forward, wondering what in Mary's name he had been into.

She was seventeen years old and she and her husband had celebrated their first wedding anniversary in July. At the time she had married Royce McDougall, six months' pregnant and looking like the Goodyear blimp, marriage had seemed every bit as blessed as Father Callahan said it was — a blessed escape hatch. Now it just seemed like a pile of kukka.

Which was, she saw with dismay, exactly what Randy had smeared all over his hands, on the wall, and in his hair.

She stood looking at him dully, holding the cold bottle in one hand.

This was what she had given up high school for, her friends for, her hopes of becoming a model for. For this crummy trailer stuck out in the Bend, Formica already peeling off the counters in strips, for a husband that worked all day at the mill and went off drinking or playing poker with his no-good gas-station buddies at night. For a kid who looked just like his no-good old man and smeared kukka all over everything.

He was screaming at the top of his lungs.

'*You shut up!*' she screamed back suddenly, and threw the plastic bottle at him. It struck his forehead and he toppled on his back in the crib, wailing and thrashing his arms. There was a red circle just below the hairline, and she felt a horrid surge of gratification, pity, and hate in her throat. She plucked him out of the crib like a rag.

'*Shut up! Shut up! Shut up!*' She had punched him twice before she could stop herself and Randy's screams of pain had become too great for sound. He lay gasping in his crib, his face purple.

'I'm sorry,' she muttered. 'Jesus, Mary, and Joseph. I'm sorry. You okay, Randy? Just a minute, Momma's going to clean you up.'

By the time she came back with a wet rag, both of Randy's eyes had swelled shut and were discoloring. But he took the bottle and when she began to wipe his face with a damp rag, he smiled toothlessly at her.

I'll tell Roy he fell off the changing table, she thought. He'll believe that. Oh God, let him believe that.

6

6:45 AM

Most of the blue-collar population of 'salem's Lot was on its way to work. Mike Ryerson was one of the few who worked in town. In the annual town report he was listed as a groundskeeper, but he was actually in charge of maintaining the town's three cemeteries. In the summer this was almost a full-time job, but even in the winter it was no walk, as some folks, such as that prissy George Middler down at the hardware store, seemed to think. He worked part-time for Carl Foreman, the Lot's undertaker, and most of the old folks seemed to poop off in the winter.

Now he was on his way out to the Burns Road in his pickup truck, which was loaded down with clippers, a battery-driven hedge-trimmer, a box of flag stands, a crowbar for lifting gravestones that might have fallen over, a ten-gallon gas can, and two Briggs & Stratton lawn mowers.

He would mow the grass at Harmony Hill this morning, and do any maintenance on the stones and the rock wall that was necessary, and this afternoon he would cross town to the Schoolyard Hill Cemetery, where school-teachers sometimes came to do rubbings, on account of an extinct colony of Shakers who had once buried their dead there. But he liked Harmony Hill best of all three. It was not as old as the Schoolyard Hill boneyard, but it was pleasant and shady. He hoped that someday he could be buried there himself — in a hundred years or so.

He was twenty-seven, and had gone through three years of college in the course of a rather checkered career. He hoped to go back someday and finish up. He was good-looking in an open, pleasant way, and he had no trouble connecting with unattached females on Saturday nights out at Dell's or in Portland. Some of them were turned off by his job, and Mike found this honestly hard to understand. It was pleasant work, there was no boss always looking over your shoulder, and the work was in the open air, under God's sky; and so what if he dug a few graves or on occasion drove Carl Foreman's funeral hack? Somebody had to do it. To his way of thinking, the only thing more natural than death was sex.

Humming, he turned off onto the Burns Road and shifted to second going up the hill. Dry dust spumed out behind him. Through the choked summer greenery on both sides of the road he could see the skeletal, leafless trunks of the trees that had burned in the big fire of '51, like old and moldering bones. There were deadfalls back in there, he knew, where a man could break his leg if he wasn't careful. Even after twenty-five years, the scar of that great burning was there. Well, that was just it. In the midst of life, we are in death.

The cemetery was at the crest of the hill, and Mike turned in the drive, ready to get out and unlock the gate . . . and then braked the truck to a shuddering stop.

The body of a dog hung head-down from the

wrought-iron gate, and the ground beneath was muddy with its blood.

Mike got out of the truck and hurried over to it. He pulled his work gloves out of his back pockets and lifted the dog's head with one hand. It came up with horrible, boneless ease, and he was staring into the blank, glazed eyes of Win Purinton's mongrel cocker, Doc. The dog had been hung on one of the gate's high spikes like a slab of beef on a meat hook. Flies, slow with the coolness of early morning, were already crawling sluggishly over the body.

Mike struggled and yanked and finally pulled it off, feeling sick to his stomach at the wet sounds that accompanied his efforts. Graveyard vandalism was an old story to him, especially around Halloween, but that was still a month and a half away and he had never seen anything like this. Usually they contented themselves with knocking over a few gravestones, scrawling a few obscenities, or hanging a paper skeleton from the gate. But if this slaughter was the work of kids, then they were real bastards. Win was going to be heartbroken.

He debated taking the dog directly back to town and showing it to Parkins Gillespie, and decided it wouldn't gain anything. He could take poor old Doc back to town when he went in to eat his lunch – not that he was going to have much appetite today.

He unlocked the gate and looked at his gloves, which were smeared with blood. The iron bars of the gate would have to be scrubbed, and it looked like he wouldn't be getting over to Schoolyard Hill this afternoon after all. He drove inside and parked, no longer humming. The zest had gone out of the day.

7

8:00 AM

The lumbering yellow school buses were making their appointed rounds, picking up the children who stood out by their mailboxes, holding their lunch buckets and skylarking. Charlie Rhodes was driving one of these buses, and his pickup route covered the Taggart Stream Road in east 'salem and the upper half of Jointner Avenue.

The kids who rode Charlie's bus were the best behaved in town — in the entire school district, for that matter. There was no yelling or horseplay or pulling pigtails on Bus 6. They goddamn well sat still and minded their manners, or they could walk the two miles to Stanley Street Elementary and explain why in the office.

He knew what they thought of him, and he had a good idea of what they called him behind his back. But that was all right. He was not going to have a lot of fool-ishness and shit-slinging on his bus. Let them save that for their spineless teachers.

The principal at Stanley Street had had the nerve to ask him if he hadn't acted 'impulsively' when he put the Durham boy off three days' running for just talking a little too loud. Charlie had just stared at him, and eventually the principal, a wet-eared little pipsqueak who had only been out of college four years, had looked away. The man in charge of the S.A.D. 21 motor pool, Dave Felsen, was an old buddy; they went all the way back to Korea together. They understood each other. They understood what was going on in the country. They understood how the kid who had been 'just talking a little too loud' on the school bus in 1958 was the kid who had been out pissing on the flag in 1968.

He glanced into the wide overhead mirror and saw Mary Kate Griegson passing a note to her little chum Brent Tenney. Little chum, yeah, right. They were banging each other by the sixth grade these days.

He pulled over, switching on his Stop flashers. Mary Kate and Brent looked up, dismayed.

'Got a lot to talk about?' he asked into the mirror. 'Good. You better get started.'

He threw open the folding doors and waited for them to get the hell off his bus.

8

9:00 AM

Weasel Craig rolled out of bed – literally. The sunshine coming in his second-floor window was blinding. His head thumped queasily. Upstairs that writer fella was already pecking away. Christ, a man would have to be nuttier than a squirrel to tap-tap-tap away like that, day in and day out.

He got up and went over to the calendar in his skivvies to see if this was the day he picked up his unemployment. No. This was Wednesday.

His hangover wasn't as bad as it had been on occasion. He had been out at Dell's until it closed at one, but he had only had two dollars and hadn't been able to cadge many beers after that was gone. Losing my touch, he thought, and scrubbed the side of his face with one hand.

He pulled on the thermal undershirt that he wore winter and summer, pulled on his green work pants, and then opened his closet and got breakfast – a bottle of warm beer for up here and a box of government-donated-commodities oatmeal for downstairs. He hated oatmeal, but he had promised the widow he would help her turn that rug, and she would probably have some other chores lined up.

He didn't mind – not really – but it was a come-down from the days when he had shared Eva Miller's bed. Her husband had died in a sawmill accident in 1959, and it was kind of funny in a way, if you could call any such horrible accident funny. In those days the sawmill had employed sixty or seventy men, and Ralph Miller had been in line for the mill's presidency.

What had happened to him was sort of funny because Ralph Miller hadn't touched a bit of machinery since 1952, seven years before, when he stepped up from foreman to the front office. That was executive gratitude for you, sure enough, and Weasel supposed that Ralph had earned it. When the big fire had swept out of the Marshes and jumped Jointner Avenue under the urging of a twenty-five-mile-an-hour east wind, it had seemed that the sawmill was certain to go. The fire departments of six neighboring townships had enough on their hands trying to save the town without sparing men for such a pissant operation as the Jerusalem's Lot Sawmill. Ralph Miller had organized the whole second shift into a fire-fighting force, and under his direction they wetted the roof and did what the entire combined fire-fighting force had been unable to do west of Jointner Avenue – he had constructed a firebreak that stopped the fire and turned it south, where it was fully contained.

Seven years later he had fallen into a shredding machine while he was talking to some visiting brass from a Massachusetts company. He had been taking them around the plant, hoping to convince them to buy in. His foot slipped in a puddle of water and son of a bitch, right into the shredder before their very eyes. Needless to say, any possibility of a deal went right down the chute with Ralph Miller. The sawmill that he had saved in 1951 closed for good in February of 1960.

Weasel looked in his water-spotted mirror and combed his white hair, which was shaggy, beautiful, and still sexy at sixty-seven. It was the only part of him that seemed to thrive on alcohol. Then he pulled on his khaki work shirt, took his oatmeal box, and went downstairs.

And here he was, almost sixteen years after all of that had happened, hiring out as a frigging housekeeper to a woman he had once bedded – and a woman he still regarded as damned attractive.

The widow fell on him like a vulture as soon as he stepped into the sunny kitchen.

'Say, would you like to wax that front banister for me after you have your breakfast, Weasel? You got time?' They both preserved the gentle fiction that he did these things as favors, and not as pay for his fourteen-dollar-a-week upstairs room.

'Sure would, Eva.'

'And that rug in the front room—'

'—has got to be turned. Yeah, I remember.'

'How's your head this morning?' She asked the question in a businesslike way, allowing no pity to enter her tone . . . but he sensed its existence beneath the surface.

'Head's fine,' he said touchily, putting water on to boil for the oatmeal.

'You were out late, is why I asked.'

'You got a line on me, is that right?' He cocked a humorous eyebrow at her and was gratified to see that she could still blush like a schoolgirl, even though they had left off any funny stuff almost nine years ago.

'Now, Ed—'

She was the only one who still called him that. To everyone else in the Lot he was just Weasel. Well, that was all right. Let them call him any old thing they wanted. The bear had caught him, sure enough.

'Never mind,' he said gruffly. 'I got up on the wrong side of the bed.'

'Fell out of it, by the sound.' She spoke more quickly than she had intended, but Weasel only grunted. He cooked and ate his hateful oatmeal, then took the can of furniture wax and rags without looking back.

Upstairs, the tap-tap of that guy's typewriter went on and on. Vinnie Upshaw, who had the room upstairs across from him, said he started in every morning at nine, went till noon, started in again at three, went until six, started in *again* at nine and went right through until midnight. Weasel couldn't imagine having that many words in your mind.

Still, he seemed a nice enough sort, and he might be good for a few beers out to Dell's some night. He had heard most of those writers drank like fish.

He began to polish the banister methodically, and fell to thinking about the widow again. She had turned this place into a boardinghouse with her husband's insurance money, and had done quite well. Why shouldn't she? She worked like a dray horse. But she must have been used to getting it regular from her husband, and after the grief had washed out of her, that need had remained. God, she had liked to do it!

In those days, '61 and '62, people had still been calling him Ed instead of Weasel, and he had still been holding the bottle instead of the other way around. He had a good job in the B&M, and one night in January of 1962 it had happened.

He paused in the steady waxing movements and looked thoughtfully out of the narrow Judas window on the second-floor landing. It was filled with the last bright foolishly golden light of summer, a light that laughed at the cold, rattling autumn and the colder winter that would follow it.

It had been part her and part him that night, and after it had happened and they were lying together in the darkness of her bedroom, she began to weep and tell him that what they had done was wrong. He told her it had been right, not knowing if it had been right or not and not caring, and there had been a norther whooping and coughing and screaming around the eaves and her room had been warm and safe and at last they had slept together like spoons in a silverware drawer.

Ah God and sonny Jesus, time was like a river and he wondered if that writer fella knew *that*.

He began to polish the banister again with long, sweeping strokes.

9

10:00 AM

It was recess time at Stanley Street Elementary School, which was the Lot's newest and proudest school building. It was a low, glassine four-classroom building that the school district was still paying for, as new and bright and modern as the Brock Street Elementary School was old and dark.

Richie Boddin, who was the school bully and proud of it, stepped out onto the playground grandly, eyes searching for that smart-ass new kid who knew all the answers in math. No new kid came waltzing into *his* school without knowing who was boss. Especially some four-eyes queer-boy teacher's pet like this one.

Richie was eleven years old and weighed 140 pounds. All his life his mother had been calling on people to see what a *huge* young man her son was. And so he knew he was big. Sometimes he fancied that he could feel the ground tremble underneath his feet when he walked. And when he grew up he was going to smoke Camels, just like his old man.

The fourth- and fifth-graders were terrified of him, and the smaller kids regarded him as a schoolyard totem. When he moved on to the seventh grade at Brock Street School, their pantheon would be empty of its devil. All this pleased him immensely.

And there was the Petrie kid, waiting to be chosen up for the recess touch football game.

'Hey!' Richie yelled.

Everyone looked around except Petrie. Every eye had

a glassy sheen on it, and every pair of eyes showed relief when they saw that Richie's rested elsewhere.

'Hey you! Four-eyes!'

Mark Petrie turned and looked at Richie. His steel-rimmed glasses flashed in the morning sun. He was as tall as Richie, which meant he towered over most of his classmates, but he was slender and his face looked defenseless and bookish.

'Are you speaking to me?'

'"Are you speaking to me?"' Richie mimicked, his voice a high falsetto. 'You sound like a queer, four-eyes. You know that?'

'No, I didn't know that,' Mark Petrie said.

Richie took a step forward. 'I bet you suck, you know that, four-eyes? I bet you suck the old hairy root.'

'Really?' His polite tone was infuriating.

'Yeah, I heard you really suck it. Not just Thursdays for you. You can't wait. Every day for you.'

Kids began to drift over to watch Richie stomp the new boy. Miss Holcomb, who was playground monitor this week, was out front watching the little kids on the swings and seesaws.

'What's your racket?' Mark Petrie asked. He was looking at Richie as if he had discovered an interesting new beetle.

'"What's your racket?"' Richie mimicked falsetto. 'I ain't got no racket. I just heard you were a big fat queer, that's all.'

'Is that right?' Mark asked, still polite. 'I heard that you were a big clumsy stupid turd, that's what I heard.'

Utter silence. The other boys gaped (but it was an interested gape; none of them had ever seen a fellow sign his own death warrant before). Richie was caught entirely by surprise and gaped with the rest.

Mark took off his glasses and handed them to the boy next to him. 'Hold these, would you?' The boy took them and goggled at Mark silently.

Richie charged. It was a slow, lumbering charge, with not a bit of grace or finesse in it. The ground trembled under his feet. He was filled with confidence and the clear, joyous urge to stomp and break. He swung his haymaker right, which would catch ole four-eyes queer-boy right in the mouth and send his teeth flying like piano keys. Get ready for the dentist, queer-boy. Here I come.

Mark Petrie ducked and sidestepped at the same instant. The haymaker went over his head. Richie was pulled halfway around by the force of his own blow, and Mark had only to stick out a foot. Richie Boddin thumped to the ground. He grunted. The crowd of watching children went 'Aaaah.'

Mark knew perfectly well that if the big, clumsy boy on the ground regained the advantage, he would be beaten up badly. Mark was agile, but agility could not stand up for long in a schoolyard brawl. In a street situation this would have been the time to run, to outdistance his slower pursuer, then turn and thumb his nose. But this wasn't the street or the city, and he knew perfectly well that if he didn't whip this big ugly turd now the harassment would never stop.

These thoughts went through his mind in a fifth of a second.

He jumped on Richie Boddin's back.

Richie grunted. The crowd went 'Aaaah' again. Mark grabbed Richie's arm, careful to get it above the shirt cuff so he couldn't sweat out of his grip, and twisted it behind Richie's back. Richie screamed in pain.

'Say uncle,' Mark told him.

Richie's reply would have pleased a twenty-year Navy man.

Mark yanked Richie's arm up to his shoulder blades, and Richie screamed again. He was filled with indignation, fright, and puzzlement. This had never happened to him before. It couldn't be happening now. Surely no four-eyes queer-boy could be sitting on his back and twisting his arm and making him scream before his subjects.

'Say uncle,' Mark repeated.

Richie heaved himself to his knees; Mark squeezed his own knees into Richie's sides, like a man riding a horse bareback, and stayed on. They were both covered with dust, but Richie was much the worse for wear. His face was red and straining, his eyes bulged, and there was a scratch on his cheek.

He tried to dump Mark over his shoulders, and Mark yanked upward on the arm again. This time Richie didn't scream. He wailed.

'Say uncle, or so help me God I'll break it.'

Richie's shirt had pulled out of his pants. His belly felt hot and scratched. He began to sob and wrench his shoulders from side to side. Yet the hateful four-eyes queer-boy stayed on. His forearm was ice, his shoulder fire.

'Get off me, you son of a whore! You don't fight fair!'

An explosion of pain.

'Say uncle.'

'No!'

He overbalanced on his knees and went facedown in the dust. The pain in his arm was paralyzing. He was eating dirt. There was dirt in his eyes. He thrashed his legs helplessly. He had forgotten about being *huge*. He had forgotten about how the ground trembled under his feet when he walked. He had forgotten that he was going to smoke Camels, just like his old man, when he grew up.

'Uncle! Uncle! Uncle!' Richie screamed. He felt that he could go on screaming uncle for hours, for days, if it would get his arm back.

'Say: "I'm a big ugly turd."'

'I'm a big ugly turd!' Richie screamed into the dirt.

'Good enough.'

Mark Petrie got off him and stepped back warily out of reach as Richie got up. His thighs hurt from squeezing them together. He hoped that all the fight was out of Richie. If not, he was going to get creamed.

Richie got up. He looked around. No one met his eyes. They turned away and went back to whatever they had been doing. That stinking Glick kid was standing next to the queer-boy and looking at him as though he were some kind of God.

Richie stood by himself, hardly able to believe how quickly his ruination had come. His face was dusty except where it had been streaked clean with his tears of rage and shame. He considered launching himself at Mark Petrie. Yet his shame and fear, new and shining and *huge*, would not allow it. Not yet. His arm ached like a rotted tooth. Son of a whoring dirty fighter. *If I ever land on you and get you down—*

But not today. He turned away and walked off and

the ground didn't tremble a bit. He looked at the ground so he wouldn't have to look anyone in the face.

Someone on the girls' side laughed – a high, mocking sound that carried with cruel clarity on the morning air.

He didn't look up to see who was laughing at him.

10

11:15 AM

The Jerusalem's Lot Town Dump had been a plain old gravel pit until it struck clay and paid out in 1945. It was at the end of a spur that led off from the Burns Road two miles beyond Harmony Hill Cemetery.

Dud Rogers could hear the faint putter and cough of Mike Ryerson's lawn mower down the road. But that sound would soon be blotted out by the crackle of flames.

Dud had been the dump custodian since 1956, and his reappointment each year at town meeting was routine and by acclamation. He lived at the dump in a neat tarpaper lean-to with a sign reading 'Dump Custodian' on the skew-hung door. He had wangled a space heater out of that skinflint board of selectmen three years ago, and had given up his apartment in town for good.

He was a hunchback with a curious cocked head that made him look as if God had given him a final petulant wrench before allowing him out into the world. His arms, which dangled apelike almost to his knees, were amazingly strong. It had taken four men to load the old hardware store floor safe into their panel truck to bring it out here when the store got its new wall job. The tires of the truck had settled appreciably when they put it in. But Dud Rogers had taken it off himself, cords standing out on his neck, veins bulging on his forehead and forearms and biceps like blue cables. He had pushed it over the east edge himself.

Dud *liked* the dump. He liked running off the kids who came here to bust bottles, and he liked directing traffic to wherever the day's dumping was going on. He liked dump-picking, which was his privilege as custodian. He supposed they sneered at him, walking across the mountains of trash in his hip waders and leather gloves, with his pistol in his holster, a sack over his shoulder, and his pocketknife in his hand. Let them sneer. There was copper core wire and sometimes whole motors with their copper wrappings intact, and copper fetched a good price in Portland. There were busted-out bureaus and chairs and sofas, things that could be fixed up and sold to the antique dealers on Route I. Dud rooked the dealers and the dealers turned around and rooked the summer people, and wasn't it just fine the way the world went round and round. He'd found a splintered spool bed with a busted frame two years back and had sold it to a faggot from Wells for two hundred bucks. The faggot had gone into ecstasies about the New England authenticity of that bed, never knowing how carefully Dud had sanded off the *Made in Grand Rapids* on the back of the headboard.

At the far end of the dump were the junked cars, Buicks and Fords and Chevies and you name it, and my God the parts people left on their machines when they were through with them. Radiators were best, but a good four-barrel carb would fetch seven dollars after it had been soaked in gasoline. Not to mention fan belts, taillights, distributor caps, windshields, steering wheels, and floor mats.

Yes, the dump was fine. The dump was Disneyland and Shangri-la all rolled up into one. But not even the money tucked away in the black box buried in the dirt below his easy chair was the best part.

The best part was the fires — and the rats.

Dud set parts of his dump on fire on Sunday and Wednesday mornings, and on Monday and Friday evenings. Evening fires were the prettiest. He loved the dusky, roseate glow that bloomed out of the green plastic bags of crap and all the newspapers and boxes. But morning fires were better for rats.

Now, sitting in his easy chair and watching the fire catch and begin to send its greasy black smoke into the air, sending the gulls aloft, Dud held his .22 target pistol loosely in his hand and waited for the rats to come out.

When they came, they came in battalions. They were big, dirty gray, pink-eyed. Small fleas and ticks jumped on their hides. Their tails dragged after them like thick pink wires. Dud loved to shoot rats.

'You buy a powerful slug o' shells, Dud,' George Middler down at the hardware store would say in his fruity voice, pushing the boxes of Remingtons across. 'Town pay for 'em?' This was an old joke. Some years back, Dud had put in a purchase order for two thousand rounds of hollow-point .22 cartridges, and Bill Norton had grimly sent him packing.

'Now,' Dud would say, 'you know this is purely a public service, George.'

There. That big fat one with the gimpy back leg was George Middler. Had something in his mouth that looked like a shredded piece of chicken liver.

'Here you go, George. Here y'are,' Dud said, and squeezed off. The .22's report was flat and undramatic, but the rat tumbled over twice and lay twitching. Hollow points, that was the ticket. Someday he was going to get a large-bore .45 or a .357 Magnum and see what that did to the little cock-knockers.

That next one now, that was that slutty little Ruthie Crockett, the one who didn't wear no bra to school and was always elbowing her chums and sniggering when Dud passed on the street. Bang. Good-by, Ruthie.

The rats scurried madly for the protection of the dump's far side, but before they were gone Dud had gotten six of them – a good morning's kill. If he went out there and looked at them, the ticks would be running off the cooling bodies like . . . like . . . why, like rats deserting a sinking ship.

This struck him as deliciously funny and he threw back his queerly cocked head and rocked back on his hump and laughed in great long gusts as the fire crept through the trash with its grasping orange fingers.

Life surely was grand.

11

12:00 noon

The town whistle went off with a great twelve-second blast, ushering in lunch hour at all three schools and welcoming the afternoon. Lawrence Crockett, the Lot's second selectman and proprietor of Crockett's Southern Maine Insurance and Realty, put away the book he had been reading (*Satan's Sex Slaves*) and set his watch by the whistle. He went to the door and hung the 'Back at One O'clock' sign from the shade pull. His routine was unvarying. He would walk up to the Excellent Café, have two cheeseburgers with the works and a cup of coffee, and watch Pauline's legs while he smoked a William Penn.

He rattled the doorknob once to make sure the lock had caught and moved off down Jointner Avenue. He paused on the corner and glanced up at the Marsten House. There was a car in the driveway. He could just make it out, twinkling and shining. It caused a thread of disquiet somewhere in his chest. He had sold the Marsten House and the long-defunct Village Washtub in a package deal over a year ago. It had been the strangest deal of his life – and he had made some strange ones in his time. The owner of the car up there was, in all probability, a man named Straker. R.T. Straker. And just this morning he had received something in the mail from this Straker.

The fellow in question had driven up to Crockett's office on a shimmering July afternoon just over a year ago. He got out of the car and stood on the sidewalk for a moment before coming inside, a tall man dressed in a sober three-piece suit in spite of the day's heat. He was as bald as a cueball and as sweatless as same. His eyebrows were a straight black slash, and the eye sockets shelved away below them to dark holes that might have been carved into the angular surface of his face with drill bits. He carried a slim black briefcase in one hand. Larry was alone in his office when Straker came in; his part-time secretary, a Falmouth girl with the most delectable set of jahoobies you ever clapped an eye to, worked for a Gates Falls lawyer on her afternoons.

The bald man sat down in the client's chair, put his

briefcase in his lap, and stared at Larry Crockett. It was impossible to read the expression in his eyes, and that bothered Larry. He liked to be able to read a man's wants in his baby blues or browns before the man even opened his mouth. This man had not paused to look at the pictures of local properties that were tacked up on the bulletin board, had not offered to shake hands and introduce himself, had not even said hello.

'How can I help you?' Larry asked.

'I have been sent to buy a residence and a business establishment in your so-fair town,' the bald man said. He spoke with a flat, uninflected tonelessness that made Larry think of the recorded announcements you got when you dialed the weather.

'Well, hey, wonderful,' Larry said. 'We have several very nice properties that might—'

'There is no need,' the bald man said, and held up his hand to stop Larry's words. Larry noted with fascination that his fingers were amazingly long – the middle finger looked four or five inches from base to tip. 'The business establishment is a block beyond the Town Office Building. It fronts on the park.'

'Yeah, I can deal with you on that. Used to be a Laundromat. Went broke a year ago. That'd be a real good location if you—'

'The residence,' the bald man overrode him, 'is the one referred to in town as the Marsten House.'

Larry had been in the business too long to show his thunderstruck feelings on his face. 'Is that so?'

'Yes. My name is Straker. Richard Throckett Straker. All papers will be in my name.'

'Very good,' Larry said. The man meant business, that much seemed clear enough. 'The asking price on the Marsten House is fourteen thousand, although I think my clients could be persuaded to take a little less. On the old washateria—'

'That is no accord. I have been authorized to pay one dollar.'

'One—?' Larry tilted his head forward the way a man will when he has failed to hear something correctly.

'Yes. Attend, please.'

Straker's long fingers undid the clasps on his brief-case, opened it, and took out a number of papers bound in a blue transparent folder.

Larry Crockett looked at him, frowning.

'Read, please. That will save time.'

Larry thumbed back the folder's plastic cover and glanced down at the first sheet with the air of a man humoring a fool. His eyes moved from left to right randomly for a moment, then riveted on something.

Straker smiled thinly. He reached inside his suit coat, produced a flat gold cigarette case, and selected a cigarette. He tamped it and then lit it with a wooden match. The harsh aroma of a Turkish blend filled the office and was eddied around by the fan.

There had been silence in the office for the next ten minutes, broken only by the hum of the fan and the muted passage of traffic on the street outside. Straker smoked his cigarette down to a shred, crushed the glowing ash between his fingers, and lit another.

Larry looked up, his face pale and shaken. 'This is a joke. Who put you up to it? John Kelly?'

'I know no John Kelly. I don't joke.'

'These papers . . . quit–claim deed . . . land title search . . . my God, man, don't you know that piece of land is worth one and a half million dollars?'

'You piker,' Straker said coldly. 'It is worth four million. Soon to be worth more, when the shopping center is built.'

'What do you want?' Larry asked. His voice was hoarse.

'I have told you what I want. My partner and I plan to open a business in this town. We plan to live in the Marsten House.'

'What sort of business? Murder Incorporated?'

Straker smiled coldly. 'A perfectly ordinary furniture business, I am afraid. With a line of rather special antiques for collectors. My partner is something of an expert in that field.'

'Shit,' Larry said crudely. 'The Marsten House you could have for eight and a half grand, the shop for sixteen. Your partner must know that. And you both must know that this town can't support a fancy furniture and antique place.'

'My partner is extremely knowledgeable on any subject in which he becomes interested,' Straker said. 'He knows that your town is on a highway which serves tourists and summer residents. These are the people with whom we expect to do the bulk of our business. However, that is no accord to you. Do you find the papers in order?'

Larry tapped his desk with the blue folder. 'They seem to be. But I'm not going to be horse-traded, no matter what you say you want.'

'No, of course not.' Straker's voice was edged with well-bred contempt. 'You have a lawyer in Boston, I believe. One Francis Walsh.'

'How do you know that?' Larry barked.

'It doesn't matter. Take the papers to him. He will confirm their validity. The land where this shopping center is to be built will be yours, on fulfillment of three conditions.'

'Ah,' Larry said, and looked relieved. 'Conditions.' He leaned back and selected a William Penn from the ceramic cigar box on his desk. He scratched a match on shoe leather and puffed. 'Now we're getting down to the bone. Fire away.'

'Number one. You will sell me the Marsten House and the business establishment for one dollar. Your client in the matter of the house is a land corporation in Bangor. The business establishment now belongs to a Portland bank. I am sure both parties will be agreeable if you make up the difference to the lowest acceptable prices. Minus your commission, of course.'

'Where do you get your information?'

'That is not for you to know, Mr Crockett. Condition two. You will say nothing of our transaction here today. Nothing. If the question ever comes up, all you know is what I have told you — we are two partners beginning a business aimed at tourists and summer people. This is very important.'

'I don't blab.'

'Nonetheless, I want to impress on you the seriousness of the condition. A time may come, Mr Crockett, when you will want to tell someone of the wonderful deal you made on this day. If you do so, I will find out. I will ruin you. Do you understand?'

'You sound like one of those cheap spy movies,' Larry said. He sounded unruffled, but underneath he felt a nasty

tremor of fear. The words *I will ruin you* had come out as
flatly as *How are you today.* It gave the statement an unpleasant
ring of truth. And how in hell did this joker know about
Frank Walsh? Not even his wife knew about Frank Walsh.

'Do you understand me, Mr Crockett?'

'Yes,' Larry said. 'I'm used to playing them close to
the vest.'

Straker offered his thin smile again. 'Of course. That
is why I am doing business with you.'

'The third condition?'

'The house will need certain renovations.'

'That's one way of puttin' it,' Larry said dryly.

'My partner plans to carry this task out himself. But
you will be his agent. From time to time there will be
requests. From time to time I will require the services of
whatever laborers you employ to bring certain things either
to the house or to the shop. You will not speak of such
services. Do you understand?'

'Yeah, I understand. But you don't come from these
parts, do you?'

'Does that have bearing?' Straker raised his eyebrows.

'Sure it does. This isn't Boston or New York. It's not
going to be just a matter of me keepin' my lip buttoned.
People are going to talk. Why, there's an old biddy over
on Railroad Street, name of Mabel Werts, who spends all
day with a pair of binoculars—'

'I don't care about the townspeople. My partner
doesn't care about the townspeople. The townspeople always
talk. They are no different from the magpies on the telephone wires. Soon they will accept us.'

Larry shrugged. 'It's your party.'

'As you say,' Straker agreed. 'You will pay for all services and keep all invoices and bills. You will be reimbursed. Do you agree?'

Larry was, as he had told Straker, used to playing them close to the vest, and he had a reputation as one of the best poker players in Cumberland County. And although he had maintained his outward calm through all of this, he was on fire inside. The deal this crazyman was offering him was the kind of thing that came along once, if ever. Perhaps the guy's boss was one of those nutty billionaire recluses who—

'Mr Crockett? I am waiting.'

'There are two conditions of my own,' Larry said.

'Ah?' Straker looked politely interested.

He rattled the blue folder. 'First, these papers have to check out.'

'Of course.'

'Second, if you're doing anything illegal up there, I don't want to know about it. By that I mean—'

But he was interrupted. Straker threw his head back and gave vent to a singularly cold and emotionless laugh.

'Did I say somethin' funny?' Larry asked, without a trace of a smile.

'Oh . . . ah . . . of course not, Mr Crockett. You must pardon my outburst. I found your comment amusing for reasons of my own. What were you about to add?'

'These renovations. I'm not going to get you anything that would leave my ass out to the wind. If you're fixing up to make moonshine or LSD or explosives for some hippie radical outfit, that's your own lookout.'

'Agreed,' Straker said. The smile was gone from his face. 'Have we a deal?'

And with an odd feeling of reluctance, Larry had said, 'If these papers check out, I guess we do at that. Although it seems like you did all the dealin' and I did all the money-makin'.'

'This is Monday,' Straker said. 'Shall I stop by Thursday afternoon?'

'Better make it Friday.'

'So it is. Very well.' He stood. 'Good day, Mr Crockett.'

The papers had checked out. Larry's Boston lawyer said the land where the Portland shopping center was to be built had been purchased by an outfit called Continental Land and Realty, which was a dummy company with office space in the Chemical Bank Building in New York. There was nothing in Continental's offices but a few empty filing cabinets and a lot of dust.

Straker had come back that Friday and Larry signed the necessary title papers. He did so with a strong taste of doubt in the back of his mouth. He had overthrown his own personal maxim for the first time: You don't shit where you eat. And although the inducement had been high, he realized as Straker put the ownership papers to the Marsten House and erstwhile Village Washtub into his briefcase that he had put himself at this man's beck and call. And the same went for his partner, the absent Mr Barlow.

As last August had passed, and as summer had slipped into fall and then fall into winter, he had begun to feel an indefinable sense of relief. By this spring he had almost managed to forget the deal he had made to get the papers which now resided in his Portland safe-deposit box.

Then things began to happen.

That writer, Mears, had come in a week and a half

ago, asking if the Marsten House was available for rental, and he had given Larry a peculiar look when he told him it was sold.

Yesterday there had been a long tube in his post office box and a letter from Straker. A note, really. It had been brief: 'Kindly have the poster which you will be receiving mounted in the window of the shop – R.T. Straker.' The poster itself was common enough, and more subdued than some. It only said: 'Opening in one week. Barlow and Straker. Fine furnishings. Selected antiques. Browsers welcome.' He had gotten Royal Snow to put it right up.

And now there was a car up there at the Marsten House. He was still looking at it when someone said at his elbow: 'Fallin' asleep, Larry?'

He jumped and looked around at Parkins Gillespie, who was standing on the corner next to him and lighting a Pall Mall.

'No,' he said, and laughed nervously. 'Just thinking.'

Parkins glanced up at the Marsten House, where the sun twinkled on chrome and metal in the driveway, then down at the old laundry with its new sign in the window. 'And you're not the only one, I guess. Always good to get new folks in town. You've met 'em, ain't you?'

'One of them. Last year.'

'Mr Barlow or Mr Straker?'

'Straker.'

'Seem like a nice enough sort, did he?'

'Hard to tell,' Larry said, and found he wanted to lick his lips. He didn't. 'We only talked business. He seemed okay.'

'Good. That's good. Come on. I'll walk up to the Excellent with you.'

When they crossed the street, Lawrence Crockett was thinking about deals with the devil.

12

1:00 PM

Susan Norton stepped into Babs' Beauty Boutique, smiled at Babs Griffen (Hal and Jack's eldest sister), and said, 'Thank goodness you could take me on such short notice.'

'No problem in the middle of the week,' Babs said, turning on the fan. 'My, ain't it close? It'll thunderstorm this afternoon.'

Susan looked at the sky, which was an unblemished blue. 'Do you think so?'

'Yeah. How do you want it, hon?'

'Natural,' Susan said, thinking of Ben Mears. 'Like I hadn't even been near this place.'

'Hon,' Babs said, closing in on her with a sigh, 'that's what they all say.'

The sigh wafted the odor of Juicy Fruit gum, and Babs asked Susan if she had seen that some folks were opening up a new furniture store in the old Village Washtub. Expensive stuff by the look of it, but wouldn't it be nice if they had a nice little hurricane lamp to match the one she had in her apartment and getting away from home and living in town was the smartest move she'd ever made and hadn't it been a nice summer? It seemed a shame it ever had to end.

13

3:00 PM

Bonnie Sawyer was lying on the big double bed in her house on the Deep Cut Road. It was a regular house, no shanty trailer, and it had a foundation and a cellar. Her husband, Reg, made good money as a car mechanic at Jim Smith's Pontiac in Buxton.

She was naked except for a pair of filmy blue panties, and she looked impatiently over at the clock on the night-stand: 3:02 − where was he?

Almost as if the thought had summoned him, the bedroom door opened the tiniest bit, and Corey Bryant peered through.

'Is it okay?' he whispered. Corey was only twenty-two, had been working for the phone company two years, and this affair with a married woman − especially a knockout like Bonnie Sawyer, who had been Miss Cumberland County of 1973 − left him feeling weak and nervous and horny.

Bonnie smiled at him with her lovely capped teeth. 'If it wasn't, honey,' she said, 'you'd have a hole in you big enough to watch TV through.'

He came tiptoeing in, his utility lineman's belt jingling ridiculously around his waist.

Bonnie giggled and opened her arms. 'I really like you, Corey. You're cute.'

Corey's eyes happened on the dark shadow beneath the taut blue nylon, and he began to feel more horny than nervous. He forgot about tiptoeing and came to her, and as they joined, a cicada began to buzz somewhere in the woods.

14

4:00 PM

Ben Mears pushed away from his desk, the afternoon's writing done. He had forgone his walk in the park so he could go to dinner at the Nortons' that night with a clear conscience, and had written for most of the day without a break.

He stood up and stretched, listening to the bones in his spine crackle. His torso was wet with sweat. He went to the cupboard at the head of the bed, pulled out a fresh towel, and went down to the bathroom to shower before everyone else got home from work and clogged the place.

He hung the towel over his shoulder, turned back to the door, and then went to the window, where something had caught his eye. Nothing in town; it was drowsing away the late afternoon under a sky that peculiar shade of deep blue that graces New England on fine late summer days.

He could look across the two-story buildings on Jointner Avenue, could see their flat, asphalted roofs, and across the park where the children now home from school lazed or biked or squabbled, and out to the northwest section of town where Brock Street disappeared behind the shoulder of that first wooded hill. His eyes traveled naturally up to the break in the woods where the Burns Road and the Brooks Road intersected in a **T** – and on up to where the Marsten House sat overlooking the town.

From here it was a perfect miniature, diminished to the size of a child's dollhouse. And he liked it that way. From here the Marsten House was a size that could be coped with. You could hold up your hand and blot it out with your palm.

There was a car in the driveway.

He stood with the towel over his shoulder, looking out at it, not moving, feeling a crawl of terror in his belly that he did not try to analyze. Two of the fallen shutters had been replaced, too, giving the house a secretive, blind look that it had not possessed before.

His lips moved silently, as if forming words no one – even himself – could understand.

15

5:00 PM

Matthew Burke left the high school carrying his briefcase in his left hand and crossed the empty parking lot to where his old Chevy Biscayne sat, still on last year's snow tires.

He was sixty-three, two years from mandatory retirement, and still carrying a full load of English classes and extracurricular activities. Fall's activity was the school play, and he had just finished readings for a three-act farce called *Charley's Problem*. He had gotten the usual glut of utter impossibles, perhaps a dozen usable warm bodies who would at least memorize their lines (and then deliver them in a deathly, trembling monotone), and three kids who showed flair. He would cast them on Friday and begin blocking next week. They would pull together between then and October 30, which was the play date. It was Matt's theory that a high school play should be like a bowl of Campbell's Alphabet Soup: tasteless but not actively offensive. The relatives would come and love it. The theater critic from the Cumberland *Ledger* would come and go into polysyllabic ecstasies, as he was paid to do over any local play. The female lead (Ruthie Crockett this year, probably) would fall in love with some other cast member and quite possibly lose her virginity after the cast party. And then he would pick up the threads of the Debate Club.

At sixty-three, Matt Burke still enjoyed teaching. He was a lousy disciplinarian, thus forfeiting any chance he might once have had to step up to administration (he was a little too dreamy-eyed to ever serve effectively as an assistant principal), but his lack of discipline had never held him back. He had read the sonnets of Shakespeare in cold, pipe-clanking classrooms full of flying airplanes and spitballs, had sat down upon tacks and thrown them away absently as he told the class to turn to page 467 in their grammars, had opened drawers to get composition paper only to discover crickets, frogs, and once a seven-foot black snake.

He had ranged across the length and breadth of the English language like a solitary and oddly complacent Ancient Mariner: Steinbeck period one, Chaucer period two, the topic sentence period three, and the function of the gerund just before lunch. His fingers were permanently yellowed with chalk dust rather than nicotine, but it was still the residue of an addicting substance.

Children did not revere or love him; he was not a Mr Chips languishing away in a rustic corner of America and waiting for Ross Hunter to discover him, but many of his students did come to respect him, and a few learned from him that dedication, however eccentric or humble, can be a noteworthy thing. He liked his work.

Now he got into his car, pumped the accelerator too much and flooded it, waited, and started it again. He tuned the radio to a Portland rock 'n' roll station and jacked the volume almost to the speaker's distortion point. He thought rock 'n' roll was fine music. He backed out of his parking slot, stalled, and started the car up again.

He had a small house out on the Taggart Stream Road, and had very few callers. He had never been married, had no family except for a brother in Texas who worked for an oil company and never wrote. He did not really miss the attachments. He was a solitary man, but solitude had in no way twisted him.

He paused at the blinking light at the intersection of Jointner Avenue and Brock Street, then turned toward home. The shadows were long now, and the daylight had taken on a curiously beautiful warmth – flat and golden, like something from a French Impressionist painting. He glanced over to his left, saw the Marsten House, and glanced again.

'The shutters,' he said aloud, against the driving beat from the radio. 'Those shutters are back up.'

He glanced in the rearview mirror and saw that there was a car parked in the driveway. He had been teaching in 'salem's Lot since 1952, and he had never seen a car parked in that driveway.

'Is someone living up there?' he asked no one in particular, and drove on.

16

6:00 PM

Susan's father, Bill Norton, the Lot's first selectman, was surprised to find that he liked Ben Mears – liked him quite a lot. Bill was a big, tough man with black hair, built like a truck, and not fat even after fifty. He had left high school for the Navy in the eleventh grade with his father's permission, and he had clawed his way up from there, picking up his diploma at the age of twenty-four on a high school equivalency test taken almost as an afterthought. He was not a blind, bullish anti-intellectual as some plain workingmen become when they are denied the level of learning that they may have been capable of, either through fate or their own doing, but he had no patience with 'art farts,' as he termed some of the doe-eyed, long-haired boys Susan had brought home from school. He didn't mind their hair or their dress. What bothered him was that none of them seemed serious-minded. He didn't share his wife's liking for Floyd Tibbits, the boy that Susie had been going around with the most since she graduated, but he didn't actively dislike him, either. Floyd had a pretty good job at the executive level in the Falmouth Grant's, and Bill Norton considered him to be moderately serious-minded. And he was a hometown boy. But so was this Mears, in a manner of speaking.

'Now, you leave him alone about that art fart business,' Susan said, rising at the sound of the doorbell. She was wearing a light green summer dress, her new casual hairdo pulled back and tied loosely with a hank of over-sized green yarn.

Bill laughed. 'I got to call 'em as I see 'em, Susie darlin'. I won't embarrass you . . . never do, do I?'

She gave him a pensive, nervous smile and went to open the door.

The man who came back in with her was lanky and agile-looking, with finely drawn features and a thick, almost greasy shock of black hair that looked freshly washed despite its natural oiliness. He was dressed in a way that impressed Bill favorably: plain blue jeans, very new, and a white shirt rolled to the elbows.

'Ben, this is my dad and mom – Bill and Ann Norton. Mom, Dad, Ben Mears.'

'Hello. Nice to meet you.'

He smiled at Mrs Norton with a touch of reserve and she said, 'Hello, Mr Mears. This is the first time we've seen a real live author up close. Susan has been *awfully* excited.'

'Don't worry; I don't quote from my own works.' He smiled again.

'H'lo,' Bill said, and heaved himself up out of his chair. He had worked himself up to the union position he now held on the Portland docks, and his grip was hard and strong. But Mears's hand did not crimp and jellyfish like that of your ordinary, garden-variety art fart, and Bill was pleased. He imposed his second testing criterion.

'Like a beer? Got some on ice out yonder.' He gestured toward the back patio, which he had built himself. Art farts invariably said no; most of them were potheads and couldn't waste their valuable consciousness juicing.

'Man, I'd love a beer,' Ben said, and the smile became a grin. 'Two or three, even.'

Bill's laughter boomed out. 'Okay, you're my man. Come on.'

At the sound of his laughter, an odd communication seemed to pass between the two women, who bore a strong resemblance to each other. Ann Norton's brow contracted while Susan's smoothed out – a load of worry seemed to have been transferred across the room by telepathy.

Ben followed Bill out onto the veranda. An ice chest

sat on a stool in the corner, stuffed with ring-tab cans of Pabst. Bill pulled a can out of the cooler and tossed it to Ben, who caught it one-hand but lightly, so it wouldn't fizz.

'Nice out here,' Ben said, looking toward the barbecue in the backyard. It was a low, businesslike construction of bricks, and a shimmer of heat hung over it.

'Built it myself,' Bill said. 'Better be nice.'

Ben drank deeply and then belched, another sign in his favor.

'Susie thinks you're quite the fella,' Norton said.

'She's a nice girl.'

'Good practical girl,' Norton added, and belched reflectively. 'She says you've written three books. Published 'em, too.'

'Yes, that's so.'

'They do well?'

'The first did,' Ben said, and said no more. Bill Norton nodded slightly, in approval of a man who had enough marbles to keep his dollars-and-cents business to himself.

'You like to lend a hand with some burgers and hot dogs?'

'Sure.'

'You got to cut the hot dogs to let the squidges out of 'em. You know about that?'

'Yeah.' He made diagonal slashes in the air with his right index finger, grinning slightly as he did so. The small slashes in natural casing franks kept them from blistering.

'You came from this neck of the woods, all right,' Bill Norton said. 'Goddamn well told. Take that bag of briquettes over there and I'll get the meat. Bring your beer.'

'You couldn't part me from it.'

Bill hesitated on the verge of going in and cocked an eyebrow at Ben Mears. 'You a serious-minded fella?' he asked.

Ben smiled, a trifle grimly. 'That I am,' he said.

Bill nodded. 'That's good,' he said, and went inside.

Babs Griffen's prediction of rain was a million miles wrong, and the backyard dinner went well. A light breeze sprang up, combining with the eddies of hickory smoke from the barbecue to keep the worst of the late-season mosquitoes away. The women cleared away the paper plates and condiments, then came back to drink a beer each and laugh as Bill, an old hand at playing the tricky wind currents, trimmed Ben 21–6 at badminton. Ben declined a rematch with real regret, pointing at his watch.

'I got a book on the fire,' he said. 'I owe another six pages. If I get drunk, I won't even be able to read what I wrote tomorrow morning.'

Susan saw him to the front gate – he had walked up from town. Bill nodded to himself as he damped the fire. He had said he was serious-minded, and Bill was ready to take him at his word. He had not come with a big case on to impress anyone, but any man who worked after dinner was out to make his mark on somebody's tree, probably in big letters.

Ann Norton, however, never quite unthawed.

17

7:00 PM

Floyd Tibbits pulled into the crushed-stone parking lot at Dell's about ten minutes after Delbert Markey, owner and bartender, had turned on his new pink sign out front. The sign said DELL'S in letters three feet high, and the apostrophe was a highball glass.

Outside, the sunlight had been leached from the sky by gathering purple twilight, and soon ground mist would begin to form in the low-lying pockets of land. The night's regulars would begin to show up in another hour or so.

'Hi, Floyd,' Dell said, pulling a Michelob out of the cooler. 'Good day?'

'Fair,' Floyd said. 'That beer looks good.'

He was a tall man with a well-trimmed sandy beard, now dressed in double-knit slacks and a casual sports jacket – his Grant's working uniform. He was second in charge of credit, and liked his work in the absent kind of way that can cross the line into boredom almost overnight. He felt himself to be drifting, but the sensation was not actively unpleasant. And there was Suze – a fine girl. She was going to come around before much longer, and then he supposed he would have to make something of himself.

He dropped a dollar bill on the bar, poured beer down the side of his glass, downed it thirstily, and refilled. The bar's only other patron at present was a young fellow in phone-company coveralls – the Bryant kid, Floyd thought. He was drinking beer at a table and listening to a moody love song on the juke.

'So what's new in town?' Floyd asked, knowing the answer already. Nothing new, not really. Someone might have showed up drunk at the high school, but he couldn't think of anything else.

'Well, somebody killed your uncle's dog. That's new.'

Floyd paused with his glass halfway to his mouth. 'What? Uncle Win's dog, Doc?'

'That's right.'

'Hit him with a car?'

'Not so you'd notice. Mike Ryerson found him. He was out to Harmony Hill to mow the grass and Doc was hangin' off those spikes atop the cemetery gate. Ripped wide open.'

'Son of a bitch!' Floyd said, astounded.

Dell nodded gravely, pleased with the impression he had made. He knew something else that was a fairly hot item in town this evening – that Floyd's girl had been seen with that writer who was staying at Eva's. But let Floyd find that out for himself.

'Ryerson brung the co'pse in to Parkins Gillespie,' he told Floyd. '*He* was of the mind that maybe the dog was dead and a bunch of kids hung it up for a joke.'

'Gillespie doesn't know his ass from a hole in the ground.'

'Maybe not. I'll tell you what *I* think.' Dell leaned forward on his thick forearms. 'I think it's kids, all right . . . hell, I *know* that. But it might be a smidge more serious than just a joke. Here, looka this.' He reached under the bar and slapped a newspaper down on it, turned to an inside page.

Floyd picked it up. The headline read SATAN WORSHIP-PERS DESECRATE FLA. CHURCH. He skimmed through it. Apparently a bunch of kids had broken into a Catholic Church in Clewiston, Florida, some time after midnight and had held some sort of unholy rites there. The altar had been desecrated, obscene words had been scrawled on the pews, the confessionals, and the holy font, and splatters of blood had been found on steps leading to the nave. Laboratory analysis had confirmed that although some of the blood was animal (goat's blood was suggested), most of it was human. The Clewiston police chief admitted there were no immediate leads.

Floyd put the paper down. 'Devil worshippers in the Lot? Come on, Dell. You've been into the cook's pot.'

'The kids are going crazy,' Dell said stubbornly. 'You see if that ain't it. Next thing you know, they'll be doing human sacrifices in Griffen's pasture. Want a refill on that?'

'No thanks,' Floyd said, sliding off his stool. 'I think I'll go out and see how Uncle Win's getting along. He loved that dog.'

'Give him my best,' Dell said, stowing his paper back under the bar – Exhibit A for later in the evening. 'Awful sorry to hear about it.'

Floyd paused halfway to the door and spoke, seemingly to the air. 'Hung him up on the spikes, did they? By Christ, I'd like to get hold of the kids who did that.'

'Devil worshippers,' Dell said. 'Wouldn't surprise me a bit. I don't know what's got into people these days.'

Floyd left. The Bryant kid put another dime in the juke, and Dick Curless began to sing 'Bury the Bottle with Me.'

18

7:30 PM

'You be home early,' Marjorie Glick said to her eldest son, Danny. 'School tomorrow. I want your brother in bed by quarter past nine.'

Danny shuffled his feet. 'I don't see why I have to take him at all.'

'You don't,' Marjorie said with dangerous pleasant-ness. 'You can always stay home.'

She turned back to the counter, where she was fresh-ening fish, and Ralphie stuck out his tongue. Danny made a fist and shook it, but his putrid little brother only smiled.

'We'll be back,' he muttered and turned to leave the kitchen, Ralphie in tow.

'By nine.'

'Okay, *okay*.'

In the living room Tony Glick was sitting in front of the TV with his feet up, watching the Red Sox and the Yankees. 'Where are you going, boys?'

'Over to see that new kid,' Danny said. 'Mark Petrie.'

'Yeah,' Ralphie said. 'We're gonna look at his . . . *electric trains*.'

Danny cast a baleful eye on his brother, but their father noticed neither the pause nor the emphasis. Doug Griffen had just struck out. 'Be home early,' he said absently.

Outside, afterlight still lingered in the sky, although sunset had passed. As they crossed the backyard Danny said, 'I ought to beat the stuff out of you, punko.'

'I'll tell,' Ralphie said smugly. 'I'll tell why you *really* wanted to go.'

'You creep,' Danny said hopelessly.

At the back of the mowed yard, a beaten path led down the slope to the woods. The Glick house was on Brock Street, Mark Petrie's on South Jointner Avenue. The path was a shortcut that saved considerable time if you were twelve and nine years old and willing to pick your way across the Crockett Brook stepping-stones. Pine needles and twigs crackled under their feet. Somewhere in the woods, a whippoor-will sang, and crickets chirred all around them.

Danny had made the mistake of telling his brother that Mark Petrie had the entire set of Aurora plastic monsters – wolfman, mummy, Dracula, Frankenstein, the mad doctor, and even the Chamber of Horrors. Their mother thought all that stuff was bad news, rotted your brains or something, and Danny's brother had immediately turned black-mailer. He was putrid, all right.

'You're putrid, you know that?' Danny said.

'I know,' Ralphie said proudly. 'What's putrid?'

'It's when you get green and squishy, like boogers.'

'Get bent,' Ralphie said. They were going down the bank of Crockett Brook, which gurgled leisurely over its gravel bed, holding a faint pearliness on its surface. Two miles east it joined Taggart Stream, which in turn joined the Royal River.

Danny started across the stepping-stones, squinting in the gathering gloom to see his footing.

'I'm gonna pushya!' Ralphie cried gleefully behind him. 'Look out, Danny, I'm gonna pushya!'

'You push me and I'll push you in the quicksand, ringmeat,' Danny said.

They reached the other bank. 'There ain't no quick-sand around here,' Ralphie scoffed, moving closer to his brother nevertheless.

'Yeah?' Danny said ominously. 'A kid got killed in the quicksand just a few years ago. I heard those old dudes that hang around the store talkin' about it.'

'Really?' Ralphie asked. His eyes were wide.

'Yeah,' Danny said. 'He went down screamin' and hollerin' and his mouth filled up with quicksand and that was it. *Raaaacccccchhhh.*'

'C'mon,' Ralphie said uneasily. It was close to full dark now, and the woods were full of moving shadows. 'Let's get out of here.'

They started up the other bank, slipping a little in the pine needless. The boy Danny had heard discussed in the store was a ten-year-old named Jerry Kingfield. He might have gone down in the quicksand screaming and hollering, but if he had, no one had heard him. He had simply disappeared in the Marshes six years ago while fishing. Some people thought quicksand, others held that a sex preevert had killed him. There were preeverts everywhere.

'They say his ghost still haunts these woods,' Danny said solemnly, neglecting to tell his little brother that the Marshes were three miles south.

'Don't, Danny,' Ralphie said uneasily. 'Not . . . not in the dark.'

The woods creaked secretively around them. The whippoorwill had ceased his cry. A branch snapped somewhere behind them, almost stealthily. The daylight was nearly gone from the sky.

'Every now and then,' Danny went on eerily, 'when some ringmeat little kid comes out after dark, it comes flapping out of the trees, the face all putrid and covered with quicksand—'

'Danny, *come on.*'

His little brother's voice held real pleading, and Danny stopped. He had almost scared himself. The trees were dark, bulking presences all around them, moving slowly in the night breeze, rubbing together, creaking in their joints.

Another branch snapped off to their left.

Danny suddenly wished they had gone by the road.

Another branch snapped.

'Danny, I'm scared,' Ralphie whispered.

'Don't be stupid,' Danny said. 'Come on.'

They started to walk again. Their feet crackled in the pine needles. Danny told himself that he didn't hear any branches snapping. He didn't hear anything except them. Blood thudded in his temples. His hands were cold. Count steps, he told himself. We'll be at Jointner Avenue in two hundred steps. And when we come back we'll go by the road, so ringmeat won't be scared. In just a minute we'll see the streetlights and feel stupid but it will be *good* to feel stupid so count steps. One . . . two . . . three . . .

Ralphie shrieked.

'I see it! I see the ghost! I SEE IT!'

Terror like hot iron leaped into Danny's chest. Wires seemed to have run up his legs. He would have turned and run, but Ralphie was clutching him.

'Where?' he whispered, forgetting that he had invented the ghost. 'Where?' He peered into the woods, half afraid of what he might see, and saw only blackness.

'It's gone now — but I saw him . . . it. Eyes. I saw eyes. Oh, Danneee—' He was blubbering.

'There ain't no ghosts, you fool. Come on.'

Danny held his brother's hand and they began to walk. His legs felt as if they were made up of ten thousand pencil erasers. His knees were trembling. Ralphie was crowding against him, almost forcing him off the path.

'It's watchin' us,' Ralphie whispered.

'Listen, I'm not gonna—'

'No, Danny. Really. Can't you *feel* it?'

Danny stopped. And in the way of children, he did feel something and knew they were no longer alone. A great hush had fallen over the woods; but it was a malefic hush. Shadows, urged by the wind, twisted languorously around them.

And Danny smelled something savage, but not with his nose.

There were no ghosts, but there *were* preeverts. They stopped in black cars and offered you candy or hung around on street corners or . . . or they followed you into the woods . . .

And then . . .

Oh and then they . . .

'Run,' he said harshly.

But Ralphie trembled beside him in a paralysis of fear. His grip on Danny's hand was as tight as baling wire. His eyes stared into the woods, and then began to widen.

'Danny?'

A branch snapped.

Danny turned and looked where his brother was looking.

The darkness enfolded them.

19

9:00 PM

Mabel Werts was a hugely fat woman, seventy-four on her last birthday, and her legs had become less and less reliable. She was a repository of town history and town gossip, and her memory stretched back over five decades of necrology, adultery, thievery, and insanity. She was a gossip but not a deliberately cruel one (although those whose stories she had sped on their back fence way might tend to disagree); she simply lived in and for the town. In a way she *was* the town, a fat widow who now went out very little, and who spent most of her time by her window dressed in a tentlike silk camisole, her yellowish-ivory hair done up in a coronet of thick, braided cables, with the telephone on her right hand and her high-powered Japanese binoculars on the left. The combination of the two – plus the time to use them fully – made her a benevolent spider sitting in the center of a communications web that stretched from the Bend to east 'salem.

She had been watching the Marsten House for want of something better to watch when the shutters to the left of the porch were opened, letting out a golden square of light that was definitely not the steady glow of electricity. She had gotten just a tantalizing glimpse of what might have been a man's head and shoulders silhouetted against the light. It gave her a queer thrill.

There had been no more movement from the house.

She thought: Now, what kind of people is it that only opens up when a body can't catch a decent glimpse of them?

She put the glasses down and carefully picked up the telephone. Two voices – she quickly identified them as Harriet Durham and Glynis Mayberry – were talking about the Ryerson boy finding Irwin Purinton's dog.

She sat quietly, breathing through her mouth, so as to give no sign of her presence on the line.

20

11:59 PM

The day trembled on the edge of extinction. The houses slept in darkness. Downtown, night lights in the hardware store and the Foreman Funeral Home and the Excellent Café threw mild electric light onto the pavement. Some lay awake – George Boyer, who had just gotten home from the three-to-eleven shift at the Gates Mill, Win Purinton, sitting and playing solitaire and unable to sleep for thinking of his Doc, whose passing had affected him much more deeply than that of his wife – but most slept the sleep of the just and the hard-working.

In Harmony Hill Cemetery a dark figure stood meditatively inside the gate, waiting for the turn of time. When he spoke, the voice was soft and cultured.

'O my father, favor me now. Lord of Flies, favor me now. Now I bring you spoiled meat and reeking flesh. I have made sacrifice for your favor. With my left hand I bring it. Make a sign for me on this ground, consecrated in your name. I wait for a sign to begin your work.'

The voice died away. A wind had sprung up, gentle, bringing with it the sigh and whisper of leafy branches and grasses and a whiff of carrion from the dump up the road.

There was no sound but that brought on the breeze. The figure stood silent and thoughtful for a time. Then it stooped and stood with the figure of a child in his arms.

'I bring you this.'

It became unspeakable.

CHAPTER FOUR
DANNY GLICK AND OTHERS

Danny and Ralphie Glick had gone out to see Mark Petrie with orders to be in by nine, and when they hadn't come home by ten past, Marjorie Glick called the Petrie house. No, Mrs Petrie said, the boys weren't there. Hadn't been there. Maybe your husband had better talk to Henry. Mrs Glick handed the phone to her husband, feeling the lightness of fear in her belly.

The men talked it over. Yes, the boys had gone by the woods path. No, the little brook was very shallow at this time of year, especially after the fine weather. No more than ankle-deep. Henry suggested that he start from his end of the path with a high-powered flashlight and Mr Glick start from his. Perhaps the boys had found a woodchuck burrow or were smoking cigarettes or something. Tony agreed and thanked Mr Petrie for his trouble. Mr Petrie said it was no trouble at all. Tony hung up and comforted his wife a little; she was frightened. He had mentally decided that neither of the boys was going to be able to sit down for a week when he found them.

But before he had even left the yard, Danny stumbled out from the trees and collapsed beside the backyard barbecue. He was dazed and slow-spoken, responding to questions ploddingly and not always sensibly. There was grass in his cuffs and a few autumn leaves in his hair.

He told his father that he and Ralphie had gone down the path through the woods, had crossed Crockett Brook by the stepping-stones, and had gotten up the other bank with no trouble. Then Ralphie began to talk about a ghost in the woods (Danny neglected to mention he had put this idea in his brother's head). Ralphie said he could see a face. Danny began to be frightened. He didn't believe in ghosts or in any kid stuff like the bogeyman, but he did think he had heard something in the dark.

What did they do then?

Danny thought they had started to walk again, holding hands. He wasn't sure. Ralphie had been whimpering about the ghost. Danny told him not to cry, because soon they would be able to see the streetlights of Jointner Avenue. It was only two hundred steps, maybe less. Then something bad had happened.

What? What was the bad thing?

Danny didn't know.

They argued with him, grew excited, expostulated. Danny only shook his head slowly and uncomprehendingly. Yes, he knew he should remember, but he couldn't. Honestly, he couldn't. No, he didn't remember falling over anything. Just . . . everything was dark. Very dark. And the next thing he remembered was lying on the path by himself. Ralphie was gone.

Parkins Gillespie said there was no point in sending men into the woods that night. Too many deadfalls. Probably the boy had just wandered off the path. He and Nolly Gardener and Tony Glick and Henry Petrie went up and down the path and along the shoulders of both South Jointner and Brock streets, hailing with battery-powered bullhorns.

Early the next morning, both the Cumberland and the state police began a coordinated search of the wood lot. When they found nothing, the search was widened. They beat the bushes for four days, and Mr and Mrs Glick wandered through the woods and fields, picking their way around the deadfalls left by the ancient fire, calling their son's name with endless and wrenching hope.

When there was no result, Taggart Stream and the Royal River were dragged. No result.

On the morning of the fifth day, Marjorie Glick woke her husband at 4:00 AM, terrified and hysterical. Danny had collapsed in the upstairs hallway, apparently on his way to the bathroom. An ambulance bore him away to Central Maine General Hospital. The preliminary diagnosis was severe and delayed emotional shock.

The doctor in charge, a man named Gorby, took Mr Glick aside.

'Has your boy ever been subject to asthma attacks?'

Mr Glick, blinking rapidly, shook his head. He had aged ten years in less than a week.

'Any history of rheumatic fever?'

'Danny? No . . . not Danny.'

'Has he had a TB skin patch during the last year?'

'TB? My boy got TB?'

'Mr Glick, we're only trying to find out—'

'Marge! Margie, come down here!'

Marjorie Glick got up and walked slowly down the corridor. Her face was pale, her hair absently combed. She looked like a woman in the grip of a deep migraine headache.

'Did Danny have a TB skin patch at school this year?'

'Yes,' she said dully. 'When he started school. No reaction.'

Gorby asked, 'Does he cough in the night?'

'No.'

'Complain of aches in the chest or joints?'

'No.'

'Painful urination?'

'No.'

'Any abnormal bleeding? Bloody noses or bloody stool or even an abnormal number of scrapes and bruises?'

'No.'

Gorby smiled and nodded. 'We'd like to keep him for tests, if we may.'

'Sure,' Tony said. 'Sure. I got Blue Cross.'

'His reactions are very slow,' the doctor said. 'We're going to do some X-rays, a marrow test, a white count—'

Marjorie Glick's eyes had slowly been widening. 'Has Danny got leukemia?' she whispered.

'Mrs Glick, that's hardly—'

But she had fainted.

2

Ben Mears was one of the 'salem's Lot volunteers who beat the bushes for Ralphie Glick, and he got nothing for his pains other than pants cuffs full of cockleburs and an aggravated case of hay fever brought on by late summer goldenrod.

On the third day of the search he came into the kitchen of Eva's ready to eat a can of ravioli and then fall into bed for a nap before writing. He found Susan Norton bustling around the kitchen stove and preparing some kind of hamburger casserole. The men just home from work were sitting around the table, pretending to talk, and ogling her – she was wearing a faded check shirt tied at the midriff and cutoff corduroy shorts. Eva Miller was ironing in a private alcove off the kitchen.

'Hey, what are you doing here?' he asked.

'Cooking you something decent before you fall away to a shadow,' she said, and Eva snorted laughter from behind the angle of the wall. Ben felt his ears burn.

'Cooks real good, she does,' Weasel said. 'I can tell. I been watchin'.'

'If you was watchin' any more, your eyes woulda fell outta their sockets,' Grover Verrill said, and cackled.

Susan covered the casserole, put it in the oven, and they went out on the back porch to wait for it. The sun was going down red and inflamed.

'Any luck?'

'No. Nothing.' He pulled a battered pack of cigarettes out of his breast pocket and lit one.

'You smell like you took a bath in Old Woodsman's,' she said.

'Fat lot of good it did.' He held out his arm and showed her a number of puffed insect bites and half-healed scratches. 'Son of a bitching mosquitoes and goddamn pricker bushes.'

'What do you think happened to him, Ben?'

'God knows.' He exhaled smoke. 'Maybe somebody crept up behind the older brother, coshed him with a sock full of sand or something, and abducted the kid.'

'Do you think he's dead?'

Ben looked at her to see if she wanted an honest answer or merely a hopeful one. He took her hand and locked his fingers through hers. 'Yes,' he said briefly. 'I think the kid is dead. No conclusive proof yet, but I think so.'

She shook her head slowly. 'I hope you're wrong. My mom and some of the other ladies have been in to sit with Mrs Glick. She's out of her mind and so is her husband. And the other boy just wanders around like a ghost.'

'Um,' Ben said. He was looking up at the Marsten House, not really listening. The shutters were closed; they would open up later on. After dark. The shutters would open after dark. He felt a morbid chill at the thought and its nearly incantatory quality.

'. . . night?'

'Hmm? Sorry.' He looked around at her.

'I said, my dad would like you to come over tomorrow night. Can you?'

'Will you be there?'

'Sure, I will,' she said, and looked at him.

'All right. Good.' He wanted to look at her – she was lovely in the sunset light – but his eyes were drawn toward the Marsten House as if by a magnet.

'It draws you, doesn't it?' she said, and the reading of his thought, right down to the metaphor, was nearly uncanny.

'Yes. It does.'

'Ben, what's this new book about?'

'Not yet,' he said. 'Give it time. I'll tell you as soon as I can. It's . . . got to work itself out.'

She wanted to say *I love you* at that precise moment, say it with the ease and lack of self-consciousness with which the thought had risen to the surface of her mind, but she bit the words off behind her lips. She did not want to say it while he was looking . . . looking up there.

She got up. 'I'll check the casserole.'

When she left him, he was smoking and looking up at the Marsten House.

3

Lawrence Crockett was sitting in his office on the morning of the twenty-second, pretending to read his Monday correspondence and keeping an eye on his secretary's jahoobies, when the telephone rang. He had been thinking about his business career in 'salem's Lot, about that small, twinkling car in the Marsten House driveway, and about deals with the devil.

Even before the deal with Straker had been consummated (that's some word, all right, he thought, and his eyes crawled over the front of his secretary's blouse), Lawrence Crockett was, without doubt, the richest man in 'salem's Lot and one of the richest in Cumberland County, although there was nothing about his office or his person to indicate it. The office was old, dusty, and lighted by two fly-specked yellow globes. The desk was an ancient rolltop, littered with papers, pens, and correspondence. A glue pot stood on one side of it and on the other was a square glass paperweight that showed pictures of his family on its different faces. Poised perilously on top of a stack of ledgers was a glass fish bowl filled with matches, and a sign on the front said, 'For Our Matchless Friends.' Except for three fireproof steel filing cabinets and the secretary's desk in a small enclosure, the office was barren.

There were, however, pictures.

Snapshots and photos were everywhere – tacked, stapled, or taped to every available surface. Some were new Polaroid prints, others were colored Kodak shots taken a few years back, still more were curled and yellowing black-and-whites, some going back fifteen years. Beneath each was a typed caption: *Fine Country Living! Six Rms.* or *Hilltop Location! Taggart Stream Road, $32,000 – Cheap! or Fit for a Squire! Ten-Rm. Farmhouse, Burns Road.* It looked like a dismal, fly-by-night operation and so it had been until 1957, when Larry Crockett, who was regarded by the better element in Jerusalem's Lot as only one step above shiftless, had decided that trailers were the wave of the future. In those dim dead days, most people thought of trailers as those cute silvery things you hooked on the back of your car when you wanted to go to Yellowstone National Park and take pictures of your wife and kids standing in front of Old Faithful. In those dim dead days, hardly anyone – even the trailer manufacturers themselves – foresaw a day when the cute silvery things would be replaced by campers, which hooked right over the bed of your Chevy pickup or which could come complete and motorized in themselves.

Larry, however, had not needed to know these things. A bush-league visionary at best, he had simply gone down to the town office (in those days he was not a selectman; in those days he couldn't have gotten elected dogcatcher) and looked up the Jerusalem's Lot zoning laws. They were tremendously satisfactory. Peering between the lines, he could see thousands of dollars. The law said you could not maintain a public dumping ground, or have more than three junked cars in your yard unless you also had a junk yard permit, or have a chemical toilet – a fancy and not very accurate term for outhouse – unless it was approved by the Town Health Officer. And that was it.

Larry had mortgaged himself to the hilt, had borrowed more, and had bought three trailers. Not cute little silvery things but long, plush, thyroidal monsters with plastic wood paneling and Formica bathrooms. He bought one-acre plots for each in the Bend, where land was cheap, had set them on cheap foundations, and had gone to work selling them. He had done so in three months, overcoming some initial resistance from people who were dubious about living in a home that resembled a Pullman car, and his profit had been close to ten thousand dollars. The wave of the future had arrived in 'salem's Lot, and Larry Crockett had been right up there shooting the curl.

On the day R.T. Straker had walked into his office, Crockett had been worth nearly two million dollars. He had done this as a result of land speculation in a great many neighboring towns (but not in the Lot; you don't shit where you eat was Lawrence Crockett's motto), based on the conviction that the mobile-home industry was going to grow like a mad bastard. It did, and my God how the money rolled in.

In 1965 Larry Crockett became the silent partner of

a contractor named Romeo Poulin, who was building a supermarket plaza in Auburn. Poulin was a veteran corner-cutter, and with his on-the-job know-how and Larry's way with figures, they made $750,000 apiece and only had to report a third of that to Uncle. It was all extremely satisfactory, and if the supermarket roof had a bad case of the leaks, well, that was life.

In 1966–68 Larry bought controlling interests in three Maine mobile-home businesses, going through any number of fancy ownership shuffles to throw the tax people off. To Romeo Poulin he described this process as going into the tunnel of love with girl A, screwing girl B in the car behind you, and ending up holding hands with girl A on the other side. He ended up buying mobile homes from himself, and these incestuous businesses were so healthy they were almost frightening.

Deals with the devil, all right, Larry thought, shuffling his papers. When you deal with him, notes come due in brimstone.

The people who bought trailers were lower-middle-class blue- or white-collar workers, people who could not raise a down payment on a more conventional house, or older people looking for ways to stretch their social security. The idea of a brand-new six-room house was something to conjure with for these people. For the elderly, there was another advantage, something that others missed but Larry, always astute, had noticed: Trailers were all on one level and there were no stairs to climb.

Financing was easy, too. A $500 down payment was usually enough to do business on. And in the bad old barracuda-financing days of the sixties, the fact that the other $9,500 was financed at 24 percent rarely struck these house-hungry people as a pitfall.

And my God! how the money rolled in.

Crockett himself had changed very little, even after playing 'Let's Make a Deal' with the unsettling Mr Straker. No fag decorator came to redo his office. He still got by with the cheap electric fan instead of air conditioning. He wore the same shiny-seat suits or glaring sports jacket combinations. He smoked the same cheap cigars and still dropped by Dell's on Saturday night to have a few beers and shoot some bumper pool with the boys. He had kept his hand in hometown real estate, which had borne two fruits: First, it had gotten him elected selectman, and second, it wrote off nicely on his income tax return, because each year's visible operation was one rung below the breakeven point. Besides the Marsten House, he was and had been the selling agent for perhaps three dozen other decrepit manses in the area. There were some good deals of course. But Larry didn't push them. The money was, after all, rolling in.

Too much money, maybe. It was possible, he supposed, to outsmart yourself. To go into the tunnel of love with girl A, screw girl B, come out holding hands with girl A, only to have both of them beat the living shit out of you. Straker had said he would be in touch and that had been fourteen months ago. Now what if—

That was when the telephone rang.

4

'Mr Crockett,' the familiar, accentless voice said.

'Straker, isn't it?'

'Indeed.'

'I was just thinkin' about you. Maybe I'm psychic.'

'How very amusing, Mr Crockett. I need a service, please.'

'I thought you might.'

'You will procure a truck, please. A big one. A rental truck, perhaps. Have it at the Portland docks tonight at seven sharp. Custom House Wharf. Two movers will be sufficient, I think.'

'Okay.' Larry drew a pad over by his right hand and scrawled: *H. Peters, R. Snow. Henry's U-Haul. 6 at latest.* He did not stop to consider how imperative it seemed to follow Straker's orders to the letter.

'There are a dozen boxes to be picked up. All save one go to the shop. The other is an extremely valuable sideboard – a Hepplewhite. Your movers will know it by its size. It is to be taken to the house. You understand?'

'Yeah.'

'Have them put it down cellar. Your men can enter through the outside bulkhead below the kitchen windows. You understand?'

'Yeah. Now, this sideboard—'

'One other service, please. You will procure five stout Yale padlocks. You are familiar with the brand Yale?'

'Everybody is. What—'

'Your movers will lock the shop's back door when they leave. At the house, they will leave the keys to all five locks on the basement table. When they leave the house, they will padlock the bulkhead door, the front and back doors, and the shed–garage. You understand?'

'Yeah.'

'Thank you, Mr Crockett. Follow all directions explicitly. Good-by.'

'Now, wait just a minute—'

Dead line.

5

It was two minutes of seven when the big orange-and-white truck with 'Henry's U-Haul' printed on the sides and back pulled up to the corrugated-steel shack at the end of Custom House Wharf at the Portland docks. The tide was on the turn and the gulls were restless with it, wheeling and crying overhead against the sunset-crimson sky.

'Christ, there's nobody here,' Royal Snow said, swigging the last of his Pepsi and dropping the empty to the floor of the cab. 'We'll get arrested for burglars.'

'There's somebody,' Hank Peters said. 'Cop.'

It wasn't precisely a cop; it was a night watchman. He shone his light in at them. 'Either of you guys Lawrence Crewcut?'

'Crockett,' Royal said. 'We're from him. Come to pick up some boxes.'

'Good,' the night watchman said. 'Come on in the office. I got an invoice for you to sign.' He gestured to Peters, who was behind the wheel. 'Back up right over there. Those double doors with the light burning. See?'

'Yeah.' He put the truck in reverse.

Royal Snow followed the night watchman into the office where a coffeemaker was burbling. The clock over the pin-up calendar said 7:04. The night watchman scrabbled through some papers on the desk and came up with a clipboard. 'Sign there.'

Royal signed his name.

'You want to watch out when you go in there. Turn on the lights. There's rats.'

'I've never seen a rat that wouldn't run from one of these,' Royal said, and swung his work-booted foot in an arc.

'These are wharf rats, sonny,' the watchman said dryly. 'They've run off with bigger men than you.'

Royal went back out and walked over to the warehouse door. The night watchman stood in the doorway of the shack, watching him. 'Look out,' Royal said to Peters. 'The old guy said there was rats.'

'Okay.' He sniggered. 'Good ole Larry Crewcut.'

Royal found the light switch inside the door and turned it on. There was something about the atmosphere, heavy with the mixed aromas of salt and wood rot and wetness, that stifled hilarity. That, and the thought of rats.

The boxes were stacked in the middle of the wide warehouse floor. The place was otherwise empty, and the collection looked a little portentous as a result. The sideboard was in the center, taller than the others, and the only one not stamped 'Barlow and Straker, 27 Jointner Avenue, Jer. Lot, Maine.'

'Well, this don't look too bad,' Royal said. He consulted his copy of the invoice and then counted boxes. 'Yeah, they're all here.'

'There are rats,' Hank said. 'Hear 'em?'

'Yeah, miserable things. I hate 'em.'

They both fell silent for a moment, listening to the squeak and patter coming from the shadows.

'Well, let's get with it,' Royal said. 'Let's put that big baby on first so it won't be in the way when we get to the store.'

'Okay.'

They walked over to the box, and Royal took out his pocketknife. With one quick gesture he had slit the brown invoice envelope taped to the side.

'Hey,' Hank said. 'Do you think we ought to—'

'We gotta make sure we got the right thing, don't we? If we screw up, Larry'll tack our asses to his bulletin board.' He pulled the invoice out and looked at it.

'What's it say?' Hank asked.

'Heroin,' Royal said judiciously. 'Two hundred pounds of the shit. Also two thousand girlie books from Sweden, three hundred gross of French ticklers—'

'Gimme that.' Hank snatched it away. 'Sideboard,' he said. 'Just like Larry told us. From London, England. Portland, Maine, P.O.E. French ticklers, my ass. Put this back.'

Royal did. 'Something funny about this,' he said.

'Yeah, you. Funny like the Italian Army.'

'No, no shit. There's no customs stamp on this fucker. Not on the box, not on the invoice envelope, not on the invoice. No stamp.'

'They probably do 'em in that ink that only shows up under a special black light.'

'They never did when I was on the docks. Christ, they stamped cargo ninety ways for Sunday. You couldn't grab a box without getting blue ink up to your elbows.'

'Good. I'm very glad. But my wife happens to go to bed very early and I had hopes of getting some tonight.'

'Maybe if we took a look inside—'

'No way. Come on. Grab it.'

Royal shrugged. They tipped the box, and something shifted heavily inside. The box was a bitch to lift. It could be one of those fancy dressers, all right. It was heavy enough.

Grunting, they staggered out to the truck and heaved it onto the hydraulic lifter with identical cries of relief. Royal stood back while Hank operated the lift. When it was even with the truck body, they climbed up and walked it inside.

There was something about the box he didn't like. It was more than the lack of customs stamp. An indefinable something. He looked at it until Hank ran down the back gate.

'Come on,' he said. 'Let's get the rest of them.'

The other boxes had regulation customs stamps, except for three that had been shipped here from inside the United States. As they loaded each box onto the truck, Royal checked it off on the invoice form and initialed it. They stacked all of the boxes bound for the new store near the back gate of the truck, away from the sideboard.

'Now, who in the name of God is going to buy all this stuff?' Royal asked when they had finished. 'A Polish rocking chair, a German clock, a spinning wheel from Ireland . . . Christ Almighty, I bet they charge a frigging fortune.'

'Tourists,' Hank said wisely. 'Tourists'll buy anything. Some of those people from Boston and New York . . . they'd buy a bag of cow-shit if it was an *old* bag.'

'I don't like that big box, neither,' Royal said. 'No customs stamp, that's a hell of a funny thing.'

'Well, let's get it where it's going.'

They drove back to 'salem's Lot without speaking, Hank driving heavy on the gas. This was one errand he wanted done. He didn't like it. As Royal had said, it was damn peculiar.

He drove around to the back of the new store, and the back door was unlocked, as Larry had said it would be. Royal tried the light switch just inside with no result.

'That's nice,' he grumbled. 'We get to unload this stuff in the goddamn dark . . . say, does it smell a little funny in here to you?'

Hank sniffed. Yes, there was an odor, an unpleasant one, but he could not have said exactly what it reminded him of. It was dry and acrid in the nostrils, like a whiff of old corruption.

'It's just been shut up too long,' he said, shining his flashlight around the long, empty room. 'Needs a good airing out.'

'Or a good burning down,' Royal said. He didn't like it. Something about the place put his back up. 'Come on. And let's try not to break our legs.'

They unloaded the boxes as quickly as they could, putting each one down carefully. Half an hour later, Royal closed the back door with a sigh of relief and snapped one of the new padlocks on it.

'That's half of it,' he said.

'The easy half,' Hank answered. He looked up toward the Marsten House, which was dark and shuttered tonight. 'I don't like goin' up there, and I ain't afraid to say so. If there was ever a haunted house, that's it. Those guys must be crazy, tryin' to live there. Probably queer for each other anyway.'

'Like those fag interior decorators,' Royal agreed. 'Probably trying to turn it into a showplace. Good for business.'

'Well, if we got to do it, let's get with it.'

They spared a last look for the crated sideboard leaning against the side of the U-Haul and then Hank pulled the back door down with a bang. He got in behind the wheel and they drove up Jointner Avenue onto the Brooks Road. A minute later the Marsten House loomed ahead of them, dark and crepitating, and Royal felt the first thread of real fear worm its way into his belly.

'Lordy, that's a creepy place,' Hank murmured. 'Who'd want to live there?'

'I don't know. You see any lights on behind those shutters?'

'No.'

The house seemed to lean toward them, as if awaiting their arrival. Hank wheeled the truck up the driveway and around to the back. Neither of them looked too closely at what the bouncing headlights might reveal in the rank grass of the backyard. Hank felt a strain of fear enter his heart that he had not even felt in Nam, although he had been scared most of his time there. That was a rational fear. Fear that you might step on a pongee stick and see your foot swell up like some noxious green balloon, fear that some kid in black p.j.'s whose name you couldn't even fit in your mouth might blow your head off with a Russian rifle, fear that you might draw a Crazy Jake on patrol that might want you to blow up everyone in a village where the Cong had been a week before. But this fear was childlike, dreamy. There was no reference point to it. A house was a house

– boards and hinges and nails and sills. There was no reason, really no reason, to feel that each splintered crack was exhaling its own chalky aroma of evil. That was just plain stupid thinking. Ghosts? He didn't believe in ghosts. Not after Nam.

He had to fumble twice for reverse, and then backed the truck jerkily up to the bulkhead leading to the cellar. The rusted doors stood open, and in the red glow of the truck's taillights, the shallow stone steps seemed to lead down into hell.

'Man, I don't dig this at *all*,' Hank said. He tried to smile and it became a grimace.

'Me either.'

They looked at each other in the wan dash lights, the fear heavy on both of them. But childhood was beyond them, and they were incapable of going back with the job undone because of irrational fear – how would they explain it in bright daylight? The job had to be done.

Hank killed the engine and they got out and walke around to the back of the truck. Royal climbed up, released the door catch, and thrust the door up on its tracks.

The box sat there, sawdust still clinging to it, squat and mute.

'God, I don't want to take that down there!' Hank Peters choked out, and his voice was almost a sob.

'Come on up,' Royal said. 'Let's get rid of it.'

They dragged the box onto the lift and let it down with a hiss of escaping air. When it was at waist level, Hank let go of the lever and they gripped it.

'Easy,' Royal grunted, backing toward the steps. 'Easy does it . . . easy . . .' In the red glow of the taillights his face was constricted and corded like the face of a man having a heart attack.

He backed down the stairs one at a time, and as the box tilted up against his chest, he felt its dreadful weight settle against him like a slab of stone. It was heavy, he would think later, but not that heavy. He and Hank had muscled bigger loads for Larry Crockett, both upstairs and down, but there was something about the atmosphere of this place that took the heart out of you and made you no good.

The steps were slimy-slick and twice he tottered on the precarious edge of balance, crying out miserably, 'Hey! For Christ's sake! Watch it!'

And then they were down. The ceiling was low above them and they carried the sideboard bent over like hags.

'Set it here!' Hank gasped. 'I can't carry it no further!'

They set it down with a thump and stepped away. They looked into each other's eyes and saw that fear had been changed to near terror by some secret alchemy. The cellar seemed suddenly filled with secret rustling noises. Rats, perhaps, or perhaps something that didn't even bear thinking of.

They bolted, Hank first and Royal Snow right behind him. They ran up the cellar steps and Royal slammed the bulkhead doors with backward sweeps of his arm.

They clambered into the cab of the U-Haul and Hank started it up and put it in gear. Royal grabbed his arm, and in the darkness his face seemed to be all eyes, huge and staring.

'Hank, we never put on those locks.'

They both stared at the bundle of new padlocks on the truck's dashboard, held together by a twist of baling wire. Hank grabbed at his jacket pocket and brought out a key ring with five new Yale keys on it, one which would fit the lock on the back door of the shop in town, four for out here. Each was neatly labeled.

'Oh, Christ,' he said. 'Look, if we come back early tomorrow morning—'

Royal unclamped the flashlight under the dashboard. 'That won't work,' he said, 'and you know it.'

They got out of the cab, feeling the cool evening breeze strike the sweat on their foreheads. 'Go do the back door,' Royal said. 'I'll get the front door and the shed.'

They separated. Hank went to the back door, his heart thudding heavily in his chest. He had to fumble twice to thread the locking arm through the hasp. This close to the house, the smell of age and wood rot was palpable. All those stories about Hubie Marsten that they had laughed about as kids began to recur, and the chant they had chased the girls with: *Watch out, watch out, watch out! Hubie'll get you if you don't . . . watch . . . OUT—*

'Hank?'

He drew in breath sharply, and the other lock dropped out of his hands. He picked it up. 'You oughtta know better than to creep up on a person like that. Did you . . . ?'

'Yeah. Hank, who's gonna go down in that cellar again and put the key ring on the table?'

'I dunno,' Hank Peters said. 'I dunno.'

'Think we better flip for it?'

'Yeah, I guess that's best.'

Royal took out a quarter. 'Call it in the air.' He flicked it.

'Heads.'

135

Royal caught it, slapped it on his forearm, and exposed it. The eagle gleamed at them dully.

'Jesus,' Hank said miserably. But he took the key ring and the flashlight and opened the bulkhead doors again.

He forced his legs to carry him down the steps, and when he had cleared the roof overhang he shone his light across the visible cellar, which took an **L**-turn thirty feet further up and went off God knew where. The flashlight beam picked out the table, with a dusty checked tablecloth on it. A rat sat on the table, a huge one, and it did not move when the beam of light struck it. It sat up on its plump haunches and almost seemed to grin.

He walked past the box toward the table. 'Hsst! Rat!'

The rat jumped down and trotted off toward the elbow-bend further up. Hank's hand was trembling now, and the flashlight beam slipped jerkily from place to place, now picking out a dusty barrel, now a decades-old bureau that had been loaded down here, now a stack of old newspapers, now—

He jerked the flashlight beam back toward the newspapers and sucked in breath as the light fell on something to the left side of them.

A shirt . . . was that a shirt? Bundled up like an old rag. Something behind it that might have been blue jeans. And something that looked like . . .

Something snapped behind him.

He panicked, threw the keys wildly on the table, and turned away, shambling into a run. As he passed the box, he saw what had made the noise. One of the aluminum bands had let go, and now pointed jaggedly toward the low roof, like a finger.

He stumbled up the stairs, slammed the bulkhead behind him (his whole body had crawled into goose flesh; he would not be aware of it until later), snapped the lock on the catch, and ran to the cab of the truck. He was breathing in small, whistling gasps like a hurt dog. He dimly heard Royal asking him what had happened, what was going on down there, and then he threw the truck into drive and screamed out, roaring around the corner of the house on two wheels, digging at the soft earth. He did not slow down until the truck was back on the Brooks Road, speeding toward Lawrence Crockett's office in town. And then he began to shake so badly he was afraid he would have to pull over.

'What was down there?' Royal asked. 'What did you see?'

'Nothin,'' Hank Peters said, and the word came out in sections divided by his clicking teeth. 'I didn't see nothin' and I never want to see it again.'

6

Larry Crockett was getting ready to shut up shop and go home when there was a perfunctory tap on the door and Hank Peters stepped back in. He still looked scared.

'Forget somethin', Hank?' Larry asked. When they had come back from the Marsten House, both looking like somebody had given their nuts a healthy tweak, he had given them each an extra ten dollars and two six-packs of Black Label and had allowed as how maybe it would be best if none of them said too much about the evening's outing.

'I got to tell you,' Hank said now. 'I can't help it, Larry. I got to.'

'Sure you do,' Larry said. He opened the bottom desk drawer, took out a bottle of Johnnie Walker, and poured them each a knock in a couple of Dixie cups. 'What's on your mind?'

Hank took a mouthful, grimaced, and swallowed it.

'When I took those keys down to put 'em on the table, I seen something. Clothes, it looked like. A shirt and maybe some dungarees. And a sneaker. I think it was a sneaker, Larry.'

Larry shrugged and smiled. 'So?' It seemed to him that a large lump of ice was resting in his chest.

'That little Glick boy was wearin' jeans. That's what it said in the *Ledger*. Jeans and a red pullover shirt and sneaks. Larry, what if—'

Larry kept smiling. The smile felt frozen on.

Hank gulped convulsively. 'What if those guys that bought the Marsten House and that store blew up the Glick kid?' There. It was out. He swallowed the rest of the liquid fire in his cup.

Smiling, Larry said, 'Maybe you saw a body, too.'

'No – no. But—'

'That'd be a matter for the police,' Larry Crockett said. He refilled Hank's cup and his hand didn't tremble at all. It was as cold and steady as a rock in a frozen brook. 'And I'd drive you right down to see Parkins. But something like this . . .' He shook his head. 'A lot of nastiness can come up. Things like you and that waitress out to Dell's . . . her name's Jackie, ain't it?'

'What the hell are you talking about?' His face had gone deadly pale.

'And they'd sure as shit find out about that dishonorable discharge of yours. But you do your duty, Hank. Do it as you see it.'

'I didn't see no body,' Hank whispered.

'That's good,' Larry said, smiling. 'And maybe you didn't see any clothes, either. Maybe they were just . . . rags.'

'Rags,' Hank Peters said hollowly.

'Sure, you know those old places. All kinds of junk in 'em. Maybe you saw some old shirt or something that was torn up for a cleaning rag.'

'Sure,' Hank said. He drained his glass a second time. 'You got a good way of looking at things, Larry.'

Crockett took his wallet out of his back pocket, opened it, and counted five ten-dollar bills out on the desk.

'What's that for?'

'Forgot all about paying you for that Brennan job last month. You should prod me about those things, Hank. You know how I forget things.'

'But you did—'

'Why,' Larry interrupted, smiling, 'you could be sitting right here and telling me something, and I wouldn't remember a thing about it tomorrow morning. Ain't that a pitiful way to be?'

'Yeah,' Hank whispered. His hand reached out trembling and took the bills; stuffed them into the breast pocket of his denim jacket as if anxious to be rid of the touch of them. He got up with such jerky hurriedness that he almost knocked his chair over. 'Listen, I got to go, Larry. I . . . I didn't . . . I got to go.'

'Take the bottle,' Larry invited, but Hank was already going out the door. He didn't pause.

Larry sat back down. He poured himself another drink. His hand still did not tremble. He did not go on shutting up shop. He had another drink, and then another. He thought about deals with the devil. And at last his phone rang. He picked it up. Listened.

'It's taken care of,' Larry Crockett said.

He listened. He hung up. He poured himself another drink.

7

Hank Peters woke up in the early hours of the next morning from a dream of huge rats crawling out of an open grave, a grave which held the green and rotting body of Hubie Marsten, with a frayed length of manila hemp around his neck. Peters lay propped on his elbows, breathing heavily, naked torso slicked with sweat, and when his wife touched his arm he screamed aloud.

8

Milt Crossen's Agricultural Store was located in the angle formed by the intersection of Jointner Avenue and Railroad Street, and most of the town's old codgers went there when it rained and the park was uninhabitable. During the long winters, they were a day-by-day fixture.

When Straker drove up in that '39 Packard – or was it a '40? – it was just misting gently, and Milt and Pat Middler were having a desultory conversation about whether Freddy Overlock's girl Judy run off in 1957 or '58. They both agreed that she had run off with that Salad-master salesman from Yarmouth, and they both agreed that he hadn't been worth a pisshole in the snow, nor was she, but beyond that they couldn't get together.

All conversation ceased when Straker walked in.

He looked around at them – Milt and Pat Middler and Joe Crane and Vinnie Upshaw and Clyde Corliss – and smiled humorlessly. 'Good afternoon, gentlemen,' he said.

Milt Crossen stood up, pulling his apron around him almost primly. 'Help you?'

'Very good,' Straker said. 'Attend over at this meat case, please.'

He bought a roast of beef, a dozen prime ribs, some hamburger, and a pound of calves' liver. To this he added some dry goods – flour, sugar, beans – and several loaves of ready-made bread.

His shopping took place in utter silence. The store's habitués sat around the large Pearl Kineo stove that Milt's father had converted to range oil, smoked, looked wisely out at the sky, and observed the stranger from the corners of their eyes.

When Milt had finished packing the goods into a large cardboard carton, Straker paid with hard cash – a twenty and a ten. He picked up the carton, tucked it under one arm, and flashed that hard, humorless smile at them again.

'Good day, gentlemen,' he said, and left.

Joe Crane tamped a load of Planter's into his corncob. Clyde Corliss hawked back and spat a mass of phlegm and chewing tobacco into the dented pail beside the stove.

Vinnie Upshaw produced his old Top cigarette roller from inside his vest, spilled a line of tobacco into it, and inserted a cigarette paper with arthritis-swelled fingers.

They watched the stranger lift the carton into the trunk. All of them knew that the carton must have weighed thirty pounds with the dry goods, and they had all seen him tuck it under his arm like a feather pillow going out. He went around to the driver's side, got in, and drove off up Jointner Avenue. The car went up the hill, turned left onto the Brooks Road, disappeared, and reappeared from behind the screen of trees a few moments later, now toy-sized with distance. It turned into the Marsten driveway and was lost from sight.

'Peculiar fella,' Vinnie said. He stuck his cigarette in his mouth, plucked a few bits of tobacco from the end of it, and took a kitchen match from his vest pocket.

'Must be one of the ones got that store,' Joe Crane said.

'Marsten House, too,' Vinnie agreed.

Clyde Corliss broke wind.

Pat Middler picked at a callus on his left palm with great interest. Five minutes passed.

'Do you suppose they'll make a go of it?' Clyde asked no one in particular.

'Might,' Vinnie said. 'They might show up right pert in the summertime. Hard to tell the way things are these days.'

A general murmur, sigh almost, of agreement.

'Strong fella,' Joe said.

'Ayuh,' Vinnie said. 'That was a thirty-nine Packard, and not a spot of rust on her.'

''Twas a forty,' Clyde said.

'The forty didn't have runnin' boards,' Vinnie said. ''Twas a thirty-nine.'

'You're wrong on that one,' Clyde said.

Five minutes passed. They saw Milt was examining the twenty Straker had paid with.

'That funny money, Milt?' Pat asked. 'That fella give you some funny money?'

'No; but look.' Milt passed it across the counter and they all stared at it. It was much bigger than an ordinary bill.

Pat held it up to the light, examined it, then turned it over. 'That's a series E twenty, ain't it, Milt?'

'Yep,' Milt said. 'They stopped makin' those forty-five or fifty years back. My guess is that'd be worth some money down to Arcade Coin in Portland.'

Pat handed the bill around and each examined it, holding it up close or far off depending on the flaws in their eyesight. Joe Crane handed it back, and Milt put it under the cash drawer with the personal checks and the coupons.

'Sure is a funny fella,' Clyde mused.

'Ayuh,' Vinnie said, and paused. 'That was a thirty-nine, though. My half brother Vic had one. Was the first car he ever owned. Bought it used, he did, in 1944. Left the oil out of her one mornin' and burned the goddamn pistons right out of her.'

'I believe it was a forty,' Clyde said, 'because I remember a fella that used to cane chairs down by Alfred, come right to your house he would, and—'

And so the argument was begun, progressing more in the silences than in the speeches, like a chess game played by mail. And the day seemed to stand still and stretch into eternity for them, and Vinnie Upshaw began to make another cigarette with sweet, arthritic slowness.

9

Ben was writing when the tap came at the door, and he marked his place before getting up to open it. It was just after three o'clock on Wednesday, September 24. The rain had ended any plans to search further for Ralphie Glick, and the consensus was that the search was over. The Glick boy was gone . . . solid gone.

He opened the door and Parkins Gillespie was standing there, smoking a cigarette. He was holding a paperback in one hand, and Ben saw with some amusement that it was the Bantam edition of *Conway's Daughter*.

'Come on in, Constable,' he said. 'Wet out there.'

'It is, a trifle,' Parkins said, stepping in. 'September's grippe weather. I always wear m' galoshes. There's some that laughs, but I ain't had the grippe since St-Lô, France, in 1944.'

'Lay your coat on the bed. Sorry I can't offer you coffee.'

'Wouldn't think of wettin' it,' Parkins said, and tapped ash in Ben's wastebasket. 'And I just had a cup of Pauline's down to the Excellent.'

'Can I do something for you?'

'Well, my wife read this . . .' He held up the book. 'She heard you was in town, but she's shy. She kind of thought maybe you might write your name in it, or somethin'.'

Ben took the book. 'The way Weasel Craig tells it,

your wife's been dead fourteen or fifteen years.'

'That so?' Parkins looked totally unsurprised. 'That Weasel, he does love to talk. He'll open his mouth too wide one day and fall right in.'

Ben said nothing.

'Do you s'pose you could sign it for me, then?'

'Delighted to.' He took a pen from the desk, opened the book to the flyleaf ('A raw slice of life!' – Cleveland *Plain Dealer*), and wrote: *Best wishes to Constable Gillespie, from Ben Mears, 9/24/75.* He handed it back.

'I appreciate that,' Parkins said, without looking at what Ben had written. He bent over and crushed out his smoke on the side of the wastebasket. 'That's the only signed book I got.'

'Did you come here to brace me?' Ben asked, smiling.

'You're pretty sharp,' Parkins said. 'I figured I ought to come and ask a question or two, now that you mention it. Waited until Nolly was off somewheres. He's a good boy, but he likes to talk, too. Lordy, the gossip that goes on.'

'What would you like to know?'

'Mostly where you were on last Wednesday evenin'.'

'The night Ralphie Glick disappeared?'

'Yeah.'

'Am I a suspect, Constable?'

'No, sir. I ain't got no suspects. A thing like this is outside my tour, you might say. Catchin' speeders out by Dell's or chasin' kids outta the park before they turn randy is more my line. I'm just nosin' here and there.'

'Suppose I don't want to tell you.'

Parkins shrugged and produced his cigarettes. 'That's your business, son.'

'I had dinner with Susan Norton and her folks. Played some badminton with her dad.'

'Bet he beat you, too. He always beats Nolly. Nolly raves up and down about how bad he'd like to beat Bill Norton just once. What time did you leave?'

Ben laughed, but the sound did not contain a great deal of humor. 'You cut right to the bone, don't you?'

'You know,' Parkins said, 'if I was one of those New York detectives like on TV, I might think you had somethin' to hide, the way you polka around my questions.'

'Nothing to hide,' Ben said. 'I'm just tired of being the stranger in town, getting pointed at in the streets, being nudged over in the library. Now you come around with this Yankee trader routine, trying to find out if I've got Ralphie Click's scalp in my closet.'

'Now, I don't think that, not at all.' He gazed at Ben over his cigarette, and his eyes had gone flinty. 'I'm just tryin' to close you off. If I thought you had anything to do with anything, you'd be down in the tank.'

'Okay,' Ben said. 'I left the Nortons around quarter past seven. I took a walk out toward Schoolyard Hill. When it got too dark to see, I came back here, wrote for two hours, and went to bed.'

'What time did you get back here?'

'Quarter past eight, I think. Around there.'

'Well, that don't clear you as well as I'd like. Did you see anybody?'

'No,' Ben said. 'No one.'

Parkins made a noncommittal grunt and walked toward the typewriter. 'What are you writin' about?'

'None of your damn business,' Ben said, and his voice

had gone tight. 'I'll thank you to keep your eyes and your hands off that. Unless you've got a search warrant, of course.'

'Kind of touchy, ain't you? For a man who means his books to be read?'

'When it's gone through three drafts, editorial correction, galley-proof corrections, final set and print, I'll personally see that you get four copies. Signed. Right now that comes under the heading of private papers.'

Parkins smiled and moved away. 'Good enough. I doubt like hell that it's a signed confession to anything, anyway.'

Ben smiled back. 'Mark Twain said a novel was a confession to everything by a man who had never done anything.'

Parkins blew out smoke and went to the door. 'I won't drip on your rug anymore, Mr Mears. Want to thank you for y'time, and just for the record, I don't think you ever saw that Glick boy. But it's my job to kind of ask round about these things.'

Ben nodded. 'Understood.'

'And you oughtta know how things are in places like 'salem's Lot or Milbridge or Guilford or any little pissant burg. You're the stranger in town until you been here twenty years.'

'I know. I'm sorry if I snapped at you. But after a week of looking for him and not finding a goddamned thing—' Ben shook his head.

'Yeah,' Parkins said. 'It's bad for his mother. Awful bad. You take care.'

'Sure,' Ben said.

'No hard feelin's?'

'No.' He paused. 'Will you tell me one thing?'

'I will if I can.'

'Where did you get that book? Really?'

Parkins Gillespie smiled. 'Well, there's a fella over in Cumberland that's got a used-furniture barn. Kind of a sissy fella, he is. Name of Gendron. He sells paperbacks a dime apiece. Had five of these.'

Ben threw back his head and laughed, and Parkins Gillespie went out, smiling and smoking. Ben went to the window and watched until he saw the constable come out and cross the street, walking carefully around puddles in his black galoshes.

10

Parkins paused a moment to look in the show window of the new shop before knocking on the door. When the place had been the Village Washtub, a body could look in here and see nothing but a lot of fat women in rollers adding bleach or getting change out of the machine on the wall, most of them chewing gum like cows with mouthfuls of mulch. But an interior decorator's truck from Portland had been here yesterday afternoon and most of today, and the place looked considerably different.

A platform had been shoved up behind the window, and it was covered with a swatch of deep nubby carpet, light green in color. Two spotlights had been installed up out of sight, and they cast soft, highlighting glows on the three objects that had been arranged in the window: a clock, a spinning wheel, and an old-fashioned cherrywood cabinet. There was a small easel in front of each piece, and a discreet price tag on each easel, and my God, would anybody in their right mind actually pay $600 for a spinning wheel when they could go down to the Value House and get a Singer for $48.95?

Sighing, Parkins went to the door and knocked.

It was opened only a second later, almost as if the new fella had been lurking behind it, waiting for him to come to the door.

'Inspector!' Straker said with a narrow smile. 'How good of you to drop by!'

'Plain old constable, I guess,' Parkins said. He lit a Pall Mall and strolled in. 'Parkins Gillespie. Pleased to meet you.' He stuck out his hand. It was gripped, squeezed gently by a hand that felt enormously strong and very dry, and then dropped.

'Richard Throckett Straker,' the bald man said.

'I figured you was,' Parkins said, looking around. The entire shop had been carpeted and was in the process of being painted. The smell of fresh paint was a good one, but there seemed to be another smell underneath it, an unpleasant one. Parkins could not place it; he turned his attention back to Straker.

'What can I do for you on this so-fine day?' Straker asked.

Parkins turned his mild gaze out the window, where the rain continued to pour down.

'Oh, nothing at all, I guess. I just came by to say how-do. More or less welcome you to the town an' wish you good luck, I guess.'

'How thoughtful. Would you care for a coffee? Some sherry? I have both out back.'

'No thanks, I can't stop. Mr Barlow around?'

'Mr Barlow is in New York, on a buying trip. I don't expect him back until at least the tenth of October.'

'You'll be openin' without him, then,' Parkins said, thinking that if the prices he had seen in the window were any indication, Straker wouldn't exactly be swamped with customers. 'What's Mr Barlow's first name, by the way?'

Straker's smile reappeared, razor-thin. 'Are you asking in your official capacity, ah . . . Constable?'

'Nope. Just curious.'

'My partner's full name is Kurt Barlow,' Straker said. 'We have worked together in both London and Hamburg. 'This' – he swept his arm around him – 'this is our retirement. Modest. Yet tasteful. We expect to make no more than a living. Yet we both love old things, fine things, and we hope to make a reputation in the area . . . perhaps even throughout your so-beautiful New England region. Do you think that would be possible, Constable Gillespie?'

'Anything's possible, I guess,' Parkins said, looking around for an ashtray. He saw none, and tapped his cigarette ash into his coat pocket. 'Anyway, I hope you'll have the best of luck, and tell Mr Barlow when you see him that I'm gonna try and get around.'

'I'll do so,' Straker said. 'He enjoys company.'

'That's fine,' Gillespie said. He went to the door, paused, looked back. Straker was looking at him intently. 'By the way, how do you like that old house?'

'It needs a great deal of work,' Straker said. 'But we have time.'

'I guess you do,' Parkins agreed. 'Don't suppose you seen any yow'uns up around there.'

Straker's brow creased. 'Yowwens?'

‘Kids,’ Parkins explained patiently. ‘You know how they sometimes like to devil new folks. Throw rocks or ring the bell an’ run away . . . that sort of thing.’

‘No,’ Straker said. ‘No children.’

‘We seem to kind have misplaced one.’

‘Is that so?’

‘Yes,’ Parkins said judiciously, ‘yes, it is. The thinkin’ now is that we may not find him. Not alive.’

‘What a shame,’ Straker said distantly.

‘It is, kinda. If you should see anything . . .’

‘I would of course report it to your office, posthaste.’ He smiled his chilly smile again.

‘That’s good,’ Parkins said. He opened the door and looked resignedly out at the pouring rain. ‘You tell Mr Barlow that I’m lookin’ forward.’

‘I certainly will, Constable Gillespie. *Ciao.*’

Parkins looked back, startled. ‘Chow?’

Straker’s smile widened. ‘Good-by, Constable Gillespie. That is the familiar Italian expression for good-by.’

‘Oh? Well, you learn somethin’ new every day, don’t you? ’By.’ He stepped out into the rain and closed the door behind him. ‘Not familiar to me, it ain’t.’ His cigarette was soaked. He threw it away.

Inside, Straker watched him up the street through the show window. He was no longer smiling.

11

When Parkins got back to his office in the Municipal Building, he called, ‘Nolly? You here, Nolly?’

No answer. Parkins nodded. Nolly was a good boy, but a little bit short on brains. He took off his coat, unbuckled his galoshes, sat down at his desk, looked up a telephone number in the Portland book, and dialed. The other end picked up on the first ring.

'FBI, Portland. Agent Hanrahan.'

'This is Parkins Gillespie. Constable at Jerusalem's Lot township. We've got us a missin' boy up here.'

'So I understand,' Hanrahan said crisply. 'Ralph Glick. Nine years old, four-three, black hair, blue eyes. What is it, kidnap note?'

'Nothin' like that. Can you check on some fellas for me?'

Hanrahan answered in the affirmative.

'First one is Benjaman Mears. M-E-A-R-S. Writer. Wrote a book called *Conway's Daughter*. The other two are sorta stapled together. Kurt Barlow. B-A-R-L-O-W. The other guy—'

'You spell that Kurt with a "c" or a "k"?' Hanrahan asked.

'I dunno.'

'Okay. Go on.'

Parkins did so, sweating. Talking to the real law always made him feel like an asshole. 'The other guy is Richard Throckett Straker. Two *t's* on the end of Throckett, and Straker like it sounds. This guy and Barlow are in the furniture and antique business. They just opened a little shop here in town. Straker claims Barlow's in New York on a buyin' trip. Straker claims the two of them worked together in London an' Hamburg. And I guess that pretty well covers it.'

'Do you suspect these people in the Glick case?'

'Right now I don't know if there even is a case. But they all showed up in town about the same time.'

'Do you think there's any connection between this guy Mears and the other two?'

Parkins leaned back and cocked an eye out the window. 'That,' he said, 'is one of the things I'd like to find out.'

12

The telephone wires make an odd humming on clear, cool days, almost as if vibrating with the gossip that is transmitted through them, and it is a sound like no other – the lonely sound of voices flying over space. The telephone poles are gray and splintery, and the freezes and thaws of winter have heaved them into leaning postures that are casual. They are not businesslike and military, like phone poles anchored in concrete. Their bases are black with tar if they are beside paved roads, and floured with dust if beside the back roads. Old weathered cleat marks show on their surfaces where linemen have climbed to fix something in 1946 or 1952 or 1969. Birds – crows, sparrows, robins, starlings – roost on the humming wires and sit in hunched silence, and perhaps they hear the foreign human sounds through their taloned feet. If so, their beady eyes give no sign. The town has a sense, not of history, but of time, and the telephone poles seem to know this. If you lay your hand against one, you can feel the vibration from the wires deep in the wood, as if souls had been imprisoned in there and were struggling to get out.

'. . . and he paid with an old twenty, Mabel, one of the big ones. Clyde said he hadn't seen one of those since the run on the Gates Bank and Trust in 1930. He was . . .'

'. . . yes, he *is* a peculiar sort of man, Evvie. I've seen him through my binocs, trundling around behind the house with a wheelbarrow. Is he up there alone, I wonder, or . . .'

'. . . Crockett might know, but he won't tell. He's keeping shut about it. He always was a . . .'

'. . . writer at Eva's. I wonder if Floyd Tibbits knows he's been . . .'

'. . . spends an awful lot of time at the library. Loretta Starcher says she never saw a fella who knew so many . . .'

'. . . she said his name was . . .'

'. . . yes, it's Straker. Mr R.T. Straker. Kenny Danles's mom said she stopped by that new place downtown and there was a genuine DeBiers cabinet in the window and they wanted *eight hundred dollars* for it. Can you imagine? So I said . . .'

'. . . funny, him coming and that little Glick boy . . .'

'. . . you don't think . . .'

'. . . no, but it *is* funny. By the way, do you still have that recipe for . . .'

The wires hum. And hum. And hum.

13

9/23/75
Name: Glick, Daniel Francis
Address: RFD # 1, Brock Road, Jerusalem's Lot, Maine 04270

Age: 12   *Sex:* Male   *Race:* Caucasian

Admitted: 9/22/75   *Admitting Person:* Anthony H. Glick
   (Father)

Symptoms: Shock, loss of memory (partial), nausea,
   disinterest in food, constipation, general loginess

Tests (see attached sheet):

   1. Tuberculosis skin patch: Neg.
   2. Tuberculosis sputum and urine: Neg.
   3. Diabetes: Neg.
   4. White cell count: Neg.
   5. Red cell count: 45% hemo.
   6. Marrow sample: Neg.
   7. Chest X-ray: Neg.

Possible diagnosis: Pernicious anemia, primary or
   secondary; previous exam shows 86% hemoglobin.
   Secondary anemia is unlikely; no history of ulcers,
   hemorrhoids, bleeding piles, et al. Differential cell
   count neg. Primary anemia combined with mental
   shock likely. Recommend barium enema and X-
   rays for internal bleeding on the off-chance, yet
   no recent accidents, father says. Also recommend
   daily dosage of vitamin B_{12} (see attached sheet).

Pending further tests, let's release him.

                              G.M. Gorby
                              Attending Physician

14

At one o'clock in the morning, September 24, the nurse stepped into Danny Glick's hospital room to give him his medication. She paused in the doorway, frowning. The bed was empty.

Her eyes jumped from the bed to the oddly wasted white bundle that lay collapsed by the foot. 'Danny?' she said.

She stepped toward him and thought, He had to go to the bathroom and it was too much for him, that's all.

She turned him over gently, and her first thought before realizing that he was dead was that the B_{12} had been helping; he looked better than he had since his admission.

And then she felt the cold flesh of his wrist and the lack of movement in the light blue tracery of veins beneath her fingers, and she ran for the nurses' station to report a death on the ward.

CHAPTER FIVE
BEN (II)

On September 25 Ben took dinner with the Nortons again. It was Thursday night, and the meal was traditional – beans and franks. Bill Norton grilled the franks on the outdoor grill, and Ann had had her kidney beans simmering in molasses since nine that morning. They ate at the picnic table and afterward they sat smoking, the four of them, talking desultorily of Boston's fading pennant chances.

There was a subtle change in the air; it was still pleasant enough, even in shirtsleeves, but there was a glint of ice in it now. Autumn was waiting in the wings, almost in sight. The large and ancient maple in front of Eva Miller's boardinghouse had already begun to go red.

There had been no change in Ben's relationship with the Nortons. Susan's liking for him was frank and clear and natural. And he liked her very much. In Bill he sensed a steadily increasing liking, held in abeyance by the subconscious taboo that affects all fathers when in the presence of men who are there because of their daughters rather than themselves. If you like another man and you are honest, you speak freely, discuss women over beer, shoot the shit about politics. But no matter how deep the potential liking, it is impossible to open up completely to a man who is dangling your daughter's potential defloration between his legs. Ben reflected that after marriage the possible had become the actual and could you become complete friends with the man who was banging your daughter night after night? There might be a moral there, but Ben doubted it.

Ann Norton continued cool. Susan had told him a little of the Floyd Tibbits situation the night before — of her mother's assumption that her son-in-law problems had been solved neatly and satisfactorily in that direction. Floyd was a known quantity; he was Steady. Ben Mears, on the other hand, had come out of nowhere and might disappear back there just as quickly, possibly with her daughter's heart in his pocket. She distrusted the creative male with an instinctive small-town dislike (one that Edward Arlington Robinson or Sherwood Anderson would have recognized at once), and Ben suspected that down deep she had absorbed a maxim: either faggots or bull studs; sometimes homicidal, suicidal, or maniacal, tend to send young girls packages containing their left ears. Ben's participation in the search for Ralphie Glick seemed to have increased her suspicions rather than allayed them, and he suspected that winning her over was an impossibility. He wondered if she knew of Parkins Gillespie's visit to his room.

He was chewing these thoughts over lazily when Ann said, 'Terrible about the Glick boy.'

'Ralphie? Yes,' Bill said.

'No, the older one. He's dead.'

Ben started. 'Who? Danny?'

'He died early yesterday morning.' She seemed surprised that the men did not know. It had been all the talk.

'I heard them talking in Milt's,' Susan said. Her hand found Ben's under the table and he took it willingly. 'How are the Glicks taking it?'

'The same way I would,' Ann said simply. 'They are out of their minds.'

Well they might be, Ben thought. Ten days ago their life had been going about its usual ordained cycle; now their family unit was smashed and in pieces. It gave him a morbid chill.

'Do you think the other Glick boy will ever show up alive?' Bill asked Ben.

'No,' Ben said. 'I think he's dead, too.'

'Like that thing in Houston two years ago,' Susan said. 'If he's dead, I almost hope they don't find him. Whoever could do something like that to a little, defense-less boy—'

'The police are looking around, I guess,' Ben said. 'Rounding up known sex offenders and talking to them.'

'When they find the guy they ought to hang him up by the thumbs,' Bill Norton said. 'Badminton, Ben?'

Ben stood. 'No thanks. Too much like you playing solitaire with me for the dummy. Thanks for the nice meal. I've got work to do tonight.'

Ann Norton lifted her eyebrow and said nothing.

Bill stood. 'How's that new book coming?'

'Good,' Ben said briefly. 'Would you like to walk down the hill with me and have a soda at Spencer's, Susan?'

'Oh, I don't know,' Ann interposed swiftly. 'After Ralphie Glick and all, I'd feel better if—'

'Momma, I'm a big girl,' Susan interposed. 'And there are streetlights all the way up Brock Hill.'

'I'll walk you back up, of course,' Ben said, almost formally. He had left his car at Eva's. The early evening had been too fine to drive.

'They'll be fine,' Bill said. 'You worry too much, Mother.'

'Oh, I suppose I do. Young folks always know best, don't they?' She smiled thinly.

'I'll just get a jacket,' Susan murmured to Ben, and turned up the back walk. She was wearing a red play skirt, thigh-high, and she exposed a lot of leg going up the steps to the door. Ben watched, knowing Ann was watching him watch. Her husband was damping the charcoal fire.

'How long do you intend to stay in the Lot, Ben?' Ann asked, showing polite interest.

'Until the book gets written, anyway,' he said. 'After that, I can't say. It's very lovely in the mornings, and the air tastes good when you breathe it.' He smiled into her eyes. 'I may stay longer.'

She smiled back. 'It gets cold in the winters, Ben. Awfully cold.'

Then Susan was coming back down the steps with a light jacket thrown over her shoulders. 'Ready? I'm going to have a chocolate. Look out, complexion.'

'Your complexion will survive,' he said, and turned to Mr and Mrs Norton. 'Thank you again.'

'Anytime,' Bill said. 'Come on over with a six-pack tomorrow night, if you want. We'll make fun of that goddamn Yastrzemski.'

'That would be fun,' Ben said, 'but what'll we do after the second inning?'

His laughter, hearty and full, followed them around the corner of the house.

2

'I don't really want to go to Spencer's,' she said as they went down the hill. 'Let's go to the park instead.'

'What about muggers, lady?' he asked, doing the Bronx for her.

'In the Lot, all muggers have to be in by seven. It's a town ordinance. And it is now exactly eight-oh-three.' Darkness had fallen over them as they walked down the hill, and their shadows waxed and waned in the streetlights.

'Agreeable muggers you have,' he said. 'No one goes to the park after dark?'

'Sometimes the town kids go there to make out if they can't afford the drive-in,' she said, and winked at him. 'So if you see anyone skulking around in the bushes, look the other way.'

They entered from the west side, which faced the Municipal Building. The park was shadowy and a little dreamlike, the concrete walks curving away under the leafy trees, and the wading pool glimmering quietly in the refracted glow from the streetlights. If anyone was here, Ben didn't see him.

They walked around the War Memorial with its long lists of names, the oldest from the Revolutionary War, the newest from Vietnam, carved under the War of 1812. There were six hometown names from the most recent conflict,

161

the new cuts in the brass gleaming like fresh wounds. He thought: This town has the wrong name. It ought to be Time. And as if the action was a natural outgrowth of the thought, he looked over his shoulder for the Marsten House, but the bulk of the Municipal Building blocked it out.

She saw his glance and it made her frown. As they spread their jackets on the grass and sat down (they had spurned the park benches without discussion), she said, 'Mom said Parkins Gillespie was checking up on you. The new boy in school must have stolen the milk money, or something like that.'

'He's quite a character,' Ben said.

'Mom had you practically tried and convicted.' It was said lightly, but the lightness faltered and let something serious through.

'Your mother doesn't care for me much, does she?'

'No,' Susan said, holding his hand. 'It was a case of dislike at first sight. I'm very sorry.'

'It's okay,' he said. 'I'm batting five hundred anyway.'

'Daddy?' She smiled. 'He just knows class when he sees it.' The smile faded. 'Ben, what's this new book about?'

'That's hard to say.' He slipped his loafers off and dug his toes into the dewy grass.

'Subject-changer.'

'No, I don't mind telling you.' And he found, surprisingly, that this was true. He had always thought of a work in progress as a child, a weak child, that had to be protected and cradled. Too much handling would kill it. He had refused to tell Miranda a word about *Conway's Daughter* or *Air Dance*, although she had been wildly curious about both of them. But Susan was different. With Miranda there had always been a directed sort of probing and her questions were more like interrogations.

'Just let me think how to put it together,' he said.

'Can you kiss me while you think?' she asked, lying back on the grass. He was forcibly aware of how short her skirt was; it had given a lot of ground.

'I think that might interfere with the thought processes,' he said softly. 'Let's see.'

He leaned over and kissed her, placing one hand lightly on her waist. She met his mouth firmly, and her hands closed over his. A moment later he felt her tongue for the first time, and he met it with his own. She shifted to return his kiss more fully, and the soft rustle of her cotton skirt seemed loud, almost maddening.

He slid his hand up and she arched her breast into it, soft and full. For the second time since he had known her he felt sixteen, a head-busting sixteen with everything in front of him six lanes wide and no hard traveling in sight.

'Ben?'

'Yes.'

'Make love to me? Do you want to?'

'Yes,' he said. 'I want that.'

'Here on the grass,' she said.

'Yes.'

She was looking up at him, her eyes wide in the dark. She said, 'Make it be good.'

'I'll try.'

'Slow,' she said. 'Slow. Slow. Here . . .'

They became shadows in the dark.

'There,' he said. 'Oh, Susan.'

3

They were walking, first aimlessly through the park, and then with more purpose toward Brock Street.

'Are you sorry?' he asked.

She looked up at him and smiled without artifice. 'No. I'm glad.'

'Good.'

They walked hand in hand without speaking.

'The book?' she asked. 'You were going to tell me about that before we were so sweetly interrupted.'

'The book is about the Marsten House,' he said slowly. 'Maybe it didn't start out to be, not wholly. I thought it was going to be about this town. But maybe I'm fooling myself. I researched Hubie Marsten, you know. He was a mobster. The trucking company was just a front.'

She was looking at him in wonder. 'How did you find that out?'

'Some from the Boston police, and more from a woman named Minella Corey, Birdie Marsten's sister. She's seventy-nine now, and she can't remember what she had for breakfast, but she's never forgotten a thing that happened before 1940.'

'And she told you—'

'As much as she knew. She's in a nursing home in New Hampshire, and I don't think anyone's really taken the time to listen to her in years. I asked her if Hubert Marsten had really been a contract killer in the Boston area – the police sure thought he was – and she nodded. "How many?" I asked her. She held her fingers up in front of her eyes and waggled them back and forth and said, "How many times can you count these?"'

'My God.'

'The Boston organization began to get very nervous about Hubert Marsten in 1927,' Ben went on. 'He was picked up for questioning twice, once by the city police and once by the Malden police. The Boston grab was for a gangland killing, and he was back on the street in two hours. The thing in Malden wasn't business at all. It was the murder of an eleven-year-old boy. The child had been eviscerated.'

'Ben,' she said, and her voice was sick.

'Marsten's employers got him off the hook – I imagine he knew where a few bodies were buried – but that was the end of him in Boston. He moved quietly to 'salem's Lot, just a retired trucking official who got a check once a month. He didn't go out much. At least, not much that we know of.'

'What do you mean?'

'I've spent a lot of time in the library looking at old copies of the *Ledger* from 1928 to 1939. Four children disappeared in that period. Not that unusual, not in a rural area. Kids get lost, and they sometimes die of exposure. Sometimes kids get buried in a gravel-pit slide. Not nice, but it happens.'

'But you don't think that's what happened?'

'I don't *know*. But I do know that *not one of those four was ever found*. No hunter turning up a skeleton in 1945 or a contractor digging one up while getting a load of gravel to make cement. Hubert and Birdie lived in that house for eleven years and the kids disappeared, and that's all anyone knows. But I keep thinking about that kid in

Malden. I think about that a lot. Do you know *The Haunting of Hill House*, by Shirley Jackson?'

'Yes.'

He quoted softly, '"And whatever walked there, walked alone." You asked what my book was about. Essentially, it's about the recurrent power of evil.'

She put her hands on his arm. 'You don't think that Ralphie Glick . . .'

'Was gobbled up by the revengeful spirit of Hubert Marsten, who comes back to life on every third year at the full of the moon?'

'Something like that.'

'You're asking the wrong person if you want to be reassured. Don't forget, I'm the kid who opened the door to an upstairs bedroom and saw him hanging from a beam.'

'That's not an answer.'

'No, it's not. Let me tell you one other thing before I tell you exactly what I think. Something Minella Corey said. She said there are evil men in the world, truly evil men. Sometimes we hear of them, but more often they work in absolute darkness. She said she had been cursed with a knowledge of two such men in her lifetime. One was Adolf Hitler. The other was her brother-in-law, Hubert Marsten.' He paused. 'She said that on the day Hubie shot her sister she was three hundred miles away in Cape Cod. She had taken a job as housekeeper for a rich family that summer. She was making a tossed salad in a large wooden bowl. It was quarter after two in the afternoon. A bolt of pain, "like lightning," she said, went through her head and she heard a shotgun blast. She fell on the floor, she claims. When she picked herself up – she was alone in the house

– twenty minutes had passed. She looked in the wooden bowl and screamed. It appeared to her that it was full of blood.'

'God,' Susan murmured.

'A moment later, everything was normal again. No headache, nothing in the salad bowl but salad. But she said she knew – she *knew* – that her sister was dead, murdered with a shotgun.'

'That's her unsubstantiated story?'

'Unsubstantiated, yes. But she's not some oily trick-ster; she's an old woman without enough brains left to lie. That part doesn't bother me, anyway. Not very much, at least. There's a large enough body of ESP data now so that a rational man laughs it off at his own expense. The idea that Birdie transmitted the facts of her death three hundred miles over a kind of psychic telegraph isn't half so hard for me to believe as the face of evil – the really monstrous face – that I sometimes think I can see buried in the outlines of that house.

'You asked me what I think. I'll tell you. I think it's relatively easy for people to accept something like telepathy or precognition or teleplasm because their willingness to believe doesn't cost them anything. It doesn't keep them awake nights. But the idea that the evil that men do lives after them is more unsettling.'

He looked up at the Marsten House and spoke slowly.

'I think that house might be Hubert Marsten's monument to evil, a kind of psychic sounding board. A supernatural beacon, if you like. Sitting there all these years, maybe holding the essence of Hubie's evil in its old, moldering bones.

'And now it's occupied again.

'And there's been another disappearance.' He turned to her and cradled her upturned face in his hands. 'You see, that's something I never counted on when I came back here. I thought the house might have been torn down, but never in my wildest dreams that it had been bought. I saw myself renting it and . . . oh, I don't know. Confronting my own terrors and evils, maybe. Playing ghost-breaker, maybe – be gone in the name of all the saints, Hubie. Or maybe just tapping into the atmosphere of the place to write a book scary enough to make me a million dollars. But no matter what, I felt that I was in control of the situation, and that would make all the difference. I wasn't any nine-year-old kid anymore, ready to run screaming from a magic-lantern show that maybe came out of my own mind and no place else. But now . . .'

'Now what, Ben?'

'Now it's occupied!' he burst out, and beat a fist into his palm. 'I'm *not* in control of the situation. A little boy has disappeared and I don't know what to make of it. It could have nothing to do with that house, but . . . I don't believe it.' The last four words came out in measured lengths.

'Ghosts? Spirits?'

'Not necessarily. Maybe just some harmless guy who admired the house when he was a kid and bought it and became . . . possessed.'

'Do you know something about—' she began, alarmed.

'The new tenant? No. I'm just guessing. But if it is the house, I'd almost rather it was possession than something else.'

'What?'

He said simply, 'Perhaps it's called another evil man.'

4

Ann Norton watched them from the window. She had called the drugstore earlier. No, Miss Coogan said, with something like glee. Not here. Haven't been in.

Where have you been, Susan? Oh, where have you been?

Her mouth twisted down into a helpless ugly grimace.

Go away, Ben Mears. Go away and leave her alone.

5

When she left his arms, she said, 'Do something important for me, Ben.'

'Whatever I can.'

'Don't mention those things to anyone else in town. Anyone.'

He smiled humorlessly. 'Don't worry. I'm not anxious to have people thinking I've been struck nuts.'

'Do you lock your room at Eva's?'

'No.'

'I'd start locking it.' She looked at him levelly. 'You have to think of yourself as under suspicion.'

'With you, too?'

'You would be, if I didn't love you.'

And then she was gone, hastening up the driveway, leaving him to look after her, stunned by all he had said and more stunned by the four or five words she had said at the end.

6

He found when he got back to Eva's that he could neither write nor sleep. He was too excited to do either. So he warmed up the Citroën, and after a moment of indecision, he drove out toward Dell's place.

It was crowded, and the place was smoky and loud. The band, a country-and-western group on trial called the Rangers, was playing a version of 'You've Never Been This Far Before,' which made up in volume for whatever it lost in quality. Perhaps forty couples were gyrating on the floor, most of them wearing blue jeans. Ben, a little amused, thought of Edward Albee's line about monkey nipples.

The stools in front of the bar were held down by construction and mill workers, each drinking identical glasses of beer and all wearing nearly identical crepe-soled work boots, laced with rawhide.

Two or three barmaids with bouffant hairdos and their names written in gold thread on their white blouses (Jackie, Toni, Shirley) circulated to the tables and booths. Behind the bar, Dell was drawing beers, and at the far end, a hawklike man with his hair greased back was making mixed drinks. His face remained utterly blank as he measured liquor into shot glasses, dumped it into his silver shaker, and added whatever went with it.

Ben started toward the bar, skirting the dance floor, and someone called out, 'Ben! Say, fella! How are you, buddy?'

Ben looked around and saw Weasel Craig sitting at a table close to the bar, a half-empty beer in front of him.

'Hello, Weasel,' Ben said, sitting down. He was relieved to see a familiar face, and he liked Weasel.

'Decided to get some night life, did you, buddy?' Weasel smiled and clapped him on the shoulder. Ben thought that his check must have come in; his breath alone could have made Milwaukee famous.

'Yeah,' Ben said. He got out a dollar and laid it on the table, which was covered with the circular ghosts of the many beer glasses that had stood there. 'How you doing?'

'Just fine. What do you think of that new band? Great, ain't they?'

'They're okay,' Ben said. 'Finish that thing up before it goes flat. I'm buying.'

'I been waitin' to hear somebody say that all night. *Jackie!*' he bawled. 'Bring my buddy here a pitcher! Budweiser!'

Jackie brought the pitcher on a tray littered with beer-soaked change and lifted it onto the table, her right arm bulging like a prize-fighter's. She looked at the dollar as if it were a new species of cockroach. 'That's a buck fawty,' she said.

Ben put another bill down. She picked them both up, fished sixty cents out of the assorted puddles on her tray, banged them down on the table, and said, 'Weasel Craig, when you yell like that you sound like a rooster gettin' its neck wrung.'

'You're beautiful, darlin',' Weasel said. 'This is Ben Mears. He writes books.'

'Meetcha,' Jackie said, and disappeared into the dimness.

Ben poured himself a glass of beer and Weasel followed

suit, filling his glass professionally to the top. The foam threatened to overspill and then backed down. 'Here's to you, buddy.'

Ben lifted his glass and drank.

'So how's that writin' goin'?'

'Pretty good, Weasel.'

'I seen you goin' round with that little Norton girl. She's a real peach, she is. You couldn't do no better there.'

'Yes, she's—'

'*Matt!*' Weasel bawled, almost startling Ben into dropping his glass. By God, he thought, he *does* sound like a rooster saying good-by to this world.

'Matt Burke!' Weasel waved wildly, and a man with white hair raised his hand in greeting and started to cut through the crowd. 'Here's a fella you ought to meet,' Weasel told Ben. 'Matt Burke's one smart son of a whore.'

The man coming toward them looked about sixty. He was tall, wearing a clean flannel shirt open at the throat, and his hair, which was as white as Weasel's, was cut in a flattop.

'Hello, Weasel,' he said.

'How are you, buddy?' Weasel said. 'Want you to meet a fella stayin' over to Eva's. Ben Mears. Writes books, he does. He's a lovely fella.' He looked at Ben. 'Me'n Matt grew up together, only he got an education and I got the shaft.' Weasel cackled.

Ben stood up and shook Matt Burke's bunched hand gingerly. 'How are you?'

'Fine, thanks. I've read one of your books, Mr Mears. *Air Dance.*'

'Make it Ben, please. I hope you liked it.'

'I liked it much better than the critics, apparently,' Matt said, sitting down. 'I think it will gain ground as time goes by. How are you, Weasel?'

'Perky,' Weasel said. 'Just as perky as ever I could be. *Jackie!*' he bawled. 'Bring Matt a glass!'

'Just wait a minute, y'old fart!' Jackie yelled back, drawing laughter from the nearby tables.

'She's a lovely girl,' Weasel said. 'Maureen Talbot's girl.'

'Yes,' Matt said. 'I had Jackie in school. Class of '71. Her mother was '51.'

'Matt teaches high school English,' Weasel told Ben. 'You and him should have a lot to talk about.'

'I remember a girl named Maureen Talbot,' Ben said. 'She came and got my aunt's wash and brought it back all folded in a wicker basket. The basket only had one handle.'

'Are you from town, Ben?' Matt asked.

'I spent some time here as a boy. With my Aunt Cynthia.'

'Cindy Stowens?'

'Yes.'

Jackie came with a clean glass, and Matt tipped beer into it. 'It really is a small world, then. Your aunt was in a senior class I taught my first year in 'salem's Lot. Is she well?'

'She died in 1972.'

'I'm sorry.'

'She went very easily,' Ben said, and refilled his glass. The band had finished its set, and the members were trouping toward the bar. The level of conversation went down a notch.

'Have you come back to Jerusalem's Lot to write a book about us?' Matt asked.

A warning bell went off in Ben's mind.

'In a way, I suppose,' he said.

'This town could do much worse for a biographer. *Air Dance* was a fine book. I think there might be another fine book in this town. I once thought I might write it.'

'Why didn't you?'

Matt smiled – an easy smile with no trace of bitterness, cynicism, or malice. 'I lacked one vital ingredient. Talent.'

'Don't you believe it,' Weasel said, refilling his glass from the dregs of the pitcher. 'Ole Matt's got a world of talent. Schoolteachin' is a wonnerful job. Nobody appreciates schoo'teachers, but they're . . .' He swayed a little in his chair, searching for completion. He was becoming very drunk. 'Salt of the earth,' he finished, took a mouthful of beer, grimaced, and stood up. 'Pardon me while I take a leak.'

He wandered off, bumping into people and hailing them by name. They passed him on with impatience or good cheer, and watching his progress to the men's room was like watching a pinball racket and bounce its way down toward the flipper buttons.

'There goes the wreck of a fine man,' Matt said, and held up one finger. A waitress appeared almost immediately and addressed him as Mr Burke. She seemed a trifle scandalized that her old English Classics teacher should be here, boozing it up with the likes of Weasel Craig. When she turned away to bring them another pitcher, Ben thought Matt looked a trifle bemused.

'I like Weasel,' Ben said. 'I get a feeling there was a lot there once. What happened to him?'

'Oh, there's no story there,' Matt said. 'The bottle got him. It got him a little more each year and now it's got all of him. He won a Silver Star at Anzio in World War II. A cynic might believe his life would have had more meaning if he had died there.'

'I'm not a cynic,' Ben said. 'I like him still. But I think I better give him a ride home tonight.'

'That would be good of you. I come out here now and then to listen to the music. I like loud music. More than ever, since my hearing began to fail. I understand that you're interested in the Marsten House. Is your book about it?'

Ben jumped. 'Who told you that?'

Matt smiled. 'How does that old Marvin Gaye song put it? I heard it through the grapevine. Luscious, vivid idiom, although the image is a bit obscure if you consider it. One conjures up a picture of a man standing with his ear cocked attentively toward a Concord or Tokay . . . I'm rambling. I ramble a great deal these days but rarely try to keep it in hand anymore. I heard from what the gentlemen of the press would call an informed source – Loretta Starcher, actually. She's the librarian at our local citadel of literature. You've been in several times to look at the Cumberland *Ledger* articles pertaining to the ancient scandal, and she also got you two true-crime books that had articles on it. By the way, the Lubert one is good – he came to the Lot and researched it himself in 1946 – but the Snow chapter is speculative trash.'

'I know,' Ben said automatically.

The waitress set down a fresh pitcher of beer and Ben suddenly had an uncomfortable image: Here is a fish swimming around comfortably and (he thinks) unobtrusively, flicking here and there amongst the kelp and the plankton. Draw away for the long view and there's the kicker: It's a goldfish bowl.

Matt paid the waitress and said, 'Nasty thing that happened up there. It's stayed in the town's consciousness, too. Of course, tales of nastiness and murder are always handed down with slavering delight from generation to generation, while students groan and complain when they're faced with a George Washington Carver or a Jonas Salk. But it's more than that, I think. Perhaps it's due to a geographical freak.'

'Yes,' Ben said, drawn in spite of himself. The teacher had just stated an idea that had been lurking below the level of his consciousness from the day he had arrived back in town, possibly even before that. 'It stands on that hill overlooking the village like – oh, like some kind of dark idol.' He chuckled to make the remark seem trivial – it seemed to him that he had said something so deeply felt in an unguarded way that he must have opened a window on his soul to this stranger. Matt Burke's sudden close scrutiny of him did not make him feel any better.

'That is talent,' he said.

'Pardon me?'

'You have said it precisely. The Marsten House has looked down on us all for almost fifty years, at all our little peccadilloes and sins and lies. Like an idol.'

'Maybe it's seen the good, too,' Ben said.

'There's little good in sedentary small towns. Mostly indifference spiced with an occasional vapid evil – or worse, a conscious one. I believe Thomas Wolfe wrote about seven pounds of literature about that.'

'I thought you weren't a cynic.'

'You said that, not I.' Matt smiled and sipped at his beer. The band was moving away from the bar, resplendent in their red shirts and glittering vests and neckerchiefs. The lead singer took his guitar and began to chord it.

'At any rate, you never answered my question. Is your new book about the Marsten House?'

'I suppose it is, in a way.'

'I'm pumping you. Sorry.'

'It's all right,' Ben said, thinking of Susan and feeling uncomfortable. 'I wonder what's keeping Weasel? He's been gone a hell of a long time.'

'Could I presume on short acquaintanceship and ask a rather large favor? If you refuse, I'll more than understand.'

'Sure, ask,' Ben said.

'I have a creative writing class,' Matt said. 'They are intelligent children, eleventh-and twelfth-graders, most of them, and I would like to present someone who makes his living with words to them. Someone who – how shall I say? – has taken the word and made it flesh.'

'I'd be more than happy to,' Ben said, feeling absurdly flattered. 'How long are your periods?'

'Fifty minutes.'

'Well, I don't suppose I can bore them too badly in that length of time.'

'Oh? I do it quite well, I think,' Matt said. 'Although I'm sure you wouldn't bore them at all. This next week?'

'Sure. Name a day and a time.'

'Tuesday? Period four? That goes from eleven o'clock until ten of twelve. No one will boo you, but I suspect you will hear a great many stomachs rumble.'

'I'll bring some cotton for my ears.'

Matt laughed. 'I'm very pleased. I will meet you at the office, if that's agreeable.'

'Fine. Do you—'

'Mr Burke?' It was Jackie, she of the heavy biceps. 'Weasel's passed out in the men's room. Do you suppose—'

'Oh? Goodness, yes. Ben, would you—'

'Sure.'

They got up and crossed the room. The band had begun to play again, something about how the kids in Muskogee still respected the college dean.

The bathroom smelled of sour urine and chlorine. Weasel was propped against the wall between two urinals, and a fellow in an army uniform was pissing approximately two inches from his right ear.

His mouth was open and Ben thought how terribly old he looked, old and ravaged by cold, impersonal forces with no gentle touch in them. The reality of his own dissolution, advancing day by day, came home to him, not for the first time, but with shocking unexpectedness. The pity that welled up in his throat like clear, black waters was as much for himself as for Weasel.

'Here,' Matt said, 'can you get an arm under him when this gentleman finishes relieving himself?'

'Yes,' Ben said. He looked at the man in the army uniform, who was shaking off in leisurely fashion. 'Hurry it up, can you, buddy?'

'Why? He ain't in no rush.'

Nevertheless, he zipped up and stepped away from the urinal so they could get in.

Ben got an arm around Weasel's back, hooked a hand in his armpit, and lifted. For a moment his buttocks pressed against the tiled wall and he could feel the vibrations from the band. Weasel came up with the limp mail sack weight of utter unconsciousness. Matt slid his head under Weasel's other arm, hooked his own arm around Weasel's waist, and they carried him out the door.

'There goes Weasel,' someone said, and there was laughter.

'Dell ought to cut him off,' Matt said, sounding out of breath. 'He knows how this always turns out.'

They went through the door into the foyer, and then out onto the wooden steps leading down to the parking lot.

'Easy,' Ben grunted. 'Don't drop him.'

They went down the stairs, Weasel's limp feet clopping on the risers like blocks of wood.

'The Citroën . . . over in the last row.'

They carried him over. The coolness in the air was sharper now, and tomorrow the leaves would be blooded. Weasel had begun to grunt deep in his throat and his head jerked weakly on the stalk of his neck.

'Can you put him to bed when you get back to Eva's?' Matt asked.

'Yes, I think so.'

'Good. Look, you can just see the rooftop of the Marsten House over the trees.'

Ben looked. Matt was right; the top angle just peeked above the dark horizon of pines, blotting out the stars at the rim of the visible world with the regular shape of human construction.

Ben opened the passenger door and said, 'Here. Let me have him.'

He took Weasel's full weight and slipped him neatly into the passenger seat and closed the door. Weasel's head lolled against the window, giving it a flattened, grotesque look.

'Tuesday at eleven?'

'I'll be there.'

'Thanks. And thanks for helping Weasel, too.' He held out his hand and Ben shook it.

He got in, started the Citroën, and headed back toward town. Once the roadhouse neon had disappeared behind the trees, the road was deserted and black, and Ben thought, These roads are haunted now.

Weasel gave a snort and a groan beside him and Ben jumped. The Citroën swerved minutely on the road.

Now, why did I think that?

No answer.

7

He opened the wing window so that it scooped cold air directly onto Weasel on the ride home, and by the time he drove into Eva Miller's dooryard, Weasel had attained a soupy semiconsciousness.

Ben led him, half stumbling, up the back porch steps and into the kitchen, which was dimly lit by the stove's fluorescent. Weasel moaned, then muttered deep in his throat, 'She's a lovely girl, Jack, and married women, they know . . . know . . .'

A shadow detached itself from the hall and it was

Eva, huge in an old quilted housecoat, her hair done up in rollers and covered with a filmy net scarf. Her face was pale and ghostly with night cream.

'Ed,' she said. 'Oh, Ed . . . you do go on, don't you?'

His eyes opened a little at the sound of her voice, and a smile touched his features. 'On and on and on,' he croaked. 'Wouldn't you know it more than the rest?'

'Can you get him up to his room?' she asked Ben.

'Yes, no sweat.'

He tightened his grip on Weasel and somehow got him up the stairs and down to his room. The door was unlocked and he carried him inside. The minute he laid him on the bed, signs of consciousness ceased and he fell into a deep sleep.

Ben paused a moment to look around. The room was clean, almost sterile, things put away with barrackslike neatness. As he began to work on Weasel's shoes, Eva Miller said from behind him, 'Never mind that, Mr Means. Go on up, if you like.'

'But he ought to be—'

'I'll undress him.' Her face was grave and full of dignified, measured sadness. 'Undress him and give him an alcohol rub to help with his hangover in the morning. I've done it before. Many times.'

'All right,' Ben said, and went upstairs without looking back. He undressed slowly, thought about taking a shower, and decided not to. He got into bed and lay looking at the ceiling and did not sleep for a long time.

CHAPTER SIX
THE LOT (II)

Fall and spring came to Jerusalem's Lot with the same suddenness of sunrise and sunset in the tropics. The line of demarcation could be as thin as one day. But spring is not the finest season in New England – it's too short, too uncertain, too apt to turn savage on short notice. Even so, there are April days which linger in the memory even after one has forgotten the wife's touch, or the feel of the baby's toothless mouth at the nipple. But by mid-May, the sun rises out of the morning's haze with authority and potency, and standing on your top step at seven in the morning with your dinner bucket in your hand, you know that the dew will be melted off the grass by eight and that the dust on the back roads will hang depthless and still in the air for five minutes after a car's passage; and that by one in the afternoon it will be up to ninety-five on the third floor of the mill and the sweat will roll off your arms like oil and stick your shirt to your back in a widening patch and it might as well be July.

But when fall comes, kicking summer out on its treacherous ass as it always does one day sometime after the midpoint of September, it stays awhile like an old friend that you have missed. It settles in the way an old friend will settle into your favorite chair and take out his pipe and light it and then fill the afternoon with stories of places he has been and things he has done since last he saw you.

It stays on through October and, in rare years, on into November. Day after day the skies are a clear, hard blue, and the clouds that float across them, always west to east, are calm white ships with gray keels. The wind begins to blow by the day, and it is never still. It hurries you along as you walk the roads, crunching the leaves that have fallen in mad and variegated drifts. The wind makes you ache in some place that is deeper than your bones. It may be that it touches something old in the human soul, a chord of race memory that says *Migrate or die – migrate or die*. Even in your house, behind square walls, the wind beats against the wood and the glass and sends its fleshless pucker against the eaves and sooner or later you have to put down what you were doing and go out and see. And you can stand on your stoop or in your dooryard at mid-afternoon and watch the cloud shadows rush across Griffen's pasture and up Schoolyard Hill, light and dark, light and dark, like the shutters of the gods being opened and closed. You can see the goldenrod, that most tenacious and pernicious and beauteous of all New England flora, bowing away from the wind like a great and silent congregation. And if there are no cars or planes, and if no one's Uncle John is out in the wood lot west of town banging away at a quail or pheasant; if the only sound is the slow beat of your own heart, you can hear another sound, and that is the sound of life winding down to its cyclic close, waiting for the first winter snow to perform last rites.

2

That year the first day of fall (real fall as opposed to calendar fall) was September 28, the day that Danny Glick was buried in the Harmony Hill Cemetery.

Church services were private, but the graveside services were open to the town and a good portion of the town turned out – classmates, the curious, and the older people to whom funerals grow nearly compulsive as old age knits their shrouds up around them.

They came up Burns Road in a long line, twisting up and out of sight over the next hill. All the cars had their lights turned on in spite of the day's brilliance. First came Carl Foreman's hearse, its rear windows filled with flowers, then Tony Glick's 1965 Mercury, its deteriorating muffler bellowing and farting. Behind that, in the next four cars, came relatives on both sides of the family, one bunch from as far away as Tulsa, Oklahoma. Others in that long, lights-on parade included: Mark Petrie (the boy Ralphie and Danny had been on their way to see the night Ralphie disappeared) and his mother and father; Richie Boddin and family; Mabel Werts in a car containing Mr and Mrs William Norton (sitting in the backseat with her cane planted between her swelled legs, she talked with unceasing constancy about other funerals she had attended all the way back to 1930); Lester Durham and his wife, Harriet; Paul Mayberry and his wife, Glynis; Pat Middler, Joe Crane, Vinnie Upshaw, and Clyde Corliss, all riding in a car driven by Milt Crossen (Milt had opened the beer cooler before they left, and they had all shared out a solemn six-pack in front of the stove); Eva Miller in a car which also contained her close friends Loretta Starcher and Rhoda Curless, who were both maiden ladies; Parkins Gillespie and his deputy, Nolly Gardener, riding in the Jerusalem's Lot police car (Parkins's Ford with a stick-on dashboard bubble); Lawrence Crockett and his sallow wife; Charles Rhodes, the sour bus driver, who went to all funerals on general principles; the Charles Griffen family, including wife and two sons, Hal and Jack, the only offspring still living at home.

Mike Ryerson and Royal Snow had dug the grave early that morning, laying strips of fake grass over the raw soil they had thrown out of the ground. Mike had lighted the Flame of Remembrance that the Glicks had specified. Mike could remember thinking that Royal didn't seem himself this morning. He was usually full of little jokes and ditties about the work at hand (cracked, off-key tenor: 'They wrap you up in a big white sheet, an' put you down at least six feet ...'), but this morning he had seemed exceptionally quiet, almost sullen. Hung over, maybe, Mike thought. He and that muscle-bound buddy of his, Peters, had certainly been slopping it up down at Dell's the night before.

Five minutes ago, when he had seen Carl's hearse coming over the hill about a mile down the road, he had swung open the wide iron gates, glancing up at the high iron spikes as he always did since he had found Doc up there. With the gates open, he walked back to the newly dug grave where Father Donald Callahan, the pastor of the Jerusalem's Lot parish, waited by the grave. He was wearing a stole about his shoulders and the book he held was open to the children's burial service. This was what they called the third station, Mike knew. The first was the house of the deceased, the second at the tiny Catholic Church, St Andrew's. Last station, Harmony Hill. Everybody out.

A little chill touched him and he looked down at the bright plastic grass, wondering why it had to be a part of every funeral. It looked like exactly what it was: a cheap imitation of life discreetly masking the heavy brown clods of the final earth.

'They're on their way, Father,' he said.

Callahan was a tall man with piercing blue eyes and a ruddy complexion. His hair was a graying steel color. Ryerson, who hadn't been to church since he turned sixteen, liked him the best of all the local witch doctors. John Groggins, the Methodist minister, was a hypocritical old poop, and Patterson, from the Church of the Latter-day Saints and Followers of the Cross, was as crazy as a bear stuck in a honey tree. At a funeral for one of the church deacons two or three years back, Patterson had gotten right down and rolled on the ground. But Callahan seemed nice enough for a Pope-lover; his funerals were calm and comforting and always short. Ryerson doubted if Callahan had gotten all those red and broken veins in his cheeks and around his nose from praying, but if Callahan did a little drinking, who was to blame him? The way the world was, it was a wonder all those preachers didn't end up in looney bins.

'Thanks, Mike,' he said, and looked up at the bright sky. 'This is going to be a hard one.'

'I guess so. How long?'

'Ten minutes, no more. I'm not going to draw out his parents' agony. There's enough of that still ahead of them.'

'Okay,' Mike said, and walked toward the rear of the graveyard. He would jump over the stone wall, go into the woods, and eat a late lunch. He knew from long experience that the last thing the grieving family and friends want to see during the third station is the resident grave-digger in his dirt-stained coveralls; it kind of put a crimp in the minister's glowing pictures of immortality and the pearly gates.

Near the back wall he paused and bent to examine a slate headstone that had fallen forward. He stood it up and again felt a small chill go through him as he brushed the dirt from the inscription:

HUBERT BARCLAY MARSTEN
October 6, 1889
August 12, 1939

The angel of Death who holdeth
The bronze Lamp beyond the golden door
Hath taken thee into dark Waters

And below that, almost obliterated by thirty-six seasons of freeze and thaw:

God Grant He Lie Still

Still vaguely troubled and still not knowing why, Mike Ryerson went back into the woods to sit by the brook and eat his lunch.

3

In the early days at the seminary, a friend of Father Callahan's had given him a blasphemous crewelwork sampler which had sent him into gales of horrified laughter at the time, but which seemed more true and less blasphemous as the years passed: *God grant me the SERENITY to accept what I cannot change, the TENACITY to change what I may, and the GOOD LUCK not to fuck up too often.* This in Old English script with a rising sun in the background.

Now, standing before Danny Glick's mourners, that old credo recurred.

The pallbearers, two uncles and two cousins of the dead boy, had lowered the coffin into the ground. Marjorie Glick, dressed in a black coat and a veiled black hat, her face showing through the mesh in the netting like cottage cheese, stood swaying in the protective curve of her father's arm, clutching a black purse as though it were a life preserver. Tony Glick stood apart from her, his face shocked and wandering. Several times during the church service he had looked around, as if to verify his presence among these people. His face was that of a man who believes he is dreaming.

The church can't stop this dream, Callahan thought. Nor all the serenity, tenacity, or good luck in the world. The fuck-up has already happened.

He sprinkled holy water on the coffin and the grave, sanctifying them for all time.

'Let us pray,' he said. The words rolled melodiously from his throat as they always had, in shine and shadow, drunk or sober. The mourners bowed their heads.

'Lord God, through your mercy those who have lived

in faith find eternal peace. Bless this grave and send your angel to watch over it. As we bury the body of Daniel Click, welcome him into your presence, and with your saints let him rejoice in you forever. We ask it through Christ our Lord. Amen.'

'Amen,' the congregation muttered, and the wind swept it away in rags. Tony Glick was looking around with wide, haunted eyes. His wife was pressing a Kleenex to her mouth.

'With faith in Jesus Christ, we reverently bring the body of this child to be buried in its human imperfection. Let us pray with confidence to God, who gives life to all things, that he will raise up this mortal body to the perfection and company of saints.'

He turned the pages of his missal. A woman in the third row of the loose horseshoe grouped around the grave had begun to sob hoarsely. A bird chirruped somewhere back in the woods.

'Let us pray for our brother Daniel Glick to our Lord Jesus Christ,' Father Callahan said, 'who told us: "I am the resurrection and the life. The man who believes in me will live even though he dies, and every living person who puts his faith in me will never suffer eternal death." Lord, you wept at the death of Lazarus, your friend: comfort us in our sorrow. We ask this in faith.'

'Lord, hear our prayer,' the Catholics answered.

'You raised the dead to life; give our brother Daniel eternal life. We ask this in faith.'

'Lord, hear our prayer,' they answered. Something seemed to be dawning in Tony Glick's eyes; a revelation, perhaps.

'Our brother Daniel was washed clean in baptism; give him fellowship with all your saints. We ask this in faith.'

'Lord, hear our prayer.'

'He was nourished with your body and blood; grant him a place at the table in your heavenly kingdom. We ask this in faith.'

'Lord, hear our prayer.'

Marjorie Glick had begun to rock back and forth, moaning.

'Comfort us in our sorrow at the death of our brother; let our faith be our consolation and eternal life our hope. We ask this in faith.'

'Lord, hear our prayer.'

He closed his missal. 'Let us pray as our Lord taught us,' he said quietly. 'Our Father who art in heaven—'

'No!' Tony Glick screamed, and propelled himself forward. 'You ain't gonna throw no dirt on my boy!'

Hands reached out to stay him, but they were belated. For a moment he tottered on the edge of the grave, and then the fake grass wrinkled and gave way. He fell into the hole and landed on the coffin with a horrid, heavy thump.

'Danny, you come outta there!' he bawled.

'Oh, *my*,' Mabel Werts said, and pressed her black silk funeral hankie to her lips. Her eyes were bright and avid, storing this the way a squirrel stores nuts for the winter.

'Danny, goddammit, you stop this fucking around!'

Father Callahan nodded at two of the pallbearers and they stepped forward, but three other men, including Parkins Gillespie and Nolly Gardener, had to step in before Glick could be gotten out of the grave, kicking and screaming and howling.

'Danny, you stop it now! You got your Momma scared! I'm gonna whip your butt for you! Lemme go! Lemme go . . . I want m'boy . . . let me go, you pricks . . . ahhh, *God*—'

'Our Father who art in heaven—' Callahan began again, and other voices joined him, lifting the words toward the indifferent shield of the sky.

'—hallowed be they name. Thy kingdom come, thy will be done—'

'Danny, you come to me, hear? *You hear me?*'

'—on earth, as it is in heaven. Give us this day our daily bread and forgive us—'

'*Dannneeee*—'

'—our trespasses, as we forgive those who trespass against us—'

'He ain't dead, he ain't dead, let go a me you miserable shitpokes—'

'—and lead us not into temptation, but deliver us from evil. Through Christ our Lord, amen.'

'He ain't dead,' Tony Glick sobbed. 'He can't be. He's only twelve fucking years old.' He began to weep heavily and staggered forward in spite of the men who held him, his face ravaged and streaming with tears. He fell on his knees at Callahan's feet and grasped his trousers with muddy hands. 'Please give me my boy back. Please don't fool me no more.'

Callahan took his head gently with both hands. 'Let us pray,' he said. He could feel Glick's wracking sobs in his thighs.

'Lord, comfort this man and his wife in their sorrow. You cleansed this child in the waters of baptism and gave him new life. May we one day join him and share heaven's joys forever. We ask this in Jesus' name, amen.'

He raised his head and saw that Marjorie Glick had fainted.

4

When they were all gone, Mike Ryerson came back and sat down on the edge of the open grave to eat his last half sandwich and wait for Royal Snow to come back.

The funeral had been at four, and it was now almost five o'clock. The shadows were long and the sun was already slanting through the tall western oaks. That frigging Royal had promised to be back by quarter of five at the latest; now where was he?

The sandwich was bologna and cheese, his favorite. All the sandwiches he made were his favorites; that was one of the advantages to being single. He finished up and dusted his hands, spraying a few bread crumbs down on the coffin.

Someone was watching him.

He felt it suddenly and surely. He stared around at the cemetery with wide, startled eyes.

'Royal? You there, Royal?'

No answer. The wind sighed through the trees, making them rustle mysteriously. In the waving shadows of the elms beyond the stone wall, he could see Hubert Marsten's marker, and suddenly he thought of Win's dog, hanging impaled on the iron front gate.

Eyes. Flat and emotionless. Watching.

Dark, don't catch me here.

He started to his feet as if someone had spoken aloud.

'Goddamn you, Royal.' He spoke the words aloud, but quietly. He no longer thought Royal was around, or even coming back. He would have to do it by himself, and it would take a long time alone.

Maybe until dark.

He set to work, not trying to understand the dread that had fallen over him, not wondering why this job that had never bothered him before was bothering him terribly now.

Moving with quick, economical gestures, he pulled the strips of fake grass away from the raw earth and folded them neatly. He laid them over his arm and took them out to his truck, parked beyond the gate, and once out of the graveyard, that nasty feeling of being watched slipped away.

He put the grass in the back of the pickup and took out a spade. He started back, then hesitated. He stared at the open grave and it seemed to mock him.

It occurred to him that the feeling of being watched had stopped as soon as he could no longer see the coffin nestled at the bottom of its hole. He had a sudden mental image of Danny Glick lying on that little satin pillow with his eyes open. No – that was stupid. They closed the eyes. He had watched Carl Foreman do it enough times. *Course we gum 'em*, Carl had said once. *Wouldn't want the corpse winkin' at the congregation, would we?*

He loaded his shovel with dirt and threw it in. It made a heavy, solid thump on the polished mahogany box, and Mike winced. The sound made him feel a little sick. He straightened up and looked around distractedly at the floral displays. A damn waste. Tomorrow the petals would be scattered all over in red and yellow flakes. Why anybody bothered was beyond him. If you were going to spend money, why not give it to the Cancer Society or the March of Dimes or even the Ladies' Aid? Then it went to some good, at least.

He threw in another shovelful and rested again.

That coffin was another waste. Nice mahogany coffin, worth a thousand bucks at least, and here he was shoveling dirt over it. The Glicks didn't have no more money than anyone else, and who puts burial insurance on kids? They were probably six miles in hock, all for a box to shovel in the ground.

He bent down, got another spadeful of earth, and reluctantly threw it in. Again that horrid, final thump. The top of the coffin was sprayed with dirt now, but the polished mahogany gleamed through, almost reproachfully.

Stop looking at me.

He got another spadeful, not a very big one, and threw it in.

Thump.

The shadows were getting very long now. He paused, looked up, and there was the Marsten House, its shutters closed blankly. The east side, the one that bid good day to the light first, looked directly down on the iron gate of the cemetery, where Doc—

He forced himself to get another spadeful of earth and throw it into the hole.

Thump.

Some of it trickled off the sides, creasing into the brass hinges. Now if anyone opened it, there would be a gritting, grating noise like opening the door to a tomb.

Stop looking at me, goddammit.

He began to bend for another spadeful, but the thought seemed too heavy and he rested for a minute. He had read once – in the *National Enquirer* or someplace – about some Texas oilman dude who had specified in his will that he be buried in a brand-new Cadillac Coupe de Ville. They did it, too. Dug the hole with a payloader and lifted the car in with a crane. People all over the country driving around in old cars held together with spit and baling wire and one of these rich pigs gets himself buried sitting behind the wheel of a ten-thousand-dollar car with all the accessories—

He suddenly jerked and took a step backward, shaking his head warily. He had almost – well – had almost been in a trance, it seemed like. That feeling of being watched was much stronger now. He looked at the sky and was alarmed to see how much light had gone out of it. Only the top story of the Marsten House was in bright sunlight now. His watch said ten past six. Christ, it had been an hour and he hadn't thrown half a dozen shovelfuls of dirt down that hole!

Mike bent to his work, trying not to let himself think. *Thump* and *thump* and *thump* and now the sound of dirt striking wood was muffled; the top of the coffin was covered and dirt was running off the sides in brown rivulets, almost up to the lock and catch.

He threw in another two spadefuls and paused.

Lock and catch?

Now, why in the name of God would anyone put a lock into a coffin? Did they think someone was going to try to get in? That had to be it. Surely they couldn't think someone would be trying to get out—

'Stop *staring* at me,' Mike Ryerson said aloud, and then felt his heart crawl up into his throat. A sudden urge to run from this place, to run straight down the road to town, filled him. He controlled it only with great effort. Just the heebie-jeebies, that's all it was. Working in a grave-yard, who wouldn't get them once in a while? It was like a fucking horror movie, having to cover up that kid, only twelve years old and his eyes wide open—

'Christ, *stop it!*' he cried, and looked wildly up toward the Marsten House. Now only the roof was in sunshine. It was six-fifteen.

After that he began to work more quickly again, bending and shoveling and trying to keep his mind completely blank. But that sense of being watched seemed to grow rather than lessen, and each shovelful of dirt seemed heavier than the last. The top of the coffin was covered now but you could still see the shape, shrouded in earth.

The Catholic prayer for the dead began to run through his mind, the way things like that will for no good reason. He had heard Callahan saying it while he was eating his dinner down by the brook. That, and the father's helpless screaming.

Let us pray for our brother Daniel Glick to our Lord Jesus Christ, who said . . .

(O my father, favor me now.)

He paused and looked blankly down into the grave. It was deep, very deep. The shadows of coming night had already pooled into it, like something viscid and alive. It was still deep. He would never be able to fill it by dark. Never.

I am the resurrection and the life. The man who believes in me will live even though he dies . . .

(Lord of Flies, favor me now.)

Yes, the eyes were open. That's why he felt watched. Carl hadn't used enough gum on them and they had flown up just like window shades and the Glick kid was staring at him. Something ought to be done about it.

. . . and every living person who puts his faith in me will never suffer eternal death . . .

(*Now I bring you spoiled meat and reeking flesh.*)

Shovel out the dirt. That was the ticket. Shovel it out and and break the lock with the shovel and open the coffin and close those awful staring eyes. He had no mortician's gum, but he had two quarters in his pocket. That would do as well. Silver. Yes, silver was what the boy needed.

The sun was above the roof of the Marsten House now, and only touched the highest and oldest spruces to the west of town. Even with the shutters closed the house seemed to stare at him.

You raised the dead to life; give our brother Daniel eternal life.

(*I have made sacrifice for your favor. With my left hand I bring it.*)

Mike Ryerson suddenly leaped into the grave and began to shovel madly, throwing dirt up and out in brown explosions. At last the blade of the shovel struck wood and he began to scrape the last of the dirt over the sides and then he was kneeling on the coffin striking at the brass lip of the lock again and again and again.

The frogs down by the brook had begun to thump, a nightjar was singing in the shadows, and somewhere close by a number of whippoorwills had begun to lift their shrilling call.

Six-fifty.

What am I doing? he asked himself. What in God's name am I doing?

He knelt there on top of the coffin and tried to think about it . . . but something on the underside of his mind was urging him to hurry, hurry, the sun was going down—

Dark, don't catch me here.

He lifted the spade over his shoulder, brought it down on the lock once more, and there was a snapping sound. It was broken.

He looked up for a moment, in a last glimmering of sanity, his face streaked and circled with dirt and sweat, the eyes staring from it in bulging white circles.

Venus glowed against the breast of the sky.

Panting, he pulled himself out of the grave, lay down full length, and fumbled for the catches on the coffin lid. He found them and pulled. The lid swung upward, gritting on its hinges just as he had imagined it would, showing at first only pink satin, and then one dark-clad arm (Danny Glick had been buried in his communion suit), then . . . then the face.

Mike's breath clogged and stopped in his throat.

The eyes were open. Just as he had known they would be. Wide open and hardly glazed at all. They seemed to sparkle with hideous life in the last, dying light of day. There was no death pallor in that face; the cheeks seemed rosy, almost juicy with vitality.

He tried to drag his eyes away from that glittering, frozen stare and was unable.

He muttered: 'Jesus—'

The sun's diminishing arc passed below the horizon.

5

Mark Petrie was working on a model of Frankenstein's monster in his room and listening to his parents down in the living room. His room was on the second floor of the farmhouse they had bought on South Jointner Avenue, and although the house was heated by a modern oil furnace now, the old second-floor grates were still there. Originally, when the house had been heated by a central kitchen stove, the warm-air grates had kept the second floor from becoming too cold – although the woman who had originally lived in this house with her dour Baptist husband from 1873 to 1896 had still taken a hot brick wrapped in flannel to bed with her – but now the grates served another purpose. They conducted sound excellently.

Although his parents were down in the living room, they might as well have been discussing him right outside the door.

Once, when his father had caught him listening at the door in their old house – Mark had only been six then – his father had told him an old English proverb: Never listen at a knothole lest you be vexed. That meant, his father said, that you may hear something about yourself that you don't like.

Well, there was another one, too. Forewarned is forearmed.

At age twelve, Mark Petrie was a little skinnier than the average and slightly delicate-looking. Yet he moved with a grace and litheness that is not the common lot of boys his age, who seem mostly made up of knees and elbows and scabs. His complexion was fair, almost milky, and his features, which would be considered aquiline later in life, now seemed a trifle feminine. It had caused him some trouble even before the Richie Boddin incident in the schoolyard, and he had determined to handle it himself. He had made an analysis of the problem. Most bullies, he had decided, were big and ugly and clumsy. They scared people by being able to hurt them. They fought dirty. Therefore, if you were not afraid of being hurt a little, and if you were willing to fight dirty, a bully might be bested. Richie Boddin had been the first full vindication of his theory. He and the bully at the Kittery Elementary School had come off even (which had been a victory of a kind; the Kittery bully, bloody but unbowed, had proclaimed to the schoolyard community at large that he and Mark Petrie were pals. Mark, who thought the Kittery bully was a dumb piece of shit, did not contradict him. He understood discretion.). Talk did no good with bullies. Hurting was the only language that the Richie Boddins of the world seemed to understand, and Mark supposed that was why the world always had such a hard time getting along. He had been sent from school that day, and his father had been very angry until Mark, resigned to his ritual whipping with a rolled-up magazine, told him that Hitler had just been a Richie Boddin at heart. That had made his father laugh like hell, and even his mother snickered. The whipping had been averted.

Now June Petrie was saying. 'Do you think it's affected him, Henry?'

'Hard . . . to tell.' And Mark knew by the pause that his father was lighting his pipe. 'He's got a hell of a poker face.'

'Still waters run deep, though.' She paused. His mother

was always saying things like still waters run deep or it's a long, long road that has no turning. He loved them both dearly, but sometimes they seemed just as ponderous as the books in the folio section of the library . . . and just as dusty.

'They were on their way to see Mark,' she resumed. 'To play with his train set . . . now one dead and one missing! Don't fool yourself, Henry. The boy feels something.'

'He's got his feet pretty solidly planted on the ground,' Mr Petrie said. 'Whatever his feelings are, I'm sure he's got them in hand.'

Mark glued the Frankenstein monster's left arm into the shoulder socket. It was a specially treated Aurora model that glowed green in the dark, just like the plastic Jesus he had gotten for memorizing all of the 119th Psalm in Sunday school class in Kittery.

'I've sometimes thought we should have had another,' his father was saying. 'Among other things, it would have been good for Mark.'

And his mother, in an arch tone: 'Not for lack of trying, dear.'

His father grunted.

There was a long pause in the conversation. His father, he knew, would be rattling through *The Wall Street Journal*. His mother would be holding a novel by Jane Austen on her lap, or perhaps Henry James. She read them over and over again, and Mark was darned if he could see the sense in reading a book more than once. You knew how it was going to end.

'D'you think it's safe to let him go in the woods behind the house?' his mother asked presently. 'They say there's quicksand somewhere in town—'

'Miles from here.'

Mark relaxed a little and glued the monster's other arm on. He had a whole table of Aurora horror monsters, arranged in a scene that he changed each time a new element was added. It was a pretty good set. Danny and Ralphie had really been coming to see that the night when . . . whatever.

'I think it's okay,' his father said. 'Not after dark, of course.'

'Well, I hope that awful funeral won't give him nightmares.'

Mark could almost see his father shrug. 'Tony Glick . . . unfortunate. But death and grief are part of living. Time he got used to the idea.'

'Maybe.' Another long pause. What was coming now? he wondered. The child is the father of the man, maybe. Or as the twig is bent the tree is shaped. Mark glued the monster onto his base, which was a grave mound with a leaning headstone in the background. 'In the midst of life we're in death. But *I* may have nightmares.'

'Oh?'

'That Mr Foreman must be quite an artist, grisly as it sounds. He really looked as if he was just asleep. That any second he might open his eyes and yawn and . . . I don't know why these people insist on torturing themselves with open–coffin services. It's . . . heathenish.'

'Well, it's over.'

'Yes, I suppose. He's a good boy, isn't he, Henry?'

'Mark? The best.'

Mark smiled.

'Is there anything on TV?'

'I'll look.'

Mark turned the rest off; the serious discussion was done. He set his model on the windowsill to dry and harden. In another fifteen minutes his mother would be calling up for him to get ready for bed. He took his pajamas out of the top dresser drawer and began to undress.

In point of fact, his mother was worrying needlessly about his psyche, which was not tender at all. There was no particular reason why it should have been; he was a typical boy in most ways, despite his economy and his gracefulness. His family was upper middle class and still upwardly mobile, and the marriage of his parents was sound. They loved each other firmly, if a little stodgily. There had never been any great trauma in Mark's life. The few school fights had not scarred him. He got along with his peers and in general wanted the same things they wanted.

If there was anything that set him apart, it was a reservoir of remoteness, of cool self-control. No one had inculcated it in him; he seemed to have been born with it. When his pet dog, Chopper, had been hit by a car, he had insisted on going with his mother to the vet's. And when the vet had said, The dog has got to be put to sleep, my boy. Do you understand why? Mark said, You're not going to put him to sleep. You're going to gas him to death, aren't you? The vet said yes. Mark told him to go ahead, but he had kissed Chopper first. He had felt sorry but he hadn't cried and tears had never been close to the surface. His mother had cried but three days later Chopper was in the dim past to her, and he would never be in the dim past for Mark. That was the value in not crying. Crying was like pissing everything out on the ground.

He had been shocked by the disappearance of Ralphie Glick, and shocked again by Danny's death, but he had not been frightened. He had heard one of the men in the store say that probably a sex pervert had gotten Ralphie. Mark knew what perverts were. They did something to you that got their rocks off and when they were done they strangled you (in the comic books, the guy getting strangled always said *Arrrgggh*) and buried you in a gravel pit or under the boards of a deserted shed. If a sex pervert ever offered him candy, he would kick him in the balls and then run like a split streak.

'Mark?' His mother's voice, drifting up the stairs.

'I am,' he said, and smiled again.

'Don't forget your ears when you wash.'

'I won't.'

He went downstairs to kiss them good night, moving lithely and gracefully, sparing one glance backward to the table where his monsters rested in tableau: Dracula with his mouth open, showing his fangs, was menacing a girl lying on the ground while the Mad Doctor was torturing a lady on the rack and Mr Hyde was creeping up on an old guy walking home.

Understand death? Sure. That was when the monsters got you.

6

Roy McDougall pulled into the driveway of his trailer at half past eight, gunned the engine of his old Ford twice, and turned the engine off. The header pipe was just about shot, the blinkers didn't work, and the sticker came up next month. Some car. Some life. The kid was howling in the house and Sandy was screaming at him. Great old marriage.

He got out of the car and fell over one of the flagstones he had been meaning to turn into a walk from the driveway to the steps since last summer.

'Shitfire,' he muttered, glowering balefully at the piece of flagging and rubbing his shin.

He was quite drunk. He had gotten off work at three and had been drinking down at Dell's ever since with Hank Peters and Buddy Mayberry. Hank had been flush just lately, and seemed intent on drinking up the whole of his dividend, whatever it had been. He knew what Sandy thought of his buddies. Well, let her get tight-assed. Begrudge a man a few beers on Saturday and Sunday even though he spent the whole week breaking his back on the goddamn picker – and getting weekend overtime to boot. Who was she to get so holy? She spent all day sitting in the house with nothing to do but take care of the place and shoot the shit with the mailman and see that the kid didn't crawl into the oven. She hadn't been watching him too close lately, anyway. Goddamn kid even fell off the changing table the other day.

Where were you?

I was holding him, Roy. He just wriggles so.

Wriggles. Yeah.

He went up to the door, still steaming. His leg hurt where he had bumped it. Not that he'd get any sympathy from *her*. So what was she doing while he was sweating his guts out for that prick of a foreman? Reading confession magazines and eating chocolate-covered cherries or watching the soap operas on the TV and eating chocolate-covered cherries or gabbing to her friends on the phone and eating chocolate-covered cherries. She was getting pimples on her ass as well as her face. Pretty soon you wouldn't be able to tell the two of them apart.

He pushed open the door and walked in.

The scene struck him immediately and forcibly, cutting through the beer haze like the flick of a wet towel: the baby, naked and screaming, blood running from his nose; Sandy holding him, her sleeveless blouse smeared with blood, looking at him over her shoulder, her face contracting with surprise and fear; the diaper on the floor.

Randy, with the discolored marks around his eyes barely fading, raised his hands as if in supplication.

'What's going on around here?' Roy asked slowly.

'Nothing, Roy. He just—'

'You hit him,' he said tonelessly. 'He wouldn't hold still for the diapers so you smacked him.'

'No,' she said quickly. 'He rolled over and bumped his nose, that's all. That's all.'

'I ought to beat the shit out of you,' he said.

'Roy, he just bumped his *nose*—'

His shoulders slumped. 'What's for dinner?'

'Hamburgs. They're burnt,' she said petulantly, and pulled the bottom of her blouse out of her Wranglers to wipe under Randy's nose. Roy could see the roll of fat she was getting. She'd never bounced back after the baby. Didn't care.

'Shut him up.'

'He isn't—'

'*Shut him up!*' Roy yelled, and Randy, who had actually been quieting down to snuffles, began to scream again.

'I'll give him a bottle,' Sandy said, getting up.

'And get my dinner.' He started to take off his denim jacket. '*Christ*, isn't this place a mess. What do you do all day, beat off?'

'*Roy!*' she said, sounding shocked. Then she giggled. Her insane burst of anger at the baby who would not hold still on his diapers so she could pin them began to be far away, hazy. It might have happened on one of her afternoon stories, or 'Medical Center.'

'Get my dinner and then pick this frigging place up.'

'All right. All right, sure.' She got a bottle out of the refrigerator and put Randy down in the playpen with it. He began to suck it apathetically, his eyes moving from mother to father in small, trapped circles.

'Roy?'

'Hmmm? What?'

'It's all over.'

'What is?'

'You know what. Do you want to? Tonight?'

'Sure,' he said. 'Sure.' And thought again: Isn't this some life. Isn't this just *some* life.

7

Nolly Gardener was listening to rock 'n' roll music on WLOB and snapping his fingers when the telephone rang. Parkins put down his crossword magazine and said, 'Cut that some, will you?'

'Sure, Park.' Nolly turned the radio down and went on snapping his fingers.

'Hello?' Parkins said.

'Constable Gillespie?'

'Yeah.'

'Agent Tom Hanrahan here, sir. I've got the information you requested.'

'Good of you to get back so quick.'

'We haven't got much of a hook for you.'

'That's okay,' Parkins said. 'What have you got?'

'Ben Mears investigated as a result of a traffic fatality in upstate New York, May 1973. No charges brought. Motorcycle smash. His wife, Miranda, was killed. Witnesses said he was moving slowly and a breath test was negative. Apparently just hit a wet spot. His politics are leftish. He was in a peace march at Princeton in 1966. Spoke at an antiwar rally in Brooklyn in 1967. March on Washington in 1968 and 1970. Arrested during a San Francisco peace march November 1971. And that's all there is on him.'

'What else?'

'Kurt Barlow, that's Kurt with a "k". He's British, but by naturalization rather than birth. Born in Germany, fled to England in 1938, apparently just ahead of the Gestapo. His earlier records just aren't available, but he's probably in his seventies. The name he was born with was Breichen. He's been in the import-export business in London since 1945, but he's elusive. Straker has been his partner since then, and Straker seems to be the fellow who deals with the public.'

'Yeah?'

'Straker is British by birth. Fifty-eight years old. His father was a cabinetmaker in Manchester. Left a fair amount of money to his son, apparently, and this Straker has done all right, too. Both of them applied for visas to spend an extended amount of time in the United States eighteen months ago. That's all we have. Except that they may be queer for each other.'

'Yeah,' Parkins said, and sighed. 'About what I thought.'

'If you'd like further assistance, we can query CID and Scotland Yard about your two new merchants.'

'No, that's fine.'

'No connection between Mears and the other two, by the way. Unless it's deep undercover.'

'Okay. Thanks.'

'It's what we're here for. If you want assistance, get in touch.'

'I will. Thank you now.'

He put the receiver back in its cradle and looked at it thoughtfully.

'Who was that, Park?' Nolly asked, turning up the radio.

'The Excellent Café. They ain't got any ham on rye. Nothin' but toasted cheese and egg salad.'

'I got some raspberry fluff in my desk if you want it.'

'No thanks,' Parkins said, and sighed again.

8

The dump was still smoldering.

Dud Rogers walked along the edge, smelling the fragrance of smoldering offal. Underfoot, small bottles crunched and powdery black ash puffed up at every step. Out in the dump's wasteland, a wide bed of coals waxed and waned with the vagaries of the wind, reminding him of a huge red eye opening and closing . . . the eye of a giant. Every now and then there was a muffled small explosion as an aerosol can or lightbulb blew up. A great many rats had come out of the dump when he lit it that morning, more rats than he had ever seen before. He had shot fully three dozen, and his pistol had been hot to the touch when he finally tucked it back in its holster. They were big bastards, too, some of them fully two feet long stretched end to end. Funny how their numbers seemed to grow or shrink depending on the year. Had something to do with the weather, probably. If it kept up, he would have to start salting poison bait around, something he hadn't had to do since 1964.

There was one now, creeping under one of the yellow sawhorses that served as fire barriers.

Dud pulled out his pistol, clicked off the safety, aimed, and fired. The shot kicked dirt in front of the rat, spraying its fur. But instead of running, it only rose up on its hind legs and looked at him, beady little eyes glittering red in the fire glow. Jesus, but some of them were bold!

'By-by, Mr Rat,' Dud said, and took careful aim.

Kapow. The rat flopped over, twitching.

Dud walked across and prodded it with one heavy work boot. The rat bit weakly at the shoe leather, its sides aspirating weakly.

'Bastard,' Dud said mildly, and crushed its head.

He hunkered down, looked at it, and found himself thinking of Ruthie Crockett, who wore no bra. When she wore one of those clingy cardigan sweaters, you could see her little nipples just as clear, made erect by the friction as they rubbed against the wool, and if a man could get ahold of those tits and rub them just a little, just a little, mind you, a slut like that would go off just like a rocket . . .

He picked the rat up by its tail and swung it like a pendulum. 'How'd you like ole Mr Rat in your pencil box, Ruthie?' The thought with its unintentional double entendre amused him, and he uttered a high-pitched giggle, his oddly off-center head nodding and dipping.

He slung the rat far out into the dump. As he did so, he swung around and caught sight of a figure – a tall, extremely thin silhouette about fifty paces to the right.

Dud wiped his hands on his green pants, hitched them up, and strolled over.

'Dump's closed, mister.'

The man turned toward him. The face that was discovered in the red glow of the dying fire was high-cheek-boned and thoughtful. The hair was white, streaked with oddly virile slashes of iron gray. The guy had it swept back from his high, waxy forehead like one of those fag concert pianists. The eyes caught and held the red glow of the embers and made them look bloodshot.

'Is it?' the man asked politely, and there was a faint accent in the words, although they were perfectly spoken. The guy might be a frog, or maybe a bohunk. 'I came to watch the fire. It is beautiful.'

'Yeah,' Dud said. 'You from around here?'

'I am a recent resident of your lovely town, yes. Do you shoot many rats?'

'Quite a few, yeah. Just lately there's millions of the little sonsa-whores. Say, you ain't the fella who bought the Marsten place, are you?'

'Predators,' the man said, crossing his hands behind his back. Dud noticed with surprise that the guy was all tricked out in a suit, vest and all. 'I love the predators of the night. The rats . . . the owls . . . the wolves. Are there wolves in this area?'

'Naw,' Dud said. 'Guy up in Durham bagged a coyote two years ago. And there's a wild-dog pack that's been runnin' deer—'

'Dogs,' the stranger said, and gestured with contempt. 'Low animals that cringe and howl at the sound of a strange step. Fit only to whine and grovel. Gut them all, I say. Gut them all!'

'Well, I never thought of it that way,' Dud said, taking a shuffling step backward. 'It's always nice to have someone come out and, you know, shoot the shit, but the dump closes at six on Sundays and it's happast nine now—'

'To be sure.'

Yet the stranger showed no sign of moving away. Dud was thinking that he had stolen a march on the rest of the town. They were all wondering who was behind that Straker guy, and he was the first to know – except maybe for Larry Crockett, who was a deep one. The next time he was in town buying shells from that prissy-faced George Middler, he would just happen to say casually: Happened to meet that new fella the other night. Who? Oh, you know. Fella that took the Marsten House. Nice enough fella. Talked a little like a bohunk.

'Any ghosts up in that old house?' he asked, when the old party showed no signs of hauling ass.

'Ghosts!' The old party smiled, and there was something very disquieting about that smile. A barracuda might smile like that. 'No; no ghosts.' He placed a faint emphasis on that last word, as if there might be something up there that was even worse.

'Well . . . gettin' late and all . . . you really ought to go now, Mister—?'

'But it's so pleasant, speaking with you,' the old party said, and for the first time he turned his full face to Dud and looked in his eyes. The eyes were wide-set, and still rimmed with the dump's sullen fire. There was no way you could look away from them, although it wasn't polite to stare. 'You don't mind if we converse a bit longer, do you?'

'No, I guess not,' Dud said, and his voice sounded far away. Those eyes seemed to be expanding, growing, until they were like dark pits ringed with fire, pits you could fall into and drown in.

'Thank you,' he said. 'Tell me . . . does the hump on your back discommode you in your job?'

'No,' Dud said, still feeling far away. He thought faintly: I be buggered if he ain't hypnotizin' me. Just like that fella at Topsham Fair . . . what was his name? Mr Mephisto. He'd put you to sleep and make you do all kinds of comical things – act like a chicken or run around like a dog or tell what happened at the birthday party you had when you were six. He hypnotized ole Reggie Sawyer and Gawd didn't we laugh . . .

'Does it perhaps inconvenience you in other ways?'

'No . . . well . . .' He looked into the eyes, fascinated.

'Come, come,' the old party's voice cajoled gently. 'We are friends, are we not? Speak to me, tell me.'

'Well . . . girls . . . you know, girls . . .'

'Of course,' the old party said soothingly. 'The girls laugh at you, do they not? They have no knowing of your manhood. Of your strength.'

'That's right,' Dud whispered. 'They laugh. *She* laughs.'

'Who is this she?'

'Ruthie Crockett. She . . . she . . .' The thought flew away. He let it. It didn't matter. Nothing mattered except this peace. This cool and complete peace.

'She makes the jokes perhaps? Snickers behind her hand? Nudges her friends when you pass?'

'Yes . . .'

'But you want her,' the voice insisted. 'Is it not so?'

'Oh yes . . .'

'You shall have her. I am sure of it.'

There was something . . . pleasant about this. Far away he seemed to hear sweet voices singing foul words. Silver chimes . . . white faces . . . Ruthie Crockett's voice. He could almost see her, hands cupping her titties, making them bulge into the V of her cardigan sweater in ripe white half-globes, whispering: *Kiss them, Dud . . . bite them . . . suck them . . .*

It was like drowning. Drowning in the old man's red-rimmed eyes.

As the stranger came closer, Dud understood everything and welcomed it, and when the pain came, it was as sweet as silver, as green as still water at dark fathoms.

9

His hand was unsteady and instead of gripping the bottle the fingers knocked it off the desk and to the carpet with a heavy thump, where it lay gurgling good scotch into the green nap.

'Shit!' said Father Donald Callahan, and reached down to pick it up before all was lost. There was, in fact, not much to lose. He set what was left on the desk again (well back from the edge) and wandered into the kitchen to look for a rag under the sink and a bottle of cleaning fluid. It would never do to let Mrs Curless find a patch of spilled scotch by the leg of his study desk. Her kind, pitying looks were too hard to take on the long, grainy mornings when you were feeling a little low—

Hung over, you mean.

Yes, hung over, very good. Let's have a little truth around here, by all means. Know the truth and it will set you free. Bully for the truth.

He found a bottle of something called E-Vap, which was not too far from the sound of violent regurgitation ('E-Vap!' croaked the old drunk, simultaneously crapping himself and blowing lunch), and took it back to the study. He was not weaving at all. Hardly at all. Watch this, Ossifer, I'm going to walk right up this white line to the stop light.

Callahan was an imposing fifty-three. His hair was silvery, his eyes a direct blue (now threaded with tiny snaps of red) surrounded by Irish laugh wrinkles, his mouth firm, his slightly cleft chin firmer still. Some mornings, looking at himself in the mirror, he thought that when he reached sixty he would throw over the priesthood, go to Hollywood, and get a job playing Spencer Tracy.

'Father Flanagan, where are you when we need you?' he muttered, and hunkered down by the stain. He squinted, read the instructions on the label of the bottle, and poured two capfuls of E-Vap onto the stain. The patch immediately turned white and began to bubble. Callahan viewed this with some alarm, and consulted the label again.

'For really tough stains,' he read aloud in the rich, rolling voice that had made him so welcome in this parish after the long, denture-clicking peregrinations of poor old Father Hume, 'allow to set for seven to ten minutes.'

He went over to the study window, which fronted on Elm Street and St Andrew's on the far side.

Well, well, he thought. Here I am, Sunday night and drunk again.

Bless me, Father, for I have sinned.

If you went slow and if you continued to work (on his long, solitary evenings, Father Callahan worked on his Notes. He had been working on the Notes for nearly seven years, supposedly for a book on the Catholic Church in New England, but he suspected now and then that the book would never be written. In point of fact, the Notes and his drinking problem had begun at the same time. Genesis I:I – 'In the beginning there was scotch, and Father Callahan said, Let there be Notes.'), you were hardly aware of the slow growth of drunkenness. You could educate your hand not to be aware of the bottle's lessening weight.

It has been at least one day since my last confession.

It was eleven-thirty, and looking out the window he saw uniform darkness, broken only by the spotlight circle of the streetlight in front of the church. At any moment Fred Astaire would dance into it, wearing a top hat, tails, spats, and white shoes, twirling a cane. He is met by Ginger Rogers. They waltz to the tune of 'I Got Dem Ol' Kozmic E-Vap Blues Again.'

He leaned his forehead against the glass, allowing the handsome face that had been, in some measure at least, his curse sag into drawn lines of distracted weariness.

I'm a drunk and I'm a lousy priest, Father.

With his eyes closed he could see the darkness of the

confessional booth, could feel his fingers sliding back the window and rolling up the shade on all the secrets of the human heart, could smell varnish and old velvet from the kneeling benches and the sweat of old men; could taste alkali traces in his saliva.

Bless me, Father,

(I broke my brother's wagon, I hit my wife, I peeked in Mrs Sawyer's window when she was undressing, I lied, I cheated, I have had lustful thoughts, I, I, I)

for I have sinned.

He opened his eyes and Fred Astaire had not appeared yet. On the stroke of midnight, perhaps. His town was asleep. Except—

He glanced up. Yes, the lights were on up *there.*

He thought of the Bowie girl — no, McDougall, her name was McDougall now — saying in her breathy little voice that she had hit her baby and when he asked how often, he could sense (could almost hear) the wheels turning in her mind, making a dozen times five, or a hundred a dozen. Sad excuse for a human being. He had baptized the baby. Randall Fratus McDougall. Conceived in the backseat of Royce McDougall's car, probably during the second feature of a drive-in double bill. Tiny screaming little thing. He wondered if she knew or guessed that he would like to reach through the little window with both hands and grasp the soul on the other side as it fluttered and twisted and squeeze it until it screamed. Your penance is six head-knocks and a good swift kick in the ass. Go your way and sin no more.

'Dull,' he said.

But there was more than dullness in the confessional; it was not that by itself that had sickened him or propelled him toward that always widening club, Associated Catholic Priests of the Bottle and Knights of the Cutty Sark. It was the steady, dead, onrushing engine of the church, bearing down all petty sins on its endless shuttle to heaven. It was the ritualistic acknowledgment of evil by a church now more concerned with social evils; atonement told in beads for elderly ladies whose parents had spoken European tongues. It was the actual presence of evil in the confessional, as real as the smell of old velvet. But it was a mindless, moronic evil from which there was no mercy or reprieve. The fist crashing into the baby's face, the tire cut open with a jackknife, the barroom brawl, the insertion of razor blades into Halloween apples, the constant, vapid qualifiers which the human mind, in all its labyrinthine twists and turns, is able to spew forth. Gentlemen, better prisons will cure this. Better cops. Better social services agencies. Better birth control. Better sterilization techniques. Better abortions. Gentlemen, if we rip this fetus from the womb in a bloody tangle of unformed arms and legs, it will never grow up to beat an old lady to death with a hammer. Ladies, if we strap this man into a specially wired chair and fry him like a pork chop in a microwave oven, he will never have an opportunity to torture any more boys to death. Countrymen, if this eugenics bill is passed, I can guarantee you that never again—

Shit.

The truth of his condition had been becoming clearer and clearer to him for some time now, perhaps for as long as three years. It had gained clarity and resolution like an out-of-focus motion picture being adjusted until every line is sharp and defined. He had been pining for a Challenge.

The new priests had theirs: racial discrimination, women's liberation, even gay liberation; poverty, insanity, illegality. They made him uncomfortable. The only socially conscious priests he felt at ease with were the ones who had been militantly opposed to the war in Vietnam. Now that their cause had become obsolete, they sat around and discussed marches and rallies the way old married couples discuss their honeymoons or their first train rides. But Callahan was neither a new priest nor an old one; he found himself cast in the role of a traditionalist who can no longer even trust his basic postulates. He wanted to lead a division in the army of – who? God, right, goodness, they were names for the same thing – into battle against EVIL. He wanted issues and battle lines and never mind standing in the cold outside supermarkets handing out leaflets about the lettuce boycott or the grape strike. He wanted to see EVIL with its cerements of deception cast aside, with every feature of its visage clear. He wanted to slug it out toe to toe with EVIL, like Muhammad Ali against Joe Frazier, the Celtics against the Knicks, Jacob against the Angel. He wanted this struggle to be pure, unhindered by the politics that rode the back of every social issue like a deformed Siamese twin. He had wanted all this since he had wanted to be a priest, and that call had come to him at the age of fourteen, when he had been inflamed by the story of St Stephen, the first Christian martyr, who had been stoned to death and who had seen Christ at the moment of his death. Heaven was a dim attraction compared to that of fighting – and perhaps perishing – in the service of the Lord.

But there were no battles. There were only skirmishes of vague resolution. And EVIL did not wear one face but many, and all of them were vacuous and more often than not the chin was slicked with drool. In fact, he was being forced to the conclusion that there was no EVIL in the world at all but only evil – or perhaps (evil). At moments like this he suspected that Hitler had been nothing but a harried bureaucrat and Satan himself a mental defective with a rudimentary sense of humor – the kind that finds feeding firecrackers wrapped in bread to seagulls unutterably funny.

The great social, moral, and spiritual battles of the ages boiled down to Sandy McDougall slamming her snot-nosed kid in the corner and the kid would grow up and slam his own kid in the corner, world without end, hallelujah, chunky peanut butter. Hail Mary, full of grace, help me win this stock-car race.

It was more than dull. It was terrifying in its consequences for any meaningful definition of life, and perhaps of heaven. What there? An eternity of church bingo, amusement park rides, and celestial drag strips?

He looked over at the clock on the wall. It was six minutes past midnight and still no sign of Fred Astaire or Ginger Rogers. Not even Mickey Rooney. But the E-Vap had had time to set. Now he would vacuum it up and Mrs Curless would not look at him with that expression of pity, and life would go on. Amen.

CHAPTER SEVEN

MATT

At the end of period three on Tuesday, Matt walked up to the office and Ben Mears was there waiting for him.

'Hi,' Matt said. 'You're early.'

Ben stood up and shook hands. 'Family curse, I guess. Say, these kids aren't going to eat me, are they?'

'Positive,' Matt said. 'Come on.'

He was a little surprised. Ben had dressed in a nice-looking sport coat and a pair of gray double-knit slacks. Good shoes that looked as if they hadn't been worn much. Matt had had other literary types into his classes and they were usually dressed in casual clothes or something downright weird. A year ago he had asked a rather well-known female poet who had done a reading at the University of Maine at Portland if she would come in the following day and talk to a class about poetry. She had shown up in pedal pushers and high heels. It seemed to be a subconscious way of saying: Look at me, I've beaten the system at its own game. I come and go like the wind.

His admiration for Ben went up a notch in comparison. After thirty-plus years of teaching, he believed that nobody beat the system or won the game, and only suckers ever thought they were ahead.

'It's a nice building,' Ben said, looking around as they walked down the hall. 'Helluva lot different from where I went to high school. Most of the windows in that place looked like loopholes.'

'First mistake,' Matt said. 'You must never call it a building. It's a "plant." Blackboards are "visual aids." And the kids are a "homogenous midteen coeducational student body."'

'How wonderful for them,' Ben said, grinning.

'It is, isn't it? Did you go to college, Ben?'

'I tried. Liberal arts. But everybody seemed to be playing an intellectual game of capture-the-flag – you too can find an ax and grind it, thus becoming known and loved. Also, I flunked out. When *Conway's Daughter* sold, I was bucking cases of Coca-Cola onto delivery trucks.'

'Tell the kids that. They'll be interested.'

'You like teaching?' Ben said.

'Sure I like it. It would have been a busted-axle forty years if I didn't.'

The late bell rang, echoing loudly in the corridor, which was empty now except for one loitering student who was wandering slowly past a painted arrow under a sign which read 'Wood Shop.'

'How's drugs here?' Ben asked.

'All kinds. Like every school in America. Ours is booze more than anything else.'

'Not marijuana?'

'I don't consider pot a problem and neither does the administration, when it speaks off the record with a few knocks of Jim Beam under its belt. I happen to know that our guidance counselor, who is one of the best in his line, isn't averse to toking up and going to a movie. I've tried it myself. The effect is fine, but it gives me acid indigestion.'

'*You* have?'

'Shhh,' Matt said. 'Big Brother is listening everywhere. Besides, this is my room.'

'Oh boy.'

'Don't be nervous,' Matt said, and led him in. 'Good morning, folks,' he said to the twenty or so students, who were eying Ben closely. 'This is Mr Ben Mears.'

2

At first Ben thought he had the wrong house.

When Matt Burke invited him for supper he was quite sure he had said the house was the small gray one after the red brick, but there was rock 'n' roll music pouring from this one in a steady stream.

He used the tarnished brass knocker, got no answer, and rapped again. This time the music was turned down and a voice that was unmistakably Matt's yelled, 'It's open! Come on in!'

He did, looking around curiously. The front door opened directly on a small living room furnished in Early American Junk Shop and dominated by an incredibly ancient Motorola TV. A KLH sound system with quad speakers was putting out the music.

Matt came out of the kitchen, outfitted in a red-and-white checked apron. The odor of spaghetti sauce wandered out after him.

'Sorry about the noise,' Matt said. 'I'm a little deaf. I turn it up.'

'Good music.'

'I've been a rock fan ever since Buddy Holly. Lovely music. Are you hungry?'

'Yeah,' Ben said. 'Thanks again for asking me. I've eaten out more since I came back to 'salem's Lot than I have in the last five years, I guess.'

'It's a friendly town. Hope you don't mind eating in the kitchen. An antique man came by a couple of months ago and offered me two hundred dollars for my dining room table. I haven't gotten around to getting another one.'

'I don't mind. I'm a kitchen eater from a long line of kitchen eaters.'

The kitchen was astringently neat. On the small four-burner stove, a pot of spaghetti sance simmered and a colander full of spaghetti stood steaming. A small drop-leaf table was set with a couple of mismatched plates and glasses which had animated cartoon figures dancing around the rims – jelly glasses, Ben thought with amusement. The last constraint of being with a stranger dropped away and he began to feel at home.

'There's Bourbon, rye, and vodka in the cupboard over the sink,' Matt said, pointing. 'There's some mixers in the fridge. Nothing too fancy, I'm afraid.'

'Bourbon and tap water will do me.'

'Go to it. I'm going to serve this mess up.'

Mixing his drink, Ben said, 'I liked your kids. They asked good questions. Tough, but good.'

'Like where do you get your ideas?' Matt asked, mimicking Ruthie Crockett's sexy little-girl lisp.

'She's quite a piece.'

'She is indeed. There's a bottle of Lancers in the icebox behind the pineapple chunks. I got it special.'

'Say, you shouldn't—'

'Oh come, Ben. We hardly see best-selling authors in the Lot every day.'

'That's a little extravagant.'

Ben finished the rest of his drink, took a plate of spaghetti from Matt, ladled sauce over it, and twirled a forkful against his spoon. 'Fantastic,' he said. 'Mamma mia.'

'But of course,' Matt said.

Ben looked down at his plate, which had emptied with amazing rapidity. He wiped his mouth a little guiltily.

'More?'

'Half a plate, if it's okay. It's great spaghetti.'

Matt brought him a whole plate. 'If we don't eat it, my cat will. He's a miserable animal. Weighs twenty pounds and waddles to his dish.'

'Lord, how did I miss him?'

Matt smiled. 'He's cruising. Is your new book a novel?'

'A fictionalized sort of thing,' Ben said. 'To be honest, I'm writing it for money. Art is wonderful, but just once I'd like to pull a big number out of the hat.'

'What are the prospects?'

'Murky,' Ben said.

'Let's go in the living room,' Matt said. 'The chairs are lumpy but more comfortable than these kitchen horrors. Did you get enough to eat?'

'Does the Pope wear a tall hat?'

In the living room Matt put on a stack of albums and went to work firing up a huge, knotted calabash pipe.

After he had it going to his satisfaction (sitting in the middle of a huge raft of smoke), he looked up at Ben.

'No,' he said. 'You can't see it from here.'

Ben looked around sharply. 'What?'

'The Marsten House. I'll bet you a nickel that's what you were looking for.'

Ben laughed uneasily. 'No bet.'

'Is your book set in a town like 'salem's Lot?'

'Town and people.' Ben nodded. 'There are a series of sex murders and mutilations. I'm going to open with one of them and describe it in progress, from start to finish, in minute detail. Rub the reader's nose in it. I was outlining that part when Ralphie Glick disappeared and it gave me . . . well, it gave me a nasty turn.'

'You're basing all of this on the the disappearances of the thirties in the township?'

Ben looked at him closely. 'You know about that?'

'Oh yes. A good many of the older residents do, too. I wasn't in the Lot then, but Mabel Werts and Glynis Mayberry and Milt Crossen were. Some of them have made the connection already.'

'What connection?'

'Come now, Ben. The connection is pretty obvious, isn't it?'

'I suppose so. The last time the house was occupied, four kids disappeared over a period of ten years. Now it's occupied again after a thirty-six-year period, and Ralphie Glick disappears right off the bat.'

'Do you think it's a coincidence?'

'I suppose so,' Ben said cautiously. Susan's words of caution were very much in his ears. 'But it's funny. I checked through the copies of the *Ledger* from 1939 to 1970 just to get a comparison. Three kids disappeared. One ran off and was later found working in Boston – he was sixteen and looked older. Another one was fished out of the Androscoggin a month later. And one was found buried off Route 116 in Gates, apparently the victim of a hit-and-run. All explained.'

'Perhaps the Glick boy's disappearance will be explained, too.'

'Maybe.'

'But you don't think so. What do you know about this man Straker?'

'Nothing at all,' Ben said. 'I'm not even sure I want to meet him. I've got a viable book working right now, and it's bound up in a certain concept of the Marsten House and inhabitants of that house. Discovering Straker to be a perfectly ordinary businessman, as I'm sure he is, might knock me off kilter.'

'I don't think that would be the case. He opened the store today, you know. Susie Norton and her mother dropped by, I understand . . . hell, most of the women in town got in long enough to get a peek. According to Dell Markey, an unimpeachable source, even Mabel Werts hobbled down. The man is supposed to be quite striking. A dandy dresser, extremely graceful, totally bald. And charming. I'm told he actually sold some pieces.'

Ben grinned. 'Wonderful. Has anyone seen the other half of the team?'

'He's on a buying trip, supposedly.'

'Why supposedly?'

Matt shrugged restlessly. 'I don't know. The whole

thing is probably perfectly on the level, but the house makes me nervous. Almost as if the two of them had sought it out. As you said, it's like an idol, squatting there on top of its hill.'

Ben nodded.

'And on top of everything else, we have another child disappearance. And Ralphie's brother, Danny. Dead at twelve. Cause of death pernicious anemia.'

'What's odd about that? It's unfortunate, of course—'

'My doctor is a young fellow named Jimmy Cody, Ben. I had him in school. He was a little heller then, a good doctor now. This is gossip, mind you. Hearsay.'

'Okay.'

'I was in for a checkup, and happened to mention that it was a shame about the Glick boy, dreadful for his parents on top of the other one's vanishing act. Jimmy said he had consulted with George Gorby on the case. The boy was anemic, all right. He said that a red cell count on a boy Danny's age should run anywhere from eighty-five to ninety-eight percent. Danny's was down to forty-five percent.'

'Wow,' Ben said.

'They were giving him B_{12} injections and calf liver and it seemed to be working fine. They were going to release him the next day. And boom, he dropped dead.'

'You don't want to let Mabel Werts get that,' Ben said. 'She'll be seeing natives with poison blowguns in the park.'

'I haven't mentioned it to anyone but you. And I don't intend to. And by the way, Ben, I believe I'd keep the subject matter of your book quiet, if I were you. If

Loretta Starcher asks what you're writing about, tell her it's architecture.'

'I've already been given that advice.'

'By Susan Norton, no doubt.'

Ben looked at his watch and stood up. 'Speaking of Susan—'

'The courting male in full plumage,' Matt said. 'As it happens, I have to go up to the school. We are reblocking the third act of the school play, a comedy of great social significance called *Charley's Problem*.'

'What is his problem?'

'Pimples,' Matt said, and grinned.

They walked to the door together, Matt pausing to pull on a faded school letter jacket. Ben thought he had the figure of an aging track coach rather than that of a sedentary English teacher – if you ignored his face, which was intelligent yet dreamy, and somehow innocent.

'Listen,' Matt said as they went out onto the stoop, 'what have you got on the stove for Friday night?'

'I don't know,' Ben said. 'I thought Susan and I might go to a movie. That's about the long and short of it around here.'

'I can think of something else,' Matt said. 'Perhaps we should form a committee of three and take a drive up to the Marsten House and introduce ourselves to the new squire. On behalf of the town, of course.'

'Of course,' Ben said. 'It would be only common courtesy, wouldn't it?'

'A rustic welcome wagon,' Matt agreed.

'I'll mention it to Susan tonight. I think she'll go for it.'

'Good.'

Matt raised his hand and waved as Ben's Citroën purred away. Ben tooted twice in acknowledgment, and then his taillights disappeared over the hill.

Matt stood on his stoop for almost a full minute after the sound of the car had died away, his hands poked into his jacket pockets, his eyes turned toward the house on the hill.

3

There was no play practice Thursday night, and Matt drove over to Dell's around nine o'clock for two or three beers. If that damn snip Jimmy Cody wouldn't prescribe for his insomnia, he would prescribe for himself.

Dell's was sparsely populated on nights when no band played. Matt saw only three people he knew: Weasel Craig, nursing a beer alone in the corner; Floyd Tibbits, with thunderclouds on his brow (he had spoken to Susan three times this week, twice on the phone and once in person, in the Norton living room, and none of the conversations had gone well); and Mike Ryerson, who was sitting in one of the far booths against the wall.

Matt walked over to the bar, where Dell Markey was polishing glasses and watching 'Ironside' on a portable TV.

'Hi, Matt. How's it going?'

'Fair. Slow night.'

Dell shrugged. 'Yeah. They got a couple of motor-cycle pictures over to the drive-in in Gates. I can't compete with that. Glass or pitcher?'

'Make it a pitcher.'

Dell drew it, cut the foam off, and added another two inches. Matt paid, and after a moment's hesitation, walked over to Mike's booth. Mike had filtered through one of Matt's English classes, like almost all the young people in the Lot, and Matt had enjoyed him. He had done above-average work with an average intelligence because he worked hard and had asked over and over about things he didn't understand until he got them. In addition to that, he had a clear, free-running sense of humor and a pleasant streak of individualism that made him a class favorite.

'Hi, Mike,' he said. 'Mind if I join you?'

Mike Ryerson looked up and Matt felt shock hit him like a live wire. His first reaction: *Drugs. Heavy drugs.*

'Sure, Mr Burke. Sit down.' His voice was listless. His complexion was a horrid, pasty white, darkening to deep shadows under his eyes. The eyes themselves seemed over-large and hectic. His hands moved slowly across the table in the tavern's semigloom like ghosts. A glass of beer stood untouched before him.

'How are you doing, Mike?' Matt poured himself a glass of beer, controlling his hands, which wanted to shake.

His life had always been one of sweet evenness, a graph with modulate highs and lows (and even those had sunk to foothills since the death of his mother thirteen years before), and one of the things that disturbed it was the miserable ends some of his students came to. Billy Royko dying in a Vietnam helicopter crash two months before the cease-fire; Sally Greer, one of the brightest and most vivacious girls he had ever had, killed by her drunken boyfriend when she told him she wanted to break up; Gary Coleman, who had gone blind due to some mysterious optic nerve degeneration; Buddy Mayberry's brother Doug, the only good kid in that whole half-bright clan, drowning at Old Orchard Beach; and drugs, the little death. Not all of them who waded into the waters of Lethe found it necessary to take a bath in it, but there were enough – kids who had made dreams their protein.

'Doing?' Mike said slowly. 'I don't know, Mr Burke. Not so good.'

'What kind of shit are you on, Mike?' Matt asked gently.

Mike looked at him uncomprehendingly.

'Dope,' Matt said. 'Bennies? Reds? Coke? Or is it—'

'I'm not on dope,' Mike said. 'I guess I'm sick.'

'Is that the truth?'

'I never did no heavy dope in my life,' Mike said, and the words seemed to be costing him a dreadful effort. 'Just grass, and I ain't had any of that for four months. I'm sick . . . been sick since Monday, I think it was. I fell asleep out at Harmony Hill Sunday night, see. Never even woke up until Monday morning.' He shook his head slowly. 'I felt crappy. I've felt crappy ever since. Worse every day, it seems like.' He sighed, and the whistle of air seemed to shake his frame like a dead leaf on a November maple.

Matt leaned forward, concerned. 'This happened after Danny Glick's funeral?'

'Yeah.' Mike looked at him again. 'I came back to finish up after everybody went home but that fucking – excuse me, Mr Burke – that Royal Snow never showed up. I waited for him a long time, and that's when I must have started to get sick, because everything after that is . . . oh, it hurts my head. It's hard to think.'

'What do you remember, Mike?'

'Remember?' Mike looked into the golden depths of his beer glass and watched the bubbles detaching themselves from the sides and floating to the surface to release their gas.

'I remember singing,' he said. 'The sweetest singing I ever heard. And a feeling like . . . like drowning. Only it was nice. Except for the eyes. The *eyes*.'

He clutched his elbows and shuddered.

'Whose eyes?' Matt asked, leaning forward.

'They were red. Oh, scary eyes.'

'Whose?'

'I don't remember. No eyes. I dreamed it all.' He pushed it away from himself. Matt could almost see him do it. 'I don't remember anything else about Sunday night. I woke up Monday morning on the ground, and at first I couldn't even get up I was so tired. But I finally did. The sun was coming up and I was afraid I'd get a sunburn. So I went down in the woods by the brook. Tired me out. Oh, awful tired. So I went back to sleep. Slept till . . . oh, four or five o'clock.' He offered a papery little chuckle. 'I was all covered with leaves when I woke up. I felt a little better, though. I got up and went back to my truck.' He passed a slow hand over his face. 'I must have finished up with the little Glick boy Sunday night, though. Funny. I don't even remember.'

'Finished up?'

'Grave was all filled in, Royal or no Royal. Sods tamped in and all. A good job. Don't remember doing it. Must have been really sick.'

'Where did you spend Monday night?'

'At my place. Where else?'

'How did you feel Tuesday morning?'

'I never woke up Tuesday morning. Slept through the whole day. Never woke up until Tuesday night.'

'How did you feel then?'

'Terrible. Legs like rubber. I tried to go get a drink of water and almost fell down. I had to go into the kitchen holding on to things. Weak as a kitten.' He frowned. 'I had a can of stew for my dinner – you know, that Dinty Moore stuff – but I couldn't eat it. Seemed like just looking at it made me feel sick to my stomach. Like when you've got an awful hangover and someone shows you food.'

'You didn't eat anything?'

'I tried, but I threw it up. But I felt a little better. I went out and walked around for a while. Then I went back to bed.' His fingers traced old beer rings on the table. 'I got scared before I went to bed. Just like a little kid afraid of the Allamagoosalum. I went around and made sure all the windows were locked. And I went to sleep with all the lights on.'

'And yesterday morning?'

'Hmmm? No . . . never got up until nine o'clock last night.' He offered the papery little chuckle again. 'I remember thinking if it kept up I'd be sleeping the clock right around. And that's what you do when you're dead.'

Matt regarded him somberly. Floyd Tibbits got up and put a quarter in the juke and began to punch up songs.

'Funny,' Mike said. 'My bedroom window was open when I got up. I must have done it myself. I had a dream . . . someone was at the window and I got up . . . got up to let him in. Like you'd get up to let in an old friend who was cold or . . . or hungry.'

'Who was it?'

'It was just a dream, Mr Burke.'

'But in the dream who was it?'

'I don't know. I was going to try and eat, but the thought of it made me want to puke.'

'What did you do?'

'I watched TV until Johnny Carson went off. I felt a lot better. Then I went to bed.'

'Did you lock the windows?'

'No.'

'And slept all day?'

'I woke up around sundown.'

'Weak?'

'I hope to tell.' He passed a hand over his face. 'I feel so low!' he cried out in a breaking voice. 'It's just the flu or something, isn't it, Mr Burke? I'm not really sick, am I?'

'I don't know,' Matt said.

'I thought a few beers would cheer me up, but I can't drink it. I took one sip and it like to gag me. The last week . . . it all seems like a bad dream. And I'm scared. I'm awful scared.' He put his thin hands to his face and Matt saw that he was crying.

'Mike?'

No response.

'Mike.' Gently, he pulled Mike's hands away from his face. 'I want you to come home with me tonight. I want you to sleep in my guest room. Will you do that?'

'All right. I don't care.' He wiped his sleeve across his eyes with lethargic slowness.

'And tomorrow I want you to come see Dr Cody with me.'

'All right.'

'Come on. Let's go.'

He thought of calling Ben Mears and didn't.

4

When Matt knocked on the door, Mike Ryerson said, 'Come in.'

Matt came in with a pair of pajamas. 'These are going to be a little big—'

'That's all right, Mr Burke. I sleep in my skivvies.'

He was standing in his shorts now, and Matt saw that his entire body was horribly pale. His ribs stood out in circular ridges.

'Turn your head, Mike. This way.'

Mike turned his head obediently.

'Mike, where did you get those marks?'

Mike's hand touched his throat below the angle of the jaw. 'I don't know.'

Matt stood restively. Then he went to the window. The catch was securely fastened, yet he rattled it back and forth with hands that were distraught. Beyond, the dark pressed against the glass heavily. 'Call me in the night if you want anything. *Anything*. Even if you have a bad dream. Will you do that, Mike?'

'Yes.'

'I mean it. *Anything*. I'm right down the hall.'

'I will.'

Hesitating, feeling there were other things he should do, he went out.

5

He didn't sleep at all, and the only thing now that kept him from calling Ben Mears was knowing that everyone at Eva's would be in bed. The boardinghouse was filled with old men, and when the phone rang late at night, it meant that someone had died.

He lay restively, watching the luminous hands of his alarm clock move from eleven-thirty to twelve. The house was preternaturally silent − perhaps because his ears were consciously attuned to catch the slightest noise. The house was an old one and built solidly, and its settling groans had mostly ceased long before. There were no sounds but the clock and the faint passage of the wind outside. No cars passed on Taggart Stream Road late on week nights.

What you're thinking is madness.

But step by step he had been forced backward toward belief. Of course, being a literary man, it had been the first thing that had come to mind when Jimmy Cody had thumbnailed Danny Glick's case. He and Cody had laughed over it. Maybe this was his punishment for laughing.

Scratches? Those marks weren't scratches. They were punctures.

One was taught that such things could not be; that things like Coleridge's 'Cristabel' or Bram Stoker's evil fairy tale were only the warp and woof of fantasy. Of course monsters existed; they were the men with their fingers on the thermonuclear triggers in six countries, the hijackers, the mass murderers, the child molesters. But not this. One knows better. The mark of the devil on a woman's breast is only a mole, the man who came back from the dead and stood at his wife's door dressed in the cerements of the grave was only suffering from locomotor ataxia, the bogeyman who gibbers and capers in the corner of a child's bedroom is only a heap of blankets. Some clergymen had proclaimed that even God, that venerable white warlock, was dead.

He was bled almost white.

No sound from up the hall. Matt thought: He is sleeping like the stones himself. Well, why not? Why had he invited Mike back to the house, if not for a good night's sleep, uninterrupted by . . . by bad dreams? He got out of bed and turned on the lamp and went to the window. From here one could just see the rooftop of the Marsten House, frosted in moonlight.

I'm frightened.

But it was worse than that; he was dead scared. His mind ran over the old protections for an unmentionable disease: garlic, holy wafer and water, crucifix, rose, running water. He had none of the holy things. He was a non-practicing Methodist, and privately thought that John Groggins was the asshole of the Western world.

The only religious object in the house was—

Softly yet clearly in the silent house the words came, spoken in Mike Ryerson's voice, spoken in the dead accents of sleep:

'Yes. Come in.'

Matt's breath stopped, then whistled out in a sound-less scream. He felt faint with fear. His belly seemed to have turned to lead. His testicles had drawn up. What in God's name had been invited into his house?

Stealthily, the sound of the hasp on the guest room

window being turned back. Then the grind of wood against wood as the window was forced up.

He could go downstairs. Run, get the Bible from the dresser in the dining room. Run back up, jerk open the door to the guest room, hold the Bible high: *In the name of the Father, the Son, and the Holy Ghost, I command you to be gone—*

But who was in there?

Call me in the night if you want anything.

But I can't, Mike. I'm an old man. I'm afraid.

Night invaded his brain and made it a circus of terrifying images which danced in and out of the shadows. Clown-white faces, huge eyes, sharp teeth, forms that slipped from the shadows with long white hands that reached for . . . for . . .

A shuddering groan escaped him, and he put his hands over his face.

I can't. I am afraid.

He could not have risen even if the brass knob on his own door had begun to turn. He was paralyzed with fear and wished crazily that he had never gone out to Dell's that night.

I am afraid.

And in the awful heavy silence of the house, as he sat impotently on his bed with his face in his hands, he heard the high, sweet, evil laugh of a child—

—and then the sucking sounds.

PART 2

THE EMPEROR OF ICE CREAM

Call the roller of big cigars,
The muscular one, and bid him whip
In kitchen cups concupiscent curds.
Let the wenches dawdle in such dress
As they are used to wear, and let the boys
Bring flowers in last month's newspapers.
Let be be finale of seem.
The only emperor is the emperor of ice cream.

Take from the dresser of deal,
Lacking the three glass knobs, that sheet
On which she embroidered three fantails once
And spread it so as to cover her face.
If her horny feet protrude, they come
To show how cold she is, and dumb.
Let the lamp affix its beam.
The only emperor is the emperor of ice cream.

– Wallace Stevens

This column has
A hole. Can you see
The Queen of the Dead?

– George Seferis

CHAPTER EIGHT
BEN (III)

The knocking must have been going on for a long time, because it seemed to echo far down the avenues of sleep as he slowly struggled up to wakefulness. It was dark outside, but when he turned to grasp the clock and bring it to his face, he knocked it onto the floor. He felt disoriented and frightened.

'Who is it?' he called out.

'It's Eva, Mr Mears. There's a phone call for you.'

He got up, pulled on his pants, and opened the door bare-chested. Eva Miller was in a white terry-cloth robe, and her face was full of the slow vulnerability of a person still two-fifths asleep. They looked at each other nakedly, and he was thinking: *Who's sick? Who's died?*

'Long-distance?'

'No, it's Matthew Burke.'

The knowledge did not relieve him as it should have done. 'What time is it?'

'Just after four. Mr Burke sounds very upset.'

Ben went downstairs and picked the phone up. 'This is Ben, Matt.'

Matt was breathing rapidly into the phone, the sound of his respiration coming in harsh little blurts. 'Can you come, Ben? Right now?'

'Yes, all right. What's the matter? Are you sick?'

'Not on the phone. Just come.'

'Ten minutes.'

'Ben?'

'Yes.'

'Have you got a crucifix? A St Christopher's medallion? Anything like that?'

'Hell no. I'm – was – a Baptist.'

'All right. Come fast.'

Ben hung up and went back upstairs quickly. Eva was standing with one hand on the newel post, her face filled with worry and indecision – on one hand wanting to know, on the other, not wanting to mix in the tenant's business.

'Is Mr Burke sick, Mr Mears?'

'He says not. He just asked me . . . say, you aren't Catholic?'

'My husband was.'

'Do you have a crucifix or a rosary or a St Christopher's medallion?'

'Well . . . my husband's crucifix is in the bedroom . . . I could . . .'

'Yes, would you?'

She went up the hall, her furry slippers scuffing at the faded strip of carpet. Ben went into his room, pulled on yesterday's shirt, and slipped his bare feet into a pair of loafers. When he came out again, Eva was standing by his door, holding the crucifix. It caught the light and threw back dim silver.

'Thank you,' he said, taking it.

'Did Mr Burke ask you for this?'

'Yes, he did.'

She was frowning, more awake now. 'He's not Catholic. I don't believe he goes to church.'

'He didn't explain to me.'

'Oh.' She nodded in a charade of understanding and gave him the crucifix. 'Please be careful of it. It has great value for me.'

'I understand that. I will.'

'I hope Mr Burke is all right. He's a fine man.'

He went downstairs and out onto the porch. He could not hold the crucifix and dig for his car keys at the same time, and instead of simply transferring it from his right hand to his left, he slipped it over his neck. The silver slipped comfortably against his shirt, and getting into the car he was hardly aware that he felt comforted.

2

Every window on the lower floor of Matt's house was lit up, and when Ben's headlights splashed across the front as he turned into the driveway, Matt opened the door and waited for him.

He came up the walk ready for almost anything, but Matt's face was still a shock. It was deadly pale, and the mouth was trembling. His eyes were wide, and they didn't seem to blink.

'Let's go in the kitchen,' he said.

Ben came in, and as he stepped inside, the hall light caught the cross lying against his chest.

'You brought one.'

'It belongs to Eva Miller. What's the matter?'

Matt repeated: 'In the kitchen.' As they passed the stairs leading to the second floor, he glanced upward and seemed to flinch away at the same time.

The kitchen table where they had eaten spaghetti was bare now except for three items, two of them peculiar: a cup of coffee, an old-fashioned clasp Bible, and a .38 revolver.

'Now, what's up, Matt? You look awful.'

'And maybe I dreamed the whole thing, but thank God you're here.' He had picked up the revolver and was turning it over restively in his hands.

'Tell me. And stop playing with that thing. Is it loaded?'

Matt put the pistol down and ran a hand through his hair. 'Yes, it's loaded. Although I don't think it would do any good . . . unless I used it on myself.' He laughed, a jagged, unhealthy sound like grinding glass.

'Stop that.'

The harshness in his voice broke the queer, fixed look in his eyes. He shook his head, not like a man propounding a negative, but the way some animals will shake themselves coming out of cold water.

'There's a dead man upstairs,' he said.

'Who?'

'Mike Ryerson. He works for the town. He's a groundskeeper.'

'Are you sure he's dead?'

'I am in my guts, even though I haven't looked in on him. I haven't dared. Because, in another way, he may not be dead at all.'

'Matt, you're not talking good sense.'

'Don't you think I know that? I'm talking nonsense and I'm thinking madness. But there was no one to call but you. In all of 'salem's Lot, you're the only person that might . . . might . . .' He shook his head and began again. 'We talked about Danny Glick.'

'Yes.'

'And how he might have died of pernicious anemia . . . what our grandfathers would have called "just wasting away."'

'Yes.'

'Mike buried him. And Mike found Win Purinton's dog impaled on the Harmony Hill Cemetery gates. I met Mike Ryerson in Dell's last night, and—'

3

'—and I couldn't go in,' he finished. 'Couldn't. I sat on my bed for nearly four hours. Then I crept downstairs like a thief and called you. What do you think?'

Ben had taken the crucifix off; now he poked at the glimmering heap of fine-link chain with a reflective finger. It was almost five o'clock and the eastern sky was rose with dawn. The fluorescent bar overhead had gone pallid.

'I think we'd better go up to your guest room and look. That's all, I think, right now.'

'The whole thing seems like a madman's nightmare now, with the light coming in the window.' He laughed shakily. 'I hope it is. I hope Mike is sleeping like a baby.'

'Well, let's go see.'

Matt firmed his lips with an effort. 'Okay.' He dropped his eyes to the table and then looked at Ben questioningly.

'Sure,' Ben said, and slipped the crucifix over Matt's neck.

'It actually does make me feel better.' He laughed self-consciously. 'Do you suppose they'll let me wear it when they cart me off to Augusta?'

Ben said, 'Do you want the gun?'

'No, I guess not. I'd stick it in the top of my pants and blow my balls off.'

They went upstairs, Ben in the lead. There was a short hall at the top, running both ways. At one end, the door to Matt's bedroom stood open, a pale sheaf of lamplight spilling out onto the orange runner.

'Down at the other end,' Matt said.

Ben walked down the hall and stood in front of the guest room door. He did not believe the monstrosity Matt had implied, but nonetheless he found himself engulfed by a wave of the blackest fright he had ever known.

You open the door and he's hanging from the beam, the face swelled and puffed and black, and then the eyes open and they're bulging in the sockets but they're SEEING you and they're glad you came—

The memory rose up in almost total sensory reference, and for the moment of its totality he was paralyzed. He could even smell the plaster and the wild odor of nesting animals. It seemed to him that the plain varnished wood door of Matt Burke's guest room stood between him and all the secrets of hell.

Then he twisted the knob and pushed the door inward. Matt was at his shoulder, and he was holding Eva's crucifix tightly.

The guest room window faced directly east, and the

top arc of the sun had just cleared the horizon. The first pellucid rays shone directly through the window, isolating a few golden motes as it fell in a shaft to the white linen sheet that was pulled up to Mike Ryerson's chest.

Ben looked at Matt and nodded. 'He's all right,' he whispered. 'Sleeping.'

Matt said tonelessly, 'The window's open. It was closed and locked. I made sure of it.'

Ben's eyes centered on the upper hem of the flaw-lessly laundered sheet that covered Mike. There was a single small drop of blood on it, dried to maroon.

'I don't think he's breathing,' Matt said.

Ben took two steps forward and then stopped. 'Mike? Mike Ryerson. Wake up, Mike!'

No response. Mike's lashes lay cleanly against his cheeks. His hair was tousled loosely across his brow, and Ben thought that in the first delicate light he was more than handsome; he was as beautiful as the profile of a Greek statue. Light color bloomed in his cheeks, and his body held none of the deathly pallor Matt had mentioned — only healthy skin tones.

'Of course he's breathing,' he said a trifle impatiently. 'Just fast asleep. Mike—' He stretched out a hand and shook Ryerson slightly. Mike's left arm, which had been crossed loosely on his chest, fell limply over the side of the bed and the knuckles rapped on the floor, like a request for entry.

Matt stepped forward and picked up the limp arm. He pressed his index finger over the wrist. 'No pulse.'

He started to drop it, remembered the grisly knocking noise the knuckles had made, and put the arm across

Ryerson's chest. It started to fall anyway, and he put it back more firmly with a grimace.

Ben couldn't believe it. He was sleeping, had to be. The good color, the obvious suppleness of the muscles, the lips half parted as if to draw breath ... unreality washed over him. He placed his wrist against Ryerson's shoulder and found the skin cool.

He moistened his finger and held it in front of those half-open lips. Nothing. Not a feather of breath.

He and Matt looked at each other.

'The marks on the neck?' Matt asked.

Ben took Ryerson's jaw in his hands and turned it gently until the exposed cheek lay against the pillow. The movement dislodged the left arm, and the knuckles rapped the floor again.

There were no marks on Mike Ryerson's neck.

4

They were at the kitchen table again. It was 5:35 AM. They could hear the lowing of the Griffen cows as they were let into their east pasturage down the hill and beyond the belt of shrubbery and underbrush that screened Taggart Stream from view.

'According to folklore, the marks disappear,' Matt said suddenly. 'When the victim dies, the marks disappear.'

'I know that,' Ben said. He remembered it both from Stoker's *Dracula* and from the Hammer films starring Christopher Lee.

'We have to put an ash stake through his heart.'

'You better think again,' Ben said, and sipped his

coffee. 'That would be damned hard to explain to a coroner's jury. You'd go to jail for desecrating a corpse at the very least. More likely to the funny farm.'

'Do you think I'm crazy?' Matt asked quietly.

With no discernible hesitation, Ben said, 'No.'

'Do you believe me about the marks?'

'I don't know. I guess I have to. Why would you lie to me? I can't see any gain for you in a lie. I suppose you'd lie if you had killed him.'

'Perhaps I did, then,' Matt said, watching him.

'There are three things going against it. First, what's your motive? Pardon me, Matt, but you're just too old for the classic ones like jealousy and money to fit very well. Second, what was your method? If it was poison, he must have gone very easily. He certainly looks peaceful enough. And that eliminates most of the common poisons right there.'

'What's your third reason?'

'No murderer in his right mind would invent a story like yours to cover up murder. It would be insane.'

'We keep coming back to my mental health,' Matt said. He sighed. 'I knew we would.'

'I don't think you're crazy,' Ben said, accenting the first word slightly. 'You seem rational enough.'

'But you're not a doctor, are you?' Matt asked. 'And crazy people are sometimes able to counterfeit sanity remarkably well.'

Ben agreed. 'So where does that put us?'

'Back to square one.'

'No. Neither one of us can afford that, because there's a dead man upstairs and pretty soon he's going to have to be explained. The constable is going to want to know what happened, and so is the medical examiner, and so is the county sheriff. Matt, could it be that Mike Ryerson was just sick with some virus all week and happened to drop dead in your house?'

For the first time since they had come back down, Matt showed signs of agitation. 'Ben, I told you what he said! I saw the marks on his neck! And I heard him invite someone into my house! Then I heard . . . God, I heard that laugh!' His eyes had taken on that peculiar blank look again.

'All right,' Ben said. He got up and went to the window, trying to set his thoughts in order. They didn't go well. As he had told Susan, things seemed to have a way of getting out of hand.

He was looking toward the Marsten House.

'Matt, do you know what's going to happen to you if you even let out a whisper of what you've told me?'

Matt didn't answer.

'People are going to start tapping their foreheads behind your back when you go by in the street. Little kids are going to get out their Halloween wax teeth when they see you coming and jump out and yell *Boo!* when you walk by their hedge. Somebody will invent a rhyme like *One, two, three, four, I'm gonna suck your blood some more.* The high school kids will pick it up and you'll hear it in the halls when you pass. Your colleagues will begin looking at you strangely. There's apt to be anonymous phone calls from people purporting to be Danny Glick or Mike Ryerson. They'll turn your life into a nightmare. They'll hound you out of town in six months.'

'They wouldn't. They know me.'

Ben turned from the window. 'Who do they know? A funny old duck who lives alone out on Taggart Stream Road. Just the fact that you're not married is apt to make them believe you've got a screw loose anyway. And what backup can I give you? I saw the body but nothing else. Even if I had, they would just say I was an outsider. They would even get around to telling each other we were a couple of queers and this was the way we got our kicks.'

Matt was looking at him with slowly dawning horror.

'One word, Matt. That's all it will take to finish you in 'salem's Lot.'

'So there's nothing to be done.'

'Yes, there is. You have a certain theory about who – or what – killed Mike Ryerson. The theory is relatively simple to prove or disprove, I think. I'm in a hell of a fix. I can't believe you're crazy, but I can't believe that Danny Glick came back from the dead and sucked Mike Ryerson's blood for a whole week before killing him, either. But I'm going to put the idea to the test. And you've got to help.'

'How?'

'Call your doctor, Cody is his name? Then call Parkins Gillespie. Let the machinery take over. Tell your story just as though you'd never heard a thing in the night. You went into Dell's and sat down with Mike. He said he'd been feeling sick since last Sunday. You invited him home with you. You went in to check him around three-thirty this morning, couldn't wake him, and called me.'

'That's all?'

'That's it. When you speak to Cody, don't even say he's dead.'

'Not dead—'

'Christ, how do we know he *is*?' Ben exploded. 'You took his pulse and couldn't find it; I tried to find his breath and couldn't do it. If I thought someone was going to shove me into my grave on that basis, I'd damn well pack a lunch. Especially if I looked as lifelike as he does.'

'That bothers you as much as it does me, doesn't it?'

'Yes, it bothers me,' Ben admitted. 'He looks like a goddamn waxwork.'

'All right,' Matt said. 'You're talking sense . . . as much as anyone can in a business like this. I guess I sounded nuts, at that.'

Ben started to deprecate, but Matt waved it off. 'But suppose . . . just hypothetically . . . that my first suspicion is right? Would you want even the remotest possibility in the back of your mind? The possibility that Mike might . . . come back?'

'As I said, that theory is easy enough to prove or disprove. And it isn't what bothers me about all this.'

'What is?'

'Just a minute. First things first. Proving or disproving it ought to be no more than an exercise in logic – ruling out possibilities. First possibility: Mike died of some disease – a virus or something. How do you confirm that or rule it out?'

Matt shrugged. 'Medical examination, I suppose.'

'Exactly. And the same method to confirm or rule out foul play. If somebody poisoned him or shot him or got him to eat a piece of fudge with a bundle of wires in it—'

'Murder has gone undetected before.'

'Sure it has. But I'll bet on the medical examiner.'

'And if the medical examiner's verdict is "unknown cause"?'

'Then,' Ben said deliberately, 'we can visit the grave after the funeral and see if he rises. If he does – which I can't conceive of – we'll know. If he doesn't, we're faced with the thing that bothers me.'

'The fact of my insanity,' Matt said slowly. 'Ben, I swear on my mother's name that those marks were there, that I heard the window go up, that—'

'I believe you,' Ben said quietly.

Matt stopped. His expression was that of a man who has braced himself for a crash that never came.

'You do?' he said uncertainly.

'To put it another way, I refuse to believe that you're crazy or had a hallucination. I had an experience once . . . an experience that had to do with that damned house on the hill . . . that makes me extremely sympathetic to people whose stories seem utterly insane in light of rational knowledge. I'll tell you about that, one day.'

'Why not now?'

'There's no time. You have those calls to make. And I have one more question. Think about it carefully. Do you have any enemies?'

'No one who qualifies for something like this.'

'An ex-student, maybe? One with a grudge?'

Matt, who knew exactly to what extent he influenced the lives of his students, laughed politely.

'Okay,' Ben said. 'I'll take your word for it.' He shook his head. 'I don't like it. First that dog shows up on the cemetery gates. Then Ralphie Glick disappears, his brother dies, and Mike Ryerson. Maybe they all tie in somehow. But this . . . I can't believe it.'

'I better call Cody's home,' Matt said, getting up. 'Parkins will be at home.'

'Call in sick at school, too.'

'Right.' Matt laughed without force. 'It will be my first sick day in three years. A real occasion.'

He went into the living room and began to make his calls, waiting at the end of each number sequence for the bell to prod sleepers awake. Cody's wife apparently referred him to Cumberland Receiving, for he dialed another number, asked for Cody, and went into his story after a short wait.

He hung up and called into the kitchen: 'Jimmy will be here in an hour.'

'Good,' Ben said. 'I'm going upstairs.'

'Don't touch anything.'

'No.'

By the time he reached the second-floor landing he could hear Matt on the phone to Parkins Gillespie, answering questions. The words melted into a background murmur as he went down the hall.

That feeling of half-remembered, half-imagined terror washed over him again as he contemplated the door to the guest room. In his mind's eye he could see himself stepping forward, pushing it open. The room looks larger, seen from a child's eye view. The body lies as they left it, left arm dangling to the floor, left cheek pressed against the pillowcase which still shows the fold lines from the linen closet. The eyes suddenly open, and they are filled with blank, animalistic triumph. The door slams shut. The left arm comes up, the hand hooked into a claw, and the lips twist into a vulpine smile that shows incisors grown wondrously long and sharp—

He stepped forward and pushed the door with tented fingers. The lower hinges squeaked slightly.

The body lay as they had left it, left arm fallen, left cheek pressed against the pillowcase—

'Parkins is coming,' Matt said from the hallway behind him, and Ben nearly screamed.

5

Ben thought how apt his phrase had been: *Let the machinery take over.* It was very much like a machine – one of those elaborate German contraptions constructed of clockwork and cogs; figures moving in an elaborate dance.

Parkins Gillespie arrived first, wearing a green tie set off by a VFW tie tack. There were still sleepy seeds in his eyes. He told them he had notified the county M.E.

'He won't be out himself, the son of a bitch,' Parkins said, tucking a Pall Mall into the corner of his seamed mouth, 'but he'll send out a deputy and a fella to take pitchers. You touch the cawpse?'

'His arm fell out of bed,' Ben said. 'I tried to put it back, but it wouldn't stay.'

Parkins looked him up and down and said nothing. Ben thought of the grisly sound the knuckles had made on the hardwood floor of Matt's guest room and felt a queasy laughter in his belly. He swallowed to keep it there.

Matt led the way upstairs, and Parkins walked around

the body several times. 'Say, you sure he's dead?' he asked finally. 'You tried to wake him up?'

James Cody, M.D., arrived next, fresh from a delivery in Cumberland. After the amenities had passed among them ('Good t'seeya,' Parkins Gillespie said, and lit a fresh cigarette), Matt led them all upstairs again. Now, if we all only played instruments, Ben thought, we could give the guy a real send-off. He felt the laughter trying to come up his throat again.

Cody turned back the sheet and frowned down at the body for a moment. With a calmness that astounded Ben, Matt Burke said, 'It reminded me of what you said about the Glick boy, Jimmy.'

'That was a privileged communication, Mr Burke,' Jimmy Cody said mildly. 'If Danny Glick's folks found out you'd said that, they could sue me.'

'Would they win?'

'No, probably not,' Jimmy said, and sighed.

'What's this about the Glick boy?' Parkins asked, frowning.

'Nothing,' Jimmy said. 'No connection.' He used his stethoscope, muttered, rolled back an eyelid, and shone a light into the glassy orb beneath.

Ben saw the pupil contract and said quite audibly, 'Christ!'

'Interesting reflex, isn't it?' Jimmy said. He let the eyelid go and it rolled shut with grotesque slowness, as if the corpse had winked at them. 'David Prine at Johns Hopkins reports pupillary contraction in some cadavers up to nine hours.'

'Now he's a scholar,' Matt said gruffly. 'Used to pull C's in Expository Writing.'

'You just didn't like to read about dissections, you old grump,' Jimmy said absently, and produced a small hammer. Nice, Ben thought. He retains his bedside manner even when the patient is, as Parkins would say, a cawpse. The dark laughter welled inside him again.

'He dead?' Parkins asked, and tapped the ash of his cigarette into an empty flower vase. Matt winced.

'Oh, he's dead,' Jimmy told him. He got up, turned the sheet back to Ryerson's feet, and tapped the right knee. The toes were moveless. Ben noticed that Mike Ryerson had yellow rings of callus on the bottoms of his feet, at the ball of the heel and at the instep. It made him think of that Wallace Stevens poem about the dead woman. 'Let it be the finale of seem,' he misquoted. 'The only emperor is the emperor of ice cream.'

Matt looked at him sharply, and for a moment his control seemed to waver.

'What's that?' Parkins asked.

'A poem,' Matt said. 'It's from a poem about death.'

'Sounds more like the Good Humor man to me,' Parkins said, and tapped his ash into the vase again.

6

'Have we been introduced?' Jimmy asked, looking up at Ben.

'You were, but only in passing,' Matt said. 'Jimmy Cody, local quack, meet Ben Mears, local hack. And vice versa.'

'He's always been clever that way,' Jimmy said. 'That's how he made all his money.'

They shook hands over the body.

'Help me turn him over, Mr Mears.'

A little squeamishly, Ben helped him turn the body on its belly. The flesh was cool, not yet cold, still pliant. Jimmy stared closely at the back, then pulled the jockey shorts down from the buttocks.

'What's that for?' Parkins asked.

'I'm trying to place the time of death by skin lividity,' Jimmy said. 'Blood tends to seek its lowest level when pumping action ceases, like any other fluid.'

'Yeah, sort of like that Drāno commercial. That's the examiner's job, ain't it?'

'He'll send out Norbert, you know that,' Jimmy said. 'And Brent Norbert was never averse to a little help from his friends.'

'Norbert couldn't find his own ass with both hands and a flashlight,' Parkins said, and flipped his cigarette butt out the open window. 'You lost your screen offa this window, Matt. I seen it down on the lawn when I drove in.'

'That so?' Matt asked, his voice carefully controlled.

'Yeah.'

Cody had taken a thermometer from his bag and now he slid it into Ryerson's anus and laid his watch on the crisp sheet, where it glittered in the strong sunlight. It was quarter of seven.

'I'm going downstairs,' Matt said in a slightly strangled voice.

'You might as well all go,' Jimmy said. 'I'll be a little while longer. Would you put on coffee, Mr Burke?'

'Sure.'

They all went out and Ben closed the door on the

scene. His last glance back would remain with him: the bright, sun-washed room, the clean sheet turned back, the gold wristwatch heliographing bright arrows of light onto the wallpaper, and Cody himself, with his swatch of flaming red hair, sitting beside the body like a steel engraving.

Matt was making coffee when Brenton Norbert, the assistant medical examiner, arrived in an elderly gray Dodge. He came in with another man who was carrying a large camera.

'Where is it?' Norbert asked.

Gillespie gestured with his thumb toward the stairs. 'Jim Cody's up there.'

'Good deal,' Norbert said. 'The guy's probably jitter-bugging by now.' He and the photographer went upstairs.

Parkins Gillespie poured cream into his coffee until it slopped into his saucer, tested it with his thumb, wiped his thumb on his pants, lit another Pall Mall, and said, 'How did you get into this, Mr Mears?'

And so Ben and Matt started their little song and dance and none of what they said was precisely a lie, but enough was left unsaid to link them together in a tenuous bond of conspiracy, and enough to make Ben wonder uneasily if he wasn't in the process of abetting either a harmless bit of kookery or something more serious, some-thing dark. He thought of Matt saying that he had called Ben because he was the only person in 'salem's Lot who might listen to such a story. Whatever Matt Burke's mental failings might be, Ben thought, inability to read character was not one of them. And that also made him nervous.

7

By nine-thirty it was over.

Carl Foreman's funeral wagon had come and taken Mike Ryerson's body away, and the fact of his passing left the house with him and belonged to the town. Jimmy Cody had gone back to his office; Norbert and the photographer had gone to Portland to talk with the county M.E.

Parkins Gillespie stood on the stoop for a moment and watched the hearse trundle slowly up the road, a cigarette dangling between his lips. 'All the times Mike drove that, I bet he never guessed how soon he'd be ridin' in the back.' He turned to Ben. 'You ain't leavin' the Lot just yet, are you? Like you to testify for the coroner's jury, if that's okay by you.'

'No, I'm not leaving.'

The constable's faded blue eyes measured him. 'I checked you through with the feds and the Maine State Police R&I in Augusta,' he said. 'You've got a clean rep.'

'That's good to know,' Ben said evenly.

'I hear it around that you're sparkin' Bill Norton's girl.'

'Guilty,' Ben said.

'She's a fine lass,' Parkins said without smiling. The hearse was out of sight now; even the hum of its engine had dwindled to a drone that faded altogether. 'Guess she don't see much of Floyd Tibbits these days.'

'Haven't you some paperwork to do, Park?' Matt prodded gently.

He sighed and cast the butt of his cigarette away. 'Sure do. Duplicate, triplicate, don't-punch-spindle-ormutilate. This job's been more trouble than a she-bitch with crabs the last couple of weeks. Maybe that old Marsten House has got a curse on it.'

Ben and Matt kept poker faces.

'Well, s'long.' He hitched his pants and walked down to his car. He opened the driver's side door and then turned back to them. 'You two ain't holdin' nothin' back on me, are you?'

'Parkins,' Matt said, 'there's nothing to hold back. He's dead.'

He looked at them a moment longer, the faded eyes sharp and glittering under his hooked brows, and then he sighed. 'I suppose,' he said. 'But it's awful goddamn funny. The dog, the Glick boy, then t'other Glick boy, now Mike. That's a year's run for a pissant little burg like this one. My old grammy used to say things ran in threes, not fours.'

He got in, started the engine, and backed out of the driveway. A moment later he was gone over the hill, trailing one farewell honk.

Matt let out a gusty sigh. 'That's over.'

'Yes,' Ben said. 'I'm beat. Are you?'

'I am, but I feel . . . weird. You know that word, the way the kids use it?'

'Yes.'

'They've got another one: spaced out. Like coming down from an acid trip or speed, when even being normal is crazy.' He scrubbed a hand across his face. 'God, you must think I'm a lunatic. It all sounds like a madman's raving in the daylight, doesn't it?'

'Yes and no,' Ben said. He put a diffident hand on Matt's shoulder. 'Gillespie is right, you know. There is something going on. And I'm thinking more and more that it has to do with the Marsten House. Other than myself, the people up there are the only new people in town. And I know I haven't done anything. Is our trip up there tonight still on? The rustic welcome wagon?'

'If you like.'

'I do. You go in and get some sleep. I'll get in touch with Susan and we'll drop by this evening.'

'All right.' He paused. 'There's one other thing. It's been bothering me ever since you mentioned autopsies.'

'What?'

'The laugh I heard – or thought I heard – was a child's laugh. Horrible and soulless, but still a child's laugh. Connected to Mike's story, does that make you think of Danny Glick?'

'Yes, of course it does.'

'Do you know what the embalming procedure is?'

'Not specifically. The blood is drained from the cadaver and replaced with some fluid. They used to use formalde-hyde, but I'm sure they've got more sophisticated methods now. And the corpse is eviscerated.'

'I wonder if all that was done to Danny?' Matt said, looking at him.

'Do you know Carl Foreman well enough to ask him in confidence?'

'Yes, I think I could find a way to do that.'

'Do it, by all means.'

'I will.'

They looked at each other a moment longer, and the glance that passed between them was friendly but inde-finable; on Matt's part the uneasy defiance of the rational man who has been forced to speak irrationalities, on Ben's a kind of ill-defined fright of forces he could not understand enough to define.

8

Eva was ironing and watching *Dialing for Dollars* when he came in. The jackpot was currently up to forty-five dollars, and the emcee was picking telephone numbers out of a large glass drum.

'I heard,' she said as he opened the refrigerator and got a Coke. 'Awful. Poor Mike.'

'It's too bad.' He reached into his breast pocket and fished out the crucifix on its fine-link chain.

'Do they know what—'

'Not yet,' Ben said. 'I'm very tired, Mrs Miller. I think I'll sleep for a while.'

'Of course you should. That upstairs room is hot at midday, even this late in the year. Take the one in the downstairs hall if you like. The sheets are fresh.'

'No, that's all right. I know all the squeaks in the one upstairs.'

'Yes, a person does get used to their own,' she said matter-of-factly. 'Why in the world did Mr Burke want Ralph's crucifix?'

Ben paused on his way to the stairs, momentarily at a loss. 'I think he must have thought Mike Ryerson was a Catholic.'

Eva slipped a new shirt on the end of her ironing board. 'He should have known better than that. After all, he had Mike in school. All his people were Lutherans.'

Ben had no answer for that. He went upstairs, pulled his clothes off, and got into bed. Sleep came rapidly and heavily. He did not dream.

9

When he woke up, it was quarter past four. His body was beaded with sweat, and he had kicked the upper sheet away. Still, he felt clear-headed again. The events of that early morning seemed to be far away and dim, and Matt Burke's fancies had lost their urgency. His job for tonight was only to humor him out of them if he could.

10

He decided that he would call Susan from Spencer's and have her meet him there. They could go to the park and he would tell her the whole thing from beginning to end. He could get her opinion on their way out to see Matt, and at Matt's house she could listen to his version and complete her judgment. Then, on to the Marsten House. The thought caused a ripple of fear in his midsection.

He was so involved in his own thoughts that he never noticed that someone was sitting in his car until the door opened and the tall form accordioned out. For a moment his mind was too stunned to command his body; it was busy boggling at what it first took to be an animated scarecrow. The slanting sun picked the figure out in detail that was sharp and cruel: the old fedora hat pulled low around the ears; the wraparound sunglasses; the ragged overcoat with the collar turned up; the heavy industrial green rubber gloves on the hands.

'Who—' was all Ben had time to get out.

The figure moved closer. The fists bunched. There was an old yellow smell that Ben recognized as that of mothballs. He could hear breath slobbering in and out.

'You're the son of a bitch that stole my girl,' Floyd Tibbits said in a grating, toneless voice. 'I'm going to kill you.'

And while Ben was still trying to clear all this through his central switchboard, Floyd Tibbits waded in.

CHAPTER NINE
SUSAN (II)

Susan arrived home from Portland a little after three in the afternoon, and came into the house carrying three crackling brown department-store bags – she had sold two paintings for a sum totaling just over eighty dollars and had gone on a small spree. Two new skirts and a cardigan top.

'Suze?' Her mother called. 'Is that you?'

'I'm home. I got—'

'Come in here, Susan. I want to talk to you.'

She recognized the tone instantly, although she had not heard it to that precise degree since her high school days, when the arguments over hem lines and boyfriends had gone on day after bitter day.

She put down her bags and went into the living room. Her mother had grown colder and colder on the subject of Ben Mears, and Susan supposed this was to be her Final Word.

Her mother was sitting in the rocker by the bay window, knitting. The TV was off. The two in conjunction were an ominous sign.

'I suppose you haven't heard the latest,' Mrs Norton

said. Her needles clicked rapidly, meshing the dark green yarn she was working with into neat rows. Someone's winter scarf. 'You left too early this morning.'

'Latest?'

'Mike Ryerson died at Matthew Burke's house last night, and who should be in attendance at the deathbed but your writer friend, Mr Ben Mears!'

'Mike . . . Ben . . . what?'

Mrs Norton smiled grimly. 'Mabel called around ten this morning and told me. Mr Burke *says* he met Mike down at Delbert Markey's tavern last night – although what a teacher is doing barhopping I don't know – and brought him home with him because Mike didn't look well. He died in the night. And no one seems to know just what Mr Mears was doing there!'

'They know each other,' Susan said absently. 'In fact, Ben says they hit it off really well . . . what happened to Mike, Mom?'

But Mrs Norton was not to be sidetracked so quickly. 'Nonetheless, there's some that think we've had a little too much excitement in 'salem's Lot since Mr Ben Mears showed his face. A little too much altogether.'

'That's foolishness!' Susan said, exasperated. 'Now, what did Mike—'

'They haven't decided that yet,' Mrs Norton said. She twirled her ball of yarn and let out slack. 'There's some that think he may have caught a disease from the little Glick boy.'

'If so, why hasn't anyone else caught it? Like his folks?'

'Some young people think they know everything,'

Mrs Norton remarked to the air. Her needles flashed up and down.

Susan got up. 'I think I'll go downstreet and see if—'

'Sit back down a minute,' Mrs Norton said. 'I have a few more things to say to you.'

Susan sat down again, her face neutral.

'Sometimes young people don't know all there is to know,' Ann Norton said. A spurious tone of comfort had come into her voice that Susan distrusted immediately.

'Like what, Mom?'

'Well, it seems that Mr Ben Mears had an accident a few years ago. Just after his second book was published. A motorcycle accident. He was drunk. His wife was killed.'

Susan stood up. 'I don't want to hear any more.'

'I'm telling you for your own good,' Mrs Norton said calmly.

'Who told you?' Susan asked. She felt none of the old hot and impotent anger, or the urge to run upstairs away from that calm, knowing voice and weep. She only felt cold and distant, as if drifting in space. 'It was Mabel Werts, wasn't it?'

'That doesn't matter. It's true.'

'Sure it is. And we won in Vietnam and Jesus Christ drives through the center of town in a go-cart every day at high noon.'

'Mabel thought he looked familiar,' Ann Norton said, 'and so she went through the back issues of her newspapers box by box—'

'You mean the scandal sheets? The ones that specialize in astrology and pictures of car wrecks and starlets' tits? Oh, what an informed source.' She laughed harshly.

'No need to be obscene. The story was right there in black and white. The woman – his wife if she really was – was riding on the backseat and he skidded on the pavement and they went smack into the side of a moving van. They gave him a breathalyzer test on the spot, the article said. Right . . . on . . . the spot.' She emphasized intensifier, preposition, and object by tapping a knitting needle against the arm of her rocker.

'Then why isn't he in prison?'

'These famous fellows always know people,' she said with calm certainty. 'There are ways to get out of everything, if you're rich enough. Just look at what those Kennedy boys have gotten away with.'

'Was he tried in court?'

'I told you, they gave him a—'

'You said that, Mother. But was he drunk?'

'I told you he was drunk!' Spots of color had begun to creep into her cheeks. 'They don't give you a breathalyzer test if you're sober! His wife died! It was just like that Chappaquiddick business! Just like it!'

'I'm going to move into town,' Susan said slowly. 'I've been meaning to tell you. I should have done it a long time ago, Mom. For both of us. I was talking to Babs Griffen, and she says there's a nice little four-room place on Sister's Lane—'

'Oh, she's offended!' Mrs Norton remarked to the air. 'Someone just spoiled her pretty picture of Mr Ben Big-shot Mears and she's just so mad she could *spit*.' This line had been particularly effective some years back.

'Mom, what's happened to you?' Susan asked a little despairingly. 'You never used to . . . to get this low—'

Ann Norton's head jerked up. Her knitting slid off her lap as she stood up, clapped her hands to Susan's shoulders, and gave her a smart shake.

'You listen to me! I won't have you running around like a common trollop with some sissy boy who's got your head all filled up with moonlight. *Do you hear me?*'

Susan slapped her across the face.

Ann Norton's eyes blinked and then opened wide in stunned surprise. They looked at each other for a moment in silence, shocked. A tiny sound came and died in Susan's throat.

'I'm going upstairs,' she said. 'I'll be out by Tuesday at the latest.'

'Floyd was here,' Mrs Norton said. Her face was still rigid from the slap. Her daughter's finger marks stood out in red, like exclamation points.

'I'm through with Floyd,' Susan said tonelessly. 'Get used to the idea. Tell your harpy friend Mabel all about it on the telephone, why don't you? Maybe then it will seem real to you.'

'Floyd loves you, Susan. This is . . . ruining him. He broke down and told me everything. He poured out his heart to me.' Her eyes shone with the memory of it. 'He broke down at the end and cried like a baby.'

Susan thought how unlike Floyd that was. She wondered if her mother could be making it up, and knew by her eyes that she was not.

'Is that what you want for me, Mom? A crybaby? Or did you just fall in love with the idea of blond-haired grandchildren? I suppose I bother you – you can't feel your job is complete until you see me married and settled down to a good man you can put your thumb on. Settled down with a fellow who'll get me pregnant and turn me into a matron in a hurry. That's the scoop, isn't it? Well, what about what *I* want?'

'Susan, you don't know what you want.'

And she said it with such absolute, convinced certainty that for a moment Susan was tempted to believe her. An image came to her of herself and her mother, standing here in set positions, her mother by her rocker and she by the door; only they were tied together by a hank of green yarn, a cord that had grown frayed and weak from many restless tuggings. Image transformed into her mother in a nimrod's hat, the band sportily pierced with many different flies. Trying desperately to reel in a large trout wearing a yellow print shift. Trying to reel it in for the last time and pop it away in the wicker creel. But for what purpose? To mount it? To eat it?

'No, Mom. I know exactly what I want. Ben Mears.'

She turned and went up the stairs.

Her mother ran after her and called up shrilly: 'You can't get a room! You haven't any money!'

'I've got a hundred in checking and three hundred in savings,' Susan replied calmly. 'And I can get a job down at Spencer's, I think. Mr Labree has offered several times.'

'All he'll care about is looking up your dress,' Mrs Norton said, but her voice had gone down an octave. Much of her anger had left her and she felt a little frightened.

'Let him,' Susan said. 'I'll wear bloomers.'

'Honey, don't be mad.' She came two steps up the stairs. 'I only want what's best for—'

'Spare it, Mom. I'm sorry I slapped you. That was

awful of me. I do love you. But I'm moving out. It's way past time. You must see that.'

'You think it over,' Mrs Norton said, now clearly sorry as well as frightened. 'I still don't think I spoke out of turn. That Ben Mears, I've seen showboats like him before. All he's interested in is—'

'No. No more.'

She turned away.

Her mother came up another step and called after her: 'When Floyd left here he was in an awful state. He—'

But the door to Susan's room closed and cut off her words.

She lay down on her bed – which had been decorated with stuffed toys and a poodle dog with a transistor radio in its belly not so long ago – and lay looking at the wall, trying not to think. There were a number of Sierra Club posters on the wall, but not so long ago she had been surrounded by posters clipped from *Rolling Stone* and *Creem* and *Crawdaddy*, pictures of her idols – Jim Morrison and John Lennon and Dave van Ronk and Chuck Berry. The ghost of those days seemed to crowd in on her like bad time exposures of the mind.

She could almost see the newsprint, standing out on the cheap pulp stock. GOING-PLACES YOUNG WRITER AND YOUNG WIFE INVOLVED IN 'MAYBE' MOTORCYCLE FATALITY. The rest in carefully couched innuendoes. Perhaps a picture taken at the scene by a local photographer, too gory for the local paper, just right for Mabel's kind.

And the worst was that a seed of doubt had been planted. Stupid. Did you think he was in cold storage before he came back here? That he came wrapped in a germ-proof cellophane bag, like a motel drinking glass? Stupid. Yet the seed had been planted. And for that she could feel something more than adolescent pique for her mother — she could feel something black that bordered on hate.

She shut the thoughts — not out but away — and put an arm over her face and drifted into an uncomfortable doze that was broken by the shrill of the telephone downstairs, then more sharply by her mother's voice calling, 'Susan! It's for you!'

She went downstairs, noticing it was just after five-thirty. The sun was in the west. Mrs Norton was in the kitchen, beginning supper. Her father wasn't home yet.

'Hello?'

'Susan?' The voice was familiar, but she could not put a name to it immediately.

'Yes, who's this?'

'Eva Miller, Susan. I've got some bad news.'

'Has something happened to Ben?' All the spit seemed to have gone out of her mouth. Her hand came up and touched her throat. Mrs Norton had come to the kitchen door and was watching, a spatula held in one hand.

'Well, there was a fight. Floyd Tibbits showed up here this afternoon—'

'Floyd!'

Mrs Norton winced at her tone.

'—and I said Mr Mears was sleeping. He said all right, just as polite as ever, but he was dressed awful funny. I asked him if he felt all right. He had on an old-fashioned overcoat and a funny hat and he kept his hands in his pockets. I never thought to mention it to Mr Mears when he got up. There's been so much excitement—'

'What happened?' Susan nearly screamed.

'Well, Floyd beat him up,' Eva said unhappily. 'Right out in my parking lot. Sheldon Corson and Ed Craig went out and dragged him off.'

'Ben. Is Ben all right?'

'I guess not.'

'What is it?' She was holding the phone very tightly.

'Floyd got in one last crack and sent Mr Mears back against that little foreign car of his, and he hit his head. Carl Foreman took him over to Cumberland Receiving, and he was unconscious. I don't know anything else. If you—'

She hung up, ran to the closet, and pulled her coat off the hanger.

'Susan, what is it?'

'That nice boy Floyd Tibbits,' Susan said, hardly aware that she had begun to cry. 'He's put Ben in the hospital.'

She ran out without waiting for a reply.

2

She got to the hospital at six-thirty and sat in an uncomfortable plastic contour chair, staring blankly at a copy of *Good Housekeeping*. And I'm the only one, she thought. How damned awful. She had thought of calling Matt Burke, but the thought of the doctor coming back and finding her gone had stopped her.

The minutes crawled by on the waiting room clock, and at ten minutes of seven, a doctor with a sheaf of papers in one hand stepped through the door and said, 'Miss Norton?'

'That's right. Is Ben all right?'

'That's not an answerable question at this point.' He saw the dread come into her face and added: 'He seems to be, but we'll want him here for two or three days. He's got a hairline fracture, multiple bruises, contusions, and one hell of a black eye.'

'Can I see him?'

'No, not tonight. He's been sedated.'

'For a minute? Please? One minute?'

He sighed. 'You can look in on him, if you like. He'll probably be asleep. I don't want you to say anything to him unless he speaks to you.'

He took her up to the third floor and then down to a room at the far end of a medicinal-smelling corridor. The man in the other bed was reading a magazine and looked up at them desultorily.

Ben was lying with his eyes closed, a sheet pulled up to his chin. He was so pale and still that for one terrified moment Susan was sure he was dead; that he had just slipped away while she and the doctor had been talking downstairs. Then she marked the slow, steady rise and fall of his chest and felt a relief so great that she swayed a little on her feet. She looked at his face closely, hardly noticing the way it had been marked. Sissy boy, her mother had called him, and Susan could see how she might have gotten that idea. His features were strong but sensitive (she wished there was a better word than 'sensitive'; that was the word you used to describe the local librarian who wrote stilted Spenserian sonnets to daffodils in his spare time; but it was the only word that fit). Only his hair seemed virile in the traditional sense. Black and heavy, it seemed almost to float above his face. The white bandage on the left side above the temple stood out in sharp, telling contrast.

I love the man, she thought. Get well, Ben. Get well and finish your book so we can go away from the Lot together, if you want me. The Lot has turned bad for both of us.

'I think you'd better leave now,' the doctor said. 'Perhaps tomorrow—'

Ben stirred and made a thick sound in his throat. His eyelids opened slowly, closed, opened again. His eyes were dark with sedation, but the knowledge of her presence was in them. He moved his hand over hers. Tears spilled out of her eyes and she smiled and squeezed his hand.

He moved his lips and she bent to hear.

'They're real killers in this town, aren't they?'

'Ben, I'm so sorry.'

'I think I knocked out two of his teeth before he decked me,' Ben whispered. 'Not bad for a writer fella.'

'Ben—'

'I think that will be enough, Mr Mears,' the doctor said. 'Give the airplane glue a chance to set.'

Ben shifted his eyes to the doctor. 'Just a minute.'

The doctor rolled his eyes. 'That's what *she* said.'

Ben's eyelids slipped down again, then came up with difficulty. He said something unintelligible.

Susan bent closer. 'What, darling?'

'Is it dark yet?'

'Yes.'

'Want you to go see . . .'

'Matt?'

He nodded. 'Tell him . . . I said for you to be told

everything. Ask him if he . . . knows Father Callahan. He'll understand.'

'Okay,' Susan said. 'I'll give him the message. You sleep now. Sleep well, Ben.'

''Kay. Love you.' He muttered something else, twice, and then his eyes closed. His breathing deepened.

'What did he say?' the doctor asked.

Susan was frowning. 'It sounded like "Lock the windows,"' she said.

3

Eva Miller and Weasel Craig were in the waiting room when she went back to get her coat. Eva was wearing an old fall coat with a rusty fur collar, obviously kept for best, and Weasel was floating in an outsized motorcycle jacket. Susan warmed at the sight of both of them.

'How is he?' Eva asked.

'Going to be all right, I think.' She repeated the doctor's diagnosis, and Eva's face relaxed.

'I'm so glad. Mr Mears seems like a very nice man. Nothing like this has ever happened at my place. And Parkins Gillespie had to lock Floyd up in the drunk tank. He didn't act drunk, though. Just sort of . . . dopey and confused.'

Susan shook her head. 'It doesn't sound like Floyd at all.'

There was a moment of uncomfortable silence.

'Ben's a lovely fella,' Weasel said, and patted Susan's hand. 'He'll be up and about in no time. You wait and see.'

'I'm sure he will be,' Susan said, and squeezed his

hand in both of hers. 'Eva, isn't Father Callahan the priest at St Andrew's?'

'Yes, why?'

'Oh . . . curious. Listen, thank you both for coming. If you could come back tomorrow—'

'We'll do that,' Weasel said. 'Sure we will, won't we, Eva?' He slipped an arm about her waist. It was a long reach, but he got there eventually.

'Yes, we will.'

Susan walked out to the parking lot with them and then drove back to Jerusalem's Lot.

4

Matt did not answer at her knock or yell *Come in!* as he usually did. Instead, a very careful voice which she hardly recognized said, 'Who is it?' very quietly from the other side.

'Susie Norton, Mr Burke.'

He opened the door and she felt real shock at the change in him. He looked old and haggard. A moment after that, she saw that he was wearing a heavy gold crucifix. There was something so strange and ludicrous about that ornate five-and-dime corpus lying against his checked flannel shirt that she almost laughed – but didn't.

'Come in. Where's Ben?'

She told him and his face grew long. 'So Floyd Tibbits of all people decides to play wronged lover, is that it? Well, it couldn't have happened at a more inopportune time. Mike Ryerson was brought back from Portland late this afternoon for burial preparations at Foreman's. And I suppose our trip up to the Marsten House will have to be put off—'

'What trip? What's this about Mike?'

'Would you like coffee?' he asked absently.

'No. I want to find out what's going on. Ben said you know.'

'That,' he said, 'is a very tall order. Easy for Ben to say I'm to tell you everything. Harder to do. But I will try.'

'What—'

He held up one hand. 'One thing first, Susan. You and your mother went down to the new shop the other day.'

Susan's brow furrowed. 'Sure. Why?'

'Can you give me your impressions of the place, and more specifically, of the man who runs it?'

'Mr Straker?'

'Yes.'

'Well, he's quite charming,' she said. 'Courtly might be an even better word. He complimented Glynis Mayberry on her dress and she blushed like a schoolgirl. And asked Mrs Boddin about the bandage on her arm . . . she spilled some hot fat on it, you know. He gave her a recipe for a poultice. Wrote it right down. And when Mabel came in . . .' She laughed a bit at the memory.

'Yes?'

'He got her a chair,' Susan said. 'Not a chair, actually, but a *chair*. More like a throne. A great carved mahogany thing. He brought it out of the back room all by himself, smiling and chatting with the other ladies all the time. But it must have weighed at least three hundred pounds. He plonked it down in the middle of the floor and escorted Mabel to it. Took her arm, you know. And she was *giggling*.

If you've seen Mabel giggling, you've seen everything. And he served coffee. Very strong but very good.'

'Did you like him?' Matt asked, watching her closely.

'This is all a part of it, isn't it?' she asked.

'It might be, yes.'

'All right, then. I'll give you a woman's reaction. I did and I didn't. I was attracted to him in a mildly sexual way, I guess. Older man, very urbane, very charming, very courtly. You know looking at him that he could order from a French menu and know what wine would go with what, not just red or white but the year and even the vineyard. Very definitely not the run of fellow you see around here. But not effeminate in the least. Lithe, like a dancer. And of course there's something attractive about a man who is so unabashedly bald.' She smiled a little defensively, knowing there was color in her cheeks, wondering if she had said more than she intended.

'But then you didn't,' Matt said.

She shrugged. 'That's harder to put my finger on. I think . . . I think I sensed a certain contempt under the surface. A cynicism. As if he were playing a certain part, and playing it well, but as if he knew he wouldn't have to pull out all the stops to fool us. A touch of condescension.' She looked at him uncertainly. 'And there seemed to be something a little bit cruel about him. I don't really know why.'

'Did anyone buy anything?'

'Not much, but he didn't seem to mind. Mom bought a little knick-knack shelf from Yugoslavia, and that Mrs Petric bought a lovely little drop-leaf table, but that was all I saw. He didn't seem to mind. Just urged people to tell their friends he was open, to come back by and not be strangers. Very Old World charming.'

'And do you think people were charmed?'

'By and large, yes,' Susan said, mentally comparing her mother's enthusiastic impression of R.T. Straker to her immediate dislike of Ben.

'You didn't see his partner?'

'Mr Barlow? No, he's in New York, on a buying trip.'

'Is he?' Matt said, speaking to himself. 'I wonder. The elusive Mr Barlow.'

'Mr Burke, don't you think you better tell me what all this is about?'

He sighed heavily.

'I suppose I must try. What you've just told me is disturbing. Very disturbing. It all fits so well . . .'

'What? What does?'

'I have to start,' he began, 'with meeting Mike Ryerson in Dell's tavern last night . . . which already seems a century ago.'

5

It was twenty after eight by the time he had finished, and they had both drunk two cups of coffee.

'I believe that's everything,' Matt said. 'And now shall I do my Napoleon imitation? Tell you about my astral conversations with Toulouse-Lautrec?'

'Don't be silly,' she said. 'There's something going on, but not what you think. You must *know* that.'

'I did until last night.'

'If no one has it in for you, as Ben suggested, then

maybe Mike did it himself. In a delirium or something.' That sounded thin, but she pushed ahead anyway. 'Or maybe you fell asleep without knowing and dreamed the whole thing. I've dozed off without knowing it before and lost a whole fifteen or twenty minutes.'

He shrugged tiredly. 'How does a person defend testimony no rational mind will accept at face value? I heard what I heard. I was not asleep. And something has me worried . . . rather badly worried. According to the old literature, a vampire cannot simply walk into a man's house and suck his blood. No. He has to be invited. But Mike Ryerson invited Danny Glick in last night. *And I invited Mike myself!*'

'Matt, has Ben told you about his new book?'

He fiddled with his pipe but didn't light it. 'Very little. Only that it's somehow connected with the Marsten House.'

'Has he told you he had a very traumatic experience in the Marsten House as a boy?'

He looked up sharply. '*In* it? No.'

'He went in on a dare. He wanted to join a club, and the initiation was for him to go into the Marsten House and bring something out. He did, as a matter of fact — but before he left, he went up to the second-floor bedroom where Hubie Marsten hung himself. When he opened the door, he saw Hubie hanging there. He opened his eyes. Ben ran. That's festered in him for twenty-four years. He came back to the Lot to try to write it out of his system.'

'Christ,' Matt said.

'He has . . . a certain theory about the Marsten House.

It springs partly from his own experience and partly from some rather amazing research he's done on Hubert Marsten—'

'His penchant for devil worship?'

She started. 'How did you know that?'

He smiled a trifle grimly. 'Not all the gossip in a small town is open gossip. There are secrets. Some of the secret gossip in 'salem's Lot has to do with Hubie Marsten. It's shared among perhaps only a dozen or so of the older people now – Mabel Werts is one of them. It was a long time ago, Susan. But even so, there is no statute of limitations on some stories. It's strange, you know. Even Mabel won't talk about Hubert Marsten with anyone but her own circle. They'll talk about his death, of course. About the murder. But if you ask about the ten years he and his wife spent up there in their house, doing God knows what, a sort of governor comes into play – perhaps the closest thing to a taboo our Western civilization knows. There have even been whispers that Hubert Marsten kidnapped and sacrificed small children to his infernal gods. I'm surprised Ben found out as much as he did. The secrecy concerning that aspect of Hubie and his wife and his house is almost tribal.'

'He didn't come by it in the Lot.'

'That explains it, then. I suspect his theory is a rather old parapsychological wheeze – that humans manufacture evil just as they manufacture snot or excrement or finger-nail parings. That it doesn't go away. Specifically, that the Marsten House may have become a kind of evil dry-cell; a malign storage battery.'

'Yes. He expressed it in exactly those terms.' She looked at him wonderingly.

He gave a dry chuckle. 'We've read the same books. And what do you think, Susan? Is there more than heaven and earth in your philosophy?'

'No,' she said with quiet firmness. 'Houses are only houses. Evil dies with the perpetration of evil acts.'

'You're suggesting that Ben's instability may enable me to lead him down the path to insanity that I am already traversing?'

'No, of course not. I don't think you're insane. But Mr Burke, you must realize—'

'Be quiet.'

He had cocked his head forward. She stopped talking and listened. Nothing . . . except perhaps a creaky board. She looked at him questioningly, and he shook his head. 'You were saying?'

'Only that coincidence has made this a poor time for him to exorcise the demons of his youth. There's been a lot of cheap talk going around town since the Marsten House was reoccupied and that store was opened . . . there's been talk about Ben himself, for that matter. Rites of exorcism have been known to get out of hand and turn on the exorcist. I think Ben needs to get out of this town and I think maybe you could use a vacation from it. Mr Burke.'

Exorcism made her think of Ben's request to mention the Catholic priest to Matt. On impulse, she decided not to. The reason he had asked was now clear enough, but it would only be adding fuel to a fire that was, in her opinion, already dangerously high. When Ben asked her – if he ever did – she would say she had forgotten.

'I know how mad it must sound,' Matt said. 'Even to me, who heard the window go up, and that laugh, and saw the screen lying beside the driveway this morning. But if it will allay your fears any, I must say that Ben's reaction to the whole thing was very sensible. He suggested we put the thing on the basis of a theory to be proved or disproved, and begin by—' He ceased again, listening.

This time the silence spun out, and when he spoke again, the soft certainty in his voice frightened her. 'There's someone upstairs.'

She listened. Nothing.

'You're imagining things.'

'I know my house,' he said softly. 'Someone is in the guest bedroom . . . there, you hear?'

And this time she did hear. The audible creak of a board, creaking the way boards in old houses do, for no good reason at all. But to Susan's ears there seemed to be something more – something unutterably sly – in that sound.

'I'm going upstairs,' he said.

'No!'

The word came out with no thought. She told herself: *Now who's sitting in the chimney corner, believing the wind in the eaves is a banshee?*

'I was frightened last night and did nothing and things grew worse. Now I am going upstairs.'

'Mr Burke—'

They had both begun to speak in undertones. Tension had wormed into her veins, making her muscles stiff. Maybe there *was* someone upstairs. A prowler.

'Talk,' he said. 'After I go, continue speaking. On any subject.'

And before she could argue, he was out of his seat

and moving toward the hall, moving with a grace that was nearly astounding. He looked back once, but she couldn't read his eyes. He began to go up the stairs.

Her mind felt dazed into unreality by the swift turn-around things had taken. Less than two minutes ago they had been discussing this business calmly, under the rational light of electric bulbs. And now she was afraid. Question: If you put a psychologist in a room with a man who thinks he's Napoleon and leave them there for a year (or ten or twenty), will you end up with two Skinner men or two guys with their hands in their shirts? Answer: Insufficient data.

She opened her mouth and said, 'Ben and I were going to drive up Route 1 to Camden on Sunday – you know, the town where they filmed *Peyton Place* – but now I guess we'll have to wait. They have the most darling little church . . .'

She found herself droning along with great facility, even though her hands were clenched together in her lap tightly enough to whiten the knuckles. Her mind was clear, still unimpressed with this talk of bloodsuckers and the undead. It was from her spinal cord, a much older network of nerves and ganglia, that the black dread emanated in waves.

6

Going up the stairs was the hardest thing Matt Burke had ever done in his life. That was all; that was it. Nothing else even came close. Except perhaps one thing.

As a boy of eight, he had been in a Cub Scout pack. The den mother's house was a mile up the road and going was fine, yes, excellent, because you walked in the late afternoon daylight. But coming home twilight had begun to fall, freeing the shadows to yawn across the road in long, twisty patterns – or, if the meeting was particularly enthusiastic and ran late, you had to walk home in the dark. Alone.

Alone. Yes, that's the key word, the most awful word in the English tongue. Murder doesn't hold a candle to it and hell is only a poor synonym . . .

There was a ruined church along the way, an old Methodist meetinghouse, which reared its shambles at the far end of a frost-heaved and hummocked lawn, and when you walked past the view of its glaring, senseless windows your footsteps became very loud in your ears and whatever you had been whistling died on your lips and you thought about how it must be inside – the overturned pews, the rotting hymnals, the crumbling altar where only mice now kept the sabbath, and you wondered what might be in there besides mice – what madmen, what monsters. Maybe they were peering out at you with yellow reptilian eyes. And maybe one night watching would not be enough; maybe some night that splintered, crazily hung door would be thrown open, and what you saw standing there would drive you to lunacy at one look.

And you couldn't explain that to your mother and father, who were creatures of the light. No more than you could explain to them how, at the age of three, the spare blanket at the foot of the crib turned into a collection of snakes that lay staring at you with flat and lidless eyes. No child ever conquers those fears, he thought. If a fear cannot be articulated, it can't be conquered. And the fears locked in small brains are much too large to pass through the orifice of the mouth. Sooner or later you found someone to walk past all the deserted meetinghouses you had to pass between grinning babyhood and grunting senility. Until tonight. Until tonight when you found out that none of the old fears had been staked – only tucked away in their tiny, child-sized coffins with a wild rose on top.

He didn't turn on the light. He mounted the steps, one by one, avoiding the sixth, which creaked. He held on to the crucifix, and his palm was sweaty and slick.

He reached the top and turned soundlessly to look down the hall. The guest room door was ajar. He had left it shut. From downstairs came the steady murmur of Susan's voice.

Walking carefully to avoid squeaks, he went down to the door and stood in front of it. The basis of all human fears, he thought. A closed door, slightly ajar.

He reached out and pushed it open.

Mike Ryerson was lying on the bed.

Moonlight flooded in the windows and silvered the room, turning it into a lagoon of dreams. Matt shook his head, as if to clear it. Almost it seemed as though he had moved backward in time, that it was the night before. He would go downstairs and call Ben because Ben wasn't in the hospital yet—

Mike opened his eyes.

They glittered for just a moment in the moonlight, silver rimmed with red. They were as blank as washed blackboards. There was no human thought or feeling in them. *The eyes are the windows of the soul*, Wordsworth had said. If so, these windows looked in on an empty room.

Mike sat up, the sheet falling from his chest, and Matt saw the heavy industrial stitchwork where the M.E. or pathologist had repaired the work of his autopsy, perhaps whistling as he sewed.

Mike smiled, and his canines and incisors were white and sharp. The smile itself was a mere flexing of the muscles around the mouth; it never touched the eyes. They retained their original dead blankness.

Mike said very clearly, '*Look at me.*'

Matt looked. Yes, the eyes were utterly blank. But very deep. You could almost see little silver cameos of yourself in those eyes, drowning sweetly, making the world seem unimportant, making fears seem unimportant—

He stepped backward and cried out, 'No! No!'

And held the crucifix out.

Whatever had been Mike Ryerson hissed as if hot water had been thrown in its face. Its arms went up as if to ward off a blow. Matt took a step into the room; Ryerson took a compensatory one backward.

'Get out of here!' Matt croaked. 'I revoke my invitation!'

Ryerson screamed, a high, ululating sound full of hate and pain. He took four shambling steps backward. The backs of the knees struck the ledge of the open window, and Ryerson tottered past the edge of balance.

'*I will see you sleep like the dead, teacher.*'

It fell outward into the night, going backward with its hands thrown out above its head, like a diver going off a high board. The pallid body gleamed like marble, in hard and depthless contrast to the black stitches that crisscrossed the torso in a Y pattern.

Matt let out a crazed, terrified wail and rushed to the window and peered out. There was nothing to be seen but the moon-gilded night – and suspended in the air below the window and above the spill of light that marked the living room, a dancing pattern of motes that might have been dust. They whirled, coalesced in a pattern that was hideously humanoid, and then dissipated into nothing.

He turned to run, and that was when the pain filled his chest and made him stagger. He clutched at it and doubled over. The pain seemed to be coming up his arm in steady, pulsing waves. The crucifix swung below his eyes.

He walked out the door holding his forearms crossed before his chest, the chain of the crucifix still caught in his right hand. The image of Mike Ryerson hanging in the dark air like some pallid high-diver hung before him.

'Mr Burke!'

'My doctor is James Cody,' he said through lips that were as cold as snow. 'It's on the phone reminder. I'm having a heart attack, I think.'

He collapsed in the upper hall, facedown.

7

She dialed the number marked beside JIMMY CODY, PILL-PUSHER. The legend was written in the neat block capitals she remembered so well from her school days. A woman's voice answered and Susan said, 'Is the doctor home? Emergency!'

'Yes,' the woman said calmly. 'Here he is.'

'Dr Cody speaking.'

'This is Susan Norton. I'm at Mr Burke's house. He's had a heart attack.'

'Who? *Matt* Burke?'

'Yes. He's unconscious. What should I—'

'Call an ambulance,' he said. 'In Cumberland that's 841–4000. Stay with him. Put a blanket over him but don't move him. Do you understand?'

'Yes.'

'I'll be there in twenty minutes.'

'Will you—'

But the phone clicked, and she was alone.

She called for an ambulance and then she was alone again, faced with going back upstairs to him.

8

She stared at the stairwell with a trepidation which was amazing to her. She found herself wishing that none of it had happened, not so that Matt could be all right, but so she would not have to feel this sick, shaken fear. Her unbelief had been total – she saw Matt's perceptions of the previous night as something to be defined in terms of her accepted realities, nothing more or less. And now that firm unbelief was gone from beneath her and she felt herself falling.

She had heard Matt's voice and had heard a terrible toneless incantation: *I will see you sleep like the dead, teacher.* The voice that had spoken those words had no more human quality than a dog's bark.

She went back upstairs, forcing her body through every step. Even the hall light did not help much. Matt lay where she had left him, his face turned sideways so the right cheek lay against the threadbare nap of the hall runner, breathing in harsh, tearing gasps. She bent and undid the top two buttons of his shirt and his breathing seemed to ease a little. Then she went into the guest bedroom to get a blanket.

The room was cool. The window stood open. The bed had been stripped except for the mattress pad, but there were blankets stacked on the top shelf of the closet. As she turned back to the hall, something on the floor near the window glittered in the moonlight and she stooped and picked it up. She recognized it immediately. A Cumberland Consolidated High School class ring. The initials engraved on the inner curve were M.C.R.

Michael Corey Ryerson.

For that moment, in the dark, she believed. She believed it all. A scream rose in her throat and she choked it unvoiced, but the ring tumbled from her fingers and lay on the floor below the window, glinting in the moonlight that rode the autumn dark.

CHAPTER TEN
THE LOT (III)

The town knew about darkness.

It knew about the darkness that comes on the land when rotation hides the land from the sun, and about the darkness of the human soul. The town is an accumulation of three parts which, in sum, are greater than the sections. The town is the people who live there, the buildings which they have erected to den or do business in, and it is the land. The people are Scotch-English and French. There are others, of course — a smattering, like a fistful of pepper thrown in a pot of salt, but not many. This melting pot never melted very much. The buildings are nearly all constructed of honest wood. Many of the older houses are saltboxes and most of the stores are false fronted, although no one could have said why. The people know there is nothing behind those façades just as most of them know that Loretta Starcher wears falsies. The land is granite-bodied and covered with a thin, easily ruptured skin of topsoil. Farming it is a thankless, sweaty, miserable, crazy business. The harrow turns up great chunks of the granite underlayer and breaks on them. In May you take out your truck as soon as the ground is dry enough to support it, and you and your boys fill it up with rocks perhaps a dozen times before harrowing and dump them in the great weed-choked pile where you have dumped them since 1955, when you first took this tiger by the balls. And when you have picked them until the dirt won't come out from under your nails when you wash and your fingers feel huge and numb and oddly large-pored, you hitch your harrow to your tractor and before you've broken two rows you bust one of the blades on a rock you missed. And putting on a new blade, getting your oldest boy to hold up the hitch so you can get at it, the first mosquito of the new season buzzes bloodthirstily past your ear with that eye-watering hum that always makes you think it's the sound loonies must hear just before they kill all their kids or close their eyes on the Interstate and put the gas pedal to the floor or tighten their toe on the trigger of the .30–.30 they just jammed into their quackers; and then your boy's sweat-slicked fingers slip and one of the other round harrow blades scrapes skin from your arm and looking around in that kind of despairing, heartless flicker of time, when it seems you could just give it all over and take up drinking or go down to the bank that holds your mortgage and declare bank-ruptcy, at that moment of hating the land and the soft suck of gravity that holds you to it, you also love it and under-stand how it knows darkness and has always known it. The land has got you, locked up solid got you, and the house, and the woman you fell in love with when you started high school (only she was a girl then, and you didn't know for shit about girls except you got one and hung on to her and she wrote your name all over her book covers and first you broke her in and then she broke you in and then neither one of you had to worry about *that* mess anymore), and the kids have got you, the kids that were started in the creaky double bed with the splintered headboard. You and she made the kids after the darkness fell – six kids, or seven, or ten. The bank has you, and the car dealership, and the Sears store in Lewiston, and John Deere in Brunswick. But most of all the town has you because you know it the way you know the shape of your wife's breast. You know who will be hanging around Crossen's store in the daytime because Knapp Shoe laid him off and you know who is having woman trouble even before *he* knows it, the way Reggie Sawyer is having it, with that phone-company kid dipping his wick in Bonnie Sawyer's barrel; you know where the roads go and where, on Friday afternoon, you and Hank and Nolly Gardener can go and park and drink a couple of six-packs or a couple of cases. You know how the ground lies and you know how to get through the Marshes in April without getting the tops of your boots wet. You know it all. And it knows you, how your crotch aches from the tractor saddle when the day's harrowing is done and how the lump on your back was just a cyst and nothing to worry about like the doctor said at first it might be, and how your mind works over the bills that come in during the last week of the month. It sees through your lies, even the ones you tell yourself, like how you are going to take the wife and the kids to Disneyland next year or the year after that, like how you can afford the payments on a new color TV if you cut cordwood next fall, like how everything is going to come out all right. Being in the town is a daily act of utter intercourse, so complete that it makes what you and your wife do in the squeaky bed look like a handshake. Being in the town is prosaic, sensuous, alcoholic. And in the dark, the town is yours and you are the town's and together you sleep like the dead, like the very stones in your north field. There is no life here but the slow death of days, and so when the evil falls on the town, its coming seems almost preordained, sweet and morphic. It is almost as though the town knows the evil was coming and the shape it would take.

The town has its secrets, and keeps them well. The people don't know them all. They know old Albie Crane's wife ran off with a traveling man from New York City – or they think they know it. But Albie cracked her skull open after the traveling man had left her cold and then he tied a block on her feet and tumbled her down the old well and twenty years later Albie died peacefully in his bed of a heart attack, just as his son Joe will die later in this story, and perhaps someday a kid will stumble on the old well where it is hidden by choked blackberry creepers and pull back the whitened, weather-smoothed boards and see that crumbling skeleton staring blankly up from the bottom of that rock-lined pit, the sweet traveling man's necklace still dangling, green and mossy, over her rib cage.

They know that Hubie Marsten killed his wife, but they don't know what he made her do first, or how it was with them in that sun-sticky kitchen in the moments before he blew her head in, with the smell of honeysuckle hanging in the hot air like the gagging sweetness of an uncovered charnel pit. They don't know that she begged him to do it.

Some of the older women in town – Mabel Werts, Glynis Mayberry, Audrey Hersey – remember that Larry McLeod found some charred papers in the upstairs fireplace, but none of them know that the papers were the accumulation of twelve years' correspondence between Hubert Marsten and an amusingly antique Austrian nobleman named Breichen, or that the correspondence of these two had commenced through the offices of a rather peculiar Boston book merchant who died an extremely nasty death in 1933, or that Hubie had burned each and every letter before hanging himself, feeding them to the fire one at a time, watching the flames blacken and char the thick, cream-colored paper and obliterate the elegant, spider-thin calligraphy. They don't know he was smiling as he did it, the way Larry Crockett now smiles over the fabulous land-title papers that reside in the safe-deposit box of his Portland bank.

They know that Coretta Simons, old Jumpin' Simons's widow, is dying slowly and horribly of intestinal cancer, but they don't know that there is better than thirty thousand dollars cash tucked away behind the dowdy sitting room wallpaper, the results of an insurance policy she collected but never invested and now, in her last extremity, has forgotten entirely.

They know that a fire burned up half of the town in that smoke-hazed September of 1951, but they don't know that it was set, and they don't know that the boy who set it graduated valedictorian of his class in 1953 and went on to make a hundred thousand dollars on Wall Street, and even if they *had* known, they would not have known the compulsion that drove him to it or the way it ate at his mind for the next twenty years of his life, until a brain embolism hustled him into his grave at the age of forty-six.

They don't know that the Reverend John Groggins has sometimes awakened in the midnight hour with horrible dreams still vivid beneath his bald pate – dreams in which he preaches to the Little Misses' Thursday Night Bible Class naked and slick, and they ready for him; or that Floyd Tibbits wandered around for all of that Friday in a sickly daze, feeling the sun lie hatefully against his strangely pallid skin, remembering going to Ann Norton only cloudily, not remembering his attack on Ben Mears at all, but remembering the cool gratitude with which he greeted the setting of the sun, the gratitude and the anticipation of something great and good;

or that Hal Griffen has six hot books hidden in the back of his closet which he masturbates over at every opportunity;

or that George Middler has a suitcase full of silk slips and bras and panties and stockings and that he sometimes pulls down the shades of his apartment over the hardware store and locks the door with both the bolt and the chain and then stands in front of the full-length mirror in the bedroom until his breath comes in short stitches and then he falls to his knees and masturbates;

or that Carl Foreman tried to scream and was unable when Mike Ryerson began to tremble coldly on the metal worktable in the room beneath the mortuary and the scream was as sightless and soundless as glass in his throat when Mike opened his eyes and sat up;

or that ten-month-old Randy McDougall did not even struggle when Danny Glick slipped through his bedroom window and plucked the baby from his crib and sank his teeth into a neck still bruised from a mother's blows.

These are the town's secrets, and some will later be known and some will never be known. The town keeps them all with the ultimate poker face.

The town cares for devil's work no more than it cares

for God's or man's. It knew darkness. And darkness was enough.

2

Sandy McDougall knew something was wrong when she woke up, but couldn't tell what. The other side of the bed was empty; it was Roy's day off, and he had gone fishing with some friends. Would be back around noon. Nothing was burning and she didn't hurt anywhere. So what could be wrong?

The sun. The sun was wrong.

It was high up on the wallpaper, dancing through the shadows cast by the maple outside the window. But Randy always woke her before the sun got up high enough to throw the maple's shadow on the wall—

Her startled eyes jumped to the clock on the dresser. It was ten minutes after nine.

Trepidation rose in her throat.

'Randy?' she called, her dressing gown billowing out behind her as she flew down the narrow hall of the trailer. 'Randy, *honey?*'

The baby's bedroom was bathed in submerged light from the one small window above the crib . . . open. But she had closed it when she went to bed. She always closed it.

The crib was empty.

'Randy?' she whispered.

And saw him.

The small body, still clad in wash-faded Dr Dentons, had been flung into the corner like a piece of garbage.

One leg stuck up grotesquely, like an inverted exclamation point.

'*Randy!*'

She fell on her knees by the body, her face marked with the harsh lines of shock. She cradled the child. The body was cool to the touch.

'Randy, honey-baby, wake up, Randy, Randy, wake up—'

The bruises were gone. All gone. They had faded overnight, leaving the small face and form flawless. His color was good. For the only time since his coming she found him beautiful, and she screamed at the sight of the beauty – a horrible, desolate sound.

'Randy! *Wake up!* Randy? Randy? Randy?'

She got up with him and ran back down the hall, the dressing gown slipping off one shoulder. The high chair still stood in the kitchen, the tray encrusted with Randy's supper of the night before. She slipped Randy into the chair, which stood in a patch of morning sunlight. Randy's head lolled against his chest and he slid sideways with a slow and terrible finality until he was lodged in the angle between the tray and one of the chair's high arms.

'Randy?' she said, smiling. Her eyes bulged from their sockets like flawed blue marbles. She patted his cheeks. 'Wake up now, Randy. Breakfast, Randy. Is oo hungwy? Please – oh Jesus, please—'

She whirled away from him and pulled open one of the cabinets over the stove and pawed through it, spilling a box of Rice Chex, a can of Chef Boy-ar-dee ravioli, a bottle of Wesson oil. The Wesson oil bottle shattered, spraying heavy liquid across the stove and floor. She found a small jar of Gerber's chocolate custard and grabbed one of the plastic Dairy Queen spoons out of the dish drainer.

'Look, Randy. Your favorite. Wake up and see the nice custard. Chocka, Randy. Chocka, chocka.' Rage and terror swept her darkly. '*Wake up!*' she screamed at him, her spittle beading the translucent skin of his brow and cheeks. '*Wake up wake up for the love of God you little shit WAKE UP!*'

She pulled the cover off the jar and spooned out some of the chocolate-flavored custard. Her hand, which knew the truth already, was shaking so badly that most of it spilled. She pushed what was left between the small slack lips, and more fell off onto the tray, making horrid plopping sounds. The spoon clashed against his teeth.

'Randy,' she pleaded. 'Stop fooling your momma.'

Her other hand stretched out, and she pulled his mouth open with a hooked finger and pushed the rest of the custard into his mouth.

'There,' said Sandy McDougall. A smile, indescribable in its cracked hope, touched her lips. She settled back in her kitchen chair, relaxing muscle by muscle. Now it would be all right. Now he would know she still loved him and he would stop this cruel trickery.

'Good?' she murmured. 'Chocka good, Wandy? Will oo make a smile for Mommy? Be Mommy's good boy and give her a smile.'

She reached out with trembling fingers and pushed up the corners of Randy's mouth.

The chocolate fell out onto the tray – plop.

She began to scream.

3

Tony Glick woke up on Saturday morning when his wife, Marjorie, fell down in the living room.

'Margie?' he called, swinging his feet out onto the floor. 'Marge?'

And after a long, long pause, she answered, 'I'm okay, Tony.'

He sat on the edge of the bed, looking blankly down at his feet. He was bare-chested and wearing striped pajama bottoms with the drawstring dangling between his legs. The hair on his head stood up in a crow's nest. It was thick black hair, and both of his sons had inherited it. People thought he was Jewish, but that dago hair should have been a giveaway, he often thought. His grandfather's name had been Gliccucchi. When someone had told him it was easier to get along in America if you had an American name, something short and snappy, Gramps had had it legally changed to Glick, unaware that he was trading the reality of one minority for the appearance of another. Tony Glick's body was wide and dark and heavily corded with muscle. His face bore the dazed expression of a man who has been punched out leaving a bar.

He had taken a leave of absence from his job, and during the past work week he had slept a lot. It went away when you slept. There were no dreams in his sleep. He turned in at seven-thirty and got up at ten the next morning and took a nap in the afternoon from two to three. The time he had gone through between the scene he had made at Danny's funeral and this sunny Saturday morning almost a week later seemed hazy and not real at all. People kept bringing food. Casseroles, preserves, cakes, pies. Margie said she didn't know what they were going to do with it. Neither of them was hungry. On Wednesday night he had tried to make love to his wife and they had both begun to cry.

Margie didn't look good at all. Her own method of coping had been to clean the house from top to bottom, and she had cleaned with a maniacal zeal that precluded all other thought. The days resounded with the clash of cleaning buckets and the whirr of the vacuum cleaner, and the air was always redolent with the sharp smells of ammonia and Lysol. She had taken all the clothes and toys, packed neatly into cartons, to the Salvation Army and the Goodwill store. When he had come out of the bedroom on Thursday morning, all those cartons had been lined up by the front door, each neatly labeled. He had never seen anything so horrible in his life as those mute cartons. She had dragged all the rugs out into the backyard, had hung them over the clothesline, and had beaten the dust out of them unmercifully. And even in Tony's bleary state of consciousness, he had noticed how pale she had seemed since last Tuesday or Wednesday; even her lips seemed to have lost their natural color. Brown shadows had insinuated themselves beneath her eyes.

These thoughts passed through his mind in less time than it takes to tell them, and he was on the verge of tumbling back into bed when she fell down again and this time did not answer his call.

He got up and padded down to the living room and saw her lying on the floor, breathing shallowly and staring with dazed eyes at the ceiling. She had been changing the living room furniture around, and everything was pulled out of position, giving the room an odd disjointed look.

Whatever was wrong with her had advanced during the night, and her appearance was bad enough to cut through his daze like a sharp knife. She was still in her robe and it had split up to mid-thigh. Her legs were the color of marble; all the tan she had picked up that summer on their vacation had faded out of them. Her hands moved like ghosts. Her mouth gaped, as if her lungs could not get enough air, and he noticed the odd prominence of her teeth but thought nothing of it. It could have been the light.

'Margie? Honey?'

She tried to answer, couldn't, and real fear shot through him. He moved to call the doctor.

He was turning to the phone when she said, 'No . . . no.' The word was repeated between a harsh gasp for air. She had struggled up to a sitting position, and the whole sun-silent house was filled with her rasping struggle for breath.

'Pull me . . . help me . . . the sun is so hot . . .'

He went to her and picked her up, shocked by the lightness of his burden. She seemed to weigh no more than a bundle of sticks.

'. . . sofa . . .'

He laid her on it, with her back propped against the armrest. She was out of the patch of sun that fell in a square through the front window and onto the rug, and her breath seemed to come a little easier. She closed her eyes for a moment, and again he was impressed by the smooth whiteness of her teeth in contrast to her lips. He felt an urge to kiss her.

'Let me call the doctor,' he said.

'No. I'm better. The sun was . . . burning me. Made me feel faint. Better now.' A little color had come back into her cheeks.

'Are you sure?'

'Yes. I'm okay.'

'You've been working too hard, honey.'

'Yes,' she said passively. Her eyes were listless.

He ran a hand through his hair, tugging at it. 'We've got to snap out of this, Margie. We've got to. You look . . .' He paused, not wanting to hurt her.

'I look awful,' she said. 'I know. I looked at myself in the bathroom mirror before I went to bed last night, and I hardly seemed to be there. For a minute I . . .' A smile touched her lips. 'I thought I could see the tub behind me. Like there was only a little of myself left and it was . . . oh, so *pale* . . .'

'I want Dr Reardon to look at you.'

But she seemed not to hear. 'I've had the most lovely dream the last three or four nights, Tony. So real. Danny comes to me in the dream. He says, "Mommy, Mommy, I'm so glad to be home!" And he says . . . says . . .'

'What does he say?' he asked her gently.

'He says . . . that he's my baby again. My own son, at my breast again. And I give him to suck and . . . and then a feeling of sweetness with an undertone of bitterness, so much like it was before he was weaned but after he was beginning to get teeth and he would nip – oh, this must sound *awful*. Like one of those psychiatrist things.'

'No,' he said. 'No.'

He knelt beside her and she put her arms around his neck and wept weakly. Her arms were cold. 'No doctor, Tony, please. I'll rest today.'

'All right,' he said. Giving in to her made him feel uneasy.

'It's such a lovely dream, Tony,' she said, speaking against his throat. The movement of her lips, the muffled hardness of her teeth beneath them, was amazingly sensual. He was getting an erection. 'I wish I could have it again tonight.'

'Maybe you will,' he said, stroking her hair. 'Maybe you will at that.'

4

'My God, don't you look good,' Ben said.

Against the hospital world of solid whites and anemic greens, Susan Norton looked very good indeed. She was wearing a bright yellow blouse with black vertical stripes and a short blue denim skirt.

'You, too,' she said, and crossed the room to him.

He kissed her deeply, and his hand slid to the warm curve of her hip and rubbed.

'Hey,' she said, breaking the kiss. 'They kick you out for that.'

'Not me.'

'No, me.'

They looked at each other.

'I love you, Ben.'

'I love you, too.'

'If I could jump in with you right now—'

'Just a second, let me pull back the spread.'

'How would I explain it to those little candy-stripers?'

'Tell them you're giving me the bedpan.'

She shook her head, smiling, and pulled up a chair. 'A lot has happened in town, Ben.'

He sobered. 'Like what?'

She hesitated. 'I hardly know how to tell you, or what I believe myself. I'm mixed up, to say the least.'

'Well, spill it and let me sort it out.'

'What's your condition, Ben?'

'Mending. Not serious. Matt's doctor, a guy named Cody—'

'No. Your mind. How much of this Count Dracula stuff do you believe?'

'Oh. That. Matt told you everything?'

'Matt's here in the hospital. One floor up in Intensive Care.'

'*What?*' He was up on his elbows. 'What's the matter with him?'

'Heart attack.'

'*Heart* attack!'

'Dr Cody says his condition is stable. He's listed as serious, but that's mandatory for the first forty-eight hours. I was there when it happened.'

'Tell me everything you remember, Susan.'

The pleasure had gone out of his face. It was watchful, intent, fine-drawn. Lost in the white room and the white sheets and the white hospital johnny, he again struck her as a man drawn to a taut, perhaps fraying edge.

'You didn't answer my question, Ben.'

'About how I took Matt's story?'

'Yes.'

'Let me answer you by saying what you think. You think the Marsten House has buggered my brain to the point where I'm seeing bats in my own belfry, to coin a phrase. Is that a fair estimate?'

'Yes, I suppose that's it. But I never thought about it in such . . . such harsh terms.'

'I know that, Susan. Let me trace the progression of my thoughts for you, if I can. It may do me some good to sort them out. I can tell from your own face that something has knocked you back a couple of steps. Is that right?'

'Yes . . . but I don't believe, *can't*—'

'Stop a minute. That word *can't* blocks up everything. That's where I was stuck. That absolute, goddamned imperative word. *Can't*. I didn't believe Matt, Susan, because such things can't be true. But I couldn't find a hole in his story any way I looked at it. The most obvious conclusion was that he had jumped the tracks somewhere, right?'

'Yes.'

'Did he seem crazy to you?'

'No. No, but—'

'Stop.' He held up his hand. 'You're thinking *can't* thoughts, aren't you?'

'I suppose I am,' she said.

'He didn't seem crazy or irrational to me, either. And we both know that paranoid fantasies or persecution complexes just don't appear overnight. They grow over a period of time. They need careful watering, care, and feeding. Have you ever heard any talk in town about Matt having a screw loose? Ever heard Matt say that someone had the knife out for him? Has he ever been involved with any dubious causes – fluoridation causes brain cancer or Sons of the American Patriots or the NLF? Has he ever expressed an inordinate amount of interest in things such as séances or astral projection or reincarnation? Ever been arrested that you know of?'

'No,' she said. 'No to everything. But Ben . . . it hurts me to say this about Matt, even to suggest it, but some people go crazy very quietly. They go crazy inside.'

'I don't think so,' he said quietly. 'There are signs. Sometimes you can't read them before, but you can afterward. If you were on a jury, would you believe Matt's testimony about a car crash?'

'Yes . . .'

'Would you believe him if he had told you he saw a prowler kill Mike Ryerson?'

'Yes, I guess I would.'

'But not this.'

'Ben, I just can't—'

'There, you said it again.' He saw her ready to protest and held up a forestalling hand. 'I'm not arguing his case, Susan. I'm only laying out my own train of thought. Okay?'

'Okay. Go on.'

'My second thought was that somebody set him up. Someone with bad blood, or a grudge.'

'Yes, that occurred to me.'

'Matt says he has no enemies. I believe him.'

'Everybody has enemies.'

'There are degrees. Don't forget the most important thing – there's a dead man wrapped up in this mess. If someone was out to get Matt, then someone must have murdered Mike Ryerson to do it.'

'Why?'

'Because the whole song and dance doesn't make much sense without a body. And yet, according to Matt's

311

story, he met Mike purely by chance. No one led him to
Dell's last Thursday night. There was no anonymous call,
no note, no nothing. The coincidence of the meeting was
enough to rule out a setup.'

'What does that leave for rational explanations?'

'That Matt dreamed the sounds of the window going
up, the laugh, and the sucking sounds. That Mike died of
some natural but unknown causes.'

'You don't believe that, either.'

'I don't believe that he dreamed hearing the window
go up. It was open. And the outside screen was lying on the
lawn. I noticed it and Parkins Gillespie noticed it. And I
noticed something else. Matt has latch-type screens on his
house – they lock on the outside, not the inside. You can't
get them off from the inside unless you pry them off with
a screwdriver or a paint scraper. Even then it would be tough.
It would leave marks. I didn't see any marks. And here's another
thing: The ground below that window was relatively soft. If
you wanted to take off a second-floor screen, you'd need to
use a ladder, and that would leave marks. There weren't any.
That's what bothers me the most. A second-floor screen
removed from the outside and no ladder marks beneath.'

They looked at each other somberly.

He resumed. 'I was running this through my head
this morning. The more I thought about it, the better Matt's
story looked. So I took a chance. I took the *can't* away for
a while. Now, tell me what happened at Matt's last night.
If it will knock all this into a cocked hat, no one is going
to be happier than I.'

'It doesn't,' she said unhappily. 'It makes it worse. He
had just finished telling me about Mike Ryerson. He said

he heard someone upstairs. He was scared, but he went.'
She folded her hands in her lap and was now holding them
tightly, as if they might fly away. 'Nothing else happened
for a little while . . . and then Matt called out, something
like he was revoking his invitation. Then . . . well, I don't
really know how to . . .'

'Go on. Don't agonize over it.'

'I think someone – someone *else* – made a kind of
hissing noise. There was a bump, as if something had fallen.'
She looked at him bleakly. 'And then I heard a voice say:
I will see you sleep like the dead, teacher. That's word for word.
And when I went in later to get a blanket for Matt I found
this.'

She took the ring out of her blouse pocket and
dropped it into his hand.

Ben turned it over, then tilted it toward the window
to let the light pick out the initials. 'M.C.R. Mike Ryerson?'

'Mike Corey Ryerson. I dropped it and then made
myself pick it up again – I thought you or Matt would
want to see it. You keep it. I don't want it back.'

'It makes you feel—?'

'Bad. Very bad.' She raised her head defiantly. 'But all
rational thought goes against this, Ben. I'd rather believe
that Matt somehow murdered Mike Ryerson and invented
that crazy vampire story for reasons of his own. Rigged
the screen to fall off. Did a ventriloquist act in that guest
room while I was downstairs, planted Mike's ring—'

'And gave himself a heart attack to make it all seem
more real,' Ben said dryly. 'I haven't given up hope of rational
explanations, Susan. I'm hoping for one. Almost praying
for one. Monsters in the movies are sort of fun, but the

thought of them actually prowling through the night isn't fun at all. I'll even grant you that the screen could have been rigged – a simple rope sling anchored on the roof would do the trick. Let's go further. Matt is something of a scholar. I suppose there are poisons that would cause the symptoms that Mike had – maybe undetectable poisons. Of course, the idea of poison is a little hard to believe because Mike ate so little—'

'You only have Matt's word for that,' she pointed out.

'He wouldn't lie, because he would know that an examination of the victim's stomach is an important part of any autopsy. And a hypo would leave tracks. But for the sake of argument, let's say it could be done. And a man like Matt could surely take something that would fake a heart attack. But where is the motive?'

She shook her head helplessly.

'Even granting some motive we don't suspect, why would he go to such Byzantine lengths, or invent such a wild cover story? I suppose Ellery Queen could explain it somehow, but life isn't an Ellery Queen plot.'

'But this . . . this other is lunacy, Ben.'

'Yes, like Hiroshima.'

'Will you stop doing that!' she whipcracked at him suddenly. 'Don't go playing the phony intellectual! It doesn't fit you! We're talking about wives' tales, bad dreams, psychosis, anything you want to call it—'

'That's shit,' he said. 'Make connections. The world is coming down around our cars and you're sticking at a few vampires.'

''Salem's Lot is my town,' she said stubbornly. 'If something is happening there, it's real. Not philosophy.'

'I couldn't agree with you more,' he said, and touched the bandage on his head with a rueful finger. 'And your ex packs a hell of a right.'

'I'm sorry. That's a side of Floyd I never saw. I can't understand it.'

'Where is he now?'

'In the town drunk tank. Parkins Gillespie told my mom he should turn him over to the county – to Sheriff McCaslin, that is – but he thought he'd wait and see if you wanted to prefer charges.'

'Do you have any feelings in the matter?'

'None whatever,' she said steadily. 'He's out of my life.'

'I'm not going to.'

She raised her eyebrows.

'But I want to talk to him.'

'About us?'

'About why he came at me wearing an overcoat, a hat, sunglasses . . . and Playtex rubber gloves.'

'*What?*'

'Well,' he said, looking at her, 'the sun was out. It was shining on him. And I don't think he liked that.'

They looked at each other wordlessly. There seemed to be nothing else on the subject to say.

5

When Nolly brought Floyd his breakfast from the Excellent Café, Floyd was fast asleep. It seemed to Nolly that it would be a meanness to wake him up just to eat a couple of

Pauline Dickens's hard-fried eggs and five or six pieces of greasy bacon, so Nolly disposed of it himself in the office and drank the coffee, too. Pauline did make nice coffee — you could say that for her. But when he brought in Floyd's lunch and Floyd was still sleeping and still in the same position, Nolly got a little scared and set the tray on the floor and went over and banged on the bars with a spoon.

'Hey! Floyd! Wake up, I got y'dinner.'

Floyd didn't wake up, and Nolly took his key ring out of his pocket to open the drunk-tank door. He paused just before inserting the key. Last week's *Gunsmoke* had been about a hard guy who pretended to be sick until he jumped the turnkey. Nolly had never thought of Floyd Tibbits as a particularly hard guy, but he hadn't exactly rocked that Mears guy to sleep.

He paused indecisively, holding the spoon in one hand and the key ring in the other, a big man whose open-throat white shirts always sweat-stained around the armpits by noon of a warm day. He was a league bowler with an average of 151 and a weekend barhopper with a list of Portland red-light bars and motels in his wallet right behind his Lutheran Ministry pocket calendar. He was a friendly man, a natural fall guy, slow of reaction and also slow to anger. For all these not inconsiderable advantages, he was not particularly agile on his mental feet and for several minutes he stood wondering how to proceed, beating on the bars with the spoon, hailing Floyd, wishing he would move or snore or do something. He was just thinking he better call Parkins on the citizen's band and get instructions when Parkins himself said from the office doorway:

'What in hell are you doin', Nolly? Callin' the hogs?'

Nolly blushed. 'Floyd won't move, Park. I'm afraid that maybe he's . . . you know, sick.'

'Well, do you think beatin' the bars with that goddamn spoon will make him better?' Parkins stepped by him and unlocked the cell.

'Floyd?' He shook Floyd's shoulder. 'Are you all r—'

Floyd fell of the chained bunk and onto the floor.

'Goddamn,' said Nolly. 'He's dead, ain't he?'

But Parkins might not have heard. He was staring down at Floyd's uncannily reposeful face. The fact slowly dawned on Nolly that Parkins looked as if someone had scared the bejesus out of him.

'What's the matter, Park?'

'Nothin',' Parkins said. 'Just . . . let's get out of here.' And then, almost to himself, he added: 'Christ, I wish I hadn't touched him.'

Nolly looked down at Floyd's body with dawning horror.

'Wake up,' Parkins said. 'We've got to get the doctor down here.'

6

It was midafternoon when Franklin Boddin and Virgil Rathbun drove up to the slatted wooden gate at the end of the Burns Road fork, two miles beyond Harmony Hill Cemetery. They were in Franklin's 1957 Chevrolet pickup, a vehicle that had been Corinthian ivory back in the first year of Ike's second term but which was now a mixture of shit brown and primer-paint red. The back of the truck was filled with what Franklin called Crappie. Once every month or so, he and Virgil took a load of Crappie to the dump, and a great deal of said Crappie consisted of empty beer bottles, empty beer cans, empty half-kegs, empty wine bottles, and empty Popov vodka bottles.

'Closed,' Franklin Boddin said, squinting to read the sign nailed to the gate. 'Well I'll be dipped in shit.' He took a honk off the bottle of Dawson's that had been resting comfortably against the bulge of his crotch and wiped his mouth with his arm. 'This is Saturday, ain't it?'

'Sure is,' Virgil Rathbun said. Virgil had no idea if it was Saturday or Tuesday. He was so drunk he wasn't even sure what month it was.

'Dump ain't closed on Saturday, is it?' Franklin asked. There was only one sign, but he was seeing three. He squinted again. All three signs said 'Closed.' The paint was barn-red and had undoubtedly come out of the can of paint that rested inside the door of Dud Rogers's caretaker shack.

'Never was closed on Saturday,' Virgil said. He swung his bottle of beer toward his face, missed his mouth, and poured a blurt of beer on his left shoulder. 'God, that hits the spot.'

'Closed,' Franklin said, with mounting irritation. 'That son of a whore is off on a toot, that's what. I'll close *him.*' He threw the truck into first gear and popped the clutch. Beer foamed out of the bottle between his legs and ran over his pants.

'Wind her, Franklin!' Virgil cried, and let out a massive belch as the pickup crashed through the gate, knocking it onto the can-littered verge of the road. Franklin shifted into second and shot up the rutted, chuck-holed road. The truck bounced madly on its worn springs. Bottles fell off the back end and smashed. Seagulls took to the air in screaming, circling waves.

A quarter of a mile beyond the gate, the Burns Road fork (now known as the Dump Road) ended in a widening clearing that was the dump. The close-pressing alders and maples gave way to reveal a great flat area of raw earth which had been scored and runneled by the constant use of the old Case bulldozer which was now parked by Dud's shack. Beyond this flat area was the gravel pit where current dumping went on. The trash and garbage, glitter-shot with bottles and aluminum cans, stretched away in gigantic dunes.

'Goddamn no-account hunchbacked pisswah, looks like he ain't plowed nor burned all the week long,' Franklin said. He jammed both feet on the brake pedal, which sank all the way to the floor with a mechanical scream. After a while the truck stopped. 'He's laid up with a case, that's what.'

'I never knew Dud to drink much,' Virgil said, tossing his empty out the window and pulling another from the brown bag on the floor. He opened it on the door latch, and the beer, crazied up from the bumps, bubbled out over his hand.

'All them hunchbacks do,' Franklin said wisely. He spat out the window, discovered it was closed, and swiped his shirtsleeve across the scratched and cloudy glass. 'We'll go see him. Might be somethin' in it.'

He backed the truck around in a huge, wandering circle and pulled up with the tailgate hanging over the latest accumulation of the Lot's accumulated throwaway. He switched off the ignition, and silence pressed in on them suddenly. Except for the restless calling of the gulls, it was complete.

'Ain't it *quiet*,' Virgil muttered.

They got out of the truck and went around to the back. Franklin unhooked the S-bolts that held the tailgate and let it drop with a crash. The gulls that had been feeding at the far end of the dump rose in a cloud, squalling and scolding.

The two of them climbed up without a word and began heaving the Crappie off the end. Green plastic bags spun through the clear air and smashed open as they hit. It was an old job for them. They were a part of the town that few tourists ever saw (or cared to) – firstly, because the town ignored them by tacit agreement, and secondly, because they had developed their own protective coloration. If you met Franklin's pickup on the road, you forgot it the instant it was gone from your rearview mirror. If you happened to see their shack with its tin chimney sending a pencil line of smoke into the white November sky, you overlooked it. If you met Virgil coming out of the Cumberland green-front with a bottle of welfare vodka in a brown bag, you said hi and then couldn't quite remember who it was you had spoken to; the face was familiar but the name just slipped your mind. Franklin's brother was Derek Boddin, father of Richie (lately deposed king of Stanley Street Elementary School), and Derek had nearly forgotten that Franklin was still alive and in town. He had progressed beyond black sheepdom; he was totally gray.

Now, with the truck empty, Franklin kicked out a last can – *clink!* – and hitched up his green work pants. 'Let's go see Dud,' he said.

They climbed down from the truck and Virgil tripped over one of his own rawhide lacings and sat down hard.

'Christ, they don't make these things half-right,' he muttered obscurely.

They walked across to Dud's tarpaper shack. The door was closed.

'Dud!' Franklin bawled. 'Hey, Dud Rogers!' He thumped the door once, and the whole shack trembled. The small hook-and-eye lock on the inside of the door snapped off, and the door tottered open. The shack was empty but filled with a sickish-sweet odor that made them look at each other and grimace — and they were barroom veterans of a great many fungoid smells. It reminded Franklin fleetingly of pickles that had lain in a dark crock for many years, until the fluid seeping out of them had turned white.

'Son of a whore,' Virgil said. 'Worse than gangrene.'

Yet the shack was astringently neat. Dud's extra shirt was hung on a hook over the bed, the splintery kitchen chair was pushed up to the table, and the cot was made up Army-style. The can of red paint, with fresh drips down the sides, was placed on a fold of newspaper behind the door.

'I'm about to puke if we don't get out of here,' Virgil said. His face had gone a whitish-green.

Franklin, who felt no better, backed out and shut the door.

They surveyed the dump, which was as deserted and sterile as the mountains of the moon.

'He ain't here,' Franklin said. 'He's back in the woods someplace, laying up snookered.'

'Frank?'

'What,' Franklin said shortly. He was out of temper.

'That door was latched on the inside. If he ain't there, how did he get out?'

Startled, Franklin turned around and regarded the shack. *Through the window,* he started to say, and then didn't. The window was nothing but a square cut into the tarpaper and buttoned up with all-weather plastic. The window wasn't large enough for Dud to squirm through, not with the hump on his back.

'Never mind,' Franklin said gruffly. 'If he don't want to share, fuck him. Let's get out of here.'

They walked back to the truck, and Franklin felt something seeping through the protective membrane of drunkenness – something he would not remember later, or want to: a creeping feeling; a feeling that something here had gone terribly awry. It was as if the dump had gained a heartbeat and that beat was slow yet full of terrible vitality. He suddenly wanted to go away very quickly.

'I don't see any rats,' Virgil said suddenly.

And there were none to be seen; only the gulls. Franklin tried to remember a time when he had brought the Crappie to the dump and seen no rats. He couldn't. And he didn't like that, either.

'He must have put out poison bait, huh, Frank?'

'Come on, let's go,' Franklin said. 'Let's get the hell out of here.'

7

After supper, they let Ben go up and see Matt Burke. It was a short visit; Matt was sleeping. The oxygen tent had been taken away, however, and the head nurse told Ben that Matt would almost certainly be awake tomorrow morning and able to see visitors for a short time.

Ben thought his face looked drawn and cruelly aged, for the first time an old man's face. Lying still, with the loosened flesh of his neck rising out of the hospital johnny, he seemed vulnerable and defenseless. If it's all true, Ben thought, these people are doing you no favors, Matt. If it's all true, then we're in the citadel of unbelief, where nightmares are dispatched with Lysol and scalpels and chemotherapy rather than with stakes and Bibles and wild mountain thyme. They're happy with their life support units and hypos and enema bags filled with barium solution. If the column of truth has a hole in it, they neither know nor care.

He walked to the head of the bed and turned Matt's head with gentle fingers. There were no marks on the skin of his neck; the flesh was blameless.

He hesitated a moment longer, then went to the closet and opened it. Matt's clothes hung there, and hooked over the closet door's inside knob was the crucifix he had been wearing when Susan visited him. It hung from a filigreed chain that gleamed softly in the room's subdued light.

Ben took it back to the bed and put it around Matt's neck.

'Here, what are you doing?'

A nurse had come in with a pitcher of water and a bedpan with a towel spread decorously over the opening.

'I'm putting his cross around his neck,' Ben said.

'Is he a Catholic?'

'He is now,' Ben said somberly.

8

Night had fallen when a soft rap came at the kitchen door of the Sawyer house on the Deep Cut Road. Bonnie Sawyer, with a small smile on her lips, went to answer it. She was wearing a short ruffled apron tied at the waist, high heels, and nothing else.

When she opened the door, Corey Bryant's eyes widened and his mouth dropped open. 'Buh,' he said. 'Buh . . . Buh . . . Bonnie?'

'What's the matter, Corey?' She put a hand on the doorjamb with light deliberation, pulling her bare breasts up to their sauciest angle. At the same time she crossed her feet demurely, modeling her legs for him.

'Jeez, Bonnie, what if it had been—'

'The man from the telephone company?' she asked, and giggled. She took one of his hands and placed it on the firm flesh of her right breast. 'Want to read my meter?'

With a grunt that held a note of desperation (the drowning man going down for the third time, clutching a mammary instead of a straw), he pulled her to him. His hands cupped her buttocks, and the starched apron crackled briskly between them.

'Oh my,' she said, wiggling against him. 'Are you going to test my receiver, Mr Telephone Man? I've been waiting for an important call all day—'

He picked her up and kicked the door shut behind him. She did not need to direct him to the bedroom. He knew his way.

'You're sure he's not going to be home?' he asked.

Her eyes gleamed in the darkness. 'Why, who can you

mean, Mr Telephone Man? Not my handsome hubby . . . he's in Burlington, Vermont.'

He put her down on the bed crossways, with her legs dangling off the side.

'Turn on the light,' she said, her voice suddenly slow and heavy. 'I want to see what you're doing.'

He turned on the bedside lamp and looked down at her. The apron had been pulled away to one side. Her eyes were heavy-lidded and warm, the pupils large and brilliant.

'Take that thing off,' he said, gesturing.

'You take it off,' she said. 'You can figure out the knots, Mr Telephone Man.'

He bent to do it. She always made him feel like a dry-mouth kid stepping up to the plate for the first time, and his hands always trembled when they got near her, as if her very flesh was transmitting a strong current into the air all around her. She never left his mind completely anymore. She was lodged in there like a sore inside the cheek which the tongue keeps poking and testing. She even cavorted through his dreams, golden-skinned, blackly exciting. Her invention knew no bounds.

'No, on your knees,' she said. 'Get on your knees for me.'

He dropped clumsily onto his knees and crawled toward her, reaching for the apron ties. She put one high-heeled foot on each shoulder. He bent to kiss the inside of her thigh, the flesh firm and slightly warm under his lips.

'That's right, Corey, that's just right, keep going up, keep—'

'Well, this is cute, ain't it?'

Bonnie Sawyer screamed.

Corey Bryant looked up, blinking and confused.

Reggie Sawyer was leaning in the bedroom doorway. He was holding a shotgun cradled loosely over his forearm, barrels pointed at the floor.

Corey felt a warm gush as his bladder let go.

'So it's true,' Reggie marveled. He stepped into the room. He was smiling. 'How about that? I owe that tosspot Mickey Sylvester a case of Budweiser. Goddamn.'

Bonnie found her voice first.

'Reggie, listen. It isn't what you think. He broke in, he was like a crazy-man, he, he was—'

'Shut up, cunt.' He was still smiling. It was a gentle smile. He was quite big. He was wearing the same steel-colored suit he had been wearing when she had kissed him good-by two hours before.

'Listen,' Corey said weakly. His mouth felt full of loose spit. 'Please. Please don't kill me. Not even if I deserve it. You don't want to go to jail. Not over this. Beat me up, I got that coming, but please don't—'

'Get up off your knees, Perry Mason,' Reggie Sawyer said, still smiling his gentle smile. 'Your fly's unzipped.'

'Listen, Mr Sawyer—'

'Oh, call me Reggie,' Reggie said, smiling gently. 'We're almost best buddies. I've even been getting your sloppy seconds, isn't that right?'

'Reggie, this isn't what you think, he raped me—'

Reggie looked at her and his smile was gentle and benign. 'If you say another word, I'm going to jam this up inside you and let you have some special airmail.'

Bonnie began to moan. Her face had gone the color of unflavored yogurt.

'Mr Sawyer . . . Reggie . . .'

'Your name's Bryant, ain't it? Your daddy's Pete Bryant, ain't he?'

Corey's head bobbed madly in agreement. 'Yeah, that's right. That's just right. Listen—'

'I used to sell him number two fuel oil when I was driving for Jim Webber,' Reggie said, smiling with gentle reminiscence. 'That was four or five years before I met this high-box bitch here. Your daddy know you're here?'

'No, sir, it'd break his heart. You can beat me up, I got that coming, but if you kill me my daddy's find out and I bet it'd kill him dead as shit and then you'd be responsible for two—'

'No, I bet he don't know. Come on out in the living room a minute. We got to talk this over. Come on.' He smiled gently at Corey to show him that he meant him no harm and then his eyes flicked to Bonnie, who was staring at him with bulging eyes. 'You stay right there, puss, or you ain't never going to know how *Secret Storm* comes out. Come on, Bryant.' He gestured with the shotgun.

Corey walked out into the living room ahead of Reggie, staggering a little. His legs were rubber. A patch between his shoulder blades began to itch insanely. That's where he's going to put it, he thought, right between the shoulder blades. I wonder if I'll live long enough to see my guts hit the wall—

'Turn around,' Reggie said.

Corey turned around. He was beginning to blubber. He didn't want to blubber, but he couldn't seem to help it. He supposed it didn't matter if he blubbered or not. He had already wet himself.

The shotgun was no longer dangling casually over Reggie's forearm. The double barrels were pointing directly at Corey's face. The twin bores seemed to swell and yawn until they were bottomless wells.

'You know what you been doin'?' Reggie asked. The smile was gone. His face was very grave.

Corey didn't answer. It was a stupid question. He did keep on blubbering, however.

'You slept with another guy's wife, Corey. That your name?'

Corey nodded, tears streaming down his cheeks.

'You know what happens to guys like that if they get caught?'

Corey nodded.

'Grab the barrel of this shotgun, Corey. Very easy. It's got a five-pound pull and I got about three on it now. So pretend . . . oh, pretend you're grabbing my wife's tit.'

Corey reached out one shaking hand and placed it on the barrel of the shotgun. The metal was cool against his flushed palm. A long, agonized groan came out of his throat. Nothing else was left. Pleading was done.

'Put it in your mouth, Corey. Both barrels. Yes, that's right. Easy! . . . that's okay. Yes, your mouth's big enough. Slip it right in there. You know all about slipping it in, don't you?'

Corey's jaws were open to their widest accommodation. The barrels of the shotgun were pushed back nearly to his palate, and his terrified stomach was trying to retch. The steel was oily against his teeth.

'Close your eyes, Corey.'

Corey only stared at him, his swimming eyes as big as tea saucers.

Reggie smiled his gentle smile again. 'Close those baby blue eyes, Corey.'

Corey closed them.

His sphincter let go. He was only dimly aware of it.

Reggie pulled both triggers. The hammers fell on empty chambers with a double *click-click*.

Corey fell onto the floor in a dead faint.

Reggie looked down at him for a moment, smiling gently, and then reversed the shotgun so the butt end was up. He turned to the bedroom.

'Here I come, Bonnie. Ready or not.'

Bonnie Sawyer began to scream.

9

Corey Bryant was stumbling up the Deep Cut Road toward where he had left his phone truck parked. He stank. His eyes were bloodshot and glassy. There was a large bump on the back of his head where he had struck it on the floor when he fainted. His boots made dragging, scuffing sounds on the soft shoulder. He tried to think about the scuffing sounds and nothing else, most notably about the sudden and utter ruin of his life. It was quarter past eight.

Reggie Sawyer had still been smiling gently when he ushered Corey out the kitchen door. Bonnie's steady, racking sobs had come from the bedroom, counterpointing his words. 'You go on up the road like a good boy, now. Get in your truck and go back to town. There's a bus that comes in from Lewiston for Boston at quarter to ten. From Boston you can get a bus to anywhere in the country. That bus stops at Spencer's. You be on it. Because if I ever see you again, I'm going to kill you. She'll be all right now. She's broke in now. She's gonna have to wear pants and long-sleeve blouses for a couple of weeks, but I didn't mark her face. You just want to get out of 'salem's Lot before you clean yourself up and start thinking you are a man again.'

And now here he was, walking up this road, about to do just what Reggie Sawyer said. He could go south from Boston . . . somewhere. He had a little over a thousand dollars saved in the bank. His mother had always said he was a very saving soul. He could wire for the money, live on it until he could get a job and begin the years-long job of forgetting this night — the taste of the gun barrel, the smell of his own shit satcheled in his trousers.

'Hello, Mr Bryant.'

Corey gave a stifled scream and stared wildly into the dark, at first seeing nothing. The wind was moving in the trees, making shadows jump and dance across the road. Suddenly his eyes made out a more solid shadow, standing by the stone wall that ran between the road and Carl Smith's back pasture. The shadow had a manlike form, but there was something . . . something . . .

'Who are you?'

'A friend who sees much, Mr Bryant.'

The form shifted and came from the shadows. In the faint light, Corey saw a middle-aged man with a black mustache and deep, bright eyes.

'You've been ill used, Mr Bryant.'

'How do you know my business?'

'I know a great deal. It's my business to know. Smoke?'

'Thanks.' He took the offered cigarette gratefully. He put it between his lips. The stranger struck a light, and in the glow of the wooden match he saw that the stranger's cheekbones were high and Slavic, his forehead pale and bony, his dark hair swept straight back. Then the light was gone and Corey was dragging harsh smoke into his lungs. It was a dago cigarette, but any cigarette was better than none. He began to feel a little calmer.

'Who are you?' he asked again.

The stranger laughed, a startlingly rich and full-bodied sound that drifted off on the slight breeze like the smoke of Corey's cigarette.

'Names!' he said. 'Oh, the American insistence on names! Let me sell you an auto because I am Bill Smith! Eat at this one! Watch that one on television! My name is Barlow, if that eases you.' And he burst into laughter again, his eyes twinkling and shining. Corey felt a smile creep onto his own lips and could scarcely believe it. His troubles seemed distant, unimportant, in comparison to the derisive good humor in those dark eyes.

'You're a foreigner, aren't you?' Corey asked.

'I am from many lands; but to me this country . . . this town . . . seems full of foreigners. You see? Eh? Eh?' He burst into that full-throated crow of laughter again, and this time Corey found himself joining in. The laughter escaped his throat under full pressure, rising a bit with delayed hysteria.

'Foreigners, yes,' he resumed, 'but beautiful, enticing foreigners, bursting with vitality, full-blooded and full of life. Do you know how beautiful the people of your country and your town are, Mr Bryant?'

Corey only chuckled, slightly embarrassed. He did

not look away from the stranger's face, however. It held him rapt.

'They have never known hunger or want, the people of this country. It has been two generations since they knew anything close to it, and even then it was like a voice in a distant room. They think they have known sadness, but their sadness is that of a child who has spilled his ice cream on the grass at a birthday party. There is no . . . how is the English? . . . attenuation in them. They spill each other's blood with great vigor. Do you believe it? Do you see?'

'Yes,' Corey said. Looking into the stranger's eyes, he could see a great many things, all of them wonderful.

'The country is an amazing paradox. In other lands, when a man eats to his fullest day after day, that man becomes fat . . . sleepy . . . piggish. But in this land . . . it seems the more you have the more aggressive you become. You see? Like Mr Sawyer. With so much; yet he begrudges you a few crumbs from his table. Also like a child at a birthday party, who will push away another baby even though he himself can eat no more. Is it not so?'

'Yes,' Corey said. Barlow's eyes were so large, and so understanding. It was all a matter of—

'It is all a matter of perspective, is it not?'

'Yes!' Corey exclaimed. The man had put his finger on the right, the exact, the perfect, word. The cigarette dropped unnoticed from his fingers and lay smoldering on the road.

'I might have bypassed such a rustic community as this,' the stranger said reflectively. 'I might have gone to one of your great and teeming cities. Bah!' He drew himself up suddenly, and his eyes flashed. 'What do I know of cities? I should be run over by a hansom crossing the street! I should choke on nasty air! I should come in contact with sleek, stupid dilettantes whose concerns are . . . what do you say? inimical? . . . yes, inimical to me. How should a poor rustic like myself deal with the hollow sophistication of a great city . . . even an American city? No! And no and no! I *spit* on your cities!'

'Oh yes!' Corey whispered.

'So I have come here, to a town which was first told of to me by a most brilliant man, a former townsman himself, now lamentably deceased. The folk here are still rich and full-blooded, folk who are stuffed with the aggression and darkness so necessary to . . . there is no English for it. *Pokol; vurderlak; eyalik.* Do you follow?'

'Yes,' Corey whispered.

'The people have not cut off the vitality which flows from their mother, the earth, with a shell of concrete and cement. Their hands are plunged into the very waters of life. They have ripped the life from the earth, whole and beating! Is it not true?'

'Yes!'

The stranger chuckled kindly and put a hand on Corey's shoulder. 'You are a good boy. A fine, strong boy. I don't think you want to leave this so-perfect town, do you?'

'No . . .' Corey whispered, but he was suddenly doubtful. Fear was returning. But surely it was unimportant. This man would allow no harm to come to him.

'And so you shall not. Ever again.'

Corey stood trembling, rooted to the spot, as Barlow's head inclined toward him.

'And you shall yet have your vengeance on those who would fill themselves while others want.'

Corey Bryant sank into a great forgetful river, and that river was time, and its waters were red.

10

It was nine o'clock and the Saturday night movie was coming on the hospital TV bolted to the wall when the phone beside Ben's bed rang. It was Susan, and her voice was barely under control.

'Ben, Floyd Tibbits is dead. He died in his cell some time last night. Dr Cody says acute anemia — but I *went* with Floyd! He had high blood pressure. That's why the Army wouldn't take him!'

'Slow down,' Ben said, sitting up.

'There's more. A family named McDougall out in the Bend. A little ten-month-old baby died out there. They took Mrs McDougall away in restraints.'

'Have you heard how the baby died?'

'My mother said Mrs Evans came over when she heard Sandra McDougall screaming, and Mrs Evans called old Dr Plowman. Plowman didn't say anything, but Mrs Evans told my mother that she couldn't see a thing wrong with the baby . . . except it was dead.'

'And both Matt and I, the crackpots, just happen to be out of town and out of action,' Ben said, more to himself than to Susan. 'Almost as if it were planned.'

'There's more.'

'What?'

'Carl Foreman is missing. And so is the body of Mike Ryerson.'

'I think that's it,' he heard himself saying. 'That has to be it. I'm getting out of here tomorrow.'

'Will they let you go so soon?'

'They aren't going to have anything to say about it.' He spoke the words absently; his mind had already moved on to another subject. 'Have you got a crucifix?'

'Me?' She sounded startled and a little amused. 'Gosh, no.'

'I'm not joking with you, Susan — I was never more serious. Is there anyplace where you can get one at this hour?'

'Well, there's Marie Boddin. I could walk—'

'No. Stay off the streets. Stay in the house. Make one yourself, even if it only means gluing two sticks together. Leave it by your bed.'

'Ben, I still don't believe this. A maniac, maybe, someone who *thinks* he's a vampire, but—'

'Believe what you want, but make the cross.'

'But—'

'Will you do it? Even if it only means humoring me?' Reluctantly: 'Yes, Ben.'

'Can you come to the hospital tomorrow around nine?'

'Yes.'

'Okay. We'll go upstairs and fill in Matt together. Then you and I are going to talk to Dr James Cody.'

She said, 'He's going to think you're crazy, Ben. Don't you know that?'

'I suppose I do. But it all seems more real after dark, doesn't it?'

'Yes,' she said softly. 'God, yes.'

For no reason at all he thought of Miranda and Miranda's dying: the motorcycle hitting the wet patch, going into a skid, the sound of her scream, his own brute panic, and the side of the truck growing and growing as they approached it broadside.

'Susan?'

'Yes.'

'Take good care of yourself. Please.'

After she hung up, he put the phone back in the cradle and stared at the TV, barely seeing the Doris Day–Rock Hudson comedy that had begun to unreel up there. He felt naked, exposed. He had no cross himself. His eyes strayed to the windows, which showed only blackness. The old, childlike terror of the dark began to creep over him and he looked at the television where Doris Day was giving a shaggy dog a bubble bath and was afraid.

11

The county morgue in Portland is a cold and antiseptic room done entirely in green tile. The floors and walls are a uniform medium green, and the ceiling is a lighter green. The walls are lined with square doors which look like large bus-terminal coin lockers. Long parallel fluorescent tubes shed a chilly neutral light over all of this. The decor is hardly inspired, but none of the clientele have ever been known to complain.

At quarter to ten on this Saturday night, two attendants were wheeling in the sheet-covered body of a young homosexual who had been shot in a downtown bar. It was the first stiff they had received that night; the highway fatals usually came in between 1:00 and 3:00 AM.

Buddy Bascomb was in the middle of a Frenchman joke that had to do with vaginal deodorant spray when he broke off in midsentence and stared down the line of locker doors M–Z. Two of them were standing open.

He and Bob Greenberg left the new arrival and hurried down quickly. Buddy glanced at the tag on the first door he came to while Bob went down to the next.

TIBBITS, FLOYD MARTIN
Sex: M
Admitted: 10/4/75
Autops. sched.: 10/5/75
Signator: J.M. Cody, M.D.

He yanked the handle set inside the door, and the slab rolled out on silent casters.

Empty.

'Hey!' Greenberg yelled up to him. 'This fucking thing is empty! Whose idea of a joke—'

'I was on the desk all the time,' Buddy said. 'No one went by me. I'd swear to it. It must have happened on Carty's shift. What's the name on that one?'

'McDougall, Randall Fratus. What does this abbreviation *inf.* mean?'

'Infant,' Buddy said dully. 'Jesus Christ, I think we're in trouble.'

12

Something had awakened him.

He lay still in the ticking dark, looking at the ceiling. A noise. Some noise. But the house was silent.

There it was again. Scratching.

Mark Petrie turned over in bed and looked through the window and Danny Glick was staring in at him through the glass, his skin gravepale, his eyes reddish and feral. Some dark substance was smeared about his lips and chin, and when he saw Mark looking at him, he smiled and showed teeth grown hideously long and sharp.

'Let me in,' the voice whispered, and Mark was not sure if the words had crossed dark air or were only in his mind.

He became aware that he was frightened – his body had known before his mind. He had never been so frightened, not even when he got tired swimming back from the float at Popham Beach and thought he was going to drown. His mind, still that of a child in a thousand ways, made an accurate judgment of his position in seconds. He was in peril of more than his life.

'Let me in, Mark. I want to play with you.'

There was nothing for that hideous entity outside the window to hold on to; his room was on the second floor and there was no ledge. Yet somehow it hung suspended in space . . . or perhaps it was clinging to the outside shingles like some dark insect.

'Mark . . . I finally came, Mark. Please . . .'

Of course. You have to invite them inside. He knew that from his monster magazines, the ones his mother was afraid might damage or warp him in some way.

He got out of bed and almost fell down. It was only then that he realized fright was too mild a word for this. Even terror did not express what he felt. The pallid face outside the window tried to smile, but it had lain in darkness too long to remember precisely how. What Mark saw was a twitching grimace – a bloody mask of tragedy.

Yet if you looked in the eyes, it wasn't so bad. If you looked in the eyes, you weren't so afraid anymore and you saw that all you had to do was open the window and say, 'C'mon in, Danny,' and then you wouldn't be afraid at all because you'd be at one with Danny and all of them and at one with *him*. You'd be—

No! That's how they get you!

He dragged his eyes away, and it took all of his willpower to do it.

'Mark, let me in! I command it! *He* commands it!'

Mark began to walk toward the window again. There was no help for it. There was no possible way to deny that voice. As he drew closer to the glass, the evil little boy's face on the other side began to twitch and grimace with eagerness. Fingernails, black with earth, scratched across the windowpane.

Think of something. Quick! Quick!

'The rain,' he whispered hoarsely. 'The rain in Spain falls mainly on the plain. In vain he thrusts his fists against the posts and still insists he sees the ghosts.'

Danny Glick hissed at him.

'Mark! Open the window!'

'Betty Bitter bought some butter—'

'The window, Mark, *he* commands it!'

'—but, says Betty, this butter's bitter.'

He was weakening. That whispering voice was seeing through his barricade, and the command was imperative. Mark's eyes fell on his desk, littered with his model monsters, now so bland and foolish—

His eyes fixed abruptly on part of the display, and widened slightly.

The plastic ghoul was walking through a plastic grave-yard and one of the monuments was in the shape of a cross.

With no pause for thought or consideration (both would have come to an adult – his father, for instance – and both would have undone him), Mark swept up the cross, curled it into a tight fist, and said loudly: 'Come on in, then.'

The face became suffused with an expression of vulpine triumph. The window slid up and Danny stepped in and took two paces forward. The exhalation from that opening mouth was fetid, beyond description: a smell of charnel pits. Cold, fish-white hands descended on Mark's shoulders. The head cocked, doglike, the upper lip curled away from those shining canines.

Mark brought the plastic cross around in a vicious swipe and laid it against Danny Glick's cheek.

His scream was horrible, unearthly . . . and silent. It echoed only in the corridors of his brain and the cham-bers of his soul. The smile of triumph on the Glick-thing's mouth became a yawning grimace of agony. Smoke spurted from the pallid flesh, and for just a moment, before the creature twisted away and half dived, half fell out the window, Mark felt the flesh yield like smoke.

And then it was over, as if it had never happened.

But for a moment the cross shone with a fierce light, as if an inner wire had been ignited. Then it dwindled away, leaving only a blue afterimage in front of his eyes.

Through the grating in the floor, he heard the distinctive click of the lamp in his parents' bedroom and his father's voice: 'What in hell was that?'

13

His bedroom door opened two minutes later, but that was still time enough to set things to rights.

'Son?' Henry Petric asked softly. 'Are you awake?'

'I guess so,' Mark answered sleepily.

'Did you have a bad dream?'

'I . . . think so. I don't remember.'

'You called out in your sleep.'

'Sorry.'

'No, don't be sorry.' He hesitated and then spoke from earlier memories of his son, a small child in a blue blanket-suit that had been much more trouble but infinitely more explicable: 'Do you want a drink of water?'

'No thanks, Dad.'

Henry Petrie surveyed the room briefly, unable to understand the trembling feeling of dread he had wakened with, and which lingered still — a feeling of disaster averted by cold inches. Yes, everything seemed all right. The window was shut. Nothing was knocked over.

'Mark, is anything wrong?'

'No, Dad.'

'Well . . . g'night, then.'

'Night.'

The door shut softly and his father's slippered feet descended the stairs. Mark let himself go limp with relief and delayed reaction. An adult might have had hysterics at this point, as a slightly younger or older child might also have done. But Mark felt the terror slip from him in almost imperceptible degrees, and the sensation reminded him of letting the wind dry you after you had been swimming on a cool day. And as the terror left, drowsiness began to come in its place.

Before drifting away entirely, he found himself reflecting – not for the first time – on the peculiarity of adults. They took laxatives, liquor, or sleeping pills to drive away their terrors so that sleep would come, and their terrors were so tame and domestic the job, the money, what the teacher will think if I can't get Jennie nicer clothes, does my wife still love me, who are my friends. They were pallid compared to the fears every child lies cheek and jowl with in his dark bed, with no one to confess to in hope of perfect understanding but another child. There is no group therapy or psychiatry or community social services for the child who must cope with the thing under the bed or in the cellar every night, the thing which leers and capers and threatens just beyond the point where vision will reach. The same lonely battle must be fought night after night and the only cure is the eventual ossification of the imaginary faculties, and this is called adulthood.

In some shorter, simpler mental shorthand, these thoughts passed through his brain. The night before, Matt Burke had faced such a dark thing and had been stricken by a heart seizure brought on by fright; tonight Mark Petrie had faced one, and ten minutes later lay in the lap of sleep, the plastic cross still grasped loosely in his right hand like a child's rattle. Such is the difference between men and boys.

CHAPTER ELEVEN
BEN (IV)

It was ten past nine on Sunday morning – a bright, sun-washed Sunday morning – and Ben was beginning to get seriously worried about Susan when the phone by his bed rang. He snatched it up.

'Where are you?'

'Relax. I'm upstairs with Matt Burke. Who requests the pleasure of your company as soon as you're able.'

'Why didn't you come—'

'I looked in on your earlier. You were sleeping like a lamb.'

'They give you knockout stuff in the night so they can steal different organs for mysterious billionaire patients,' he said. 'How's Matt?'

'Come up and see for yourself,' she said, and before she could do more than hang up, he was getting into his robe.

2

Matt looked much better, rejuvenated, almost. Susan was sitting by his bed in a bright blue dress, and Matt raised a hand in salute when Ben walked in. 'Drag up a rock.'

Ben pulled over one of the hideously uncomfortable hospital chairs and sat down. 'How you feeling?'

'A lot better. Weak, but better. They took the I.V. out of my arm last night and gave me a poached egg for breakfast this morning. Gag. Previews of the old folks home.'

Ben kissed Susan lightly and saw a strained kind of composure on her face, as if everything was being held together by fine wire.

'Is there anything new since you called last night?'

'Nothing I've heard. But I left the house around seven and the Lot wakes up a little later on Sunday.'

Ben shifted his gaze to Matt. 'Are you up to talking this thing over?'

'Yes, I think so,' he said, and shifted slightly. The gold cross Ben had hung around his neck flashed prominently. 'By the way, thank you for this. It's a great comfort, even though I bought it on the remaindered shelf at Woolworth's Friday afternoon.'

'What's your condition?'

'"Stabilized" is the fulsome term young Dr Cody used when he examined me late yesterday afternoon. According to the EKG he took, it was strictly a minor-league heart attack . . . no clot formation.' He harrumphed. 'Should hope for his sake it wasn't. Coming just a week after the checkup he gave me, I'd sue his sheepskin off the wall for breach of promise.' He broke off and looked levelly at Ben. 'He said he'd seen such cases brought on by massive shock. I kept my lip zipped. Did I do right?'

'Just right. But things have developed. Susan and I are going to see Cody today and spill everything. If he doesn't sign the committal papers on me right away, we'll send him to you.'

'I'll give him an earful,' Matt said balefully. 'Snot-nosed little son of a bitch won't let me have my pipe.'

'Has Susan told you what's been happening in Jerusalem's Lot since Friday night?'

'No. She said she wanted to wait until we were all together.'

'Before she does, will you tell me exactly what happened at your house?'

Matt's face darkened, and for a moment the mask of convalescence fluttered. Ben glimpsed the old man he had seen sleeping the day before.

'If you're not up to it—'

'No, of course I am. I must be, if half of what I suspect is true.' He smiled bitterly. 'I've always considered myself a bit of a free thinker, not easily shocked. But it's amazing how hard the mind can try to block out some-thing it doesn't like or finds threatening. Like the magic slates we had as boys. If you didn't like what you had drawn, you had only to pull the top sheet up and it would disappear.'

'But the line stayed on the black stuff underneath forever,' Susan said.

'Yes.' He smiled at her. 'A lovely metaphor for the interaction of the conscious and unconscious mind. A pity Freud was stuck with onions. But we wander.' He looked at Ben. 'You've heard this once from Susan?'

'Yes, but—'

'Of course. I only wanted to be sure I could dispense with the background.'

He told the story in a nearly flat, inflectionless voice, pausing only when a nurse entered on whisper-soft crepe soles to ask him if he would like a glass of ginger ale. Matt told her it would be wonderful to have a ginger ale, and he sucked on the flexible straw at intervals as he finished. Ben noticed that when he got to the part about Mike going out the window backward, the ice cubes clinked slightly in the glass as he held it. Yet his voice did not waver; it retained the same even, slightly inflected tones that he undoubtedly used in his classes. Ben thought, not for the first time, that he was an admirable man.

There was a brief pause when he had finished, and Matt broke it himself.

'And so,' he said. 'You who have seen nothing with your own eyes, what think you of this hearsay?'

'We talked that over for quite a while yesterday,' Susan said. 'I'll let Ben tell you.'

A little shy, Ben advanced each of the reasonable explanations and then knocked it down. When he mentioned the screen that fastened on the outside, the soft ground, the lack of ladder feet impressions, Matt applauded.

'Bravo! A sleuth!'

Matt looked at Susan. 'And you, Miss Norton, who used to write such well-organized themes with paragraphs like building blocks and topic sentences for mortar? What do you think?'

She looked down at her hands, which were folding a pleat of her dress, and then back up at him. 'Ben lectured me on the linguistic meanings of *can't* yesterday, so I won't use that word. But it's very difficult for me to believe that vampires are stalking 'salem's Lot, Mr Burke.'

'If it can be arranged so that secrecy will not be breached, I will take a polygraph test,' he said softly.

She colored a little. 'No, no – don't misunderstand me, please. I'm convinced that something is going on in town. Something . . . horrible. But . . . this . . .'

He put his hand out and covered hers with it. 'I understand that, Susan. But will you do something for me?'

'If I can.'

'Let us . . . the three of us . . . proceed on the premise that all of this is real. Let us keep that premise before us as fact until – and *only* until – it can be disproved. The scientific method, you see? Ben and I have already discussed ways and means of putting the premise to the test. And no one hopes more than I that it can be disproved.'

'But you don't think it will be, do you?'

'No,' he said softly. 'After a long conversation with myself, I've reached my decision. I believe what I saw.'

'Let's put questions of belief and unbelief behind us for the minute,' Ben said. 'Right now they're moot.'

'Agreed,' Matt said. 'What are your ideas about procedure?'

'Well,' Ben said, 'I'd like to appoint you Researcher General. With your background, you're uniquely well fitted for the job. And you're off your feet.'

Matt's eyes gleamed as they had over Cody's perfidy in declaring his pipe off-limits. 'I'll have Loretta Starcher on the phone when the library opens. She'll have to bring the books down in a wheelbarrow.'

'It's Sunday,' Susan reminded. 'Library's closed.'

'She'll open it for me,' Matt said, 'or I'll know the reason why.'

'Get anything and everything that bears on the subject,' Ben said. 'Psychological as well as pathological and mythic. You understand? The whole works.'

'I'll start a notebook,' Matt rasped. 'Before God, I will!' He looked at them both. 'This is the first time since I woke up in here that I feel like a man. What will you be doing?'

'First, Dr Cody. He examined both Ryerson and Floyd Tibbits. Perhaps we can persuade him to exhume Danny Glick.'

'Would he do that?' Susan asked Matt.

Matt sucked at his ginger ale before answering. 'The Jimmy Cody I had in class would have, in a minute. He was an imaginative, open-minded boy who was remarkably resistant to cant. How much of an empiricist college and med school may have made of him, I don't know.'

'All of this seems roundabout to me,' Susan said. 'Especially going to Dr Cody and risking a complete rebuff. Why don't Ben and I just go up to the Marsten House and have done with it? That was on the docket just last week.'

'I'll tell you why,' Ben said. 'Because we are proceeding on the premise that all this is real. Are you so anxious to put your head in the lion's mouth?'

'I thought vampires slept in the daytime.'

'Whatever Straker may be, he's not a vampire,' Ben said, 'unless the old legends are completely wrong. He's been highly visible in the daytime. At best we'd be turned away as trespassers with nothing learned. At worst, he might overpower us and keep us there until dark. A wakeup snack for Count Comic Book.'

'Barlow?' Susan asked.

Ben shrugged. 'Why not? That story about the New York buying expedition is a little too good to be true.'

The expression in her eyes remained stubborn, but she said nothing more.

'What will you do if Cody laughs you off?' Matt asked. 'Always assuming he doesn't call for the restraints immediately.'

'Off to the graveyard at sunset,' Ben said. 'To watch Danny Glick's grave. Call it a test case.'

Matt half rose from his reclining position. 'Promise me that you'll be careful. Ben, promise me!'

'We will,' Susan said soothingly. 'We'll both positively clank with crosses.'

'Don't joke,' Matt muttered. 'If you'd seen what I have—' He turned his head and looked out the window, which showed the sun-shanked leaves of an alder and the autumn-bright sky beyond.

'If she's joking, I'm not,' Ben said. 'We'll take all precautions.'

'See Father Callahan,' Matt said. 'Make him give you some holy water . . . and if possible, some of the wafer.'

'What kind of man is he?' Ben asked.

Matt shrugged. 'A little strange. A drunk, maybe. If he is, he's a literate, polite one. Perhaps chafing a little under the yoke of enlightened Popery.'

'Are you sure that Father Callahan is a . . . that he drinks?' Susan asked, her eyes a trifle wide.

'Not positive,' Matt said. 'But an ex-student of mine, Brad Campion, works in the Yarmouth liquor store and he says Callahan's a regular customer. A Jim Beam man. Good taste.'

'Could he be talked to?' Ben asked.

'I don't know. I think you must try.'

'Then you don't know him at all?'

'No, not really. He's writing a history of the Catholic Church in New England, and he knows a great deal about the poets of our so-called golden age – Whittier, Longfellow, Russell, Holmes, that lot. I had him in to speak to my American Lit students late last year. He has a quick, acerbic mind – the students enjoyed him.'

'I'll see him,' Ben said, 'and follow my nose.'

A nurse peeked in, nodded, and a moment later Jimmy Cody entered with a stethoscope around his neck.

'Disturbing my patient?' he asked amiably.

'Not half so much as you are,' Matt said. 'I want my pipe.'

'You can't have it,' Cody said absently, reading Matt's chart.

'Goddamn quack,' Matt muttered.

Cody put the chart back and drew the green curtain that went around the bed on a C-shaped steel runner overhead. 'I'm afraid I'll have to ask you two to step out in a moment. How is your head, Mr Mears?'

'Well, nothing seems to have leaked out.'

'You heard about Floyd Tibbits?'

'Susan told me. I'd like to speak to you, if you have a moment after your rounds.'

'I can make you the last patient on my rounds, if you like. Around eleven.'

'Fine.'

Cody twitched the curtain again. 'And now, if you and Susan would excuse us—'

'Here we go, friends, into isolation,' Matt said. 'Say the secret word and win a hundred dollars.'

The curtain came between Ben and Susan and the bed. From beyond it they heard Cody say: 'The next time I have you under gas I think I'll take out your tongue and about half of your prefrontal lobe.'

They smiled at each other, the way young couples will when they are in sunshine and there is nothing seriously the matter with their works, and the smiles faded almost simultaneously. For a moment they both wondered if they might not be crazy.

3

When Jimmy Cody finally came into Ben's room, it was twenty after eleven and Ben began, 'What I wanted to talk to you about—'

'First the head, then the talk.' He parted Ben's hair gently, looked at something, and said, 'This'll hurt.' He pulled off the adhesive bandage and Ben jumped. 'Hell of a lump,' Cody said conversationally, and then covered the wound with a slightly smaller dressing.

He shone a light into Ben's eyes, then tapped his left knee with a rubber hammer. With sudden morbidity, Ben wondered if it was the same one he had used on Mike Ryerson.

'All that seems to be satisfactory,' he said, putting his things away. 'What's your mother's maiden name?'

'Ashford,' Ben said. They had asked him similar questions when he had first recovered consciousness.

'First-grade teacher?'

'Mrs Perkins. She rinsed her hair.'

'Father's middle name?'

'Merton.'

'Any dizziness or nausea?'

'No.'

'Experience of strange odors, colors, or—'

'No, no, and no. I feel fine.'

'I'll decide that,' Cody said primly. 'Any instance of double vision?'

'Not since the last time I bought a gallon of Thunderbird.'

'All right,' Cody said. 'I pronounce you cured through the wonders of modern science and by virtue of a hard head. Now, what was on your mind? Tibbits and the little McDougall boy, I suppose. I can only tell you what I told Parkins Gillespie. Number one, I'm glad they've kept it out of the papers, one scandal per century is enough in a small town. Number two, I'm damned if I know who'd want to do such a twisted thing. It can't have been a local person. We've got our share of the weirdies, but—'

He broke off, seeing the puzzled expressions on their faces. 'You don't know? Haven't heard?'

'Heard what?' Ben demanded.

'It's rather like something by Boris Karloff out of Mary Shelley. Someone snatched the bodies from the Cumberland County Morgue in Portland last night.'

'Jesus Christ,' Susan said. Her lips made the words stiffly.

'What's the matter?' Cody asked, suddenly concerned. 'Do you know something about this?'

'I'm starting to really think we do,' Ben said.

4

It was ten past noon when they had finished telling everything. The nurse had brought Ben a lunch tray, and it stood untouched by his bed.

The last syllable died away, and the only sound was the rattle of glasses and cutlery coming through the half-open door as hungrier patients on the ward ate.

'Vampires,' Jimmy Cody said. Then: 'Matt Burke, of all people. That makes it awfully hard to laugh off.'

Ben and Susan kept silent.

'And you want me to exhume the Glick kid,' he ruminated. 'Jesus jumped-up Christ in a sidecar.'

Cody took a bottle out of his bag and tossed it to Ben, who caught it. 'Aspirin,' he said. 'Ever use it?'

'A lot.'

'My dad used to call it the good doctor's best nurse. Do you know how it works?'

'No,' Ben said. He turned the bottle of aspirin idly in his hands, looking at it. He did not know Cody well enough to know what he usually showed or kept hidden, but he was sure that few of his patients saw him like this – the boyish, Norman Rockwell face overcast with thought and introspection. He didn't want to break Cody's mood.

'Neither do I. Neither does anybody else. But it's good for headache and arthritis and the rheumatism. We don't know what any of those are, either. Why should your head ache? There are no nerves in your brain. We know that aspirin is very close in chemical composition to LSD, but why should one cure the ache in the head and the other cause the head to fill up with flowers? Part of the reason we don't understand is because we don't really know what the brain is. The best-educated doctor in the world is standing on a low island in the middle of a sea of ignorance. We rattle our medicine sticks and kill our chickens and read messages in blood. All of that works a surprising amount of time. White magic. *Bene gris-gris.* My med school profs would tear their hair if they could hear me say that. Some of them tore it when I told them I was going into general practice in rural Maine. One of them told me that Marcus Welby always lanced the boils on the patient's ass during station identification. But I never wanted to be Marcus Welby.' He smiled. 'They'd roll on the ground and have fits if they knew I was going to request an exhumation order on the Glick boy.'

'You'll do it?' Susan said, frankly amazed.

'What can it hurt? If he's dead, he's dead. If he's not, then I'll have something to stand the AMA convention on its ear next time. I'm going to tell the county M.E. that I want to look for signs of infectious encephalitis. It's the only sane explanation I can think of.'

'Could that actually be it?' she asked hopefully.

'Damned unlikely.'

'What's the earliest you could do it?' Ben asked.

'Tomorrow, tops. If I have to hassle around, Tuesday or Wednesday.'

'What should he look like?' Ben asked. 'I mean . . .'

'Yes, I know what you mean. The Glicks wouldn't have the boy embalmed, would they?'

'No.'

'It's been a week?'

'Yes.'

'When the coffin is opened, there's apt to be a rush

of gas and a rather offensive smell. The body may be bloated. The hair will have grown down over his collar — it continues to grow for an amazing period of time — and the fingernails will also be quite long. The eyes will almost certainly have fallen in.'

Susan was trying to maintain an expression of scientific impartiality and not succeeding very well. Ben was glad he hadn't eaten lunch.

'The corpse will not have begun radical mortification,' Cody went on in his best recitation voice, 'but enough moisture may be present to encourage growth on the exposed cheeks and hands, possibly a mossy substance called—' He broke off. 'I'm sorry. I'm grossing you out.'

'Some things may be worse than decay,' Ben remarked, keeping his voice carefully neutral. 'Suppose you find none of those signs? Suppose the body is as natural-looking as the day it was buried? What then? Pound a stake through his heart?'

'Hardly,' Cody said. 'In the first place, either the M.E. or his assistant will have to be there. I don't think even Brent Norbert would regard it professional of me to take a stake out of my bag and hammer it through a child's corpse.'

'What will you do?' Ben asked curiously.

'Well, begging Matt Burke's pardon, I don't think that will come up. If the body was in such a condition, it would undoubtedly be brought to the Maine Medical Center for an extensive post. Once there, I would dally about my examination until dark . . . and observe any phenomena that might occur.'

'And if he rises?'

'Like you, I can't conceive of that.'

'I'm finding it more conceivable all the time,' Ben said grimly. 'Can I be present when all this happens – if it does?'

'That might be arranged.'

'All right,' Ben said. He got out of bed and walked toward the closet where his clothes were hanging. 'I'm going to—'

Susan giggled, and Ben turned around. 'What?'

Cody was grinning. 'Hospital johnnies have a tendency to flap in the back, Mr Mears.'

'Oh hell,' Ben said, and instinctively reached around to pull the johnny together. 'You better call me Ben.'

'And on that note,' Cody said, rising, 'Susan and I will exit. Meet us downstairs in the coffee shop when you're decent. You and I have some business this afternoon.'

'We do?'

'Yes. The Glicks will have to be told the encephalitis story. You can be my colleague if you like. Don't say anything. Just stroke your chin and look wise.'

'They're not going to like it, are they?'

'Would you?'

'No,' Ben said. 'I wouldn't.'

'Do you need their permission to get an exhumation order?' Susan asked.

'Technically, no. Realistically, probably. My only experience with the question of exhuming corpses has been in Medical Law II. But I think if the Glicks are set strongly enough against it, they could force us to a hearing. That would lose us two weeks to a month, and once we got there I doubt if my encephalitis theory would hold up.' He paused and looked at them both. 'Which leads us to the thing that disturbs me most about this, Mr Burke's story aside. Danny Glick is the only corpse we have a marker for. All the others have disappeared into thin air.'

5

Ben and Jimmy Cody got to the Glick home around one-thirty. Tony Glick's car was sitting in the driveway, but the house was silent. When no one answered the third knock, they crossed the road to the small ranch-style house that sat there — a sad, prefab refugee of the 1950s held up on one end by a rusty pair of house jacks. The name on the mailbox was Dickens. A pink lawn flamingo stood by the walk, and a small cocker spaniel thumped his tail at their approach.

Pauline Dickens, waitress and part owner of the Excellent Café, opened the door a moment or two after Cody rang the bell. She was wearing her uniform.

'Hi, Pauline,' Jimmy said. 'Do you know where the Glicks are?'

'You mean you don't *know*?'

'Know what?'

'Mrs Glick died early this morning. They took Tony Glick to Central Maine General. He's in shock.'

Ben looked at Cody. Jimmy looked like a man who had been kicked in the stomach.

Ben took up the slack quickly. 'Where did they take her body?'

Pauline ran her hands across her hips to make sure her uniform was right. 'Well, I spoke to Mabel Werts on the phone an hour ago, and she said Parkins Gillespie was going to take the body right up to that Jewish fellow's funeral home in Cumberland. On account of no one knows where Carl Foreman is.'

'Thank you,' Cody said slowly.

'Awful thing,' she said, her eyes straying to the empty house across the road. Tony Glick's car sat in the driveway like a large and dusty dog that had been chained and then abandoned. 'If I was a superstitious person, I'd be afraid.'

'Afraid of what, Pauline?' Cody asked.

'Oh . . . things.' She smiled vaguely. Her fingers touched a small chain hung around her neck.

A St Christopher's medal.

6

They were sitting in the car again. They had watched Pauline drive off to work without speaking.

'Now what?' Ben asked finally.

'It's a balls-up,' Jimmy said. 'The Jewish fellow is Maury Green. I think maybe we ought to drive over to Cumberland. Nine years ago Maury's boy almost drowned at Sebago Lake. I happened to be there with a girlfriend, and I gave the kid artificial respiration. Got his motor going again. Maybe this is one time I ought to trade on somebody's goodwill.'

'What good will it do? The M.E. will have taken her body for autopsy or postmortem or whatever they call it.'

'I doubt it. It's Sunday, remember? The M.E. will be out in the woods someplace with a rock hammer – he's an amateur geologist. Norbert – do you remember Norbert?'

Ben nodded.

'Norbert is supposed to be on call, but he's erratic. He's probably got the phone off the hook so he can watch the Packers and the Patriots. If we go up to Maury Green's funeral parlor now, there's a pretty fair chance the body will be there unclaimed until after dark.'

'All right,' Ben said. 'Let's go.'

He remembered the call he was to have made on Father Callahan, but it would have to wait. Things were going very fast now. Too fast to suit him. Fantasy and reality had merged.

7

They drove in silence until they were on the turnpike, each lost in his own thoughts. Ben was thinking about what Cody had said at the hospital. Carl Foreman gone. The bodies of Floyd Tibbits and the McDougall baby gone – disappeared from under the noses of two morgue attendants. Mike Ryerson was also gone, and God knew who else. How many people in 'salem's Lot could drop out of sight and not be missed for a week . . . two weeks . . . a month? Two hundred? Three? It made the palms of his hands sweaty.

'This is beginning to seem like a paranoid's dream,' Jimmy said, 'or a Gahan Wilson cartoon. The scariest part of this whole thing, from an academic point of view, is the relative ease with which a vampire colony could be founded – always if you grant the first one. It's a bedroom town for Portland and Lewiston and Gates Falls, mostly. There's no in-town industry where a rise in absenteeism would be noticed. The schools are three-town consolidated, and if the absence list starts getting a little longer, who notices? A lot of people go to church over in Cumberland, a lot more don't go at all. And TV has pretty well put the kibosh on the old neighborhood get-togethers, except for the duffers who hang around Milt's store. All this could be going on with great effectiveness behind the scenes.'

'Yeah,' Ben said. 'Danny Glick infects Mike. Mike infects . . . oh, I don't know. Floyd, maybe. The McDougall baby infects . . . his father? Mother? How are they? Has anyone checked?'

'Not my patients. I assume Dr Plowman would have been the one to call them this morning and tell them about their son's disappearance. But I have no real way of knowing if he actually called or actually got in contact with them if he did.'

'They should be checked on,' Ben said. He began to feel harried. 'You see how easily we could end up chasing our tails? A person from out of town could drive through the Lot and not know a thing was wrong. Just another one-horse town where they roll up the sidewalks at nine. But who knows what's going on in the houses, behind drawn shades? People could be lying in their beds . . . or propped in closets like brooms . . . down in cellars . . . waiting for the sun to go down. And each sunrise, less people out on the streets. Less every day.' He swallowed and heard a dry click in his throat.

'Take it easy,' Jimmy said. 'None of this is proven.'

'The proof is piling up in drifts,' Ben retorted. 'If we were dealing in an accepted frame of reference – with a possible outbreak of typhoid or A_2 flu, say – the whole town would be in quarantine by now.'

'I doubt that. You don't want to forget that only one person has actually *seen* anything.'

'Hardly the town drunk.'

'He'd be crucified if a story like this got out,' Jimmy said.

'By whom? Not by Pauline Dickens, that's for sure. She's ready to start nailing hex signs on her door.'

'In an era of Watergate and oil depletion, she's an exception,' Jimmy said.

They drove the rest of the way without conversation. Green's Mortuary was at the north end of Cumberland, and two hearses were parked around back, between the rear door of the nondenominational chapel and a high board fence. Jimmy turned off the ignition and looked at Ben. 'Ready?'

'I guess.'

They got out.

8

The rebellion had been growing in her all afternoon, and around two o'clock it burst its bonds. They were going at it stupidly, taking the long way around the barn to prove something that was (sorry, Mr Burke) probably a lot of horseshit anyway. Susan decided to go up to the Marsten House now, this afternoon.

She went downstairs and picked up her pocketbook. Ann Norton was baking cookies and her father was in the living room, watching the Packers–Patriots game.

'Where are you going?' Mrs Norton asked.

'For a drive.'

'Supper's at six. See if you can be back on time.'

'Five at the latest.'

She went out and got into her car, which was her proudest possession – not because it was the first one she'd ever owned outright (although it was), but because she had paid for it (almost, she amended; there were six payments left) from her own work, her own talent. It was a Vega hatchback, now almost two years old. She backed it carefully out of the garage and lifted a hand briefly to her mother, who was looking out the kitchen window at her. The break was still between them, not spoken of, not healed. The other quarrels, no matter how bitter, had always knit up in time; life simply went on, burying the hurts under a bandage of days, not ripped off again until the next quarrel, when all the old grudges and grievances would be brought out and counted up like high-scoring cribbage hands. But this one seemed complete, it had been a total war. The wounds were beyond bandaging. Only amputation remained. She had already packed most of her things, and it felt right. This had been long overdue.

She drove out along Brock Street, feeling a growing sense of pleasure and purpose (and a not unpleasant underlayer of absurdity) as the house dropped behind her. She was going to take positive action, and the thought was a tonic to her. She was a forthright girl, and the events of the weekend had bewildered her, left her drifting at sea. Now she would row!

She pulled over onto the soft shoulder outside the village limits, and walked out into Carl Smith's west pasture to where a roll of red-painted snow fence was curled up, waiting for winter. The sense of absurdity was magnified now, and she couldn't help grinning as she bent one of the pickets back and forth until the flexible wire holding it to the others snapped. The picket formed a natural stake, about three feet long, tapering to a point. She carried it back to the car and put it in the backseat, knowing intellectually what it was for (she had seen enough Hammer films at the drive-in on double dates to know you had to pound a stake into a vampire's heart), but never pausing to wonder if she would be able to hammer it through a man's chest if the situation called for it.

She drove on, past the town limits and into Cumberland. On the left was a small country store that stayed open on Sundays, where her father got the Sunday *Times*. Susan remembered a small display case of junk jewelry beside the counter.

She bought the *Times*, and then picked out a small gold crucifix. Her purchases came to four-fifty, and were rung up by a fat counterman who hardly turned from the TV, where Jim Plunkett was being thrown for a loss.

She turned north on the County Road, a newly surfaced stretch of two-lane blacktop. Everything seemed fresh and crisp and alive in the sunny afternoon, and life seemed very dear. Her thoughts jumped from that to Ben. It was a short jump.

The sun came out from behind a slowly moving cumulus cloud, flooding the road with brilliant patches of dark and light as it streamed through the overhanging trees. On a day like this, she thought, it was possible to believe there would be happy endings all around.

About five miles up County, she turned off onto the Brooks Road, which was unpaved once she recrossed the town line into 'salem's Lot. The road rose and fell and wound through the heavily wooded area northwest of the village, and much of the bright afternoon sunlight was cut off. There were no houses or trailers out here. Most of the land was owned by a paper company most renowned for asking patrons not to squeeze their toilet paper. The verge of the road was marked every one hundred feet with no-hunting and no-trespassing signs. As she passed the turnoff which led to the dump, a ripple of unease went through her. On this gloomy stretch of road, nebulous possibilities seemed more real. She found herself wondering – not for the first time – why any normal man would buy the wreck of a suicide's house and then keep the windows shuttered against the sunlight.

The road dipped sharply and then rose steeply up the western flank of Marsten's Hill. She could make out the peak of the Marsten House roof through the trees.

She parked at the head of a disused wood-road at the bottom of the dip and got out of the car. After a moment's hesitation, she took the stake and hung the crucifix around her neck. She still felt absurd, but not half so absurd as she was going to feel if someone she knew happened to drive by and see her marching up the road with a snow-fence picket in her hand.

Hi, Suze, where you headed?

Oh, just up to the old Marsten place to kill a vampire. But I have to hurry because supper's at six.

She decided to cut through the woods.

She stepped carefully over a ruinous rock wall at the foot of the road's ditch, and was glad she had worn slacks. Very much *haute couture* for fearless vampire killers. There were nasty brambles and deadfalls before the woods actually started.

In the pines it was at least ten degrees cooler, and gloomier still. The ground was carpeted with old needles, and the wind hissed through the trees. Somewhere, some small animal crashed off through the underbrush. She suddenly realized that if she turned to her left, a walk of no more than half a mile would bring her into the Harmony Hill Cemetery, if she were agile enough to scale the back wall.

She toiled steadily upward, going as quietly as possible. As she neared the brow of the hill, she began to catch glimpses of the house through the steadily thinning screen of branches – the blind side of the house in relation to the village below. And she began to be afraid. She could not put her finger on any precise reason, and in that way it was like the fear she had felt (but had already largely forgotten) at Matt Burke's house. She was fairly sure that no one could hear her, and it was broad daylight – but the fear was there, a steadily oppressive weight. It seemed to be welling into her consciousness from a part of her brain that was usually silent and probably as obsolete as her appendix. Her pleasure in the day was gone. The sense that she was playing was gone. The feeling of decisiveness was gone. She found herself thinking of those same drive-in horror movie epics where the heroine goes venturing up the narrow attic stairs to see what's frightened poor old Mrs Cobham so, or down into some dark, cobwebby cellar where the walls are rough, sweating stone – symbolic womb – and she, with her date's arm comfortably around her, thinking: *What a silly bitch . . . I'd never do that!* And here she was, doing it, and she began to grasp how deep the division between the human cerebrum and the human midbrain had become; how the cerebrum can force one on and on in spite of the warnings given by that instinctive part, which is so similar in physical construction to the brain of the alligator. The cerebrum could force one on and on, until the attic door was flung open in the face of some grinning horror or one looked into a half-bricked alcove in the cellar and saw—

STOP!

She threw the thoughts off and found that she was sweating. All at the sight of an ordinary house with its shutters closed. You've got to stop being stupid, she told herself. You're going to go up there and spy the place out, that's all. From the front yard you can see your own house. Now, what in God's name could happen to you in sight of your own house?

Nonetheless, she bent over slightly and took a tighter grip on the stake, and when the screening trees became too thin to offer much protection, she dropped to her hands and knees and crawled. Three or four minutes later, she had come as far as it was possible without breaking cover. From her spot behind a final stand of pines and a spray of junipers, she could see the west side of the house and the creepered tangle of honeysuckle, now autumn-barren. The grass of summer was yellow but still knee-high. No effort had been made to cut it.

A motor roared suddenly in the stillness, making her heart rise into her throat. She controlled herself by hooking her fingers into the ground and biting hard on her lower lip. A moment later an old black car backed into sight, paused at the head of the driveway, and then turned out onto the road and started away toward town. Before it drew out of sight, she saw the man quite clearly: large bald head, eyes sunken so deeply you could really see nothing of them but the sockets, and the lapels and collar of a dark suit. Straker. On his way in to Crossen's store, perhaps.

She could see that most of the shutters had broken slats. All right, then. She would creep up and peek through and see what there was to see. Probably nothing but a house in the first stages of a long renovation process, new plastering under way, new papering perhaps, tools and ladders and buckets. All about as romantic and supernatural as a TV football game.

But still: the fear.

It rose suddenly, emotion overspilling logic and the bright Formica reason of the cerebrum, filling her mouth with a taste like black copper.

And she knew someone was behind her even before the hand fell on her shoulder.

9

It was almost dark.

Ben got up from the wooden folding chair, walked over to the window that looked out on the funeral parlor's back lawn, and saw nothing in particular. It was quarter to seven, and evening's shadows were very long. The grass was still green despite the lateness of the year, and he supposed that the thoughtful mortician would endeavor to keep it so until snow covered it. A symbol of continuing life in the midst of the death of the year. He found the thought inordinately depressing and turned from the view.

'I wish I had a cigarette,' he said.

'They're killers,' Jimmy told him without turning around. He was watching a Sunday night wildlife program on Maury Green's small Sony. 'Actually, so do I. I quit when the surgeon general did his number on cigarettes ten years ago. Bad P.R. not to. But I always wake up grabbing for the pack on the nightstand.'

'I thought you quit.'

'I keep it there for the same reason some alcoholics keep a bottle of scotch on the kitchen shelf. Willpower, son.'

Ben looked at the clock: 6:47. Maury Green's Sunday paper said sundown would officially arrive at 7:02 EST.

Jimmy had handled everything quite neatly. Maury Green was a small man who had answered the door in an unbuttoned black vest and an open-collar white shirt. His sober, inquiring expression had changed to a broad smile of welcome.

'*Shalom*, Jimmy!' he cried. 'It's good to see you! Where you been keeping yourself?'

'Saving the world from the common cold,' Jimmy said, smiling, as Green wrung his hand. 'I want you to meet a very good friend of mine. Maury Green, Ben Mears.'

Ben's hand was enveloped in both of Maury's. His eyes glistened behind the black-rimmed glasses he wore. '*Shalom*, also. Any friend of Jimmy's, and so on. Come on in, both of you. I could call Rachel—'

'Please don't,' Jimmy said. 'We've come to ask a favor. A rather large one.'

Green glanced more closely at Jimmy's face. '"A rather large one,"' he jeered softly. 'And why? What have you ever done for me, that my son should graduate third in his class from Northwestern? Anything, Jimmy.'

Jimmy blushed. 'I did what anyone would have done, Maury.'

'I'm not going to argue with you,' Green said. 'Ask.

What is it that has you and Mr Mears so worried? Have you been in an accident?'

'No. Nothing like that.'

He had taken them into a small kitchenette behind the chapel, and as they talked, he brewed coffee in a battered old pot that sat on a hot plate.

'Has Norbert come after Mrs Glick yet?' Jimmy asked.

'No, and not a sign of him,' Maury said, putting sugar and cream on the table. 'That one will come by at eleven tonight and wonder why I'm not here to let him in.' He sighed. 'Poor lady. Such tragedy in one family. And she looks so sweet, Jimmy. That old poop Reardon brought her in. She was your patient?'

'No,' Jimmy said. 'But Ben and I . . . we'd like to sit up with her this evening, Maury. Right downstairs.'

Green paused in the act of reaching for the coffeepot. 'Sit up with her? Examine her, you mean?'

'No,' Jimmy said steadily. 'Just sit up with her.'

'You're joking?' He looked at them closely. 'No, I see you're not. Why would you want to do that?'

'I can't tell you that, Maury.'

'Oh.' He poured the coffee, sat down with them, and sipped. 'Not too strong. Very nice. Has she got something? Something infectious?'

Jimmy and Ben exchanged a glance.

'Not in the accepted sense of the word,' Jimmy said finally.

'You'd like me to keep my mouth shut about this, eh?'

'Yes.'

'And if Norbert comes?'

'I can handle Norbert,' Jimmy said. 'I'll tell him

370

Reardon asked me to check her for infectious encephalitis. He'll never check.'

Green nodded. 'Norbert doesn't know enough to check his watch, unless someone asks him.'

'Is it okay, Maury?'

'Sure, sure. I thought you said a big favor.'

'It's bigger than you think, maybe.'

'When I finish my coffee, I'll go home and see what horror Rachel has produced for my Sunday dinner. Here is the key. Lock up when you go, Jimmy.'

Jimmy tucked it away in his pocket. 'I will. Thanks again, Maury.'

'Anything. Just do me one favor in return.'

'Sure. What?'

'If she says anything, write it down for posterity.' He began to chuckle, saw the identical look on their faces, and stopped.

10

It was five to seven. Ben felt tension begin to seep into his body.

'Might as well stop staring at the clock,' Jimmy said. 'You can't make it go any faster by looking at it.'

Ben started guiltily.

'I doubt very much that vampires — if they exist at all — rise at almanac sunset,' Jimmy said. 'It's never full dark.'

Nonetheless he got up and shut off the TV, catching a wood duck in mid-squawk.

Silence descended on the room like a blanket. They were in Green's workroom, and the body of Marjorie Glick was on a stainless-steel table equipped with gutters and foot stirrups that could be raised or depressed. It reminded Ben of the tables in hospital delivery rooms.

Jimmy had turned back the sheet that covered her body when they entered and had made a brief examination. Mrs Glick was wearing a burgundy-colored quilted housecoat and knitted slippers. There was a Band-Aid on her left shin, perhaps covering a shaving nick. Ben looked away from it, but his eyes were drawn back again and again.

'What do you think?' Ben had asked.

'I'm not going to commit myself when another three hours will probably decide one way or the other. But her condition is strikingly similar to that of Mike Ryerson – no surface lividity, no sign of rigor or incipient rigor.' And he had pulled the sheet back and would say no more.

It was 7:02.

Jimmy suddenly said, 'Where's your cross?'

Ben started. 'Cross? Jesus, I don't have one!'

'You were never a Boy Scout,' Jimmy said, and opened his bag. 'I, however, always come prepared.'

He brought out two tongue depressors, stripped off the protective cellophane, and bound them together at right angles with a twist of Red Cross tape.

'Bless it,' he said to Ben.

'What? I can't . . . I don't know how.'

'Then make it up,' Jimmy said, and his pleasant face suddenly appeared strained. 'You're the writer; you'll have to be the metaphysician. For Christ's sake, hurry. I think something is going to happen. Can't you feel it?'

And Ben could. Something seemed to be gathering in the slow purple twilight, unseen as yet, but heavy and electric. His mouth had gone dry, and he had to wet his lips before he could speak.

'In the name of the Father, the Son, and the Holy Ghost.' Then he added, as an afterthought: 'In the name of the Virgin Mary, too. Bless this cross and . . . and . . .'

Words rose to his lips with sudden, eerie surety.

'The Lord is my shepherd,' he spoke, and the words fell into the shadowy room as stones would have fallen into a deep lake, sinking out of sight without a ripple. 'I shall not want. He maketh me to lie down in green pastures: He leadeth me beside the still waters. He restoreth my soul.'

Jimmy's voice joined his own, chanting.

'He leadeth me in the paths of righteousness for his name's sake. Yea, though I walk through the valley of the shadow of death, I will fear no evil—'

It seemed hard to breathe properly. Ben found that his whole body had crawled into goose flesh, and the short hairs on the nape of his neck had begun to prickle, as if they were rising into hackles.

'Thy rod and thy staff they comfort me. Thou preparest a table before me in the presence of mine enemies: thou anointest my head with oil; my cup runneth over. Surely goodness and mercy shall—'

The sheet covering Marjorie Glick's body had begun to tremble. A hand fell out below the sheet and the fingers began to dance jaggedly on the air, twisting and turning.

'My Christ, am I *seeing* this?' Jimmy whispered. His face had gone pale and his freckles stood out like spatters on a windowpane.

'—follow me all the days of my life,' Ben finished. 'Jimmy, look at the cross.'

The cross was glowing. The light spilled over his hand in an elvish flood.

A slow, choked voice spoke in the stillness, as grating as shards of broken crockery: '*Danny?*'

Ben felt his tongue cleave to the roof of his mouth. The form under the sheet was sitting up. Shadows in the darkening room moved and slithered.

'*Danny, where are you, darling?*'

The sheet fell from her face and crumpled in her lap.

The face of Marjorie Glick was a pallid, moonlike circle in the semi-dark, punched only by the black holes of her eyes. She saw them, and her mouth juddered open in an awful, cheated snarl. The fading glow of daylight flashed against her teeth.

She swung her legs over the side of the table; one of the slippers fell off and lay unheeded.

'Sit right there!' Jimmy told her. 'Don't try to move.'

Her answer was a snarl, a dark silver sound, doglike. She slid off the table, staggered, and walked toward them. Ben caught himself looking into those punched eyes and wrenched his gaze away. There were black galaxies shot with red in there. You could see yourself, drowning and liking it.

'Don't look in her face,' he told Jimmy.

They were retreating from her without thought, allowing her to force them toward the narrow hall which led to the stairs.

'Try the cross, Ben.'

He had almost forgotten he had it. Now he held it up, and the cross seemed to flash with brilliance. He had to squint against it. Mrs Glick made a hissing, dismayed noise and threw her hands up in front of her face. Her features seemed to draw together, twitching and writhing like a nest of snakes. She tottered a step backward.

'That's got her!' Jimmy yelled.

Ben advanced on her, holding the cross out before him. She hooked one hand into a claw and made a swipe at it. Ben dipped it below her hand and then thrust it at her. A ululating scream came from her throat.

For Ben, the rest took on the maroon tones of nightmare. Although worse horrors were to come, the dreams of the following days and nights were always of driving Marjorie Glick back toward that mortician's table, where the sheet that had covered her lay crumpled beside one knitted slipper.

She retreated unwillingly, her eyes alternating between the hateful cross and an area on Ben's neck to the right of the chin. The sounds that were wrenched out of her were inhuman gibberings and hissings and glottals, and there was something so blindly reluctant in her withdrawal that she began to seem like some giant, lumbering insect. Ben thought: If I didn't have this cross out front, she would rip my throat open with her nails and gulp down the blood that spurted out of the jugular and carotid like a man just out of the desert and dying of thirst. She would bathe in it.

Jimmy had cut away from his side, and was circling her to the left. She didn't see him. Her eyes were fixed only on Ben, dark and filled with hatred . . . filled with fear.

Jimmy circled the mortician's table, and when she backed around it, he threw both arms around her neck with a convulsive yell.

She gave a high, whistling cry and twisted in his grip. Ben saw Jimmy's nails pull away a flap of her skin at the shoulder, and nothing welled out – the cut was like a lipless mouth. And then, incredibly, she threw him across the room. Jimmy crashed into the corner, knocking Maury Green's portable TV off its stand.

She was on him in a flash, moving in a hunched, scrabbling run that was nearly spiderlike. Ben caught a shadow-scrawled glimpse of her falling on top of him, ripping at his collar, and then the sideward predatory lunge of her head, the yawning of her jaws, as she battened on him.

Jimmy Cody screamed – the high, despairing scream of the utterly damned.

Ben threw himself at her, stumbling and nearly falling over the shattered television on the floor. He could hear her harsh breathing, like the rattle of straw, and below that, the revolting sound of smacking, champing lips.

He grabbed her by the collar of her housecoat and yanked her upward, forgetting the cross momentarily. Her head came around with frightening swiftness. Her eyes were dilated and glittering, her lips and chin slicked with blood that was black in this near-total darkness.

Her breath in his face was foul beyond measure, the breath of tombs. As if in slow motion, he could see her tongue lick across her teeth.

He brought the cross up just as she jerked him forward into her embrace, her strength making him feel like something made of rags. The rounded point of the tongue depressor that formed the cross's downstroke struck her under the chin – and then continued upward with no fleshy resistance. Ben's eyes were stunned by a flash of not-light that happened not before his eyes but seemingly behind them. There was the hot and porcine smell of burning flesh. Her scream this time was full-throated and agonized. He sensed rather than saw her throw herself backward, stumble over the television, and fall on the floor, one white arm thrown outward to break her fall. She was up again with wolflike agility, her eyes narrowed in pain, yet still filled with her insane hunger. The flesh of her lower jaw was smoking and black. She was snarling at him.

'Come on, you bitch,' he panted. 'Come on, come on.'

He held the cross out before him again, and backed her into the corner at the far left of the room. When he got her there, he was going to jam the cross through her forehead.

But even as her back pressed the narrowing walls, she uttered a high, squealing giggle that made him wince. It was like the sound of a fork being dragged across a porcelain sink.

'Even now one laughs! Even now your circle is smaller!'

And before his eyes her body seemed to elongate and become translucent. For a moment he thought she was still there, laughing at him, and then the white glow of the streetlamp outside was shining on bare wall, and there was only a fleeting sensation on his nerve endings, which seemed to be reporting that she had seeped into the very pores of the wall, like smoke.

She was gone.

And Jimmy was screaming.

11

He flicked on the overhead bar of fluorescents and turned to look at Jimmy, but Jimmy was already on his feet, holding his hands to the side of his neck. The fingers were sparkling scarlet.

'She *bit* me!' Jimmy howled. 'Oh God-Jesus, she *bit* me!'

Ben went to him, tried to take him in his arms, and Jimmy pushed him away. His eyes rolled madly in their sockets.

'Don't touch me. I'm unclean.'

'Jimmy—'

'Give me my bag. Jesus, Ben, I can feel it in there. I can feel it working in me. *For Christ's sake, give me my bag!*'

It was in the corner. Ben got it, and Jimmy snatched it. He went to the mortician's table and set the bag on it. His face was death pale, shining with sweat. The blood pulsed remorselessly from the torn gash in the side of his neck. He sat down on the table and opened the bag and swept through it, his breath coming in whining gasps through his open mouth.

'She *bit* me,' he muttered into the bag. 'Her mouth . . . oh God, her dirty filthy *mouth* . . .'

He pulled a bottle of disinfectant out of the bag and sent the cap spinning across the tiled floor. He leaned back, supporting himself on one arm, and upended the bottle over his throat, and it splashed the wound, his slacks, the table. Blood washed away in threads. His eyes closed and he screamed once, then again. The bottle never wavered.

'Jimmy, what can I—'

'In a minute,' Jimmy muttered. 'Wait. It's better, I think. Wait, just wait—'

He tossed the bottle away and it shattered on the floor. The wound, washed clean of the tainted blood, was clearly visible. Ben saw there was not one but two puncture wounds not far from the jugular, one of them horribly mangled.

Jimmy had pulled an ampoule and a hypo from the bag. He stripped the protective covering from the needle and jabbed it through the ampoule. His hands were shaking so badly he had to make two thrusts at it. He filled the needle and held it out to Ben.

'Tetanus,' he said. 'Give it to me. Here.' He held his arm out, rotated to expose the armpit.

'Jimmy, that'll knock you out.'

'No. No, it won't. Do it.'

Ben took the needle and looked questioningly into Jimmy's eyes. He nodded. Ben injected the needle.

Jimmy's body tensed like spring steel. For a moment he was a sculpture in agony, every tendon pulled out into sharp relief. Little by little he began to relax. His body shuddered in reaction, and Ben saw that tears had mixed with the sweat on his face.

'Put the cross on me,' he said. 'If I'm still dirty from her, it'll . . . it'll do something to me.'

'Will it?'

'I'm sure it will. When you were going after her, I looked up and I wanted to go after *you*. God help me, I did. And I looked at that cross and I . . . my belly wanted to heave up.'

Ben put the cross on his neck. Nothing happened. Its glow – if there had been a glow at all – was entirely gone. Ben took the cross away.

'Okay,' Jimmy said. 'I think that's all we can do.' He rummaged in his bag again, found an envelope containing two pills, and crushed them into his mouth. 'Dope,' he said. 'Great invention. Thank God I used the john before that

. . . before it happened. I think I pissed myself, but it only came to about six drops. Can you bandage my neek?'

'I think so,' Ben said.

Jimmy handed him gauze, adhesive tape, and a pair of surgical scissors. Bending to put the bandage on, he saw that the skin around the wounds had gone an ugly, congealed red. Jimmy flinched when he pressed the bandage gently into place.

He said: 'For a couple of minutes there, I thought I was going to go nuts. Really, clinically nuts. Her lips on me . . . biting me . . .' His throat rippled as he swallowed. 'And when she was doing it, I *liked* it, Ben. That's the hellish part. I actually had an erection. Can you believe it? If you hadn't been here to pull her off, I would have . . . would have let her . . .'

'Never mind,' Ben said.

'There's one more thing I have to do that I don't like.'

'What's that?'

'Here. Look at me a minute.'

Ben finished the bandage and drew back a little to look at Jimmy. 'What—'

And suddenly Jimmy slugged him. Stars rocketed up in his brain and he took three wandering steps backward and sat down heavily. He shook his head and saw Jimmy getting carefully down from the table and coming toward him. He groped madly for the cross, thinking: This is what's known as an O. Henry ending, you stupid shit, you stupid, stupid—

'You all right?' Jimmy was asking him. 'I'm sorry, but it's a little easier when you don't know it's coming.'

'What the Christ—?'

Jimmy sat down beside him on the floor. 'I'm going

to tell you our story,' he said. 'It's a damned poor one, but I'm pretty sure Maury Green will back it up. It will keep my practice, and keep us both out of jail or some asylum . . . and at this point, I'm not so concerned about those things as I am about staying free to fight these . . . things, whatever you want to call them, another day. Do you understand that?'

'The thrust of it,' Ben said. He touched his jaw and winced. There was a knot to the left of his chin.

'Somebody barged in on us while I was examining Mrs Glick,' Jimmy said. 'The somebody coldcocked you and then used me for a punching bag. During the struggle, the somebody bit me to make me let him go. That's all either of us remembers. *All*. Understand?'

Ben nodded.

'The guy was wearing a dark CPO coat, maybe blue, maybe black, and a green or gray knitted cap. That's all you saw. Okay?'

'Have you ever thought about giving up doctoring in favor of a career in creative writing?'

Jimmy smiled. 'I'm only creative in moments of extreme self-interest. Can you remember the story?'

'Sure. And I don't think it's as poor as you might believe. After all, hers isn't the first body that's disappeared lately.'

'I'm hoping they'll add that up. But the county sheriff is a lot more on the ball than Parkins Gillespie ever thought of being. We have to watch our step. Don't embellish the story.'

'Do you suppose anyone in officialdom will begin to see the pattern in all this?'

Jimmy shook his head. 'Not a chance in the world. We're going to have to bumble through this on our own. And remember that from this point on, we're criminals.'

Shortly after, he went to the phone and called Maury Green, then County Sheriff Homer McCaslin.

12

Ben got back to Eva's at about fifteen minutes past midnight and made himself a cup of coffee in the deserted downstairs kitchen. He drank it slowly, reviewing the night's events with all the intense recall of a man who has just escaped falling from a high ledge.

The county sheriff was a tall, balding man. He chewed tobacco. He moved slowly, but his eyes were bright with observation. He had pulled an enormous battered notebook on a chain from his hip pocket, and an old thick-barreled fountain pen from under his green wool vest. He had questioned Ben and Jimmy while two deputies dusted for fingerprints and took pictures. Maury Green stood quietly in the background, throwing a puzzled look at Jimmy from time to time.

What had brought them to Green's Mortuary?

Jimmy took that one, reciting the encephalitis story.

Did old Doc Reardon know about it?

Well, no. Jimmy thought it would be best to make a quiet check before mentioning it to anyone. Doc Reardon had been known to be, well, overly chatty on occasion.

What about this encephawhatzis? Did the woman have it?

No, almost certainly not. He had finished his examination before the man in the CPO coat burst in. He (Jimmy) would not be willing – or able – to state just how the woman *had* died, but it certainly wasn't of encephalitis.

Could they describe this fella?

They answered in terms of the story they had worked out. Ben added a pair of brown work boots just so they wouldn't sound too much like Tweedledum and Tweedledee.

McCaslin asked a few more questions, and Ben was just beginning to feel that they were going to get out of it unscathed when McCaslin turned to him and asked:

'What are you doing in this, Mears? You ain't no doctor.'

His watchful eyes twinkled benignly. Jimmy opened his mouth to answer, but the sheriff quieted him with a single hand gesture.

If the purpose of McCaslin's sudden shot had been to startle Ben into a guilty expression or gesture, it failed. He was too emotionally wrung out to react much. Being caught in a misstatement did not seem too shattering after what had gone before. 'I'm a writer, not a doctor. I write novels. I'm writing one currently where one of the important secondary characters is a mortician's son. I just wanted a look into the back room. I hitched a ride with Jimmy here. He told me he would rather not reveal his business, and I didn't ask.' He rubbed his chin, where a small, knotted bump had risen. 'I got more than I bargained for.'

McCaslin looked neither pleased nor disappointed in Ben's answer. 'I should say you did. You're the fella that wrote *Conway's Daughter*, ain't you?'

'Yes.'

'My wife read part of that in some woman's magazine.

383

Cosmopolitan, I think. Laughed like hell. I took a look and couldn't see nothing funny in a little girl strung out on drugs.'

'No,' Ben said, looking McCaslin in the eye. 'I didn't see anything funny about it, either.'

'This new book the one they say you been workin' on up to the Lot?'

'Yes.'

'P'raps, you'd like Moe Green here to read it over,' McCaslin remarked. 'See if you got the undertakin' parts right.'

'That section isn't written yet,' Ben said. 'I always research before I write. It's easier.'

McCaslin shook his head wonderingly. 'You know, your story sounds just like one of those Fu Manchu books. Some guy breaks in here an' overpowers two strong men an' makes off with the body of some poor woman who died of unknown causes.'

'Listen, Homer—' Jimmy began.

'Don't you Homer me,' McCaslin said. 'I don't like it. I don't like any part of it. This encephalitis is catchin', ain't it?'

'Yes, it's infectious,' Jimmy said warily.

'An' you still brought this writer along? Knowin' she might be infected with somethin' like that?'

Jimmy shrugged and looked angry. 'I don't question your professional judgments, Sheriff. You'll just have to bear with mine. Encephalitis is a fairly low-grade infection which gains slowly in the human bloodstream. I felt there would be no danger to either of us. Now, wouldn't you be better off trying to find out who carted away Mrs Glick's body

– Fu Manchu or otherwise – or are you just having fun questioning us?'

McCaslin fetched a deep sigh from his not inconsiderable belly, flipped his notebook closed, and stored it in the depths of his hip pocket again. 'Well, we'll put the word out, Jimmy. Doubt if we'll get much on this unless the kook comes out of the woodwork again – if there ever was a kook, which I doubt.'

Jimmy raised his eyebrows.

'You're lyin' to me,' McCaslin said patiently. 'I know it, these deputies know it, prob'ly even ole Moe knows it. I don't know how much you're lyin' – a little or a lot – but I know I can't *prove* you're lyin' as long as you both stick to the same story. I could take you both down to the cooler, but the rules say I gotta give you one phone call, an' even the greenest kid fresh out of law school could spring you on what I got, which could best be described as Suspicion of Unknown Hanky-panky. An' I bet your lawyer ain't fresh out of law school, is he?'

'No,' Jimmy said. 'He's not.'

'I'd take you down just the same and put you to the inconvenience except I get a feelin' you ain't lyin' because you did somethin' against the law.' He hit the pedal at the foot of the stainless-steel waste can by the mortician's table. The top banged up and McCaslin shot a brown stream of tobacco juice into it. Maury Green jumped. 'Would either of you like to sort of revise your story?' he asked quietly, and the back-country twang was gone from his voice. 'This is serious business. We've had four deaths in the Lot, and all four bodies are gone. I want to know what's happening.'

'We've told you everything we know,' Jimmy said

with quiet firmness. He looked directly at McCaslin. 'If we could tell you more, we would.'

McCaslin looked back at him, just as keenly. 'You're scared shitless,' he said. 'You and this writer, both of you. You look the way some of the guys in Korea looked when they brought 'em back from the front lines.'

The deputies were looking at them. Ben and Jimmy said nothing.

McCaslin sighed again. 'Go on, get out of here. I want you both down to my office tomorrow by ten to make statements. If you ain't there by ten, I'll send a patrol car out to get you.'

'You won't have to do that,' Ben said.

McCaslin looked at him mournfully and shook his head. 'You ought to write books with better sense. Like the guy who writes those Travis McGee stories. A man can sink his teeth into one of those.'

13

Ben got up from the table and rinsed his coffee cup at the sink, pausing to look out the window into the night's blackness. What was out there tonight? Marjorie Glick, reunited with her son at last? Mike Ryerson? Floyd Tibbits? Carl Foreman?

He turned away and went upstairs.

He slept the rest of the night with the desk lamp on and left the tongue-depressor cross that had vanquished Mrs Glick on the table by his right hand. His last thought before sleep took him was to wonder if Susan was all right, and safe.

CHAPTER TWELVE
MARK

___

When he first heard the distant snapping of twigs, he crept behind the trunk of a large spruce and stood there, waiting to see who would show up. *They* couldn't come out in the daytime, but that didn't mean *they* couldn't get people who could; giving them money was one way, but it wasn't the only way. Mark had seen that guy Straker in town, and his eyes were like the eyes of a toad sunning itself on a rock. He looked like he could break a baby's arm and smile while he did it.

He touched the heavy shape of his father's target pistol in his jacket pocket. Bullets were no good against *them* – except maybe silver ones – but a shot between the eyes would punch that Straker's ticket, all right.

His eyes shifted downward momentarily to the roughly cylindrical shape propped against the tree, wrapped in an old piece of toweling. There was a woodpile behind his house, half a cord of yellow ash stove lengths which he and his father had cut with the McCulloch chain saw in July and August. Henry Petrie was methodical, and each length, Mark knew, would be within an inch of three feet, one way or the other. His father knew the proper length just as he knew that winter followed fall and that yellow ash would burn longer and cleaner in the living room fireplace.

His son, who knew other things, knew that ash was for men – things like *him*. This morning, while his mother and father were out on their Sunday bird walk, he had taken one of the lengths and whacked one end into a rough point with his Boy Scout hatchet. It was rough, but it would serve.

He saw a flash of color and shrank back against the tree, peering around the rough bark with one eye. A moment later he got his first clear glimpse of the person climbing the hill. It was a girl. He felt a sense of relief mingled with disappointment. No henchman of the devil there; that was Mr Norton's daughter.

His gaze sharpened again. She was carrying a stake of her own! As she drew closer, he felt an urge to laugh bitterly – a piece of snow fence, that's what she had. Two swings with an ordinary tool box hammer would split it right in two.

She was going to pass his tree on the right. As she drew closer, he began to slide carefully around his tree to the left, avoiding any small twigs that might pop and give him away. At last the synchronized little movement was done; her back was to him as she went on up the hill toward the break in the trees. She was going very carefully, he noted with approval. That was good. In spite of the silly snow fence stake, she apparently had some idea of what she was getting into. Still, if she went much further, she was going to be in trouble. Straker was at home. Mark had been here since twelve-thirty, and he had seen Straker go out to the driveway and look down the road and then go back into the house. Mark had been trying to make up his mind on what to do himself when this girl had entered things, upsetting the equation.

Perhaps she was going to be all right. She had stopped behind a screen of bushes and was crouching there, just looking at the house. Mark turned it over in his mind. Obviously she knew. How didn't matter, but she would not have had even that pitiful stake with her if she didn't know. He supposed he would have to go up and warn her that Straker was still around, and on guard. She probably didn't have a gun, not even a little one like his.

He was pondering how to make his presence known to her without having her scream her head off when the motor of Straker's car roared into life. She jumped visibly, and at first he was afraid she was going to break and run, crashing through the woods and advertising her presence for a hundred miles. But then she hunkered down again, holding on to the ground like she was afraid it would fly away from her. She's got guts even if she is stupid, he thought approvingly.

Straker's car backed down the driveway — she would have a much better view from where she was; he could only see the Packard's black roof — hesitated for a moment, and then went off down the road toward town.

He decided they had to team up. Anything would be better than going up to that house alone. He had already sampled the poison atmosphere that enveloped it. He had felt it from a half a mile away, and it thickened as you got closer.

Now he ran lightly up the carpeted incline and put

his hand on her shoulder. He felt her body tense, knew she was going to scream, and said, 'Don't yell. It's all right. It's me.'

She didn't scream. What escaped was a terrified exhalation of air. She turned around and looked at him, her face white. 'W-Who's me?'

He sat down beside her. 'My name is Mark Petrie. I know you; you're Sue Norton. My dad knows your dad.'

'Petrie . . . ? Henry Petrie?'

'Yes, that's my father.'

'What are you doing here?' Her eyes were moving continually over him, as if she hadn't been able to take in his actuality yet.

'The same thing you are. Only that stake won't work. It's too . . .' He groped for a word that had checked into his vocabulary through sight and definition but not by use. 'It's too flimsy.'

She looked down at her piece of snow fence and actually blushed. 'Oh, that. Well, I found that in the woods and . . . and thought someone might fall over it, so I just—'

He cut her adult temporizing short impatiently: 'You came to kill the vampire, didn't you?'

'Wherever did you get that idea? Vampires and things like that?'

He said somberly, 'A vampire tried to get me last night. It almost did, too.'

'That's absurd. A big boy like you should know better than to make up—'

'It was Danny Glick.'

She recoiled, her eyes wincing as if he had thrown a

mock punch instead of words. She groped out, found his arm, and held it. Their eyes locked. 'Are you making this up, Mark?'

'No,' he said, and told his story in a few simple sentences.

'And you came here alone?' she asked when he had finished. 'You believed it and came up here alone?'

'Believed it?' He looked at her, honestly puzzled. 'Sure I believed it. I saw it, didn't I?'

There was no response to that, and suddenly she was ashamed of her instant doubt (no, doubt was too kind a word) of Matt's story and of Ben's tentative acceptance.

'How come you're here?'

She hesitated a moment and then said, 'There are some men in town who suspect that there is a man in that house whom no one has seen. That he might be a . . . a . . .' Still she could not say the word, but he nodded his understanding. Even on short acquaintance, he seemed quite an extraordinary little boy.

Abridging all that she might have added, she said simply, 'So I came to look and find out.'

He nodded at the stake. 'And brought that to pound through him?'

'I don't know if I could do that.'

'I could,' he said calmly. 'After what I saw last night. Danny was outside my window, holding on like a great big fly. And his teeth . . .' He shook his head, dismissing the nightmare as a businessman might dismiss a bankrupt client.

'Do your parents know you're here?' she asked, knowing they must not.

'No,' he said matter-of-factly. 'Sunday is their nature day. They go on bird walks in the mornings and do other things in the afternoon. Sometimes I go and sometimes I don't. Today they went for a ride up the coast.'

'You're quite a boy,' she said.

'No, I'm not,' he said, his composure unruffled by the praise. 'But I'm going to get rid of *him*.' He looked up at the house.

'Are you sure—'

'Sure I am. So're you. Can't you *feel* how bad he is? Doesn't that house make you afraid, just looking at it?'

'Yes,' she said simply, giving in to him. His logic was the logic of nerve endings, and unlike Ben's or Matt's, it was resistless.

'How are we going to do it?' she asked, automatically giving over the leadership of the venture to him.

'Just go up there and break in,' he said. 'Find him, pound the stake – *my* stake – through his heart, and get out again. He's probably down cellar. They like dark places. Did you bring a flashlight?'

'No.'

'Damn it, neither did I.' He shuffled his sneakered feet aimlessly in the leaves for a moment. 'Probably didn't bring a cross either, did you?'

'Yes, I did,' Susan said. She pulled the link chain out of her blouse and showed him. He nodded and then pulled a chain out of his own shirt.

'I hope I can get this back before my folks come home,' he said gloomily. 'I crooked it from my mother's jewelry box. I'll catch hell if she finds out.' He looked around. The shadows had lengthened even as they talked, and they both felt an impulse to delay and delay.

'When we find him, don't look in his eyes,' Mark told her. 'He can't move out of his coffin, not until dark, but he can still hook you with his eyes. Do you know anything religious by heart?'

They had started through the bushes between the woods and the unkempt lawn of the Marsten House.

'Well, the Lord's Prayer—'

'Sure, that's good. I know that one, too. We'll both say it while I pound the stake in.'

He saw her expression, revolted and half flagging, and he took her hand and squeezed it. His self-possession was disconcerting. 'Listen, we have to. I bet he's got half the town after last night. If we wait any longer, he'll have it all. It will go fast, now.'

'After last night?'

'I dreamed it,' Mark said. His voice was still calm, but his eyes were dark. 'I dreamed of them going to houses and calling on phones and begging to be let in. Some people knew, way down deep they knew, but they let them in just the same. Because it was easier to do that than to think something so bad might be real.'

'Just a dream,' she said uneasily.

'I bet there's a lot of people lying around in bed today with the curtains closed or the shades drawn, wondering if they've got a cold or the flu or something. They feel all weak and fuzzy-headed. They don't want to eat. The idea of eating makes them want to puke.'

'How do you know so much?'

'I read the monster magazines,' he said, 'and go to see the movies when I can. Usually I have to tell my mom

I'm going to see Walt Disney. And you can't trust all of it. Sometimes they just make stuff up so the story will be bloodier.'

They were at the side of the house. Say, we're quite a crew, we believers, Susan thought. An old teacher half-cracked with books, a writer obsessed with his childhood nightmares, a little boy who has taken a postgraduate course in vampire lore from the films and the modern penny-dreadfuls. And me? Do I really believe? Are paranoid fantasies catching?

She believed.

As Mark had said, this close to the house it was just not possible to scoff. All the thought processes, the act of conversation itself, were overshadowed by a more funda-mental voice that was screaming *danger! danger!* in words that were not words at all. Her heartbeat and respiration were up, yet her skin was cold with the capillary-dilating effect of adrenaline, which keeps the blood hiding deep in the body's wells during moments of stress. Her kidneys were tight and heavy. Her eyes seemed preternaturally sharp, taking in every splinter and paint flake on the side of the house. And all of this had been triggered by no external stimuli at all: no men with guns, no large and snarling dogs, no smell of fire. A deeper watchman than her five senses had been wakened after a long season of sleep. And there was no ignoring it.

She peered through a break in the lower shutters. 'Why, they haven't done a thing to it,' she said almost angrily. 'It's a mess.'

'Let me see. Boost me up.'

She laced her fingers together so he could look

through the broken slats and into the crumbling living room of the Marsten House. He saw a deserted, boxy parlor with a thick patina of dust on the floor (many footprints had been tracked through it), peeling wallpaper, two or three old easy chairs, a scarred table. There were cobwebs festooned in the room's upper corners, near the ceiling.

Before she could protest, he had rapped the hook-and-eye combination that held the shutter closed with the blunt end of his stake. The lock fell to the ground in two rusty pieces, and the shutters creaked outward an inch or two.

'Hey!' she protested. 'You shouldn't—'

'What do you want to do? Ring the doorbell?'

He accordioned back the right-hand shutter and rapped one of the dusty, wavy panes of glass. It tinkled inward. The fear leaped up in her, hot and strong, making a coppery taste in her mouth.

'We can still run,' she said, almost to herself.

He looked down at her and there was no contempt in his glance – only an honesty and a fear that was as great as her own. 'You go if you have to,' he said.

'No. I don't have to.' She tried to swallow away the obstruction in her throat and succeeded not at all. 'Hurry it up. You're getting heavy.'

He knocked the protruding shards of glass out of the pane he had broken, switched the stake to his other hand, then reached through and unlatched the window. It moaned slightly as he pushed it up, and then the way was open.

She let him down and they looked wordlessly at the window for a moment. Then Susan stepped forward, pushed the right-hand shutter open all the way, and put her hands on the splintery windowsill preparatory to boosting herself up. The fear in her was sickening with its greatness, settled in her belly like a horrid pregnancy. At last, she understood how Matt Burke had felt as he had gone up the stairs to whatever waited in his guest room.

She had always consciously or unconsciously formed fear into a simple equation: fear = unknown. And to solve the equation, one simply reduced the problem to simple algebraic terms, thus: unknown = creaky board (or whatever), creaky board = nothing to be afraid of. In the modern world all terrors could be gutted by simple use of the transitive axiom of equality. Some fears were justified, of course (you don't drive when you're too plowed to see, don't extend the hand of friendship to snarling dogs, don't go parking with boys you don't know – how did the old joke go? Screw or walk?), but until now she had not believed that some fears were larger than comprehension, apocalyptic and nearly paralyzing. This equation was insoluble. The act of moving forward at all became heroism.

She boosted herself with a smooth flex of muscles, swung one leg over the sill, and then dropped to the dusty parlor floor and looked around. There was a smell. It oozed out of the walls in an almost visible miasma. She tried to tell herself it was only plaster rot, or the accumulated damp guano of all the animals that had nested behind those broken lathings – woodchucks, rats, perhaps even a raccoon or two. But it was more. The smell was deeper than animal-stink, more entrenched. It made her think of tears and vomit and blackness.

'Hey,' Mark called softly. His hands waved above the windowsill. 'A little help.'

She leaned out, caught him under the armpits, and dragged him up until he had caught a grip on the windowsill. Then he jackknifed himself in neatly. His sneakered feet thumped the carpet, and then the house was still again.

They found themselves listening to the silence, fascinated by it. There did not even seem to be the faint, high hum that comes in utter stillness, the sound of nerve endings idling in neutral. There was only a great dead soundlessness and the beat of blood in their own ears.

And yet they both knew, of course. They were not alone.

2

'Come on,' he said. 'Let's look around.' He clutched the stake very tightly and for just a moment looked longingly back at the window.

She moved slowly toward the hall and he came after her. Just outside the door there was a small end table with a book on it. Mark picked it up.

'Hey,' he said. 'Do you know Latin?'

'A little, from high school.'

'What's this mean?' He showed her the binding.

She sounded the words out, a frown creasing her forehead. Then she shook her head. 'Don't know.'

He opened the book at random, and flinched. There was a picture of a naked man holding a child's gutted body toward something you couldn't see. He put the book down, glad to let go of it – the stretched binding felt uncomfortably familiar under his hand – and they went down the hallway toward the kitchen together. The shadows were more prominent here. The sun had gotten around to the other side of the house.

'Do you smell it?' he asked.

'Yes.'

'It's worse back here, isn't it?'

'Yes.'

He was remembering the cold-pantry his mother had kept in the other house, and how one year three bushel baskets of tomatoes had gone bad down there in the dark. This smell was like that, like the smell of tomatoes decaying into putrescence.

Susan whispered: 'God, I'm so scared.'

His hand groped out, found hers, and they locked tightly.

The kitchen linoleum was old and gritty and pocked, worn black in front of the old porcelain-tub sink. A large, scarred table stood in the middle of the floor, and on it was a yellow plate, a knife and fork, and a scrap of raw hamburger.

The cellar door was standing ajar.

'That's where we have to go,' he said.

'Oh,' she said weakly.

The door was open just a crack, and the light did not penetrate at all. The tongue of darkness seemed to lick hungrily at the kitchen, waiting for night to come so it could swallow it whole. That quarter inch of darkness was hideous, unspeakable in its possibilities. She stood beside Mark, helpless and moveless.

Then he stepped forward and pulled the door open and stood for a moment, looking down. She saw a muscle jump beneath his jaw.

'I think—' he began, and she heard something behind her and turned, suddenly feeling slow, feeling too late. It was Straker. He was grinning.

Mark turned, saw, and tried to dive around him. Straker's fist crashed into his chin and he knew no more.

3

When Mark came to, he was being carried up a flight of stairs – not the cellar stairs, though. There was not that feeling of stone enclosure, and the air was not so fetid. He allowed his eyelids to unclose themselves a tiny fraction, letting his head still loll limply on his neck. A stair landing coming up . . . the second floor. He could see quite clearly. The sun was not down yet. Thin hope, then.

They gained the landing, and suddenly the arms holding him were gone. He thumped heavily onto the floor, hitting his head.

'Do you not think I know when someone is playing the possum, young master?' Straker asked him. From the floor he seemed easily ten feet tall. His bald head glistened with a subdued elegance in the gathering gloom. Mark saw with growing terror that there was a coil of rope around his shoulder.

He grabbed for the pocket where the pistol had been.

Straker threw back his head and laughed. 'I have taken the liberty of removing the gun, young master. Boys should not be allowed weapons they do not understand . . . any more than they should lead young ladies to houses where their commerce has not been invited.'

'What did you do with Susan Norton?'

Straker smiled. 'I have taken her where she wished to go, my boy. Into the cellar. Later, when the sun goes down, she will meet the man she came here to meet. You will meet him yourself, perhaps later tonight, perhaps tomorrow night. He may give you to the girl, of course . . . but I rather think he'll want to deal with you himself. The girl will have friends of her own, some of them perhaps meddlers like yourself.'

Mark lashed out with both feet at Straker's crotch, and Straker sidestepped liquidly, like a dancer. At the same moment he kicked his own foot out, connecting squarely with Mark's kidneys.

Mark bit his lips and writhed on the floor.

Straker chuckled. 'Come, young master. To your feet.'

'I . . . I can't.'

'Then crawl,' Straker said contemptuously. He kicked again, this time striking the large muscle of the thigh. The pain was dreaful, but Mark clenched his teeth together. He got to his knees, and then to his feet.

They progressed down the hall toward the door at the far end. The pain in his kidneys was subsiding to a dull ache. 'What are you going to do with me?'

'Truss you like a spring turkey, young master. Later, after my Master holds intercourse with you, you will be set free.'

'Like the others?'

Straker smiled.

As Mark pushed open the door and stepped into the room where Hubert Marsten had committed suicide, something odd seemed to happen in his mind. The fear did not fall away from it, but it seemed to stop acting as a brake on his thoughts, jamming all productive signals. His thoughts began to flicker past with amazing speed, not in words or precisely in images, but in a kind of symbolic shorthand. He felt like a lightbulb that has suddenly received a surge of power from no known source.

The room itself was utterly prosaic. The wallpaper hung in strips, showing the white plaster and Sheetrock beneath. The floor was heavily dusted with time and plaster, but there was only one set of footprints in it, suggesting someone had come up once, looked around, and left again. There were two stacks of magazines, a cast-iron cot with no spring or mattress, and a small tin plate with a faded Currier & Ives design that had once blocked the stove hole in the chimney. The window was shuttered, but enough light filtered dustily through the broken slats to make Mark think there might be an hour of daylight left. There was an aura of old nastiness about the room.

It took perhaps five seconds to open the door, see these things, and cross to the center of the room where Straker told him to stop. In that short period, his mind raced along three tracks and saw three possible outcomes to the situation he found himself in.

On one, he suddenly sprinted across the room toward the shuttered window and tried to crash through both glass and shutter like a Western movie hero, taking the drop to whatever lay below with blind hope. In one mental eye he saw himself crashing through only to fall onto a rusty pile of junked farm machinery, twitching away the last seconds of his life impaled on blunt harrow blades like a bug on a pin. In the other eye he saw himself crashing through the glass and into the shutter which trembled but did not break. He saw Straker pulling him back, his clothes torn, his body lacerated and bleeding in a dozen places.

On the second track, he saw Straker tie him up and leave. He saw himself trussed on the floor, saw the light fading, saw his struggles become more frenzied (but just as useless), and heard, finally, the steady tread on the stairs of one who was a million times worse than Straker.

On the third track, he saw himself using a trick he had read about last summer in a book on Houdini. Houdini had been a famous magician who had escaped jail cells, chained boxes, bank vaults, steamer trunks thrown into rivers. He could get out of ropes, police handcuffs, and Chinese finger-pullers. And one of the things the book said he did was hold his breath and tighten his hands into fists when a volunteer from the audience was trying him up. You bulged your thighs and forearms and neck muscles, too. If your muscles were big, you had a little slack when you relaxed them. The trick then was to relax completely, and go at your escape slowly and surely, never letting panic hurry you up. Little by little, your body would give you sweat for grease, and that helped, too. The book made it sound very easy.

'Turn around,' Straker said. 'I am going to tie you up. While I tie you up, you will not move. If you move, I take this' – he cocked his thumb before Mark like a hitchhiker – 'and pop your right eye out. Do you understand?'

Mark nodded. He took a deep breath, held it, and bunched all his muscles.

Straker threw his coil of rope over one of the beams. 'Lie down,' he said.

Mark did.

He crossed Mark's hands behind his back and bound them tightly with the rope. He made a loop, slipped it around Mark's neck, and tied it in a hangman's knot. 'You're made fast to the very beam my Master's friend and sponsor in this country hung himself from, young master. Are you flattered?'

Mark grunted, and Straker laughed. He passed the rope through Mark's crotch, and he groaned as Straker took up the slack with a brutal jerk.

He chuckled with monstrous good nature. 'So your jewels hurt? They will not for long. You are going to lead an ascetic's life, my boy – a long, long life.'

He banded the rope over Mark's taut thighs, made the knot tight, banded it again over his knees, and again over his ankles. Mark needed to breathe very badly now, but he held on stubbornly.

'You're trembling, young master,' Straker said mockingly. 'Your body is all in hard little knots. Your flesh is white – but it will be whiter! Yet you need not be so afraid. My Master has the capacity for kindness. He is much loved, right here in your own town. There is only a little sting, like the doctor's needle, and then sweetness. And later on you will be let free. You will go see your mother and father, yes? You will see them after they sleep.'

He stood up and looked down at Mark benignly. 'I will say good-by for a bit now, young master. Your lovely consort is to be made comfortable. When we meet again, you will like me better.'

He left, slamming the door behind him. A key rattled in the lock. And as his feet descended the stairs, Mark let out his breath and relaxed his muscles with a great, whooping sigh.

The ropes holding him loosened — a little.

He lay moveless, collecting himself. His mind was still flying with that same unnatural, exhilarating speed. From his position, he looked across the swelled, uneven floor to the iron cot frame. He could see the wall beyond it. The wallpaper was peeled away from that section and lay beneath the cot frame like a discarded snakeskin. He focused on a small section of the wall and examined it closely. He flushed everything else from his mind. The book on Houdini said that concentration was all-important. No fear or taint of panic must be allowed in the mind. The body must be completely relaxed. And the escape must take place in the mind before a single finger did so much as twitch. Every step must exist concretely in the mind.

He looked at the wall, and minutes passed.

The wall was white and bumpy, like an old drive-in movie screen. Eventually, as his body relaxed to its greatest degree, he began to see himself projected there, a small boy wearing a blue T-shirt and Levi's jeans. The boy was on his side, arms pulled behind him, wrists nestling the small of the back above the buttocks. A noose looped around his neck, and any hard struggling would tighten that running slipknot inexorably until enough air was cut off to black out the brain.

He looked at the wall.

The figure there had begun to move cautiously, although he himself lay perfectly still. He watched all the movements of the simulacrum raptly. He had achieved a level of concentration necessary to the Indian fakirs and yogis, who are able to contemplate their toes or the tips of their noses for days, the state of certain mediums who levitate tables in a state of unconsciousness or extrude long tendrils of teleplasm from the nose, the mouth, the fingertips. His state was close to sublime. He did not think of Straker or the fading daylight. He no longer saw the gritty floor, the cot frame, or even the wall. He only saw the boy, a perfect figure which went through a tiny dance of carefully controlled muscles.

He looked at the wall.

And at last he began to move his wrists in half circles, toward each other. At the limit of each half circle, the thumb sides of his palms touched. No muscles moved but those in his lower forearms. He did not hurry. He looked at the wall.

As sweat rose through his pores, his wrists began to turn more freely. The half circles became three-quarters. At the limit of each, the backs of his hands pressed together. The loops holding them had loosened a tiny bit more.

He stopped.

After a moment had passed, he began to flex his thumbs against his palms and press his fingers together in a wriggling motion. His face was utterly expressionless, the plaster face of a department store dummy.

Five minutes passed. His hands were sweating freely now. The extreme level of his concentration had put him in partial control of his own sympathetic nervous system, another device of yogis and fakirs, and he had, unknowingly, gained some control over his body's involuntary functions. More sweat trickled from his pores than his careful movements could account for. His hands had become oily. Droplets fell from his forehead, darkening the white dust on the floor.

He began to move his arms in an up-and-down piston motion, using his biceps and back muscles now. The noose tightened a little, but he could feel one of the loops holding his hands beginning to drag lower on his right palm. It was sticking against the pad of the thumb now, and that was all. Excitement shot through him and he stopped at once until the emotion had passed away completely. When it had, he began again. Up-down. Up-down. Up-down. He gained an eighth of an inch at a time. And suddenly, shockingly, his right hand was free.

He left it where it was, flexing it. When he was sure it was limber, he eased the fingers under the loop holding the left wrist and tented them. The left hand slid free.

He brought both hands around and put them on the floor. He closed his eyes for a moment. The trick now was to not think he had it made. The trick was to move with great deliberation.

Supporting himself with his left hand, he let his right roam over the bumps and valleys of the knot which secured the noose at his neck. He saw immediately that he would have to nearly choke himself to free it – and he was going to tighten the pressure on his testicles, which already throbbed dully.

He took a deep breath and began to work on the knot. The rope tightened by steady degrees, pressing into his neck and crotch. Prickles of coarse hemp dug into his throat like miniature tattoo needles. The knot defied him for what seemed an endless time. His vision began to fade under the onslaught of large black flowers that burst into soundless bloom before his eyes. He refused to hurry. He wiggled the knot steadily, and at last felt new slack in it.

For a moment the pressure on his groin tightened unbearably, and then with a convulsive jerk, he threw the noose over his head and the pain lessened.

He sat up and hung his head over, breathing raggedly, cradling his wounded testicles in both hands. The sharp pain became a dull, pervading ache that made him feel nauseated.

When it began to abate a little, he looked over at the shuttered window. The light coming through the broken slats had faded to a dull ocher – it was almost sundown. And the door was locked.

He pulled the loose loop of rope over the beam, and set to work on the knots that held his legs. They were maddeningly tight, and his concentration had begun to slip away from him as reaction set in.

He freed his thighs, the knees, and after a seemingly endless struggle, his ankles. He stood up weakly among the harmless loops of rope and staggered. He began to rub his thighs.

There was a noise from below: footsteps.

He looked up, panicky, nostrils dilating. He hobbled over to the window and tried to lift it. Nailed shut, with rusted tenpennies bent over the cheap wood of the half sill like staples.

The feet were coming up the stairs.

He wiped his mouth with his hand and stared wildly around the room. Two bundles of magazines. A small tin plate with a picture of an 1890s summer picnic on the back. The iron cot frame.

He went to it despairingly and pulled up one end. And some distant gods, perhaps seeing how much luck he had manufactured by himself, doled out a little of their own.

The steps had begun down the hall toward the door when he unscrewed the steel cot leg to its final thread and pulled it free.

4

When the door opened, Mark was standing behind it with the bed leg upraised, like a wooden Indian with a tomahawk.

'Young master, I've come to—'

He saw the empty coils of rope and froze for perhaps one full second in utter surprise. He was halfway through the door.

To Mark, things seemed to have slowed to the speed of a football maneuver seen in instant replay. He seemed to have minutes rather than bare seconds to aim at the one-quarter skull circumference visible beyond the edge of the door.

He brought the leg down with both hands, not as hard as he could – he sacrificed some force for better aim. It struck Straker just above the temple, as he started to turn to look behind the door. His eyes, open wide, squeezed shut in pain. Blood flew from the scalp wound in an amazing spray.

Straker's body recoiled and he stumbled backward into the room. His face was twisted into a terrifying grimace. He reached out and Mark hit him again. This time the pipe struck his bald skull just above the bulge of the forehead, and there was another gout of blood.

He went down bonelessly, his eyes rolling up in his head.

Mark skirted the body, looking at it with eyes that were bulging and wide. The end of the bed leg was painted with blood. It was darker than Technicolor movie blood. Looking at it made him feel sick, but looking at Straker made him feel nothing.

I killed him, he thought. And on the heels of that: *Good. Good.*

Straker's hand closed around his ankle.

Mark gasped and tried to pull his foot away. The hand held fast like a steel trap and now Straker was looking up at him, his eyes cold and bright through a dripping mask of blood. His lips were moving, but no sound came out. Mark pulled harder, to no avail. With a half groan, he began to hammer at Straker's clutching hand with the bed leg. Once, twice, three times, four. There was the awful pencil sound of snapping fingers. The hand loosened, and he pulled free with a yank that sent him stumbling out through the doorway and into the hall.

Straker's head had dropped to the floor again, but his mangled hand opened and closed on the air with tene-brous vitality, like the jerking of a dog's paws in dreams of cat-chasing.

The bed leg fell from his nerveless fingers and he backed away, trembling. Then panic took him and he turned and fled down the stairs, leaping two or three at a time on his numb legs, his hand skimming the splintered banister.

The front hall was shadow-struck, horribly dark.

He went into the kitchen, casting lunatic, shying

glances at the open cellar door. The sun was going down in a blazing mullion of reds and yellows and purples. In a funeral parlor sixteen miles distant, Ben Mears was watching the clock as the hands hesitated between 7:01 and 7:02.

Mark knew nothing of that, but he knew the vampire's time was imminent. To stay longer meant confrontation on top of confrontation; to go back down into that cellar and try to save Susan meant induction into the ranks of the Undead.

Yet he went to the cellar door and actually walked down the first three steps before his fear wrapped him in almost physical bonds and would allow him to go no further. He was weeping, and his body was trembling wildly, as if with ague.

'Susan!' he screamed. 'Run!'

'M-Mark?' Her voice, sounding weak and dazed. 'I can't see. It's dark—'

There was a sudden booming noise, like a hollow gunshot, followed by a profound and soulless chuckle.

Susan screamed . . . a sound that trailed away to a moan and then to silence.

Still he paused, on feather-feet that trembled to blow him away.

And from below came a friendly voice, amazingly like his father's: 'Come down, my boy. I admire you.'

The power in the voice alone was so great that he felt the fear ebbing from him, the feathers in his feet turning to lead. He actually began to grope down another step before he caught hold of himself — and the catching hold took all the ragged discipline he had left.

'Come down,' the voice said, closer now. It held,

beneath the friendly fatherliness, the smooth steel of command.

Mark shouted down: 'I know your name! It's Barlow!' And fled.

By the time he reached the front hall the fear had come on him full again, and if the door had not been unlocked he might have burst straight through the center of it, leaving a cartoon cutout of himself behind.

He fled down the driveway (much like that long-ago boy Benjaman Mears) and then straight down the center of the Brooks Road toward town and dubious safety. Yet might not the king vampire come after him, even now?

He swerved off the road and made his way blunderingly through the woods, splashing through Taggart Stream and falling in a tangle of burdocks on the other side, and finally out into his own backyard.

He walked through the kitchen door and looked through the arch into the living room to where his mother, with worry written across her face in large letters, was talking into the telephone with the directory open on her lap.

She looked up and saw him, and relief spread across her face in a physical wave.

'—here he is—'

She set the phone into its cradle without waiting for a response and walked toward him. He saw with greater sorrow than she would have believed that she had been crying.

'Oh, Mark . . . where have you been?'

'He's home?' His father called from the den. His face, unseen, was filling with thunder.

'*Where have you been?*' She caught his shoulders and shook them.

'Out,' he said wanly. 'I fell down running home.'

There was nothing else to say. The essential and defining characteristic of childhood is not the effortless merging of dream and reality, but only alienation. There are no words for childhood's dark turns and exhalations. A wise child recognizes it and submits to the necessary consequences. A child who counts the cost is a child no longer.

He added: 'The time got away from me. It—'

Then his father, descending upon him.

5

Some time in the darkness before Monday's dawn.

Scratching at the window.

He came up from sleep with no pause, no intervening period of drowsiness or orientation. The insanities of sleep and waking had become remarkably similar.

The white face in the darkness outside the glass was Susan's.

'Mark . . . let me in.'

He got out of bed. The floor was cold under his bare feet. He was shivering.

'Go away,' he said tonelessly. He could see that she was still wearing the same blouse, the same slacks. I wonder if *her* folks are worried, he thought. If they've called the police.

'It's not so bad, Mark,' she said, and her eyes were flat and obsidian. She smiled, showing her teeth, which shone in sharp relief below her pale gums. 'It's ever so nice. Let me in, I'll show you. I'll kiss you, Mark. I'll kiss you all over like your mother never did.'

'Go away,' he repeated.

'One of us will get you sooner or later,' she said. 'There are lots more of us now. Let it be me, Mark. I'm . . . I'm hungry.' She tried to smile, but it turned into a nightshade grimace that made his bones cold.

He held up his cross and pressed it against the window.

She hissed, as if scalded, and let go of the window frame. For a moment she hung suspended in air, her body becoming misty and indistinct. Then, gone. But not before he saw (or thought he saw) a look of desperate unhappiness on her face.

The night was still and silent again.

There are lots more of us now.

His thoughts turned to his parents, sleeping in thoughtless peril below him, and dread gripped his bowels.

Some men knew, she had said, or suspected.

Who?

The writer, of course. The one she dated. Mears, his name was. He lived at Eva's boardinghouse. Writers knew a lot. It would be him. And he would have to get to Mears before she did—

He stopped on his way back to bed.

If she hadn't already.

CHAPTER THIRTEEN

FATHER CALLAHAN

On that same Sunday evening, Father Callahan stepped hesitantly into Matt Burke's hospital room at quarter to seven by Matt's watch. The bedside table and the counterpane itself were littered with books, some of them dusty with age. Matt had called Loretta Starcher at her spinster's apartment and had not only gotten her to open the library on Sunday, but had gotten her to deliver the books in person. She had come in at the head of a procession made up of three hospital orderlies, each loaded down. She had left in something of a huff because he refused to answer questions about the strange conglomeration.

Father Callahan regarded the schoolteacher curiously. He looked worn, but not so worn or wearily shocked as most of the parishioners he visited in similar circumstances. Callahan found that the common first reaction to news of cancer, strokes, heart attacks, or the failure of some major organ was one of betrayal. The patient was astounded to find that such a close (and, up to now at least, fully understood) friend as one's own body could be so sluggard as to lie down on the job. The reaction which followed close

414

on the heels of the first was the thought that a friend who would let one down so cruelly was not worth having. The conclusion that followed these reactions was that it didn't matter if *this* friend was worth having or not. One could not refuse to speak to one's traitorous body, or get up a petition against it, or pretend that one was not at home when it called. The final thought in this hospital-bed train of reasoning was the hideous possibility that one's body might not be a friend at all, but an enemy implacably dedicated to destroying the superior force that had used it and abused it ever since the disease of reason set in.

Once, while in a fine drunken frenzy, Callahan had sat down to write a monograph on the subject for *The Catholic Journal*. He had even illustrated it with a fiendish editorial-page cartoon, which showed a brain poised on the highest ledge of a skyscraper. The building (labeled 'The Human Body') was in flames (which were labeled 'Cancer' – although they might have been a dozen others). The cartoon was titled 'Too Far to Jump.' During the next day's enforced bout with sobriety, he had torn the prospective monograph to shreds and burned the cartoon – there was no place in Catholic doctrine for either, unless you wanted to add a helicopter labeled 'Christ' that was dangling a rope ladder. Nonetheless, he felt that his insights had been true ones, and the result of such sickbed logic on the part of the patient was usually acute depression. The symptoms included dulled eyes, slow responses, sighs fetched from deep within the chest cavity, and sometimes tears at the sight of the priest, that black crow whose function was ultimately predicated on the problem the fact of mortality presented to the thinking being.

Matt Burke showed none of this depression. He held

out his hand, and when Callahan shook it, he found the grip surprisingly strong.

'Father Callahan. Good of you to come.'

'Pleased to. Good teachers, like a wife's wisdom, are pearls beyond price.'

'Even agnostic old bears like myself?'

'Especially those,' Callahan said, riposting with pleasure. 'I may have caught you at a weak moment. There are no atheists in the foxholes, I've been told, and precious few agnostics in the Intensive Care ward.'

'I'm being moved soon, alas.'

'Pish-posh,' Callahan said. 'We'll have you Hail Marying and Our Fathering yet.'

'That,' Matt said 'is not as far-fetched as you might think.'

Father Callahan sat down, and his knee bumped the bedstand as he drew his chair up. A carelessly piled stack of books cascaded into his lap. He read the titles aloud as he put them back.

'*Dracula. Dracula's Guest. The Search for Dracula. The Golden Bough. The Natural History of the Vampire* – natural? *Hungarian Folk Tales. Monsters of the Darkness. Monsters in Real Life. Peter Kurtin, Monster of Düsseldorf.* And . . .' He brushed a thick patina of dust from the last cover and revealed a spectral figure poised menacingly above a sleeping damsel. '*Varney the Vampyre, or, The Feast of Blood.* Goodness – required reading for convalescent heart attack patients?'

Matt smiled. 'Poor old *Varney*. I read it a long time ago for a class report in Eh-279 at the university . . . Romantic Lit. The professor, whose idea of fantasy began with *Beowulf* and ended with *The Screwtape Letters*, was quite shocked. I got a D plus on the report and a written command to elevate my sights.'

'The case of Peter Kurtin is interesting enough, though,' Callahan said. 'In a repulsive sort of way.'

'You know his history?'

'Most of it, yes. I took an interest in such things as a divinity student. My excuse to the highly skeptical elders was that, in order to be a successful priest, one had to plumb the depths of human nature as well as aspire to its heights. All eyewash, actually. I just liked a shudder as well as the next one. Kurtin, I believe, murdered two of his playmates as a young boy by drowning them – he simply gained possession of a small float anchored in the middle of a wide river and kept pushing them away until they tired and went under.'

'Yes,' Matt said. 'As a teenager, he twice tried to kill the parents of a girl who refused to go walking with him. He later burned down their house. But that is not the part of his, uh, career that I'm interested in.'

'I guessed not, from the trend of your reading matter.' He picked a magazine off the coverlet which showed an incredibly endowed young woman in a skintight costume who was sucking the blood of a young man. The young man's expression seemed to be an uneasy combination of extreme terror and extreme lust. The name of the magazine – and of the young woman, apparently – was *Vampirella*. Callahan put it down, more intrigued than ever.

'Kurtin attacked and killed over a dozen women,' Callahan said. 'Mutilated many more with a hammer. If it was their time of the month, he drank their discharge.'

Matt Burke nodded again. 'What's not so generally

known,' he said, 'is that he also mutilated animals. At the height of his obsession, he ripped the heads from the bodies of two swans in Düsseldorf's central park and drank the blood which gushed from their necks.'

'Has all this to do with why you wanted to see me?' Callahan asked. 'Mrs Curless told me you said it was a matter of some importance.'

'Yes, it does and it is.'

'What might it be, then? If you've meant to intrigue me, you've certainly succeeded.'

Matt looked at him calmly. 'A good friend of mine, Ben Mears, was to have gotten in touch with you today. Your housekeeper said he had not.'

'That's so. I've seen no one since two o'clock this afternoon.'

'I have been unable to reach him. He left the hospital in the company of my doctor, James Cody. I have also been unable to reach him. I have likewise been unable to reach Susan Norton, Ben's lady friend. She went out early this afternoon, promising her parents she would be in by five. They are worried.'

Callahan sat forward at this. He had a passing acquaintance with Bill Norton, who had once come to see him about a problem that had to do with some Catholic coworkers.

'You suspect something?'

'Let me ask you a question,' Matt said. 'Take it very seriously and think it over before you answer. Have you noticed anything out of the ordinary in town just lately?'

Callahan's original impression, now almost a certainty, was that this man was proceeding very carefully indeed, not wanting to frighten him off by whatever was on his mind. Something sufficiently outrageous was suggested by the litter of books.

'Vampires in 'salem's Lot?' he asked.

He was thinking that the deep depression which followed grave illness could sometimes be avoided if the person afflicted had a deep enough investment in life: artists, musicians, a carpenter whose thoughts centered on some half-completed building. The interest could just as well be linked to some harmless (or not so harmless) psychosis, perhaps incipient before the illness.

He had spoken at some length with an elderly man named Horris from Schoolyard Hill who had been in the Maine Medical Center with advanced cancer of the lower intestine. In spite of pain which must have been excruciating, he had discoursed with Callahan in great and lucid detail concerning the creatures from Uranus who were infiltrating every walk of American life. 'One day the fella who fills your gas tank down at Sonny's Amoco is just Joe Blow from Falmouth,' this bright-eyed, talking skeleton told him, 'and the next day it's a Uranian who just *looks* like Joe Blow. He even has Joe Blow's memories and speech patterns, you see. Because Uranians eat alpha waves . . . smack, smack, smack!' According to Horris, he did not have cancer at all, but an advanced case of laser poisoning. The Uranians, alarmed at his knowledge of their machinations, had decided to put him out of the way. Horris accepted this, and was prepared to go down fighting. Callahan made no effort to disabuse him. Leave that to well-meaning but thickheaded relatives. Callahan's experience was that psychosis, like a good knock of Cutty Sark, could be extremely beneficial.

So now he simply folded his hands and waited for Matt to continue.

Matt said, 'It's difficult to proceed as it is. It's going to be more difficult still if you think I'm suffering from sickbed dementia.'

Startled by hearing his thoughts expressed just as he had finished thinking them, Callahan kept his poker face only with difficulty – although the emotion that would have come through would not have been disquiet but admiration.

'On the contrary, you seem extremely lucid,' he said.

Matt sighed. 'Lucidity doesn't presuppose sanity – as you well know.' He shifted in bed, redistributing the books that lay around him. 'If there is a God, He must be making me do penance for a life of careful academicism – of refusing to plant an intellectual foot on any ground until it had been footnoted in triplicate. Now for the second time in one day, I'm compelled to make the wildest declarations without a shred of proof to back them up. All I can say in defense of my own sanity is that my statements can be either proved or disproved without too much difficulty, and hope that you will take me seriously enough to make the test before it's too late.' He chuckled. '*Before it's too late.* Sounds straight out of the thirties' pulp magazines, doesn't it?'

'Life is full of melodrama,' Callahan remarked, reflecting that if it were so, he had seen precious little of it lately.

'Let me ask you again if you have noticed anything – *anything* – out of the way or peculiar this weekend.'

'To do with vampires, or—'

'To do with anything.'

Callahan thought it over. 'The dump's closed,' he said finally. 'But the gate was broken off, so I drove in anyway.' He smiled. 'I rather enjoy taking my own garbage to the dump. It's so practical and humble that I can indulge my elitist fantasies of a poor but happy proletariat to the fullest. Dud Rogers wasn't around, either.'

'Anything else?'

'Well . . . the Crocketts weren't at mass this morning, and Mrs Crockett hardly ever misses.'

'More?'

'Poor Mrs Glick, of course—'

Matt got up on one elbow. 'Mrs Glick? What about her?'

'She's dead.'

'Of what?'

'Pauline Dickens seemed to think it was a heart attack,' Callahan said, but hesitatingly.

'Has anyone else died in the Lot today?' Ordinarily, it would have been a foolish question. Deaths in a small town like 'salem's Lot were generally spread apart, in spite of the higher proportion of elderly in the population.

'No,' Callahan said slowly. 'But the mortality rate has certainly been high lately, hasn't it? Mike Ryerson . . . Floyd Tibbits . . . the McDougall baby . . .'

Matt nodded, looking tired. 'Passing strange,' he said. 'Yes. But things are reaching the point where they'll be able to cover up for each other. A few more nights and I'm afraid . . . afraid . . .'

'Let's stop beating around the bush,' Callahan said.

'All right. There's been rather too much of that already, hasn't there?'

He began to tell his story from beginning to end, weaving in Ben's and Susan's and Jimmy's additions as he went along, holding back nothing. By the time he had finished, the evening's horror had ended for Ben and Jimmy. Susan Norton's was just beginning.

2

When he finished, Matt allowed a moment of silence and then said, 'So. Am I crazy?'

'You're determined that people will think you so, anyway,' Callahan said, 'in spite of the fact that you seem to have convinced Mr Mears and your own doctor. No, I don't think you're crazy. After all, I am in the business of dealing with the supernatural. If I may be allowed a small pun, it is my bread and wine.'

'But—'

'Let me tell you a story. I won't vouch for its truth, but I will vouch for my own belief that it *is* true. It concerns a good friend of mine, Father Raymond Bissonette, who has been ministering to a parish in Cornwall for some years now – along the so-called Tin Coast. Do you know of it?'

'Through reading, yes.'

'Some five years ago he wrote me that he had been called to an out-of-the-way corner of his parish to conduct a funeral service for a girl who had just "pined away." The girl's coffin was filled with wild roses, which struck Ray as unusual. What he found downright grotesque was the fact that her mouth had been propped open with a stick and then filled with garlic and wild thyme.'

'But those are—'

'Traditional protections against the rising of the Undead, yes. Folk remedies. When Ray inquired, he was told quite matter-of-factly by the girl's father that she had been killed by an incubus. You know the meaning?'

'A sexual vampire.'

'The girl had been betrothed to a young man named Bannock, who had a large strawberry-colored birthmark on the side of his neck. He was struck and killed by a car on his way home from work two weeks before the wedding. Two years later, the girl became engaged to another man. She broke it off quite suddenly during the week before the banns were to be cried for the second time. She told her parents and friends that John Bannock had been coming to her in the night and she had been unfaithful with him. Her present lover, according to Ray, was more distressed by the thought that she might have become mentally unbalanced than by the possibility of demon visitation. Nonetheless, she wasted away, died, and was buried in the old ways of the church.

'All of that did not occasion Ray's letter. What did was an occurrence some two months after the girl's burial. While he was on an early morning walk, Ray spied a young man standing by the girl's grave – a young man with a strawberry-colored birthmark on his neck. Nor is that the end of the story. He had gotten a Polaroid camera from his parents the Christmas before and had amused himself by snapping various views of the Cornish countryside. I have some of them in a picture album at the rectory – they're quite good. The camera was around his neck that morning, and he took several snaps of the young man.

When he showed them around the village, the reaction was quite amazing. One old lady fell down in a faint, and the dead girl's mother began to pray in the street.

'But when Ray got up the next morning, the young man's figure had completely faded out of the pictures, and all that was left were several views of the local churchyard.'

'And you believe that?' Matt asked.

'Oh yes. And I suspect most people would. The ordinary fellow isn't half so leery of the supernatural as the fiction writers like to make out. Most writers who deal in that particular subject, as a matter of fact, are more hard-headed about spirits and demons and boogies than your ordinary man in the street. Lovecraft was an atheist. Edgar Allan Poe was sort of a half-assed transcendentalist. And Hawthorne was only conventionally religious.'

'You're amazingly conversant on the subject,' Matt said.

The priest shrugged. 'I had a boy's interest in the occult and the outré,' he said, 'and as I grew older, my calling to the priesthood enhanced rather than retarded it.' He sighed deeply. 'But lately I've begun to ask myself some rather hard questions about the nature of evil in the world.' With a twisted smile he added, 'It's spoiled a lot of the fun.'

'Then . . . would you investigate a few things for me? And would you be averse to taking along some holy water and a bit of the Host?'

'You're treading on uneasy theological ground now,' Callahan said with genuine gravity.

'Why?'

'I'm not going to say no, not at this point,' Callahan

said. 'And I ought to tell you that if you'd gotten a younger priest, he probably would have said yes almost at once, with few if any qualms at all.' He smiled bitterly. 'They view the trappings of the church as symbolic rather than practical – like a shaman's headdress and medicine stick. This young priest might decide you were crazy, but if shaking a little holy water around would ease your craziness, fine and dandy. I can't do that. If I should proceed to make your investigations in a neat Harris tweed with nothing under my arm but a copy of Sybil Leek's *The Sensuous Exorcist* or whatever, that would be between you and me. But if I go with the Host . . . then I go as an agent of the Holy Catholic Church, prepared to execute what I would consider the most spiritual rites of my office. Then I go as Christ's representative on earth.' He was now looking at Matt seriously, solemnly. 'I may be a poor excuse for a priest – at times I've thought so – a bit jaded, a bit cynical, and just lately suffering a crisis of . . . what? faith? identity? . . . but I still believe enough in the awesome, mystical, and apotheotic power of the church which stands behind me to tremble a bit at the thought of accepting your request lightly. The church is more than a bundle of ideals, as these younger fellows seem to believe. It's more than a spiritual Boy Scout troop. The church is a Force . . . and one does not set a Force in motion lightly.' He frowned severely at Matt. 'Do you understand that? Your understanding is vitally important.'

'I understand.'

'You see, the overall concept of evil in the Catholic Church has undergone a radical change in this century. Do you know what caused it?'

425

'I imagine it was Freud.'

'Very good. The Catholic Church began to cope with a new concept as it marched into the twentieth century: evil with a small "e." With a devil that was not a red-horned monster complete with spiked tail and cloven hooves, or a serpent crawling through the garden – although that is a remarkably apt psychological image. The devil, according to the Gospel According to Freud, would be a gigantic composite id, the subconscious of all of us.'

'Surely a more stupendous concept than red-tailed boogies or demons with such sensitive noses that they can be banished with one good fart from a constipated churchman,' Matt said.

'Stupendous, of course. But impersonal. Merciless. Untouchable. Banishing Frend's devil is as impossible as Shylock's bargain – to extract a pound of flesh without spilling a drop of blood. The Catholic Church has been forced to reinterpret its whole approach to evil – bombers over Cambodia, the war in Ireland and the Middle East, cop-killings and ghetto riots, the billion smaller evils loosed on the world each day like a plague of gnats. It is in the process of shedding its old medicine-man skin and reemerging as a socially active, socially conscious body. The inner city rap-center ascendant over the confessional. Communion playing second fiddle to the civil rights movement and urban renewal. The church has been in the process of planting both feet in this world.'

'Where there are no witches or incubi or vampires,' Matt said, 'but only child-beating, incest, and the rape of the environment.'

'Yes.'

Matt said deliberately, 'And you hate it, don't you?'

'Yes,' Callahan said quietly. 'I think it's an abomination. It's the Catholic Church's way of saying that God isn't dead, only a little senile. And I guess that's my answer, isn't it? What do you want me to do?'

Matt told him.

Callahan thought it over and said, 'You realize it flies in the face of everything I just told you?'

'On the contrary, I think it's your chance to put your church – *your* church – to the test.'

Callahan took a deep breath. 'Very well, I agree. On one condition.'

'What would that be?'

'That all of us who go on this little expedition first go to the shop this Mr Straker is managing. That Mr Mears, as spokesman, should speak to him frankly about all of this. That we all have a chance to observe his reactions. And finally, that he should have his chance to laugh in our faces.'

Matt was frowning. 'It would be warning him.'

Callahan shook his head. 'I believe the warning would be of no avail if the three of us – Mr Mears, Dr Cody, and myself – still agreed that we should move ahead regardless.'

'All right,' Matt said. 'I agree, contingent on the approval of Ben and Jimmy Cody.'

'Fine.' Callahan sighed. 'Will it hurt you if I tell you that I hope this is all in your mind? That I hope this man Straker does laugh in our faces, and with good reason?'

'Not in the slightest.'

'I do hope it. I have agreed to more than you know. It frightens me.'

'I am frightened, too,' Matt said softly.

427

3

But walking back to St Andrew's, he did not feel frightened at all. He felt exhilarated, renewed. For the first time in years he was sober and did not crave a drink.

He went into the rectory, picked up the telephone, and dialed Eva Miller's boardinghouse. 'Hello? Mrs Miller? May I speak with Mr Mears? . . . He's not. Yes, I see . . . No, no message. I'll call tomorrow. Yes, good-by.'

He hung up and went to the window.

Was Mears out there someplace, drinking beer on a country road, or could it be that everything the old schoolteacher had told him was true?

If so . . . if so . . .

He could not stay in the house. He went out on the back porch, breathing in the brisk, steely air of October, and looked into the moving darkness. Perhaps it wasn't all Freud after all. Perhaps a large part of it had to do with the invention of the electric light, which had killed the shadows in men's minds much more effectively than a stake through a vampire's heart – and less messily, too.

The evil still went on, but now it went on in the hard, soulless glare of parking-lot fluorescents, of neon tubing, of hundred-watt bulbs by the billions. Generals planned strategic air strikes beneath the no-nonsense glow of alternating current, and it was all out of control, like a kid's soapbox racer going downhill with no brakes: *I was following my orders.* Yes, that was true, patently true. We were all soldiers, simply following what was written on our walking papers. But where were the orders coming from, ultimately? *Take me to your leader.* But where is his office?

I was just following orders. The people elected me. But who elected the people?

Something flapped overhead and Callahan looked up, startled out of his confused revery. A bird? A bat? Gone. Didn't matter.

He listened for the town and heard nothing but the whine of telephone wires.

The night the kudzu gets your fields, you sleep like the dead.

Who wrote that? Dickey?

No sound; no light but the fluorescent in front of the church where Fred Astaire had never danced and the faint waxing and waning of the yellow warning light at the crossroads of Brock Street and Jointner Avenue. No baby cried.

The night the kudzu gets your fields, you sleep like—

The exultation had faded away like a bad echo of pride. Terror struck him around the heart like a blow. Not terror for his life or his honor or that his housekeeper might find out about his drinking. It was a terror he had never dreamed of, not even in the tortured days of his adolescence.

The terror he felt was for his immortal soul.

PART 3

THE DESERTED VILLAGE

I heard a voice, crying from the deep:
Come join me, baby, in my endless sleep.
 – Old rock 'n' roll song

And travelers now within that valley
Through the red-litten windows see
Vast forms that move fantastically
To a discordant melody;
While, like a rapid ghastly river,
Through the pale door,
A hideous throng rush out forever
And laugh – but smile no more.
 – Edgar Allan Poe,
 '*The Haunted Palace*'

Tell you now that the whole town is empty.
 – Bob Dylan

CHAPTER FOURTEEN
THE LOT (IV)

From the 'Old Farmer's Almanac':
Sunset on Sunday, October 5, 1975, at 7:02 PM, sunrise on Monday, October 6, 1975, at 6:49 AM. The period of darkness on Jerusalem's Lot during that particular rotation of the Earth, thirteen days after the vernal equinox, lasted eleven hours and forty-seven minutes. The moon was new. The day's verse from the Old Farmer was: 'See less sun, harvest's night done.'

From the Portland Weather Station:
High temperature for the period of darkness was 62°, reported at 7:05 PM. Low temperature was 47°, reported at 4:06 AM. Scattered clouds, precipitation zero. Winds from the northwest at five to ten miles per hour.

From the Cumberland County police blotter:
Nothing.

2

No one pronounced Jerusalem's Lot dead on the morning of October 6; no one knew it was. Like the bodies of previous days, it retained every semblance of life.

Ruthie Crockett, who had lain pale and ill in bed all weekend, was gone on Monday morning. The disappearance went unreported. Her mother was down cellar, lying behind her shelves of preserves with a canvas tarpaulin pulled over her body, and Larry Crockett, who woke up very late indeed, simply assumed that his daughter had gotten herself off to school. He decided not to go into the office that day. He felt weak and washed out and light-headed. Flu, or something. The light hurt his eyes. He got up and pulled down the shades, yelping once when the sunlight fell directly on his arm. He would have to replace that window some day when he felt better. Defective window glass was no joke. You could come home on a sunshiny day, find your house burning away six licks to the minute, and those insurance pricks in the home office called it spontaneous combustion and wouldn't pay up. When he felt better was time enough. He thought about a cup of coffee and felt sick to his stomach. He wondered vaguely where his wife was, and then the subject slipped out of his mind. He went back to bed, fingering a funny little shaving nick just under his chin, pulled the sheet over his wan cheek, and went back to sleep.

His daughter, meanwhile, slept in enameled darkness within an abandoned freezer close to Dud Rogers – in the night world of her new existence, she found his advances among the heaped mounds of garbage very acceptable.

Loretta Starcher, the town librarian, had also disappeared, although there was no one in her disconnected spinster's life to remark it. She now resided on the dark and musty third floor of the Jerusalem's Lot Public Library.

The third floor was always kept locked (she had the only key, always worn on a chain around her neck) except when some special supplicant could convince her that he was strong enough, intelligent enough, and *moral* enough to receive a special dispensation.

Now she rested there herself, a first edition of a different kind, as mint as when she had first entered the world. Her binding, so to speak, had never even been cracked.

The disappearance of Virgil Rathbun also went unnoticed. Franklin Boddin woke up at nine o'clock in their shack, noticed vaguely that Virgil's pallet was empty, thought nothing of it, and started to get out of bed and see if there was a beer. He fell back, all rubber legs and reeling head.

Christ, he thought, drifting into sleep again. *What was we into last night? Sterno?*

And beneath the shack, in the cool of twenty seasons' fallen leaves and among a galaxy of rusted beer cans popped down through the gaping floorboards in the front room, Virgil lay waiting for night. In the dark clay of his brain there were perhaps visions of a liquid more fiery than the finest scotch, more quenching than the finest wine.

Eva Miller missed Weasel Craig at breakfast but thought little of it. She was too busy directing the flow to and from the stove as her tenants rustled up their breakfasts and then stumbled forth to look another work week in the eye. Then she was too busy putting things to rights and washing the plates of that damned Grover Verrill and that no good Mickey Sylvester, both of whom had been consistently ignoring the 'Please wash up your dishes' sign taped over the sink for years.

But as the silence crept back into the day and the

frantic bulge of breakfast work merged into the steady routine of things to be done, she missed him again. Monday was garbage-collection day on Railroad Street, and Weasel always took the big green bags of rubbish out to the curb for Royal Snow to pick up in his dilapidated old International Harvester truck. Today the green bags were still out on the back steps.

She went to his room and knocked gently. 'Ed?'

There was no response. On another day she would have assumed his drunkenness and simply have put the bags out herself, her lips slightly more compressed than usual. But this morning a faint thread of disquiet wormed into her, and she turned the doorknob and poked her head in. 'Ed?' she called softly.

The room was empty. The window by the head of the bed was open, the curtains fluttering randomly in and out with the vagaries of the light breeze. The bed was wrinkled and she made it without thinking, her hands doing their own work. Stepping over to the other side, her right loafer crunched in something. She looked down and saw Weasel's horn-backed mirror, shattered on the floor. She picked it up and turned it over in her hands, frowning. It had been his mother's, and he had once turned down an antique dealer's offer of ten dollars for it. And that had been after he started drinking.

She got the dustpan from the hall closet and brushed up the glass with slow, thoughtful gestures. She knew Weasel had been sober when he went to bed the night before, and there was no place he could buy beer after nine o'clock, unless he had hitched a ride out to Dell's or into Cumberland.

She dumped the fragments of broken mirror into Weasel's wastebasket, seeing herself reflected over and over for a brief second. She looked into the wastebasket but saw no empty bottle there. Secret drinking was really not Ed Craig's style, anyway.

Well. He'll turn up.

But going downstairs, the disquiet remained. Without consciously admitting it to herself she knew that her feelings for Weasel went a bit deeper than friendly concern.

'Ma'am?'

She started from her thoughts and regarded the stranger in her kitchen. The stranger was a little boy, neatly dressed in corduroy pants and a clean blue T-shirt. *Looks like he fell off his bike.* He looked familiar, but she couldn't quite pin him down. From one of the new families out on Jointer Avenue, most likely.

'Does Mr Ben Mears live here?'

Eva began to ask why he wasn't in school, then didn't. His expression was very serious, even grave. There were blue hollows under his eyes.

'He's sleeping.'

'May I wait?'

Homer McCaslin had gone directly from Green's Mortuary to the Norton home on Brock Street. It was eleven o'clock by the time he got there. Mrs Norton was in tears, and while Bill Norton seemed calm enough, he was chain-smoking and his face looked drawn.

McCaslin agreed to put the girl's description on the wire. Yes, he would call as soon as he heard something. Yes, he would check the hospitals in the area, it was part of the routine (so was the morgue). He privately thought the girl might have gone off in a tiff. The mother admitted they had quarreled and that the girl had been talking of moving out.

Nonetheless, he cruised some of the back roads, one ear comfortably cocked to the crackle of static coming from the radio slung under the dash. At a few minutes past midnight, coming up the Brooks Road toward town, the spotlight he had trained on the soft shoulder of the road glinted off metal − a car parked in the woods.

He stopped, backed up, got out. The car was parked partway up an old disused wood-road. Chevy Vega, light brown, two years old. He pulled his heavy chained notebook out of his back pocket, paged past the interview with Ben and Jimmy, and trained his light on the license number Mrs Norton had given him. It matched. The girl's car, all right. That made things more serious. He laid his hand on the hood. Cool. It had been parked for a while.

'Sheriff?'

A light, carefree voice, like tinkling bells. Why had his hand dropped to the butt of his gun?

He turned and saw the Norton girl, looking incredibly beautiful, walking toward him hand in hand with a stranger − a young man with black hair unfashionably combed straight back from his forehead. McCaslin shone the flashlight at his face and had the oddest impression that the light was shining right through it without illuminating it in the slightest. And although they were walking, they left no tracks in the soft dirt. He felt fear and warning kindle in his nerves, his hand tightened on his revolver . . . and then loosened. He clicked off his flashlight and waited passively.

'Sheriff,' she said, and now her voice was low, caressing.

'How good of you to come,' the stranger said.

They fell on him.

Now his patrol car was parked far out on the rutted and brambled dead end of the Deep Cut Road, with hardly a twinkle of chrome showing through the heavy strands of juniper, bracken, and Lolly-come-see-me. McCaslin was curled up in the trunk. The radio called him at regular intervals unheeded.

Later that same morning Susan paid a short visit to her mother but did little damage; like a leech that had fed well on a slow swimmer, she was satisfied. Still, she had been invited in and now she could come and go as she pleased. There would be a new hunger tonight . . . every night.

Charles Griffen had wakened his wife at a little after five on that Monday morning, his face long and chiseled into sardonic lines by his anger. Outside, the cows were bawling unmilked with full udders. He summed up the work of the night in six words:

'Those damned boys have run off.'

But they had not. Danny Glick had found and battened upon Jack Griffen and Jack had gone to his brother Hal's room and had finally ended his worries of school and books and unyielding fathers forever. Now both of them lay in the center of a huge pile of loose hay in the upper mow, with chaff in their hair and sweet motes of pollen dancing in the dark and tideless channels of their noses. An occasional mouse scampered across their faces.

Now the light had spilled across the land, and all evil things slept. It was to be a beautiful autumn day, crisp and clear and filled with sunshine. By and large the town (not knowing it was dead) would go off to their jobs with no inkling of the night's work. According to the Old Farmer, sunset Monday night would come at 7:00 P M sharp.

The days shortened, moving toward Halloween, and beyond that, winter.

3

When Ben came downstairs at quarter to nine, Eva Miller said from the sink, 'There's someone waiting to see you on the porch.'

He nodded and went out the back door, still in his slippers, expecting to see either Susan or Sheriff McCaslin. But the visitor was a small, economical boy sitting on the top step of the porch and looking out over the town, which was coming slowly to its Monday morning vitality.

'Hello?' Ben said, and the boy turned around quickly.

They looked at each other for no great space of time, but for Ben the moment seemed to undergo a queer stretching, and a feeling of unreality swept him. The boy reminded him physically of the boy he himself had been, but it was more than that. He seemed to feel a weight settle onto his neck, as if in a curious way he sensed the more-than-chance coming together of their lives. It made him think of the day he had met Susan in the park, and how their light, get-acquainted conversation had seemed queerly heavy and fraught with intimations of the future.

Perhaps the boy felt something similar, for his eyes widened slightly and his hand found the porch railing, as if for support.

'You're Mr Mears,' the boy said, not questioning.

'Yes. You have the advantage, I'm afraid.'

'My name is Mark Petrie,' the boy said. 'I have some bad news for you.'

And I bet he does, too, Ben thought dismally, and tried to tighten his mind against whatever it might be – but when it came, it was a total, shocking surprise.

'Susan Norton is one of *them*,' the boy said. 'Barlow got her at the house. But I killed Straker. At least, I think I did.'

Ben tried to speak and couldn't. His throat was locked.

The boy nodded, taking charge effortlessly. 'Maybe we could go for a ride in your car and talk. I don't want anyone to see me around. I'm playing hooky and I'm already in dutch with my folks.'

Ben said something – he didn't know what. After the motorcycle accident that had killed Miranda, he had picked himself up off the pavement shaken but unhurt (except for a small scratch across the back of his left hand, mustn't forget that, Purple Hearts had been awarded for less) and the truck driver had walked over to him, casting two shadows in the glow of the streetlight and the headlamps of the truck – he was a big, balding man with a pen in the breast pocket of his white shirt, and stamped in gold letters on the barrel of the pen he could read 'Frank's Mobil Sta' and the rest was hidden by the pocket, but Ben had guessed shrewdly that the final letters were 'tion,' elementary, my dear Watson, elementary. The truck driver had said something to Ben, he didn't remember what, and then he took Ben's arm gently, trying to lead him away. He saw one of Miranda's flat-heeled shoes lying near the large rear wheels of the moving van and had shaken the trucker off and started toward it and the trucker had taken two steps after him and said, *I wouldn't do that, buddy.* And Ben had looked up at him dumbly, unhurt except for the small scratch across the back of his left hand, wanting to tell the trucker that five minutes ago this hadn't happened, wanting to tell the trucker that in some parallel world he and Miranda had taken a left at the corner one block back and were riding into an entirely different future. A crowd was gathering, coming out of a liquor store on one corner and a small milk-and-sandwich bar on the other. And he had begun to feel then what he was feeling now: the complex and awful mental and physical interaction that is the beginning of acceptance, and the only counterpart to that feeling is rape. The stomach seems to drop. The lips become numb. A thin foam forms on the roof of the mouth. There is a ringing noise in the ears. The skin on the testicles seems to crawl and tighten. The mind goes through a turning away, a hiding of its face, as from a light too brilliant to bear. He had shaken off the well-meaning truck driver's hands a second time and had walked over to the shoe. He picked it up. He turned it over. He placed his hand inside it, and the insole was still warm from her foot. Carrying it, he had gone two steps further and had seen her sprawled legs under the truck's front wheels, clad in the yellow Wranglers she had pulled on with such careless and laughing ease back at the apartment. It was impossible to believe that the girl who had pulled on those slacks was dead, yet the acceptance was there, in his belly, his mouth, his balls. He had groaned aloud, and that was when the tabloid photographer had snapped his picture for Mabel's paper.

One shoe off, one shoe on. People looking at her bare foot as if they had never seen one before. He had taken two steps away and leaned over and—

'I'm going to be sick,' he said.

'That's all right.'

Ben stepped behind his Citroën and doubled over, holding on to the door handle. He closed his eyes, feeling darkness wash over him, and in the darkness Susan's face appeared, smiling at him and looking at him with those lovely deep eyes. He opened his eyes again. It occurred to him that the kid might be lying, or mixed up, or an out-and-out psycho. Yet the thought brought him no hope. The kid was not set up like that. He turned back and looked into the kid's face and read concern there – nothing else.

'Come on,' he said.

The boy got in the car and they drove off. Eva Miller watched them go from the kitchen window, her brow creased. Something bad was happening. She felt it, was filled with it, the same way she had been filled with an obscure and cloudy dread on the day her husband died.

She got up and dialed Loretta Starcher. The phone rang over and over without answer until she put it back in the cradle. Where could she be? Certainly not at the library. It was closed Mondays.

She sat, looking pensively at the telephone. She felt that some great disaster was in the wind – perhaps something as terrible as the fire of '51.

At last she picked up the phone again and called Mabel Werts, who was filled with the gossip of the hour and eager for more. The town hadn't known such a weekend in years.

4

Ben drove aimlessly and without direction as Mark told his story. He told it well, beginning with the night Danny Glick had come to his window and ending with his nocturnal visitor early this morning.

'Are you sure it was Susan?' he asked.

Mark Petrie nodded.

Ben pulled an abrupt U-turn and accelerated back up Jointner Avenue.

'Where are you going? To the—'

'Not there. Not yet.'

5

'Wait. Stop.'

Ben pulled over and they got out together. They had been driving slowly down the Brooks Road, at the bottom of Marsten's Hill. The wood-road where Homer McCaslin had spotted Susan's Vega. They had both caught the glint of sun on metal. They walked up the disused road together, not speaking. There were deep and dusty wheel ruts, and the grass grew high between them. A bird twitted somewhere.

They found the car shortly.

Ben hesitated, then halted. He felt sick to his stomach again. The sweat on his arms was cold.

'Go look,' he said.

Mark went down to the car and leaned in the driver's side window. 'Keys are in it,' he called back.

Ben began to walk toward the car and his foot kicked

something. He looked down and saw a .38 revolver lying in the dust. He picked it up and turned it over in his hands. It looked very much like a police issue revolver.

'Whose gun?' Mark asked, walking toward him. He had Susan's keys in his hand.

'I don't know.' He checked the safety to be sure it was on, and then put the gun in his pocket.

Mark offered him the keys and Ben took them and walked toward the Vega, feeling like a man in a dream. His hands were shaking and he had to poke twice before he could get the right key into the trunk slot. He twisted it and pulled the back deck up without allowing himself to think.

They looked in together. The trunk held a spare tire, a jack, and nothing else. Ben felt his breath come out in a rush.

'Now?' Mark asked.

Ben didn't answer for a moment. When he felt that his voice would be under control, he said, 'We're going to see a friend of mine named Matt Burke, who is in the hospital. He's been researching vampires.'

The urgency in the boy's gaze remained. 'Do you believe me?'

'Yes,' Ben said, and hearing the word on the air seemed to confirm it and give it weight. It was beyond recall. 'Yes, I believe you.'

'Mr Burke is from the high school, isn't he? Does he know about this?'

'Yes. So does his doctor.'

'Dr Cody?'

'Yes.'

They were both looking at the car as they spoke, as if it were a relic of some dark, lost race which they had discovered in these sunny woods to the west of town. The trunk gaped open like a mouth, and as Ben slammed it shut, the dull thud of its latching echoed in his heart.

'And after we talk,' he said, 'we're going up to the Marsten House and get the son of a bitch who did this.'

Mark looked at him without moving. 'It may not be as easy as you think. She will be there, too. She's *his* now.'

'He's going to wish he never saw 'salem's Lot,' he said softly. 'Come on.'

6

They arrived at the hospital at nine-thirty, and Jimmy Cody was in Matt's room. He looked at Ben, unsmiling, and then his eyes flicked to Mark Petrie with curiosity.

'I've got some bad news for you, Ben. Sue Norton has disappeared.'

'She's a vampire,' Ben said flatly, and Matt grunted from his bed.

'Are you sure of that?' Jimmy asked sharply.

Ben cocked his thumb at Mark Petrie and introduced him. 'Mark here had a little visit from Danny Glick on Saturday night. He can tell you the rest.'

Mark told it from beginning to end, just as he had told Ben earlier.

Matt spoke first when he had finished. 'Ben, there are no words to say how sorry I am.'

'I can give you something if you need it,' Jimmy said.

'I know what medicine I need, Jimmy. I want to move against this Barlow today. Now. Before dark.'

'All right,' Jimmy said. 'I've canceled all my calls. And I phoned the county sheriff's office. McCaslin is gone, too.'

'Maybe that explains this,' Ben said, and took the pistol out of his pocket and dropped it onto Matt's bedside table. It looked strange and out of place in the hospital room.

'Where did you get this?' Jimmy asked, picking it up.

'Out by Susan's car.'

'Then I can guess. McCaslin went to the Norton house sometime after he left us. He got the story on Susan, including the make, model, and license number of her car. Went out cruising some of the back roads, just on the off-chance. And—'

Broken silence in the room. None of them needed it filled.

'Foreman's is still closed,' Jimmy said. 'And a lot of the old men who hang around Crossen's have been complaining about the dump. No one has seen Dud Rogers for a week.'

They looked at each other bleakly.

'I spoke with Father Callahan last night,' Matt said. 'He has agreed to go along, providing you two – plus Mark, of course – will stop at this new shop and talk to Straker first.'

'I don't think he'll be talking to anyone today,' Mark said quietly.

'What did you find out about *them*?' Jimmy asked Matt. 'Anything useful?'

'Well, I think I've put some of the pieces together.

Straker must be this thing's human watchdog and body-guard . . . a kind of human familiar. He must have been in town long before Barlow appeared. There were certain rites to be performed, in propitiation of the Dark Father. Even Barlow has his Master, you see.' He looked at them somberly. 'I rather suspect no one will ever find a trace of Ralphie Glick. I think he was Barlow's ticket of admission. Straker took him and sacrificed him.'

'Bastard,' Jimmy said distantly.

'And Danny Glick?' Ben asked.

'Straker bled him first,' Matt said. 'His Master's gift. First blood for the faithful servant. Later, Barlow would have taken over that job himself. But Straker performed another service for his Master before Barlow ever arrived. Do any of you know what?'

For a moment there was silence, and then Mark said quite distinctly, 'The dog that man found on the cemetery gate.'

'What?' Jimmy said. 'Why? Why would he do that?'

'The white eyes,' Mark said, and then looked questioningly at Matt, who was nodding with some surprise.

'All last night I nodded over these books, not knowing we had a scholar in our midst.' The boy blushed a little. 'What Mark says is exactly right. According to several of the standard references on folklore and the supernatural, one way to frighten a vampire away is to paint white "angel eyes" over the real eyes of a black dog. Win's Doc was all black except for two white patches. Win used to call them his headlights − they were directly over his eyes. He let the dog run at night. Straker must have spotted it, killed it, and then hung it on the cemetery gate.'

'And how about this Barlow?' Jimmy asked. 'How did he get to town?'

Matt shrugged. 'I have no way of telling. I think that we must assume, in line with the legends, that he is old . . . very old. He may have changed his name a dozen times, or a thousand. He may have been a native of almost every country in the world at one time or another, although I suspect his origins may have been Romanian or Magyar or Hungarian. It doesn't really matter how he got to town anyway . . . although I wouldn't be surprised to find out Larry Crockett had a hand in it. He's here. That's the important thing.

'Now, here is what you must do: Take a stake when you go. And a gun, in case Straker is still alive. Sheriff McCaslin's revolver will serve the purpose. The stake must pierce the heart or the vampire may rise again. Jimmy, you can check that. When you have staked him you must cut off his head, stuff the mouth with garlic, and turn it face-down in the coffin. In most vampire fiction, Hollywood and otherwise, the staked vampire mortifies almost instantly into dust. This may not happen in real life. If it doesn't, you must weight the coffin and throw it into running water. I would suggest the Royal River. Do you have questions?'

There were none.

'Good. You must each carry a vial of holy water and a bit of the Host. And you must each have Father Callahan hear your confession before you go.'

'I don't think any of us are Catholic,' Ben said.

'I am,' Jimmy said. 'Nonpracticing.'

'Nonetheless, you will make a confession and an act

of contrition. Then you go pure, washed in Christ's blood
. . . clean blood, not tainted.'

'All right,' Ben said.

'Ben, had you slept with Susan? Forgive me, but—'

'Yes,' he said.

'Then you must pound the stake – first into Barlow,
then into *her*. You are the only person in this little party
who has been hurt personally. You will act as her husband.
And you mustn't falter. You'll be releasing her.'

'All right,' he said again.

'Above all' – his glance swept all of them – '*you must
not look in his eyes!* If you do, he'll catch you and turn you
against the others, even at the expense of your own life.
Remember Floyd Tibbits! That makes it dangerous to carry
a gun, even if it's necessary. Jimmy, you take it, and hang
back a little. If you have to examine either Barlow or Susan,
give it to Mark.'

'Understood,' Jimmy said.

'Remember to buy garlic. And roses, if you can. Is
that little flower shop in Cumberland still open, Jimmy?'

'The Northern Belle? I think so.'

'A white rose for each of you. Tie them in your hair
or around your neck. And I'll repeat myself – don't look
in his eyes! I could keep you here and tell you a hundred
other things, but you better go along. It's ten o'clock
already, and Father Callahan may be having second thoughts.
My best wishes and my prayers go with you. Praying is
quite a trick for an old agnostic like me, too. But I don't
think I'm as agnostic as I once was. Was it Carlyle who
said that if a man dethrones God in his heart, then Satan
must ascend to His position?'

No one answered, and Matt sighed. 'Jimmy, I want a closer look at your neck.'

Jimmy stepped to the bedside and lifted his chin. The wounds were obviously punctures, but they had both scabbed over and seemed to be healing nicely.

'Any pain? Itching?' Matt asked.

'No.'

'You were very lucky,' he said, looking at Jimmy soberly.

'I'm starting to think I was luckier than I'll ever know.'

Matt leaned back in his bed. His face looked drawn, the eyes deeply socketed. 'I will take the pill Ben refused, if you please.'

'I'll tell one of the nurses.'

'I'll sleep while you go about your work,' Matt said. 'Later there is another matter . . . well, enough of that.' His eyes shifted to Mark. 'You did a remarkable thing yesterday, boy. Foolish and reckless, but remarkable.'

'*She* paid for it,' Mark said quietly, and clasped his hands together in front of him. They were trembling.

'Yes, and you may have to pay again. Any of you, or all of you. Don't underestimate him! And now, if you don't mind, I'm very tired. I was reading most of the night. Call me the very minute the work is done.'

They left. In the hall Ben looked at Jimmy and said, 'Did he remind you of anyone?'

'Yes,' Jimmy said. 'Van Helsing.'

7

At quarter past ten, Eva Miller went down cellar to get two jars of corn to take to Mrs Norton who, according to Mabel Werts, was in bed. Eva had spent most of September in a steamy kitchen, toiling over her canning operations, blanching vegetables and putting them up, putting paraffin plugs in the tops of Ball jars to cover homemade jelly. There were well over two hundred glass jars neatly shelved in her spick-and-span dirt-floored basement – canning was one of her great joys. Later in the year, as fall drifted into winter and the holidays neared, she would add mincemeat.

The smell struck her as soon as she opened the cellar door.

'Gosh'n fishes,' she muttered under her breath, and went down gingerly, as if wading into a polluted pool. Her husband had built the cellar himself, rock-walling it for coolness. Every now and then a muskrat or woodchuck or mink would crawl into one of the wide chinks and die there. That was what must have happened, although she could never recall a stink this strong.

She reached the lower floor and went along the walls, squinting in the faint overhead glow of the two sixty-watt bulbs. Those should be replaced with seventy-fives, she thought. She got her preserves, neatly labeled CORN in her own careful blue script (a slice of red pepper on the top of every one), and continued her inspection, even squeezing into the space behind the huge, multi-duct furnace. Nothing.

She arrived back at the steps leading up to her kitchen and stared around, frowning, hands on hips. The large cellar was much neater since she had hired two of Larry Crockett's boys to build a tool shed behind her house two years ago. There was the furnace, looking like an Impressionist sculpture of the goddess Kali with its score of pipes twisting off in all directions; the storm windows that she would have to get on soon now that October had come and heating was so dear; the tarpaulin-covered pool table that had been Ralph's. She had the felt carefully vacuumed each May, although no one had played on it since Ralph had died in 1959. Nothing much else down here now. A box of paperbacks she had collected for the Cumberland Hospital, a snow shovel with a broken handle, a pegboard with some of Ralph's old tools hanging from it, a trunk containing drapes that were probably all mildewed by now.

Still, the stink persisted.

Her eyes fixed on the small half-door that led down to the root cellar, but she wasn't going down there, not today. Besides, the walls of the root cellar were solid concrete. Unlikely that an animal could have gotten in there. Still—

'Ed?' she called suddenly, for no reason at all. The flat sound of her voice scared her.

The word died in the dimly lit cellar. Now, why had she done that? What in God's name would Ed Craig be doing down here, even if there *was* a place to hide? Drinking? Offhand, she couldn't think of a more depressing place in town to drink than here in her cellar. More likely he was off in the woods with that good-for-nothing friend of his, Virge Rathbun, guzzling someone's dividend.

Yet she lingered a moment longer, sweeping her gaze around. The rotten stink was awful, just awful. She hoped she wouldn't have to have the place fumigated.

With a last glance at the root cellar door, she went back upstairs.

8

Father Callahan heard them out, all three, and by the time he was brought up to date, it was a little after eleven-thirty. They were sitting in the cool and spacious sitting room of the rectory, and the sun flooded in the large front windows in bars that looked thick enough to slice. Watching the dust motes that danced dreamily in the sun shafts, Callahan was reminded of an old cartoon he had seen somewhere. Cleaning woman with a broom is staring in surprise down at the floor, she has swept away part of her shadow. He felt a little like that now. For the second time in twenty-four hours he had been confronted with a stark impossiblity – only now the impossiblity had corroboration from a writer, a seemingly levelheaded little boy, and a doctor whom the town respected. Still, an impossibility was an impossibility. You couldn't sweep away your own shadow. Except that it seemed to have happened.

'This would be much easier to accept if you could have arranged for a thunderstorm and a power failure,' he said.

'It's quite true,' Jimmy said. 'I assure you.' His hand went to his neck.

Father Callahan got up and pulled something out of Jimmy's black bag – two truncated baseball bats with sharpened points. He turned one of them over in his hands and said, 'Just a moment, Mrs Smith. This won't hurt a bit.'

No one laughed.

Callahan put the stakes back, went to the window, and looked out at Jointner Avenue. 'You are all very persuasive,' he said. 'And I suppose I must add one little piece which you now do not have in your possession.'

He turned back to them.

'There is a sign in the window of the Barlow and Straker Furniture Shop,' he said. 'It says, "Closed Until Further Notice." I went down this morning myself promptly at nine o'clock to discuss Mr Burke's allegations with your mysterious Mr Straker. The shop is locked, front and back.'

'You have to admit that jibes with what Mark says,' Ben remarked.

'Perhaps. And perhaps it's only chance. Let me ask you again: Are you sure you must have the Catholic Church in this?'

'Yes,' Ben said. 'But we'll proceed without you if we have to. If it comes to that, I'll go alone.'

'No need of that,' Father Callahan said, rising. 'Follow me across to the church, gentlemen, and I will hear your confessions.'

9

Ben knelt awkwardly in the darkened mustiness of the confessional, his mind whirling, his thoughts inchoate. Flicking through them was a succession of surreal images: Susan in the park; Mrs Glick backing away from the makeshift tongue-depressor cross, her mouth an open, writhing wound; Floyd Tibbits coming out of his car in a lurch, dressed like a scarecrow, charging him; Mark Petrie leaning in the window of Susan's car. For the first and only time, the possibility that all of this might be a dream occurred to him, and his tired mind clutched at it eagerly.

His eye fell on something in the corner of the confessional, and he picked it up curiously. It was an empty Junior Mints box, fallen from the pocket of some little boy, perhaps. A touch of reality that was undeniable. The cardboard was real and tangible under his fingers. This nightmare was real.

The little sliding door opened. He looked at it but could see nothing beyond. There was a heavy screen in the opening.

'What should I do?' he asked the screen.

'Say, "Bless me, Father, for I have sinned."'

'Bless me, Father, for I have sinned,' Ben said, his voice sounding strange and heavy in the enclosed space.

'Now tell me your sins.'

'All of them?' Ben asked, appalled.

'Try to be representative,' Callahan said, his voice dry. 'I know we have something to do before dark.'

Thinking hard and trying to keep the Ten Commandments before him as a kind of sorting screen, Ben began. It didn't become easier as he went along. There was no sense of catharsis – only the dull embarrassment that went with telling a stranger the mean secrets of his life. Yet he could see how this ritual could become compulsive: as bitterly compelling as strained rubbing alcohol for the chronic drinker or the pictures behind the loose board in the bathroom for an adolescent boy. There was something medieval about it, something accursed – a ritual act of regurgitation. He found himself remembering a scene from the Bergman picture *The Seventh Seal*, where a crowd of ragged penitents proceeds through a town stricken with the black plague. The penitents were scourging themselves with birch branches, making themselves bleed. The hatefulness of baring himself this way (and perversely, he would not allow himself to lie, although he could have done so quite convincingly) made the day's purpose real in the final sense, and he could almost see the word 'vampire' printed on the black screen of his mind, not in scare movie-poster print, but in small, economical letters that were made to be a woodcut or scratched on a scroll. He felt helpless in the grip of this alien ritual, out of joint with his time. The confessional might have been a direct pipeline to the days when werewolves and incubi and witches were an accepted part of the outer darkness and the church the only beacon of light. For the first time in his life he felt the slow, terrible beat and swell of the ages and saw his life as a dim and glimmering spark in an edifice which, if seen clearly, might drive all men mad. Matt had not told them of Father Callahan's conception of his church as a Force, but Ben would have understood that now. He could feel the Force in this fetid little box, beating in on him, leaving him naked and contemptible. He felt it as no Catholic, raised to confession since earliest childhood, could have.

When he stepped out, the fresh air from the open doors struck him thankfully. He wiped at his neck with the palm of his hand and it came away sweaty.

Callahan stepped out. 'You're not done yet,' he said.

Wordlessly, Ben stepped back inside, but did not kneel. Callahan gave him an act of contrition – ten Our Fathers and ten Hail Marys.

'I don't know that one,' Ben said.

'I'll give you a card with the prayer written on it,' the voice on the other side of the screen said. 'You can say them to yourself while we ride over to Cumberland.'

Ben hesitated a moment. 'Matt was right, you know. When he said it was going to be harder than we thought. We're going to sweat blood before this is over.'

'Yes?' Callahan said – polite or just dubious? Ben couldn't tell. He looked down and saw he was still holding the Junior Mints box. He had crushed it to a shapeless pulp with the convulsive squeezing of his right hand.

10

It was nearing one o'clock when they all got in Jimmy Cody's large Buick and set off. None of them spoke. Father Donald Callahan was wearing his full gown, a surplice, and a white stole bordered with purple. He had given them each a small tube of water from the Holy Font, and had blessed them each with the sign of the cross. He held a small silver pyx on his lap which contained several pieces of the Host.

They stopped at Jimmy's Cumberland office first, and Jimmy left the motor idling while he went inside. When he came out, he was wearing a baggy sport coat that concealed the bulge of McCaslin's revolver and carrying an ordinary Craftsman hammer in his right hand.

Ben looked at it with some fascination and saw from the tail of his eye that Mark and Callahan were also staring. The hammer had a blue steel head and a perforated rubber handgrip.

'Ugly, isn't it?' Jimmy remarked.

Ben thought of using that hammer on Susan, using it to ram a stake between her breasts, and felt his stomach flip over slowly, like an airplane doing a slow roll.

'Yes,' he said, and moistened his lips. 'It's ugly, all right.'

They drove to the Cumberland Stop and Shop. Ben and Jimmy went into the supermarket and picked up all the garlic that was displayed along the vegetable counter – twelve boxes of the whitish-gray bulbs. The checkout girl raised her eyebrows and said, 'Glad I ain't going on a long ride with you boys t'night.'

Going out, Ben said idly, 'I wonder what the basis of garlic's effectiveness against them is? Something in the Bible, or an ancient curse, or—'

'I suspect it's an allergy,' Jimmy said.

'Allergy?'

Callahan caught the last of it and asked for a repetition as they drove toward the Northern Belle Flower Shop.

'Oh yes, I agree with Dr Cody,' he said. 'Probably is an allergy . . . if it works as a deterrent at all. Remember, that's not proved yet.'

'That's a funny idea for a priest,' Mark said.

'Why? If I must accept the existence of vampires (and it seems I must, at least for the time being), must I also accept them as creatures beyond the bounds of all natural laws? Some, certainly. Folklore says they can't be seen in mirrors, that they can transform themselves into bats or wolves or birds – the so-called psychopompos – that they can narrow their bodies and slip through the tiniest cracks. Yet we know they see, and hear, and speak . . . and they most certainly taste. Perhaps they also know discomfort, pain—'

'And love?' Ben asked, looking straight ahead.

'No,' Jimmy answered. 'I suspect that love is beyond them.' He pulled into a small parking lot beside an L-shaped flower shop with an attached greenhouse.

A small bell tinkled over the door when they went in, and the heavy aroma of flowers struck them. Ben felt sickened by the cloying heaviness of their mixed perfumes, and was reminded of funeral parlors.

'Hi there.' A tall man in a canvas apron came toward them, holding an earthen flowerpot in one hand.

Ben had only started to explain what they wanted when the man in the apron shook his head and interrupted.

'You're late, I'm afraid. A man came in last Friday and bought every rose I had in stock — red, white, and yellow. I'll have no more until Wednesday at least. If you'd care to order—'

'What did this man look like?'

'Very striking,' the proprietor said, putting his pot down. 'Tall, totally bald. Piercing eyes. Smoked foreign cigarettes, by the smell. He had to take the flowers out in three armloads. He put them in the back of a very old car, a Dodge, I think—'

'Packard,' Ben said. 'A black Packard.'

'You know him, then.'

'In a manner of speaking.'

'He paid cash. Very unusual, considering the size of the order. But perhaps if you get in touch with him, he would sell you—'

'Perhaps,' Ben said.

In the car again, they talked it over.

'There's a shop in Falmouth—' Father Callahan began doubtfully.

'No!' Ben said. 'No!' And the raw edge of hysteria in his voice made them all look around. 'And when we got to Falmouth and found that Straker had been there, too? What then? Portland? Kittery? *Boston?* Don't you realize what's happening? He's foreseen us! *He's leading us by the nose!*'

'Ben, be reasonable,' Jimmy said. 'Don't you think we ought to at least—'

'Don't you remember what Matt said? 'You mustn't go into this feeling that because he can't rise in the daytime he can't harm you.' Look at your watch, Jimmy.'

Jimmy did. 'Two-fifteen,' he said slowly, and looked up at the sky as if doubting the truth on the dial. But it was true; now the shadows were going the other way.

'He's anticipated us,' Ben said. 'He's been four jumps ahead every mile of the way. Did we – could we – actually think that *he* would be blissfully unaware of us? That *he* never took the possibility of discovery and opposition into account? We have to go *now*, before we waste the rest of the day arguing about how many angels can dance on the head of a pin.'

'He's right,' Callahan said quietly. 'I think we had better stop talking and get going.'

'Then *drive*,' Mark said urgently.

Jimmy pulled out of the flower-shop parking lot fast, screeching the tires on the pavement. The proprietor stared after them, three men, one of them a priest, and a little boy who sat in a car with M.D. plates and shouted at each other of total lunacies.

11

Cody came at the Marsten House from the Brooks Road, on the village's blind side, and Donald Callahan, looking at it from this new angle, thought: Why, it actually *looms* over the town. Strange I never saw it before. It must have perfect elevation there, perched on its hill high above the crossroads of Jointner Avenue and Brock Street. Perfect elevation and a very nearly 360° view of the township itself. It was a huge and rambling place, and with the shutters closed it took on an uncomfortable, overlarge configuration in the mind; it became a sarcophaguslike monolith, an evocation of doom.

And it was the site of both suicide and murder, which meant it stood on unhallowed ground.

He opened his mouth to say so, and then thought better of it.

Cody turned off onto the Brooks Road, and for a moment the house was blotted out by trees. Then they thinned, and Cody was turning into the driveway. The Packard was parked just outside the garage, and when Jimmy turned off the car, he drew McCaslin's revolver.

Callahan felt the atmosphere of the place seize him at once. He took a crucifix – his mother's – from his pocket and slipped it around his neck with his own. No bird sang in these fall-denuded trees. The long and ragged grass seemed even drier and more dehydrated than the end of the season warranted; the ground itself seemed gray and used up.

The steps leading up to the porch were warped crazily, and there was a brighter square of paint on one of the porch posts where a no-trespassing sign had recently been taken down. A new Yale lock glittered brassily below the old rusted bolt on the front door.

'A window, maybe, like Mark—' Jimmy began hesitantly.

'No,' Ben said. 'Right through the front door. We'll break it down if we have to.'

'I don't think that will be necessary,' Callahan said, and his voice did not seem to be his own. When they got out, he led them without stopping to think about it. An eagerness – the old eagerness he was sure had gone forever – seemed to seize him as he approached the door. The house seemed to lean around them, to almost ooze its evil from the cracked pores of its paint. Yet he did not hesitate. Any thought of temporizing was gone. In the last moments he did not lead them so much as he was impelled.

'In the name of God the Father!' he cried, and his voice took on a hoarse, commanding note that made them all draw closer to him. 'I command the evil to be gone from this house! Spirits, depart!' And without being aware he was going to do it, he smote the door with the crucifix in his hand.

There was a flash of light – afterward they all agreed there had been – a pungent whiff of ozone, and a crackling sound, as if the boards themselves had screamed. The curved fanlight above the door suddenly exploded outward, and the large bay window to the left that overlooked the lawn coughed its glass onto the grass at the same instant. Jimmy cried out. The new Yale lock lay on the boards at their feet, welded into an almost unrecognizable mass. Mark bent to poke it and then yelped.

'Hot,' he said.

463

Callahan withdrew from the door, trembling. He looked down at the cross in his hand. 'This is, without a doubt, the most amazing thing that's ever happened to me in my life,' he said. He glanced up at the sky, as if to see the very face of God, but the sky was indifferent.

Ben pushed at the door and it swung open easily. But he waited for Callahan to go in first. In the hall Callahan looked at Mark.

'The cellar,' he said. 'You get to it through the kitchen. Straker's upstairs. But –' He paused, frowning. 'Something's different. I don't know what. Something's not the same as it was.'

They went upstairs first, and even though Ben was not in the lead, he felt a prickle of very old terror as they approached the door at the end of the hall. Here, almost a month to the day after he had come back to 'salem's Lot, he was to get his second look into that room. When Callahan pushed the door open, he glanced upward . . . and felt the scream well up in his throat and out of his mouth before he could stop it. It was high, womanish, hysterical.

But it was not Hubert Marsten hanging from the overhead beam, or his spirit.

It was Straker, and he had been hung upside down like a pig in a slaughtering pen, his throat ripped wide open. His glazed eyes stared at them, through them, past them.

He had been bled white.

12

'Dear God,' Father Callahan said. 'Dear God.'

They advanced slowly into the room, Callahan and

Cody a bit in the lead, Ben and Mark behind, pressed together.

Straker's feet had been bound together; then he had been hauled up and tied there. It occurred to Ben in a distant part of his brain that it must have taken a man with enormous strength to haul Straker's dead weight up to a point where his dangling hands did not quite touch the floor.

Jimmy touched the forehead with his inner wrist, then held one of the dead hands in his own. 'He's been dead for maybe eighteen hours,' he said. He dropped the hand with a shudder. 'My God, what an awful way to . . . I can't figure this out. Why – who—'

'Barlow did it,' Mark said. He looked at Straker's corpse with unflinching eyes.

'And Straker screwed up,' Jimmy said. 'No eternal life for him. But why like this? Hung upside down?'

'It's as old as Macedonia,' Father Callahan said. 'Hanging the body of your enemy or betrayer upside down so his head faces earth instead of heaven. St Paul was cruci-fied that way, on an X-shaped cross with his legs broken.'

Ben spoke, and his voice sounded old and dusty in his throat. 'He's still diverting us. He has a hundred tricks. Let's go.'

They followed him back down the hall, back down the stairs, into the kitchen. Once there, he deferred to Father Callahan again. For a moment they just looked at each other, and then at the cellar door that led downward, just as twenty-five-odd years ago he had taken a set of stairs upward, to face an overwhelming question.

13

When the priest opened the door, Mark felt the rank, rotten odor assail his nostrils again — but that was also different. Not so strong. Less malevolent.

The priest started down the stairs. Still, it took all his willpower to continue down after Father Callahan into that pit of the dead.

Jimmy had produced a flashlight from his bag and clicked it on. The beam illuminated the floor, crossed to one wall, and swung back. It paused for a moment on a long crate, and then the beam fell on a table.

'There,' he said. 'Look.'

It was an envelope, clean and shining in all this dingy darkness, a rich yellow vellum.

'It's a trick,' Father Callahan said. 'Better not touch it.'

'No,' Mark spoke up. He felt both relief and disappointment. 'He's not here. He's gone. That's for us. Full of mean things, probably.'

Ben stepped forward and picked the envelope up. He turned it over in his hands twice — Mark could see in the glow of Jimmy's flashlight that his fingers were trembling — and then he tore it open.

There was one sheet inside, rich vellum like the envelope, and they crowded around. Jimmy focused his flashlight on the page, which was closely written in an elegant, spider-thin hand. They read it together, Mark a little more slowly than the others.

October 4
My Dear Young Friends,

How lovely of you to have stopped by!

I am never averse to company; it has been one of my great joys in a long and often lonely life. Had you come in the evening, I should have welcomed you in person with the greatest of pleasure. However, since I suspected you might choose to arrive during daylight hours, I thought it best to be out.

I have left you a small token of my appreciation; someone very near and dear to one of you is now in the place where I occupied my days until I decided that other quarters might be more congenial. She is very lovely, Mr Mears — very toothsome, if I may be permitted a small bon mot. I have no further need of her and so I have left her for you to — how is your idiom? — to warm up for the main event. To whet your appetites, if you like. Let us see how well you like the appetizer to the main course you contemplate, shall we?

Master Petrie, you have robbed me of the most faithful and resourceful servant I have ever known. You have caused me, in an indirect fashion, to take part in his ruination, have caused my own appetites to betray me. You sneaked up behind him, doubtless. I am going to enjoy dealing with you. Your parents first, I think. Tonight . . . or tomorrow night . . . or the next. And then you. But you shall enter my church as choirboy castratum.

And Father Callahan — have they persuaded you to come? I thought so. I have observed you at some length since I arrived in Jerusalem's Lot . . . much as a good chess player will study the games of his opposition, am I correct?

The Catholic Church is not the oldest of my opponents, though! I was old when it was young, when its members hid in the catacombs of Rome and painted fishes on their chests so they could tell one from another. I was strong when this simpering club of bread-eaters and wine-drinkers who venerate the sheep-savior was weak. My rites were old when the rites of your church were unconceived. Yet I do not underestimate. I am wise in the ways of goodness as well as those of evil. I am not jaded.

And I will best you. How? you say. Does not Callahan hear the symbol of White? Does not Callahan move in the day as well as the night? Are there not charms and potions, both Christian and pagan, which my so-good friend Matthew Burke has informed me and my compatriots of? Yes, yes, and yes. But I have lived longer than you. I am crafty. I am not the serpent, but the father of serpents.

Still, you say, this is not enough. And it is not. In the end, 'Father' Callahan, you will undo yourself. Your faith in the White is weak and soft. Your talk of love is presumption. Only when you speak of the bottle are you informed.

My good, good friends — Mr Mears; Mr Cody; Master Petrie; Father Callahan — enjoy your stay. The Médoc is excellent, procured for me especially by the late owner of this house, whose personal company I was never able to enjoy. Please be my guests if you still have a taste for wine after you have finished the work at hand. We will meet again, in person, and I shall convey my felicitations to each of you at that time in a more personal way.

Until then, adieu.

BARLOW.

Trembling, Ben let the letter fall to the table. He looked at the others. Mark stood with his hands clenched into fists, his mouth frozen in the twist of someone who has bitten something rotten; Jimmy, his oddly boyish face drawn and pale; Father Donald Callahan, his eyes alight, his mouth drawn down in a trembling bow.

And one by one, they looked up at him.

'Come on,' he said.

They went around the corner together.

14

Parkins Gillespie was standing on the front step of the brick Municipal Building, looking through his high-powered Zeiss binoculars when Nolly Gardener drove up in the town's police car and got out, hitching up his belt and picking out his seat at the same time.

'What's up, Park?' he asked, walking up the steps.

Parkins gave him the glasses wordlessly and flicked one callused thumb at the Marsten House.

Nolly looked. He saw that old Packard, and parked in front of it, a new tan Buick. The gain on the binoculars wasn't quite high enough to pick off the plate number. He lowered his glasses. 'That's Doc Cody's car, ain't it?'

'Yes, I believe it is.' Parkins inserted a Pall Mall between his lips and scratched a kitchen match on the brick wall behind him.

'I never seen a car up there except that Packard.'

'Yes, that's so,' Parkins said meditatively.

'Think we ought to go up there and have a look?' Nolly spoke with a marked lack of his usual enthusiasm.

He had been a lawman for five years and was still entranced with his own position.

'No,' Parkins said, 'I believe we'll just leave her alone.' He took his watch out of his vest and clicked up the scrolled silver cover like a trainman checking an express. Just 3:41. He checked his watch against the clock on the town hall and then tucked it back into place.

'How'd all that come out with Floyd Tibbits and the little McDougall baby?' Nolly asked.

'Dunno.'

'Oh,' Nolly said, momentarily nonplussed. Parkins was always taciturn, but this was a new high for him. He looked through the glasses again: no change.

'Town seems quiet today,' Nolly volunteered.

'Yes,' Parkins said. He looked across Jointner Avenue and the park with his faded blue eyes. Both the avenue and the park were deserted. They had been deserted most of the day. There was a remarkable lack of mothers strolling babies or idlers around the War Memorial.

'Funny things been happening,' Nolly ventured.

'Yes,' Parkins said, considering.

As a last gasp, Nolly fell back on the one bit of conversational bait that Parkins had never failed to rise to: the weather. 'Clouding up,' he said. 'Be rain by tonight.'

Parkins studied the sky. There were mackerel scales directly overhead and a building bar of clouds to the south-west. 'Yes,' he said, and threw the stub of his cigarette away.

'Park, you feelin' all right?'

Parkins Gillespie considered it.

'Nope,' he said.

'Well, what in hell's the matter?'

'I believe,' Gillespie said, 'that I'm scared shitless.'

'What?' Nolly floundered. 'Of what?'

'Dunno,' Parkins said, and took his binoculars back. He began to scan the Marsten House again while Nolly stood speechless beside him.

15

Beyond the table where the letter had been propped, the cellar made an L-turn, and they were now in what once had been a wine cellar. Hubert Marsten must have been a bootlegger indeed, Ben thought. There were small and medium casks covered with dust and cobwebs. One wall was covered with a crisscrossed wine rack, and ancient magnums still peered forth from some of the diamond-shaped pigeonholes. Some of them had exploded, and where sparkling burgundy had once waited for some discerning palate, the spider now made his home. Others had undoubtedly turned to vinegar; that sharp odor drifted in the air, mingled with that of slow corruption.

'No,' Ben said, speaking quietly, as a man speaks a fact. 'I can't.'

'You must,' Father Callahan said. 'I'm not telling you it will be easy, or for the best. Only that you must.'

'I *can't!*' Ben cried, and this time the words echoed in the cellar.

In the center, on a raised dais and spotlighted by Jimmy's flashlight, Susan Norton lay still. She was covered from shoulders to feet in a drift of simple white linen, and when they reached her, none of them had been able to speak. Wonder had swallowed words.

In life she had been a cheerfully pretty girl who had missed the turn to beauty somewhere (perhaps by inches), not through any lack in her features but — just possibly — because her life had been so calm and unremarkable. But now she had achieved beauty. Dark beauty.

Death had not put its mark on her. Her face was blushed with color, and her lips, innocent of makeup, were a deep and glowing red. Her forehead was pale but flawless, the skin like cream. Her eyes were closed, and the dark lashes lay sootily against her cheeks. One hand was curled at her side, and the other was thrown lightly across her waist. Yet the total impression was not of angelic loveliness but a cold, disconnected beauty. Something in her face — not stated but hinted at — made Jimmy think of the young Saigon girls, some not yet thirteen, who would kneel before soldiers in the alleys behind the bars, not for the first time or the hundredth. Yet with those girls, the corruption hadn't been evil but only a knowledge of the world that had come too soon. The change in Susan's face was quite different — but he could not have said just how.

Now Callahan stepped forward and pressed his fingers against the springiness of her left breast. 'Here,' he said. 'The heart.'

'No,' Ben repeated. 'I can't.'

'Be her lover,' Father Callahan said softly. 'Better, be her husband. You won't hurt her, Ben. You'll free her. The only one hurt will be you.'

Ben looked at him dumbly. Mark had taken the stake from Jimmy's black bag and held it out wordlessly. Ben took it in a hand that seemed to stretch out for miles.

If I don't think about it when I do it, then maybe—

But it would be impossible not to think about it. And suddenly a line came to him from *Dracula*, that amusing bit of fiction that no longer amused him in the slightest. It was Van Helsing's speech to Arthur Holmwood when Arthur had been faced with this same dreadful task: *We must go through bitter waters before we reach the sweet.*

Could there be sweetness for any of them, ever again?

'Take it away!' he groaned. 'Don't make me do this—'

No answer.

He felt a cold, sick sweat spring out on his brow, his cheeks, his forearms. The stake that had been a simple baseball bat four hours before seemed infused with eerie heaviness, as if invisible yet titanic lines of force had converged on it.

He lifted the stake and pressed it against her left breast, just above the last fastened button of her blouse. The point made a dimple in her flesh, and he felt the side of his mouth begin to twitch in an uncontrollable tic.

'She's not dead,' he said. His voice was hoarse and thick. It was his last line of defense.

'No,' Jimmy said implacably. 'She's Undead, Ben.' He had shown them; had wrapped the blood-pressure cuff around her still arm and pumped it. The reading had been 00/00. He had put his stethoscope on her chest, and each of them had listened to the silence inside her.

Something was put into Ben's other hand – years later he still did not remember which of them had put it there. The hammer. The Craftsman hammer with the rubber perforated grip. The head glimmered in the flashlight's glow.

'Do it quickly,' Callahan said, 'and go out into the daylight. We'll do the rest.'

We must go through bitter waters before we reach the sweet.

'God forgive me,' Ben whispered.

He raised the hammer and brought it down.

The hammer struck the top of the stake squarely, and the gelatinous tremor that vibrated up the length of ash would haunt him forever in his dreams. Her eyes flew open, wide and blue, as if from the very force of the blow. Blood gushed upward from the stake's point of entry in a bright and astonishing flood, splashing his hands, his shirt, his cheeks. In an instant the cellar was filled with its hot, coppery odor.

She writhed on the table. Her hands came up and beat madly at the air like birds. Her feet thumped an aimless, rattling tattoo on the wood of the platform. Her mouth yawned open, revealing shocking, wolflike fangs, and she began to peal forth shriek after shriek, like hell's clarion. Blood gushed from the corners of her mouth in freshets.

The hammer rose and fell: again . . . again . . . again.

Ben's brain was filled with the shrieks of large black crows. It whirled with awful, unremembered images. His hands were scarlet, the stake was scarlet, the remorselessly rising and falling hammer was scarlet. In Jimmy's trembling hands the flashlight became stroboscopic, illuminating Susan's crazed, lashing face in spurts and flashes. Her teeth sheared through the flesh of her lips, tearing them to ribbons. Blood splattered across the fresh linen sheet which Jimmy had so neatly turned back, making patterns like Chinese ideograms.

And then, suddenly, her back arched like a bow, and her mouth stretched open until it seemed her jaws must break. A huge explosion of darker blood issued forth from the wound the stake had made – almost black in this chancy, lunatic light: heart's blood. The scream that welled from the sounding chamber of that gaping mouth came from all the subcellars of deepest race memory and beyond that, to the moist darknesses of the human soul. Blood suddenly boiled from her mouth and nose in a tide . . . and something else. In the faint light it was only a suggestion, a shadow, of something leaping up and out, cheated and ruined. It merged with the darkness and was gone.

She settled back, her mouth relaxing, closing. The mangled lips parted in a last, susurrating pulse of air. For a moment the eyelids fluttered and Ben saw, or fancied he saw, the Susan he had met in the park, reading his book.

It was done.

He backed away, dropping the hammer, holding his hands out before him, a terrified conductor whose symphony has run riot.

Callahan put a hand on his shoulder. 'Ben—'

He fled.

He stumbled going up the stairs, fell, and crawled toward the light at the top. Childhood horror and adult horror had merged. If he looked over his shoulder, he would see Hubie Marsten (or perhaps Straker) only a hand's breadth behind, grinning out of his puffed and greenish face, the rope embedded deep into his neck – the grin revealing fangs instead of teeth. He screamed once, miserably.

Dimly, he heard Callahan cry out, 'No, let him go—'

He burst through the kitchen and out the back door.

The back porch steps were gone under his feet and he pitched headlong into the dirt. He got to his knees, crawled, got to his feet, and cast a glance behind him.

Nothing.

The house loomed without purpose, the last of its evil stolen away. It was just a house again.

Ben Mears stood in the great silence of the weed-chocked backyard, his head thrown back, breathing in great white snuffles of air.

16

In the fall, night comes like this in the Lot:

The sun loses its thin grip on the air first, turning it cold, making it remember that winter is coming and winter will be long. Thin clouds form, and the shadows lengthen out. They have no breadth, as summer shadows have; there are no leaves on the trees or fat clouds in the sky to make them thick. They are gaunt, mean shadows that bite the ground like teeth.

As the sun nears the horizon, its benevolent yellow begins to deepen, to become infected, until it glares an angry inflamed orange. It throws a variegated glow over the horizon – a cloud-congested caul that is alternately red, orange, vermilion, purple. Sometimes the clouds break apart in great, slow rafts, letting through beams of inno-cent yellow sunlight that are bitterly nostalgic for the summer that has gone by.

This is six o'clock, the supper hour (in the Lot, dinner is eaten at noon and the lunch buckets that men grab from counters before going out the door are known as dinner pails). Mabel Werts, the unhealthy fat of old age hanging doughily on her bones, is sitting down to a broiled breast of chicken and a cup of Lipton tea, the phone by her elbow. In Eva's the men are getting together whatever they have to get together: TV dinners, canned corned beef, canned beans which are woefully unlike the beans their mothers used to bake all Saturday morning and afternoon years ago, spaghetti dinners, or reheated hamburgers picked up at the Falmouth McDonald's on the way home from work. Eva sits at the table in the front room, irritably playing gin rummy with Grover Verrill, and snapping at the others to wipe up their grease and to stop that damn slopping around. They cannot remember ever having seen her this way, cat-nervous and feisty. But they know what the matter is, even if she does not.

Mr and Mrs Petrie eat sandwiches in their kitchen, trying to puzzle out the call they have just received, a call from the local Catholic priest, Father Callahan: *Your son is with me. He's fine. I will have him home shortly. Good-by.* They have debated calling the local lawman, Parkins Gillespie, and have decided to wait a bit longer. They have sensed some sort of change in their son, who has always been what his mother likes to call A Deep One. Yet the specters of Ralphie and Danny Glick hang over them, un-acknowledged.

Milt Crossen is having bread and milk in the back of his store. He has had damned little appetite since his wife died back in '68. Delbert Markey, proprietor of Dell's, is working his way methodically through the five hamburgers which he has fried himself on the grill. He eats them with mustard and heaps of raw onions, and will complain most of the night to anyone who will listen that his goddamn acid indigestion is killing him. Father Callahan's housekeeper, Rhoda Curless, eats nothing. She is worried about the Father, who is out someplace ramming the roads. Harriet Durham and her family are eating pork chops. Carl Smith, a widower since 1957, has one boiled potato and a bottle of Moxie. The Derek Boddins are having an Armour Star ham and brussels sprouts. *Yechhh*, says Richie Boddin, the deposed bully. Brussels sprouts. You eat 'em or I'll clout your ass backward, Derek says. He hates them himself.

Reggie and Bonnie Sawyer are having a rib roast of beef, frozen corn, french-fried potatoes, and for dessert a chocolate bread pudding with hard sauce. These are all Reggie's favorites. Bonnie, her bruises just beginning to fade, serves silently with downcast eyes. Reggie eats with steady, serious attention, killing three cans of Bud with the meal. Bonnie eats standing up. She is still too sore to sit down. She hasn't much appetite, but she eats anyway, so Reggie won't notice and say something. After he beat her up on that night, he flushed all her pills down the toilet and raped her. And has raped her every night since then.

By quarter of seven, most meals have been eaten, most after-dinner cigarettes and cigars and pipes smoked, most tables cleared. Dishes are being washed, rinsed, and stacked in drainers. Young children are being packed into Dr Dentons and sent into the other room to watch game shows on TV until bedtime.

Roy McDougall, who has burned the shit out of a fry pan full of veal steaks, curses and throws them — fry pan and all — into the swill. He puts on his denim jacket and sets out for Dell's, leaving his goddamn good-for-nothing pig of a wife to sleep in the bedroom. Kid's dead, wife's slacking off, supper's burned to hell. Time to get drunk. And maybe time to haul stakes and roll out of this two-bit town.

In a small upstairs flat on Taggart Street, which runs a short distance from Jointner Avenue to a dead end behind the Municipal Building, Joe Crane is given a left-handed gift from the gods. He has finished a small bowl of Shredded Wheat and is sitting down to watch the TV when he feels a large and sudden pain paralyze the left side of his chest and his left arm. He thinks: *What's this? Ticker?* As it happens, this is exactly right. He gets up and makes it halfway to the telephone before the pain suddenly swells and drops him in his tracks like a steer hit with a hammer. His small color TV babbles on and on, and it will be twenty-four hours before anyone finds him. His death, which occurs at 6:51 PM, is the only natural death to occur in Jerusalem's Lot on October 6.

By 7:00 the panoply of colors on the horizon has shrunk to a bitter orange line on the western horizon, as if furnace fires had been banked beyond the edge of the world. In the east the stars are already out. They gleam steadily, like fierce diamonds. There is no mercy in them at this time of year, no comfort for lovers. They gleam in beautiful indifference.

For the small children, bedtime is come. Time for the babies to be packed into their beds and cribs by parents who smile at their cries to be let up a little longer, to leave the light on. They indulgently open closet doors to show there is nothing in there.

And all around them, the bestiality of the night rises on tenebrous wings. The vampire's time has come.

17

Matt was dozing lightly when Jimmy and Ben came in, and he snapped awake almost immediately, his hand tightening on the cross he held in his right hand.

His eys touched Jimmy's, moved to Ben's ... and lingered.

'What happened?'

Jimmy told him briefly. Ben said nothing.

'Her body?'

'Callahan and I put it facedown in a crate that was down cellar, maybe the same crate Barlow came to town in. We threw it into the Royal River not an hour ago. Filled the box with stones. We used Straker's car. If anyone noticed it by the bridge, they'll think of him.'

'You did well. Where's Callahan? And the boy?'

'Gone to Mark's house. His parents have to be told everything. Barlow threatened them specifically.'

'Will they believe?'

'If they don't, Mark will have his father call you.'

Matt nodded. He looked very tired.

'And Ben,' he said. 'Come here. Sit on my bed.'

Ben came obediently, his face blank and dazed. He sat down and folded his hands neatly in his lap. His eyes were burned cigarette holes.

'There's no comfort for you,' Matt said. He took one of Ben's hands in his own. Ben let him, unprotesting. 'It doesn't matter. Time will comfort you. She is at rest.'

'He played us for fools,' Ben said hollowly. 'He mocked us, each in turn. Jimmy, give him the letter.'

Jimmy gave Matt the envelope. He stripped the heavy sheet of stationery from the envelope and read it carefully, holding the paper only inches from his nose. His lips moved slightly. He put it down and said, 'Yes. It is him. His ego is larger than even I imagined. It makes me want to shiver.'

'He left her for a joke,' Ben said hollowly. '*He* was gone, long before. Fighting him is like fighting the wind. We must seem like bugs to him. Little bugs scurrying around for his amusement.'

Jimmy opened his mouth to speak, but Matt shook his head slightly.

'That is far from the truth,' he said. 'If he could have taken Susan with him, he would have. He wouldn't give up his Undead just for jokes when there are so few of them! Step back a minute, Ben, and consider what you've done to him. Killed his familiar, Straker. By his own admission, even forced him to participate in the murder by reason of his insatiable appetite! How it must have terrified him to wake from his dreamless sleep and find that a young boy, unarmed, had slain such a fearsome creature.'

He sat up in bed with some difficulty. Ben had turned his head and was looking at him with the first interest he had shown since the others had come out of the house to find him in the backyard.

'Maybe that's not the greatest victory,' Matt mused. 'You've driven him from his house, his chosen home. Jimmy said that Father Callahan sterilized the cellar with holy water and has sealed all the doors with the Host. If he goes there again, he'll die . . . *and he knows it.*'

'But he got away,' Ben said. 'What does it matter?'

'He got away,' Matt echoed softly. 'And where did he sleep today? In the trunk of a car? In the cellar of one of his victims? Perhaps in the basement of the old Methodist Church in the Marshes which burned down in the fire of '51? Wherever it was, do you think he liked it, or felt safe there?'

Ben didn't answer.

'Tomorrow, you'll begin to hunt,' Matt said, and his hands tightened over Ben's. 'Not just for Barlow, but for all the little fish — and there will be a great many little fish after tonight. *Their* hunger is never satisfied. They'll eat until they're glutted. The nights are his, but in the daytime you will hound him and hound him until he takes fright and flees or until you drag him, staked and screaming, into the sunlight!'

Ben's head had come up at this speech. His face had taken on an animation that was close to ghastly. Now a small smile touched his mouth. 'Yes, that's good,' he whispered. 'Only tonight instead of tomorrow. Right now—'

Matt's hand shot out and clutched Ben's shoulder with surprising, sinewy strength. 'Not tonight. Tonight we're going to spend together — you and I and Jimmy and Father Callahan and Mark and Mark's parents. *He* knows now . . . he's afraid. Only a madman or a saint would dare to approach Barlow when he is awake in his mother-night. And none of us are either.' He closed his eyes and said softly, 'I'm beginning to know him, I think. I lie in this hospital bed and play Mycroft Holmes, trying to outguess him by putting myself in his place. He has lived for centuries, and he is brilliant. But he is also an egocentric, as his letter shows. Why not? His ego has grown the way a pearl does, layer by layer, until it is huge and poisonous. He's filled with pride. It must be vaunting indeed. And his thirst for revenge must be overmastering, a thing to be trembled at, but perhaps also a thing to be used.'

He opened his eyes and looked solemnly at them both. He raised the cross before him. 'This will stop *him*, but it may not stop someone he can use, the way he used Floyd Tibbits. I think he may try to eliminate some of us tonight . . . some of us or all of us.'

He looked at Jimmy.

'I think bad judgment was used in sending Mark and Father Callahan to the house of Mark's parents. They could have been called from here and summoned, knowing nothing. Now we are split . . . and I am especially worried for the boy. Jimmy, you had better call them . . . call them now.'

'All right.' He got up.

Matt looked at Ben. 'And you will stay with us? Fight with us?'

'Yes,' Ben said hoarsely. 'Yes.'

Jimmy left the room, went down the hall to the nurses' station, and found the Petries' number in the book. He dialed it rapidly and listened with sick horror as the sirening sound of a line out of service came through the earpiece instead of a ringing tone.

'He's got them,' he said.

The head nurse glanced up at the sound of his voice and was frightened by the look on his face.

18

Henry Petrie was an educated man. He had a B.S. from Northeastern, a master's from Massachusetts Tech, and a Ph.D. in economics. He had left a perfectly good junior college teaching position to take an administrative post with the Prudential Insurance Company, as much out of curiosity as from any hope of monetary gain. He had wanted to see if certain of his economic ideas worked out as well in practice as they did in theory. They did. By the following summer, he hoped to be able to take the CPA test, and two years after that, the bar examination. His current goal was to begin the 1980s in a high federal government economics post. His son's fey streak had not come from Henry Petrie; his father's logic was complete and seamless, and his world was machined to a point of almost total precision. He was a registered Democrat who had voted for Nixon in the 1972 elections not because he believed Nixon was honest — he had told his wife many times that he considered Richard Nixon to be an unimaginative little crook with all the finesse of a shoplifter in Woolworth's — but because the opposition was a crack-brained sky pilot who would bring down economic ruin on the country. He had viewed the counterculture of the late sixties with calm tolerance born of the belief that it would collapse harmlessly because it had no monetary base upon which to stand. His love for his wife and son was not beautiful — no one would ever write a poem to the passion of a man who balled his socks before his wife — but it was sturdy and unswerving. He was a straight arrow, confident in himself and in the natural laws of physics, mathematics, economics, and (to a slightly lesser degree) sociology.

He listened to the story told by his son and the village abbé, sipping a cup of coffee and prompting them with lucid questions at points where the thread of narration became tangled or unclear. His calmness increased, it seemed, in direct ratio to the story's grotesqueries and to his wife June's growing agitation. When they had finished it was almost five minutes of seven. Henry Petrie spoke his verdict in four calm, considered syllables.

'Impossible.'

Mark sighed and looked at Callahan and said, 'I told you.' He *had* told him, as they drove over from the rectory in Callahan's old car.

'Henry, don't you think we—'

'Wait.'

That and his hand held up (almost casually) stilled her at once. She sat down and put her arm around Mark, pulling him slightly away from Callahan's side. The boy submitted.

Henry Petrie looked at Father Callahan pleasantly. 'Let's see if we can't work this delusion or whatever it is out like two reasonable men.'

'That may be impossible,' Callahan said with equal pleasantness, 'but we'll certainly try. We are here, Mr Petrie, specifically because Barlow has threatened you and your wife.'

'Did you actually pound a stake through that girl's body this afternoon?'

'I did not. Mr Mears did.'

'Is the corpse still there?'

'They threw it in the river.'

'If that much is true,' Petrie said, 'you have involved my son in a crime. Are you aware of that?'

'I am. It was necessary. Mr Petrie, if you'll simply call Matt Burke's hospital room—'

'Oh, I'm sure your witnesses will back you up,' Petrie said, still smiling that faint, maddening smile. 'That's one of the fascinating things about this lunacy. May I see the letter this Barlow left you?'

Callahan cursed mentally. 'Dr Cody has it.' He added as an afterthought: 'We really ought to ride over to the Cumberland Hospital. If you talk to—'

Petrie was shaking his head.

'Let's talk a little more first. I'm sure your witnesses are reliable, as I've indicated. Dr Cody is our family physician, and we all like him very much. I've also been given to understand that Matthew Burke is above reproach . . . as a teacher, at least.'

'But in spite of that?' Callahan asked.

'Father Callahan, let me put it to you. If a dozen reliable witnesses told you that a giant ladybug had lumbered through the town park at high noon singing "Sweet Adeline" and waving a Confederate flag, would you believe it?'

'If I was sure the witnesses were reliable, and if I was sure they weren't joking, I would be far down the road to belief, yes.'

Still with the faint smile, Petrie said, 'That is where we differ.'

'Your mind is closed,' Callahan said.

'No – simply made up.'

'It amounts to the same thing. Tell me, in the company you work for do they approve of executives making decisions on the basis of internal beliefs rather than external facts? That's not logic, Petrie; that's cant.'

Petrie stopped smiling and stood up. 'Your story is disturbing, I'll grant you that. You've involved my son in something deranged, possibly dangerous. You'll all be lucky if you don't stand in court for it. I'm going to call your people and talk to them. Then I think we had all better go to Mr Burke's hospital room and discuss the matter further.'

'How good of you to bend a principle,' Callahan said dryly.

Petrie went into the living room and picked up the telephone. There was no answering open hum; the line was bare and silent. Frowning slightly, he jiggled the cut-off buttons. No response. He set the phone in its cradle and went back to the kitchen.

'The phone seems to be out of order,' he said.

He saw the instant look of fearful understanding that passed between Callahan and his son, and was irritated by it.

'I can assure you,' he said a little more sharply than he had intended, 'that the Jerusalem's Lot telephone service needs no vampires to disrupt it.'

The lights went out.

19

Jimmy ran back to Matt's room.

'The line's out at the Petrie house. I think he's there. Goddamn, we were so *stupid*—'

Ben got off the bed. Matt's face seemed to squeeze

and crumple. 'You see how he works?' he muttered. 'How smoothly? If only we had another hour of daylight, we could but we don't. It's done.'

'We have to go out there,' Jimmy said.

'No! You must not! For fear of your lives and mine, you must not.'

'But they—'

'*They are on their own!* What is happening — or has happened — will be done by the time you get out there!'

They stood near the door, indecisive.

Matt struggled, gathered his strength, and spoke to them quietly but with force.

'His ego is great, and his pride is great. These might be flaws we can put to our use. But his mind is also great, and we must respect it and allow for it. You showed me his letter — he speaks of chess. I've no doubt he's a superb player. Don't you realize that he could have donehis work at that house without cutting the telephone line? He did it because he wants you to know one of white's pieces is in check! He understands forces, and he understands that it becomes easier to conquer if the forces are split and in confusion. You gave him the first move by default because you forgot that — the original group was split in two. If you go haring off to the Petries' house, the group is split in three. I'm alone and bedridden; easy game in spite of crosses and books and incantations. All he needs to do is send one of his almost-Undead here to kill me with a gun or a knife. And that leaves only you and Ben, rushing pell-mell through the night to your own doom. Then 'salem's Lot is his. Don't you see it?'

Ben spoke first. 'Yes,' he said.

Matt slumped back. 'I'm not speaking out of fear for my life, Ben. You have to believe that. Not even for fear of your lives. I'm afraid for the town. No matter what else happens, someone must be left to stop him tomorrow.'

'Yes. And he's not going to have me until I've had revenge for Susan.'

A silence fell among them.

Jimmy Cody broke it. 'They may get away anyway,' he said meditatively. 'I think he's underestimated Callahan, and I know damned well he's underestimated the boy. That kid is one cool customer.'

'We'll hope,' Matt said, and closed his eyes.

They settled down to wait.

20

Father Donald Callahan stood on one side of the spacious Petrie kitchen, holding his mother's cross high above his head, and it spilled its ghostly effulgence across the room. Barlow stood on the other side, near the sink, one hand pinning Mark's hands behind his back, the other slung around his neck. Between them, Henry and June Petrie lay sprawled on the floor in the shattered glass of Barlow's entry.

Callahan was dazed. It had all happened with such swiftness that he could not take it in. At one moment he had been discussing the matter rationally (if maddeningly) with Petrie, under the brisk, no-nonsense glow of the kitchen lights. At the next, he had been plunged into the insanity that Mark's father had denied with such calm and understanding firmness.

His mind tried to reconstruct what had happened.

Petrie had come back and told them the phone was out. Moments later they had lost the lights. June Petrie screamed. A chair fell over. For several moments all of them had stumbled around in the new dark, calling out to each other. Then the window over the sink had crashed inward, spraying glass across the kitchen counter and onto the linoleum floor. All this had happened in a space of thirty seconds.

Then a shadow had moved in the kitchen, and Callahan had broken the spell that held him. He clutched at the cross that hung around his neck, and even as his flesh touched it, the room was lit with its unearthly light.

He saw Mark, trying to drag his mother toward the arch which led into the living room. Henry Petrie stood beside them, his head turned, his calm face suddenly slack-jawed with amazement at this totally illogical invasion. And behind him, looming over them, a white, grinning face like something out of a Frazetta painting, which split to reveal long, sharp fangs — and red, lurid eyes like furnace doors to hell. Barlow's hands flew out (Callahan had just time to see how long and sensitive those livid fingers were, like a concert pianist's) and then he had seized Henry Petrie's head in one hand, June's in the other, and had brought them together with a grinding, sickening crack. They had both dropped down like stones, and Barlow's first threat had been carried out.

Mark had uttered a high, keening scream and threw himself at Barlow without thought.

'And here you are!' Barlow had boomed good-naturedly in his rich, powerful voice. Mark attacked without thought and was captured instantly.

Callahan moved forward, holding his cross up.

Barlow's grin of triumph was instantly transformed into a rictus of agony. He fell back toward the sink, dragging the boy in front of him. Their feet crunched in the broken glass.

'In God's name—' Callahan began.

At the name of the Deity, Barlow screamed aloud as if he had been struck by a whip, his mouth open in a downward grimace, the needle fangs glimmering within. The cords of muscle on his neck stood out in stark, etched relief. 'No closer!' he said. 'No closer, shaman! Or I sever the boy's jugular and carotid before you can draw a breath!' As he spoke, his upper lip lifted from those long, needle-like teeth, and as he finished, his head made a predatory downward pass with adder's speed, missing Mark's flesh by a quarter-inch.

Callahan stopped.

'Back up,' Barlow commanded, now grinning again. 'You on your side of the board and I on mine, eh?'

Callahan backed up slowly, still holding the cross before him at eye level, so that he looked over its arms. The cross seemed to thrum with chained fire, and its power coursed up his forearm until the muscles bunched and trembled.

They faced each other.

'Together at last!' Barlow said, smiling. His face was strong and intelligent and handsome in a sharp, forbidding sort of way – yet, as the light shifted, it seemed almost effeminate. Where had he seen a face like that before? And it came to him, in this moment of the most extreme terror he had ever known. It was the face of Mr Flip, his own personal bogeyman, the thing that hid in the closet during the days and came out after his mother closed the bedroom door. He was not allowed a night-light — both his mother and his father had agreed that the way to conquer these childish fears was to face them, not toady to them — and every night, when the door snicked shut and his mother's footsteps padded off down the hall, the closet door slid open a crack and he could sense (or actually *see?*) the thin white face and burning eyes of Mr Flip. And here he was again, out of the closet, staring over Mark's shoulder with his clown-white face and glowing eyes and red, sensual lips.

'What now?' Callahan said, and his voice was not his own at all. He was looking at Barlow's fingers, those long, sensitive fingers, which lay against the boy's throat. There were small blue blotches on them.

'That depends. What will you give for this miserable wretch?' He suddenly jerked Mark's wrists high behind his back, obviously hoping to punctuate his question with a scream, but Mark would not oblige. Except for the sudden whistle of air between his set teeth, he was silent.

'You'll scream,' Barlow whispered, and his lips had twisted into a grimace of animal hate. 'You'll scream until your throat *bursts!*'

'Stop that!' Callahan cried.

'And should I?' The hate was wiped from his face. A darkly charming smile shone forth in its place. 'Should I reprieve the boy, save him for another night?'

'Yes!'

Softly, almost purring, Barlow said, 'Then will you throw away your cross and face me on even terms — black against white? Your faith against my own?'

'Yes,' Callahan said, but a trifle less firmly.

'Then do it!' Those full lips became pursed, anticipatory. The high forehead gleamed in the weird fairy light that filled the room.

'And trust you to let him go? I would be wiser to put a rattlesnake in my shirt and trust it not to bite me.'

'But I trust you . . . look!'

He let Mark go and stood back, both hands in the air, empty.

Mark stood still, unbelieving for a moment, and then ran to his parents without a backward look at Barlow.

'Run, Mark!' Callahan cried. 'Run!'

Mark looked up at him, his eyes huge and dark. 'I think they're dead—'

'RUN!'

Mark got slowly to his feet. He turned around and looked at Barlow.

'Soon, little brother,' Barlow said, almost benignly. 'Very soon now you and I will—'

Mark spit in his face.

Barlow's breath stopped. His brow darkened with a depth of fury that made his previous expressions seem like what they might well have been: mere playacting. For a moment Callahan saw a madness in his eyes blacker than the soul of murder.

'*You spit on me*,' Barlow whispered. His body was trembling, nearly rocking with his rage. He took a shuddering step forward like some awful blind man.

'*Get back!*' Callahan screamed, and thrust the cross forward.

Barlow cried out and threw his hands in front of his

face. The cross flared with preternatural, dazzling brilliance, and it was at that moment that Callahan might have banished him if he had dared to press forward.

'I'm going to kill you,' Mark said.

He was gone, like a dark eddy of water.

Barlow seemed to grow taller. His hair, swept back from his brow in the European manner, seemed to float around his skull. He was wearing a dark suit and a wine-colored tie, impeccably knotted, and to Callahan he seemed part and parcel of the darkness that surrounded him. His eyes glared out of their sockets like sly and sullen embers.

'Then fulfill your part of the bargain, shaman.'

'I'm a *priest!*' Callahan flung at him.

Barlow made a small, mocking bow. '*Priest,*' he said, and the word sounded like a dead haddock in his mouth.

Callahan stood indecisive. Why throw it down? Drive him off, settle for a draw tonight, and tomorrow—

But a deeper part of his mind warned. To deny the vampire's challenge was to risk possibilities far graver than any he had considered. If he dared not throw the cross aside, it would be as much as admitting . . . admitting . . . what? If only things weren't going so fast, if one only had time to think, to reason it out—

The cross's glow was dying.

He looked at it, eyes widening. Fear leaped into his belly like a confusion of hot wires. His head jerked up and he stared at Barlow. He was walking toward him across the kitchen and his smile was wide, almost voluptuous.

'Stay back,' Callahan said hoarsely, retreating a step. 'I command it, in the name of God.'

Barlow laughed at him.

The glow in the cross was only a thin and guttering light in a cruciform shape. The shadows had crept across the vampire's face again, masking his features in strangely barbaric lines and triangles under the sharp cheekbones.

Callahan took another step backward, and his buttocks bumped the kitchen table, which was set against the wall.

'Nowhere left to go,' Barlow murmured sadly. His dark eyes bubbled with infernal mirth. 'Sad to see a man's faith fail. Ah, well . . .'

The cross trembled in Callahan's hand and suddenly the last of its light vanished. It was only a piece of plaster that his mother had bought in a Dublin souvenir shop, probably at a scalper's price. The power it had sent ramming up his arm, enough power to smash down walls and shatter stone, was gone. The muscles remembered the thrumming but could not duplicate it.

Barlow reached from the darkness and plucked the cross from his fingers. Callahan cried out miserably, the cry that had vibrated in the soul – but never the throat – of that long-ago child who had been left alone each night with Mr Flip peering out of the closet at him from between the shutters of sleep. And the next sound would haunt him for the rest of his life: two dry snaps as Barlow broke the arms of the cross, and a meaningless thump as he threw it on the floor.

'God *damn* you!' he cried out.

'It's too late for such melodrama,' Barlow said from the darkness. His voice was almost sorrowful. 'There is no need of it. You have forgotten the doctrine of your own church, is it not so? The cross . . . the bread and wine . . . the confessional . . . only symbols. Without faith, the cross is only wood, the bread baked wheat, the wine sour grapes. If you had cast the cross away, you should have beaten me another night. In a way, I hoped it might be so. It has been long since I have met an opponent of any real worth. The boy makes ten of you, false priest.'

Suddenly, out of the darkness, hands of amazing strength gripped Callahan's shoulders.

'You would welcome the oblivion of my death now, I think. There is no memory for the Undead; only the hunger and the need to serve the Master. I could make use of you. I could send you among your friends. Yet is there need of that? Without you to lead them, I think they are little. And the boy will tell them. One moves against them at this time. There is, perhaps, a more fitting punishment for you, false priest.'

He remembered Matt saying: *Some things are worse than death.*

He tried to struggle away, but the hands held him in a viselike grip. Then one hand left him. There was the sound of cloth moving across bare skin, and then a scraping sound.

The hands moved to his neck.

'Come, false priest. Learn of a true religion. Take *my* communion.'

Understanding washed over Callahan in a ghastly flood.

'No! Don't . . . don't—'

But the hands were implacable. His head was drawn forward, forward, forward.

'Now, priest,' Barlow whispered.

And Callahan's mouth was pressed against the reeking

flesh of the vampire's cold throat, where an open vein pulsed. He held his breath for what seemed like aeons, twisting his head wildly and to no avail, smearing the blood across his cheeks and forehead and chin like war paint.

Yet at last, he drank.

21

Ann Norton got out of her car without bothering to take the keys, and began to walk across the hospital parking lot toward the bright lights of the lobby. Overhead, clouds had blotted out the stars and soon it would begin to rain. She didn't look up to see the clouds. She walked stolidly, looking straight in front of her.

She was a very different-looking woman from the lady Ben Mears had met on that first evening Susan had invited him to take dinner with her family. That lady had been medium-tall, dressed in a green wool dress that did not scream of money but spoke of material comfort. That lady had not been beautiful but she had been well groomed and pleasant to look at; her graying hair had been permed not long since.

This woman wore only carpet slippers on her feet. Her legs were bare, and with no Supp-hose to mask them, the varicose veins bulged prominently (although not as prominently as before; some of the pressure had been taken off them). She was wearing a ragged yellow dressing gown over her negligee; her hair was blown in errant sheafs by the rising wind. Her face was pallid, and heavy brown circles lay beneath her eyes.

She had told Susan, had warned her about that man

Mears and his friends, had warned her about the man who had murdered her. Matt Burke had put him up to it. They had been in cahoots. Oh yes. She knew. *He* had told her.

She had been sick all day, sick and sleepy and nearly unable to get out of bed. And when she had fallen into a heavy slumber after noon, while her husband was off answering questions for a silly missing persons report, *he* had come to her in a dream. His face was handsome and commanding and arrogant and compelling. His nose was hawklike, his hair swept back from his brow, and his heavy, fascinating mouth masked strangely exciting white teeth that showed when *he* smiled. And his eyes . . . they were red and hypnotic. When *he* looked at you with those eyes, you could not look away . . . and you didn't want to.

He had told her everything, and what she must do — and how she could be with her daughter when it was done, and with so many others . . . and with *him*. Despite Susan, it was *him* she wanted to please, so *he* would give her the thing she craved and needed: the touch; the penetration.

Her husband's .38 was in her pocket.

She entered the lobby and looked toward the reception desk. If anyone tried to stop her, she would take care of them. Not by shooting, no. No shot must be fired until she was in Burke's room. *He* had told her so. If they got to her and stopped her before she had done the job, *he* would not come to her, to give her burning kisses in the night.

There was a young girl at the desk in a white cap and uniform, working a crossword in the soft glow of the lamp over her main console. An orderly was just going down the hall, his back to them.

The duty nurse looked up with a trained smile when she heard Ann's footsteps, but it faded when she saw the hollow-eyed woman who was approaching her in night-clothes. Her eyes were blank yet oddly shiny, as if she were a wind-up toy someone had set in motion. A patient, perhaps, who had gone wandering.

'Ma'am, if you—'

Ann Norton drew the .38 from the pocket of her wrapper like some creaky gunslinger from beyond time. She pointed it at the duty nurse's head and told her, 'Turn around.'

The nurse's mouth worked silently. She drew in breath with a convulsive heave.

'Don't scream. I'll kill you if you do.'

The air wheezed out. The nurse had gone very pale.

'Turn around now.'

The nurse got up slowly and turned around. Ann Norton reversed the .38 and prepared to bring the butt down on the nurse's head with all the strength she had.

At that precise moment, her feet were kicked out from under her.

22

The gun went flying.

The woman in the ragged yellow dressing gown did not scream but began to make a high whining noise in her throat, almost keening. She scrambled after it like a crab, and the man who was behind her, looking bewildered and frightened, also darted after it. When he saw that she would get to it first, he kicked it across the lobby rug.

'Hey!' he yelled. 'Hey, help!'

Ann Norton looked over her shoulder and hissed at him, her face pulled into a cheated scrawl of hate, and then scrambled after the gun again. The orderly had come back, on the run. He looked at the scene with blank amazement for a moment, and then picked up the gun that lay almost at his feet.

'For Christ's sake,' he said. 'This thing is load—'

She attacked him. Her hands, hooked into claws, pinwheeled across his face, dragging red stripes across the surprised orderly's forehead and right cheek. He held the gun up out of her reach. Still keening, she clawed for it.

The bewildered man came up from behind and grabbed her. He would say later that it was like grabbing a bag of snakes. The body beneath the dressing gown was hot and repulsive, every muscle twitching and writhing.

As she struggled to get free, the orderly popped her one flush on the jaw. Her eyes rolled up to the whites and she collapsed.

The orderly and the bewildered man looked at each other.

The nurse at the reception desk was screaming. Her hands were clapped to her mouth, giving the screams a unique foghorn effect.

'What kind of a hospital do you people run here, anyhow?' the bewildered man asked.

'Christ if I know,' the orderly said. 'What the hell happened?'

'I was just coming in to visit my sister. She had a baby. And this kid walks up to me and says a woman just went in with a gun. And—'

'What kid?'

The bewildered man who had come to visit his sister looked around. The lobby was filling with people, but all of them were above drinking age.

'I don't see him now. But he was here. That gun loaded?'

'It sure is,' the orderly said.

'What kind of a hospital do you people run here, anyhow?' the bewildered man asked again.

23

They had seen two nurses run past the door toward the elevators and heard a vague shout down the stairwell. Ben glanced at Jimmy and Jimmy shrugged imperceptibly. Matt was dozing with his mouth open.

Ben closed the door and turned off the lights. Jimmy crouched by the foot of Matt's bed, and when they heard footsteps hesitate outside the door, Ben stood beside it, ready. When it opened and a head poked through, he grabbed it in a half nelson and jammed the cross he held in the other hand into the face.

'Let me *go!*'

A hand reached up and beat futilely at his chest. A moment later the overhead light went on. Matt was sitting up in bed, blinking at Mark Petrie, who was struggling in Ben's arms.

Jimmy came out of his crouch and ran across the room. He seemed almost ready to embrace the boy when he hesitated. 'Lift your chin.'

Mark did, showing all three of them his unmarked neck.

Jimmy relaxed. 'Boy, I've never been so glad to see anyone in my life. Where's the Father?'

'Don't know,' Mark said somberly. 'Barlow caught me . . . killed my folks. They're dead. My folks are dead. He beat their heads together. He killed my folks. Then he had me and he said to Father Callahan that he would let me go if Father Callahan would promise to throw away his cross. He promised. I ran. But before I ran, I spit on him. I spit on him and I'm going to kill him.'

He swayed in the doorway. There were bramble marks on his forehead and cheeks. He had run through the forest along the path where Danny Glick and his brother had come to grief so long before. His pants were wet to the knees from his flight through Taggart Stream. He had hitched a ride, but couldn't remember who he had hitched it with. The radio had been playing, he remembered that.

Ben's tongue was frozen. He did not know what to say.

'You poor boy,' Matt said softly. 'You poor, brave boy.'

Mark's face began to break up. His eyes closed and his mouth twisted and strained. 'My muh-muh-*mother*—'

He staggered blindly and Ben caught him in his arms, enfolded him, rocked him as the tears came and raged against his shirt.

24

Father Donald Callahan had no idea how long he walked in the dark. He stumbled back toward the downtown area along Jointner Avenue, never heeding his car, which he had left parked in the Petries' driveway. Sometimes he wandered in the middle of the road, and sometimes he staggered along the sidewalk. Once a car bore down on him, its headlights great shining circles; its horn began to blare and it swerved at the last instant, tires screaming on the pavement. Once he fell in the ditch. As he approached the yellow blinking light, it began to rain.

There was no one on the streets to mark his passage; 'salem's Lot had battened down for the night, even tighter than usual. The diner was empty, and in Spencer's Miss Coogan was sitting by her cash register and reading a confession magazine off the rack in the frosty glow of the overhead fluorescents. Outside, under the lighted sign showing the blue dog in mid-flight, a red neon sign said:

BUS

They were afraid, he supposed. They had every reason to be. Some inner part of themselves had absorbed the danger, and tonight doors were locked in the Lot that had not been locked in years . . . if ever.

He was on the streets alone. And he alone had nothing to fear. It was funny. He laughed aloud, and the sound of it was like wild, lunatic sobbing. No vampire would touch him. Others, perhaps, but not him. The Master had marked him, and he would walk free until the Master claimed his own.

St Andrew's loomed above him.

He hesitated, then walked up the path. He would pray. Pray all night, if necessary. Not to the new God, the God of ghettos and social conscience and free lunches, but the old God, who had proclaimed through Moses not to suffer a witch to live and who had given it unto his own son to raise from the dead. A second chance, God. All my life for penance. Only . . . a second chance.

He stumbled up the wide steps, his gown muddy and bedraggled, his mouth smeared with Barlow's blood.

At the top he paused a moment, and then reached for the handle of the middle door.

As he touched it, there was a blue flash of light and he was thrown backward. Pain lanced his back, then his head, then his chest and stomach and shins as he fell head over heels down the granite steps to the walk.

He lay trembling in the rain, his hand afire.

He lifted it before his eyes. It was burned.

'Unclean,' he muttered. 'Unclean, unclean, O God, so unclean.'

He began to shiver. He slid his arms around his shoulders and shivered in the rain and the church loomed behind him, its doors shut against him.

25

Mark Petrie sat on Matt's bed, in exactly the spot Ben had occupied when Ben and Jimmy had come in. Mark had dried his tears with his shirtsleeve, and although his eyes were puffy and bloodshot, he seemed to have himself in control.

'You know, don't you,' Matt asked him, 'that 'salem's Lot is in a desperate situation?'

Mark nodded.

'Even now, *his* Undead are crawling over it,' Matt said somberly. 'Taking others to themselves. They won't get them all — not tonight — but there is dreadful work ahead of you tomorrow.'

'Matt, I want you to get some sleep,' Jimmy said. 'We'll be here, don't worry. You don't look good. This has been a horrible strain on you—'

'My town is disintegrating almost before my eyes and you want me to sleep?' His eyes, seemingly tireless, flashed out of his haggard face.

Jimmy said stubbornly, 'If you want to be around for the finish, you better save something back. I'm telling you that as your physician, goddammit.'

'All right. In a minute.' He looked at all of them. 'Tomorrow the three of you must go back to Mark's house. You're going to make stakes. A great many of them.'

The meaning sank home to them.

'How many?' Ben asked softly.

'I would say you'll need three hundred at least. I advise you to make five hundred.'

'That's impossible,' Jimmy said flatly. 'There can't be that many of them.'

'The Undead are thirsty,' Matt said simply. 'It's best to be prepared. You will go together. You dare not split up, even in the daytime. It will be like a scavenger hunt. You must start at one end of town and work toward the other.'

'We'll never be able to find them all,' Ben objected. 'Not even if we could start at first light and work through until dark.'

'You've got to do your best, Ben. People may begin to believe you. Some will help, if you show them the truth of what you say. And when dark comes again, much of *his* work will be undone.' He sighed. 'We have to assume that

Father Callahan is lost to us. That's bad. But you must press on, regardless. You'll have to be careful, all of you. Be ready to lie. If you're locked up, that will serve *his* purpose well. And if you haven't considered it, you might do well to consider it now: There is every possibility that some of us or all of us may live and triumph only to stand trial for murder.'

He looked each of them in the face. What he saw there must have satisfied him, because he turned his attention wholly to Mark again.

'You know what the most important job is, don't you?'

'Yes,' Mark said. 'Barlow has to be killed.'

Matt smiled a trifle thinly. 'That's putting the cart before the horse, I'm afraid. First we have to find him.' He looked closely at Mark. 'Did you see anything tonight, hear anything, smell anything, touch anything, that might help us locate him? Think carefully before you answer! You know better than any of us how important it is!'

Mark thought. Ben had never seen anyone take a command quite so literally. He lowered his chin into the palm of his hand and shut his eyes. He seemed to be quite deliberately going over every nuance of the night's encounter.

At last he opened his eyes, looked around at them briefly, and shook his head. 'Nothing.'

Matt's face fell, but he did not give up. 'A leaf clinging to his coat, maybe? A cattail in his pants cuff? Dirt on his shoes? Any loose thread that he has allowed to dangle?' He smote the bed helplessly. 'Jesus Christ Almighty, is he seamless like an egg?'

Mark's eyes suddenly widened.

'What?' Matt said. He grasped the boy's elbow. 'What is it? What have you thought of?'

'Blue chalk,' Mark said. 'He had one arm hooked around my neck, like this, and I could see his hand. He had long white fingers and there were smears of blue chalk on two of them. Just little ones.'

'Blue chalk,' Matt said thoughtfully.

'A school,' Ben said. 'It must be.'

'Not the high school,' Matt said. 'All our supplies come from Dennision and Company in Portland. They supply only white and yellow. I've had it under my finger-nails and on my coats for years.'

'Art classes?' Ben asked.

'No, only graphic arts at the high school. They use inks, not chalk. Mark, are you sure it was—'

'Chalk,' he said, nodding.

'I believe some of the science teachers use colored chalk, but where is there to hide at the high school? You saw it – all on one level, all enclosed in glass. People are in and out of the supply closets all day. That is also true of the furnace room.'

'Backstage?'

Matt shrugged. 'It's dark enough. But if Mrs Rodin takes over the class play for me – the students call her Mrs Rodan after a quaint Japanese science fiction film – that area would be used a great deal. It would be a horrible risk for him.'

'What about the grammar schools?' Jimmy asked. 'They must teach drawing in the lower grades. And I'd bet a hundred dollars that colored chalk is one of the things they keep on hand.'

Matt said, 'The Stanley Street Elementary School was built with the same bond money as the high school. It is also modernistic, filled to capacity, and built on one level. Many glass windows to let in the sun. Not the kind of building our target would want to frequent at all. They like old buildings, full of tradition, dark, dingy, like—'

'Like the Brock Street School,' Mark said.

'Yes.' Matt looked at Ben. 'The Brock Street School is a wooden frame building, three stories and a basement, built at about the same time as the Marsten House. There was much talk in the town when the school bond issue was up for a vote that the school was a fire hazard. It was one reason our bond issue passed. There had been a schoolhouse fire in New Hampshire two or three years before—'

'I remember,' Jimmy murmured. 'In Cobbs' Ferry, wasn't it?'

'Yes. Three children were burned to death.'

'Is the Brock Street School still used?' Ben asked.

'Only the first floor. Grades one through four. The entire building is due to be phased out in two years, when they put the addition on the Stanley Street School.'

'Is there a place for Barlow to hide?'

'I suppose so,' Matt said, but he sounded reluctant. 'The second and third floors are full of empty classrooms. The windows have been boarded over because so many children threw stones through them.'

'That's it, then,' Ben said. 'It must be.'

'It sounds good,' Matt admitted, and he looked very tired indeed now. 'But it seems too simple. Too transparent.'

'Blue chalk,' Jimmy murmured. His eyes were far away.

'I don't know,' Matt said, sounding distracted. 'I just don't know.'

Jimmy opened his black bag and brought out a small bottle of pills. 'Two of these with water,' he said. 'Right now.'

'No. There's too much to go over. There's too much—'

'Too much for us to risk losing you,' Ben said firmly. 'If Father Callahan *is* gone, you're the most important of all of us now. Do as he says.'

Mark brought a glass of water from the bathroom, and Matt gave in with some bad grace.

It was quarter after ten.

Silence fell in the room. Ben thought that Matt looked fearfully old, fearfully used. His white hair seemed thinner, drier, and a lifetime of care seemed to have stamped itself on his face in a matter of days. In a way, Ben thought, it was fitting that when trouble finally came to him – great trouble – it should come in this dreamlike, darkly fantastical form. A lifetime's existence had prepared him to deal in symbolic evils that sprang to light under the reading lamp and disappeared at dawn.

'I'm worried about him,' Jimmy said softly.

'I thought the attack was mild,' Ben said. 'Not really a heart attack at all.'

'It was a mild occlusion. But the next one won't be mild. It'll be major. This business is going to kill him if it doesn't end quickly.' He took Matt's hand and fingered the pulse gently, with love. 'That,' he said, 'would be a tragedy.'

They waited around his bedside, sleeping and watching

by turns. He slept the night away, and Barlow did not put in an appearance. He had business elsewhere.

26

Miss Coogan was reading a story called 'I Tried to Strangle Our Baby' in *Real Life Confessions* when the door opened and her first customer of the evening came in.

She had never seen things so slow. Ruthie Crockett and her friends hadn't even been in for a soda at the fountain – not that she missed *that* crowd – and Loretta Starcher hadn't stopped in for *The New York Times*. It was still under the counter, neatly folded. Loretta was the only person in Jerusalem's Lot who bought the *Times* (she pronounced it that way, in italics) regularly. And the next day she would put it out in the reading room.

Mr Labree hadn't come back from his supper, either, although there was nothing unusual about that. Mr Labree was a widower with a big house out on Schoolyard Hill near the Griffens, and Miss Coogan knew perfectly well that he didn't go home for his supper. He went out to Dell's and ate hamburgers and drank beer. If he wasn't back by eleven (and it was quarter of now), she would get the key out of the cash drawer and lock up herself. Wouldn't be the first time, either. But they would all be in a pretty pickle if someone came in needing medicine badly.

She sometimes missed the after-movie rush that had always come about this time before they had demolished the old Nordica across the street – people wanting ice-cream sodas and frappés and malteds, dates holding hands and talking about homework assignments. It had been hard, but it had been *wholesome*, too. Those children hadn't been like Ruthie Crockett and her crowd, sniggering and flaunting their busts and wearing jeans tight enough to show the line of their panties – if they were wearing any. The reality of her feelings for those bygone patrons (who, although she had forgotten it, had irritated her just as much) was fogged by nostalgia, and she looked up eagerly when the door opened, as if it might be a member of the class of '64 and his girl, ready for a chocolate fudge sundae with extra nuts.

But it was a man, a grown-up man, someone she knew but could not place. As he carried his suitcase down to the counter, something in his walk or the motion of his head identified him for her.

'Father Callahan!' she said, unable to keep the surprise out of her voice. She had never seen him without his priest suit on. He was wearing plain dark slacks and a blue chambray shirt, like a common mill-worker.

She was suddenly frightened. The clothes he wore were clean and his hair was neatly combed, but there was something in his face, something—

She suddenly remembered the day, twenty years ago, when she had come from the hospital where her mother had died of a sudden stroke – what the old-timers called a shock. When she had told her brother, he had looked something like Father Callahan did now. His face had a haggard, doomed look, and his eyes were blank and stunned. There was a burned-out look in them that made her uncomfortable. And the skin around his mouth looked red and irritated, as if he had overshaved or rubbed it for a long period of time with a washcloth, trying to get rid of a bad stain.

'I want to buy a bus ticket,' he said.

That's it, she thought. Poor man, someone's died and he just got the call down at the directory, or whatever they call it.

'Certainly,' she said. 'Where—'

'What's the first bus?'

'To where?'

'Anywhere,' he said, throwing her theory into shambles.

'Well . . . I don't . . . let me see . . .' She fumbled out the schedule, and looked at it, flustered. 'There's a bus at eleven-ten that connects with Portland, Boston, Hartford, and New Y—'

'That one,' he said. 'How much?'

'For how long – I mean, how far?' She was thoroughly flustered now.

'All the way,' he said hollowly, and smiled. She had never seen such a dreadful smile on a human face, and she flinched from it. *If he touches me*, she thought, *I'll scream. Scream blue murder.*

'T-th-that would be to New York City,' she said. 'Twenty-nine dollars and seventy-five cents.'

He dug his wallet out of his back pocket with some difficulty, and she saw that his right hand was bandaged. He put a twenty and two ones before her, and she knocked a whole pile of blank tickets onto the floor taking one off the top of the stack. When she finished picking them up, he had added five more ones and a pile of change.

She wrote the ticket as fast as she could, but nothing

would have been fast enough. She could feel his dead gaze on her. She stamped it and pushed it across the counter so she wouldn't have to touch his hand.

'Y-you'll have to wait outside, Father C-Callahan. I've got to close in about five minutes.' She scraped the bills and change into the cash drawer blindly, making no attempt to count it.

'That's fine,' he said. He stuffed the ticket into his breast pocket. Without looking at her he said, 'And the Lord set a mark upon Cain, that whosoever found him should not kill him. And Cain went out from the face of the Lord, and dwelt as a fugitive on the earth, at the east side of Eden. That's Scripture, Miss Coogan. The hardest scripture in the Bible.'

'Is that so?' she said. 'I'm afraid you'll have to go outside, Father Callahan. I . . . Mr Labree is just in back a minute and he doesn't like . . . doesn't like me to . . . to . . .'

'Of course,' he said, and turned to go. He stopped and looked around at her. She flinched before those wooden eyes. 'You live in Falmouth, don't you, Miss Coogan?'

'Yes—'

'Have your own car?'

'Yes, of course. I really have to ask you to wait for the bus outside—'

'Drive home quickly tonight, Miss Coogan. Lock all your car doors and don't stop for anybody. *Anybody.* Don't even stop if it's someone you know.'

'I *never* pick up hitchhikers,' Miss Coogan said right-eously.

'And when you get home, stay away from Jerusalem's

Lot,' Callahan went on. He was looking at her fixedly. 'Things have gone bad in the Lot now.'

She said faintly, 'I don't know what you're talking about, but you'll have to wait for the bus outside.'

'Yes. All right.'

He went out.

She became suddenly aware of how quiet the drug-store was, how utterly quiet. Could it be that no one – *no* one – had come in since it got dark except Father Callahan? It was. No one at all.

Things have gone bad in the Lot now.

She began to go around and turn off the lights.

27

In the Lot the dark held hard.

At ten minutes to twelve, Charlie Rhodes was awakened by a long, steady honking. He came awake in his bed and sat bolt upright.

His bus!

And on the heels of that:

The little bastards!

The children had tried things like this before. He knew them, the miserable little sneaks. They had let the air out of his tires with matchsticks once. He hadn't seen who did it, but he had a damned good idea. He had gone to that damned wet-ass principal and reported Mike Philbrook and Audie James. He had known it was them – who had to see?

Are you sure it was them, Rhodes?

I told you, didn't I?

514

And there was nothing that fucking mollycoddle could do; he *had* to suspend them. Then the bastard had called him to the office a week later.

Rhodes, we suspended Andy Garvey today.

Yeah? Not surprised. What was he up to?

Bob Thomas caught him letting the air out of his bus tires. And he had given Charlie Rhodes a long, cold, measuring look.

Well, so what if it had been Garvey instead of Philbrook and James? They all hung around together, they were all creeps, they all deserved to have their nuts in the grinder.

Now, from outside, the maddening sound of his horn, running down the battery, really laying on it:

WHONK, WHONNK, WHOONNNNNNNNNK—

'You sons of whores,' he whispered, and slid out of bed. He dragged his pants on without using the light. The light would scare the little scumbags away, and he didn't want that.

Another time, someone had left a cow pie on his driver's seat, and he had a pretty good idea of who had done that, too. You could read it in their eyes. He had learned that standing guard at the repple depple in the war. He had taken care of the cow-pie business in his own way. Kicked the little son of a whore off the bus three day's running, four miles from home. The kid finally came to him crying.

I ain't done nothin', Mr Rhodes. Why you keep kickin' me off?

You call puttin' a cow flop on my seat nothin'?

No, that wasn't me. Honest to God it wasn't.

Well, you had to hand it to them. They could lie to their own mothers with a clear and smiling face, and they probably did it, too. He had kicked the kid off two more nights and then he had confessed, by the Jesus. Charlie kicked him off once more – one to grow on, you might say – and then Dave Felsen down at the motor pool told him he better cool it for a while.

WHONNNNNNNNNNNNNNNNNNNK—

He grabbed his shirt and then got the old tennis racket standing in the corner. By Christ, he was going to whip some ass tonight!

He went out the back door and around the house to where he kept the big yellow bus parked. He felt tough and coldly competent. This was infiltration, just like the Army.

He paused behind the oleander bush and looked at the bus. Yes, he could see them, a whole bunch of them, darker shapes behind the night-darkened glass. He felt the old red rage, the hate of them like hot ice, and his grip on the tennis racket tightened until it trembled in his hand like a tuning fork. They had busted out – six, seven, eight – eight windows on *his* bus!

He slipped behind it and then crept up the long yellow side to the passenger door. It was folded open. He tensed, and suddenly sprang up the steps.

'All right! Stay where you are! Kid, lay off that goddamn horn or I'll—'

The kid sitting in the driver's seat with both hands plastered on the horn ring turned to him and smiled crazily. Charlie felt a sickening drop in his gut. It was Richie Boddin. He was white – just as white as a sheet – except for the black chips of coal that were his eyes, and his lips, which were ruby red.

And his teeth—

Charlie Rhodes looked down the aisle.

Was that Mike Philbrook? Audie James? God Almighty, the Griffen boys were down there! Hal and Jack, sitting near the back with hay in their hair. *But they don't ride on my bus!* Mary Kate Griegson and Brent Tenney, sitting side by side. She was in a nightgown, he in blue jeans and a flannel shirt that was on backward and inside out, as if he had forgotten how to dress himself.

And Danny Glick. But – oh, Christ – he was *dead;* dead for *weeks!*

'You,' he said through numb lips. 'You kids—'

The tennis racket slid from his hand. There was a wheeze and a thump as Richie Boddin, still smiling that crazy smile, worked the chrome lever that shut the folding door. They were getting out of their seats now, all of them.

'No,' he said, trying to smile. 'You kids . . . you don't understand. It's me. It's Charlie Rhodes. You . . . you . . .' He grinned at them without meaning, shook his head, held out his hands to show them they were just ole Charlie Rhodes's hands, blameless, and backed up until his back was jammed against the wide tinted glass of the wind-shield.

'Don't,' he whispered.

They came on, grinning.

'Please don't.'

And fell on him.

28

Ann Norton died on the short elevator trip from the first floor of the hospital to the second. She shivered once, and a small trickle of blood ran from the corner of her mouth.

'Okay,' one of the orderlies said. 'You can turn off the siren now.'

29

Eva Miller had been dreaming.

It was a strange dream, not quite a nightmare. The fire of '51 was raging under an unforgiving sky that shaded from pale blue at the horizons to a hot and merciless white overhead. The sun glared from this inverted bowl like a glinting copper coin. The acrid smell of smoke was everywhere, all business activity had stopped and people stood in the streets, looking southwest, toward the Marshes, and northwest, toward the woods. The smoke had been in the air all morning, but now, at one in the afternoon, you could see the bright arteries of fire dancing in the green beyond Griffen's pasture. The steady breeze that had allowed the flames to jump one firebreak now brought a steady fall of white ash over the town like summer snow.

Ralph was alive, off trying to save the sawmill. But it was all mixed up because Ed Craig was with her and she had never even met Ed until the fall of 1954.

She was watching the fire from her upstairs bedroom window, and she was naked. Hands touched her from behind, rough brown hands on the smooth whiteness of her hips, and she knew it was Ed, although she could not see even a ghost of his reflection in the glass.

Ed, she tried to say. *Not now. It's too early. Not for almost nine years.*

But his hands were insistent, running over her belly, one finger toying with the cup of her navel, then both hands slipping up to catch her breasts with brazen knowledge.

She tried to tell him they were in the window, anyone out there in the street could look over his shoulder and see them, but the words would not come out and then his lips were on her arm, her shoulder, then fastening with firm and lustful insistence on her neck. She felt his teeth and he was biting her, sucking and biting, drawing blood, and she tried to protest again: *Don't give me a hickey, Ralph will see—*

But it was impossible to protest and she no longer even wanted to. She no longer cared who looked around and saw them, naked and brazen.

Her eyes drifted dreamily to the fire as his lips and teeth worked against her neck, and the smoke was very black, as black as night, obscuring that hot gunmetal sky, turning day to night; yet the fire moved inside it in those pulsing scarlet threads and blossoms – rioting flowers in a midnight jungle.

And then it *was* night and the town was gone but the fire still raged in the blackness, shifting through fascinating, kaleidoscopic shapes until it seemed that it limned a face in blood – a face with a hawk nose, deep-set, fiery eyes, full and sensuous lips partially hidden by a heavy mustache, and hair swept back from the brow like a musician's.

'The Welsh dresser,' a voice said distantly, and she knew it was *his*. 'The one in the attic. That will do nicely, I think. And then we'll fix the stairs . . . it's wise to be prepared.'

The voice faded. The flames faded.

There was only the darkness, and she in it, dreaming or beginning to dream. She thought dimly that the dream would be sweet and long, but bitter underneath and without light, like the waters of Lethe.

Another voice – Ed's voice. 'Come on, darlin'. Get up. We have to do as he says.'

'Ed? Ed?'

His face looked over hers, not drawn in fire, but looking terribly pale and strangely empty. Yet she loved him again . . . more than ever. She yearned for his kiss.

'Come on, Eva.'

'Is it a dream, Ed?'

'No . . . not a dream.'

For a moment she was frightened, and then there was no more fear. There was knowing instead. With the knowing came the hunger.

She glanced into the mirror and saw only her bedroom reflected, empty and still. The attic door was locked and the key was in the bottom drawer of the dresser, but it didn't matter. No need for keys now.

They slipped between the door and the jamb like shades.

30

At three in the morning the blood runs slow and thick, and slumber is heavy. The soul either sleeps in blessed ignorance of such an hour or gazes about itself in utter despair. There is no middle ground. At three in the morning the gaudy paint is off that old whore, the world, and she has no nose and a glass eye. Gaiety becomes hollow and brittle, as in Poe's castle surrounded by the Red Death. Horror is destroyed by boredom. Love is a dream.

Parkins Gillespie shambled from his office desk to the coffeepot, looking like a very thin ape that had been sick with a wasting illness. Behind him, a game of solitaire was laid out like a clock. He had heard several screams in the night, the strange, jagged beating of a horn on the air, and once, running feet. He had not gone out to investigate any of these things. His lined and socketed face was haunted by the things he thought were going on out there. He was wearing a cross, a St Christopher's medal, and a peace sign around his neck. He didn't know exactly why he had put them on, but they comforted him. He was thinking that if he could get through this night, he would go far away tomorrow and leave his badge on the shelf, by his key ring.

Mabel Werts was sitting at her kitchen table, a cold cup of coffee in front of her, the shades pulled down for the first time in years, the lens caps on her binoculars. For the first time in sixty years she did not want to see things, or hear them. The night was rife with a deadly gossip she did not want to listen to.

Bill Norton was on his way to the Cumberland Hospital in response to a telephone call (made while his wife was still alive), and his face was wooden and unmoving. The windshield wipers clicked steadily against the rain, which was coming down more heavily now. He was trying not to think about anything.

There were others in the town who were either sleeping or waking untouched. Most of the untouched were single people without relatives or close friends in the town. Many of them were unaware that anything had been happening.

Those that were awake, however, had turned on all their lights, and a person driving through town (and several cars did pass, headed for Portland or points south) might have been struck by this small village, so much like the others along the way, with its odd salting of fully lit dwellings in the very graveyard of morning. The passerby might have slowed to look for a fire or an accident, and seeing neither, speeded up and dismissed it from mind.

Here is the peculiar thing: None of those awake in Jerusalem's Lot knew the truth. A handful might have suspected, but even their suspicions were as vague and unformed as three-month fetuses. Yet they had gone unhesitatingly to bureau drawers, attic boxes, or bedroom jewel collections to find whatever religious hex symbols they might possess. They did this without thinking, the way a man driving a long distance alone will sing without knowing he sings. They walked slowly from room to room, as if their bodies had become glassy and fragile, and they turned on all the lights, and they did not look out their windows.

That above all else. They did not look out their windows.

No matter what noises or dreadful possibilities, no matter how awful the unknown, there was an even worse thing: to look the Gorgon in the face.

31

The noise penetrated his sleep like a nail being bludgeoned into heavy oak; with exquisite slowness, seemingly fiber by fiber. At first Reggie Sawyer thought he was dreaming of carpentry, and his brain, in the shadow land between sleeping and waking, obliged with a slow-motion memory fragment of him and his father nailing clapboards to the sides of the camp they had built on Bryant Pond in 1960.

This faded into a muddled idea that he was not dreaming at all, but actually hearing a hammer at work. Disorientation followed, and then he was awake and the blows were falling on the front door, someone dropping his fist against the wood with metronomelike regularity.

His eyes first jerked to Bonnie, who was lying on her side, an S-shaped hump under the blankets. Then to the clock: 4:15.

He got up, slipped out of the bedroom, and closed the door behind him. He turned on the hall light, started down toward the door, and then paused. An internal set of hackles had risen.

Sawyer regarded his front door with mute, head-cocked curiosity. No one knocked at 4:15. If someone in the family croaked, they called on the telephone, but they didn't come knocking.

He had been in Vietnam for seven months in 1968, a very hard year for American boys in Vietnam, and he had seen combat. In those days, coming awake had been as sudden as the snapping of fingers or the clicking on of a lamp; one minute you were a stone, the next you were awake in the dark. The habit had died in him almost as soon as he had been shipped back to the States, and he had been proud of that, although he never spoke of it. He was no machine, by Jesus. Push button A and Johnny wakes up, push button B and Johnny kills some slants.

But now, with no warning at all, the muzziness and cottonheadedness of sleep fell off him like a snakeskin and he was cold and blinking.

Someone was out there. The Bryant kid, likely, liquored up and packing iron. Ready to do or die for the fair maiden.

He went into the living room and crossed to the gunrack over the fake fireplace. He didn't turn on a light; he knew his way around by touch perfectly well. He took down his shotgun, broke it, and the hall light gleamed dully on brass casings. He went back to the living room doorway and poked his head out into the hall. The pounding went on monotonously, with regularity but no rhythm.

'Come on in,' Reggie Sawyer called.

The pounding stopped.

There was a long pause and then the doorknob turned, very slowly, until it had reached full cock. The door opened and Corey Bryant stood there.

Reggie felt his heart falter for an instant. Bryant was dressed in the same clothes he had been wearing when Reggie sent him down the road, only now they were ripped and mud-stained. Leaves clung to his pants and shirt. A streak of dirt across his forehead accentuated his pallor.

'Stop right there,' Reggie said, lifting the shotgun and clicking off the safety. 'This time it's loaded.'

But Corey Bryant plodded forward, his dull eyes fixed

on Reggie's face with an expression that was worse than hate. His tongue slid out and slicked his lips. His shoes were clotted with heavy mud that had been mixed to a black glue by the rain, and clods dropped off onto the hall floor as he came forward. There was something unforgiving and remorseless in that walk, something that impressed the watching eye with a cold and dreadful lack of mercy. The mud-caked heels clumped. There was no command that would stop them or plea that would stay them.

'Take two more steps and I'll blow your fucking head off,' Reggie said. The words came out hard and dry. The guy was worse than drunk. He was off his rocker. He knew with sudden clarity that he was going to have to shot him.

'Stop,' he said again, but in a casual, offhand way.

Corey Bryant did not stop. His eyes were fixed on Reggie's face with the dead and sparkling avidity of a stuffed moose. His heels clumped solemnly on the floor.

Bonnie screamed behind him.

'Go on in the bedroom,' Reggie said. He stepped out into the hallway to get between them. Bryant was only two paces away now. One limp, white hand was reaching out to grasp the twin barrels of the Stevens.

Reggie pulled both triggers.

The blast was like a thunderclap in the narrow hallway. Fire licked momentarily from both barrels. The stink of burned powder filled the air. Bonnie screamed again, piercingly. Corey's shirt shredded and blackened and parted, not so much perforated as disintegrated. Yet when it blew open, divorced from its buttons, the fish whiteness of his chest and abdomen was incredibly unmarked. Reggie's frozen eyes received an impression that the flesh was not really flesh at all, but something as insubstantial as a gauze curtain.

Then the shotgun was slapped from his hands, as if from the hands of a child. He was gripped and thrown against the wall with teeth-rattling force. His legs refused to support him and he fell down, dazed. Bryant walked past him, toward Bonnie. She was cringing in the doorway, but her eyes were on his face, and Reggie could see the heat in them.

Corey looked back over his shoulder and grinned at Reggie, a huge and moony grin, like that offered to tourists by cow skulls in the desert. Bonnie was holding her arms out. They trembled. Over her face, terror and lust seemed to pass like alternating flashes of sunshine and shadow.

'Darling,' she said.

Reggie screamed.

32

'Hey,' the bus driver said. 'This is Hartford, Mac.'

Callahan looked out the wide, polarized window at the strange country, made even stranger by the first seeping light of morning. In the Lot they would be going back now, back into their holes.

'I know,' he said.

'We got a twenty-minute rest stop. Don't you want to go in and get a sandwich or something?'

Callahan fumbled his wallet out of his pocket with his bandaged hand and almost dropped it. Oddly, the burned hand didn't seem to hurt much anymore; it was only numb. It would have been better if there had been pain. Pain was at least real. The taste of death was in his mouth, a moronic, mealy taste like a spoiled apple. Was that all? Yes. That was bad enough.

He held out a twenty. 'Can you get me a bottle?'

'Mister, the rules—'

'And keep the change, of course. A pint would be fine.'

'I don't need nobody cutting up on my bus, mister. We'll be in New York in two hours. You can get what you want there. Anything.'

I think you are wrong, friend, Callahan thought. He looked into the wallet again to see what was there. A ten, two fives, a single. He added the ten to the twenty and held it out in his bandaged hand.

'A pint would be fine,' he said. 'And keep the change, of course.'

The driver looked from the thirty dollars to the dark, socketed eyes, and for one terrible moment thought he was holding conversation with a living skull, a skull that had somehow forgotten how to grin.

'Thirty dollars for a pint? Mister, you're crazy.' But he took the money, walked to the front of the empty bus, then turned back. The money had disappeared. 'But don't you go cutting up on me. I don't need nobody cutting up on my bus.'

Callahan nodded like a very small boy accepting a deserved reprimand.

The bus driver looked at him a moment longer, then got off.

Something cheap, Callahan thought. Something that will burn the tongue and sizzle the throat. Something to take away that bland, sweet taste . . . or at least allay it until he could find a place to begin drinking in earnest. To drink and drink and drink—

He thought then that he might break down, begin to cry. There were no tears. He felt very dry, and completely empty. There was only . . . that taste.

Hurry, driver.

He went on looking out the window. Across the street, a teenaged boy was sitting on a porch stoop with his head folded into his arms. Callahan watched him until the bus pulled out again, but the boy never moved.

33

Ben felt a hand on his arm and swam upward to wakefulness. Mark, near his right ear, said, 'Morning.'

He opened his eyes, blinked twice to clear the gum out of them, and looked out the window at the world. Dawn had come stealing through a steady autumn rain that was neither heavy nor light. The trees which ringed the grassy pavilion on the hospital's north side were half denuded now, and the black branches were limned against the gray sky like giant letters in an unknown alphabet. Route 30, which curved out of town to the east, was as shiny as sealskin – a car passing with its taillights still on left baleful red reflections on the macadam.

Ben stood up and looked around. Matt was sleeping, his chest rising and falling in regular but shallow respiration. Jimmy was also asleep, stretched out in the room's one lounge chair. There was an undoctor-like stubble on the planes of his cheeks, and Ben ran a palm across his own face. It rasped.

'Time to get going, isn't it?' Mark asked.

Ben nodded. He thought of the day ahead of them and all its potential hideousness, and shied away from it. The only way to get through it would be without thinking more than ten minutes ahead. He looked into the boy's face, and the stony eagerness he saw there made him feel queasy. He went over and shook Jimmy.

'Huh!' Jimmy said. He thrashed in his chair like a swimmer coming up from deep water. His face twitched, his eyes fluttered open, and for a moment they showed blank terror. He looked at them both unreasoningly, without recognition.

Then recognition came, and his body relaxed. 'Oh. Dream.'

Mark nodded in perfect understanding.

Jimmy looked out the window and said 'Daylight' the way a miser might say *money*. He got up and went over to Matt, took his wrist and held it.

'Is he all right?' Mark asked.

'I think he's better than he was last night,' Jimmy said. 'Ben, I want the three of us to leave by way of the service elevator in case someone noticed Mark last night. The less risk, the better.'

'Will Mr Burke be okay alone?' Mark asked.

'I think so,' Ben said. 'We'll have to trust to his ingenuity, I guess. Barlow would like nothing better than to have us tied up another day.'

They tiptoed down the corridor and used the service elevator. The kitchen was just cranking up at this hour — almost quarter past seven. One of the cooks looked up, waved a hand, and said, 'Hi, Doc.' No one else spoke to them.

'Where first?' Jimmy asked. 'The Brock Street School?'

'No,' Ben said. 'Too many people until this afternoon. Do the little ones get out early, Mark?'

'They go until two o'clock.'

'That leaves plenty of daylight,' Ben said. 'Mark's house first. Stakes.'

34

As they drew closer to the Lot, an almost palpable cloud of dread formed in Jimmy's Buick, and conversation lagged. When Jimmy pulled off the turnpike at the large green reflectorized sign that read ROUTE 12 JERUSALEM'S LOT CUMBERLAND CUMBERLAND CTR, Ben thought that this was the way he and Susan had come home after their first date – she had wanted to see something with a car chase in it.

'It's gone bad,' Jimmy said. His boyish face looked pale and frightened and angry. 'Christ, you can almost smell it.'

And you could, Ben thought, although the smell was mental rather than physical: a psychic whiff of tombs.

Route 12 was nearly deserted. On the way in they passed Win Purinton's milk truck, parked off the road and deserted. The motor was idling, and Ben turned it off after looking in the back. Jimmy glanced at him inquiringly as he got back in. Ben shook his head. 'He's not there. The engine light was on, and it was almost out of gas. Been idling there for hours.' Jimmy pounded his leg with a closed fist.

But as they entered town, Jimmy said in an almost absurdly relieved tone, 'Look there. Crossen's is open.'

It was. Milt was out front, fussing a plastic drop cover over his rack of newspapers, and Lester Silvius was standing next to him, dressed in a yellow slicker.

'Don't see the rest of the crew, though,' Ben said.

Milt glanced up at them and waved, and Ben thought he saw lines of strain on both men's faces. The 'Closed' sign was still posted inside the door of Foreman's Mortuary. The hardware store was also closed, and Spencer's was locked and dark. The diner was open, and after they had passed it, Jimmy pulled his Buick up to the curb in front of the new shop. Above the show window, simple gold-faced letters spelled out the name: 'Barlow and Straker – Fine Furnishings.' And taped to the door, as Callahan had said, a sign which had been hand-lettered in a fine script which they all recognized from the note they had seen the day before: 'Closed until further notice.'

'Why are you stopping here?' Mark asked.

'Just on the off-chance that he might be holing up inside,' Jimmy said. 'It's so obvious he might figure we'd overlook it. And I think that sometimes customs men put an okay on boxes they've checked through. They write it on with chalk.'

They went around to the back, and while Ben and Mark hunched their shoulders against the rain, Jimmy poked one overcoated elbow through the glass in the back door until they could all climb inside.

The air was noxious and stale, the air of a room shut up for centuries rather than days. Ben poked his head out into the showroom, but there was no place to hide out there. Sparsely furnished, there was no sign that Straker had been replenishing his stock.

'Come here!' Jimmy called hoarsely, and Ben's heart leaped into his throat.

Jimmy and Mark were standing by a long crate which Jimmy had partly pried open with the claw end of his hammer. Looking in, they could see one pale hand and a dark sleeve.

Without thinking, Ben attacked the crate. Jimmy was fumbling at the far end with the hammer.

'Ben,' Jimmy said, 'you're going to cut your hands. You—'

He hadn't heard. He snapped boards off the crate, regardless of nails and splinters. They had him, they had the slimy night-thing, and he would pound the stake into him as he had pounded it into Susan, he would—

He snapped back another piece of the cheap wooden crating and looked into the dead, moon-pallid face of Mike Ryerson.

For a moment there was utter silence, and then they all let out their breath . . . it was as if a soft wind had coursed through the room.

'What do we do now?' Jimmy asked.

'We better get out to Mark's house first,' Ben said. His voice was dull with disappointment. 'We know where he is. We don't even have a finished stake yet.'

They put the splintered strips of wood back helter-skelter.

'Better let me look at those hands,' Jimmy said. 'They're bleeding.'

'Later,' Ben said. 'Come on.'

They went back around the building, all of them wordlessly glad to be back in the open air, and Jimmy drove the Buick up Jointner Avenue and into the residential part of town, just outside the skimpy business district. They arrived at Mark's house perhaps sooner than any of them would have liked.

Father Callahan's old sedan was parked behind Henry Petrie's sensible Pinto runabout in the circular Petrie driveway. At the sight of it, Mark sucked in his breath and looked away. All color had drained out of his face.

'I can't go in there,' he muttered. 'I'm sorry. I'll wait in the car.'

'Nothing to be sorry for, Mark,' Jimmy said.

He parked, turned off the ignition, and got out. Ben hesitated a minute, then put a hand on Mark's shoulder. 'Are you going to be all right?'

'Sure.' But he did not look all right. His chin was trembling and his eyes looked hollow. He suddenly turned to Ben and the hollowness was gone from the eyes and they were filled with simple pain, swimming with tears. 'Cover them up, will you? If they're dead, cover them up.'

'Sure I will,' Ben said.

'It's better this way,' Mark said. 'My father . . . he would have made a very successful vampire. Maybe as good as Barlow, in time. He . . . he was good at everything he tried. Maybe too good.'

'Try not to think too much,' Ben said, hating the lame sound of the words as they left his mouth. Mark looked up at him and smiled wanly.

'The woodpile's around in the back,' Mark said. 'You can go faster if you use my father's lathe down in the basement.'

'All right,' Ben said. 'Be easy, Mark. As easy as you can.'

But the boy was looking away now, swiping at his eyes with his arm.

He and Jimmy went up the back steps and inside.

35

'Callahan's not here,' Jimmy said flatly. They had gone through the entire house.

Ben forced himself to say it. 'Barlow must have gotten him.'

He looked at the broken cross in his hand. It had been around Callahan's neck yesterday. It was the only trace of him they had found. It had been lying next to the bodies of the Petries, who were very dead indeed. Their heads had been crushed together with force enough to literally shatter the skulls. Ben remembered the unnatural strength Mrs Glick had displayed and felt sick.

'Come on,' he said to Jimmy. 'We've got to cover them up. I promised.'

36

They took the dustcover from the couch in the living room and covered them with that. Ben tried not to look at or think about what they were doing, but it was impossible. When the job was done, one hand – the cultivated, lacquered nails revealed it to be June Petrie's – protruded from under the gaily patterned dustcover, and he poked it underneath with his toe, grimacing in an effort to keep his stomach under control. The shapes of the bodies under the cover were undeniable and unmistakable, making him think of news photos from Vietnam — battlefield dead and soldiers carrying dreadful burdens in black rubber sacks that looked absurdly like golf bags.

They went downstairs, each with an armload of yellow ash stove lengths.

The cellar had been Henry Petrie's domain, and it reflected his personality perfectly: Three high-intensity lights had been hung in a straight line over the work area, each shaded with a wide metal shell that allowed the light to fall with strong brilliance on the planer, the jigsaw, the bench saw, the lathe, the electric sander. Ben saw that he had been building a bird hotel, probably to place in the backyard next spring, and the blueprint he had been working from was neatly laid out and held at each corner with machined metal paperweights. He had been doing a competent but uninspired job, and now it would never be finished. The floor was neatly swept, but a pleasantly nostalgic odor of sawdust hung in the air.

'This isn't going to work at all,' Jimmy said.

'I know that,' Ben said.

'The woodpile,' Jimmy snorted, and let the wood fall from his arms in a lumbering crash. The stove lengths rolled wildly on the floor like jackstraws. He uttered a high, hysterical laugh.

'Jimmy—'

But his laugh cut across Ben's attempt to speak like jags of piano wire. 'We're going to go out and end the scourge with a pile of wood from Henry Petrie's back lot. How about some chair legs or baseball bats?'

'Jimmy, what else can we do?'

Jimmy looked at him and got himself under control with a visible effort. 'Some treasure hunt,' he said. 'Go forty paces into Charles Griffen's north pasture and look under the large rock. Ha. Jesus. We can get out of town. We can do that.'

'Do you want to quit? Is that what you want?'

'No. But it isn't going to be just today, Ben. It's going to be weeks before we get them all, if we ever do. Can you stand that? Can you stand doing . . . doing what you did to Susan a thousand times? Pulling them out of their closets and their stinking little bolt holes screaming and struggling, only to pound a stake into their chest cavities and smash their hearts? Can you keep that up until November without going nuts?'

Ben thought about it and met a blank wall: utter incomprehension.

'I don't know,' he said.

'Well, what about the kid? Do you think he can take it? He'll be ready for the fucking nut hatch. And Matt will be dead. I'll guarantee you that. And what do we do when the state cops start nosing around to find out what in hell happened to 'salem's Lot? What do we tell them? 'Pardon me while I stake this bloodsucker'? What about that, Ben?'

'How the hell should I know? Who's had a chance to stop and think this thing out?'

They realized simultaneously that they were standing nose to nose, yelling at each other. 'Hey,' Jimmy said. 'Hey.'

Ben dropped his eyes. 'I'm sorry.'

'No, my fault. We're under pressure . . . what Barlow

would undoubtedly call an end game.' He ran a hand through his carroty hair and looked around aimlessly. His eye suddenly lit on something beside Petrie's blueprint and he picked it up. It was a black grease pencil.

'Maybe this is the best way,' he said.

'What?'

'You stay here, Ben. Start turning out stakes. If we're going to do this, it's got to be scientific. You're the production department. Mark and I will be research. We'll go through the town, looking for them. We'll find them, too, just the way we found Mike. I can mark the locations with this grease pencil. Then, tomorrow, the stakes.'

'Won't they see the marks and move?'

'I don't think so. Mrs Glick didn't look as though she was connecting too well. I think they move more on instinct than real thought. They might wise up after a while, start hiding better, but I think at first it would be like shooting fish in a barrel.'

'Why don't I go?'

'Because I know the town, and the town knows me – like they knew my father. The live ones in the Lot are hiding in their houses today. If you come knocking, they won't answer. If I come, most of them will. I know some of the hiding places. I know where the winos shack up out in the Marshes and where the pulp roads go. You don't. Can you run that lathe?'

'Yes,' Ben said.

Jimmy was right, of course. Yet the relief he felt at not having to go out and face *them* made him feel guilty.

'Okay. Get going. It's after noon now.'

Ben turned to the lathe, then paused. 'If you want to

wait a half hour, I can give you maybe half a dozen stakes to take with you.'

Jimmy paused a moment, then dropped his eyes. 'Uh, I think tomorrow . . . tomorrow would be . . .'

'Okay,' Ben said. 'Go on. Listen, why don't you come back around three? Things ought to be quiet enough around that school by then so we can check it out.'

'Good.'

Jimmy stepped away from Petrie's shop area and started for the stairs. Something – a half thought or perhaps inspiration – made him turn. He saw Ben across the basement, working under the bright glare of those three lights, hung neatly in a row.

Something . . . and it was gone.

He walked back.

Ben shut off the lathe and looked at him. 'Something else?'

'Yeah,' Jimmy said. 'On the tip of my tongue. But it's stuck there.'

Ben raised his eyebrows.

'When I looked back from the stairs and saw you, something clicked. It's gone now.'

'Important?'

'I don't know.' He shuffled his feet purposelessly, wanting it to come back. Something about the image Ben had made, standing under those work lights, bent over the lathe. No good. Thinking about it only made it seem more distant.

He went up the stairs, but paused once more to look back. The image was hauntingly familiar, but it wouldn't come. He went through the kitchen and out to the car. The rain had faded to drizzle.

37

Roy McDougall's car was standing in the driveway of the trailer lot on the Bend Road, and seeing it there on a weekday made Jimmy suspect the worst.

He and Mark got out, Jimmy carrying his black bag. They mounted the steps and Jimmy tried the bell. It didn't work and so he knocked instead. The pounding roused no one in the McDougall trailer or in the neighboring one twenty yards down the road. There was a car in that driveway, too.

Jimmy tried the storm door and it was locked. 'There's a hammer in the backseat of the car,' he said.

Mark got it, and Jimmy smashed the glass of the storm door beside the knob. He reached through and unsnapped the catch. The inside door was unlocked. They went in.

The smell was definable instantly, and Jimmy felt his nostrils cringe against it and try to shut it out. The smell was not as strong as it had been in the basement of the Marsten House, but it was just as basically offensive – the smell of rot and deadness. A wet, putrefied stink. Jimmy found himself remembering when, as boys, he and his buddies had gone out on their bikes during spring vacation to pick up the returnable beer and soft-drink bottles the retreating snows had uncovered. In one of those (an Orange Crush bottle) he saw a small, decayed field mouse which had been attracted by the sweetness and had then been unable to get out. He had gotten a whiff of it and had immediately turned away and thrown up. This smell was plangently like that – sickish sweet and decayed sour, mixed together and fermenting wildly. He felt his gorge rise.

'They're here,' Mark said. 'Somewhere.'

They went through the place methodically – kitchen, dining nook, living room, the two bedrooms. They opened closets as they went. Jimmy thought they had found something in the master bedroom closet, but it was only a heap of dirty clothes.

'No cellar?' Mark asked.

'No, but there might be a crawl space.'

They went around to the back and saw a small door that swung inward, set into the trailer's cheap concrete foundation. It was fastened with an old padlock. Jimmy knocked it off with five hard blows of the hammer, and when he pushed the half-trap open, the smell hit them in a ripe wave.

'There they are,' Mark said.

Peering in, Jimmy could see three sets of feet, like corpses lined up on a battlefield. One set wore work boots, one wore knitted bedroom slippers, and the third set – tiny feet indeed – were bare.

Family scene, Jimmy thought crazily. *Reader's Digest*, where are you when we need you? Unreality washed over him. The baby, he thought. How are we supposed to do that to a little baby?

He made a mark with the black grease pencil on the trap and picked up the broken padlock. 'Let's go next door,' he said.

'Wait,' Mark said. 'Let me pull one of them out.'

'Pull . . . ? Why?'

'Maybe the daylight will kill them,' Mark said. 'Maybe we won't have to do that with the stakes.'

Jimmy felt hope. 'Yeah, okay. Which one?'

'Not the baby,' Mark said instantly. 'The man. You catch one foot.'

'All right,' Jimmy said. His mouth had gone cotton-dry, and when he swallowed there was a click in his throat.

Mark wriggled in on his stomach, the dead leaves that had drifted in crackling under his weight. He seized one of Roy McDougall's work boots and pulled. Jimmy squirmed in beside him, scraping his back on the low over-hang, fighting claustrophobia. He got hold of the other boot and together they pulled him out into the lessening drizzle and white light.

What followed was almost unbearable. Roy McDougall began to writhe as soon as the light struck him full, like a man who has been disturbed in sleep. Steam and moisture came from his pores, and the skin underwent a slight sagging and yellowing. Eyeballs rolled behind the thin skin of his closed lids. His feet kicked slowly and dreamily in the wet leaves. His upper lip curled back, showing upper incisors like those of a large dog – a German shepherd or a collie. His arms thrashed slowly, the hands clenching and unclenching, and when one of them brushed Mark's shirt, he jerked back with a disgusted cry.

Roy turned over and began to hunch slowly back into the crawl space, arms and knees and face digging grooves in the rain-softened humus. Jimmy noted that a hitching, Cheyne-Stokes type of respiration had begun as soon as the light struck the body; it stopped as soon as McDougall was wholly in shadow again. So did the mois-ture extrusion.

When he had reached his previous resting place, McDougall turned over and lay still.

'Shut it,' Mark said in a strangled voice. 'Please shut it.'

Jimmy closed the trap and replaced the hammered lock as well as he could. The image of McDougall's body, struggling in the wet, rotted leaves like a dazed snake, remained in his mind. He did not think there would ever be a time when it was not within hand's reach of his memory — even if he lived to be a hundred.

38

They stood in the rain, trembling, looking at each other. 'Next door?' Mark asked.

'Yes. They'd be the logical ones for the McDougalls to attack first.'

They went across, and this time their nostrils picked up the telltale odor of rot in the dooryard. The name below the doorbell was Evans. Jimmy nodded. David Evans and family. He worked as a mechanic in the auto department of Sears in Gates Falls. He had treated him a couple of years ago, for a cyst or something.

This time the bell worked, but there was no response. They found Mrs Evans in bed. The two children were in a bunk bed in a single bedroom, dressed in identical pajamas that featured characters from the Pooh stories. It took longer to find Dave Evans. He had hidden himself away in the unfinished storage space over the small garage.

Jimmy marked a check inside a circle on the front door and the garage door. 'We're doing good,' he said. 'Two for two.'

Mark said diffidently, 'Could you hold on a minute or two? I'd like to wash my hands.'

'Sure,' Jimmy said. 'I'd like that, too. The Evanses won't mind if we use their bathroom.'

They went inside, and Jimmy sat down in one of the living room chairs and closed his eyes. Soon he heard Mark running water in the bathroom.

On the darkened screen of his eyes he saw the mortician's table, saw the sheet covering Marjorie Glick's body start to tremble, saw her hand fall out and begin its delicate toe dance on the air—

He opened his eyes.

This trailer was in nicer condition than the McDougalls', neater, taken care of. He had never met Mrs Evans, but it seemed she must have taken pride in her home. There was a neat pile of the dead children's toys in a small storage room, a room that had probably been called the laundry room in the mobile home dealer's original brochure. Poor kids, he hoped they'd enjoyed the toys while there had still been bright days and sunshine to enjoy them in. There was a tricycle, several large plastic trucks and a play gas station, one of those caterpillars on wheels (there must have been some dandy fights over that), a toy pool table.

He started to look away and then looked back, startled.

Blue chalk.

Three shaded lights in a row.

Men walking around the green table under the bright lights, cueing up, brushing the grains of blue chalk off their fingertips—

'Mark!' he shouted, sitting bolt upright in the chair.

'Mark!' And Mark came running with his shirt off, to see what the matter was.

39

An old student of Matt's (class of '64, A's in literature, C's in composition) had dropped by to see him around two-thirty, had commented on the stacks of arcane literature, and had asked Matt if he was studying for a degree in the occult. Matt couldn't remember if his name was Herbert or Harold.

Matt, who had been reading a book called *Strange Disappearances* when Herbert-or-Harold walked in, welcomed the interruption. He was waiting for the phone to ring even now, although he knew the others could not safely enter the Brock Street School until after three o'clock. He was desperate to know what had happened to Father Callahan. And the day seemed to be passing with alarming rapidity – he had always heard that time passed slowly in the hospital. He felt slow and foggy, an old man at last.

He began telling Herbert-or-Harold about the town of Momson, Vermont, whose history he had just been reading. He had found it particularly interesting because he thought the story, if true, might be a precursor of the Lot's fate.

'Everyone disappeared,' he told Herbert-or-Harold, who was listening with polite but not very well masked boredom. 'Just a small town in the upcountry of northern Vermont, accessible by Interstate Route 2 and Vermont Route 19. Population of 312 in the census of 1920. In August of 1923 a woman in New York got worried because her sister hadn't written her for two months. She and her husband took a ride out there, and they were the first to break the story to the newspapers, although I don't doubt that the locals in the surrounding area had known about the disappearance for some time. The sister and her husband were gone, all right, and so was everyone else in Momson. The houses and the barns were all standing, and in one place supper had been put on the table. The case was rather sensational at the time. I don't believe that I would care to stay there overnight. The author of this book claims the people in the neighboring townships tell some odd stories . . . ha'ants and goblins and all that. Several of the outlying barns have hex signs and large crosses painted on them, even to this day. Look, here's a photograph of the general store and ethyl station and feed-and-grain store − what served in Momson as downtown. What do you suppose ever happened there?'

Herbert-or-Harold looked at the picture politely. Just a little town with a few stores and a few houses. Some of them were falling down, probably from the weight of snow in the winter. Could be any town in the country. Driving through most of them, you wouldn't know if anyone was alive after eight o'clock when they rolled up the sidewalks. The old man had certainly gone dotty in his old age. Herbert-or-Harold thought about an old aunt of his who had become convinced in the last two years of her life that her daughter had killed her pet parakeet and was feeding it to her in the meat loaf. Old people got funny ideas.

'Very interesting,' he said, looking up. 'But I don't think . . . Mr Burke? Mr Burke, is something wrong? Are you . . . nurse! Hey, *nurse!*'

Matt's eyes had grown very fixed. One hand gripped the top sheet of the bed. The other was pressed against his chest. His face had gone pallid, and a pulse beat in the center of his forehead.

Too soon, he thought. *No, too soon—*

Pain, smashing into him in waves, driving him down into darkness. Dimly he thought: *Watch that last step, it's a killer.*

Then, falling.

Herbert-or-Harold ran out of the room, knocking over his chair and spilling a pile of books. The nurse was already coming, nearly running herself.

'It's Mr Burke,' Herbert-or-Harold told her. He was still holding the book, with his index finger inserted at the picture of Momson, Vermont.

The nurse nodded curtly and entered the room. Matt was lying with his head half off the bed, his eyes closed.

'Is he—?' Herbert-or-Harold asked timidly. It was a complete question.

'Yes, I think so,' the nurse answered, at the same time pushing the button that would summon the ECV unit. 'You'll have to leave now.'

She was calm again now that all was known, and had time to regret her lunch, left half-eaten.

40

'But there's no pool hall in the Lot,' Mark said. 'The closest one is over in Gates Falls. Would he go there?'

'No,' Jimmy said. 'I'm sure he wouldn't. But some people have pool tables or billiard tables in their houses.'

'Yes, I know that.'

'There's something else,' Jimmy said. 'I can almost get it.'

He leaned back, closed his eyes, and put his hands over them. There was something else, and in his mind he associated it with plastic. Why plastic? There were plastic toys and plastic utensils for picnics and plastic drop covers to put over your boat when winter came—

And suddenly a picture of a pool table draped in a large plastic dustcover formed in his mind, complete with sound track, a voiceover that was saying, *I really ought to sell it before the felt gets mildew or something – Ed Craig says it might mildew – but it was Ralph's . . .*

He opened his eyes. 'I know where he is,' he said. 'I know where Barlow is. He's in the basement of Eva Miller's boardinghouse.' And it was true; he knew it was. It felt incontrovertibly right in his mind.

Mark's eyes flashed brilliantly. 'Let's go get him.'

'Wait.'

He went to the phone, found Eva's number in the book, and dialed it swiftly. It rang with no answer. Ten rings, eleven, a dozen. He put it back in its cradle, frightened. There had been at least ten roomers at Eva's, many of them old men, retired. There was always someone around. Always before this.

He looked at his watch. It was quarter after three and time was racing, racing.

'Let's go,' he said.

'What about Ben?'

Jimmy said grimly, 'We can't call. The line's out at your house. If we go straight to Eva's, there'll be plenty of daylight left if we're wrong. If we're right, we'll come back and get Ben and stop his fucking clock.'

'Let me put my shirt on again,' Mark said, and ran down the hall to the bathroom.

41

Ben's Citroën was still sitting in Eva's parking lot, now plastered with wet leaves from the elms that shaded the square of gravel. The wind had picked up but the rain had stopped. The sign that said 'Eva's Rooms' swung and squeaked in the gray afternoon. The house had an eerie silence about it, a waiting quality, and Jimmy made a mental connection and was chilled by it. It was just like the Marsten House. He wondered if anyone had ever committed suicide here. Eva would know, but he didn't think Eva would be talking . . . not anymore.

'It would be perfect,' he said aloud. 'Take up residence in the local boardinghouse and then surround yourself with your children.'

'Are you sure we shouldn't get Ben?'

'Later. Come on.'

They got out of the car and walked toward the porch. The wind pulled at their clothes, riffled their hair. All the shades were drawn, and the house seemed to brood over them.

'Can you smell it?' Jimmy asked.

'Yes. Thicker than ever.'

'Are you up to this?'

'Yes,' Mark said firmly. 'Are you?'

'I hope to Christ I am,' Jimmy said.

They went up the porch steps and Jimmy tried the door. It was unlocked. When they stepped into Eva Miller's compulsively neat big kitchen, the odor smote them both, like an open garbage pit — yet dry, as with the smoke of years.

Jimmy remembered his conversation with Eva — it had been almost four years ago, just after he had begun practicing. Eva had come in for a checkup. His father had had her for a patient for years, and when Jimmy took his place, even running things out of the same Cumberland office, she had come to him without embarrassment. They had spoken of Ralph, dead twelve years even then, and she had told him that Ralph's ghost was still in the house — every now and then she would turn up something new and temporarily forgotten in the attic or a bureau drawer. And of course there was the pool table in the basement. She said that she really ought to get rid of it; it was just taking up space she could use for something else. But it had been Ralph's, and she just couldn't bring herself to take out an ad in the paper or call up the local radio 'Yankee Trader' program.

Now they walked across the kitchen to the cellar door, and Jimmy opened it. The stench was thick, nearly overpowering. He thumbed the light switch but got no response. He would have broken that, of course.

'Look around,' he told Mark. 'She's got to have a flashlight, or candles.'

Mark began nosing around, pulling open drawers and looking into them. He noticed that the knife rack over the sink was empty, but thought nothing of it at the time. His heart was thudding with painful slowness, like a muffled drum. He recognized the fact that he was now on the far, ragged edges of his endurance, at the outer limits. His mind did not seem to be thinking, but only reacting. He kept seeing movement at the corners of his eyes and jerking his head around to look, seeing nothing. A war veteran might have recognized the symptoms which signaled the onset of battle fatigue.

He went out into the hall and looked through the dresser there. In the third drawer he found a long four-cell flashlight. He took it back to the kitchen. 'Here it is, J—'

There was a rattling noise, followed by a heavy thump.

The cellar door stood open.

And the screams began.

42

When Mark stepped back into the kitchen of Eva's Rooms, it was twenty minutes of five. His eyes were hollow, and his T-shirt was smeared with blood. His eyes were stunned and slow.

Suddenly he shrieked.

The sound came roaring out of his belly, up the dark passage of his throat, and through his distended jaws. He shrieked until he felt some of the madness begin to leave his brain. He shrieked until his throat cracked and an awful pain lodged in his vocal cords like a sliver of bone. And even when he had externalized all the fear, the horror, the rage, the disappointment that he could, that awful pressure remained, coming up out of the cellar in waves – the knowledge of Barlow's presence somewhere down there – and now it was close to dark.

He went outside onto the porch and breathed great gasps of the windy air. Ben. He had to get Ben. But an odd sort of lethargy seemed to have wrapped his legs in lead. What was the use? Barlow was going to win. They had been crazy to go against him. And now Jimmy had paid the full price, as well as Susan and the Father.

The steel in him came up. *No. No. No.*

He went down the porch steps on trembling legs and got into Jimmy's Buick. The keys hung in the ignition.

Get Ben. Try once more.

His legs were too short to reach the pedals. He pulled the seat up and twisted the key. The engine roared. He put the gearshift lever in drive and put his foot on the gas. The car leaped forward. He slammed his foot down on the power brake and was thrown painfully into the steering wheel. The horn honked.

I can't drive it!

And he seemed to hear his father saying in his logical, pedantic voice: You must be careful when you learn to drive, Mark. Driving is the only means of transportation that is not fully regulated by federal law. As a result, all the operators are amateurs. Many of these amateurs are suicidal. Therefore, you must be extremely careful. You use the gas pedal like there was an egg between it and your foot. When you're driving a car with an automatic transmission, like ours, the left foot is not used at all. Only the right is used; first brake and then gas.

He let his foot off the brake and the car crawled forward down the driveway. It bumped over the curb and he brought it to a jerky stop. The windshield had fogged up. He rubbed it with his arm and only smeared it more.

'Screw it,' he muttered.

He started up jerkily and performed a wide, drunken U-turn, driving over the far curb in the process, and set off for his house. He had to crane his neck to see over the steering wheel. He fumbled out with his right hand and turned on the radio and played it loud. He was crying.

43

Ben was walking down Jointner Avenue toward town when Jimmy's tan Buick came up the road, moving in jerks and spasms, weaving drunkenly. He waved at it and it pulled over, bounced the left front wheel over the curb, and came to a stop.

He had lost track of time making the stakes, and when he looked at his watch, he had been startled to see that it was nearly ten minutes past four. He had shut down the lathe, taken a couple of the stakes, put them in his belt, and gone upstairs to use the telephone. He had only put his hand on it when he remembered it was out.

Badly worried now, he ran outside and looked in both cars, Callahan's and Petrie's. No keys in either. He could have gone back and searched Henry Petrie's pockets, but the thought was too much. He had set off for town at a fast walk, keeping an eye peeled for Jimmy's Buick. He had been intending to go straight to the Brock Street School when Jimmy's car came into sight.

He ran around to the driver's seat and Mark Petrie was sitting behind the wheel . . . alone. He looked at Ben numbly. His lips worked but no sound came out.

'What's the matter? Where's Jimmy?'

'Jimmy's dead,' Mark said woodenly. 'Barlow thought ahead of us again. He's in the basement of Mrs Miller's boardinghouse somewhere. Jimmy's there, too. I went down to help him and I couldn't get back out. Finally I got a board that I could crawl up, but at first I thought I was going to be trapped down there . . . until s-s-sunset . . .'

'What happened? What are you talking about?'

'Jimmy figured out the blue chalk, you see? While we were at a house in the Bend. Blue chalk. Pool tables. There's a pool table in the cellar at Mrs Miller's, it belonged to her husband. Jimmy called the boardinghouse and there was no answer so we drove over.'

He lifted his tearless face to Ben's.

'He told me to look around for a flashlight because the cellar light switch was broken, just like at the Marsten House. So I started to look around. I . . . I noticed that all the knives in the rack over the sink were gone, but I didn't think anything of it. So in a way I killed him. I did it. It's my fault, all my fault, all my—'

Ben shook him: two brisk snaps. 'Stop it, Mark. Stop it!'

Mark put his hands to his mouth, as if to catch the hysterical babble before it could flow out. His eyes stared hugely at Ben over his hands.

At last he went on: 'I found a flashlight in the hall dresser, see. And that was when Jimmy fell, and he started to scream. He – I would have fallen, too, but he warned me. The last thing he said was *Look out, Mark.*'

'What was it?' Ben demanded.

'Barlow and the others just took the stairs away,' Mark said in a dead, listless voice. 'Sawed the stairs off after the second one going down. They left a little more of the railing so it looked like . . . looked like . . .' He shook his head. 'In the dark, Jimmy just thought they were there. You see?'

'Yes,' Ben said. He saw. It made him feel sick. 'And the knives?'

'Set all around on the floor underneath,' Mark whispered. '*They* pounded the blades through these thin plywood squares and then knocked off the handles so they would sit flat with the blades pointing . . . pointing.'

'Oh,' Ben said helplessly. 'Oh, Christ.' He reached down and took Mark by the shoulders. 'Are you sure he's dead, Mark?'

'Yes. He . . . he was stuck in half a dozen places. The blood . . .'

Ben looked at his watch. It was ten minutes of five. Again he had that feeling of being crowded, of running out of time.

'What are we going to do now?' Mark asked remotely.

'Go into town. Talk to Matt on the phone and then talk to Parkins Gillespie. We'll finish Barlow before dark. We've got to.'

Mark smiled a small, morbid smile. 'Jimmy said that, too. He said we were going to stop his clock. But he keeps beating us. Better guys than us must have tried, too.'

Ben looked down at the boy and got ready to do something nasty.

'You sound scared,' he said.

'I *am* scared,' Mark said, not rising to it. 'Aren't you?'

'I'm scared,' Ben said, 'but I'm mad, too. I lost a girl I liked one hell of a lot. I loved her, I guess. We both lost

Jimmy. You lost your mother and father. They're lying in your living room under a dustcover from your sofa.' He pushed himself to a final brutality. 'Want to go back and look?'

Mark winced away from him, his face horrified and hurting.

'I want you with me,' Ben said more softly. He felt a germ of selfdisgust in his stomach. He sounded like a football coach before the big game. 'I don't care who's tried to stop him before. I don't care if Attila the Hun played him and lost. I'm going to have my shot. I want you with me. I need you.' And that was the truth, pure and naked.

'Okay,' Mark said. He looked down into his lap, and his hands found each other and entwined in distraught pantomime.

'Dig your feet in,' Ben said.

Mark looked at him hopelessly. 'I'm trying,' he said.

44

Sonny's Exxon station on outer Jointner Avenue was open and Sonny James (who exploited his country-music name-sake with a huge color poster in the window beside a pyramid of oil cans) came out to wait on them himself. He was a small, gnomelike man whose receding hair was lawnmowered into a perpetual crew cut that showed his pink scalp.

'Hey there, Mr Mears, howya doin'? Where's your Citrowan?'

'Laid up, Sonny. Where's Pete?' Pete Cook was Sonny's part-time help, and lived in town. Sonny did not.

'Never showed up today. Don't matter. Things been slow, anyway. Town seems downright dead.'

Ben felt dark, hysterical laughter in his belly. It threatened to boil out of his mouth in a great and rancid wave.

'Want to fill it up?' he managed. 'Want to use your phone.'

'Sure. Hi, kid. No school today?'

'I'm on a field trip with Mr Mears,' Mark said. 'I had a bloody nose.'

'I guess to God you did. My brother used to get 'em. They're a sign of high blood pressure, boy. You want to watch out.' He strolled to the back of Jimmy's car and took off the gas cap.

Ben went inside and dialed the pay phone beside the rack of New England road maps.

'Cumberland Hospital, which department?'

'I'd like to speak with Mr Burke, please. Room 402.'

There was an uncharacteristic hesitation, and Ben was about to ask if the room had been changed when the voice said:

'Who is this, please?'

'Benjaman Mears.' The possibility of Matt's death suddenly loomed up in his mind like a long shadow. Could that be? Surely not — that would be too much. 'Is he all right?'

'Are you a relative?'

'No, a close friend. He isn't—'

'Mr Burke died at 3:07 this afternoon, Mr Mears. If you'd like to hold for just a minute, I'll see if Dr Cody has come in yet. Perhaps he could . . .'

The voice went on but Ben had ceased hearing it,

556

although the receiver was still glued to his ear. The realization of how much he had been depending on Matt to get them through the rest of this nightmare afternoon crashed home with sickening weight. Matt was dead. Congestive heart failure. Natural causes. It was as if God Himself had turned His face away from them.

Just Mark and I now.

Susan, Jimmy, Father Callahan, Matt. All gone.

Panic seized him and he grappled with it silently.

He put the receiver back into its cradle without thinking about it, guillotining a question half-asked.

He walked back outside. It was ten after five. In the west the clouds were breaking up.

'Comes to just three dollars even,' Sonny told him brightly. 'That's Doc Cody's car, ain't it? I see them M.D. plates and it always makes me think of this movie I seen, this story about a bunch of crooks and one of them would always steal cars with M.D. plates because—'

Ben gave him three one-dollar bills. 'I've got to split, Sonny. Sorry. I've got trouble.'

Sonny's face crinkled up. 'Gee, I'm sorry to hear that, Mr Mears. Bad news from your editor?'

'I guess you could say that.' He got behind the wheel, shut the door, pulled out, and left Sonny looking after him in his yellow foul-weather slicker.

'Matt's dead, isn't he?' Mark asked, watching him.

'Yes. Heart attack. How did you know?'

'Your face. I saw your face.'

It was 5:15.

45

Parkins Gillespie was standing on the small covered porch of the Municipal Building, smoking a Pall Mall and looking out at the western sky. He turned his attention to Ben Mears and Mark Petrie reluctantly. His face looked sad and old, like the glasses of water they bring you in cheap diners.

'How are you, Constable?' Ben asked.

'Tolerable,' Parkins allowed. He considered a hang-nail on the leathery are of skin that bordered his thumb-nail. 'Seen you truckin' back and forth. Looked like the kid was drivin' up from Railroad Street by hisself this last time. That so?'

'Yes,' Mark said.

'Almost got clipped. Fella goin' the other way missed you by a whore's hair.'

'Constable,' Ben said, 'we want to tell you what's been happening around here.'

Parkins Gillespie spat out the stub of his cigarette without raising his hands from the rail of the small covered porch. Without looking at either of them, he said calmly, 'I don't want to hear it.'

They looked at him dumbfounded.

'Nolly didn't show up today,' Parkins said, still in that calm, conversational voice. 'Somehow don't think he will. He called in late last night and said he'd seen Homer McCaslin's car out on the Deep Cut Road – I think it was the Deep Cut he said. He never called back in.' Slowly, sadly, like a man under water, he dipped into his shirt pocket and reached another Pall Mall out of it.

He rolled it reflectively between his thumb and finger. 'These fucking things are going to be the death of me,' he said.

Ben tried again. 'The man who took the Marsten House, Gillespie. His name is Barlow. He's in the basement of Eva Miller's boardinghouse right now.'

'That so?' Parkins said with no particular surprise. 'Vampire, ain't he? Just like in all the comic books they used to put out twenty years ago.'

Ben said nothing. He felt more and more like a man lost in a great and grinding nightmare where clockwork ran on and on endlessly, unseen, but just below the surface of things.

'I'm leavin' town,' Parkins said. 'Got my stuff all packed up in the back of the car. I left my gun and the bubble and my badge in on the shelf. I'm done with lawin'. Goin' t'see my sister in Kittery, I am. Figure that's far enough to be safe.'

Ben heard himself say remotely, 'You gutless creep. You cowardly piece of shit. This town is still alive and you're running out on it.'

'It ain't alive,' Parkins said, lighting his smoke with a wooden kitchen match. 'That's why *he* came here. It's dead, like him. Has been for twenty years or more. Whole country's goin' the same way. Me and Nolly went to a drive-in show up in Falmouth a couple of weeks ago, just before they closed her down for the season. I seen more blood and killin's in that first Western than I seen both years in Korea. Kids was eatin' popcorn and cheerin' 'em on.' He gestured vaguely at the town, now lying unnaturally gilded in the broken rays of the westering sun, like a dream village. 'They prob'ly like bein' vampires. But not me; Nolly'd be in after me tonight. I'm goin'.'

Ben looked at him helplessly.

'You two fellas want to get in that car and hit it out of here,' Parkins said. 'This town will go on without us . . . for a while. Then it won't matter.'

Yes, Ben thought. *Why don't we do that?*

Mark spoke the reason for both of them. 'Because he's bad, mister. He's really bad. That's all.'

'Is that so?' Parkins said. He nodded and puffed his Pall Mall. 'Well, okay.' He looked up toward the Consolidated High School. 'Piss-poor attendance today, from the Lot, anyway. Buses runnin' late, kids out sick, office phonin' houses and not gettin' any answer. The attendance officer called me, and I soothed him some. He's a funny little bald-headed fella who thinks he knows what he's doing. Well, the teachers are there, anyway. They come from out of town, mostly. They can teach each other.'

Thinking of Matt, Ben said, 'Not all of them are from out of town.'

'It don't matter,' Parkins said. His eyes dropped to the stakes in Ben's belt. 'You going to try to do that fella up with one of those?'

'Yes.'

'You can have my riot gun if you want it. That gun, it was Nolly's idea. Nolly liked to go armed, he did. Not even a bank in town so's he could hope someone would rob it. He'll make a good vampire though, once he gets the hang of it.'

Mark was looking at him with rising horror, and Ben knew he had to get him away. This was the worst of all.

'Come on,' he said to Mark. 'He's done.'

'I guess that's it,' Parkins said. His pale, crinkle-caught eyes surveyed the town. 'Surely is quiet. I seen Mabel Werts, peekin' out with her glasses, but I don't guess there's much to peek at, today. There'll be more tonight, likely.'

They went back to the car. It was almost 5:30.

46

They pulled up in front of St Andrew's at quarter of six. Lengthening shadows fell from the church across the street to the rectory, covering it like a prophecy. Ben pulled Jimmy's bag out of the backseat and dumped it out. He found several small ampoules, and dumped their contents out the window, saving the bottles.

'What are you doing?'

'We're going to put holy water in these,' Ben said. 'Come on.'

They went up the walk to the church and climbed the steps. Mark, about to open the middle door, paused and pointed. 'Look at that.'

The handle was blackened and pulled slightly out of shape, as if a heavy electric charge had been pushed through it.

'Does that mean anything to you?' Ben asked.

'No. No, but . . .' Mark shook his head, pushing an unformed thought away. He opened the door and they went in. The church was cool and gray and filled with the endless pregnant pause that all empty altars of faith, white and black, have in common.

561

The two ranks of pews were split by a wide central aisle, and flanking this, two plaster angels stood cradling bowls of holy water, their calm and sweetly knowing faces bent, as if to catch their own reflections in the still water.

Ben put the ampoules in his pocket. 'Bathe your face and hands,' he said.

Mark looked at him, troubled. 'That's sac – sacri—'

'Sacrilege? Not this time. Go ahead.'

They dunked their hands in the still water and then splashed it over their faces, the way a man who has just wakened will splash cold water into his eyes to shock the world back into them.

Ben took the first ampoule out of his pocket and was filling it when a shrill voice cried. 'Here! Here now! What are you doing?'

Ben turned around. It was Rhoda Curless, Father Callahan's housekeeper, who had been sitting in the first pew and twisting a rosary helplessly between her fingers. She was wearing a black dress, and her slip hung below the hem. Her hair was in disarray; she had been pulling her fingers through it.

'Where's the Father? What are you doing?' Her voice was reedy and thin, close to hysteria.

'Who are you?' Ben asked.

'Mrs Curless. I'm Father Callahan's housekeeper. Where's the Father? What are you doing?' Her hands came together and began to war with each other.

'Father Callahan is gone,' Ben said, as gently as he could.

'Oh.' She closed her eyes. 'Was he getting after whatever ails this town?'

'Yes,' Ben said.

'I knew it,' she said. 'I didn't have to ask. He's a strong, good man of the cloth. There were always those who said he'd never be man enough to fill Father Bergeron's shoes, but he filled 'em. They were too small for him, as it turned out.'

She opened her eyes wide and looked at them. A tear spilled from her left, and ran down her cheek. 'He won't be back, will he?'

'I don't know,' Ben said.

'They talked about his drinkin',' she said, as though she hadn't heard. 'Was there ever an Irish priest worth his keep who didn't tip the bottle? None of that mollycod-dlin' wet-nursin' church-bingo-prayer-basket for him. He was more'n that!' Her voice rose toward the vaulted ceiling in a hoarse, almost challenging cry. 'He was a *priest*, not some holy alderman!'

Ben and Mark listened without speech or surprise. There was no surprise left on this dream-struck day; there was not even the capacity for it. They no longer saw them-selves as doers or avengers or saviors; the day had absorbed them. Helplessly, they were only living.

'Was he strong when last you saw him?' she demanded, peering at them. The tears magnified the gimlet lack of compromise in her eyes.

'Yes,' Mark said, remembering Callahan in his mother's kitchen, holding his cross aloft.

'And are you about his work now?'

'Yes,' Mark said again.

'Then be about it,' she snapped at them. 'What are you waiting for?' And she left them, walking down the center aisle in her black dress, the solitary mourner at a funeral that hadn't been held here.

47

Eva's again — and at the last. It was ten minutes after six. The sun hung over the western pines, peering out of the broken clouds like blood.

Ben drove into the parking lot and looked curiously up at his room. The shade was not drawn and he could see his typewriter standing sentinel, and beside it, his pile of manuscript and the glass globe paperweight on top of it. It seemed amazing that he could see all those things from here, see them clearly, as if everything in the world was sane and normal and ordered.

He let his eyes drop to the back porch. The rocking chairs where he and Susan had shared their first kiss stood side by side, unchanged. The door which gave ingress to the kitchen stood open, as Mark had left it.

'I can't,' Mark muttered. 'I just can't.' His eyes were wide and white. He had drawn up his knees and was now crouched on the seat.

'It's got to be both of us,' Ben said. He held out two of the ampoules filled with holy water. Mark twitched away from them in horror, as if touching them would admit poison through his skin. 'Come on,' Ben said. He had no arguments left. 'Come on, come on.'

'No.'

'Mark?'

'No!'

'Mark, I need you. You and me, that's all that's left.'

'I've done enough!' Mark cried. 'I can't do any more! *Can't you understand I can't look at him?*'

'Mark, it has to be the two of us. Don't you know that?'

Mark took the ampoules and curled them slowly against his chest. 'Oh boy,' he whispered. 'Oh boy, oh boy.' He looked at Ben and nodded. The movement of his head was jerky and agonized. 'Okay,' he said.

'Where's the hammer?' he asked as they got out.

'Jimmy had it.'

'Okay.'

They walked up the porch steps in the strengthening wind. The sun glared red through the clouds, dyeing everything. Inside, in the kitchen, the stink of death was palpable and wet, pressing against them like granite. The cellar door stood open.

'I'm so scared,' Mark said, shuddering.

'You better be. Where's that flashlight?'

'In the cellar. I left it when . . .'

'Okay.' They stood at the mouth of the cellar. As Mark had said, the stairs looked intact in the sunset light. 'Follow me,' Ben said.

48

Ben thought quite easily: *I'm going to my death.*

The thought came naturally, and there was no fear or regret in it. Inward-turning emotions were lost under the overwhelming atmosphere of evil that hung over this place. As he slipped and scraped his way down the board Mark had set up to get out of the cellar, all he felt was an unnatural glacial calm. He saw that his hands were glowing, as if wreathed in ghost gloves. It did not surprise him.

Let be be finale of seem. The only emperor is the emperor of ice cream. Who had said that? Matt? Matt was dead. Susan was dead. Miranda was dead. Wallace Stevens was dead, too. *I wouldn't look at that, if I were you.* But he had looked. That's what you looked like when it was over. Like something smashed and broken that had been filled with different-colored fluids. It wasn't so bad. Not so bad as *his* death. Jimmy had been carrying McCaslin's pistol; it would still be in his coat pocket. He would take it, and if sunset came before they could get to Barlow . . . first the boy, and then himself. Not good, but better than *his* death.

He dropped to the cellar floor and then helped Mark down. The boy's eyes flashed to the dark, curled thing on the floor and then skipped away.

'I can't look at that,' he said huskily.

'That's all right.'

Mark turned away and Ben knelt down. He swept away a number of the lethal plywood squares, the knife blades thrust through them glittering like dragon's teeth. Gently, then, he turned Jimmy over.

I wouldn't look at that, if I were you.

'Oh, Jimmy,' he tried to say, and the words broke open and bled in his throat. He cradled Jimmy in the curve of his left arm and pulled Barlow's blades out of him with his right hand. There were six of them, and Jimmy had bled a great deal.

There was a nearly folded stack of living room drapes on a corner shelf. He took them over to Jimmy and spread them over his body after he had the gun and the flashlight and the hammer.

He stood up and tried the flashlight. The plastic lens cover had cracked, but the bulb still worked. He flashed it around. Nothing. He shone it under the pool table. Bare. Nothing behind the furnace. Racks of preserves, and a wallboard hung with tools. The amputated stairs, pushed over in the far corner so they would be out of sight from the kitchen. They looked like a scaffold leading nowhere.

'Where is he?' Ben muttered. He glanced at his watch, and the hands stood at 6:23. When was sunset? He couldn't remember. Surely no later than 6:55. That gave them a bare half hour.

'Where is he?' he cried out. 'I can *feel* him, but where is he?'

'There!' Mark cried, pointing with one glowing hand. 'What's that?'

Ben centered the light on it. A Welsh dresser. 'It's not big enough,' he said to Mark. 'And it's flush against the wall.'

'Let's look behind it.'

Ben shrugged. They crossed the room to the Welsh dresser and each took a side. He felt a trickle of building excitement. Surely the odor or aura or atmosphere or whatever you wanted to call it was thicker here, more offensive?

Ben glanced up at the open kitchen door. The light was dimmer now. The gold was fading out of it.

'It's too heavy for me,' Mark panted.

'Never mind,' Ben said. 'We're going to tip it over. Get your best hold.'

Mark bent over it, his shoulder against the wood. His eyes looked fiercely out of his glowing face. 'Okay.'

They threw their combined weight against it and the Welsh dresser went over with a bonelike crash as Eva Miller's long-ago wedding china shattered inside.

'I *knew* it!' Mark cried triumphantly.

There was a small door, chest-high, set into the wall where the Welsh dresser had been. A new Yale padlock secured the hasp.

Two hard swings of the hammer convinced him that the lock wasn't going to give. 'Jesus Christ,' he muttered softly. Frustration welled up bitterly in his throat. To be balked like this at the end, balked by a five-dollar padlock—

No. He would bite through the wood with his teeth if he had to.

He shone the flashlight around, and its beam fell on the neatly hung tool board to the right of the stairs. Hung on two of its steel pegs was an ax with a rubber cover masking its blade.

He ran across, snatched it off the wallboard, and pulled the rubber cover from the blade. He took one of the ampoules from his pocket and dropped it. The holy water ran out on the floor, beginning to glow immediately. He got another one, twisted the small cap off, and doused the blade of the ax. It began to glimmer with eldritch fairy-light. And when he set his hands on the wooden haft, the grip felt incredibly good, incredibly *right*. Power seemed to have welded his flesh into its present grip. He stood holding it for a moment, looking at the shining blade, and some curious impulse made him touch it to his forehead. A hard sense of sureness clasped him, a feeling of inevitable rightness, of *whiteness*. For the first time in weeks he felt he was no longer groping through fogs of belief and unbelief, sparring with a partner whose body was too insubstantial to sustain blows.

Power, humming up his arms like volts.

The blade glowed brighter.

'Do it!' Mark pleaded. 'Quick! Please!'

Ben Mears spread his feet, slung the ax back, and brought it down in a gleaming are that left an afterimage on the eye. The blade bit wood with a booming, portentous sound and sunk to the haft. Splinters flew.

He pulled it out, the wood screaming against the steel. He brought it down again ... again ... again. He could feel the muscles of his back and arms flexing and meshing, moving with a sureness and a studied heat that they had never known before. Each blow sent chips and splinters flying like shrapnel. On the fifth blow the blade crashed through to emptiness and he began hacking the hole wider with a speed that approached frenzy.

Mark stared at him, amazed. The cold blue fire had crept down the ax handle and spread up his arms until he seemed to be working in a column of fire. His head was twisted to one side, the muscles of his neck corded with strain, one eye open and glaring, the other squeezed shut. The back of his shirt had split between the straining wings of his shoulder blades, and the muscles writhed beneath the skin like ropes. He was a man taken over, possessed, and Mark saw without knowing (or having to know) that the possession was not in the least Christian; the good was more elemental, less refined. It was ore, like something coughed up out of the ground in naked chunks. There was nothing finished about it. It was Force; it was Power; it was whatever moved the greatest wheels of the universe.

The door to Eva Miller's root cellar could not stand before it. The ax began to move at a nearly blinding speed; it became a ripple, a descending are, a rainbow from over Ben's shoulder to the splintered wood of the last door.

He dealt it a final blow and slung the ax away. He held his hands up before his eyes. They blazed.

He held them out to Mark, and the boy flinched.

'I love you,' Ben said.

They clasped hands.

49

The root cellar was small and cell-like, empty except for a few dusty bottles, some crates, and a dusty bushel basket of very old potatoes that were sprouting eyes in every direction – and the bodies. Barlow's coffin stood at the far end, propped up against the wall like a mummy's sarcophagus, and the crest on it blazed coldly in the light they carried with them like St Elmo's fire.

In front of the coffin, leading up to it like railroad ties, were the bodies of the people Ben had lived with and broken bread with: Eva Miller, and Weasel Craig beside her; Mabel Mullican from the room at the end of the second-floor hall; John Snow, who had been on the county and could barely walk down to the breakfast table with his arthritis; Vinnie Upshaw; Grover Verrill.

They stepped over them and stood by the coffin. Ben glanced down at his watch; it was 6:40.

'We're going to take it out there,' he said. 'By Jimmy.'

'It must weigh a ton,' Mark said.

'We can do it.' He reached out, almost tentatively, and then grasped the upper right corner of the coffin. The crest glittered like an impassioned eye. The wood was crawlingly unpleasant to the touch, smooth and stonelike with years. There seemed to be no pores in the wood, no small imperfections for the fingers to recognize and mold to. Yet it rocked easily. One hand did it.

He tipped it forward with a small push, feeling the great weight held in check as if by invisible counterweights. Something thumped inside. Ben took the weight of the coffin on one hand.

'Now,' he said. 'Your end.'

Mark lifted and the end of the coffin came up easily. The boy's face filled with pleased amazement. 'I think I could do it with one finger.'

'You probably could. Things are finally running our way. But we have to be quick.'

They carried the coffin through the shattered door. It threatened to stick at its widest point, and Mark lowered his head and shoved. It went through with a wooden scream.

They carried it across to where Jimmy lay, covered with Eva Miller's drapes.

'Here he is, Jimmy,' Ben said. 'Here the bastard is. Set it down, Mark.'

He glanced at his watch again. 6:45. Now the light coming through the kitchen door above them was an ashy gray.

'Now?' Mark asked.

They looked at each other over the coffin.

'Yes,' Ben said.

Mark came around and they stood together in front of the coffin's locks and seals. They bent together, and the locks split as they touched them, making a sound like thin, snapping clapboards. They lifted.

Barlow lay before them, his eyes glaring upward.

He was a young man now, his black hair vibrant and lustrous, flowing over the satin pillow at the head of his narrow apartment. His skin glowed with life. The cheeks were as ruddy as wine. His teeth curved out over his full lips, white with strong streaks of yellow, like ivory.

'He—' Mark began, and never finished.

Barlow's red eyes rolled in their sockets, filling with a hideous life and mocking triumph. They locked with Mark's eyes and Mark gaped down into them, his own eyes growing blank and far away.

'Don't look at him!' Ben cried, but it was too late.

He knocked Mark away. The boy whined deep in his throat and suddenly attacked Ben. Taken by surprise, Ben staggered backward. A moment later the boy's hands were in his coat pocket, digging for Homer McCaslin's pistol.

'Mark! Don't—'

But the boy didn't hear. His face was as blank as a washed blackboard. The whining went on and on in his throat, the sound of a very small trapped animal. He had both hands around the pistol. They struggled for it, Ben trying to rip it from the boy's grasp and keep it pointed away from both of them.

'Mark!' he bellowed. 'Mark, wake up! For Christ's sake—'

The muzzle jerked down toward his head and the

gun went off. He felt the slug pass by his temple. He wrapped his hands around Mark's and kicked out with one foot. Mark staggered backward, and the gun clattered on the floor between them. The boy leaped at it, whining, and Ben punched him in the mouth with all the strength he had. He felt the boy's lips mash back against his teeth and cried out as if he himself had been hit. Mark slipped to his knees, and Ben kicked the gun away. Mark tried to go after it crawling, and Ben hit him again.

With a tired sigh, the boy collapsed.

The strength had left him now, and the sureness. He was only Ben Mears again, and he was afraid.

The square of light in the kitchen doorway had faded to thin purple; his watch said 6:51.

A huge force seemed to be dragging at his head, commanding· him to look at the rosy, gorged parasite in the coffin beside him.

Look and see me, puny man. Look upon Barlow, who has passed the centuries as you have passed hours before a fireplace with a book. Look and see the great creature of the night whom you would slay with your miserable little stick. Look upon me, scribbler. I have written in human lives, and blood has been my ink. Look upon me and despair!

Jimmy, I can't do it. It's too late, he's too strong for me—
LOOK AT ME!

It was 6:53.

Mark groaned on the floor. 'Mom? Momma, where are you? My head hurts . . . it's dark . . .'

He shall enter my service castratum . . .

Ben fumbled one of the stakes from his belt and dropped it. He cried out miserably, in utter despair. Outside, the sun had deserted Jerusalem's Lot. Its last rays lingered on the roof of the Marsten House.

He snatched the stake up. But where was the hammer? *Where was the fucking hammer?*

By the root cellar door. He had swung at the padlock with it.

He scrambled across the cellar and picked it up where it lay.

Mark was half sitting, his mouth a bloody gash. He wiped a hand across it and looked dazedly at the blood. 'Momma!' he cried. 'Where's my mother?'

6:55 now. Light and darkness hung perfectly balanced.

Ben ran back across the darkening cellar, the stake clutched in his left hand, the hammer in his right.

There was a booming, triumphant laugh. Barlow was sitting up in his coffin, those red eyes flashing with hellish triumph. They locked with Ben's, and he felt the will draining away from him.

With a mad, convulsive yell, he raised the stake over his head and brought it down in a whistling arc. Its razored point sheared through Barlow's shirt, and he felt it strike into the flesh beneath.

Barlow screamed. It was an eerie, hurt sound, like the howl of a wolf. The force of the stake slamming home drove him back into the coffin on his back. His hands rose out of it, hooked into claws, waving crazily.

Ben brought the hammer down on the top of the stake, and Barlow screamed again. One of his hands, as cold as the grave, seized Ben's left hand, which was locked around the stake.

Ben wriggled into the coffin, his knees planted on

Barlow's knees. He stared down into the hate and pain-driven face.

'*Let me GO!*' Barlow cried.

'Here it comes, you bastard,' Ben sobbed. 'Here it is, leech. Here it is for you.'

He brought the hammer down again. Blood splashed upward in a cold gush, blinding him momentarily. Barlow's head lashed from side to side on the satin pillow.

'*Let me go, you dare not, you dare not, you dare not do this—*'

He brought the hammer down again and again. Blood burst from Barlow's nostrils. His body began to jerk in the coffin like a stabbed fish. The hands clawed at Ben's cheeks, pulling long gouges in his skin.

'*LET ME GOOOOOOOOOOOOOOOOO—*'

He brought the hammer down on the stake once more, and the blood that pulsed from Barlow's chest turned black.

Then, dissolution.

It came in the space of two seconds, too fast to ever be believed in the daylight of later years, yet slow enough to recur again and again in nightmares, with awful stop-motion slowness.

The skin yellowed, coarsened, blistered like old sheets of canvas. The eyes faded, filmed white, fell in. The hair went white and fell like a drift of feathers. The body inside the dark suit shriveled and retreated. The mouth widened gapingly as the lips drew back and drew back, meeting the nose and disappearing in an oral ring of jutting teeth. The fingernails went black and peeled off, and then there were only bones, still dressed with rings, clicking and clenching like castanets. Dust puffed through the fibers of the linen shirt. The bald and wrinkled head became a skull. The pants, with nothing to fill them out, fell away to broomsticks clad in black silk. For a moment a hideously animated scarecrow writhed beneath him, and Ben lunged out of the coffin with a strangled cry of horror. But it was impossible to tear the gaze away from Barlow's last metamorphosis; it hypnotized. The fleshless skull whipped from side to side on the satin pillow. The nude jawbone opened in a soundless scream that had no vocal cords to power it. The skeletal fingers danced and clicked on the dark air like marionettes.

Smells struck his nose and then vanished, each in a tight little puff: gas; putrescence, horrid and fleshy; a moldy library smell; acrid dust; then nothing. The twisting, protesting finger bones shredded and flaked away like pencils. The nasal cavity of the skull widened and met the oral cavity. The empty eye sockets widened in a fleshless expression of surprise and horror, met, and were no more. The skull caved in like an ancient Ming vase. The clothes settled flat and became as neutral as dirty laundry.

And still there was no end to its tenacious hold on the world — even the dust billowed and writhed in tiny dust devils within the coffin. And then, suddenly, he felt the passage of something which buffeted past him like a strong wind, making him shudder. At the same instant, every window of Eva Miller's boardinghouse blew outward.

'Look out, Ben!' Mark screamed. 'Look out!'

He whirled over on his back and saw them coming out of the root cellar — Eva, Weasel, Mabel, Grover, and the others. Their time was on the world.

Mark's screams echoed in his ears like great fire bells, and he grabbed the boy by the shoulders.

'The holy water!' he yelled into Mark's tormented face. *'They can't touch us!'*

Mark's cries turned to whimpers.

'Go up the board,' Ben said. 'Go on.' He had to turn the boy to face it, and then slap his bottom to make him climb. When he was sure the boy was going up, he turned back and looked at them, the Undead.

They were standing passively some fifteen feet away, looking at him with a flat hate that was not human.

'You killed the Master,' Eva said, and he could almost believe there was grief in her voice. 'How could you kill the Master?'

'I'll be back,' he told her. 'For all of you.'

He went up the board, climbing bent over, using his hands. It groaned under his weight, but held. At the top, he spared one glance back down. They were gathered around the coffin now, looking in silently. They reminded him of the people who had gathered around Miranda's body after the accident with the moving van.

He looked around for Mark, and saw him lying by the porch door, on his face.

50

Ben told himself that the boy had just fainted, and nothing more. It might be true. His pulse was strong and regular. He gathered him in his arms and carried him out to the Citroën.

He got behind the wheel and started the engine. As

577

he pulled out onto Railroad Street, delayed reaction struck him like a physical blow, and he had to stifle a scream.

They were in the streets, the walking dead.

Cold and hot, his head full of a wild roaring sound, he turned left on Jointner Avenue and drove out of 'salem's Lot.

CHAPTER FIFTEEN
BEN AND MARK

Mark woke up a little at a time, letting the Citroën's steady hum bring him back without thought or memory. At last he looked out the window, and fright took him in rough hands. It was dark. The trees at the sides of the road were vague blurs, and the cars that passed them had their parking lights and headlights on. A gagging, inarticulate groan escaped him, and he clawed at his neck for the cross that still hung there.

'Relax,' Ben said. 'We're out of town. It's twenty miles behind us.'

The boy reached over him, almost making him swerve, and locked the driver's side door. Whirling, he locked his own door. Then he crouched slowly down in a ball on his side of the seat. He wished the nothingness would come back. The nothingness was nice. Nice nothingness with no nasty pictures in it.

The steady sound of the Citroën's engine was soothing. *Mmmmmmmmmmmm.* Nice. He closed his eyes.

'Mark?'

Safer not to answer.

'Mark, are you all right?'

Mmmmmmmmmmmmmmmmm.

'—mark—'

Far away. That was all right. Nice nothingness came back, and shades of gray swallowed him.

2

Ben checked them into a motel just across the New Hampshire state line, signing the register Ben Cody and Son, scrawling it. Mark walked into the room holding his cross out. His eyes darted from side to side in their sockets like small, trapped beasts. He held the cross until Ben had closed the door, locked it, and hung his own cross from the doorknob. There was a color TV and Ben watched it for a while. Two African nations had gone to war. The President had a cold but it wasn't considered serious. And a man in Los Angeles had gone berserk and shot fourteen people. The weather forecast was for rain – snow flurries in northern Maine.

3

'Salem's Lot slept darkly, and the vampires walked its streets and country roads like a trace memory of evil. Some of them had emerged enough from the shadows of death to have regained some rudimentary cunning. Lawrence Crockett called up Royal Snow and invited him over to the office to play some cribbage. When Royal pulled up front and walked in, Lawrence and his wife fell on him. Glynis Mayberry called Mabel Werts, said she was frightened, and asked if she could come over and spend the evening with her until her husband got back from Waterville. Mabel agreed with almost pitiful relief, and when she opened the door ten minutes later, Glynis was standing there stark naked, her purse over her arm, grinning with huge, ravenous incisors. Mabel had time to scream, but only once. When Delbert Markey stepped out of his deserted tavern just after eight o’clock, Carl Foreman and a grinning Homer McCaslin stepped out of the shadows and said they had come for a drink. Milt Crossen was visited at his store just after closing time by a number of his most faithful customers and oldest cronies. And George Middler visited several of the high school boys who bought things at his store and always had looked at him with a mixture of scorn and knowledge; and his darkest fantasies were satisfied.

Tourists and through-travelers still passed by on Route 12, seeing nothing of the Lot but an Elks billboard and a thirty-five-mile-an-hour speed sign. Outside of town they went back up to sixty and perhaps dismissed it with a single thought: Christ, what a dead little place.

The town kept its secrets, and the Marsten House brooded over it like a ruined king.

4

Ben drove back the next day at dawn, leaving Mark in the motel room. He stopped at a busy hardware store in Westbrook and bought a spade and a pick.

’Salem’s Lot lay silent under a dark sky from which rain had not yet begun to fall. Few cars moved on the streets. Spencer’s was open but now the Excellent Café was shut up, all the green blinds drawn, the menus removed from the windows, the small daily special chalkboard erased clean.

The empty streets made him feel cold in his bones, and an image came to mind, an old rock 'n' roll album with a picture of a transvestite on the front, profile shot against a black background, the strangely masculine face bleeding with rouge and paint; title: 'They Only Come Out at Night.'

He went to Eva's first, climbed the stairs to the second floor, and pushed the door to his room open. Just the same as he had left it, the bed unmade, an open roll of Life Savers on his desk. There was an empty tin wastebasket under the desk and he pulled it out into the middle of the floor.

He took his manuscript, threw it in, and made a paper spill of the title page. He lit it with his Cricket, and when it flared up he tossed it in on top of the drift of type-written pages. The flame tasted them, found them good, and began to crawl eagerly over the paper. Corners charred, turned upward, blackened. Whitish smoke began to billow out of the wastebasket, and without thinking about it, he leaned over his desk and opened the window.

His hand found the paperweight – the glass globe that had been with him since his boyhood in this nighted town – grabbed unknowing in a dreamlike visit to a monster's house. Shake it up and watch the snow float down.

He did it now, holding it up before his eyes as he had as a boy, and it did its old, old trick. Through the floating snow you could see a little gingerbread house with a path leading up to it. The gingerbread shutters were closed, but as an imaginative boy (as Mark Petrie was now), you could fancy that one of the shutters was being folded back (as indeed, one of them seemed to be folding back now) by a long white hand, and then a pallid face would be looking out at you, grinning with long teeth, inviting you into this house beyond the world in its slow and endless fantasyland of false snow, where time was a myth. The face was looking out at him now, pallid and hungry, a face that would never look on daylight or blue skies again.

It was his own face.

He threw the paperweight into the corner and it shattered.

He left without waiting to see what might leak out of it.

5

He went down into the cellar to get Jimmy's body, and that was the hardest trip of all. The coffin lay where it had the night before, empty even of dust. Yet . . . not entirely empty. The stake was in there, and something else. He felt his gorge rise. Teeth. Barlow's teeth – all that was left of him. Ben reached down, picked them up – and they twisted in his hand like tiny white animals, trying to come together and bite.

With a disgusted cry he threw them outward, scattering them.

'God,' he whispered, rubbing his hand against his shirt. 'Oh, my dear God. Please let that be the end. Let it be the end of him.'

6

Somehow he managed to get Jimmy, still bundled up in Eva's drapes, out of the cellar. He tucked the bundle into the trunk of Jimmy's Buick and then drove out to the Petrie house, the pick and shovel resting next to Jimmy's black bag in the backseat. In a wooded clearing behind the Petrie house and close to the babble of Taggart Stream, he spent the rest of the morning and half the afternoon digging a wide grave four feet deep. Into it he put Jimmy's body and the Petries, still wrapped in the sofa dustcover.

He began filling in the grave of these clean ones at two-thirty. He began to shovel faster and faster as the light began its long drain from the cloudy sky. Sweat that was not wholly from exertion condensed on his skin.

The hole was filled in by four. He tamped in the sods as well as he could, and drove back to town with the earth-clotted pick and shovel in the trunk of Jimmy's car. He parked it in front of the Excellent Café, leaving the keys in the ignition.

He paused for a moment, looking around. The deserted business buildings with their false fronts seemed to lean crepitatingly over the street. The rain, which had started around noon, fell softly and slowly, as if in mourning. The little park where he had met Susan Norton was empty and forlorn. The shades of the Municipal Building were drawn. A 'Be back soon' sign hung in the window of Larry Crockett's Insurance and Real Estate office with hollow jauntiness. And the only sound was soft rain.

He walked up toward Railroad Street, his heels clicking emptily on the sidewalk. When he got to Eva's, he paused by his car for a moment, looking around for the last time. Nothing moved.

The town was dead. All at once he knew it for sure and true, just as he had known for sure that Miranda was dead when he had seen her shoe lying in the road.

He began to cry.

He was still crying when he drove past the Elks sign, which read: 'You are now leaving Jerusalem's Lot, a nice little town. Come again!'

He got on the turnpike. The Marsten House was blotted out by the trees as he went down the feeder ramp. He began to drive south toward Mark, toward his life.

EPILOGUE

Among these decimated villages
Upon this headland naked to the south wind
With the trail of mountains before us, hiding you,
Who will reckon up our decision to forget?
Who will accept our offering at this end of autumn?
                                    – George Seferis

            Now she's eyeless.
            The snakes she held once
            Eat up her hands.
                        – George Seferis

'SALEM'S LOT

From a scrapbook kept by Ben Mears (all clippings from the Portland Press-Herald):

November 19, 1975 (p. 27):

JERUSALEM'S LOT – The Charles V. Pritchett family, who bought a farm in the Cumberland County town of Jerusalem's Lot only a month ago, are moving out because things keep going bump in the night, according to Charles and Amanda Pritchett, who moved here from Portland. The farm, a local landmark on School-yard Hill, was previously owned by Charles Griffen. Griffen's father was the owner of Sunshine Dairy, Inc., which was absorbed by the Slewfoot Dairy Corporation in 1962. Charles Griffen, who sold the farm through a Portland realtor for what Pritchett called 'a bargain basement price,' could not be reached for comment. Amanda Pritchett first told her husband about the 'funny noises' in the hayloft shortly after . . .

January 4, 1976 (p. 1):

JERUSALEM'S LOT – A bizare car crash occurred last night or early this morning in the small southern

Maine town of Jerusalem's Lot. Police theorize from skid marks found near the scene that the car, a late-model sedan, was traveling at an excessive speed when it left the road and struck a Central Maine Power utility pole. The car was a total wreck, but although blood was found on the front seat and the dashboard, no passengers have yet been found. Police say that the car was registered to Mr Gordon Phillips of Scarborough. According to a neighbor, Phillips and his family had been on their way to see relatives in Yarmouth. Police theorize that Phillips, his wife, and their two children may have wandered off in a daze and become lost. Plans for a search have been . . .

February 14, 1976 (p. 4):
CUMBERLAND — Mrs Fiona Coggins, a widow who lived alone on the Smith Road in West Cumberland, was reported missing this morning to the Cumberland County sheriff's office by her niece, Mrs Gertrude Hersey. Mrs Hersey told police officers that her aunt was a shut-in and is in poor health. Sheriff's deputies are investigating, but claim that at this point it is impossible to say what . . .

February 27, 1976 (p. 6):
FALMOUTH — John Farrington, an elderly farmer and lifelong Falmouth resident, was found dead in his barn early this morning by his son-in-law, Frank Vickery. Vickery said Farrington was lying facedown outside a low haymow, a pitchfork near one hand. County Medical Examiner David Rice says

Farrington apparently died of a massive hemorrhage, or perhaps internal bleeding . . .

May 20, 1976 (p. 17):
PORTLAND – Cumberland County game wardens have been instructed by the Maine State Wildlife Service to be on the lookout for a wild dog pack that may be running in the Jerusalem's Lot-Cumberland-Falmouth area. During the last month, several sheep have been found dead with their throats and bellies mangled. In some cases, sheep have been disembow-eled. Deputy Game Warden Upton Pruitt said, 'As you know, this situation has worsened a good deal in southern Maine . . .'

May 29, 1976 (p. 1):
JERUSALEM'S LOT – Possible foul play is suspected in the disappearance of the Daniel Holloway family, who had moved into a house on the Taggart Stream Road in this small Cumberland Country township recently. Police were alerted by Daniel Holloway's grandfather, who became alarmed at the repeated failure of anyone to answer his telephone calls.

The Holloways and their two children moved onto the Taggart Stream Road in April, and had complained to both friends and relatives of hearing 'funny noises' after dark.

Jerusalem's Lot has been at the center of several strange occurrences during the last several months, and a great many families have . . .

June 4, 1976 (p. 2):

CUMBERLAND – Mrs Elaine Tremont, a widow who owns a small house on the Back Stage Road in the western part of this small Cumberland County village, was admitted to Cumberland Receiving Hospital early this morning with a heart attack. She told a reporter from this paper that she had heard a scratching noise at her bedroom window while she was watching television, and looked up to see a face peering in at her.

'It was grinning,' Mrs Tremont said. 'It was horrible. I've never been so frightened in my life. And since that family was killed just a mile away on the Taggart Stream Road, I've been frightened all the time.'

Mrs Tremont referred to the Daniel Holloway family, who disappeared from their Jerusalem's Lot residence some time early last week. Police said the connection was being investigated, but . . .

2

The tall man and the boy arrived in Portland in mid-September and stayed at a local motel for three weeks. They were used to heat, but after the dry climate of Los Zapatos, they both found the high humidity enervating. They both swam in the motel pool a great deal and watched the sky a great deal. The man got the Portland *Press-Herald* every day, and now the copies were fresh, unmarked by time or dog urine. He read the weather forecasts and he watched for items concerning Jerusalem's Lot. On the ninth day of their stay in Portland, a man in Falmouth disappeared. His dog was found dead in the yard. Police were looking into it.

The man rose early on October 6 and stood in the forecourt of the motel. Most of the tourists were gone now, back to New York and New Jersey and Florida, to Ontario and Nova Scotia, to Pennsylvania and California. The tourists left their litter and their summer dollars and the natives to enjoy their state's most beautiful season.

This morning there was something new in the air. The smell of exhaust from the main road was not so great. There was no haze on the horizon, and no ground fog lying milkily around the legs of the billboard in the field across the way. The morning sky was very clear, and the air was chill. Indian summer seemed to have left overnight.

The boy came out and stood beside him.

The man said: 'Today.'

3

It was almost noon when they got to the 'salem's Lot turnoff, and Ben was reminded achingly of the day he had arrived here determined to exorcise all the demons that had haunted him, and confident of his success. That day had been warmer than this, the wind had not been so strong out of the west, and Indian summer had only been beginning. He remembered two boys with fishing poles. The sky today was a harder blue, colder.

The car radio proclaimed that the fire index was at five, its second-highest reading. There had been no significant rainfall in southern Maine since the first week of September. The deejay on WJAB cautioned drivers to crush their smokes and then played a record about a man who was going to jump off a water tower for love.

They drove down Route 12 past the Elks sign and were on Jointner Avenue. Ben saw at once that the blinker was dark. No need of a warning light now.

Then they were in town. They drove through it slowly, and Ben felt the old fear drop over him, like a coat found in the attic which has grown tight but still fits. Mark sat rigidly beside him, holding a vial of holy water brought all the way from Los Zapatos. Father Gracon had presented him with it as a going-away present.

With the fear came memories: almost heartbreaking.

They had changed Spencer's Sundries to a LaVerdiere's, but it had fared no better. The closed windows were dirty and bare. The Grey-hound bus sign was gone. A for-sale sign had fallen askew in the window of the Excellent Café, and all the counter stools had been uprooted and ferried away to some more prosperous lunchroom. Up the street the sign over what had once been a Laundromat still read 'Barlow and Straker – Fine Furnishings,' but now the gilt letters were tarnished and they looked out on empty sidewalks. The show window was empty, the deep-pile carpet dirty. Ben thought of Mike Ryerson and wondered if he was still lying in the crate in the back room. The thought made his mouth dry.

Ben slowed at the crossroads. Up the hill he could see the Norton house, the grass grown long and yellow in front and behind it, where Bill Norton's brick barbecue had stood. Some of the windows were broken.

Further up the street he pulled in to the curb and looked into the park. The War Memorial presided over a junglelike growth of bushes and grass. The wading pool had been choked by summer waterweeds. The green paint on the benches was flaked and peeling. The swing chains had rusted, and to ride in one would produce squealing noises unpleasant enough to spoil the fun. The slippery slide had fallen over and lay with its legs sticking stiffly out, like a dead antelope. And perched in one corner of the sandbox, a floppy arm trailing on the grass, was some child's forgotten Raggedy Andy doll. Its shoe-button eyes seemed to reflect a black, vapid horror, as if it had seen all the secrets of darkness during its long stay in the sandbox. Perhaps it had.

He looked up and saw the Marsten House, its shutters still closed, looking down on the town with rickety malevolence. It was harmless now, but after dark . . . ?

The rains would have washed away the wafer with which Callahan had sealed it. It could be theirs again if they wanted it, a shrine, a dark lighthouse overlooking this shunned and deadly town. Did they meet up there? he wondered. Did they wander, pallid, through its nighted halls and hold revels, twisted services to the Maker of their Maker?

He looked away, cold.

Mark was looking at the houses. In most of them the shades were drawn; in others, uncovered windows looked in on empty rooms. They were worse than those decently closed, Ben thought. They seemed to look out at these daylight interlopers with the vapid stares of mental defectives.

'They're in those houses,' Mark said tightly. 'Right now, in all those houses. Behind the shades. In beds and closets and cellars. Under the floors. Hiding.'

'Take it easy,' Ben said.

The village dropped behind them. Ben turned onto the Brooks Road and they drove past the Marsten House – its shutters still sagging, its lawn a complex maze of knee-high witch grass and goldenrod.

Mark pointed, and Ben looked. A path had been beaten across the grass, beaten white. It cut across the lawn from the road to the porch. Then it was behind them, and he felt a loosening in his chest. The worst had been faced and was behind them.

Far out on the Burns Road, not too far distant from the Harmony Hill graveyard, Ben stopped the car and they got out. They walked into the woods together. The undergrowth snapped harshly, dryly, under their feet. There was a gin-sharp smell of juniper berries and the sound of late locusts. They came out on a small, knoll-like prominence of land that looked down on a slash through the woods where the Central Maine Power lines twinkled in the day's cool windiness. Some of the trees were beginning to show color.

'The old-timers say this is where it started,' Ben said. 'Back in 1951. The wind was blowing from the west. They think maybe a guy got careless with a cigarette. One little cigarette. It took off across the Marshes and no one could stop it.'

He took a package of Pall Malls from his pocket, looked at the emblem thoughtfully – *in hoc signo vinces* – and then tore the cellophane top off. He lit one and shook out the match. The cigarette tasted surprisingly good, although he had not smoked in months.

'They have their places,' he said. 'But they could lose

them. A lot of them could be killed . . . or destroyed. That's a better word. But not all of them. Do you understand?'

'Yes,' Mark said.

'They're not very bright. If they lose their hiding places, they'll hide badly the second time. A couple of people just looking in obvious places could do well. Maybe it could be finished in 'salem's Lot by the time the first snow flew. Maybe it would never be finished. No guarantee, one way or the other. But without . . . something . . . to drive them out, to upset them, there would be no chance at all.'

'Yes.'

'It would be ugly and dangerous.'

'I know that.'

'But they say fire purifies,' Ben said reflectively. 'Purification should count for something, don't you think?'

'Yes,' Mark said again.

Ben stood up. 'We ought to go back.'

He flicked the smoldering cigarette into a pile of dead brush and old brittle leaves. The white ribbon of smoke rose thinly against the green background of junipers for two or three feet, and then was pulled apart by the wind. Twenty feet away, downwind, was a large, jumbled deadfall.

They watched the smoke, transfixed, fascinated.

It thickened. A tongue of flame appeared. A small popping noise issued from the pile of dead brush as twigs caught.

'Tonight they won't be running sheep or visiting farms,' Ben said softly. 'Tonight they'll be on the run. And tomorrow—'

'You and me,' Mark said, and closed his fist. His face

was no longer pale; bright color glowed there. His eyes flashed.

They went back to the road and drove away.

In the small clearing overlooking the power lines, the fire in the brush began to burn more strongly, urged by the autumn wind that blew from the west.

October 1972
June 1975

ONE FOR THE ROAD

It was quarter past ten and Herb Tooklander was thinking of closing for the night when the man in the fancy over-coat and the white, staring face burst into Tookey's Bar, which lies in the northern part of Falmouth. It was the tenth of January, just about the time most folks are learning to live comfortably with all the New Year's resolutions they broke, and there was one hell of a northeaster blowing outside. Six inches had come down before dark and it had been going hard and heavy since then. Twice we had seen Billy Larribee go by high in the cab of the town plow, and the second time Tookey ran him out a beer – an act of pure charity my mother would have called it, and my God knows she put down enough of Tookey's beer in her time. Billy told him they were keeping ahead of it on the main road, but the side ones were closed and apt to stay that way until next morning. The radio in Portland was forecasting another foot and a forty-mile-an-hour wind to pile up the drifts.

There was just Tookey and me in the bar, listening to the wind howl around the eaves and watching it dance the fire around on the hearth. 'Have one for the road, Booth,' Tookey says, 'I'm gonna shut her down.'

He poured me one and himself one and that's when the door cracked open and this stranger staggered in, snow up to his shoulders and in his hair, like he had rolled around in confectioner's sugar. The wind billowed a sand-fine sheet of snow in after him.

'Close the door!' Tookey roars at him. 'Was you born in a barn?'

I've never seen a man who looked that scared. He was like a horse that's spent an afternoon eating fire nettles. His eyes rolled toward Tookey and he said, 'My wife – my daughter—' and he collapsed on the floor in a dead faint.

'Holy Joe,' Tookey says. 'Close the door, Booth, would you?'

I went and shut it, and pushing it against the wind was something of a chore. Tookey was down on one knee holding the fellow's head up and patting his cheeks. I got over to him and saw right off that it was nasty. His face was fiery red, but there were gray blotches here and there, and when you've lived through winters in Maine since the time Woodrow Wilson was President, as I have, you know those gray blotches mean frosbite.

'Fainted,' Tookey said. 'Get the brandy off the back bar, will you?'

I got it and came back. Tookey had opened the fellow's coat. He had come around a little, his eyes were half open and he was muttering something too low to catch.

'Pour a capful,' Tookey says.

'Just a cap?' I ask him.

'That stuff's dynamite,' Tookey says. 'No sense over-loading his carb.'

I poured out a capful and looked at Tookey. He nodded. 'Straight down the hatch.'

I poured it down. It was a remarkable thing to watch. The man trembled all over and began to cough. His face got redder. His eyelids, which had been at half-mast, flew up like window shades. I was a bit alarmed, but Tookey only sat him up like a big baby and clapped him on the back.

The man started to retch, and Tookey clapped him again.

'Hold on to it,' he says, 'that brandy comes dear.'

The man coughed some more, but it was diminishing now. I got my first good look at him. City fellow, all right, and from somewhere south of Boston, at a guess. He was wearing kid gloves, expensive but thin. There were probably some more of those grayish-white patches on his hands, and he would be lucky not to lose a finger or two. His coat was fancy, all right; a three-hundred-dollar job if ever I'd seen one. He was wearing tiny little boots that hardly came up over his ankles, and I began to wonder about his toes.

'Better,' he said.

'All right,' Tookey said. 'Can you come over to the fire?'

'My wife and my daughter,' he said. 'They're out there . . . in the storm.'

'From the way you came in, I didn't figure they were at home watching the TV,' Tookey said. 'You can tell us by the fire as easy as here on the floor. Hook on, Booth.'

He got to his feet, but a little groan came out of him and his mouth twisted down in pain. I wondered about his toes again, and I wondered why God felt he had to make fools from New York City who would try driving around in southern Maine at the height of a northeast blizzard. And I wondered if his wife and his little girl were dressed any warmer than him.

We hiked him across to the fireplace and got him sat down in a rocker that used to be Missus Tookey's favorite until she passed on in '74. It was Missus Tookey that was responsible for most of the place, which had been written up in *Down East* and the *Sunday Telegram* and even once in the Sunday supplement of the Boston *Globe*. It's really more of a public house than a bar, with its big wooden floor, pegged together rather than nailed, the maple bar, the old barn-raftered ceiling, and the monstrous big field-stone hearth. Missus Tookey started to get some ideas in her head after the *Down East* article came out, wanted to start calling the place Tookey's Inn or Tookey's Rest, and I admit it has sort of a Colonial ring to it, but I prefer plain old Tookey's Bar. It's one thing to get uppish in the summer, when the state's full of tourists, another thing altogether in the winter, when you and your neighbors have to trade together. And there had been plenty of winter nights, like this one, that Tookey and I had spent all alone together, drinking scotch and water or just a few beers. My own Victoria passed on in '73, and Tookey's was a place to go where there were enough voices to mute the steady ticking of the deathwatch beetle – even if there was just Tookey and me, it was enough. I wouldn't have felt the same about it if the place had been Tookey's Rest. It's crazy but it's true.

We got this fellow in front of the fire and he got the shakes harder than ever. He hugged onto his knees and his teeth clattered together and a few drops of clear mucus spilled off the end of his nose. I think he was starting to realize that another fifteen minutes out there might have been enough to kill him. It's not the snow, it's the wind-chill factor. It steals your heat.

'Where did you go off the road?' Tookey asked him.

'S-six miles s-s-south of h-here,' he said.

Tookey and I stared at each other, and all of a sudden I felt cold. Cold all over.

'You sure?' Tookey demanded. 'You came six miles through the snow?'

He nodded. 'I checked the odometer when we came through t-town. I was following directions . . . going to see my wife's s-sister . . . in Cumberland . . . never been there before . . . we're from New Jersey . . .'

New Jersey. If there's anyone more purely foolish than a New Yorker, it's a fellow from New Jersey.

'Six miles, you're sure?' Tookey demanded.

'Pretty sure, yeah. I found the turnoff but it was drifted in . . . it was . . .'

Tookey grabbed him. In the shifting glow of the fire his face looked pale and strained, older than his sixty-six years by ten. 'You made a right turn?'

'Right turn, yeah. My wife—'

'Did you see a sign?'

'Sign?' He looked up at Tookey blankly and wiped the end of his nose. 'Of course I did. It was on my instruc-tions. Take Jointner Avenue through Jerusalem's Lot to the 295 entrance ramp.' He looked from Tookey to me and back to Tookey again. Outside, the wind whistled and howled and moaned through the caves. 'Wasn't that right, mister?'

'The Lot,' Tookey said, almost too soft to hear. 'Oh my God.'

'What's wrong?' the man said. His voice was rising. 'Wasn't that right? I mean, the road looked drifted in, but I thought . . . if there's a town there, the plows will be out and . . . and then I . . .'

He just sort of tailed off.

'Booth,' Tookey said to me, low. 'Get on the phone. Call the sheriff.'

'Sure,' this fool from New Jersey says, 'that's right. What's wrong with you guys, anyway? You look like you saw a ghost.'

Tookey said, 'No ghosts in the Lot, mister. Did you tell them to stay in the car?'

'Sure I did,' he said, sounding injured. 'I'm not crazy.'

Well, you couldn't have proved it by me.

'What's your name?' I asked him. 'For the sheriff.'

'Lumley,' he says. 'Gerard Lumley.'

He started in with Tookey again, and I went across to the telephone. I picked it up and heard nothing but dead silence. I hit the cutoff buttons a couple of times. Still nothing.

I came back. Tookey had poured Gerard Lumley another tot of brandy, and this one was going down him a lot smoother.

'Was he out?' Tookey asked.

'Phone's dead.'

'Hot damn,' Tookey says, and we look at each other. Outside the wind gusted up, throwing snow against the windows.

Lumley looked from Tookey to me and back again.

'Well, haven't either of you got a car?' he asked. The anxiety was back in his voice. 'They've got to run the engine to run the heater. I only had about a quarter of a tank of gas, and it took me an hour and a half to . . . Look, will you *answer* me?' He stood up and grabbed Tookey's shirt.

'Mister,' Tookey says, 'I think your hand just ran away from your brains, there.'

Lumley looked at his hand, at Tookey, then dropped it. 'Maine,' he hissed. He made it sound like a dirty word about somebody's mother. 'All right,' he said. 'Where's the nearest gas station? They must have a tow truck—'

'Nearest gas station is in Falmouth Center,' I said. 'That's three miles down the road from here.'

'Thanks,' he said, a bit sarcastic, and headed for the door, buttoning his coat.

'Won't be open, though,' I added.

He turned back slowly and looked at us.

'What are you talking about, old man?'

'He's trying to tell you that the station in the Center belongs to Billy Larribee and Billy's out driving the plow, you damn fool,' Tookey says patiently. 'Now why don't you come back here and sit down, before you bust a gut?'

He came back, looking dazed and frightened. 'Are you telling me you can't . . . that there isn't . . . ?'

'I ain't telling you nothing,' Tookey says. 'You're doing all the telling, and if you stopped for a minute, we could think this over.'

'What's this town, Jerusalem's Lot?' he asked. 'Why was the road drifted in? And no lights on anywhere?'

I said, 'Jerusalem's Lot burned out three years back.'

'And they never rebuilt?' He looked like he didn't believe it.

'It appears that way,' I said, and looked at Tookey. 'What are we going to do about this?'

'Can't leave them out there,' he said.

I got closer to him. Lumley had wandered away to look out the window into the snowy night.

'What if they've been got at?' I asked.

'That may be,' he said. 'But we don't know it for sure. I've got my Bible on the shelf. You still wear your Pope's medal?'

I pulled the crucifix out of my shirt and showed him. I was born and raised Congregational, but most folks who live around the Lot wear something – crucifix, St Christopher's medal, rosary, something. Because two years ago, in the span of one dark October month, the Lot went bad. Sometimes, late at night, when there were just a few regulars drawn up around Tookey's fire, people would talk it over. Talk around it is more like the truth. You see, people in the Lot started to disappear. First a few, then a few more, then a whole slew. The schools closed. The town stood empty for most of a year. Oh, a few people moved in – mostly damn fools from out of state like this fine specimen here – drawn by the low property values, I suppose. But they didn't last. A lot of them moved out a month or two after they'd moved in. The others . . . well, they disappeared. Then the town burned flat. It was at the end of a long dry fall. They figure it started up by the Marsten House on the hill that overlooked Jointner Avenue, but no one knows how it started, not to this day. It burned out of control for three days. After that, for a time, things were better. And then they started again.

I only heard the word 'vampires' mentioned once. A crazy pulp truck driver named Richie Messina from over Freeport way was in Tookey's that night, pretty well liquored up. 'Jesus Christ,' this stampeder roars, standing up about nine feet tall in his wool pants and his plaid shirt and his leather-topped boots. 'Are you all so damn afraid to say it out? Vampires! That's what you're all thinking, ain't it? Jesus-jumped-up-Christ in a chariot-driven sidecar! Just like a bunch of kids scared of the movies! You know what there is down there in 'salem's Lot? Want me to tell you? Want me to tell you?'

'Do tell, Richie,' Tookey says. It had got real quiet in the bar. You could hear the fire popping, and outside the soft drift of November rain coming down in the dark. 'You got the floor.'

'What you got over there is your basic wild dog pack,' Richie Messina tells us. 'That's what you got. That and a lot of old women who love a good spook story. Why, for eighty bucks I'd go up there and spend the night in what's left of that haunted house you're all so worried about. Well, what about it? Anyone want to put it up?'

But nobody would. Richie was a loudmouth and a mean drunk and no one was going to shed any tears at his wake, but none of us were willing to see him go into 'salem's Lot after dark.

'Be screwed to the bunch of you,' Richie says. 'I got my four-ten in the trunk of my Chevy, and that'll stop anything in Falmouth, Cumberland, *or* Jerusalem's Lot. And that's where I'm goin'.'

He slammed out of the bar and no one said a word for a while. Then Lamont Henry says, real quiet, 'That's the last time anyone's gonna see Richie Messina. Holy God.' And Lamont, raised to be a Methodist from his mother's knee, crossed himself.

'He'll sober off and change his mind,' Tookey said, but he sounded uneasy. 'He'll be back by closin' time, makin' out it was all a joke.'

But Lamont had the right of that one, because no one ever saw Richie again. His wife told the state cops she thought he'd gone to Florida to beat a collection agency, but you could see the truth of the thing in her eyes — sick, scared eyes. Not long after, she moved away to Rhode Island. Maybe she thought Richie was going to come after her some dark night. And I'm not the man to say he might not have done.

Now Tookey was looking at me and I was looking at Tookey as I stuffed my crucifix back into my shirt. I never felt so old or so scared in my life.

Tookey said again, 'We can't just leave them out there, Booth.'

'Yeah. I know.'

We looked at each other for a moment longer, and then he reached out and gripped my shoulder. 'You're a good man, Booth.' That was enough to buck me up some. It seems like when you pass seventy, people start forgetting that you are a man, or that you ever were.

Tookey walked over to Lumley and said, 'I've got a four-wheel-drive Scout. I'll get it out.'

'For God's sake, man, why didn't you say so before?' He had whirled around from the window and was staring angrily at Tookey. 'Why'd you have to spend ten minutes beating around the bush?'

Tookey said, very softly, 'Mister, you shut your jaw. And if you get urge to open it, you remember who made that turn onto an unplowed road in the middle of a goddamned blizzard.'

He started to say something, and then shut his mouth. Thick color had risen up in his cheeks. Tookey went out to get his Scout out of the garage. I felt around under the bar for his chrome flask and filled it full of brandy. Figured we might need it before this night was over.

Maine blizzard – ever been out in one?

The snow comes flying so thick and fine that it looks like sand and sounds like that, beating on the sides of your car or pickup. You don't want to use your high beams because they reflect off the snow and you can't see ten feet in front of you. With the low beams on, you can see maybe fifteen feet. But I can live with the snow. It's the wind I don't like, when it picks up and begins to howl, driving the snow into a hundred weird flying shapes and sounding like all the hate and pain and fear in the world. There's death in the throat of a snowstorm wind, white death – and maybe something beyond death. That's no sound to hear when you're tucked up all cozy in your own bed with the shutters bolted and the doors locked. It's that much worse if you're driving. And we were driving smack into 'salem's Lot.

'Hurry up a little, can't you?' Lumley asked.

I said, 'For a man who came in half frozen, you're in one hell of a hurry to end up walking again.'

He gave me a resentful, baffled look and didn't say

anything else. We were moving up the highway at a steady twenty-five miles an hour. It was hard to believe that Billy Larribee had just plowed this stretch an hour ago; another two inches had covered it, and it was drifting in. The strongest gusts of wind rocked the Scout on her springs. The headlights showed a swirling white nothing up ahead of us. We hadn't met a single car.

About ten minutes later Lumley gasps: 'Hey! What's that?'

He was pointing out my side of the car; I'd been looking dead ahead. I turned, but was a shade too late. I thought I could see some sort of slumped form fading back from the car, back into the snow, but that could have been imagination.

'What was it? A deer?' I asked.

'I guess so,' he says, sounding shaky. 'But its eyes — they looked red.' He looked at me. 'Is that how a deer's eyes look at night?' He sounded almost as if he were pleading.

'They can look like anything,' I say, thinking that might be true, but I've seen a lot of deer at night from a lot of cars, and never saw any set of eyes reflect back red.

Tookey didn't say anything.

About fifteen minutes later, we came to a place where the snowbank on the right of the road wasn't so high because the plows are supposed to raise their blades a little when they go through an intersection.

'This looks like where we turned,' Lumley said, not sounding too sure about it. 'I don't see the sign—'

'This is it,' Tookey answered. He didn't sound like himself at all. 'You can just see the top of the signpost.'

'Oh. Sure.' Lumley sounded relieved. 'Listen, Mr

Tooklander, I'm sorry about being so short back there. I was cold and worried and calling myself two hundred kinds of fool. And I want to thank you both—'

'Don't thank Booth and me until we've got them in this car,' Tookey said. He put the Scout in four-wheel drive and slammed his way through the snowbank and onto Jointner Avenue, which goes through the Lot and out to 295. Snow flew up from the mudguards. The rear end tried to break a little bit, but Tookey's been driving through snow since Hector was a pup. He jockeyed it a bit, talked to it, and on we went. The headlights picked out the bare indication of other tire tracks from time to time, the ones made by Lumley's car, and then they would disappear again. Lumley was leaning forward, looking for his car. And all at once Tookey said, 'Mr Lumley.'

'What?' He looked around at Tookey.

'People around these parts are kind of superstitious about 'salem's Lot,' Tookey says, sounding easy enough – but I could see the deep lines of strain around his mouth, and the way his eyes kept moving from side to side. 'If your people are in the car, why, that's fine. We'll pack them up, go back to my place, and tomorrow, when the storm's over, Billy will be glad to yank your car out of the snowbank. But if they're not in the car—'

'Not in the car?' Lumley broke in sharply. 'Why wouldn't they be in the car?'

'If they're not in the car,' Tookey goes on, not answering, 'we're going to turn around and drive back to Falmouth Center and whistle for the sheriff. Makes no sense to go wallowing around at night in a snowstorm anyway, does it?'

'They'll be in the car. Where else would they be?'

I said, 'One other thing, Mr Lumley. If we should see anybody, we're not going to talk to them. Not even if they talk to us. You understand that?'

Very slow, Lumley says, 'Just what are these superstitions?'

Before I could say anything – God alone knows what I would have said – Tookey broke in. 'We're there.'

We were coming up on the back end of a big Mercedes. The whole hood of the thing was buried in a snowdrift, and another drift had socked in the whole left side of the car. But the taillights were on and we could see exhaust drifting out of the tailpipe.

'They didn't run out of gas, anyway,' Lumley said.

Tookey pulled up and pulled on the Scout's emergency brake. 'You remember what Booth told you, Lumley.'

'Sure, sure.' But he wasn't thinking of anything but his wife and daughter. I don't see how anybody could blame him, either.

'Ready, Booth?' Tookey asked me. His eyes held on mine, grim and gray in the dashboard lights.

'I guess I am,' I said.

We all got out and the wind grabbed us, throwing snow in our faces. Lumley was first, bending into the wind, his fancy topcoat billowing out behind him like a sail. He cast two shadows, one from Tookey's headlights, the other from his own taillights. I was behind him, and Tookey was a step behind me. When I got to the trunk of the Mercedes, Tookey grabbed me.

'Let him go,' he said.

'Janey! Francie!' Lumley yelled. 'Everything okay?' He

pulled open the driver's-side door and leaned in. 'Everything—'

He froze to a dead stop. The wind ripped the heavy door right out of his hand and pushed it all the way open.

'Holy God, Booth,' Tookey said, just below the scream of the wind. 'I think it's happened again.'

Lumley turned back toward us. His face was scared and bewildered, his eyes wide. All of a sudden he lunged toward us through the snow, slipping and almost falling. He brushed me away like I was nothing and grabbed Tookey.

'How did you know?' he roared. 'Where are they? What the hell is going on here?'

Tookey broke his grip and shoved past him. He and I looked into the Mercedes together. Warm as toast it was, but it wasn't going to be for much longer. The little amber low-fuel light was glowing. The big car was empty. There was a child's Barbie doll on the passenger's floormat. And a child's ski parka was crumpled over the seatback.

Tookey put his hands over his face . . . and then he was gone. Lumley had grabbed him and shoved him right back into the snowbank. His face was pale and wild. His mouth was working as if he had chewed down on some bitter stuff he couldn't yet unpucker enough to spit out. He reached in and grabbed the parka.

'Francie's coat?' he kind of whispered. And then loud, bellowing: '*Francie's coat!*' He turned around, holding it in front of him by the little fur-trimmed hood. He looked at me, blank and unbelieving. 'She can't be out without her coat on, Mr Booth. Why . . . why . . . she'll freeze to death.'

'Mr Lumley—'

He blundered past me, still holding the parka, shouting: '*Francie! Janey! Where are you? Where are youuu?*'

I gave Tookey my hand and pulled him onto his feet. 'Are you all—'

'Never mind me,' he says. 'We've got to get hold of him, Booth.'

We went after him as fast as we could, which wasn't very fast with the snow hip-deep in some places. But then he stopped and we caught up to him.

'Mr Lumley—' Tookey started, laying a hand on his shoulder.

'This way,' Lumley said. 'This is the way they went. Look!'

We looked down. We were in a kind of dip here, and most of the wind went right over our heads. And you could see two sets of tracks, one large and one small, just filling up with snow. If we had been five minutes later, they would have been gone.

He started to walk away, his head down, and Tookey grabbed him back. 'No! No, Lumley!'

Lumley turned his wild face up to Tookey's and made a fist. He drew it back . . . but something in Tookey's face made him falter. He looked from Tookey to me and then back again.

'She'll freeze,' he said, as if we were a couple of stupid kids. 'Don't you get it? She doesn't have her jacket on and she's only seven years old—'

'They could be anywhere,' Tookey said. 'You can't follow those tracks. They'll be gone in the next drift.'

'What do you suggest?' Lumley yells, his voice high

and hysterical. 'If we go back to get the police, she'll freeze to death! Francie *and* my wife!'

'They may be frozen already,' Tookey said. His eyes caught Lumley's. 'Frozen, or something worse.'

'What do you mean?' Lumley whispered. 'Get it straight, goddamn it! Tell me!'

'Mr Lumley,' Tookey says, 'there's something in the Lot—'

But I was the one who came out with it finally, said the word I never expected to say. 'Vampires, Mr Lumley. Jerusalem's Lot is full of vampires. I expect that's hard for you to swallow—'

He was staring at me as if I'd gone green. 'Loonies,' he whispers. 'You're a couple of loonies.' Then he turned away, cupped his hands around his mouth, and bellowed, *'FRANCIE! JANEY!'* He started floundering off again. The snow was up to the hem of his fancy coat.

I looked at Tookey. 'What do we do now?'

'Follow him,' Tookey says. His hair was plastered with snow, and he did look a little bit loony. 'I can't just leave him out here, Booth. Can you?'

'No,' I say. 'Guess not.'

So we started to wade through the snow after Lumley as best we could. But he kept getting further and further ahead. He had his youth to spend, you see. He was breaking the trail, going through that snow like a bull. My arthritis began to bother me something terrible, and I started to look down at my legs, telling myself: A little further, just a little further, keep goin', damn it, keep goin' . . .

I piled right into Tookey, who was standing spread-legged in a drift. His head was hanging and both of his hands were pressed to his chest.

'Tookey,' I say, 'you okay?'

'I'm all right,' he said, taking his hands away. 'We'll stick with him, Booth, and when he fags out he'll see reason.'

We topped a rise and there was Lumley at the bottom, looking desperately for more tracks. Poor man, there wasn't a chance he was going to find them. The wind blew straight across down there where he was, and any tracks would have been rubbed out three minutes after they was made, let alone a couple of hours.

He raised his head and screamed into the night: *'FRANCIE! JANEY! FOR GOD'S SAKE!'* And you could hear the desperation in his voice, the terror, and pity him for it. The only answer he got was the freight-train wail of the wind. It almost seemed to be laughin' at him, saying: I took them Mister New Jersey with your fancy car and camel's-hair topcoat. *I took them and I rubbed out their tracks and by morning I'll have them just as neat and frozen as two strawberries in a deepfreeze . . .*

'Lumley!' Tookey bawled over the wind. 'Listen, you never mind vampires or boogies or nothing like that, but you mind this! You're just making it worse for them! We got to get the—'

And then there *was* an answer, a voice coming out of the dark like little tinkling silver bells, and my heart turned cold as ice in a cistern.

'Jerry . . . Jerry, is that you?'

Lumley wheeled at the sound. And then *she* came, drifting out of the dark shadows of a little copse of trees like a ghost. She was a city woman, all right, and right then she seemed like the most beautiful woman I had ever seen. I felt like I wanted to go to her and tell her how glad I was she was safe after all. She was wearing a heavy green pullover sort of thing, a poncho, I believe they're called. It floated all around her, and her dark hair streamed out in the wild wind like water in a December creek, just before the winter freeze stills it and locks it in.

Maybe I did take a step toward her, because I felt Tookey's hand on my shoulder, rough and warm. And still – how can I say it? – I *yearned* after her, so dark and beautiful with that green poncho floating around her neck and shoulders, as exotic and strange as to make you think of some beautiful woman from a Walter de la Mare poem.

'Janey!' Lumley cried. *'Janey!'* He began to struggle through the snow toward her, his arms outstretched.

'No!' Tookey cried. '*No, Lumley!*'

He never even looked . . . but she did. She looked up at us and grinned. And when she did, I felt my longing, my yearning turn to horror as cold as the grave, as white and silent as bones in a shroud. Even from the rise we could see the sullen red glare in those eyes. They were less human than a wolf's eyes. And when she grinned you could see how long her teeth had become. She wasn't human anymore. She was a dead thing somehow come back to life in this black howling storm.

Tookey made the sign of the cross at her. She flinched back . . . and then grinned at us again. We were too far away, and maybe too scared.

'Stop it!' I whispered. 'Can't we stop it?'

'Too late, Booth!' Tookey says grimly.

Lumley had reached her. He looked like a ghost himself, coated in snow like he was. He reached for her . . . and then he began to scream. I'll hear that sound in my dreams, that man screaming like a child in a nightmare. He tried to back away from her, but her arms, long and bare and as white as the snow, snaked out and pulled him to her. I could see her cock her head and then thrust it forward—

'Booth!' Tookey said hoarsely. 'We're got to get out of here!'

And so we ran. Ran like rats, I suppose some would say, but those who would weren't there that night. We fled back down along our own trail, falling down, getting up again, slipping and sliding. I kept looking back over my shoulder to see if that woman was coming after us, grinning that grin and watching us with those red eyes.

We got back to the Scout and Tookey doubled over, holding his chest. 'Tookey!' I said, badly scared. 'What—'

'Ticker,' he said. 'Been bad for five years or more. Get me around in the shotgun seat, Booth, and then get us the hell out of here.'

I hooked an arm under his coat and dragged him around and somehow boosted him up and in. He leaned his head back and shut his eyes. His skin was waxy-looking and yellow.

I went back around the hood of the truck at a trot, and I damned near ran into the little girl. She was just standing there beside the driver's side door, her hair in pigtails, wearing nothing but a little bit of a yellow dress.

'Mister,' she said in a high, clear voice, as sweet as

morning mist, 'won't you help me find my mother? She's gone and I'm so cold—'

'Honey,' I said, 'honey, you better get in the truck. Your mother's—'

I broke off, and if there was ever a time in my life I was close to swooning, that was the moment. She was standing there, you see, but she was standing *on top* of the snow and there were no tracks, not in any direction.

She looked up at me then, Lumley's daughter, Francie. She was no more than seven years old, and she was going to be seven for an eternity of nights. Her little face was a ghastly corpse white, her eyes a red and silver that you could fall into. And below her jaw I could see two small punctures like pinpricks, their edges horribly mangled.

She held out her arms at me and smiled. 'Pick me up, mister,' she said softly. 'I want to give you a kiss. Then you can take me to my mommy.'

I didn't want to, but there was nothing I could do. I was leaning forward, my arms outstretched. I could see her mouth opening, I could see the little fangs inside the pink ring of her lips. Something slipped down her chin, bright and silvery, and with a dim, distant, faraway horror, I realized she was drooling.

Her small hands clasped themselves around my neck and I was thinking: Well, maybe it won't be so bad, not so bad, maybe it won't be so awful after a while – when something black flew out of the Scout and struck her on the chest. There was a puff of strange-smelling smoke, a flashing glow that was gone an instant later, and then she was backing away, hissing. Her face was twisted into a vulpine mask of rage, hate, and pain. She turned sideways and then . . . and then she was gone. One moment she was there, and the next there was a twisting knot of snow that looked a little bit like a human shape. Then the wind tattered it away across the fields.

'Booth!' Tookey whispered. 'Be quick, now!'

And I was. But not so quick that I didn't have time to pick up what he had thrown at that little girl from hell. His mother's Douay Bible. That was some time ago. I'm a sight older now, and I was no chicken then. Herb Tooklander passed on two years ago. He went peaceful, in the night. The bar is still there, some man and his wife from Waterville bought it, nice people, and they've kept it pretty much the same. But I don't go by much. It's different somehow with Tookey gone.

Things in the Lot go on pretty much as they always have. The sheriff found that fellow Lumley's car the next day, out of gas, the battery dead. Neither Tookey nor I said anything about it. What would have been the point? And every now and then a hitchhiker or a camper will disappear around there someplace, up on Schoolyard Hill or out near the Harmony Hill cemetery. They'll turn up the fellow's packsack or a paperback book all swollen and bleached out by the rain or snow, or some such. But never the people.

I still have bad dreams about that stormy night we went out there. Not about the woman so much as the little girl, and the way she smiled when she held her arms up so I could pick her up. So she could give me a kiss. But I'm an old man and the time comes soon when dreams are done.

You may have an occasion to be traveling in southern Maine yourself one of these days. Pretty part of the countryside. You may even stop by Tookey's Bar for a drink. Nice place. They kept the name just the same. So have your drink, and then my advice to you is to keep right on moving north. Whatever you do, don't go up that road to Jerusalem's Lot.

Especially not after dark.

There's a little girl somewhere out there. And I think she's still waiting for her good-night kiss.

JERUSALEM'S LOT

Oct. 2, 1850.

DEAR BONES,

How good it was to step into the cold, draughty hall here at Chapelwaite, every bone in an ache from that abominable coach, in need of instant relief from my distended bladder – and to see a letter addressed in your own inimitable scrawl propped on the obscene little cherry-wood table beside the door! Be assured that I set to deciphering it as soon as the needs of the body were attended to (in a coldly ornate downstairs bathroom where I could see my breath rising before my eyes).

I'm glad to hear that you are recovered from the *miasma* that has so long set in your lungs, although I assure you that I do sympathize with the moral dilemma the cure has affected you with. An ailing abolitionist healed by the sunny climes of slave-struck Florida! Still and all, Bones, I ask you as a friend who has also walked in the valley of the shadow, *to take all care of yourself* and venture not back to Massachusetts until your body gives you leave. Your fine mind and incisive pen cannot serve us if you are clay, and if the Southern zone is a healing one, is there not poetic justice in that?

Yes, the house is quite as fine as I had been led to believe by my cousin's executors, but rather more sinister. It sits atop a huge and jutting point of land perhaps three miles north of Falmouth and nine miles north of Portland. Behind it are some four acres of grounds, gone back to the wild in the most formidable manner imaginable — junipers, scrub vines, bushes, and various forms of creeper climb wildly over the picturesque stone walls that separate the estate from the town domain. Awful imitations of Greek statuary peer blindly through the wrack from atop various hillocks — they seem, in most cases, about to lunge at the passer-by. My Cousin Stephen's tastes seem to have run the gamut from the unacceptable to the downright horrific. There is an odd little summer-house which has been nearly buried in scarlet sumac and a grotesque sundial in the midst of what must once have been a garden. It adds the final lunatic touch.

But the view from the parlour more than excuses this; I command a dizzying view of the rocks at the foot of Chapelwaite Head and the Atlantic itself. A huge, bellied bay-window looks out on this, and a huge, toad-like secretary stands beside it. It will do nicely for the start of that novel which I have talked of so long [and no doubt tiresomely].

To-day has been gray with occasional splatters of rain. As I look out all seems to be a study in slate —

the rocks, old and worn as Time itself, the sky, and of course the sea, which crashes against the granite fangs below with a sound which is not precisely sound but vibration — I can feel the waves with my feet even as I write. The sensation is not a wholly unpleasant one.

I know you disapprove my solitary habits, dear Bones, but I assure you that I am fine and happy. Calvin is with me, as practical, silent, and as dependable as ever, and by midweek I am sure that between the two of us we shall have straightened our affairs and made arrangement for necessary deliveries from town — and a company of cleaning women to begin blowing the dust from this place!

I will close — there are so many things as yet to be seen, rooms to explore, and doubtless a thousand pieces of execrable furniture to be viewed by these tender eyes. Once again, my thanks for the touch of familiar brought by your letter, and for your continuing regard.

Give my love to your wife, as you both have mine.

CHARLES.

Oct. 6, 1850.

DEAR BONES,

Such a place this is!

It continues to amaze me — as do the reactions of the townfolk in the closest village to my occupancy. That is a queer little place with the picturesque name of Preacher's Corners. It was there that Calvin contracted for the weekly provisions. The other errand, that of securing a sufficient supply of cord-wood for the winter, was likewise taken care of. But Cal returned with gloomy countenance, and when I asked him what the trouble was, he replied grimly enough:

'They think you mad, Mr Boone!'

I laughed and said that perhaps they had heard of the brain fever I suffered after my Sarah died — certainly I spoke madly enough at that time, as you could attest.

But Cal protested that no-one knew anything of me except through my Cousin Stephen, who contracted for the same services as I have now made provision for. 'What was said, sir, was that anyone who would live in Chapelwaite must be either a lunatic or run the risk of becoming one.'

This left me utterly perplexed, as you may imagine, and I asked who had given him this amazing communication. He told me that he had been referred to a sullen and rather besotted pulp-logger named Thompson, who owns four hundred acres of pine, birch, and spruce, and who logs it with the help of his five sons, for sale to the mills in Portland and to house-holders in the immediate area.

When Cal, all unknowing of his queer prejudice, gave him the location to which the wood was to be brought, this Thompson stared at him with his mouth ajaw and said that he would send his sons with the wood, in the good light of the day, and by the sea road.

Calvin, apparently misreading my bemusement for

distress, hastened to say that the man reeked of cheap whiskey and that he had then lapsed into some kind of nonsense about a deserted village and Cousin Stephen's relations – and worms! Calvin finished his business with one of Thompson's boys, who, I take it was rather surly and none too sober or freshly-scented himself. I take it, there has been some of this reaction in Preacher's Corners itself, at the general store where Cal spoke with the shop-keeper, although this was more of the gossipy, behind-the-hand type.

None of this has bothered me much; we know how rustics dearly love to enrich their lives with the smell of scandal and myth, and I suppose poor Stephen and his side of the family are fair game. As I told Cal, a man who has fallen to his death almost from his own front porch is more than likely to stir talk.

The house itself is a constant amazement. Twenty-three rooms Bones! The wainscotting which panels the upper floors and the portrait gallery is mildewed but still stout. While I stood in my late cousin's upstairs bedroom, I could hear the rats scuttering behind it, and big ones they must be, from the sound they make – almost like people walking there. I should hate to encounter one in the dark; or even in the light, for that matter. Still, I have noted neither holes nor droppings. Odd.

The upper gallery is lined with bad portraits in frames which must be worth a fortune. Some bear a resemblance to Stephen as I remember him. I believe I have correctly identified my Uncle Henry Boone and his wife, Judith; the others are unfamiliar. I suppose one of them may be my own notorious grandfather, Robert. But Stephen's side of the family is all but unknown to me, for which I am heartily sorry. The same good humour that shone in Stephen's letters to Sarah and me, the same light of high intellect shines in these portraits, bad as they are. For what foolish reasons families fall out! A rifled *escritoire*, hard words between brothers now dead three generations, and blameless descendants are needlessly estranged. I cannot help reflecting upon how fortunate it was that you and John Petty succeeded in contacting Stephen when it seemed I might follow my Sarah through the Gates – and upon how unfortunate it was that chance should have robbed us of a face-to-face meeting. How I would have loved to hear him defend the ancestral statuary and furnishings!

But do not let me denigrate the place to an extreme. Stephen's taste was not my own, true, but beneath the veneer of his additions there are pieces [a number of them shrouded by dust-covers in the upper chambers] which are true masterworks. There are beds, tables, and heavy, dark scrollings done in teak and mahogany, and many of the bedrooms and receiving chambers, the upper study and small parlour, hold a somber charm. The floors are rich pine that glow with an inner and secret light. There is dignity here; dignity and the weight of years. I cannot yet say I like it, but I do respect it. I am eager to watch it change as we revolve through the changes of this northern clime.

Lord, I run on! Write soon, Bones. Tell me what progress you make, and what news you hear from

Petty and the rest. And please do not make the mistake of trying to persuade any new Southern acquaintances as to your views *too forcibly* – I understand that not all are content to answer merely with their mouths, as is our long-winded *friend*, Mr Calhoun.

Yr. affectionate friend,

CHARLES.

Oct. 16, 1850.

DEAR RICHARD,

Hello, and how are you? I have thought about you often since I have taken up residence here at Chapelwaite, and had half-expected to hear from you – and now I receive a letter from Bones telling me that I'd forgotten to leave my address at the club! Rest assured that I would have written eventually anyway, as it sometimes seems that my true and loyal friends are all I have left in the world that is sure and completely normal. And, Lord, how spread we've become! You in Boston, writing faithfully for *The Liberator* [to which I have also sent my address, incidentally], Hanson in England on another of his confounded *jaunts*, and poor old Bones in the very *lions' lair*, recovering his lungs.

It goes as well as can be expected here, Dick, and be assured I will render you a full account when I am not quite as pressed by certain events which are extant here – I think your legal mind may be quite intrigued by certain happenings at Chapelwaite and in the area about it.

But in the meantime I have a favour to ask, if you will entertain it. Do you remember the historian you introduced me to at Mr Clary's fund-raising dinner for the cause? I believe his name was Bigelow. At any rate, he mentioned that he made a hobby of collecting odd bits of historical lore which pertained to the very area in which I am now living. My favour, then, is this: Would you contact him and ask him what facts, bits of folklore, or *general rumour* – if any – he may be conversant with about a small, deserted village called JERUSALEM'S LOT, near a township called Preacher's Corners, on the Royal River? The stream itself is a tributary of the Androscoggin, and flows into that river approximately eleven miles above that river's emptying place near Chapelwaite. It would gratify me intensely, and, more important, may be a matter of some moment.

In looking over this letter I feel I have been a bit short with you, Dick, for which I am heartily sorry. But be assured I will explain myself shortly, and until that time I send my warmest regards to your wife, two fine sons, and, of course, to yourself.

Yr. affectionate friend,

CHARLES.

Oct. 16, 1850.

DEAR BONES,

I have a tale to tell you which seems a little strange [and even disquieting] to both Cal and me – see what you think. If nothing else, it may serve to amuse you while you battle the mosquitoes!

Two days after I mailed my last to you, a group of four young ladies arrived from the Corners under the supervision of an elderly lady of intimidatingly-competent visage named Mrs Cloris, to set the place in order and to remove some of the dust that had been causing me to sneeze seemingly at every other step. They all seemed a little nervous as they went about their chores; indeed, one flighty miss uttered a small screech when I entered the upstairs parlour as she dusted.

I asked Mrs Cloris about this [she was dusting the downstairs hall with grim determination that would have quite amazed you, her hair done up in an old faded bandanna, and she turned to me and said with an air of determination: 'They don't like the house, and I don't like the house, sir, because it has always been a *bad* house.'

My jaw dropped at this unexpected bit, and she went on in a kindlier tone: 'I do not mean to say that Stephen Boone was not a fine man, for he was; I cleaned for him every second Thursday all the time he was here, as I cleaned for his father, Mr Randolph Boone, until he and his wife disappeared in eighteen and sixteen. Mr Stephen was a good and kindly man, and so you seem, sir (if you will pardon my bluntness; I know no other way to speak), but the house is *bad* and it always *has been*, and no Boone has ever been happy here since your grandfather Robert and his brother Philip fell out over stolen [and here she paused, almost guiltily] items in seventeen and eighty-nine.'

Such memories these folks have, Bones!

Mrs Cloris continued: 'The house was built in unhappiness, has been lived in with unhappiness, there has been blood spilt on its floors [as you may or may not know, Bones, my Uncle Randolph was involved in an accident on the cellar stairs which took the life of his daughter Marcella; he then took his own life in a fit of remorse. The incident is related in one of Stephen's letters to me, on the sad occasion of his dead sister's birthday], there has been disappearance and accident.

'I have worked here, Mr Boone, and I am neither blind nor deaf. I've heard awful sounds in the walls, sir, awful sounds — thumpings and crashings and once a strange wailing that was half laughter. It fair made my blood curdle. It's a dark place, sir.' And there she halted, perhaps afraid she had spoken too much.

As for myself, I hardly knew whether to be offended or amused, curious or merely matter-of-fact. I'm afraid that amusement won the day. 'And what do you suspect, Mrs Cloris? Ghosts rattling chains?'

But she only looked at me oddly. 'Ghosts there may be. But it's not ghosts in the walls. It's not ghosts that wail and blubber like the damned and crash and blunder away in the darkness. It's—'

'Come, Mrs Cloris,' I prompted her. 'You've come this far. Now can you finish what you've begun?'

The strangest expression of terror, pique, and — I would swear to it — religious awe passed over her face. 'Some die not,' she whispered. 'Some live in the twilight shadows between to serve Him!'

And that was the end. For some minutes I continued to tax her, but she grew only more obstinate and would say no more. At last I desisted, fearing she might gather herself up and quit the premises.

This is the end of one episode, but a second occurred the following evening. Calvin had laid a fire downstairs and I was sitting in the living-room, drowsing over a copy of *The Intelligencer* and listening to the sound of wind-driven rain on the large bay-window. I felt comfortable as only one can on such a night, when all is miserable outside and all is warmth and comfort inside; but a moment later Cal appeared at the door, looking excited and a bit nervous.

'Are you awake, sir?' he asked.

'Barely,' I said. 'What is it?'

'I've found something upstairs I think you should see,' he responded, with the same air of suppressed excitement.

I got up and followed him. As we climbed the wide stairs, Calvin said: 'I was reading a book in the upstairs study – a rather strange one – when I heard a noise in the wall.'

'Rats,' I said. 'Is that all?'

He paused on the landing, looking at me solemnly. The lamp he held cast weird, lurking shadows on the dark draperies and on the half-seen portraits that seemed now to leer rather than smile. Outside the wind rose to a brief scream and then subsided grudgingly.

'Not rats,' Cal said. 'There was a kind of blundering,

thudding sound from behind the book-cases, and then a horrible gurgling – horrible, sir. And scratching, as if something were struggling to get out . . . to get at me!'

You can imagine my amazement, Bones. Calvin is not the type to give way to hysterical flights of imagination. It began to seem that there was a mystery here after all – and perhaps an ugly one indeed.

'What then?' I asked him. We had resumed down the hall, and I could see the light from the study spilling forth onto the floor of the gallery. I viewed it with some trepidation; the night seemed no longer comfortable.

'The scratching noise stopped. After a moment the thudding, shuffling sounds began again, this time moving away from me. It paused once, and I swear I heard a strange, almost inaudible laugh! I went to the book-case and began to push and pull, thinking there might be a partition, or a secret door.'

'You found one?'

Cal paused at the door to the study. 'No – but I found this!'

We stepped in and I saw a square black hole in the left case. The books at that point were nothing but dummies, and what Cal had found was a small hiding place. I flashed my lamp within it and saw nothing but a thick fall of dust, dust which must have been decades old.

'There was only this,' Cal said quietly, and handed me a yellowed foolscap. The thing was a map, drawn in spider-thin strokes of black ink – the map of a town or village. There were perhaps seven buildings, and one, clearly marked with a steeple, bore this legend beneath it: *The Worm That Doth Corrupt*.

In the upper left corner, to what would have been the northwest of this little village, an arrow pointed. Inscribed beneath it: *Chapelwaite*.

Calvin said: 'In town, sir, someone rather superstitiously mentioned a deserted village called Jerusalem's Lot. It's a place they steer clear of.'

'But this?' I asked, fingering the odd legend below the steeple.

'I don't know.'

A memory of Mrs Cloris, adamant yet fearful, passed through my mind. 'The Worm . . .' I muttered.

'Do you know something, Mr Boone?'

'Perhaps . . . it might be amusing to have a look for this town tomorrow, do you think, Cal?'

He nodded, eyes lighting. We spent almost an hour after this looking for some breach in the wall behind the cubby-hole Cal had found, but with no success. Nor was there a recurrence of the noises Cal had described.

We retired with no further adventure that night.

On the following morning Calvin and I set out on our ramble through the woods. The rain of the night before had ceased, but the sky was somber and lowering. I could see Cal looking at me with some doubtfulness and I hastened to reassure him that should I tire, or the journey prove too far, I would not hesitate to call a halt to the affair. We had equipped ourselves with a picnic lunch, a fine Buckwhite compass, and, of course, the odd and ancient map of Jerusalem's Lot.

It was a strange and brooding day; not a bird seemed to sing nor an animal to move as we made our way through the great and gloomy stands of pine to the south and east. The only sounds were those of our own feet and the steady pound of the Atlantic against the headlands. The smell of the sea, almost preternaturally heavy, was our constant companion.

We had gone no more than two miles when we struck an overgrown road of what I believe were once called the 'corduroy' variety; this tended in our general direction and we struck off along it making brisk time. We spoke little. The day, with its still and ominous quality, weighed heavily on our spirits.

At about eleven o'clock we heard the sound of rushing water. The remnant of road took a hard turn to the left, and on the other side of a boiling, slaty little stream, like an apparition, was Jerusalem's Lot!

The stream was perhaps eight feet across, spanned by a moss-grown footbridge. On the far side, Bones, stood the most perfect little village you might imagine, understandably weathered, but amazingly preserved. Several houses, done in that austere yet commanding form for which the Puritans were justly famous, stood clustered near the steeply-sheared bank. Further beyond, along a weed-grown thoroughfare, stood three or four of what might have been primitive business establishments, and beyond that, the spire of the church marked on the map, rising up to the gray sky and looking grim beyond description with its peeled paint and tarnished, leaning cross.

'The town is well named,' Cal said softly beside me.

We crossed to the town and began to poke through it – and this is where my story grows slightly amazing, Bones, so prepare yourself!

The air seemed leaden as we walked among the buildings; weighted, if you will. The edifices were in a state of decay – shutters torn off, roofs crumbled under the weight of heavy snows gone by, windows dusty and leering. Shadows from odd corners and warped angles seemed to sit in sinister pools.

We entered an old and rotting tavern first – somehow it did not seem right that we should invade any of those houses to which people had retired when they wished privacy. An old and weather-scrubbed sign above the splintered door announced that this had been the BOAR'S HEAD INN AND TAVERN. The door creaked hellishly on its one remaining hinge, and we stepped into the shadowed interior. The smell of rot and mould was vaporous and nearly over-powering. And beneath it seemed to lie an even deeper smell, a slimy and pestiferous smell, a smell of ages and the decay of ages. Such a stench as might issue from corrupt coffins or violated tombs. I held my handkerchief to my nose and Cal did likewise. We surveyed the place.

'My God, sir—' Cal said faintly.

'It's never been touched,' I finished for him.

As indeed it had not. Tables and chairs stood about

like ghostly guardians of the watch, dusty, warped by the extreme changes in temperature which the New England climate is known for, but otherwise perfect – as if they had waited through the silent, echoing decades for those long gone to enter once more, to call for a pint or a dram, to deal cards and light clay-pipes. A small square mirror hung beside the rules of the tavern, *unbroken*. Do you see the significance, Bones? Small boys are noted for exploration and vandalism; there is not a 'haunted' house which stands with windows intact, no matter how fearsome the eldritch inhabitants are rumoured to be; not a shadowy graveyard without at least one tombstone upended by young pranksters. Certainly there must be a score of young pranksters in Preacher's Corners, not two miles from Jerusalem's Lot. Yet the inn-keeper's glass [which must have cost him a nice sum] was intact – as were the other fragile items we found in our pokings. The only damage in Jerusalem's Lot has been done by impersonal Nature. The implication is obvious: Jerusalem's Lot is a shunned town. But why? I have a notion, but before I even dare hint at it, I must proceed to the unsettling conclusion of our visit.

We went up to the sleeping quarters and found beds made up, pewter water-pitchers neatly placed beside them. The kitchen was likewise untouched by anything save the dust of the years and that horrible, sunken stench of decay. The tavern alone would be an antiquarian's paradise; the wondrously queer kitchen stove alone would fetch a pretty price at Boston auction.

'What do you think, Cal?' I asked when we had emerged again into the uncertain daylight.

'I think it's bad business, Mr Boone,' he replied in his doleful way, 'and that we must see more to know more.'

We gave the other shops scant notice — there was a hostelry with mouldering leather goods still hung on rusted flatnails, a chandler's, a warehouse with oak and pine still stacked within, a smithy.

We entered two houses as we made our way toward the church at the center of the village. Both were perfectly in the Puritan mode, full of items a collector would give his arm for, both deserted and full of the same rotten scent.

Nothing seemed to live or move in all of this but ourselves. We saw no insects, no birds, not even a cobweb fashioned in a window corner. Only dust.

At last we reached the church. It reared above us, grim, uninviting, cold. Its windows were black with the shadows inside, and any Godliness or sanctity had departed from it long ago. Of that I am certain. We mounted the steps, and I placed my hand on the large iron door-pull. A set, dark look passed from myself to Calvin and back again. I opened the portal. How long since that door had been touched? I would say with confidence that mine was the first in fifty years; perhaps longer. Rust-clogged hinges screamed as I opened it. The smell of rot and decay which smote us was nearly palpable. Cal made a gagging sound in his throat and twisted his head involuntarily for clearer air.

'Sir,' he asked, 'are you sure that you are—?'

'I'm fine,' I said calmly. But I did not feel calm, Bones, no more than I do now. I believe, with Moses, with Jereboam, with Increase Mather, and with our own Hanson [when he is in a philosophical *temperament*], that there are spiritually noxious places, buildings where the milk of the cosmos has become sour and rancid. This church is such a place; I would swear to it.

We stepped into a long vestibule equipped with a dusty coat rack and shelved hymnals. It was windowless. Oil-lamps stood in niches here and there. An unremarkable room, I thought, until I heard Calvin's sharp gasp and saw what he had already noticed.

It was an obscenity.

I daren't describe that elaborately-framed picture further than this: that it was done after the fleshy style of Rubens; that it contained a grotesque travesty of a madonna and child; that strange, half-shadowed creatures sported and crawled in the background.

'Lord,' I whispered.

'There's no Lord here,' Calvin said, and his words seemed to hang in the air. I opened the door leading into the church itself, and the odor became a miasma, nearly overpowering.

In the glimmering half-light of afternoon the pews stretched ghost-like to the altar. Above them was a high, oaken pulpit and a shadow-struck narthex from which gold glimmered.

With a half-sob Calvin, that devout Protestant, made the Holy Sign, and I followed suit. For the gold was a large, beautifully-wrought cross — but it was hung upside down, symbol of Satan's Mass.

'We must be calm,' I heard myself saying. 'We must be calm, Calvin. We must be calm.'

But a shadow had touched my heart, and I was afraid as I had never been. I have walked beneath death's umbrella and thought there was none darker. But there is. There is.

We walked down the aisle, our footfalls echoing above and around us. We left tracks in the dust. And at the altar there were other tenebrous *objets d'art*. I will not, cannot, let my mind dwell upon them.

I began to mount to the pulpit itself.

'Don't, Mr Boone!' Cal cried suddenly. 'I'm afraid—'

But I had gained it. A huge book lay open upon the stand, writ both in Latin and crabbed runes which looked, to my unpractised eye, either Druidic or pre-Celtic. I enclose a card with several of the symbols, redrawn from memory.

I closed the book and looked at the words stamped into the leather: *De Vermis Mysteriis*. My Latin is rusty, but serviceable enough to translate: *The Mysteries of the Worm*.

As I touched it, that accursed church and Calvin's white, upturned face seemed to swim before me. It seemed that I heard low, chanting voices, full of hideous yet eager fear — and below that sound, another, filling the bowels of the earth. An hallucination, I doubt it not — but at the same moment, the church was filled with a very real sound, which I can only

643

describe as a huge and macabre *turning* beneath my feet. The pulpit trembled beneath my fingers; the desecrated cross trembled on the wall.

We exited together, Cal and I, leaving the place to its own darkness, and neither of us dared look back until we had crossed the rude planks spanning the stream. I will not say we defiled the nineteen hundred years man has spent climbing upward from a hunkering and superstitious savage by actually running; but I would be a liar to say that we strolled.

That is my tale. You mustn't shadow your recovery by fearing that the fever has touched me again; Cal can attest to all in these pages, up to and including the hideous *noise*.

So I close, saying only that I wish I might see you [knowing that much of my bewilderment would drop away immediately], and that I remain your friend and admirer,

CHARLES.

Oct. 17, 1850.

DEAR GENTLEMEN:

In the most recent edition of your catalogue of household items (i.e., Summer, 1850), I noticed a preparation which is titled Rat's Bane. I should like to purchase one (1) 5-pound tin of this preparation at your stated price of thirty cents ($.30). I enclose return postage. Please mail to: Calvin McCann, Chapelwaite, Preacher's Corners, Cumberland County, Maine.

Thank you for your attention in this matter.

I remain, dear Gentlemen,

CALVIN MCCANN.

Oct. 19, 1850.

DEAR BONES,

Developments of a disquieting nature.

The noises in the house have intensified, and I am growing more to the conclusion that rats are not all that move within our walls. Calvin and I went on another fruitless search for hidden crannies or passages, but found nothing. How poorly we would fit into one of Mrs Radcliffe's romances! Cal claims, however, that much of the sound emanates from the cellar, and it is there we intend to explore tomorrow. It makes me no easier to know that Cousin Stephen's sister met her unfortunate end there.

Her portrait, by the by, hangs in the upstairs gallery. Marcella Boone was a sadly pretty thing, if the artist got her right, and I do know she never married. At times I think that Mrs Cloris was right that it *is* a bad house. It has certainly held nothing but gloom for its past inhabitants.

But I have more to say of the redoubtable Mrs Cloris, for I have had this day a second interview with her. As the most level-headed person from the Corners that I have met thus far, I sought her out this afternoon, after an unpleasant interview which I will relate.

The wood was to have been delivered this morning, and when noon came and passed and no wood with it, I decided to take my daily walk into the town itself. My object was to visit Thompson, the man with whom Cal did business.

It has been a lovely day, full of the crisp snap of bright autumn, and by the time I reached the Thompsons' homestead [Cal, who remained home to poke further through Cousin Stephen's library, gave me adequate directions] I felt in the best mood that these last few days have seen, and quite prepared to forgive Thompson's tardiness with the wood.

The place was a massive tangle of weeds and fallen-down buildings in need of paint; to the left of the barn a huge sow, ready for November butchering, grunted and wallowed in a muddy sty, and in the littered yard between house and out-buildings a woman in a tattered gingham dress was feeding chickens from her apron. When I hailed her, she turned a pale and vapid face toward me.

The sudden change in expression from utter, doltish emptiness to one of frenzied terror was quite wonderful to behold. I can only think she took me for Stephen himself, for she raised her hand in the prong-fingered sign of the evil eye and screamed. The chicken-feed scattered on the ground and the fowls fluttered away, squawking.

Before I could utter a sound, a huge, hulking figure of a man clad only in long-handled under-wear lumbered out of the house with a squirrel-rifle in one hand and a jug in the other. From the red light in his eye and unsteady manner of walking, I judged that this was Thompson the Woodcutter himself.

'A Boone!' he roared. 'G— d—n your eyes!' He dropped the jug a-rolling and also made the Sign.

'I've come,' I said with as much equanimity as I could muster under the circumstances, 'because the wood has not. According to the agreement you struck with my man—'

'G— d—n your man too, say I!' And for the first time I noticed that beneath his bluff and bluster he was deadly afraid. I began seriously to wonder if he mightn't actually use his rifle against me in his excitement.

I began carefully: 'As a gesture of courtesy, you might—'

'G— d—n your courtesy!'

'Very well then,' I said with as much dignity as I could muster. 'I bid you good day until you are more in control of yourself.' And with this I turned away and began down the road to the village.

'Don'tchee come back!' he screamed after me. 'Stick wi' your evil up there! Cursed! Cursed! Cursed!' He pelted a stone at me, which struck my shoulder. I would not give him the satisfaction of dodging.

So I sought out Mrs Cloris, determined to solve the mystery of Thompson's enmity, at least. She is a widow [and none of your confounded *matchmaking*, Bones; she is easily fifteen years my senior, and I'll not see forty again] and lives by herself in a charming little cottage at the ocean's very door-step. I found the lady hanging out her wash, and she seemed genuinely pleased to see me. I found this a great relief; it is vexing almost beyond words to be branded pariah for no understandable reason.

'Mr Boone,' said she, offering a half-curtsey. 'If you've come about washing, I take none in past September. My rheumatiz pains me so that it's trouble enough to do my own.'

'I wish laundry *was* the subject of my visit. I've come for help, Mrs Cloris. I must know all you can tell me about Chapelwaite and Jerusalem's Lot and why the townfolk regard me with such fear and suspicion!'

'Jerusalem's Lot! You know about *that*, then.'

'Yes,' I replied, 'and visited it with my companion a week ago.'

'God!' She went pale as milk, and tottered. I put out a hand to steady her. Her eyes rolled horribly, and for a moment I was sure she would swoon.

'Mrs Cloris, I am sorry if I have said anything to—'

'Come inside,' she said. 'You must know. Sweet Jesu, the evil days have come again!'

She would not speak more until she had brewed strong tea in her sunshiny kitchen. When it was before us, she looked pensively out at the ocean for a time. Inevitably, her eyes and mine were drawn to the jutting brow of Chapelwaite Head, where the house looked out over the water. The large bay-window glittered in the rays of the westering sun like a diamond. The view was beautiful but strangely disturbing. She suddenly turned to me and declared vehemently:

'Mr Boone, you must leave Chapelwaite immediately!'

I was flabbergasted.

'There has been an evil breath in the air since you took up residence. In the last week — since you set foot in the accursed place — there have been omens and portents. A caul over the face of the moon; flocks of whippoorwills which roost in the cemeteries; an unnatural birth. You *must* leave!'

When I found my tongue, I spoke as gently as I could. 'Mrs Cloris, these things are dreams. You must know that.'

'Is it a dream that Barbara Brown gave birth to a child with no eyes? Or that Clifton Brockett found a flat, pressed trail five feet wide in the woods beyond Chapelwaite *where all had withered and gone white?* And can you, who have visited Jerusalem's Lot, say with truth that nothing still lives there?'

I could not answer; the scene in that hideous church sprang before my eyes.

She clamped her gnarled hands together in an effort to calm herself. 'I know of these things only from my mother and her mother before her. Do you know the history of your family as it applies to Chapelwaite?'

'Vaguely,' I said. 'The house has been the home of Philip Boone's line since the 1780s; his brother, Robert, my grandfather, located in Massachusetts after an argument over stolen papers. Of Philip's side I know little, except that an unhappy shadow fell over it, extending from father to son to grandchildren — Marcella died in a tragic accident and Stephen fell to his death. It was his wish that Chapelwaite become the home of me and mine, and that the family rift thus be mended.'

'Never to be mended,' she whispered. 'You know nothing of the original quarrel?'

'Robert Boone was discovered rifling his brother's desk.'

'Philip Boone was mad,' she said. 'A man who trafficked with the unholy. The thing which Robert Boone *attempted* to remove was a profane Bible writ in the old tongues – Latin, Druidic, others. A hellbook.'

'*De Vermis Mysteriis.*'

She recoiled as if struck. 'You know of it?'

'I have seen it . . . touched it.' It seemed again she might swoon. A hand went to her mouth as if to stifle an outcry. 'Yes; in Jerusalem's Lot. On the pulpit of a corrupt and desecrated church.'

'Still there; still there, then.' She rocked in her chair. 'I had hoped God in His wisdom had cast it into the pit of hell.'

'What relation had Philip Boone to Jerusalem's Lot?'

'Blood relation,' she said darkly. 'The Mark of the Beast was on him, although he walked in the clothes of the Lamb. And on the night of October 31, 1789, Philip Boone disappeared . . . and the entire populace of that damned village with him.'

She would say little more; in fact, seemed to know little more. She would only reiterate her pleas that I leave, giving as reason something about 'blood calling to blood' and muttering about 'those who *watch* and those who *guard*.' As twilight drew on she seemed to grow more agitated rather than less, and to placate her I promised that her wishes would be taken under strong consideration.

I walked home through lengthening, gloomy shadows, my good mood quite dissipated and my head spinning with questions which still plague me. Cal greeted me with the news that our noises in the walls have grown worse still – as I can attest at this moment. I try to tell myself that I hear only rats, but then I see the terrified, earnest face of Mrs Cloris.

The moon has risen over the sea, bloated, full, the colour of blood, staining the ocean with a noxious shade. My mind turns to that church again and

(here a line is struck out)

But you shall not see that, Bones. It is too mad. It is time I slept, I think. My thoughts go out to you.

Regards,

CHARLES.

(The following is from the pocket journal of Calvin McCann.)

Oct. 20, '50

Took the liberty this morning of forcing the lock which binds the book closed; did it before Mr Boone arose. No help; it is all in cypher. A simple one, I believe. Perhaps I may break it as easily as the lock. A diary, I am certain, the hand oddly like Mr Boone's own. Whose book, shelved in the most obscure corner of this library and locked across the pages? It seems old, but how to tell? The corrupting air has largely been kept from its pages. More later, if time; Mr Boone set upon looking about the cellar. Am afraid these dreadful goings-on will be too much for his chancy health yet. I must try to persuade him—

But he comes.

Oct. 20, 1850.

BONES,

I can't write I cant [sic] write of this yet I I I

(From the pocket journal of Calvin McCann)

Oct. 20, '50

As I had feared, his health has broken—

Dear God our Father Who art in Heaven!

Cannot bear to think of it; yet it is planted, burned on my brain like a tin-type; that horror in the cellar—!

Alone now; half-past eight o'clock; house silent but

Found him swooned over his writing table; he still sleeps; yet for those few moments how nobly he acquitted himself while I stood paralyzed and shattered!

His skin is waxy, cool. Not the fever again, God be thanked. I daren't move him or leave him to go to the village. And if I did go, who would return with me to aid him? Who would come to this cursed house?

O, the cellar! The things in the cellar that have haunted our walls!

Oct. 22, 1850.

DEAR BONES,

I am myself again, although weak, after thirty-six hours of unconsciousness. Myself again ... what a grim and bitter joke! I shall never be myself again, never. I have come face to face with an insanity and a horror beyond the limits of human expression. And the end is not yet.

If it were not for Cal, I believe I should end my life this minute. He is one island of sanity in all this madness.

You shall know it all.

We had equipped ourselves with candles for our cellar exploration, and they threw a strong glow that was quite adequate – hellishly adequate! Calvin tried to dissuade me, citing my recent illness, saying that the most we should probably find would be some healthy rats to mark for poisoning.

I remained determined, however; Calvin fetched a sigh and answered: 'Have it as you must then, Mr Boone.'

The entrance to the cellar is by means of a trap in the kitchen floor [which Cal assures me he has since stoutly boarded over], and we raised it only with a great deal of straining and lifting.

A foetid, overpowering smell came up out of the darkness, not unlike that which pervaded the deserted town across the Royal River. The candle I held shed its glow on a steeply-slanting flight of stairs leading down into darkness. They were in a terrible state of repair – in one place an entire riser missing, leaving

653

only a black hole – and it was easy enough to see how the unfortunate Marcella might have come to her end there.

'Be careful, Mr Boone!' Cal said; I told him I had no intention of being anything but, and we made the descent.

The floor was earthen, the walls of stout granite, and hardly wet. The place did not look like a rat haven at all, for there were none of the things rats like to make their nests in, such as old boxes, discarded furniture, piles of paper, and the like. We lifted our candles, gaining a small circle of light, but still able to see little. The floor had a gradual slope which seemed to run beneath the main living-room and the dining-room – i.e., to the west. It was in this direction we walked. All was in utter silence. The stench in the air grew steadily stronger, and the dark about us seemed to press like wool, as if jealous of the light which had temporarily deposed it after so many years of undisputed dominion.

At the far end, the granite walls gave way to a polished wood which seemed totally black and without reflective properties. Here the cellar ended, leaving what seemed to be an alcove off the main chamber. It was positioned at an angle which made inspection impossible without stepping around the corner.

Calvin and I did so.

It was as if a rotten spectre of this dwelling's sinister past had risen before us. A single chair stood in this alcove, and above it, fastened from a hook in one of the stout overhead beams, was a decayed noose of hemp.

'Then it was here that he hung himself,' Cal muttered. 'God!'

'Yes . . . with the corpse of his daughter lying at the foot of the stairs behind him.'

Cal began to speak; then I saw his eyes jerked to a spot behind me; then his words became a scream.

How, Bones, can I describe the sight which fell upon our eyes? How can I tell you of the hideous tenants within our walls?

The far wall swung back, and from that darkness a face leered – a face with eyes as ebon as the Styx itself. Its mouth yawned in a toothless, agonized grin; one yellow, rotted hand stretched itself out to us. It made a hideous, mewling sound and took a shambling step forward. The light from my candle fell upon it—

And I saw the livid rope-burn about its neck!

From beyond it something else moved, something I shall dream of until the day when all dreams cease: a girl with a pallid, mouldering face and a corpse-grin; a girl whose head lolled at a lunatic angle.

They wanted us; I know it. And I know they would have drawn us into that darkness and made us their own, had I not thrown my candle directly at the thing in the partition, and followed it with the chair beneath that noose.

After that, all is confused darkness. My mind has drawn the curtain. I awoke, as I have said, in my room with Cal at my side.

If I could leave, I should fly from this house of

horror with my night-dress flapping at my heels. But I cannot. I have become a pawn in a deeper, darker drama. Do not ask how I know; I only do. Mrs Cloris was right when she spoke of blood calling to blood; and how horribly right when she spoke of those who *watch* and those who *guard*. I fear that I have wakened a Force which has slept in the tenebrous village of Jerusalem's Lot for half a century, a Force which has slain my ancestors and taken them in unholy bondage as *nosferatu* – the Undead. And I have greater fears than these, Bones, but I still see only in part. If I knew . . . if I only knew all!

CHARLES.

Postscriptum – And of course I write this only for myself; we are isolated from Preacher's Corners. I daren't carry my taint there to post this, and Calvin will not leave me. Perhaps, if God is good, this will reach you in some manner.

C.

(From the pocket journal of Calvin McCann)

Oct. 23, '50

He is stronger to-day; we talked briefly of the *apparitions* in the cellar; agreed they were neither hallucinations nor of an *ectoplasmic* origin, but *real*. Does Mr Boone suspect, as I do, that they have gone? Perhaps; the noises are still; yet all is ominous yet, o'ercast with a dark pall. It seems we wait in the deceptive Eye of the Storm . . .

'SALEM'S LOT

Have found a packet of papers in an upstairs bedroom, lying in the bottom drawer of an old roll-top desk. Some correspondence & receipted bills lead me to believe the room was Robert Boone's. Yet the most interesting document is a few jottings on the back of an advertisement for gentlemen's beaver hats. At the top is writ:

Blessed are the meek.

Below, the following apparent nonsense is writ:

b k e d s h d e r m t h e s e a k
e l m s o e r a r e s h a m d e d

I believe 'tis the key of the locked and coded book in the library. The cypher above is certainly a rustic one used in the War for Independence known as the *Fence-Rail*. When one removes the 'nulls' from the second bit of scribble, the following is obtained:

b e s d r t e e k
l s e a e h m e

Read up and down rather than across, the result is the original quotation from the Beatitudes.

Before I dare show this to Mr Boone, I must be sure of the book's contents . . .

Oct. 24, 1850.

DEAR BONES,

An amazing occurrence — Cal, always close-mouthed until absolutely sure of himself [a rare and admirable human trait!], has found the diary of my Grandfather Robert. The document was in a code which Cal himself has broken. He modestly declares that the discovery was an accident, but I suspect that perseverance and hard work had rather more to do with it.

At any rate, what a somber light it sheds on our mysteries here!

The first entry is dated June 1, 1789, the last October 27, 1789 — four days before the cataclysmic disappearance of which Mrs Cloris spoke. It tells a tale of deepening obsession — nay, of madness — and makes hideously clear the relationship between Great-uncle Philip, the town of Jerusalem's Lot, and the book which rests in that desecrated church.

The town itself, according to Robert Boone, pre-dates Chapelwaite [built in 1782] and Preacher's Corners [known in those days as Preacher's Rest and founded in 1741]; it was founded by a splinter group of the Puritan faith in 1710, a sect headed by a dour religious fanatic named James Boon. What a start that name gave me! That this Boon bore relation to my family can hardly be doubted, I believe. Mrs Cloris could not have been more right in her superstitious belief that familial bloodline is of crucial importance in this matter; and I recall with terror her answer to my question about Philip and *his* relationship to

Jerusalem's Lot. 'Blood relation,' said she, and I fear that it is so.

The town became a settled community built around the church where Boon preached – or held court. My grandfather intimates that he also held commerce with any number of ladies from the town, assuring them that this was God's way and will. As a result, the town became an anomaly which could only have existed in those isolated and queer days when belief in witches and the Virgin Birth existed hand in hand: an interbred, rather degenerate religious village controlled by a half-mad preacher whose twin gospels were the Bible and de Goudge's sinister *Demon Dwellings*, a community in which rites of exorcism were held regularly; a community of incest and the insanity and physical defects which so often accompany that sin. I suspect [and believe Robert Boone must have also] that one of Boon's bastard offspring must have left [or have been spirited away from] Jerusalem's Lot to seek his fortune to the south – and thus founded our present lineage. I do know, by my own family reckoning, that our clan supposedly originated in that part of Massachusetts which has so lately become this Sovereign State of Maine. My great-grandfather, Kenneth Boone, became a rich man as a result of the then-flourishing fur trade. It was his money, increased by time and wise investment, which built this ancestral home long after his death in 1763. His sons, Philip and Robert, built Chapelwaite. *Blood calls to blood*, Mrs Cloris said. Could it be that Kenneth was born of James Boon, fled the madness of his father and his father's town, only to have his sons, all-unknowing, build the Boone home *not two miles from the Boon beginnings?* If 'tis true, does it not seem that some huge and invisible Hand has guided us?

According to Robert's diary, James Boon was ancient in 1789 – and he must have been. Granting him an age of twenty-five in the year of the town's founding, he would have been one hundred and four, a prodigious age. The following is quoted direct from Robert Boone's diary:

August 4, 1789.
To-day for the first time I met this Man with whom my Brother has been so unhealthily taken; I must admit this Boon controls a strange Magnetism which upset me Greatly. He is a veritable Ancient, white-bearded, and dresses in a black Cassock which struck me as somehow obscene. More disturbing yet was the Fact that he was surrounded by Women, as a Sultan would be surrounded by his Harem; and P. assures me he is active yet, although at least an Octogenarian . . .

The Village itself I had visited only once before, and will not visit again; its Streets are silent and filled with the Fear the old Man inspires from his Pulpit: I fear also that Like has mated with Like, as so many of the Faces are similar. It seemed that each way I turned I beheld the old Man's Visage . . . all are so wan; they seem Lack-Luster, as if sucked dry of all Vitality, I beheld Eyeless and Noseless Children, Women who wept and gibbered and pointed at

*the Sky for no Reason, and garbled talk from the Scriptures
with talk of Demons; . . .*

*P. wished me to stay for Services, but the thought of that
sinister Ancient in the Pulpit before an Audience of this Town's
interbred Populace repulsed me and I made an Excuse . . .*

The entries preceding and following this tell of Philip's
growing fascination with James Boon. On September 1,
1789, Philip was baptized into Boon's church. His brother
says: 'I am aghast with Amaze and Horror – my Brother
has changed before my very Eyes – he even seems to grow
to resemble the wretched Man.'

First mention of the book occurs on July 23. Robert's
diary records it only briefly: 'P. returned from the smaller
Village to-night with, I thought, a rather wild Visage. Would
not speak until Bedtime, when he said that Boon had
enquired after a Book titled *Mysteries of the Worm*. To please
P. I promised to write Johns & Goodfellow a letter of
enquiry; P. almost fawningly Grateful.'

On August 12, this notation: 'Rec'd two Letters in
the Post today . . . one from Johns & Goodfellow in Boston.
They have Note of the Tome in which P. has expressed an
Interest. Only five Copies extant in this Country. The
Letter is rather cool; odd indeed. Have known Henry
Goodfellow for Years.'

August 13:
*P. insanely excited by Goodfellow's letter; refuses to say why.
He would only say that Boon is exceedingly anxious to
obtain a Copy. Cannot think why, since by the Title it
seems only a harmless gardening Treatise . . .*

*Am worried for Philip; he grows stranger to me Daily.
I wish now we had not returned to Chapelwaite. The Summer
is hot, oppressive, and filled with Omens . . .*

There are only two further mentions of the infamous
book in Robert's diary [he seems not to have realized the
true importance of it, even at the end]. From the entry of
September 4:

*I have petitioned Goodfellow to act as P.'s Agent in the
matter of the Purchase, although my better Judgement cries
against It. What use to demur? Has he not his own Money,
should I refuse? And in return I have extracted a Promise
from Philip to recant this noisome Baptism . . . yet he is
so Hectic; nearly Feverish; I do not trust him. I am hopelessly at Sea in this Matter . . .*

Finally, September 16:

*The Book arrived to-day, with a note from Goodfellow
saying he wishes no moe of my Trade . . . P. was excited to
an unnatural Degree; all but snatched the Book from my
Hands. It is writ in bastard Latin and a Runic Script of
which I can read Nothing. The Thing seemed almost warm
to the Touch, and to vibrate in my Hands, as if it contained
a huge Power . . . I reminded P. of his Promise to Recant
and he only laughed in an ugly, crazed Fashion and waved
that Book in my Face, crying over and over again: 'We have
it! We have it! The Worm! The Secret of the Worm!'*

*He is now fled, I suppose to his mad Benefactor, and I
have not seen him more this Day . . .*

Of the book there is no more, but I have made certain deductions which seem at least probable. First, that this book was, as Mrs Cloris has said, the subject of the falling-out between Robert and Philip; second, that it is a repository of unholy incantation, possibly of Druidic origin [many of the Druidic blood-rituals were preserved in print by the Roman conquerors of Britain in the name of scholarship, and many of these infernal cook-books are among the world's forbidden literature]; third, that Boon and Philip intended to use the book for their own ends. Perhaps, in some twisted way, they intended good, but I do not believe it. I believe they had long before bound themselves over to whatever faceless powers exist beyond the rim of the Universe; powers which may exist beyond the very fabric of Time. The last entries of Robert Boone's diary lend a dim glow of approbation to these speculations, and I allow them to speak for themselves.

October 26, 1789.

A terrific Babble in Preacher's Corners to-day; Frawley, the Blacksmith, seized my Arm and demanded to know 'What your Brother and that mad Antichrist are into up there.' Goody Randall claims there have been Signs in the sky of great impending Disaster. A Cow has been born with two Heads.

As for Myself, I know not what impends; perhaps 'tis my Brother's Insanity. His Hair has gone Gray almost Overnight, his Eyes are great blood-shot Circles from which the pleasing light of Sanity seems to have departed. He grins and whispers, and, for some Reason of his Own, has begun to haunt our Cellar when not in Jerusalem's Lot.

The Whippoorwills congregate about the House and upon the Grass; their combined Calling from the Mist blends with the Sea into an uneartbly Shriek that predudes all thought of Sleep.

October 27, 1789.

Followed P. this Evening when he departed for Jerusalem's Lot, keeping a safe Distance to avoid Discovery. The cursed Whippoorwills flock through the Woods, filling all with a deathly, psycho-pompotic Chant. I dared not cross the Bridge; the Town all dark except for the Church, which was litten with a ghastly red Glare that seemed to transform the high, peak'd Windows into the Eyes of the Inferno. Voices rose and fell in a Devil's Litany, sometimes laughing, sometimes sobbing. The very Ground seem'd to swell and groan beneath me, as if it bore an awful Weight, and I fled, amaz'd and full of Terror, the hellish, screaming Cries of the Whippoorwills dinning in my ears as I ran through those shadow-riven Woods.

All tends to the Climax, yet unforeseen. I dare not sleep for the Dreams that come, yet not remain awake for what lunatic Terrors may come. The night is full of awful Sounds and I fear—

And yet I feel the urge to go again, to watch, to see. It seems that Philip himself calls me, and the old Man.

The Birds cursed

cursed cursed

Here the diary of Robert Boone ends.

Yet you must notice, Bones, near the conclusion, that he claims Philip himself seemed to call him. My final conclusion is formed by these lines, by the talk of Mrs Cloris and the others, but most of all by those terrifying figures in the cellar, dead yet alive. Our line is yet an unfortunate one, Bones. There is a curse over us which refuses to be buried; it lives a hideous shadow-life in this house and that town. And the culmination of the cycle is drawing close again. I am the last of the Boone blood. I fear that something knows this, and that I am at the nexus of an evil endeavor beyond all sane understanding. The anniversary is All Saints' Eve, one week from today.

How shall I proceed? If only you were here to counsel me, to help me! If only you were here!

I must know all; I must return to the shunned town. May God support me!

CHARLES.

(From the pocket journal of Calvin McCann)

Oct. 25, '50

Mr Boone has slept nearly all this day. His face is pallid and much thinner. I fear recurrence of his fever is inevitable.

While refreshing his water carafe I caught sight of two unmailed letters to Mr Granson in Florida. He plans to return to Jerusalem's Lot; 'twill be the killing of him if I allow it. Dare I steal away to Preacher's Corners and hire a buggy? I must, and yet what if he wakes? If I should return and find him gone?

The noises have begun in our walls again. Thank God he still sleeps! My mind shudders from the import of this.

Later

I brought him his dinner on a tray. He plans on rising later, and despite his evasions, I know what he plans; yet I go to Preacher's Corners. Several of the sleeping-powders prescribed to him during his late illness remained with my things; he drank one with his tea, all-unknowing. He sleeps again.

To leave him with the Things that shamble behind our walls terrifies me; to let him continue even one more day within these walls terrifies me even more greatly. I have locked him in.

God grant he should still be there, safe and sleeping, when I return with the buggy!

Still later

Stoned me! Stoned me like a wild and rabid dog! Monsters and fiends! These, that call themselves *men!* We are prisoners here—

The birds, the whippoorwills, have begun to gather.

October 26, 1850.

DEAR BONES,

It is nearly dusk, and I have just wakened, having slept nearly the last twenty-four hours away. Although Cal has said nothing, I suspect he put a sleeping-powder in my tea, having gleaned my intentions. He is a good and faithful friend, intending only the best and I shall say nothing.

Yet my mind is set. Tomorrow is the day. I am calm, resolved, but also seem to feel the subtle onset of the fever again. If it is so, it *must* be tomorrow. Perhaps tonight would be better still; yet not even the fires of Hell itself could induce me to set foot in that village by shadow-light.

Should I write no more, may God bless and keep you, Bones.

CHARLES.

Postscriptum – The birds have set up their cry, and the horrible shuffling sounds have begun again. Cal does not think I hear, but I do.

C.

(From the pocket journal of Calvin McCann)

Oct. 27, '50
5 AM

He is impersuadable. Very well. I go with him.

November 4, 1850.

DEAR BONES,

Weak, yet lucid. I am not sure of the date, yet my almanac assures me by tide and sunset that it must be correct. I sit at my desk, where I sat when I first wrote you from Chapelwaite, and look out over the dark sea from which the last of the light is rapidly fading. I shall never see more. This night is my night; I leave it for whatever shadows be.

How it heaves itself at the rocks, this sea! It throws clouds of sea-foam at the darkling sky in banners, making the floor beneath me tremble. In the window-glass I see my reflection, pallid as any vampire's. I have been without nourishment since the twenty-seventh of October, and should have been without water, had not Calvin left the carafe beside my bed on that day.

O, Cal! He is no more, Bones. He is gone in my place, in the place of this wretch with his pipe-stem arms and skull face who I see reflected back in the darkened glass. And yet he may be the more fortunate; for no dreams haunt him as they have haunted me these last days – twisted shapes that lurk in the nightmare corridors of delirium. Even now my hands tremble; I have splotched the page with ink.

Calvin confronted me on that morning just as I was about to slip away – and I thinking I had been so crafty. I had told him that I had decided we must leave, and asked him if he would go to Tandrell, some ten miles distant, and hire a trap where we were less notorious. He agreed to make the hike and I watched him leave by the sea-road. When he was out of sight I quickly made myself ready, donning both coat and muffler [for the weather had turned frosty; the first touch of coming winter was on that morning's cutting breeze]. I wished briefly for a gun, then laughed at myself for the wish. What avails guns in such a matter?

I let myself out by the pantry-way, pausing for a last look at sea and sky; for the smell of the fresh air against the putrescence I knew I should smell soon enough; for the sight of a foraging gull wheeling below the clouds.

I turned – and there stood Calvin McCann.

'You shall not go alone,' said he; and his face was as grim as ever I have seen it.

'But, Calvin—' I began.

'No, not a word! We go together and do what we must, or I return you bodily to the house. You are not well. You shall not go alone.'

It is impossible to describe the conflicting emotions that swept over me: confusion, pique, gratefulness – yet the greatest of them was love.

We made our way silently past the summer-house and the sundial, down the weed-covered verge and into the woods. All was dead still – not a bird sang nor a wood-cricket chirruped. The world seemed cupped in a silent pall. There was only the ever-present smell of salt, and from far away, the faint tang of wood smoke. The woods were a blazoned riot of colour, but, to my eye, scarlet seemed to predominate all.

Soon the scent of salt passed, and another, more sinister odour took its place; that rottenness which I have mentioned. When we came to the leaning bridge which spanned the Royal, I expected Cal to ask me again to defer, but he did not. He paused, looked at that grim spire which seemed to mock the blue sky above it, and then looked at me. We went on.

We proceeded with quick yet dread footsteps to James Boon's church. The door still hung ajar from our latter exit, and the darkness within seemed to leer at us. As we mounted the steps, brass seemed to fill my heart; my hand trembled as it touched the door-handle and pulled it. The smell within was greater, more noxious than ever.

We stepped into the shadowy ante-room and, with no pause, into the main chamber.

It was a shambles.

Something vast had been at work in there, and a mighty destruction had taken place. Pews were overturned and heaped like jack-straws. The wicked cross lay against the east wall, and a jagged hole in the plaster above it testified to the force with which it had been hurled. The oil-lamps had been ripped from their high fixtures, and the reek of whale-oil mingled with the terrible stink which pervaded the town. And down the center aisle, like a ghastly bridal path, was a trail of black ichor, mingled with sinister tendrils of blood. Our eyes followed it to the pulpit – the only untouched thing in view. Atop it, staring at us from across that blasphemous Book with glazed eyes, was the butchered body of a lamb.

'God,' Calvin whispered.

We approached, keeping clear of the slime on the floor. The room echoed back our footsteps and seemed to transmute them into the sound of gigantic laughter.

We mounted the narthex together. The lamb had not been torn or eaten; it appeared, rather, to have been *squeezed* until its blood-vessels had forcibly ruptured. Blood lay in thick and noisome puddles on the lectern itself, and about the base of it . . . *yet on the book it was transparent, and the crabbed runes could be read through it, as through coloured glass!*

'Must we touch it?' Cal asked, unfaltering.

'Yes. I must have it.'

'What will you do?'

'What should have been done sixty years ago. I am going to destroy it.'

We rolled the lamb's corpse away from the book; it struck the floor with a hideous, lolling thud. The blood-stained pages now seemed alive with a scarlet glow of their own.

My ears began to ring and hum; a low chant seemed to emanate from the walls themselves. From the twisted look on Cal's face I knew he heard the same. The floor beneath us trembled, as if the familiar which haunted this church came now unto us, to protect its own. The fabric of sane space and time seemed to twist and crack; the church seemed filled with spectres and litten with the hell-glow of eternal cold fire. It seemed that I saw James Boon, hideous and misshapen, cavorting around the supine body of a woman, and my Grand-uncle Philip behind him, an acolyte in a black, hooded cassock, who held a knife and a bowl.

'Deum vobiscum magna vermis—'

The words shuddered and writhed on the page before me, soaked in the blood of sacrifice, prize of a creature that shambles beyond the stars—

A blind, interbred congregation swaying in mindless, daemoniac praise; deformed faces filled with hungering, nameless anticipation—

And the Latin was replaced by an older tongue, ancient when Egypt was young and the Pyramids unbuilt, ancient when this Earth still hung in an unformed, boiling firmament of empty gas:

'*Gyyagin vardar Yogsoggoth! Verminis! Gyyagin! Gyyagin! Gyyagin!*'

The pulpit began to rend and split, pushing upward—

Calvin screamed and lifted an arm to shield his face. The narthex trembled with ahuge, tenebrous motion like a ship wracked in a gale. I snatched up the book and held it away from me; it seemed filled with the heat of the sun and I felt that I should be cindered, blinded.

'Run!' Calvin screamed. 'Run!'

But I stood frozen and the alien presence filled me like an ancient vessel that had waited for years – for generations!

'*Gyyagin vardar!*' I screamed. 'Servant of Yog-soggoth, the Nameless One! The Worm from beyond Space! Star-Eater! Blinder of Time! *Verminis!* Now comes the Hour of Filling, the Time of Rending! *Verminis! Alyah! Alyah! Gyyagin!*'

Calvin pushed me and I tottered, the church whirling before me, and fell to the floor. My head crashed against the edge of an upturned pew, and red fire filled my head – yet seemed to clear it.

I groped for the sulphur matches I had brought.

Subterranean thunder filled the place. Plaster fell. The rusted bell in the steeple pealed a choked devil's carillon in sympathetic vibration.

My match flared. I touched it to the book just as the pulpit exploded upward in a rending explosion of wood. A huge black maw was discovered beneath; Cal tottered on the edge his hands held out, his face distended in a wordless scream that I shall hear forever.

And then there was a huge surge of gray, vibrating flesh. The smell became a nightmare tide. It was a huge outpouring of a viscid, pustulant jelly, a huge and awful form that seemed to skyrocket from the very bowels of the ground. And yet, with a sudden horrible comprehension which no man can have known, I perceived *that it was but one ring, one segment, of a monster worm that had existed eyeless for years in the chambered darkness beneath that abominated church!*

The book flared alight in my hands, and the Thing seemed to scream soundlessly above me. Calvin was struck glancingly and flung the length of the church like a doll with a broken neck.

It subsided – the thing subsided, leaving only a huge and shattered hole surrounded with black slime, and a great screaming, mewling sound that seemed to fade through colossal distances and was gone.

I looked down. The book was ashes.

I began to laugh, then to howl like a struck beast.

All sanity left me, and I sat on the floor with blood streaming from my temple, screaming and gibbering into those unhallowed shadows while Calvin sprawled in the far corner, staring at me with glazing, horror-struck eyes.

I have no idea how long I existed in that state. It is beyond all telling. But when I came again to my faculties, shadows had drawn long paths around me and I sat in twilight. Movement had caught my eye, movement from the shattered hole in the narthex floor.

A hand groped its way over the riven floor-boards.

My mad laughter choked in my throat. All hysteria melted into numb bloodlessness.

With terrible, vengeful slowness, a wracked figure pulled itself up from darkness, and a half-skull peered at me. Beetles crawled over the fleshless forehead. A rotted cassock clung to the askew hollows of mouldered collar-bones. Only the eyes lived – red, insane pits that glared at me with more than lunacy; they glared with the empty life of the pathless wastes beyond the edges of the Universe.

It came to take me down to darkness.

That was when I fled, screeching, leaving the body of my lifelong friend unheeded in that place of dread. I ran until the air seemed to burst like magma in my lungs and brain. I ran until I had gained this possessed and tainted house again, and my room, where I collapsed and have lain like a dead man until to-day. I ran because even in my crazed state, and even in the shattered ruin of that dead-yet-animated shape, *I had seen the family resemblance.* Yet not of Philip or of Robert, whose likenesses hang in the upstairs gallery. *That rotted visage belonged to James Boon, Keeper of the Worm!*

He still lives somewhere in the twisted, lightless wanderings beneath Jerusalem's Lot and Chapelwaite – and *It* still lives. The burning of the book thwarted *It*, but there are other copies.

Yet I am the gateway, and I am the last of the Boone blood. For the good of all humanity I must die . . . and break the chain forever.

I go to the sea now, Bones. My journey, like my story, is at an end. May God rest you and grant you all peace.

CHARLES

The odd series of papers above was eventually received by Mr Everett Granson, to whom they had been addressed. It is assumed that a recurrence of the unfortunate brain fever which struck him originally following the death of his wife in 1848 caused Charles Boone to lose his sanity and murder his companion and longtime friend, Mr Calvin McCann.

The entries in Mr McCann's pocket journal are a fascinating exercise in forgery, undoubtedly perpetrated by Charles Boone in an effort to reinforce his own paranoid delusions.

In at least two particulars, however, Charles Boone is proved wrong. First, when the town of Jerusalem's Lot was 'rediscovered' (I use the term historically, of course), the floor of the narthex, although rotted, showed no sign of explosion or huge damage. Although the ancient pews *were* overturned and several windows shattered, this can be assumed to be the work of vandals from neighboring towns over the years. Among the older residents of Preacher's Corners and Tandrell there is still some idle rumor about Jerusalem's Lot (perhaps, in his day, it was this kind of harmless folk legend which started Charles Boone's mind on its fatal course), but this seems hardly relevant.

Second, Charles Boone was not the last of his line. His grandfather, Robert Boone, sired at least two bastards. One died in infancy. The second took the Boone name and located in the town of Central Falls, Rhode Island. I am the final descendant of this offshoot of the Boone line; Charles Boone's second cousin, removed by three generations. These papers have been in my committal for ten years. I offer them for publication on the occasion of my residence in the Boone ancestral home, Chapelwaite, in the hope that the reader will find sympathy in his heart for Charles Boone's poor, misguided soul. So far as I can tell, he was correct about only one thing: this place badly needs the services of an exterminator.

There are some huge rats in the walls, by the sound.

Signed,
James Robert Boone
October 2, 1971.

DELETED SCENES

In Susan (I), *after Ben and Susan depart before their date in the evening, the original manuscript reads:*

And yet, the horror was on its way even then, and not so far distant: the horror was docking at Portland Harbor, only twenty miles away. Neither of them had mentioned the Marsten House, which brooded over the north end of town like the humped shoulders of some Gothic spinster, but either might have; it had been vacant for years – over twenty of them. The great forest fire of 1951 had burned almost to its very yard before the wind had changed, leaving it to stand at the lip of all that great charring.

It had stood more years, and still more: the FOR SALE sign had been replaced three times, and the last time it had been allowed to whiten in the sun until it was unreadable. Then a gale in the Fall of 1960 had ripped it completely away, leaving only the sheriff's NO TRESPASSING signs, which were replaced with machinelike regularity each Spring and Fall.

A full year ago, a new sign had been nailed up on the peeling boards beside the ramshackle from porch, and this sign said: SOLD.

In The Lot (I) *after Ben Mears contemplates the Marsten House at 4 o'clock, King has the following passage:*

He hung the towel over his shoulder, turned back to the door – and froze, staring out the window. Something was different out there, different than it had been yesterday.

Not in the town, certainly; it drowsed away the late afternoon under a sky of that peculiar shade of deep blue that graces New England on particularly fine days in late September.

He could look across the two-story buildings on Momson Avenue, see their flat, asphalted roofs, across the park where the children now home from school lazed or biked or squabbled, and out to the northwest section of town where Brock Street disappeared beyond the shoulder of that first wooded hill. His eye followed up naturally to the break in the woods where the Burns Road cut through, and to the Marsten House which sat overlooking the town.

The shutters were closed.

When he had come back to Momson ['Salem's Lot], one of the things that had made him decide to stay and write the book that had been increasingly on his mind had been the close correspondence between his memory of the Marsten House and its actuality, twenty-four years later. It was still unpainted, still leaning and ominous and seemingly pregnant with awful things (and perhaps the suicide-murder perpetrated by Hubie Marsten was only the least of them) that had transpired within its walls. The upstairs windows were still like vacant eyes peering forth from under steep angled eaves like eyebrows – eyes that had been cataracted with patched and faded green shades. The glass in those windows had been long since broken with small boys' stones, of course, but that added rather than detracted from the overall impression of idiot malignancy.

The shutters had always hung leaningly beside the windows, accordioned back and held with rusty eyehook latches. It seemed to Ben that they had been flakingly green in 1951 (the house itself had been a peeled and ruinous white), but now all the color was gone from them, and like the house, they were a uniform and weatherbeaten gray.

But they had been pulled shut.

He stood with the towel over his shoulder, looking out at it, not moving, feeling a crawl of fear in his belly that he did not try to analyze. He had thought occupancy could only destroy the fragile splice of child-memory and adult-reality that was so important to the book he was writing, unless it was his own occupancy – a thought that still made him feel fear-sick. The new owner would re-shingle, or cut the lawn, or tear off the old ivy trellis and repaint. But the closing of the shutters in the daytime had added something unreckoned with, something he most emphatically didn't like.

In The Lot (1), *section 20 (11:59 PM), when Straker sacrifices the body of Ralphie Glick, King's original passages read:*

In the Burns Road cemetery, a dark figure stood meditatively inside the gate, waiting for the turn of time, for the instant of midnight when God hides His face.

'O my father,' the figure said, its voice soft and cultured, flavored with a faint and unidentifiable accent, 'favor me now. Lord of Flies, Prince of Darkness, favor me now. Now I bring you spoiled meat and reeking flesh. Blood I bring, the water of life. With my left hand I bring it. Make a sign for me on this ground, consecrated in your name. I wait a sign to begin your work.'

The voice died away. A wind sprang up, gentle, bringing with it the sigh and whisper of leafy branches and grasses, and a whiff of corruption from the dump at the end of the road.

A blue light began to glow at the far end of the cemetery, and intensified. In its glow, the figure's countenance was discovered: elderly, with sunken eyes, and strangely heavy, almost negroid lips. The hair, swept back from the forehead, was pure white.

The blue glow intensified, grew searing, and took on a hunched, shifting shape that seemed to stretch up and up, beyond the close and hemming horizon of trees, to the sky itself.

A Voice said: *'What do you bring me?'*

'This.'

The figure stooped, and then stood with the sleeping figure of a child in his arms.

'It is well.'

The figure bowed.

'Consummate your act, and grow strong.'

It became unspeakable.

The chapter Danny Glick and Others (*which King originally had titled* Straker) *features the scene where Royal Snow and Hank Peters bring the crate with Barlow's coffin down cellar of the Marsten House. In the first draft, there is no Barlow and Straker antique store and only one box is delivered. When Hank delivers the locks, he sees a rat on the table. The original passage features more rats. Grisly scenes of rats are not so frequent in the published novel:*

The beam steadied. Hank sucked in breath and felt the room go hazy around him.

Rats.

Hundreds of them, possibly thousands, all of them massed in ranks and platoons at that elbow bend. Staring at him, their V-shaped upper lips lifted to show the sharp incisors beneath. Their eyes glared at him.

He panicked, threw the keys wildly on the table, and turned away, shambling into a run. Again that queer odor of putrefaction seemed to fill his nostrils, the smell of age and wet and rotting flesh. He had to get away from it.

His flashlight beam struck the box, and he would have screamed if he had had the strength. That was what was making that queer wooden thumping noise. It was rocking back and forth, and the wood seemed to be straining, bulging. As his eyes took it in, one of the aluminum bands split and flew upward, making a shadow on the wall like a clutching hand . . .

He ran.

In Danny Glick and Others, *at the end of the chapter when the nurse finds Danny dead, there is another section with the doctor reporting on him, and the vampiric condition of Danny is revealed much earlier.*

'Dead,' he said, and began to pull the sheet up over the oddly calm face.

Her hand stopped him. 'Doctor?'

'Yes?' He blinked at her mildly. He was a thin,

intense-looking resident named Burke, and he was losing his hair rapidly.

'Those scratches on his neck are gone.'

He looked. 'Yes,' he said indifferently, and covered the face of Danny Glick with the sheet. 'Healed, probably.'

'I thought he was alive,' she said, and gripped her elbows to restrain a very un-R.N.-like shiver. 'I thought he got up and opened the window and fainted. He looks like a . . . a waxwork.'

'Really?' he said without interest, and turned away. 'It's a condition that sometimes predates rigor mortis. Known in the argot as mortician's complexion.'

'God,' she muttered.

They went out.

Under the sheet, Danny Glick opened flat obsidian eyes and smiled. The teeth discovered by that smile were white and cruelly sharp.

After Ben and Susan make love in the park in Ben (II), *they have a different discussion, a longer one, about the nature of the Marsten House and evil.*

'The book?' she asked. 'You were going to tell me about that before we were so sweetly interrupted.'

'The book is about what happened to me at the Marsten House,' he said slowly. 'I can see it from my window. And the paperweight I use to hold down my manuscript is the snow-dome I had in my hand when I ran out of there.'

'Ben, that sounds morbid. Morbid as hell.' Her face was sober, and the flat glow of the streetlights milked her tan, making her look pallid.

'It is,' he said. 'But didn't I tell you writing was an act of exorcism? I'm writing this one out of my nightmares, and I wouldn't mind if I milked that reservoir dry. You know, the other three books were all quite cheerful . . . *Conway's Daughter* especially. They all had happy endings. Do you know what Brewster at the *The New York Times* said about the conclusion of *Air Dance?* "Ben Mears reminds one of a mentally regressive street-performer doing a tap-dance on the gallows of the American prison system."'

'I thought it was lovely,' she said indignantly. 'Just because you're not willing to go around and cry doom like Camus or Salinger or John Updike—'

'Do you remember when those hoods shot John Stennis in Washington, D.C.?' he asked.

'Sure,' she said, puzzled by the abrupt change in direction.

'They held him up outside his house and after he handed over his wallet and watch, one of them said, "We're going to shoot you anyway." Then they did it. That's always haunted me. Or Capote's book, *In Cold Blood.* I was nineteen when I read it, and the image of Perry Smith going around and blowing the Clutter's heads off is as clear now as it was then. Can you imagine what it would feel like to be lying on the floor with your hands tied behind you and to see a man coming toward you with a shotgun, and knowing what he was going to do?'

'Ben, you're giving me the creeps.'

'I'm sorry,' he said. 'This is hardly the place, is it?' He gestured at the dark around them.

'Go ahead,' she said. 'It's very important to me.'

'Why?'

'Because it is to you.'

He looked over to the right, and there was the Marsten House. The shutters had been pulled back – they were closed all day, every day – and the light shone out of the downstairs windows in rectangles.

'Those are kerosene lamps, aren't they?' he asked.

'Yes . . . I think so.'

'Do you ever wonder who is up there?' he asked.

'Everyone in town wonders.'

He laughed. 'I suppose they do. I wonder if Mabel Werts has got the straight dope yet?'

She chuckled throatily. 'If she did, my mother would have it, too. You can bet Mabel's bending every effort, though.'

'The book is set in a town like Momson,' he said, 'and the people are like Momson people. There is a series of sex murders and mutilations. I'm going to describe one of the crimes in progress, from beginning to end, in minute detail. I'm going to rub the reader's nose in it. I was outlining that part when Ralphie Glick disappeared. That's why . . . well, it gave me a nasty turn.'

'I can understand that. Ben, is it necessary to be so . . . so clinical about violence?'

'I don't know,' he said honestly. 'It does to me, in this book.'

'Suppose you encourage somebody to commit a similar crime?'

'Do you mean like the kid who saw *Psycho* and then ran out and killed his grandmother?'

'Yes, something like that.'

'I'd like to think he would have killed her anyway,' he

said. 'That's brutal, I suppose. What I mean is I wish she hadn't been killed at all, but since she was, I hope Hitchcock isn't an accessory after the fact. You know, people used to argue that drugstore pornography, stuff like *Beach Blanket Gang-Bang*, encouraged sex crimes. Then the government did a study and said that was full of shit. Most sex criminals are Eagle scout types with severe repression problems – like the old inquisitors who used to stretch teenage blondes on the rack and run their hands all over their bodies, searching for witch's tits and marks of the devil – then reaming out their vaginas with red-hot pokers. The kid who masturbates in the bathroom over a skin magazine doesn't want to run out and rape a six-year-old and then cut her up. A shy, retiring bank clerk who has no sex outlets at all and who broods in his room night after night may.'

'In other words, if a man is going to do it, he'll do it regardless.'

'I distrust generalizations like that,' he said. 'If *The Night Creature* is published and six months later a series of crimes with the same M.O. crops up, I'd lose a lot of sleep. A writer who won't take moral responsibility may be a good writer, but he's a shitty human being in my book. And I think there are some writers who have made mistakes in judgment. In *Airport*, Arthur Hailey tells you how to make a suitcase bomb. There's a lovely description of how to hot-wire a car in *Texas Whirlwind*, by Norman Sullivan. There are others, too.'

They had arrived at her house, and stood by the mailbox. The lights downstairs were on, shining out on the lawn, and looking in the front bay window, Ben could see Ann Norton rocking and knitting something.

'What's the rest of it?' she asked.

'Well, the house. The guy who lives there is a recluse, has been for years. People start to suspect he's the killer. They go up there and find out he's hung himself in the upstairs bedroom. A note is found. I'm sorry, the note says. God forgive me for what I've done.

'The killings stop . . . for a while. Then they begin again. The town sheriff begins to think, you know, that the real murderer killed the old man and wrote the note to throw the scent. He gets a court order and the body is exhumed. But it's gone.'

'It's awful, all right,' she said.

'People begin to suspect something supernatural . . . even the sheriff can't get the idea out of his mind. The book's hero is a kid named Jamie Atwood. He goes up to the house because he wants to join the big kid's club—'

'The hero is Ben Mears,' she said.

He bowed. 'Every author makes a guest appearance in every book, Susan. There, that's three generalizations about writers, and I told you that first day I'd only make one. That's breach of promise.'

'Never mind that. What happens?'

'The old man is up there, awful and rotted, a real horror. Rope still dangling from his neck. It turns out in the end that the real murderer – the town librarian – killed the old man just as the sheriff thought, and then went one step further. Dug up the body, cut off the head, and—'

'Yes,' she said. 'Ben, you're like a stranger to me. Do you know that? I'm scared of you.'

'We'd all be scared if we knew what was swept under the carpet of each other's minds,' he said. 'Do you know what made Poe great? And Machen and Lovecraft? A direct pipeline to the old subconscious. To the fears and twisted needs that swim around down there like phosphorescent fish. That's what I'm after. And I'm getting it.'

'Does Jamie live?' she asked.

'No,' he said softly. 'He's the mad librarian's last victim.'

'Well I think that's awful,' she said, sounding upset. 'Where's the redeeming social merit in all that?'

'I don't know,' he said. 'Where's the redeeming social merit in *Psycho*?'

'We're not talking about *Psycho*,' she said stiffly.

'True,' he said. 'I don't know about social merit – I've always thought that was a crock. Morality is the only way to judge art. Art that trades on what happens to be socially acceptable is only pop art, and who wants to spend their life painting pictures of soup cans, even if you can sell them for a thousand bucks a crack? I think *The Night Creature* is going to be an extremely moral book, at least by my own code. The portrait of the killer is drawn in blood. He's the most detestable human being imaginable . . . he makes me a little sick just to write about him. But that isn't the worth of the book. That's not what I'm writing about.'

'Then what is?'

'The town,' he said, and his eyes gleamed. 'The town and the madness that spreads over it and poisons it. I'm writing about mindless evil – the worst kind of all, because there's no escape from it. No begging, no pleading, no logic will get you out of it. I'm writing about those hoods saying we're going to shoot you anyway. About Perry Smith walking from room to room and shooting human beings as if they were chickens. About Charles Starkwether and Charles Manson and Charles Witman. I'm writing about the mindless violence that wants to rip all of our lives to pieces. Have you ever seen Lon Chaney in *The Phantom of the Opera*?'

'Yes; at B.U. It gave me nightmares.'

'Then you know the scene where the girl creeps up behind him while he's playing that great organ and pulls the mask off and she sees what a monster he is . . . I want to do that. I want to rip the mask off and show people that the Grand Guiginol lives on the corner of your own street . . . and in your own house.'

At the end of The Lot (II), *after we meet Donald Callahan and before the chapter on Matt, King has this section on the town, completely excised from the published novel:*

The town slept.

The cities sleep uneasily, like paranoiacs who spend their days in fear and their exhausted nights fleeing crooked shadows to that final hotel room where, as Auden says, it has been waiting all the time under one naked lightbulb. Their sleep is marred by the rising screams of the squad-car sirens, by the endless neon, by taxis that cruise restlessly like yellow wolves. Their sleep is sweating, fearful, yet vital.

But the town sleeps like a stone, like the dead.

Shops stand closed and dark, and there are only two night-lights: the sign which says POLICE and the lighted circle around the Bulova clock in the small window of Carl Foreman's Funeral Home. The clock hands stand at quarter of one.

Ben Mears slept, and the Nortons, and Hal Griffen, flat on his back with his mouth open, schoolbooks on his desk, untouched all the weekend which had so lately become Monday morning. Win Purinton slept, and his new puppy — given to him by the boys at the dairy — slept in Doe's old basket in the pantry, with a two-dollar alarm clock tucked in beside him to ease the loneliness that even dogs can feel. Eva Miller slept in her widow's bed, twisting laboriously through the night in a slow and subconscious dance of love; and above her, Weasel Craig slept the slow and heavy sleep of wine.

When you come from the city to the town you lie wakeful in the absence of noise at first. You wait for something to break it: the cough of shattering glass, the squeal of tires blistering against the pavement, perhaps a scream. But there is nothing but the unearthly hum of the telephone wires and so you wait and wait and then sleep badly. But when the town gets you, you sleep like the town and the town sleeps deep in its blood, like a bear.

Yet it did not sleep quite so completely as it had, because on the hill above town the lights shone from the Marsten House, as if the eye of the dark itself had opened and disclosed a fearful yellow pupil.

When Ben comes over for dinner at Matthew Burke's house, right after mixing his bourbon and water, and before eating spaghetti, he speaks of his financial state with Matt.

. . . as Ben sat down in the steel-legged kitchen chair with his drink, he found himself telling Matt Burke what he had not even told Susan: his financial state, which was far from rock steady.

'Yeah,' he said, '*Conway's Daughter* did all right; for somebody, anyway. I got an advance of $3,000 against royalties and another three in royalties. The publisher and I split 50–50 on the paperback sale and the movie option, which was picked up by Columbia – and then put back down again when they couldn't get Robert Mitchum to play Conway.'

'50–50's not usual, is it?' Matt asked, sitting down.

'No, but it's not bad for a first novel, which usually dies in the road anyway. And considering I wasn't agented, I thought I'd done pretty well. I came out with about eighteen thousand dollars, and I put half of it right into some safe stock. Which I'm now selling off, chunk by chunk.'

'But the other books—'

'Well, I got a good advance on *Air Dance*, and the advance sales were good. The contract was a hell of a lot better, too, but the critics gave it both barrels and it didn't move very well after that. And just after it came out someone I – I liked a lot died, and I stopped noticing where the money was going for a while. I ended up in Las Vegas. I dropped the last of the advance money on number 16, red, and then rented a cabin in the most Godforsaken western California valley you ever saw. Didn't see anybody for weeks at a time. Wrote *Billy Said Keep Going* in two months. Holt House, which published the first two, turned it down.'

Ben finished the rest of his drink, took a plate of spaghetti from Matt, and thanked him. He ladled sauce over it and twirled a forkful against his spoon. 'Fantastic,' he said. 'Mama mia.'

'But of course,' Matt said. 'What happened then?'

Ben shrugged. 'When the script finally got back to me, I was in Mexico, living it up. And all of a sudden I realized I couldn't afford to live it up. I traded the Pontiac GT I'd bought after the paperback sale of *Air Dance* for the Citroën I'm driving now, and crept back across the border.

'That was what happened on the outside. Inside I was in shock. All my life I wanted to be a writer – not an author but a *writer* – and after I finally had it made, I started feeling it all slip through my fingers. I was in shock. Coming up through Texas on one of those long, straight stretches, I put the car up to ninety and started to feed the pages of Billy through the wing window. I had some crazy idea that I'd leave a trail of words all the way from the goddamn border to New York City, where I was going to throw my damn stupid editor out of his office window. After I'd fed about seventy-five pages, I suddenly came to my senses and hit the brakes with both feet . . . I left rubber for a quarter of a mile and damn near killed myself. I pulled over onto the shoulder and spent the rest of the day cruising back the way I came, picking them up. I got one hell of a sunburn, but I got all of them but six pages. I rewrote those in an El Paso hotel room and they're in the book. Better, I think.'

'I haven't read that one,' Matt said. 'It's still—'

'—on reserve at the library,' Ben finished for him, grinning. 'Mrs Starcher told me. Susan hasn't had a chance to read it and she claims it's driving her nuts. Apparently it's been in great demand since I came to Momson. No place else but here, anyway.' He laughed again, a sound that was almost a tuneless bark.

'You got it published, at any rate.'

'Yes, and the critics were a little kinder – although there was still plenty for them to pick apart, apparently. After Holt, Doubleday and Lippincott both turned it down before Putnam's picked it up. I'm not sure how much they spent on promotion, but I'm sure you could have bought a bunch of bananas with it, if not the cereal to go with it.'

'It died?'

'Not immediately, in spite of all that. It sold a fair number of copies, but the paperback deal is pretty horrible. They're promoting it sort of as a sequel to *Conway's Daughter* even though the two books have absolutely nothing in common.'

Also in the chapter on Matt, there is a deleted scene in which Matt has a physical checkup with Dr Cody, and they discuss the Glick case and it is here that Matt mentions Dracula. *This scene does not appear in the published novel but is referenced several times in it.*

Matt's doctor was Jimmy Cody, a boy whom he had had in English some ten years before. Then he had been a little heller, but he seemed to have grown up nicely in medical school. Even his pimples were gone.

He sat on Jimmy's examining table and allowed himself to be poked and prodded and fingered while Jimmy asked him how things were going down at the old jail. Matt told him that things were fine; all the irons nicely hot and the manacles well-oiled.

Jimmy laughed. 'You can put your shirt on, Mr Burke. You'll go another forty before you even need an oil change.'

'That's what they all say,' Matt told him, a little

grumpily. He had confessed having some trouble with insomnia and Jimmy, referring to him by the old honorific of 'Mr' all the time, had cheerfully refused to prescribe. Just wait, he told himself balefully, buttoning his shirt. Wait until you're sixty, fellow, and the high point of your day is having a good crap for the first time in a week.

Aloud he said, 'It's a shame about Danny Glick.'

'Funny you should mention that,' said Jimmy. 'I was at the hospital the night he died. Was called in for consultation, in fact. I was the Glicks' family doctor.' He shook his head. 'I've been thinking of writing the case up for one of the journals. Damn strange.'

'I don't suppose you can talk about it.'

'You're trustworthy enough,' Jimmy said. 'Just keep away from Mabel Werts and Ann Norton, if you please. They'd be seeing natives with poison blowguns in the bushes.'

Matt laughed.

'The kid was found over by the window of his room. The nurse said he must have gotten up, opened it, and then collapsed. She called a doctor in – Dr Berry in fact – and Berry pronounced him dead. He noted a condition which is known somewhat unfairly as mortician's complexion, and it's not that rare, but . . . I examined Danny Glick the day before. He had an anemic condition, an acutely anemic condition.' Jimmy shook his head and twiddled his stethoscope absently. 'It was bad enough so I had set up a series of tests for the big C.'

'Leukemia?' Matt asked.

'Yes – it was the only thing that fit. But I've never heard of a case of mortician's complexion in conjunction with anemia. And rigor mortis was late and extremely shallow, which is a condition most common with people who are prone to hypertension – high blood pressure.'

'Did he have a previous history of anemia?'

'Hell, no! I gave him a physical myself when he went out for little league baseball. That also tends to make me think that the kid was maybe developing leukemia. The tests he was given when he was admitted show negative, but they were general diagnostic tests, not very conclusive. If the boy had lived one more day . . .' He trailed off for a moment. 'Anyway, I'm in correspondence with three heavy heads in the area. If the condition has been noted before in pm leukemia patients, I think that will solve it. I still might write it up, though.'

He shook his head. 'The mother and father went into hysterics when they saw him, and I can't blame them. That kid didn't look any more dead than, well, than you do. He looked ready to get right up and start shagging flies.'

'His father made that very clear at the funeral,' Matt said. 'I don't suppose Danny had any innocent-looking marks on his neck?'

Jimmy Cody had been rearranging medicine samples in a glass case, and now he looked around sharply.

'Why, now that you mention it, the boy *did* have a couple of small scratches just above the carotid vein. How did you know that?'

Matt smiled, although he felt a superstitious uneasiness in spite of himself, and felt the crawl of hard bumps up his forearms – somewhere a goose was walking across his grave. But he certainly was not going to show Jimmy Cody that feeling.

'It seems to me you have a little more technical literature to read, Jimmy. I recommend the public library. A man
by the name of Bram Stoker described all of Danny Glick's
symptoms almost seventy-five years ago.'

'Are you kidding me?'

'I certainly hope so,' Matt said. 'The name of the
book is *Dracula*.'

*In Chapter 8 (Ben [III]), there are several scenes which failed
to make it to the finished book. Here are a few:*

When he woke up, it was quarter after four. His body
was beaded with sweat, and he had kicked the upper sheet
away. Still, he felt clearheaded again. The events of that
early morning seemed to be far away and dim, and Matt
Burke's fancies seemed no more than a harmless, antique
whimsey.

Still, Mike Bush [Ryerson] was dead. That was a fact.

He went down the hall to the shower with a towel
slung over his shoulder, and Weasel looked out of his room.
His eyes were bleary, and he was holding a gallon jug of
zinfandel red by the neck.

'Ben, how are you, buddy?'

'All right, Weasel.'

'Come on in an' have a drink. Awful thing about
Mike Bush. I knew his mom well. She was a lovely woman.'

'Maybe later, Weasel. I want to get a shower.'

'Sure, buddy. Say—'

Ben, who had gotten to the bathroom door, looked
back over his shoulder.

'I heard ol' Mabel Werts blabbing her jowls to Joe
Crane when I was down to the store, an' she was saying

that maybe both Mike and that poor little Glick boy might have had some rare disease—'

'That's bullshit, Weasel.'

'Yeah . . . still, you shower good, buddy. You never know what germs dead people have.'

Ben went in and shut the door. Undressing, he reflected that the telephone was the most primitive form of communication in a small town. The comment Matt Burke had made to Jimmy Cody had been enough to set the ball rolling. Like that game they played on rainy days when they were kids – Whisper. Start off with 'Frankie Winchell has pimples' and by the time it got to the other side of the room you had 'Francis Waylon is pregnant.' Parkins Gillespie whispers to his wife, his wife whispers to Ann Norton, Ann whispers to Mabel Werts, and Mabel sends it into the streets in a fright-wig.

He turned on the showerhead.

When he went downstairs, Eva said: 'Matt Burke called about an hour ago. Wants you to call him back. He said there was no hurry.'

'Okay.'

Several of the oldsters who roomed at Eva's were eating their supper at the table – beans and sardines – and asked him to sit down and tell them about Mike. Ben did, not because he wanted to tell his story again, but because he was curious to find how far the rumors had gotten.

'I heard they may throw a quarantine over us,' Grover Verrill said, holding a sardine by its tail for a moment before popping it into his toothless mouth.

'Where did you hear that?' Ben asked.

'Joe Crane was tellin' it down at Crossen's,' Grover said, and looked over at Vinnie Upshaw. 'Ain't you been down there today?'

'No; goddamn leg's tighter'n a tick. May go down this evenin'.'

'Why would they want to throw a quarantine?' Mabe Mullican asked.

'They think he may have had one of them funny diseases,' Grover said. 'The berryberries or Hong Kong mumps or some shit like that,' he added sagely.

'Think he mighta caught it off that Glick kid, do they?' Mabe asked.

'Well, as Joe told it—'

Ben slipped away to the phone in the hall and dialed Matt's number. The other end was picked up after a single ring. 'Hello? Ben?'

'Yes.'

'I talked to Carl Foreman.'

'What did he say?'

'Daniel Glick was cosmeticized, but not embalmed. The father wouldn't allow it.'

'Which means he . . .' Ben suddenly became aware that he could be heard in the kitchen.

Matt mistook his reticence for the delicacy they had both shown when approaching the subject.

'It means that Danny Glick *could* be Undead. He *could* have sucked Mike Bush's blood.' His voice rose a note. 'We're talking about vampires, Ben. And all the old legends say they can only be stopped by three things: sunlight, holy artifacts, or a stake through the heart. I don't know about the others – perhaps the Torah would stop a Jewish vampire

697

– but I suspect evisceration would substitute nicely for the stake. *But Danny Glick was not eviscerated! He was not embalmed! He could be—*'

'Settle down,' Ben said.

'Yes,' Matt said. 'Yes, I'm sorry for that. Are there people close enough to hear?'

'Yes.'

'You're coming over tonight?'

'Yes.'

'Good. Good.' The relief in Matt's voice was nearly tangible. 'Can you see how important it is that Mike Bush is given . . . everything?'

'Yes.'

'There's another matter, too. Something I just thought of.'

'What?'

'Not over the phone. Will you be here . . . before dark?'

'Yes, okay.' Ben hesitated, and then said what had been on his mind. 'I may bring Susan with me.'

'Do you mean tell her?'

'Is it a bad idea?'

'I don't know . . . no, that might be all right. If you think it's best, all right.'

'Okay,' Ben said. 'Maybe I'll bring her and the three of us can . . . can discuss things.'

'All right, Ben. I'm sorry if I sounded hysterical.'

'No, you didn't. I'll see you, Matt.'

'Okay. Good-by.'

'By.'

Ben hung up thoughtfully. The fears were not so

distant or so curiously antique now. The word they had both avoided – even the night before – had been spoken.

Vampire.

From the German word *wampyre*, meaning devil. Night-creature, pallid as the moon. Seriocomic hero of a thousand poorly-photographed B-pictures, destined to their own nighttime living death at drive-in theaters across the United States. Mainstay of the comic books of the 50s, when Ben had grown up, and now of the 70s, when he had returned to the place of his growing-up.

Vampire.

Dweller in cold marble tombs and crypts of earth and stone. Propitiating its own legend, even in the face of cold science, thriving even in an age of rockets, computers, DNA analysis. Flittering into ten thousand bedrooms of the mind, where voluptuous teenage girls lay in the grip of nightmares with their nightgowns twisted above their alabaster thighs.

Vampire.

The old men – and Eva – were looking at him, but he hardly noticed them going out. The word clanged in his mind like a churchyard bell.

In the original ending to Susan (II), Count Barlow (who is called Sarlinov in the original manuscript) and Straker meet out near the end of town to discuss how the novel's heroes had been faring.

The Deep Cut Road skirts the marshes to the south-west of the town's center, and then winds crazily through a series of folded ridges and sudden, knife-cut dips, and here the country was so wild that even the ubiquitous trailers were left behind. It was here that the big fire of 1951 burned at its most feverish, destructive pitch, and the growth has come back and formed into fervid tangles and nightmare patterns which lurch over and under huge dead-falls like a drunkard's stagger. This country continues for only five miles or so, but it is five miles of the wildest land in the area. Now, with much of the fall foliage dashed from the trees and the wildly-leaning trunks painted by the moonlight, the woods looked like nothing so much as a three-dimensional maze constructed by a madman.

At nearly midnight on that Friday night, a black Packard – either a '39 or a '40 – was parked somewhere along this stretch of road, idling quietly. The exhaust drew a wavering line in the dark. A tall shadow – Straker – stood with one foot on the driver's side running board, smoking one of his Turkish cigarettes.

Something stirred in the air, darker even than the pines that formed the scene's backdrop. A large crow, or perhaps a bat. Its form seemed to shift, elongate, and change. For a moment it seemed oddly insubstantial, as if it might disappear altogether. And then there was a second shadow, standing beside the first.

'Our father has been kind,' Straker remarked.

'Be it ever so,' remarked the other. His hair was now a vigorous black, with the faintest speckles of gray at the temples. 'Mr Ben Mears?'

'In the hospital.'

'And Mr Tibbits?'

'In the constable's lock-up. Mr Bush will attend to him later.'

'Burke is out of the way?'

'Yes. Not dead, but also in the hospital. He had a heart attack.'

'It is sufficient. He had the most knowledge; and a certain . . . persuasiveness.'

'But no zealotry.'

'Ah, no.' The figure with the vigorous black hair laughed softly. He did not in the least look like Bela Lugosi or Christopher Lee. 'No zealotry there.'

'Is Master Glick—'

'Master Glick is about his business. Yes. Yes, indeed.' The dark man laughed again.

Straker asked humbly: 'Is it my time yet?'

'Almost, my good servant. It is almost time.'

'Our father is kind,' Straker said, and there was the faintest touch of resignation in his voice.

'Be it ever so.'

Together, in the darkness, they seemed to merge into a single shadow.

In The Lot (III), *we have this scene of Ruthie Crockett being visited by Dud Rogers, and another of the McDougall baby visiting his mother.*

Ruthie Crockett's shortie nightgown had twisted up above her thighs, showing a darker patch at their juncture that had been there for less than two years. Her perfect adolescent breasts rose and fell slowly in her deep sleep.

It took a long time for the soft beating on her window to awaken her, and even then she never woke fully. It was in a dream that she saw the oddly cocked head and behind it the twisted, hunched back of Dud Rogers.

His eyes glittered over her, filling with the night-reality of her slumbrous vitality, so deep that even in deepest sleep no cool hint of mortality could touch it. Her breasts pressed against each other in milky curves at the bodice of her nightdress.

'Ruthie . . . please, Ruthie, let me in a minute. Let me in.'

And she, still dreaming of the boy who had just the previous evening parked with her and run his hands over her body until it seemed ready to shriek aloud with painful pleasure, seemed to see his clear face and his straight back instead of Dud's, and as she slid the window open and held out her sleeping arms, the flame leaped up in her like coal oil splashed into an open hearth and his arms were around her and there were no negatives now, negatives were swept away, impossible. His lips found the soft column of her throat, and for a single, darkly enchanted moment, she could hear the soft and eager champing of his tongue against her skin, laving it, preparing it for some unknown and unexpected entry.

His teeth dented against her throat . . . paused . . . pierced.

Orgasm shook her. Fierce, alien, compelling beyond all compulsion. And again. And again. So, on and on, down dark hallways, until all thought of her flesh was lost, drowned in a sweet green singing that rose and rose, bearing her down into darkness, unbearable in its sweet repulsiveness.

In her dream, her son had come back to her.

She lay in her own bed again, because Roy had taken her home. He had driven her home heavily sedated, sitting on the far right-hand side of the front seat with her hands in her lap. Roy asked her if she would like something to eat. She said no thank you. Her eyes, moving listlessly around the dining nook of the trailer and the living room beyond, saw that all sign of the baby was gone: Playpen, toy basket, Raggedy Andy doll, the caterpillar, the high chair where she had tried to feed him back to life.

No thank you, she had said, I want to go to sleep.

And now in this dream Randy was scratching at the window and she rushed to let him in because it was night and cold and her baby boy was naked.

She opened the window and he crawled into her arms – never mind how he got up to that high window, it doesn't matter in dreams – and nuzzled at her neck like a little puppy dog.

And he was cold, so cold – but alive, not like this morning. His eyes were open and they were so pretty that you could hardly look away from them and he had been cutting new teeth, too.

Come to bed, baby, cover up warm with Momma.

And as she pulled the blankets over them a heavy sweetness – fulfillment – came to her and it was all right again because this was real and the rest had been a dream.

But you're so *cold*, she said, hugging Randy to her, and her body heat did not seem to bring any vitality to him.

Teeth, nuzzling her neck.

Is oo hungwy? Want Momma to fix oo a wittle snackie?

But too hard to get up. And surely she was meant to nourish her own, and let him grow strong. She was going to be a good mother from now on. Such a scare she had had!

Leaning back on her pillow, drowsing off, she gave her son suck. In a last moment of belated fright, of near reality, she glanced over at the mirror which ran the length of her dressing table and in the glimmering light saw her own ecstatic face, eyes burning with a dark love that verged on fanaticism, and her arms cradling – nothing.

Her eyes searched for him in the crook of the arm and found him, her son with his tiny body lying on the swell of her breast, his working mouth pressed to her throat.

I'm never going to hit you again, Randy, she thought, just before drowsing off.

Never again.

In Chapter 12 (Mark), *both Mark and Susan explore the Marsten House, plotting to kill Barlow. However, in the published novel, the house is still a shambles when Susan peers in the window. In the original manuscript, there has been some renovation, detailed below:*

She peered in through the break in the shutters. 'Wow,' she murmured.

'What is it?' he asked anxiously. Even standing on tiptoe, he wasn't quite tall enough to peer in.

She tried stumblingly to explain. Of course, neither of them knew that Parker [Larry] Crockett, feeling more and more like a man in the devil's power, had been acting on Straker's orders – orders that unvaryingly specified pick-up and delivery after dark. The invoices and bills of lading were always correct to the final letter, and payment was always to be made in cash – and Straker calculated with devilish accuracy, including sums for tipping porters and drivers. Drivers were hard to find, also. The harried Crockett found himself having to cast further and further afield for haulers and he found none that would do the job more than once. Royal Snow had laughed in his face and said, 'I wouldn't go back to that hell-house for a million bucks. Not if you drove the million up to my back door in a pickup. Get someone else.'

The triumph of owning the hot property downstate had even gone a bit sour in his mouth. Looking at the duly-executed papers in his safe-deposit box somehow didn't compensate for the looks on the country-boys' faces when they came into his office to collect Straker's money. Parker knew that some of the deliveries were paintings – even when crated and covered with brown paper, the shape and feel of a painting was unmistakable. He suspected that the other crates, some of them picked up at the Portland docks, some at the Gates Falls railhead, contained furniture.

On Friday evening, the two men Parker had hired from Harlow had not returned – instead, Straker had shown up, driving the U-Haul.

'Where are those two guys?' Parker had asked. 'I got their money . . .' He indicated the sealed white envelopes with a finger that shook slightly. Straker made that happen, damn him. For the first time in his long and not-so-straight business life, Parker Crockett felt manipulated, and he did not like it.

'They were curious,' Straker said, smiling his wolfish smile. 'Like Bluebeard's wife.'

'Where are they?' Parker asked again, aware that he was afraid Straker might tell him the truth.

'I've paid them,' Straker said. 'You needn't worry. You can keep that, if you like,' he added carelessly. There was two hundred dollars in each envelope.

Parker said deliberately: 'If the State Police or Homer McCaslin shows up here, I want you to know I'm not going to cover up a goddamned thing. You've exceeded our agreement.'

Straker had thrown back his head and roared out his humorless, black laughter. 'You are a precious man, Mr Crockett. Precious. You needn't fear the authorities. Indeed, no.' The mockery of humor disappeared from his face like a dream. 'If you must fear anything, fear your own curiosity. Do not be like those two dirt-grubbers tonight . . . or Bluebeard's wife. There is a saying in our country: he who knows little is a sparrow; and the sparrows abide.'

And Parker Crockett asked no more questions. His daughter was sick in bed, and he asked no questions about that, either.

Looking through those dusty, broken slats was like looking through a science fiction time-lens into some stately Victorian mansion after the family had gone to Brighton for the summer. The walls were covered with a heavy, silken paper, wine-colored. Several wing chairs stood about, and a deep green velour sofa. In the alcove just off the main living room she could see a huge mahogany rolltop desk. Over it, in a heavily-scrolled frame, was a reproduction of Rembrandt's *Boy at his Studies* – of course, it had to be a reproduction, didn't it? Sliding doors, half-open, fronted the hallway that led past the stairwell and down toward the kitchen where Hubert Marsten's wife had met her end. In the passage's brown depths, she could see the crystal glimmer of a chandelier.

She stepped away fighting an urge to rub her eyes.

It was so unlike the Marsten House of town rumor, or the stories passed from mouth to horrified mouth around the Girl Scout campfires that it was almost indecent. And all the changes had been made invisibly, it seemed.

'What is it?' Mark hissed again. 'Is it *him?*'

'No,' she said. 'The house, it . . . it's been redone,' she finished lamely.

'Sure,' he said, in perfect understanding. '*They* like to have all *their* stuff. Why shouldn't they? They've got tons of money and gold.'

She boosted herself up with a smooth flex of her muscles, and suddenly thought of Ben telling her about the hoods who had stuck up John Stennis: *We're going to shoot you anyway.*

She dropped lightly to the carpet, which was smooth and soft and deep. Across the room, a grandfather clock with its wonderfully convoluted works in an oblong glass case, ticked away the minutes. The highly polished pendulum made a sunstreak on the opposing wall. There was an open humidor by one of the wing chairs, and beside it, an old-looking book with a calfskin binding. A black satin bookmark was placed into it perhaps three quarters of the way through. The overhead light fixture was a wonderfully convoluted thing composed of oblique prisms.

There were no mirrors in the room.

'Hey,' Mark hissed. His hands waved above the windowsill. 'Help me get up.'

She leaned out, caught him under the armpits, and dragged him up until he could catch a grip on the sill.

Then he jackknifed himself in neatly. His sneakered feet thumped to the carpet, and then the house was still again.

They found themselves listening to the silence, fascinated by it. There did not even seem to be the faint, high hum in the ears that comes in utter stillness, the sound of nerve-endings idling in neutral. There was only a great dead soundlessness. And that wasn't right because—

She looked wildly across the room.

The clock had stopped. The pendulum hung straight down.

The cellar door was standing ajar.

'That's where we have to go,' he said.

'Oh,' she said weakly. 'Oh.'

The door was open just a crack, and the light did not penetrate at all. The tongue of darkness seemed to lick at the kitchen, hungrily, waiting for night to come so it could swallow it whole. That quarter inch of darkness was hideous, unspeakable in its possibilities. She stood beside Mark, helpless and moveless.

Then he moved forward and pulled the door open, and she felt her legs fall in behind him.

His fingers found a light switch and thumbed it back and forth several times.

'Busted,' he muttered. '*That's* no surprise.' He reached into his back pocket and brought out a greasy, crooked candle that had been slightly flattened by its trip in Mark's back pocket. He turned to her and made himself offer: 'Look, maybe you better stay up here and keep a watch out for Straker.'

'No,' she said. 'I'm coming.'

It did not occur to either of them that the time had come to go back, to get Ben and perhaps even Jimmy Cody, to come back here with powerful eight-cell flashlights and shotguns. They were beyond reality; they had gone around the bend that so many discuss so lightly at parties where the electric lights are on and shadows are kept sensibly under tables and locked in closets.

He lit the candle and they went through the door.

The throat of the stairway was narrow stone, the steps themselves dusty and old. The candle flame danced and fluttered in the noisome exhalation from below.

Now she heard something: the faint whisk and patter of many small feet. She pressed her lips together to still the sound that wanted to come between them – it might have been a scream.

'Rats,' he said. 'You scared of rats?'

'No,' she lied.

They went down.

She counted the steps – thirteen of them. Didn't they say that the old English gallows had thirteen steps? Only of course that was going up, not down.

(Ben had mentioned *Psycho*, what was that line from the book, not Hitchcock's movie? *You've made your grave and now you have to lie in it. Only it wasn't a grave, it was a bed.* Or Poe: *My God, I had walled the monster up in the tomb!* Or nameless hoodlums on a Washington, D.C. street: *We're going to kill you anyway.*)

They stepped on the hard-packed earth floor, and Mark held the candle up. The ceiling was low; the top of Susan's head nearly brushed the cobwebby beams. In the glow of the candle they could see moving shadows in the darkness, and every now and again the ruby glint of an eye. There was an old table covered by a piece of oilcloth, and beside it stood an opened crate, with aluminum retaining bands snapped. The smell of rot and putridity was thick in the throat, nearly overwhelming.

'Take your cross in your hand,' he said.

She fumbled it out of her blouse and held it tightly. Closed in her fist, it seemed to be the only warmth in a cold world. She began to feel a little better, a little comforted. She looked down at her tightly curled hand and saw a faint, luminous glow escaping between her fingers in rays.

'It's glowing,' she whispered.

'Yes. We don't have to worry about the rats. Come on. This way.'

They began to walk forward, single file, toward the long southern spread of the cellar. She could see that it took an L-turn up ahead, and knew that whatever they had come for would reach its culmination beyond that turn. She looked aside and felt her blood cool in her veins.

The rats were everywhere, seemingly millions of them, two and three deep, squirming over each other in their eagerness. She saw some as big as small cats. Their beady eyes stared at them with cold impudence. They had left a small pathway for them, about two feet across, and were closing in behind them as the Red Sea had closed behind Moses.

One of them darted forward and nipped at Mark's foot and without thought she thrust her crucifix at it, hissing. The rat squealed and scrabbled off into the darkness, a brown elastic sock fiber hanging from its jaw.

They stopped at the cellar's elbow-bend. 'Remember,' he told her. 'Don't look at his eyes. No matter what happens.'

'Yes . . . all right.'

He took her hand again. 'I'm scared,' he said. 'I couldn't ever do this again.'

'It's too late to go back, isn't it?'

'Yes. I . . . I think it is.'

'Then go on, Mark. We'll do what we have to.' She was stunned by the calmness which seemed to flow from her own voice.

They were around the corner, and a warm carrion breeze immediately whiffed out the candle, plunging them into utter, womblike darkness. She screamed; was unable to help it. In her ears was the sound of the rats, squeaking and rustling and drawing closer with tenebrous eagerness.

'Hold your cross up!' Mark shouted.

She did.

Its glow spilled forth with an effulgent, unearthly radiance that was brighter by far than the candle that now lay at Mark's feet. It spilled off these crumbled brick walls with a frosty luminescence which was deeply comforting. The rats squealed and scampered.

Mark, also holding up his cross, was looking around. 'Judas Priest!' he muttered.

Hubert Marsten must have been a bootlegger indeed, Susan thought. They stood at the mouth of what must once have been an extensive wine cellar (Poe again: *For the love of God, Montressor*—!), full of casks covered with dust and cobwebs, and lined with crisscrossing wine holders. From some of these, ancient magnums still peeked forth. Some of them had popped their corks, and where sparkling burgundy had once waited for some discerning palate, the spider now made his home. Others would have turned to vinegar. Still others might be good, still waiting . . . waiting for . . .

She shifted her eyes up. The wine cellar opened out to an underground dais, freshly hung with circular velvet drapes. Unlit black tapers stood about. On the far wall, a cross with broken arms hung upside down. Obscene statues stood to either side of the main podium – and on it rested a huge coffin of banded oak, and on top of it was an embossed coat of arms with a wolf rampant, and one word:

SARLINOV.

This was it, then. True – all true. The word echoed dismally into the depths of her mind, as if through channels of fog. She felt waves of faintness sweep over her, and her cross wavered. She felt frozen in indecision, unable to move. It would be so much simpler, so blessed, to just wait here . . . wait here until the world turned into *his* nighted sphere above them.

'Now!' Mark shouted at her. 'Now!'

'No,' she whispered weakly. 'I can't. Let me alone.' The scene wavered and danced in front of her eyes, as if seen from behind a burning haze of heat. The statues which flanked the coffin, statues she faintly recognized as the Holy Family in unthinkable postures, seemed to writhe and move.

'Our Father, who art in Heaven . . .' he began.

'No . . . no . . .'

His hand flashed out, and her head rocked back. One eye watered and twitched.

This section is from Father Callahan's chapter, when he is talking to Matt Burke. This scene was omitted from the final novel but still carries peripheral interest.

'I'm not going to say no, not at this point,' Callahan said. 'But I want you to understand my position. Let me make three points, and then I'll ask you if you have changed your mind. Agreed?'

'Yes.'

'Okay. One: During the black plague which covered Europe during the Middle Ages, vampire hysteria was roughly equal to the flying saucer hysteria of a few years ago in this country. People in many cases observed the unquiet dead writhing on the carts of the dead-wagons that went through the streets, collecting plague victims, and in many cases, a traveler passing a cemetery would see a hand clawing up through the earth, followed by the mud-clotted, wild-eyed face of what the illiterate, frightened "man-in-the-street" of the day quite reasonably took to be an Undead. In the countries of Eastern Europe, the peasants recently converted to Catholicism besieged their priests, begging them to do something about the vampires that were abroad in the countryside. Most priests had never heard of such a thing, but were loath to admit it. Many of them, therefore, blessed the rite of vampire-killing forthwith. Are you following?'

'Yes.'

'Good. Then imagine you are Joe Smithov, a typical Romanian peasant. You are stricken with the black plague, and for two weeks you thrash in a delirium of fever. At last it breaks, and you plunge down into a cooling, restorative unconsciousness. At this point you are pronounced dead by an unlettered country quack who held a mirror in front of your mouth for four seconds and then felt for your pulse by pressing his ear to your stomach. Still unconscious, you are piled into a rude coffin by frightened relatives, and carried to the local graveyard, where you are buried in a shallow pit. Later, you awake to the horror of all horrors: buried alive! Perhaps you scream. Perhaps you are able to pull away one of the boards and thrust an arm up through the loose earth, waving wildly. And then . . . blessed rescue! You hear the shovels, then see the good light of day again. Instead of stale air, the fresh, sweet breeze of God's heaven. And then . . . what's this? A delegation with an ash stake, tied with ceremonial red ribbons. Two men hold you down, screaming and begging. A third places the stake against your chest. A fourth holds a mallet, ready to send your blood-sucking soul back to Father Satan. And behind this delegation, who should you see with your dying gaze but the village priest, reading the rite of exorcism and sprinkling everything in sight with holy water! Fade out. Not pretty, is it?'

'No.'

'The church is desperately ashamed of the whole episode – they use it as a case in point whenever someone in its body shows a sign of jumping to conclusions – of proceeding on the basis of two hundred years' study rather than five hundred.'

In the scene when Ben, Mark, Cody and Callahan come into the Marsten House cellar, they are greeted with a tape recording of Barlow's voice, rather than the handwritten note that is in the finished novel.

When the priest opened the door, Mark felt the rank,

rotten odor assail his nostrils again — but that, also, was different. Not so strong. Less . . . less malevolent.

The priest started down the stairs, and his cross did not glow as theirs had done the day before. Still, it took all his willpower to continue down after them into that pit of horror.

Jimmy had produced a flashlight from his bag and clicked it on. The beam illuminated again the old table, the dusty, monolithic coal furnace with its many projecting pipes like tentacles, the overturned crate. Yet there was no squirming tide of rats, no ominous sensation of moving to meet a dark force of illimitable power and cold hate. And somehow that frightened him more than anything else, although he could not have told why.

'Around the corner,' he said, his voice flat and dead in the enclosed space.

Holding the crucifix high, Callahan advanced. And now, at last, the crucifix he held aloft began to glow belatedly. As he turned the corner, he thundered: 'In the name of God the Father—' His words clogged suddenly in his throat, and a huge, monstrous chuckle smote their ears.

Mark screamed: 'It's *him*, it's *him!*'

'A recording!' Callahan shouted. 'Some kind of tape! I felt a wire across my chest—'

'Hello, my young friends!' the voice boomed. It was gentle, mocking, jeering. 'How lovely of you to have dropped in.'

Ben darted forward, ignoring the coldness which rose in him at that reptilian voice. He swept his hands in the empty air, found a length of something very like piano wire, and followed it on a diagonal from the corner.

'I am never averse to company — it has always been one of my great joys,' the voice continued, booming hollowly in the dark and rank smelling cellar. 'Had you come in the evening, I should have welcomed you in person . . . however, since I suspected you might come in daylight, I thought it might be best to be out.' The chuckle again, booming and racketing, heart-freezing. It struck a familiar cord in Jimmy Cody, and he isolated it. As a young boy, crouching in front of a very large Zenith radio in his father's house, he had heard a chuckle much like that echo from the vocal cords of the Shadow.

Ben found the tape recorder, sitting on a high shelf to the left of the wine cellar's entrance. It was a modern Wollensak reel-to-reel, the piano wire tightly snubbed around the spring-loaded PLAY/RECORD button.

'I have left you a token of my appreciation,' the voice continued, becoming soft and caressing. 'Someone very near and dear to one of you is now in the place where I occupied my days until yesterday . . . you are there, aren't you, Mr Mears?'

Ben jumped and regarded the tape recorder as if it were a snake that had just bitten him.

'I do not need her,' the voice said with frightening indifference. 'I have left her for you to — how is the idiom? — to warm up for the main event. To whet your appetite, if you like. Let us see how well you like the appetizer to the main course you contemplate.'

'Turn it off!' Jimmy cried.

'No!' Ben shouted. 'He may say something about—'

'—want to say something special to one of you,' the

voice continued, and it had become silky with menace. 'Young Master Petrie.'

Mark stiffened.

'Master Petrie, in some way unknown to me, you have robbed me of the most faithful and resourceful servant I have ever known – and that covers a long, long period of time. How dare you?' the voice asked, rage creeping in. 'Did you sneak up behind him and push him? You cowardly little whelp, *how dare you?*'

Mark bared his teeth unconsciously at the voice. His hands had doubled up into fists.

'I am going to enjoy dealing with you,' the voice continued, still rising. 'Your parents first, I think. Tonight . . . or tomorrow night . . . or the next. And then you. But you shall enter my church as a choirboy *castratum*. I take the blood not from your neck, but from your very manhood: the testicles. I send you into the outer darknesses of my service unshod, eh? Eh?' The voice pealed off into laughter, but even to Father Callahan's ear, frozen with wonder and fear, the laughter sounded false, brassy with rage . . . and uncertainty. What a turn it must have given him to rise on Sunday evening and find his right arm had been cut off!

'Father Callahan?' the voice asked teasingly, and he jumped as Ben had a moment earlier. 'Are you there? *Pardonez-moi*, I cannot see you. Have they persuaded you to come? Perhaps so. I have observed you at some length since I arrived in Momson . . . much as a good chess player will study the games of his opposition, eh? The Catholic Church is not yet the oldest of my adversaries, no! I was old even when *it* was young, this claque which you and your fellows venerate so for its antiquity. This simpering club of bread-eaters and wine-drinkers who venerate the sheep-savior. Yet I do not underestimate. I am wise in the ways of goodness as well as evil. I am not jaded. Even now I love the game as well as the prize, so I do not underestimate.

'So how do I see you? Better, perhaps, than you see yourself. Braver. How is your word? Courage? No. Spanish is *machismo*. Much-man. More than courage. Thinking, also. Coolness. When coupled with white magic, that is much. These others . . . *fut*, I spit on them. When I am ready, I will take them one by one and break them. It is only you I fear, coupled to your Church. How is this, that I feel fear? It is also *machismo*. You yourself fear, even now when it is not me but only my voice in this box, is it not so?'

Yes, Callahan thought. Yes, yes. I know fear. So much that it seems like the first ever in my life.

'It is wise to fear one's opponent,' the bodiless voice comforted him. 'This is how we live in the world.

'Yet I will best you,' the voice added, almost as an afterthought. 'How? you say. Do I not bear the symbol of White? Can I not move in the day as well as the night? Are there not charms and potions, both Christian and pagan, which my so-good friend Matthew Burke has informed me of? Yes, yes, and yes. But I have lived longer than you. I am crafty. I am not the serpent, but the father of serpents.

'Still, you say, this is not enough. And it is not. In the end, it is your own wretched faith that will undo you. It is weak . . . soft . . . rotten. It is no longer a defense against the evils that are in your world, if it ever was. You your-self, acolyte and preserver of the flame, doubt the worth of the flame that you guard. You preach of love and there is no love. I spit on love!' He cried it, his voice rising in a sudden and wrenching flight that held notes of madness. 'Love, the talisman of White! What is it? Words and pressings of flesh and barnyard copulation! The rest is mere presumption! *It has failed!*' And now that voice, as resourceful as a cathedral organ, had taken on accents of triumph, and it was impossible to tell if they were real or counterfeit.

'Always you assume good is greater than evil, but it is not so. Goodness, dear Father Callahan, requires the act of faith. Evil requires only that one wait. It is loose in the world, as omnipresent as the wind. You know that, but you do not know of good. And when the moment comes, it will be check to the king . . . *and black wins all!*'

The voice rose to a scream that made them all flinch, and then the voice was silent. The tape spooled on vacantly for a sheaf of moments, and then another voice spoke – Susan's voice. The cool, clear accents were the same, complete to the faint Maine accent of slurred r's. Yet for all that, it was a travesty, a husk, a bad imitation, a talking doll speaking in Susan's voice.

'Come to me, Ben. Let me fuck you. Wait until dark and I'll fuck you. Fuck-fuck-fuck. Father Callahan, too. Would you like a piece of it, Father? Let me slip my hand under that black robe and start to—'

Ben pulled the tape recorder off the shelf, barely aware that he was screaming. Something inside it popped and flared and the words ran down to a grotesquely deepening basso, and still he didn't, couldn't stop. He kicked it, sending one of the reels flying, unreeling tape. He chased it, kicked it again, chased it, kicked it again, chased it—

Hands on his shoulders, shaking him. 'Ben, stop it! Stop it! Stop it!'

He glanced up, dazed. Jimmy's face in front of his, contorted. Weeping?

'I'm sorry,' he said, his voice dull and distant in his own ears. 'Sorry.'

He looked around. Mark, his fists still balled, his mouth frozen in the twist of someone who has bitten something rotten; Jimmy, his oddly boyish face streaked with sweat and tears; Father Donald Callahan, his face pallid and drawn into an agonized rictus. And they were all looking at him.

Later, when Barlow has Callahan cornered in the Petrie kitchen, the published novel takes a different turn; the original plays out below.

The cross's glow was dying.

He looked at it, eyes widening. Fear leaped into his belly like a confusion of hot wires. His head jerked up and he stared at Sarlinov. He was coming forward, his smile wide, almost voluptuous.

'Stay back,' Callahan said hoarsely, retreating a step. 'I command it, in the name of God.'

Sarlinov laughed at him.

The glow in the cross was only a thin and guttering light in a cruciform shape. The shadows had crept across the vampire's face again, masking his features in strangely barbaric lines and triangles under the sharp cheekbones.

Callahan took another step backward, and his buttocks bumped the kitchen table, which was set against the wall.

'Nowhere left to go,' Sarlinov murmured sadly, but

his dark eyes bubbled with infernal mirth. 'Sad to see a man's faith fail. Ah, well . . .'

The cross trembled in his hand and suddenly all its light was gone. It was only a piece of plaster that his mother had bought in a Dublin souvenir shop, probably at a scalper's price. The power it had sent ramming up his arm, enough power, seemingly, to smash down walls and shatter stones, was gone. The muscles remembered the thrumming but could not duplicate it.

Sarlinov's voice came out of the dark – Callahan shifted his eyes with frenzied futility to locate its position exactly and couldn't. Sarlinov was toying with him now, playing cat-and-mouse.

Can he hear my heart beating? Callahan wondered. Like a rabbit, caught in a trap? I pray to God not.

'It is the malaise of you Americans,' Sarlinov's voice said from a new place. 'You believe in toothpastes and the spray for armpits and for wonderful pills, but you do not believe in Powers. Instead, you have grown rich on darkness, like a fat pig that has grown fat on garbage. It is ripe, swelled, ready to be bled.'

God, Callahan thought, I'm begging, pleading, for You to get me out of this. Not for myself but for . . . for . . .

Yet there was no intensity to his thoughts, none of the feeling of *transmitting* that had come to him as a young man; no feeling that the words were going further than the cage of his skull.

Something clattered to the floor.

The cross.

'Ah, you've dropped it,' Sarlinov said, and now he was

far to the right of where Callahan had expected him, nearly behind him. 'But it doesn't matter; you've forgotten the doctrine of your own church, is it not so? The cross . . . or the flag . . . or the bread and wine . . . others . . . only symbols. Without faith, the cross is only wood, the flag cloth, the bread baked wheat, the wine sour grapes. Is it not so? If you had dropped it before, you should have beaten me yet another night. I rather suspected you would. In a way, I had hoped it might be so. It has been long since I met an opponent of any real worth.'

Another silence, dreadful. There was no sound of movement, none. The vampire was more silent than a cat in its deadly stalk.

Callahan suddenly began to grope on the table, running his hands lightly across its surface, his fingers trying to remember where it was, the knife Mrs Petrie had used to cut the sandwiches.

He remembered Matt saying, *Some things are worse than death.*

His fingertips read breadcrumbs like braille, slid over a plate, touched the rim of a coffee cup. Where was it? Where? For the love of God!

And as he touched it and his fingers closed around the wooden handle, Sarlinov spoke again, almost at his elbow.

'But there must be an end to talking now,' Sarlinov said with real regret. 'There must be—'

'*In God's name!*' Callahan cried, and swung the knife in a great, rising arc.

Light suddenly streamed from the blade in bright effulgence. Sarlinov's words were broken off into a jagged scream, and for one split second, Callahan could see the blazing knife-blade mirrored in each of his nighted eyes.

The blade grazed his forehead, and blood streamed forth in a welling stream.

'It's too late, shaman!' Sarlinov snarled. 'You pay a thousand times for your flawed belief, and for daring to cut me—'

And with no thought (he was, after all, a thinking man), Callahan plunged the knife into his own chest, not feeling it, seeing the impotent fury in the thing's eyes – but it dared not come near.

He withdrew the blade, and plunged it in again, with all that remained of his flagging strength. As thought began to ebb, he realized that his faith – some of it – had come back and he might have cheated himself of victory in his final, instinctive effort to save his soul from the hell of the Undead; and that was the most serious denial of faith of all.

Then thought was gone and he fell forward on the half of the knife and he closed his eyes and let himself go off to see what gods there were.

This scene occurs when Jimmy and Ben are driving back into Momson.

As they drew closer to Momson, an almost palpable cloud formed just above their heads, like the ones that used to form over the heads of Huey, Dewie, and Louie in the old Donald Duck comic books when they were angry. When Jimmy pulled off the turnpike at the large green reflectorized sign that read ROUTE 12 MOMSON CUMBER-LAND CUMBERLAND CTR Ben reflected that this was the way he and Susan had come home after their first date — she had wanted to see something with a car chase in it — and he had told her about the childhood experience that had finally gotten him pregnant with book. That book seemed very pale now.

'It's gone bad,' Jimmy said. His boyish face looked pale and frightened and angry. 'Christ, you can almost smell it.'

And you could, although the smell was mental rather than physical; a psychic whiff of tombs.

Route 12 was nearly deserted. On the way in, they passed Win Purinton's milk truck, and he lifted his hand in a puzzled, bemused kind of wave. They passed a few fast-moving cars going the other way, obviously transients. The houses on outer Momson Avenue had a deserted, shut-up look.

As they entered town, Jimmy said in an almost absurdly relieved tone: 'Look there. Crossen's is open.'

It was. Milt was out front, gassing up a car with a New Hampshire license plate, and Grover Verrill was standing next to him, dressed in a yellow lobsterman's slicker.

'Don't see the rest of the crew, though,' Jimmy added.

Milt glanced up at them and waved, and Ben thought he saw lines of strain on both old men's faces. The CLOSED sign was still posted inside the door of Foreman's Mortuary. The hardware store was also closed. The diner was open, however; as they flashed by, Ben caught a glimpse of Pauline Dickens serving someone coffee. The rest of the place looked empty.

The local police car was pulled up by the Municipal

Building and Parkins Gillespie, also in a slicker, was standing beside it. He did not wave, but watched them go by with hooded eyes.

The downtown streets were empty – not unusual in itself; it was a small town, and it was raining – but many shades were drawn, giving the town a brooding, secret look.

'They've been at it, all right,' Ben said.

Later, they enter the Petrie house and encounter the remains of Callahan.

'Good dear Christ,' Jimmy whispered. His arms turned to water; the bats went crashing over the floor like swollen pick-up sticks.

Ben only stared, frozen.

The bodies of Mr and Mrs Petrie lay where they had fallen, undisturbed. But Sarlinov had vented his full fury on Callahan, who had branded him and then cheated him at the moment of his victory.

His headless corpse was nailed to the dining room door, in a hideous parody of the crucifixion.

Ben closed his eyes, tried to swallow, and found nothing to swallow on. His mouth was like glass. Think of it as a cut of meat at the delicatessen, he told himself sickly. Think of it as—

He dropped his own armload and ran for the sink.

Faintly, he heard Jimmy cry out in a choked voice: 'What kind of a man is he?'

Ben raised himself on trembling arms and ran water into the sink. As if from a great distance, he heard his voice say: 'Not a man at all.'

The truth of it finally struck home to both of them,

725

with a great and iron weight, like the slamming of a huge door.

When Jimmy and Mark begin working on taking care of the vampires, they manage more than pulling Roy McDougall out into the sun, as this section shows:

Roy McDougall's car was standing in the driveway of the trailer lot on the Bend Road, and seeing it there on a weekday made Jimmy suspect the worst.

He and Mark got out into the rain without a word. Jimmy took his black bag, and Mark brought several of the freshly sharpened stakes and a hammer with a two-pound head from the trunk. Jimmy mounted the rickety steps and tried the bell. It didn't work, and so he knocked instead. The pounding roused no one, either in the McDougall trailer or in the neighboring one twenty yards down – although there was a car in that yard, also.

Jimmy tried the storm door, and it was locked. 'Give me that hammer,' he said.

Mark handed it over, and Jimmy smashed the glass to the right of the knob, whacking it out with two solid blows. He reached through and unsnapped the catch. The inside door was unlocked. They went in.

The smell was definable instantly – a dead giveaway. Jimmy felt his nostrils cringe against it, to try (unsuccessfully) to shut it out. The smell was not as strong as it had been in the basement of the Marsten House, but it was just as basically offensive – the smell of rot, of deadness. A wet, putrefied smell. Jimmy found himself suddenly remembering when, as boys, he and his buddies had gone out on their bikes during spring vacation to pick up the returnable beer and soft drink bottles the retreating snow had uncovered. In one of these (an Orange Crush bottle) he saw a small, decayed field mouse which had been attracted by the sweetness, perhaps, and had then been unable to get out. He had gotten a whiff of it and had immediately turned away and thrown up. This smell was plangently like that — sickish sweet and decayed sour mixed together and fermenting wildly. He felt his gorge rise.

'They're here,' Mark said.

They went through the place methodically — kitchen, dining nook, living room, each bedroom. They opened closets as they went. Jimmy thought they had found something in the master bedroom closet, but it was only a heap of dirty clothes.

'No cellar?' Mark asked.

'No . . . but there might be a crawl space.'

They went around the back and saw the small door that swung inward set into the trailer's rudimentary foundation. It was fastened with a padlock. Jimmy knocked it off with five hard blows from the hammer, and when he pushed open the half-trap, the smell hit them in a wave of corruption.

'There they are,' Mark said.

Peering in, Jimmy could just see three sets of feet, like corpses lined up on a battlefield. One set wore work boots, one wore knitted slippers, and the third set — tiny feet indeed — were bare.

Family scene, he thought crazily. Norman Rockwell, where are you? Unreality washed over him. The baby, he thought. How am I supposed to do this to a little baby? *Matt would do it.* I'm not Matt. I'm a doctor. I'm supposed to be a healer, not a . . . *You are healing. You're giving them back their souls so they can leave whatever awful place they're in.*

'I'm smaller,' Mark said. 'I'll go in.'

He dropped to his knees and wriggled through the half-trap.

'Get the . . . the little one first,' Jimmy heard himself saying. 'Let's get that over with.'

Mark grabbed Randy McDougall's ankles and pulled him out.

He was naked and dirty, his small body scratched and the knees lacerated to the point of horror. God knows where the fever in his body had caused him to crawl on them. As soon as the daylight struck his body, his eyelids fluttered and he began to writhe.

Mark gave him a last convulsive jerk out of the half-trap and then stood away, his face a writhing mask of revulsion and grim vengeance.

The baby writhed on the drifts of wet leaves like a fish hooked and pulled up on the bank. Tiny mewling noises escaped its throat as the light burned it. Inside the crawl space, his mother stirred and moaned and made an inarticulate cry. Her feet and hands were twitching, Jimmy saw, as if an electric current had been passed through them.

Randy screamed, lips peeling back over baby teeth that had suddenly developed into puppy fangs, sharp enough to rip skin.

'Hold him,' he said to Mark.

Mark hesitated for a moment. The thought of touching the thing they had dragged out of the darkness showed on his face. Then he dropped to his knees and pinned the arms.

Jimmy had taken his stethoscope, and now he put the earpieces in place, and he applied the pick-up to that twisting chest. Randy's small head lashed from side to side, gnashing at the air. His eyelids twitched with the roll of the eyes in their sockets.

No heartbeat.

'In the name of God,' Jimmy said, and brought the stake down with both hands in a hard, sweeping curve.

It was very quick.

The body jerked upward, the eyelids flew open, and then the body settled back tiredly and was still. Only a dead little boy remained in front of them . . . but one that had been dead for a week, and unembalmed. The body swelled in front of them, and suddenly a ghastly, noxious burp escaped the mouth, and they both turned away from it. The cheeks sagged, and the eyes fell inward.

Mark gave a horrified little cry and turned away, but Jimmy felt comforted. He had seen this: it was a normal (although accelerated) process – decay. Nature reclaiming her component parts. Full circle. Something inside him loosened, and he could believe that, even if they were not doing God's work, that they were doing nature's.

'Are you all right?' he asked Mark. 'Can you keep going?'

'Yes.' He turned and looked at Jimmy with wan, horrified eyes. 'It's not like the movies, is it?'

'No.'

He glanced down at the small corpse. It had caught up with itself, and was finished. The blood which had gushed from around the stake had clotted, then powdered. The entry wound itself looked shriveled and old. He touched

the stake and it wiggled easily, with none of the tension
he would have found in, say, the handle of a knife planted
in a new corpse. The tissues had relaxed like old rubber
bands.

He looked at Mark and said: 'Poor kid. He's not
pretty, but this is the way he should be. This is right.'

Mark nodded. 'Yes. I know that. It's only hard for a
minute.' He looked at the other two, in their pitiful mock–
grave. 'How are we going to handle them? If they thrash,
I can't hold them.'

'I will, if you can drive the stake. Can you do that?'

'Yes.'

Jimmy crawled in, holding his breath against the
stench, and pulled out Sandy McDougall. Mark used the
hammer quickly and mercifully. Roy McDougall was more
difficult. He had been a strong man, in the prime of his
life, and his thrashings and buckings were like a maddened
horse. The predatory lungings of his bared teeth were
frightening. A square strike on the wrist could sever the
hand completely. Mark made two false starts; one nick in
the shoulder and one stroke that dug a shallow channel
across McDougall's rib cage. Both of them unleashed freshets
of blood, and his screams attained a horrible, foghorn
quality that unnerved Jimmy almost totally.

In panicky desperation, Jimmy threw himself across
Roy McDougall's stomach and thighs and yelled: 'Quick!
Hit him now!'

Mark brought the stake down and smashed it into
the flesh with one heavy blow from the hammer. For a
moment McDougall's thrashings intensified, tossing Jimmy
off as if he were a piece of chaff, and then he trembled all

over and lay still. One of his hands closed tightly, clutching a useless fistful of leaves, and they both watched it, fascinated, until it loosened.

'Let's drag them back inside there,' Jimmy said.

'Shouldn't we take them to the river——?'

'We'll leave the stakes in them. I think that will do it; they're only Undead, and their hearts are destroyed. And if we have to take time to do that with each of them, we'll never get done.'

They dragged them back into the crawl space, and Jimmy drove a strong twig through the hasp of the broken lock to hold it shut.

They stood in the rain again, soaked and bloody. 'We'll have to get rid of the bodies eventually,' Jimmy said. 'I'm not going to jail for this if I can help it.'

'The next trailer?' Mark asked.

'Yes. They would be the logical ones for the McDougalls to attack first.'

They went across, and this time their nostrils picked up the telltale odor of rot even in the dooryard. Not even the steady autumn rain could lay it.

The name below the doorbell was Evans. Jimmy nodded. Yes, the husband's name was David Evans. He worked in the auto department of Grant's in Gates Falls. He had treated him a couple years ago. A cyst, or something.

This time the bell worked, but there was no response. They found Mrs Evans in bed, white and still, and dispatched her. The white sheets were drenched. The two children were in a single bedroom, both dressed in pajamas. Jimmy used his stethoscope and found nothing. The stakes did their work, and now he found using them little different from using a scalpel or a bone-saw. Even horror had its limits.

Mark found David Evans, hidden away in the unfinished storage space over their small garage. He was dressed in neat mechanic's greens and his mouth was crusted with blood that had dried in two streams from the corners of his mouth. Perhaps his children's blood.

'Let's put them all up here,' Jimmy said.

They did, checking the road carefully for cars before carrying each sheet-wrapped body across the space between the house and garage. When the town hall noon whistle went off, sending its shriek up to the gray, membranous sky, they both jumped and then looked at each other sheepishly.

Mark looked at his red-gloved hands with loathing. 'Can we use the shower?' he asked Jimmy. 'I feel . . . you know . . .'

'Yes,' Jimmy said. 'I want to call Ben, anyway. We—' He snapped his fingers. 'The phone's out at your house. Christ, why didn't I think of that? As soon as we clean up, we'd better go back.'

They went inside, and Jimmy sat down in one of the living room chairs and closed his eyes. Soon he heard Mark running water in the bathroom.

On the darkened screen of his eyes he saw Randy McDougall twisting and writhing on the wet leaves, saw the stake falling, saw his stomach swell with gas—

He opened his eyes.

This trailer was in nicer condition than the McDougalls', neater. He had never known Mrs Evans, but it seemed she must have taken pride in her home. There was a neat pile of the dead children's toys in a small storage room, a room that had probably been called the laundry room in the mobile home dealer's original brochure. Poor kids, he hoped they'd enjoyed the toys while there had still been bright days and sunshine to enjoy them in, before they arrived at their final quarters – the shoddy upstairs of a half-finished second-story garage. There wa a tricycle, several large trucks and a play gas station, one of those caterpillars on wheels (there must have been some dandy fights over that!), a toy pool table—

Blue chalk.

Three shaded lights in a row.

Men walking around the green table under the bright lights, cueing up, brushing the grains of blue chalk off their fingertips—

'That's it!' he shouted, sitting bolt upright in the chair, and Mark came running, half undressed for the shower, to see what the matter was.

In this section, Jimmy enters Eva's basement to confirm that Barlow is hiding there. In the novel, he opens the cellar door and steps down, and, as the published text says, 'the screams began.' In the original manuscript, this part is exactly the same, but the reason the screams begin is completely different:

Jimmy told himself he would only go to the foot of the stairs; he could use his lighter and see if the pool table was still there. He went down slowly, using the railing, breathing through his mouth to cut the smell. At the bottom, he flicked the wheel of the Zippo and the lighter flamed. He saw the pool table.

And he saw the rats.

The cellar was full of them. Every inch of floor space and shelf space was covered by the squirming bodies. They had tumbled whole rows of Eva's carefully-made preserves on the floor and they had smashed, leaving rich, splattered deposits of food. They were not eating now; they had been waiting for him . . . or for someone. Sarlinov's daytime guards. And at the flash of light, they attacked, wave after wave of them.

He screamed a warning to Mark and then turned to go back up the steps. A half-dozen huge dump rats that had been crouched on the small utility shelf hung over the steps threw themselves at his face, biting and clawing for purchase. He dropped the lighter and screamed again, this time not in warning but in pain and terror.

Rats crawled across his shoes and swarmed up his legs toward his waist, their sharp teeth and claws sinking through the cloth of his trousers and into flesh.

He staggered up two steps, beating at them with his hands. One of them snuffled through his hair and peered over Jimmy's forehead and into his eyes; the nose wriggled, and the rodent teeth flashed as he slashed at Jimmy's eyes.

Jimmy felt a great, flaring pain. He struck the rat away. His right foot slipped through the hole between two of the unbacked stairs and he fell forward, sealing his doom. Pain bloomed and he heard the muffled snap as his right ankle twisted, then broke.

I've had it, he thought. But like this . . . oh, God!

'Mark, run!' he screamed. 'Get Ben! Get—'

A rat squirmed into his mouth, back feet digging at his chin. He bit at it, tore at it, and the rat squealed and writhed. The fetid taste of it filled his mouth. He ripped it away, beat more of them off, and began to crawl up the stairs.

Mark went to the door and saw something coming painfully up the steps on its hands and knees. It was brown and writhing with feet and tails and eyes. He saw a flash of something that looked like Jimmy's shirt.

He went down two steps and held out his hand. A rat jumped on it and crawled up his arm like lightning, black eyes glaring. He struck it off.

The brown, writhing thing heaved itself to its feet and Mark screamed and put his hands to his temples. Jimmy Cody's face was shredding before his eyes. One eye socket was dark and lightless; a rat was spread-eagled across his left cheek, chewing at his ear. They were crawling in and out of his shirt and now two brown rivers of them were moving up to where Mark stood. In a moment they would be on him.

'Get Ben!' the brown, writhing thing that had been James Cody, M.D., screamed. 'Run! Run! R—'

He swayed, threw out his arms, and fell backward into the stairwell with a final, despairing scream.

The rats that had been coming for Mark paused and looked around, sitting up on their haunches and looking down, their paws held out in front of them – as if in applause.

Mark hesitated just a moment, swaying, unable to look away.

The thing that had fallen at the foot of the stairs twisted, writhed, screamed, tried to rise again, fell back, was dreadfully silent.

He could hear cloth being ripped and torn.

The rats began scurrying up toward him, their bodies plump and horribly well-fed. Not dump rats any longer. Graveyard rats.

When the first one reached him, he kicked out, smashing its head, sending it flying. Then he turned, walked up the two steps to the kitchen, and closed the door firmly.

In this scene, Ben and Mark have to chase away the rats before getting Barlow; flit guns and jugs of holy water help them.

They walked slowly through the hissing rain toward the porch. Rats carpeted the steps. They squeaked and thumped on the boards. A line of them were perched up on the red porch railings, like spectators at a racetrack.

'Be gone in the name of God,' Ben said conversationally, and pumped the handle of the flit gun. A thin spray, nearly invisible in the rain, clouded toward the rats on the steps. The effect was immediate and amazing. The rats squealed and writhed and scampered upward, some of them twisting and biting at their own flanks, as if suddenly infested with hungry fleas.

'It works,' he said. 'Go back and get one stake and the hammer.'

Mark ran back to the car. Ben started up the porch steps. After two more squirts, all the rats broke ranks and fled. Some jumped over the railing and were gone; most streamed back inside.

Mark ran up the steps to where Ben stood. He had unbuttoned his shirt and tucked the stake and the hammer inside, against his skin. His face was pallid, and a hectic blotch of red stood out on each cheek like a fever-sign.

The kitchen was overrun with them. They crawled across Eva Miller's neat red-and-white checked oilcloth with their tails dragging; sat upon the shelves, hissing and squeaking; scampered across the burners of the big electric stove. The sink was full of them, a writhing, twisting mass.

'They're—' Ben began, and a rat leaped onto his head, twisting and biting. He staggered, and all the rats surged forward eagerly.

Mark screamed and pumped his flit-gun at Ben's head. The aerosolsized drops of water were cool and soothing; the rat fell, twisting, to the floor and ran off, squealing.

'I'm so scared,' Mark said, shuddering.

'You better be. Where's that flashlight?'

'At the . . . bottom of the cellar stairs. I dropped it when Jimmy . . .'

'Okay.' They stood at the mouth of the cellar. A steady, eager rustling noise came up from the darkness below, and a tenebrous squeaking and squealing, as if from the throat of a catacomb.

'Oh Ben, do we have to?' the boy groaned.

Ben said: 'Did Christ have to walk to Calvary?'

They started down.

Ben thought: I'm going to my death. The thought came easily and naturally, and there was no regret in it. Any fine emotion such as regret was buried beneath a vast white glacier of fear. He had felt like this once before, when he and a friend had split a tab of acid. You entered a strange jungle world where you suddenly found you did not want to go; a jungle inhabited by exotic beasts. You were no longer in control of you, not for a while. The colors and sounds and images formed whether you wanted them to or not. Filled with an alien presence, you were driven on wings of fear, higher and higher, willy-nilly, never knowing when the overwhelming question might be presented to you for half-mad inspection.

Let be be the finale of seem. The only emperor is the emperor of ice cream. Who said that? Matt? When? Matt was dead. Wallace Stevens was dead. Susan was dead. Miranda was dead. *I wouldn't look at that, if I were you.* The driver of the truck that had squashed Miranda's head to a bloody pumpkin had said that. Perhaps he was dead, too. And he might be dead soon himself. And the might part of it seemed very weak indeed. Again he thought: I'm going to my death.

They reached the bottom, and the rats closed in. They stood back to back, working the flit guns. The rats drew back, then broke in confusion. Ben saw the flashlight and picked it up. The glass lens had cracked, but the bulb was intact. He turned it on and flashed it around. It caught the pool table first, mummified in plastic, and then a dark, huddled shape lying on the concrete floor in a puddle of something that might have been oil.

'Stay here,' he said, and walked carefully over and flashed a light down on what remained of Jimmy Cody after a thousand rats had finished with him.

I wouldn't look at that, if I were you.

'Oh, Jimmy,' he tried to say, and the words broke open and bled in his throat.

There was a neatly folded stack of living room drapes

on a corner shelf. He took one of them and threw it over Jimmy's body. Dark flowers blossomed on it.

The rats were creeping in again. He sprayed them wildly, running at them, and they squealed and fled from him.

'Don't do that!' Mark called, frightened. 'Half of it's gone already!'

Ben stopped, trembling. He flashed the light around; nothing. He shone it under the pool table. Bare. No room behind the furnace.

'Where is he?' he muttered.

Shelves, preserves smashed on the floor, a Welsh dresser against the far wall—

He swung the flashlight back and focused on it.

The rats had retreated to their thickest concentration there; they crawled over it and around it in profusion, their small buckshot eyes casting back the light with a reddish sheen.

'That wasn't here before,' he said. 'Let's move it.'

They walked across to it, and this time it took both of them spraying before the rats split their ranks and moved away in two wings. Yet they would not go far, although several of them had gone into twisting, snarling convulsions from the spray that had fallen on them. The stairs leading up to the kitchen were blocked, Ben saw with cold horror; choked with rats. If the flit guns ran dry—

They couldn't push it and still hold on to their hand-sprayers. 'Hell with that,' Ben said. 'Let's tip it over.'

They both grabbed the back with one hand.

'Now,' Ben grunted, and they threw their shoulders into it. The Welsh dresser went over with a bonelike rattle and crash as Eva Miller's long-ago wedding china shattered inside. The rats hurried forward, squeaking, and they drove them back again.

There was a small door, chest-high, set into the wall where the Welsh dresser had been. A new Yale padlock secured the hasp.

'Give me the hammer,' Ben said, and Mark handed it over. His eyes were rolling and jerking in an effort to follow the steady encroachment of the rats.

Two hard swings at the lock convinced him that it wasn't going to give. 'Jesus,' he muttered softly. Frustration welled up bitterly in his throat. He held up the flit gun and looked at it. Three-quarters empty. There were two nearly-full cans of holy water out in Jimmy Cody's car, but it could have been a million miles away. To be balked like this—

No. He would bite through the wood with his teeth, if he had to.

He shone the flashlight around, and its beam fell on a neat Peg-Board hung with tools to the right of the stairs. Hung on two steel pegs was an ax with a rubber cover masking its blade.

He started across to it, and the rats closed in.

'For the love of Jesus!' he cried at them, and it seemed they flinched. He made it to the Peg-Board, took the ax down, and turned back. The rats had closed the path behind him, a solid sea of them. Mark stood backed up against the door to the root cellar, the flit gun held tightly in both hands.

Ben steeled himself and started back, kicking the rats out of the way, spraying them when he had to. They squeaked and chittered and bit. One ran up inside the cuff of his pants and bit his ankle through the sock. He kicked it loose violently and it flew through the air, twisting and still biting, now at nothingness.

'Keep them away from me,' he said to Mark, and slipped the rubber envelope off the blade. It glittered wickedly even in the dim light. Without thinking, he held the ax head up to the height of his forehead, offering it to something he could not see. 'Be my strength,' he said, and there was nothing corny to the words, and also nothing prayerlike or petitioning or fainting. The words came out as a simple command, and to Mark, the rats seemed to shrink back for a moment, as if in horror.

The ax blade glimmered with a tracery of that eldritch fairy-light that Ben had seen before at Green's Mortuary and in the cellar beneath the Marsten House. At the same time, power seemed to streak down the wooden handle to where his hands clasped it. He stood holding it for a moment, looking at the blade, and a sense of curious sureness gripped him, the feeling of a man who has bet on a fighter who has his opponent staggering and clinching in the third round. For the first time in two weeks, he felt he was no longer groping through fogs of belief and unbelief, sparring with a partner whose body was too insubstantial to sustain blows.

Power, humming up his arms like volts.

The blade glowed brighter.

'Do it,' Mark said. 'Quick! Please!' He dropped his empty flit gun to the floor and the glass barrel shattered. He took Ben's and began to spray again.

Ben Mears spread his feet, slung the ax back, and

brought it down in a flashing are that left an afterimage on the eye, like a time exposure. The blade bit wood with a booming, portentous sound and sunk to the haft. Splinters flew.

The rest of this section reads almost identical to the published novel.

In this section, the last of the deleted scenes of the published novel, they stake Barlow. In the original manuscript, they take Sarlinov's coffin outside and let the sun do the work:

They let it go together, and Sarlinov's coffin settled to the wet autumn earth. They looked at each other over it.

'Now?' Mark said. He walked around, and they stood side by side, in front of the coffin's locks and seals.

'Yes,' Ben said.

They bent together, and the locks split as they touched them, making a sound like thin, snapping clapboards. They lifted.

Sarlinov was a young man now, his hair black and vibrant and lustrous, flowing over the satin pillow at the head of his narrow apartment. His skin glowed with life; the cheeks were as ruddy as wine. His teeth curved over his full lips, white with streaks of strong yellow, like ivory.

'He—' Mark began, and never finished.

The light struck him.

The eyes flew open, the lids rising like frightened window shades, and the chest hitched and air was suddenly pulled in with a terrible, windy inhalation that was nearly a scream. The mouth opened, revealing all the teeth and the tongue writhing among them like a red animal caught in a cage of snakes.

The shriek that erupted with the ebb of breath was awful, piercing, never to be forgotten – nailed to the brain in a sonic pattern of hellishness. The body writhed in the coffin like a stabbed fish. The teeth champed at the lips, the hands reached up blindly to hide the light, clawed the skin into bloody chevrons.

Then, dissolution.

It came in the space of two seconds, too fast to ever be fully believed in the daylight of later years, yet slow enough to recur again and again in nightmares, with awful stop-motion slowness.

The skin yellowed, coarsened, blistered, cracked like old sheets of canvas. The eyes faded, filmed white, fell in. The hair went white and fell like a drift of feathers. The body inside the dark suit shriveled and fell inward. The mouth widened gapingly as the lips drew back and drew back, meeting the nose and disappearing into an oral ring of jutting teeth. The fingernails blackened and fell off, and then there were only bones, still dressed with rings, clicking and clenching like castanets. Dust puffed through the fibers of the linen shirt. The bald and wrinkled head became a skull; the pants, with nothing to fill them out, fell away to broomsticks. For a moment a hideously animated scarecrow writhed before them. The fleshless skull whipped from side to side; the nude jawbone opened in a soundless scream that had no vocal cords to power it. The skeletal fingers rose and clicked in a marionette dance of repulsion.

Smells struck their noses and then vanished in tight little puffs: gas, putrescence, a moldy library smell, dust, then nothing. The twisting, protesting finger bones shredded and flaked away like pencils. The empty eye sockets widened in a fleshless expression of surprise and horror, met, and were no more. The skull caved in like an ancient Ming vase. The clothes settled flat and became as neutral as dirty laundry.

And still there was no end to its tenacious hold on the world; even the dust billowed and writhed in tiny dust devils within the coffin. And then, suddenly, they felt the passage of something between them which buffeted them like a strong wind, making them stagger backward. The limbs of the elm were suddenly whipped to a groaning frenzy by a wind from nowhere, a wind that departed as quickly as it had come. It was over. All that remained were the dark clothes and a ring of moldering teeth.

AFTERWORD

I first read *Dracula* when I was nine or ten – around 1957, this would have been. I can't remember why I wanted to read it, something some kid at school had said, or perhaps some vampire movie on John Zacherley's *Shock Theater*, but I did, and my mother brought it home from the Stratford Public Library and passed it over without comment. My brother, David, and I were both precocious readers, and our mother encouraged us greatly by forbidding us only a little. Quite often she would hand us a book one of us had requested, adding 'That's trash' in a tone which suggested she knew that the news wouldn't stop us; might, on the contrary, actually encourage us. Besides, she knew that trash has its place.

To Nellie Ruth Pillsbury King, *The Blackboard Jungle* was trash; *The Bat*, by Mary Roberts Rinehart, was trash; *The Amboy Dukes*, by Irving Shulman, was *serious* trash. None of these books were forbidden to us, however. A very few others were. These our mother described as 'bad trash,' and *Dracula* wasn't one of them. The only three in that category I can remember for sure were *Peyton Place*, *Kings Row*, and *Lady Chatterley's Lover*. I had read all of these by the age of thirteen and enjoyed them all . . . but none of them could match Bram Stoker's novel of old horrors colliding with modern technology and investigative techniques. That one was in a class by itself.

I remember that Stratford Library book clearly and with great affection. It had that comfortably sprung, lived-in look that library books with a lively circulation always get; bent page corners, a dab of mustard on page 331, a whiff of some reader's spilled after-dinner whiskey on page 468. Only library books speak with such wordless eloquence of the power good stories hold over us; how good stories abide, unchanged and mutely wise, while we poor humans grow older and slower.

'You might not like it,' my mother said. 'It looks like nothing but letters to me.'

Dracula was my first encounter with the epistolary novel as well as one of my earlier forays into adult fiction, and turned out to be comprised not just of letters but of diary entries, newspaper cuttings, and Dr Seward's exotic 'phonograph diary,' kept on wax cylinders. And after the original strangeness of reading such a patchwork wore off, I loved the form. There was a kind of justified snoopiness to it which exerted tremendous appeal. I loved the story, too. There were plenty of frightening sections – Jonathan Harker's growing realization that he has been imprisoned in the Count's castle, the bloody staking of Lucy Westenra in her tomb, the burning of Mina Murray Harker's forehead with the holy wafer – but what I responded to most strongly (I was only nine or ten, remember) was the intrepid band of adventurers which takes off in blind, brave pursuit of Count Dracula, hounding him first out of England, then back to Europe, and finally to his native Transylvania, where the issue is resolved at sunset. When I discovered J. R. R. Tolkien's *Rings* trilogy ten years later, I thought, 'Shit, this is just a slightly sunnier version of Stoker's *Dracula*, with Frodo playing Jonathan Harker, Gandalf playing Abraham Van Helsing, and Sauron playing the Count himself.' I think *Dracula* was the first fully satisfying adult novel I ever read, and I suppose it is no surprise that it marked me so early and so indelibly.

A year or two later (by this time my mother and my brother and I had left Connecticut and moved back to our native Maine), I discovered a cache of comic books (with torn-off covers) for sale in a local notions store called The Kennebec Fruit Company. These could be had for a nickel apiece. Some were *Classics Illustrated* (bad), some were *Donald Ducks* (good), and a great many were E.C. titles such as *Tales from the Crypt* and *The Vault of Horror* (best of all). In these comics I discovered a new breed of vampire, both cruder than Stoker's Count and more physically monstrous. These were pale, paranoid nightmares with gigantic fangs and fleshy red lips. They did not sip delicately, as Count Dracula sipped at the ever-more-wasted veins of Lucy Westenra; the E.C. vampires created by Al Feldstein and brought most gruesomely to life by the pen of Graham 'Ghastly' Ingels were prone to *tearing* and *ripping* and *shredding*. In one story, vampires running a restaurant actually installed *spigots* in the necks of their dying victims, suspending them upside down and drinking splurting red streams of hot plasma like kids quaffing from the backyard hose. And the victims didn't just moan or sigh, like Lucy in her maiden's bed; they were more apt to scream in long strings of repeated E's and Y's and G's, making sounds – *'Eeeeeeahh!' 'Arrgggggh!' 'Eyyyyyyyyggghh!'* – that looked like terrible phlegmy expectorations. These vampires did not just scare me; they fucking *terrified* me, chasing me through my dreams with their lips peeled back to show their monstrous cannibal teeth.

My mother didn't approve of the E.C.'s, but neither did she take them away; they were trash, and she often said so, but they were apparently not *bad* trash. Eventually I gave them up on my own (as she probably knew I would, and all the quicker if I wasn't nagged about it), but those vampires remained with me all the same, as vivid and as vital in their own way as Stoker's Count. Perhaps even more vivid and vital because, unlike Count Dracula, they were *American* vampires. Some of them drove cars . . . went out on dates . . . and there were the ones that owned the vampire restaurant (where, I remember, one of the specials was French Fried Scabs). Why, if owning a goddam beanery wasn't good old American free enterprise, what was?

I reencountered *Dracula* in 1971, when I was teaching a high school English class called Fantasy and Science Fiction. I came back to it with some trepidation, knowing that a book read – not just read but studied and taught, even at the high school level – at twenty-four looks a lot different than one read at the age of nine or ten. Usually smaller. But the great ones only get bigger and cast longer shadows. *Dracula*, although created by a man who never wrote much else of lasting worth in his life (a few short stories, such as 'The Judge's House,' still bear scrutiny), is one of the great ones. My students enjoyed it, and I'd say I enjoyed it even more than they did.

One night, the second time through the adventures of the sanguinary Count (I only taught high school for two years), I wondered out loud to my wife what might have happened if Drac had appeared not in turn-of-the-century London but in the America of the 1970s. 'Probably he'd land in New York and be killed by a taxicab, like Margaret Mitchell in Atlanta,' I added, laughing.

My wife, who has been responsible for all of my greatest successes, did not join my laughter. 'What if he came here, to Maine?' she asked. 'What if he came to the country? After all, isn't that where his castle was? In the Transylvanian countryside?'

That was really all it took. My mind lit up with possibilities, some hilarious, some horrible. I saw how such a man – such a *thing* – could operate with lethal ease in a small town; the locals would be very similar to the peasants he had known and ruled back home, and with the help of a couple of greedy Kiwanis types like real estate agent Larry Crockett, he would soon become what he had always been: the *boyar*, the master.

I saw more, as well: how Stoker's aristocratic vampire might be combined with the fleshy leeches of the E.C. comics, creating a pop-cult hybrid that was part nobility and part bloodthirsty dope, like the zombies in George Romero's *Night of the Living Dead*. And, in the post-Vietnam America I inhabited and still loved (often against my better instincts), I saw a metaphor for everything that was wrong with the society around me, where the rich got richer and the poor got welfare . . . if they were lucky.

I also wanted to tell a tale that inverted *Dracula*. In Stoker's novel, the optimism of Victorian England shines through everything like the newly invented electric light. Ancient evil comes to the city and is sent scatting (not without some struggle, it is true) by thoroughly modern vampire-hunters who use blood transfusions and stenography and typewriting machines. My novel could look through the other end of the telescope, at a world where electric lights and modern inventions would actually aid the incubus, by rendering belief in him all but impossible. Even Father Callahan, the man of God, cannot really believe in Mr Barlow – no, not even when the evidence appears before his very eyes – and so Callahan is sent hence, into the land of Nod which lies to the east of Eden (in *'Salem's Lot*, Detroit serves as a stand-in for Nod). I thought that, in my story, the vampires would probably win, and good luck to them. Drive those cars, boys. Run that restaurant. WELCOME TO JERUSALEM'S LOT, BLOOD SAUSAGE OUR SPECIALTY.

The story didn't quite turn out that way – as you will see for yourself – because some of my human characters turned out to be stronger than I had expected. It took a certain amount of courage to allow them to grow toward each other as they wanted to do, but I found that courage. If I ever won a single battle as a novelist, that was probably it. Writers have found it so much easier to imagine doom in the years since World War II (and especially in the years since Vietnam), easier to imagine characters who grow smaller as a result of their trials rather than bigger. Ben Mears, I discovered, wanted to be big. Wanted, in fact, to be a hero. I let him be what he wanted to be. I have never been sorry.

'Salem's Lot was originally published by Doubleday

in 1975. It is dated in many ways (I have always been more a writer of the moment than I wanted to be), but I still like it well enough to number it among my favorites. I like the picture it draws of a small New England town; I like its sense of deepening menace; I like its strong, intended echoes of *Dracula* and of the EC comics where the vampires ripped and snarked and tore instead of sipping delicately like wine-snobs at a vicarage tasting party. Most of all I like the moment where it takes off like a big-ass bird into a world where all the rules have become moot and anything is possible. *Carrie*, the book which came before it, seems almost fey by comparison. There is more confidence here, more willingness to be funny ('The world is falling down around our ears and you're sticking at a few vampires,' one of the characters says), more pushing of the envelope. In a way, this book was my coming-out party.

The woman who brought me *Dracula* from the Stratford Public Library never saw *'Salem's Lot*. By the time the first draft was completed, she was too ill to read much – she who read with such enjoyment over the course of her life – and by the time it was published, she was dead. If she had read it, I like to think she would have finished the last hundred pages in one of her marathon chain-smoking readathons, then laughed, put it aside (not without some affection), and pronounced it trash.

But maybe not *bad* trash.

Longboat Key, Florida
February 24, 1999

STEPHEN KING
LISEY'S STORY

Every marriage has two hearts, one light and one dark.

Lisey knew it when she first fell for Scott. And now he's dead, she knows it for sure.

Lisey was the light to Scott Landon's dark for twenty-five years. As his wife, only she saw the truth behind the public face of the famous author – that he was a haunted man whose bestselling novels were based on a terrifying reality.

Now Scott has gone, Lisey wants to lock herself away with her memories. But the fans have other ideas. And when the sinister threats begin, Lisey realises that, just as Scott depended on her strength – her light – to live, so she will have to draw on his darkness to survive.

'A psychological thriller of extraordinary sensitivity that takes the reader deep into the dark places in us all'
– *Independent on Sunday*

'A consummate and compassionate novel – one of King's very best' – *Guardian*

HODDER